SINS *of* EMPIRE

By Brian McClellan

Gods of Blood and Powder
Sins of Empire

The Powder Mage Trilogy
Promise of Blood
The Crimson Campaign
The Autumn Republic

Forsworn (novella)
Servant of the Crown (novella)
Murder at the Kinnen Hotel (novella)
Ghosts of the Tristan Basin (novella)
In the Field Marshal's Shadow (collection)

SINS *of* EMPIRE

GODS OF BLOOD
AND POWDER

BRIAN
McCLELLAN

www.orbitbooks.net

Copyright © 2017 by Brian McClellan
Cover design by Lauren Panepinto
Cover illustration by Thom Tenery
Cover copyright © 2017 by Hachette Book Group, Inc.
Map illustration by Isaac Stewart

Orbit
Hachette Book Group
1290 Avenue of the Americas
New York, NY 10104
orbitbooks.net

First Edition: March 2017

Orbit is an imprint of Hachette Book Group.
The Orbit name and logo are trademarks of Little, Brown Book Group Limited.

The Hachette Speakers Bureau provides a wide range of authors for speaking events. To find out more, go to www.hachettespeakersbureau.com or call (866) 376-6591.

ISBNs: 978-0-316-40721-2 (hardcover), 978-0-316-37512-2 (ebook)

Printed in the United States of America

LSC-H

10 9 8 7 6 5 4 3 2 1

For Marlene Napalo,
high school English,
for reading and reviewing my early derivative garbage
full of dwarves, elves, and dragons, even though I'm sure
you had far better things to do over Christmas break.

And for William Prueter,
high school Latin,
for teaching me to think outside the box and work hard.
And because I know winding up at the front of a
fantasy novel will irritate you.

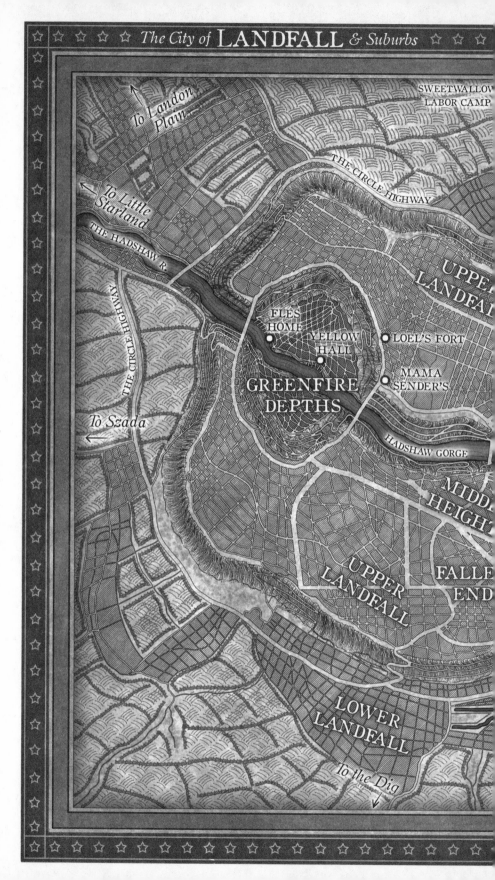

SWEETWALLOW
LABOR CAMP

To Landon
Plain

THE CIRCLE HIGHWAY

To Little
Starland

THE HADSHAW R.

UPPER
LANDFALL

FLES
HOME

YELLOW
HALL

LOEL'S FORT

THE CIRCLE HIGHWAY

MAMA
SENDER'S

GREENFIRE
DEPTHS

To Szada

HADSHAW GORGE

MIDDLE
HEIGHTS

UPPER
LANDFALL

FALLEN
END

LOWER
LANDFALL

To the Dig

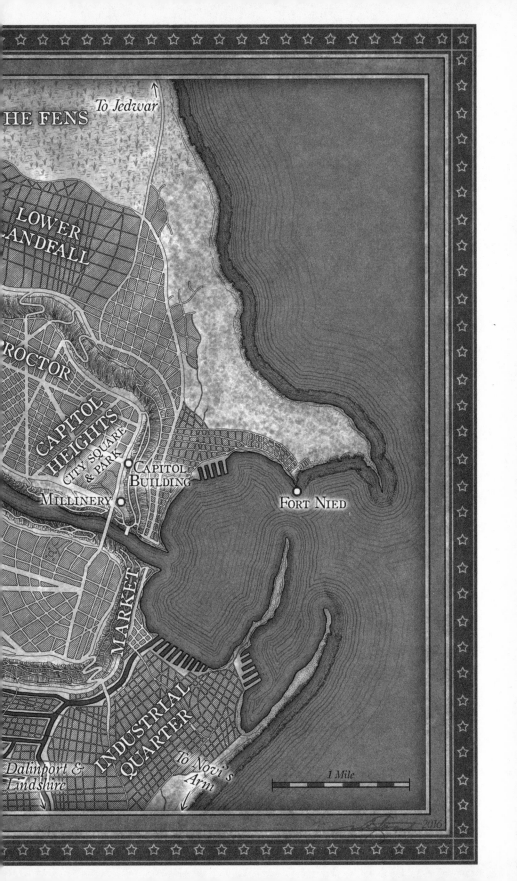

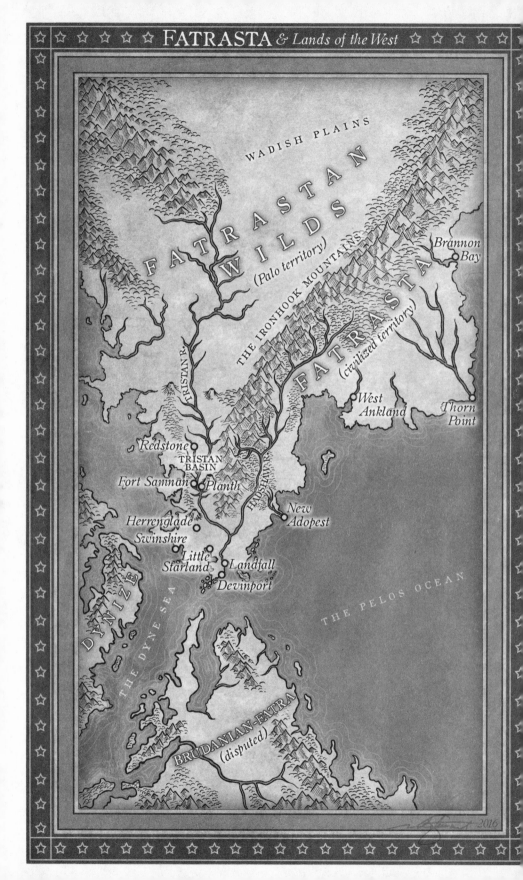

SINS *of* EMPIRE

PROLOGUE

Privileged Robson paused with one foot on the muddy highway and the other on the step of his carriage, his hawkish nose pointed into the hot wind of the Fatrastan countryside. The air was humid and rank, and the smell of distant city smokestacks clung to the insides of his nostrils. Onlookers, he considered, might comment to one another that he looked like a hound testing the air—though only a fool would compare a Privileged sorcerer to a lowly dog anywhere within earshot—and they wouldn't be entirely wrong.

Privileged sorcery was tuned to the elements and the Else, giving Robson and any of his brother or sister Privileged a deep and unrivaled understanding of the world. Such an understanding, a sixth sense, provided him an invaluable advantage in any number of situations. But in this particular case, it gave Robson nothing more than a vague hint of unease, a cloudy premonition that caused a tingling sensation in his fingertips.

He remained poised on the carriage step for almost a full minute before finally lowering himself to the ground.

The countryside was empty, floodplains and farmland rolling

toward the horizon to the south and west. A salty wind blew off the ocean to the east, and to the north the Fatrastan capital of Landfall sat perched atop a mighty, two-hundred-foot limestone plateau. The city was less than two miles away, practically within spitting distance, and the presence of the Lady Chancellor's secret police meant that it was very unlikely that any threat was approaching from that direction.

Robson remained beside his carriage, pulling on his gloves and flexing his fingers as he tested his access to the Else. He could feel the usual crackle and spark of sorcery just out of reach, waiting to be tamed, and allowed a small smile at the comfort it brought him. Perhaps he was being foolish. The only thing capable of challenging a Privileged was a powder mage, and there were none of *those* in Landfall. What else could possibly cause such disquiet?

He scanned the horizon a second and third time, reaching out with his senses. There was nothing out there but a few farmers and the usual highway traffic passing along on the other side of his carriage. He tugged at the Else with a twitch of his middle finger, pulling on the invisible thread until he'd brought enough power into this world to create a shield of hardened air around his body.

One could never be too careful.

"I'll just be a moment, Thom," he said to his driver, who was already nodding off in the box.

Robson's boots squelched as he followed a muddy track away from the highway and toward a cluster of dirty tents. A work camp had been set up a few hundred yards away from the road in the center of a trampled cotton field, occupying the top of a small rise, and a small army of laborers hauled soil from a pit at the center of the camp.

Robson's unease continued to grow as he approached the camp, but he pushed it aside, forcing a cold smile on his face as an older man left the ring of tents and came out to greet him.

"Privileged Robson," the man said, bowing several times before offering his hand. "My name is Cressel. Professor Cressel. I'm the head of the excavation. Thank you so much for coming on such short notice."

Robson shook Cressel's hand, noting the way the professor flinched when he touched the embroidered fabric of Robson's gloves. Cressel was a thin man, stooped from years of bending over books, square spectacles perched on the tip of his nose and only a wisp of gray hair remaining on his head. Over sixty years old, he was almost twenty years Robson's senior and a respected faculty member at Landfall University. Robson practically towered over him.

Cressel snatched his hand back as soon as he was able, clenching and unclenching his fingers as he looked pensively toward the highway. He was, from all appearances, an awfully flighty man.

"I was told it was important," Robson said.

Cressel stared at him for several moments. "Oh. Yes! Yes, it's very important. At least, I think so."

"You think so? I'm having supper with the Lady Chancellor herself in two hours and you *think* this is important?"

A bead of sweat appeared on Cressel's forehead. "I'm so sorry, Privileged. I didn't know, I . . ."

"I'm already here," Robson said, cutting off the old professor. "Just get to the point."

As they drew closer to the camp Robson noted a dozen or so guards, carrying muskets and truncheons, forming a loose cordon around the perimeter. There were more guards inside, distinguished by the yellow jackets they wore, overlooking the laborers.

Robson didn't entirely approve of work camps. The laborers tended to be unreliable, slow, and weak from malnourishment, but Fatrasta was a frontier city and received more than its fair share of criminals and convicts shipped over from the Nine. Lady Chancellor Lindet had long ago decided the only thing to do with them was let them earn their freedom in the camps. It gave the city enough labor for the dozens of public works projects, and to lend out to private organizations including, in this case, Landfall University.

"Do you know what we're doing here?" Cressel asked.

"Digging up another one of those Dynize relics, I heard." The damned things were all over the place, ancient testaments to a bygone civilization that had retreated from this continent well before anyone from the Nine actually arrived. They jutted from the center of parks, provided foundations for buildings, and, if some rumors were to be believed, there was an entire city's worth of stone construction buried beneath the floodplains that surrounded Landfall. Some of the artifacts still retained traces of ancient sorcery, making them of special interest to scholars and Privileged.

"Right. Quite right. The point," Cressel said, wringing his hands. "The point, Privileged Robson, is that we've had six workers go mad since we reached the forty-foot mark of the artifact."

Robson tore his mind away from the logistics of the labor camp and glanced at Cressel. "Mad, you say?"

"Stark, raving mad," Cressel confirmed.

"Show me the artifact."

Cressel led him toward the center of the camp, where they came upon an immense pit in the ground. It was about twenty yards across and nearly as deep, and at its center was an eight-foot-squared obelisk surrounded by scaffolding. Beneath a flaking coat of mud, the obelisk was made of smooth, light gray limestone carved, no doubt, from the quarry at the center of the Landfall Plateau. Robson recognized the large letters on its side as Old Dynize, not an uncommon sight on the ruins that dotted the city.

Robson felt his stomach turn. The sorcery crackling at the edges of his senses seemed to shy away, as if repulsed by the very presence of the obelisk. "It looks entirely ordinary," he said, removing a handkerchief and blowing his nose to hide the tremble in his fingers. "Just another old rock the Dynize left behind."

"That's what we think, too," Cressel agreed, adjusting his mud-splattered spectacles. "There is very little unique about this artifact, except for the fact that it is so far from the ancient city center."

"If there's nothing special about it, why are you bothering to dig it up?" Robson asked petulantly.

"It sank into the soft soil of the floodplains. Aside from the water, we thought it would be a very easy dig."

"And is it?"

"So far," Cressel said. He hesitated, and then said, "Until the madness set in, that is."

"What happened?"

"The workers." Cressel gestured toward the stream of laborers hauling baskets of rubble up the wooden ramps at the edges of the excavation site. "We estimate the artifact is about eighty feet tall—probably the longest of its kind in the city. Last week, about sixty feet down, or rather twenty feet from the bottom, we found some unusual writing. That very day, one of the laborers went mad."

"Correlation is not causation," Robson said, not bothering to hide the impatience in his voice.

"True, true. We assumed it was just heatstroke at first. But it happened again the next day. Then the next. And every day since. By the sixth we decided to call on you because, well, you've been very keen on the university and we thought…"

"I could do you a favor," Robson finished sourly. He made a mental note to make his annual donations to the university a few thousand krana smaller. Best not to let them think him overly generous. He liked the university, was fascinated by their search for knowledge both past and future, but they'd overstepped their bounds this time. He was a busy man. "What do you mean by 'unusual writing'?" he asked.

"It's not written in Old Dynize. In fact, no one at the university recognized the language. Here, you should come down and see it." Cressel immediately began descending one of the ramps leading into the excavation pit. "I would appreciate a Privileged's perspective on this."

Robson's skin crawled, and he remained rooted to the ground, dread sinking to the pit of his stomach like a ball of lead. He couldn't quite place the source of his misgivings. Ancient ruins on this continent were *always* marked with Old Dynize. Finding a different language written on one of these obelisks might have historical significance, but surely a matter of translation shouldn't leave him with such trepidation.

He wondered if his senses were trying to warn him off from something. It would be easy enough to tell Cressel no. He could order the dig closed, the obelisk destroyed by gunpowder or sorcery.

But Privileged didn't maintain their reputations by being timid, so he followed Cressel down into the depths of the dig.

Laborers scurried out of their way as Cressel led Robson across the rickety scaffolding until they were standing beside the obelisk, staring at a spot only a few feet from the bottom of the pit. One of the stone's smooth faces bore an intricate inscription. It had been meticulously cleaned of soil, revealing an almost-white face covered in flowing letters entirely unfamiliar to Robson's eyes.

He peered at the letters for several moments. "Have there been any patterns in the madness?" he asked absently. Behind them, the soft thumping sound of laborers hacking at the soil with mattocks and shovels reverberated through the pit.

"It appears to affect only those who spend the better part of the day down here," Cressel said. "When the third case happened, I suspended faculty or camp guards from descending into the pit unless it was an emergency."

But not the laborers, Robson noted. Oh well. *Someone* had to suffer in the pursuit of knowledge.

Robson tilted his head to one side, beginning to see repeated patterns in the flowing letters. As Cressel mentioned, this was indeed a script of some kind. *But what language?* A Privileged of Robson's age was as learned in a broad selection of studies as most professors were in their own fields but Robson had never seen anything like this.

The writing was ancient. Older than the Dynize script surrounding it, which was one of the oldest languages known to modern linguistics. Slowly, hesitantly, Robson lifted his hand. He reached out for the Else, grasping for the wild sorcery from beyond this world. The sorcery once again shied away, and he had to wrestle to keep it close at hand in case he needed it in a pinch. There was something sinister about this obelisk, and he would not be caught unawares.

When he was certain he'd prepared himself against any sort of backlash, he touched his gloved fingertips to the plaque.

A vision stabbed through Robson's mind. He saw a man, a familiar face wreathed in golden curls, hands held out as if to cradle the world. Whiteness surrounded the figure, brilliant and unforgiving, and Robson was not entirely sure whether the man was creating the whiteness or being consumed by it.

Robson jerked his fingertips back and the vision was gone. He found himself shaking violently, his clothes soaked with sweat, as Cressel looked on in shock.

Robson rubbed his hands together, noting that the fingertips of his right glove were gone, seared away, though his fingers were unhurt. He left Cressel standing on the platform, dumbfounded, as he ran up the ramps and through the camp, sprinting all the way back to his carriage.

"Thom!"

The snoozing driver jolted awake. "My lord?"

"Thom, I need you to take a message to the Lady Chancellor. Give it to her in person, without anyone else present."

"Yes, my lord! What is the message?"

"Tell her that I've found it."

Thom scratched his head. "Is that it?"

"Yes!" Robson said. "That's all you need to know for your own safety. Now go!"

He watched the carriage cut across the highway, nearly running a train of pack mules off the road and leaving a cursing merchant in its wake. Robson pulled out his handkerchief and dabbed his forehead, only to find that his handkerchief was also soaked with sweat.

"Privileged!"

Robson turned to find that the old professor had caught up.

"Privileged," Cressel wheezed. "What's happening? Are you all right?"

"Yes, yes, I'm fine." Robson waved him off and began striding back toward the camp. Cressel fell in beside him.

"But, sir, you look like you've seen a ghost!"

Robson considered the brief vision, his brow furrowing as he let it hang in his mind for a few moments. "No," he said. "Not a ghost. I've seen God."

CHAPTER 1

Fort Samnan was in ruins.

The largest fortification on the western branch of the Tristan River, Samnan's twenty-foot palisade of split cypress trunks enclosed a sizable trading town and wooden motte that held a community center and several administration buildings. Forty-foot guard towers overlooked the river on one side and a few hundred acres of cleared, drained farmland on the other.

The fort stood as a monument to civilization in the center of the biggest piece of swampland in the world, which made Vlora all the more saddened to see it in its current state.

The mighty doors lay broken just inside walls that had been breached in a dozen places by artillery. Most of the towers were nothing but smoldering remains, and the shelled motte had been reduced to splinters. Smoke rose over the fort, billowing a thousand feet high into the hot, humid afternoon sky.

The aftermath of a battle rarely elicited horror within her. No career soldier could view battle after battle with horror and keep her sanity for very long but for Vlora there was always a sort of melancholy there, masking the shock. It tugged at the back of her mind and stifled the urge to celebrate a fight well won.

Vlora tasted the familiar tang of smoke on her tongue and spit into the mud, watching soldiers in their crimson and blue jackets as they drifted in and out of the haze. The men cleared away the dead, inventoried the weapons, set up surgeries, and counted the prisoners. It was done quickly, efficiently, without looting, rape, or murder, and for that Vlora felt a flash of pride. But her eyes lingered on the bodies, wondering what the final tally would be on both sides of the conflict.

Vlora worked her way through what remained of the gatehouse, stepping over the shattered timber that had once been the fort doors, pausing to let two soldiers pass with a stretcher held between them. She sucked nervously on her teeth as she got her first view of the trading town inside the fort. Some of the buildings had escaped the shelling, but the rest had fared little better than the motte.

Frontier forts were built to have modern weapons and light artillery on the inside, with Palo arrows and outdated muskets on the outside. Not the other way around.

Out of the corner of her eye she caught sight of a soldier creeping out from a half-ruined building, a small box under one arm. She tilted her head, feeling more bemused than angry, and struggled to remember his name. "Private Dobri!" she finally called out.

The soldier, a little man with an oversize nose and long fingers, leapt a foot into the air. He whirled toward Vlora, attempting to hide the box behind his back.

"Ma'am!" he said, snapping a salute and managing to drop the box. A few cups and a load of silverware spilled onto the street.

Vlora eyed him for a long moment, letting him stew in his discomfort. "You looking for the owner of that fine silver, Dobri?"

Dobri's eyes widened. He held the salute, eyes forward, and Vlora could make out just the slightest tremble. She approached him sidelong, ignoring the silver, and did a quick circuit around him. He wore the same uniform as her, a blood-red jacket and pants with dark blue stripes and cuffs. It had gold buttons and a brass pin at the lapel of muskets crossed behind a shako—the symbol of the Riflejack Mercenary Company. The uniform was dusty, with soot stains on his trousers and arms. He opened his mouth, closed it, then gave a defeated sigh. "No, Lady Flint. I was stealing it."

"Well," Vlora said. "At least you remembered how little I like a liar." She considered the situation for a few moments. The battle had been short but fierce, and Dobri had been one of the first of her soldiers through the walls once their artillery had battered down the gates. He was a brave soldier, if light-fingered. "Give the silver to the quartermaster for inventory, then tell Colonel Olem you volunteer for latrine duty for the next three weeks. I wouldn't suggest telling him why, unless you want to end up in front of a firing squad."

"Yes, Lady Flint."

"The Riflejacks do not steal," Vlora said. "We're mercenaries, not thieves. Dismissed."

She watched Dobri gather the silver and then scramble toward the quartermaster's tent outside the fort walls. She wondered if she should have made an example of him—she did have the moniker "Flint" to uphold, after all. But the men had been on the frontier for almost a year. Sympathy and discipline needed to be handed out equally, or she'd wind up with a mutiny on her hands.

"General Flint!"

She turned, finding a young sergeant approaching from the direction of the demolished motte. "Sergeant Padnir, what can I help you with?"

The sergeant saluted. "Colonel Olem's asking for your presence, ma'am. He says it's urgent."

Vlora scowled. Padnir was pale, despite the heat, and had a nervous look in his eyes. He was a levelheaded man in his late twenties, just a few years younger than her, one of the many soldiers under her command to be forged during the Adran-Kez War. Something must have gone wrong for him to get so worked up. "Of course. Just making my rounds. I'll come immediately."

She followed the sergeant down the street, turning onto the main thoroughfare of the town. She paused once to examine the line of prisoners, all kneeling on the side of the road, a handful of soldiers guarding them. Every one of them was a Palo—Fatrastan natives with bright red hair and pale freckled skin. At a glance she could tell that they were villagers, not warriors.

This particular group had seized Fort Samnan, declaring that the fort was on their land and forbidding the Fatrastan government from passing through the area. They'd killed a few dozen settlers and torched some farmhouses, but not much else. It was fairly mild as far as insurrections went.

The Fatrastan government had responded by sending Vlora and the Riflejack Mercenary Company to put down the rebels. It wasn't the first time Vlora had put down an insurrection on the frontier—the Fatrastans paid well, after all—and she didn't think it would be the last.

A few of the faces glanced up at her, staring vacantly. Some of them glared, a few cursed in Palo as she walked past. She ignored them.

She didn't like fighting the Palo, who tended to be passionate, underfunded, and out-armed. That meant a lot of guerrilla warfare, with leaders like the elusive Red Hand causing disproportionate damage to any Fatrastan army with the bad luck to get singled out. Pitched battles—like the siege of Fort Samnan—turned into a damned slaughter in the other direction.

As far as Vlora saw it, the poor fools had a point. This *was* their land. They'd been here since the Dynize left this place almost a thousand years ago, long before the Kressians came over from the Nine and started colonizing Fatrasta. Unfortunately for them, the

Palo couldn't afford to hire the Riflejacks, while the Fatrastan government could.

Vlora left the prisoners behind and found Colonel Olem just a few moments later, on the opposite side of the destroyed motte. At forty-five, the colonel was beginning to show his age, streaks of gray creeping into his sandy beard. Vlora thought it made him look distinguished. He wore the same red and blue uniform as his comrades with only the single silver star at his lapel, opposite the crossed muskets and shako, to mark his rank. An unlit cigarette hung out of one corner of his mouth.

"Colonel," Vlora said.

"Flint," Olem responded without looking up. Technically, he was Vlora's second officer. In reality, they were both retired generals of the Adran Army and co-owners of the Riflejack Mercenary Company, putting them on equal footing. He preferred the formality of just being "Colonel" Olem, but she deferred to his judgment just as often as he did to hers.

Olem sat back on his haunches, hands on his knees, looking perplexed.

The corpse of an old Palo man lay stretched out before him. The body was bent, with freckled skin as wrinkled as a prune, and still bleeding from multiple gunshot and bayonet wounds. At least two dozen bodies in Riflejack uniforms lay scattered around the corpse. Throats and stomachs had been slashed. A pair of rifles had been snapped clean in two.

"What happened here?"

"Your guess is as good as mine," Olem said. He stood up and struck a match on his belt, shielding the flame from the breeze. He lit his cigarette, puffing moodily as he eyed the corpse of the old man at their feet.

Vlora gazed at the bodies of her soldiers. She named them silently in her head—Forlin, Jad, Wellans. The list went on. They were all privates, and she didn't know any of them well, but they were still her men. "Who's this son of a bitch?" she asked, gesturing at the Palo corpse.

"No idea."

"Did *he* do this?"

"Seems so," Olem said. "We already dragged off fifteen wounded."

Vlora chewed on that information for a moment, trying to catch up. It didn't make any sense. Palo tended to be scrappy fighters, but they dropped like anyone else against trained soldiers with bayonets fixed. "How did"—she did a quick count—"a single old man inflict almost forty casualties on the best damned infantry on the continent?"

"That," Olem said, "is a really good question."

"And…?" She gave him a long, annoyed look. It was one that sent most of her men scrambling. Olem, as usual, seemed unaffected.

"The boys say he moved too fast for the eye to follow. Like…" Olem paused, meeting her eyes. "Like a powder mage."

Vlora reached out with her sorcerous senses, probing into the Else. As a powder mage she could feel every powder charge and horn within hundreds of yards, each of them showing up in her mind's eye like points on a map. She focused on the body. The old man didn't have an ounce of powder on him, but she could sense a sort of subtle sorcery around him the likes of which she'd never felt. Further examination gave her a headache, and she closed her third eye.

"Well," she told Olem, "he wasn't a powder mage. There's something… sorcerous about him, but I can't pin it down."

"I didn't feel it," he responded. He had his own Knack, a minor sorcery that allowed him to go without sleep. But his ability to see into the Else was not as strong as hers.

Vlora knelt next to the body, giving it a second look *without* sorcery. The old man's hair had long since faded from red to white, and his gnarled hands still clutched a pair of polished bone axes. Most Palo dressed for their surroundings—buckskins on the frontier, suits or trousers in the city. This warrior, however, wore thick, dark leathers that didn't come from any mammal. The skin was ridged, tough to the touch, textured like a snake.

"You ever seen anybody wear an outfit like this before?"

"It's swamp dragon leather," Olem observed. "I've seen satchels and boots, but the stuff is damned expensive. Hard to tan. Nobody wears a whole suit." He ashed his cigarette. "And I've definitely never seen a Palo fight like this. Might be cause for concern."

"Maybe," Vlora said, feeling suddenly shaken. Being stuck in the swamps with the swamp dragons, snakes, bugs, and Palo was bad enough. But out here, the Riflejacks had always been at the top of the food chain. Until now. She ran her fingers over the leather. The stuff appeared to make an effective armor, thick enough to turn a knife or even a bayonet thrust. "It's like a uniform," she muttered.

"Rumors are going to spread," Olem said. "Should I put a stop to idle talk?"

"No," Vlora said. "Let the men gossip. But give them an order. If they see somebody wearing an outfit like this, they're to form ranks and keep him at the end of their bayonets. And send someone running for me."

Olem's brow wrinkled. "You think you could fight someone capable of cutting through this many infantry?" he asked.

"No idea. But I'll be damned if I let some Palo yokel carve through my men like a holiday ham. I can at least put a bullet in his head from thirty paces."

"And if there's more than one?"

Vlora glared at him.

"Right," Olem said, finishing his cigarette and crushing the butt underfoot. "Form line, call for General Flint."

Vlora and Olem stood in silence for several minutes, watching as the rest of the corpses were carted off and the fires finally put out by the bucket brigade. Messengers dropped reports off to Olem, and a flagpole was raised above one of the few remaining fort towers. The

Fatrastan flag, sunflower yellow with green corners, was run up it along with the smaller, red and blue standard of the Riflejacks.

Vlora watched as a woman on horseback rode through the shattered fort gate and guided her horse through the crowds and the chaos of the battle cleanup. The woman examined her surroundings with a jaded, casual air, a sneer on her lips for the Palo prisoners on their knees in the street. Vlora didn't know the woman, but she recognized the yellow uniform well enough—it matched the flag her men had just run up the pole. Fatrastan military.

The rider came to a stop in front of Vlora and Olem, looking down on them with a fixed scowl. No salute. Not even a hello.

"You General Flint?" the woman asked.

"Who wants to know?" Vlora responded.

"Message from Lady Chancellor Lindet," the woman said. She pulled an envelope from her jacket and held it out. Olem took it from her, tearing it open with one finger and smoothing the paper against his stomach. The woman turned her horse around without a word and immediately rode back down the street, heading for the fort gate.

Fatrastan soldiers tended to be arrogant pricks, but Vlora had seldom seen one so rude. She tapped the butt of her pistol. "Would it be terribly unprofessional of me to shoot her hat off?"

"Yes," Olem said without looking up from the letter.

"Damned Fatrastan army needs to show more respect to the people doing their dirty work."

"Console yourself with the fact that you make far more money than she does," Olem said. "Here, you'll want to see this."

Vlora turned her attention to the letter in his hand. "What is it?"

"Trouble in Landfall," he said. "We've been recalled. We're to head to the city immediately."

Vlora's first thought was to do a little dance. Landfall might be hot and fetid, but at least it was a modern city. She could have a real meal, go to the theater, and even take a bath. No more of this damned swamp or—she glanced at the body of the little old man that was only now being removed—its dragon-skin-wearing Palo.

Her relief, however, was quickly squashed by a creeping suspicion. "What kind of trouble?" she asked.

"Doesn't say."

"Of course it doesn't." Vlora chewed on her bottom lip. "Finish the cleanup," she said, "and send the prisoners to Planth with a regiment of our boys. Tell everyone else we're leaving at first light."

Vlora waited by the Tristan River while her men boarded the waiting keelboats that had been sent to retrieve them. Heading downriver by keelboat would get them to Landfall in just a few days, but she wondered what could be so urgent that they needed to be recalled in such a manner. It made her nervous, but she put that in the back of her mind and turned to the box in her lap.

It was an old hat box, something she'd had since she was a teenager, and it was filled with letters from a former lover now long dead and gone. Taniel Two-shot had been a childhood friend, an adopted brother, even her fiancé at one point, but he'd also been a hero of the Fatrastan Revolution. Eleven years ago he'd fought for Fatrastan independence from the Kez through these very swamps, creeping through the channels with his musket, killing Privileged sorcerers and officers.

They were both Adrans, foreigners to this place, and the experiences Taniel wrote to her about had become a wealth of information for her own career in mercenary work on this blasted continent.

"They've sent us enough keelboats for the infantry only," a voice suddenly said.

Vlora jumped, reaching to hide the letters, but stopped herself. It was only Olem, and there were no secrets between them. "And what do we do with our dragoons and cuirassiers?"

Olem crushed the butt of his cigarette under his boot, peering at the letters in her lap. "I'll have Major Gustar bring them along. It'll take them about a week longer to arrive in Landfall, so let's hope we don't need them sooner. Are those Taniel's letters?"

"Yes," she said, flipping through them absently. The loss of her cavalry, even for a week, was an irritating prospect. "Looking to see if he ever mentioned any crazy Palo warriors wearing swamp dragon leathers."

"Seems like something that would have stood out," Olem said. He sat down beside her in the grass, watching as a new keelboat pulled up to load more soldiers. Behind them, Fort Samnan still smoldered.

Vlora felt a pang of nostalgia. The letters were a constant reminder of a past life—for both her *and* Olem. "I would have thought so, but I wanted to check anyway."

"Probably a good idea," Olem agreed. "The Palo liked him, didn't they?"

"He's still a damned legend, even after all this time," Vlora said, hoping she didn't sound too sour. Every mention of Taniel put her on edge. Their history had been a . . . turbulent one.

"Do you think he would have fought for Fatrastan independence if he had known the Fatrastans would go on to treat the Palo like that?" Olem asked, jerking his head toward Fort Samnan.

"Maybe. Maybe not." Vlora had some qualms about what she did for a living. But mercenary work couldn't always be choosy. "He got into that war to kill Kez. Came out of it . . ." Vlora's eyes narrowed involuntarily as she remembered the redheaded companion Taniel had brought back from his travels. "Well." She snapped the hat box shut. "Nothing useful in here, not regarding that Palo warrior anyway." She got to her feet and offered Olem a hand. "Let's go to Landfall."

CHAPTER 2

M ichel Bravis sat at the back of an empty pub, nursing a warm beer at six o'clock in the morning. Outside he could hear the local teamsters already at work hauling cotton and grain down to the docks, cursing the heat with every other breath. He wondered if there was a single person who actually *liked* summer in Landfall, but decided such a thing would be an affront against every god that ever existed.

He had spent most of his life in Landfall. He'd grown into a man during the revolution, worked the docks conning merchants and tourists during the reconstruction, and now as he approached thirty he served in the Lady Chancellor's secret police—or, as they were more widely known, the Blackhats. *I would think,* he thought to himself bitterly, *that I would have learned to head north for the summers.*

He took a long sip of beer, checking his pocket watch. Eleven minutes past. Mornings, summer, and people being late. A perfect trifecta to put him in a foul mood.

And once in a foul mood in this blasted heat, he'd stay that way for the rest of the day.

He forced a grin on his face and displayed it to the empty bar. "You don't have to be in a bad mood," he said. "Cheer up. It could be worse. You could be outside."

"Good point," he replied to himself, taking on a serious air. "Besides, we've got beer on tap in here, and the owner won't be around until noon."

"You," he said in his happy voice, draining the rest of his beer and heading behind the bar to refill his glass, "are going to get very drunk."

"Yes. Yes I am."

He often wondered what people thought when they overheard him speaking to himself. Probably that he was a mad fool. But circumstance had often found him alone as a young man, and speaking aloud helped him gather his thoughts and stave off boredom on the long, hot Fatrastan nights. Besides, in his line of work it was best to keep people at arm's length.

He was on his third beer when the door finally opened and a young man appeared. He peeked inside hesitantly, his legs braced as if to run, and then glanced over his shoulder before calling out, "Hello?"

"Yeah, I'm over here," Michel said, waving. "You're late."

"I couldn't find the place."

"Stupid excuse."

"Pardon?"

Michel held up his beer, examining the young man through the glass. Young man? A boy, more like it. Couldn't be older than sixteen, barely even a scruff of beard on his chin. He was short for his age, a little bit overweight, but with the kind of plain face that could disappear into the crowd. Not all that different from Michel, which wasn't surprising. It was, after all, the first thing the Blackhats looked for in a spy.

"A stupid excuse," Michel repeated. The young man wore high-legged trousers, a flat-cut jacket, and a scarf in the style of a poor man's cravat. The outfit was three years out of date, and it irritated Michel. "Not being able to find an address makes you look either a fool or an asshole. Both of those can come in useful at one time or another, but not as often as you'd think. Nobody likes a fool *or* an asshole, and the first thing you need to be is likable, or else you won't blend in anywhere."

The young man cast a confused glance around the bar, his eyes slightly wide as if he'd stumbled onto the lair of a crazy person. "Are you Mickle?" he asked.

"Michel," Michel corrected, putting an emphasis on the second half of the name. "Me-Kell. My name doesn't rhyme with 'pickle.'"

"Right," the young man said slowly. "I'm Dristan. Are you the guy who's supposed to teach me how to be a spy?"

"Likable people," Michel continued, ignoring the question, "are informed. They say please and thank you. They ask for directions. They are punctual. You're going to be all these things, or you're not going to be able to do your job. At best, the people you're sent to observe will reject you. At worst, they'll find out you're not who you claim to be and kill you very slowly." Michel sighed, finishing his beer and telling himself he shouldn't drink another one. "You're not a spy," he said. "You're going to be what we call a 'passive informant.' You'll become someone else, immersing yourself entirely into a life that is not your own, and leak information about unrest, crimes, and plots against the government to your handler."

Dristan looked more than a little pensive. He remained standing, uncertain of himself, still seeming like he might run at any moment.

Michel continued: "Don't dress like a lower-class dandy. It makes you memorable, and you rarely want to be memorable. Wear short trousers and a light-colored shirt. Maybe a flatcap. You can never go wrong dressing like a common laborer." Michel whirled his finger in the direction of Dristan's head. "That look you have on your face: that hesitant, nervous thing. You want to start practicing *not* making that face. It's suspicious. Now, tell me your name."

"I told you I'm Dristan."

"No," Michel said, slamming the palm of his hand on the table. Dristan jumped. "Tell me your name."

"I'm Dri..." Dristan paused. "My name is, uh, Plinnith."

He catches on quicker than most of the people I teach to do this. "Plinnith? What kind of a name is Plinnith? That's a stupid name."

"Hey, I've heard it around before!" Dristan protested.

Michel rolled his eyes. "Plinnith is a stupid name," he repeated slowly. "What kind is it?"

Dristan stared at him as if wondering what, exactly, he was asking for, before his eyes suddenly lit up. "Oh, oh! Plinnith. It's Brudanian."

"That where you're from?" Michel asked, continuing the mock interrogation.

"I'm not. My, um, my mother was Brudanian. Came from a fishing village there."

"Oh yeah? My best friend is from a fishing village in Brudania. Maybe it's the same place."

"I don't remember the name," Dristan answered.

"Oh, that's too bad. What are you doing in Landfall, Plinnith?"

"Dad was a farmer out near Redstone. He died last fall, so Mom's sent me to the capital for work."

Michel continued to fire questions at the boy, going on for almost five minutes, needling him for details that normal people wouldn't possibly ask for before he finally gave it a rest. He dropped the pretense, poured himself another beer, and said, "Not half-bad."

The boy beamed back at him.

"Not great, either," Michel continued. "I didn't believe a damned word of it."

"But you already know I'm not a farmer's son named Plinnith!" Dristan protested.

"Do I?" Michel shrugged. "You have no idea what I know. It's your job to convince me you're the person you say you are." He swirled the beer around, wishing for the thousandth time that there was a better way to do this. Kids came off the street all the time, looking to join the Blackhats. Most of them became low-level enforcers, roughing up anyone who spoke out against the Lady Chancellor. The smart ones might become political liaisons or pencil-pushers. The rest became informants, spying on the very population the Lady Chancellor governed.

Informants had the most dangerous job and got the least amount of training. What good was an informant, after all, if anyone spotted them hanging around with a known Blackhat? The best they could expect was a few days in an out-of-the-way spot with someone like Michel—an experienced informant who'd lived long enough to become a bureaucrat. People knew Michel was a Blackhat, of course. They just didn't know he'd climbed the ranks by selling out his neighbors.

"Look," Michel said. "It's all about relating to people."

"What do you mean?" Dristan asked.

"You and me, we're Kressians, right? I mean, we call ourselves Fatrastan, but even if we were born here our grandparents were born in the Nine. Follow?"

"I think?"

"Now, our grandparents might have hated each other back in the old country. Maybe yours were Kez, mine were Adran. Mortal enemies. But once they'd come over the ocean they now had something in common. So they put aside their old hatreds and now they just call themselves Fatrastans. Right?"

Dristan didn't look impressed. "I suppose..."

Michel cut him off. "They *related*. They found out what they had in common and worked together. During the revolution all of us who considered ourselves Fatrastan worked with the Palo against the Kez. Another instance of relating against a common enemy."

"But Fatrastans and Palo hate each other now."

"Sure. Because loyalties change once they're no longer convenient. Remember, informants have to blend in. The loyalties you wear on your sleeve have to match the people around you. It's a kind of theatrics, and a good actor will tell you that the best way to get into a character's head will be by relating to them, even if they're the villain. To inform on enemies of the state, you have to think like one; to become one." He made an expansive gesture. "That's spycraft, summed up."

"I thought we weren't spies."

" 'Informantcraft' isn't a word," Michel said. He squinted around the bar, scrunching his face, and considered another drink. Maybe just half a glass.

"You seem older than you look," Dristan observed.

Michel headed around the bar toward the tap. "It's because I know what I'm about. Learn confidence—or at least how to feign it—and everyone will assume you're ten years older than you really are. Helps to know your craft, too, and in this case my craft is keeping an eye on the Lady Chancellor's people." Michel put the glass up against the barrel, holding it there for several moments before opening the tap.

Dristan seemed like a good kid. He might just be smart enough to make it through a few years of spying. Michel would give him an extra day or two of training, but he'd already decided to give Silver Rose Salacia—the person who would be Dristan's handler—the thumbs-up. Unfortunately, in this line of work *toss them in the bay and hope they learn to swim* was the most efficient method of training. "What do you get out of this?" he asked, filling a second beer and sliding it down the bar to Dristan.

"I get a Rose, don't I?"

The Roses were the Blackhat badge of authority, medallions that gave them their names—an Iron or Bronze Rose indicated a low rank, Brass or Silver a mid-rank, and Gold—well, Gold Roses were the Blackhat elites, privy to all the secrets and machinations of the Fatrastan government. They ran the country on behalf of the Lady Chancellor and held the wealth of the continent in their palms. Everyone coveted the Gold Roses. Few got them.

But even getting an Iron Rose could be a huge step up for someone from the slums like Dristan. If Dristan survived a mission or two he might jump straight up to a Brass Rose.

"Other than the Rose," Michel said.

Dristan took a drink, looking down at his hands for a long moment, then said, "The Blackhats will take care of my sisters. Keep them fed, housed, out of the whorehouses. They'll take care of them even if I die, so long as I remain loyal."

Michel nodded. It was a common enough story. A lot of horrible shit was said about the Blackhats—most of it true—but they always took care of their own. "A piece of advice for you," he said. "You've got a life right now, a family, happy memories?" He held out his hand, pointing to invisible objects on his palm.

"Yeah."

"When you go into cover, you have to become someone else entirely. Don't think about your old life, not even for a second, or you may betray yourself in a weak moment. Eat, sleep, breathe, even *think* like Plinnith the farmer's son, or whoever the pit you become." He made a fist. "Take all those happy thoughts and put them into a little marble in the back corner of your brain and don't even look at it until the job is finished. I'm not an informant anymore—just a midlevel Blackhat serving at her Lady Chancellor's pleasure—but I was in your spot once. The marble trick is how I got through it."

"You were a spy—er, an informant?"

"Why do you think I'm sitting here telling you all this? I've been undercover three times, which is twice too many for someone operating in a single city. It's a miracle nobody recognized me those second and third stints. But it also means I've done this a lot, so I get a few hours to pass on my experience to somebody like you."

"Why did you do it?"

Michel considered the question for a moment. "Like you, I did it for the Rose." He looped a thumb through the cord around his neck and showed Dristan the silver medallion that dangled against his chest at all times. "I also did it for Fatrasta," he said honestly. "Because I wanted to make a difference."

"Did you make a difference?"

"When you finish your first assignment, come and find me. I'll tell you about the Powder Mage Affair." Michel looked at his half-full glass and set it on the bar, more than a little annoyed with himself. Four glasses of beer before seven in the morning was excessive, even by his standards. There was a sudden thump, bringing Michel's head around, and the door to the pub suddenly opened.

A familiar face peered in. It was a man in a black, long-sleeved shirt with a row of black buttons up the left breast and matching black trousers—the typical uniform of the Lady Chancellor's secret police. He was missing a button from his left cuff, which irritated Michel to no end. He wore a Brass Rose openly pinned to his shirt. "Agent Bravis, sir," he said.

"Son of a…Damn it, Warsim, this is a safe house. I train people here. People see you coming in here, wearing that, at this hour and…" Michel swore to himself several more times. His foul mood was just finally starting to turn for the better and Warsim had to show up and ruin his favorite safe house. "What the pit is it?"

Warsim ducked his head, grimacing. "Sorry, sir. I didn't have much of a choice. You've been summoned to the grand master's office. Fidelis Jes wants to see you."

"Why?" Michel was taken aback. He wasn't a Gold Rose. He had no dealings with the grand master. A cold sweat broke out on the back of his neck. "Me? He asked for me by name?"

"That's what I was told."

Michel pushed away his beer and desperately hoped he'd have time to sober up. Pit, he *was* sober now. Being called into the grand master's office was like being dunked in the bay. "Right. What time?"

"You have an appointment for eight fifteen."

Michel checked his watch and glanced over at Dristan. "Get out of here," he said. "Lesson canceled."

"Should I come back tomorrow?"

"No. If things work out, I'll come find you soon and we'll get you back in training."

"And if not?"

Michel double-checked his watch. The grand master. Bloody pit. "Forget we ever spoke."

CHAPTER 3

P rogress."

It was an unimposing word, and not even that particularly fun to say, but it was bandied about in the newspapers so much that you'd think it was the name of Fatrasta's new god. As if Fatrasta, a land of bickering immigrants, a twice-stolen nation of industrialized robbery, would ever spawn its own god. Landfall, the capital city of Fatrasta, would chew up a god and spit it out and it would barely make the newspapers.

Styke sat squeezed on an uncomfortable wooden bench in a narrow hallway. There were half a dozen others on the same bench—broken, beaten men who looked twenty years older than their age. They stared at the floor or the ceiling, avoiding eye contact, either praying or buried in their own desperate thoughts. Light streamed in through a high, barred window, and someone with a rickety cough hacked out their lungs in a nearby room.

On Styke's lap was a worn, four-month-old newspaper, with PROGRESS emblazoned across the front of the first page. He considered the word for several minutes and thought of ripping the paper up as a way to vent the disgust it caused in him, but it was hard enough to get a newspaper in the labor camps and he'd traded a week's tobacco ration for this one.

Instead, he produced a semi-carved piece of wood, clutching it as tightly as he could manage with his mangled left hand. With his right he began working at the wood with a small knife he'd stolen from the mess hall, thumb on the back of the blade, shaving bits off mechanically as he read.

The newspaper reported Adran mercenaries hard at work "taming the frontier." Landfall was to open three more labor camps around the city to accommodate convicts shipped over from the Nine. Riots had broken out in the Palo quarter over the public hanging of a young radical. Trade had still not normalized with Kez, despite their civil war ending six years ago.

Styke snorted. The world, as he determined from the contents of any newspaper he could get his hands on, had changed little in the ten years since his sentencing. It was still filled with the greedy, violent, poor, angry, and not much else. He shifted his attention from the paper to the carving in his hand, whittling details into the soft pine for the next several minutes.

He held his handiwork up to the morning light. It wasn't a bad little canoe, if he did say so himself. It was as long as his palm, thin and sleek, the outside covered in Palo markings. Certainly well done despite a dull knife and a crippled hand. He blew shavings off the back of his arm, then folded his newspaper and forced himself to stand, scowling as it took his right leg just a few seconds too long to obey his command.

He walked to the door leading into the courtyard and opened it a crack. Just outside waiting on the stoop was a young girl, though one might have easily mistaken her for a boy behind the mask of grime and filth that came from living in a labor camp. She was barefoot, wearing an old shirt of Styke's that had to be tied at the neck and waist to keep it from falling off. She looked like a starving sparrow with half its feathers plucked out.

"Celine," he whispered.

The girl perked up, turning her head. "Ben! You get out?" she asked excitedly.

Styke shook his head. "Haven't even gone inside yet," he responded. "Here." He slipped the canoe through the crack before a guard could notice the door was open. "It might be a couple hours."

"I'll wait."

Styke closed the door quietly and limped back to his seat, suppressing a groan as he lowered himself onto the hard bench. One of the other inmates glanced toward the door, then over at him, but quickly lowered his gaze.

Only a few minutes passed before a door opened at the far end of the hallway and a guard appeared. Styke couldn't remember his name, but he knew he'd served in the Kez army as military police back before the war. He was a big man, taller than most with forearms as big around as powder kegs. The guard looked out across the sorry lot on the bench and whirled his truncheon absently. He wore the same sunflower-yellow smocks as the other guards, a facsimile of the Fatrastan military jackets that Styke himself used to wear.

He glared at Styke. "You," he said. "Convict 10642. You're up."

Styke climbed to his feet and limped toward the guard.

"Hurry it up there," the guard said. "I haven't got all day."

I wonder, Styke thought to himself, *what you'd look like without arms.*

"Pit," the guard breathed as Styke came up beside him, "you're a big one, aren't you?"

Styke averted his gaze. He knew what kind of attention his size attracted. It was never good, not here. Guards liked to make examples of the biggest inmates to keep everyone else in line.

I could squash you like a bug. The thought came unbidden,

and Styke quickly suppressed it. No room for that kind of thinking here. He was a model inmate, and he'd continue to be until his time was done, or else he'd be here until they worked him to death. A brief memory flashed through his mind—blood-spattered gauntlets on his fists, sword in hand, belting out a lancer's hymn as he waded, unhorsed, through enemy grenadiers, each one as big as this arrogant guard. He blinked, and the vision was gone.

The guard finally took a step back and held the door open for Styke, directing him down another dusty hall with only a single window. "First door on the right."

Styke followed the instructions and soon found himself in a small, brick room. It reminded him of a confessional at a Kresim church, though instead of a wicker screen between him and the next room over, there was a thick, iron grate over the window. Above it was a sign in broad letters that said PAROLE. The room was well lit, probably so the judge could get a good look at the monster he was about to let loose on the world.

"Please sit," a voice said from behind the iron grate.

Styke sat on a low wooden stool, nervously listening to it creak beneath his bulk.

Several moments of silence followed, until Styke lifted his gaze from the floor to peer through the iron grate. He'd been through this process twice before now, and he knew the song and dance. Parole judges were simply whichever senior prison administrator had the time for you, meaning that the difference between freedom and another two years of hard labor depended heavily on whether they'd gotten up on the right side of the bed that morning.

What Styke saw on the other side of the grate made his heart sing.

"Raimy?" he asked.

Four-thumb Raimy wasn't much to look at. She was a middle-aged woman, small and unimposing, with a pair of spectacles dangling on a chain around her neck, and dressed in what passed for a smart suit in the labor camps. She was the camp accountant and quarter-master. Being one of the few inmates who could read, write, and do sums, Styke had helped her with the books on more than one occasion. He liked the quiet of her office, where Celine could play on the floor and he could stay out of trouble.

Raimy coughed. She shuffled through her papers, picked up her pencil, and promptly fumbled, letting it roll across the desk and onto the floor. Instead of retrieving it, she carefully plucked a new one from her front jacket pocket and tested the tip.

"Benjamin," she said.

"How's it going, Raimy?" he asked.

She gave him a wan smile. "Cough's bad. You know the dust on these dry days. How's your knee?"

Styke shrugged. "Hurts. Friend of mine got that cough once, back during the war. He added honey to his whiskey. Didn't clear it up completely, but it sure made him less miserable."

"I'll keep that in mind." She cleared her throat, the sound turning into a coughing fit, then shuffled through her papers once more before continuing on in a formal tone. "Convict 10642, Benjamin Styke. Your ten-year parole hearing has begun. Is there anyone to speak for you?"

Styke glanced around the tiny room. "I'm not allowed letters or outside communication, so I'm not sure if anyone even knows I'm still alive."

"I see," Raimy said. She checked a box on the paper in front of her, muttering, "no advocates," before continuing on in her formal tone. "Benjamin Styke, you were sentenced to the firing squad for disobeying orders from your superior officer during the revolution. Your sentence was reduced by the grace of the Lady Chancellor to twenty years of hard labor. Is this correct?"

"I wouldn't say reduced," Styke said, holding up his mangled hand and spreading the fingers as well as he could. "They gave it two goes before deciding it would be easier to have me dig trenches than soak up bullets."

Raimy's eyes widened and the formal tone disappeared. "Two volleys from the firing squad? I had no idea."

"That was my crime," he confirmed, lowering his hand. "And my sentence."

Raimy coughed, dropped another pencil, and fetched a new one before checking a box. "Right. Well, Mr. Styke, I've spent the last hour reviewing your case. You've gone seven years since a violent incident and five since any marks have been made against your record. Considering the, uh"—she cleared her throat—"average life span of an inmate at Sweetwallow Labor Camp is only about six years, I'd say you've done very well for yourself."

Styke found himself sitting on the edge of the stool, ignoring the protests from his bad knee as he leaned forward. "Have I been granted parole?" he breathed, not daring to show the elation growing inside him.

"I think..." Raimy was cut off by a sudden knock on the door on her side of the grate. She frowned, setting her pencil down carefully, and stood up to answer it. "One moment," she told him, then stepped outside.

Styke could hear muted voices on the other side of the room, but nothing loud enough to understand. The voices suddenly grew louder, until Raimy broke into a coughing fit. Silence followed, then Raimy came back inside the room.

She had another piece of paper in her hand, and she carefully set it flat on the table, then slid it beneath the rest of his file. She stared at the desk, one finger drumming nervously.

Styke didn't know what this meant, but it couldn't be good. He was almost falling off his stool now, and wanted to reach through the iron grate and shake her. "Parole," he said helpfully.

Raimy seemed to snap out of her reverie and looked up at him, smiling. "Ah, where was I? Yes, well, I have good news and bad news, Mr. Styke. The bad news is that I must, in good conscience, deny you parole." She continued on quickly: "The good news is that I am able to offer you a transfer to a labor camp with a less… dangerous reputation. Soft labor, as some of us like to call it." She let out a nervous chuckle, coughed, and continued: "The beds will be softer, the hours shorter, and the facilities better."

Styke stared, his heart falling. "Another labor camp?" he asked flatly. He felt in shock, as if he'd been punched in the gut. "This is my life. Do you think I care if my bed is a little softer?"

A bead of sweat rolled down Raimy's temple.

"I know you can let me out," Styke said, slapping the wall with his good hand. The sound made Raimy jump. "I know it's up to your discretion. I've kept my head down for ten years. I've taken beatings without a protest, I've starved when the gruel is thin. Bloody pit, I taught you to read after you faked your way into a job as the camp quartermaster. I thought we were friends, Raimy."

Raimy remained still. Her hands lay flat on the table, her eyes straight ahead like a deer caught in the garden. Her only movement was a violent tremble moving up and down her body. "I'm sorry," she said quietly.

"Sorry? Sorry for what?"

"I didn't know you were *that* Ben Styke."

"What do you mean by *that* Ben Styke? How many of us do you think there are?" Styke stood up, barely feeling the twinge in his knee through the anger. His head grazed the ceiling of the parole cell. For some reason, the tremble going through Raimy's body made him even angrier. They'd spent countless days together in her unguarded office, even had a few laughs together. She'd *flirted* with him. And now she was shaking, terrified, even though she was behind an iron grate? "Are we friends?" he demanded.

"Yes," Raimy squeaked.

Styke wrapped his good hand and the two working fingers of

his bad hand around the bars of the grate. He tightened his grip and, with one solid yank, ripped it out of the wall. Raimy's mouth fell open but she remained transfixed as he set the grate to one side and leaned in over her desk, fishing through her papers until he came to the last one.

It was a note on stationery from the office of the Lady Chancellor. It had three sentences:

Mad Ben Styke, formerly Colonel Styke of the Mad Lancers, is a violent murderer guilty of several war crimes. He must be denied parole. Make it convincing.

It was signed by Fidelis Jes, head of the Lady Chancellor's secret police.

Styke could hear someone yelling in the hallway. They'd heard the racket, and the yelling was soon followed by the pounding footsteps of the guards. Styke crumpled up the note and flicked it into Raimy's face. "You can stop your damned trembling, then. I don't hurt my friends."

He turned away from her, spreading his arms wide, and waited for the first guard to come through the door.

CHAPTER 4

Michel was in a tiny, out-of-the-way neighborhood called
Proctor, about a mile and a half west of the docks and
two hundred feet above them in the very center of the Landfall
Plateau. Favored by pensioned veterans and small immigrant families, Proctor wasn't a great part of town, but it wasn't a slum like
Greenfire Depths, either. Most people couldn't find it on a map,
and that made it a good place to stay out of trouble. Or in Michel's
case, keep someone else out of trouble.

Fidelis Jes wants to see you.

The words frayed Michel's nerves in a way that very few sentences could. It was just an hour after canceling his training session, and he paused to read the note Warsim had handed him. It
was on embossed stationery marked with a Platinum Rose. No
mistaking that signature. Only two people in Fatrasta had a Platinum Rose—Fidelis Jes, and the Lady Chancellor herself.

What could the grand master want with a Silver Rose? Michel
had seen Fidelis Jes on many occasions at headquarters. They'd

even exchanged a few words. But Michel had never been summoned to his office.

Perhaps, he reasoned, it was a mistake. Or perhaps he'd be meeting with someone else in the grand master's office. A niggling fear in the back of his head told him that he'd let something slip to the wrong person and he was to be brought up on charges against the state. He wanted to dismiss it as a ridiculous notion, but not even the most loyal Blackhat was beyond reproach. Surely, he decided, he'd have woken up in a cell if that were the case.

"The wrong word at the wrong time," he muttered to himself, "can lose you your head in this city."

He smiled reassuringly at his reflection in a nearby shop window. "You're a damned good Blackhat. You'll be fine."

"Says you. Look, just take care of this thing and then you can go get your face stomped in by the grand master."

He checked his pocket watch. His meeting with the grand master was in forty-five minutes. He'd want to be early but, he thought as he eyed the house across the street, there were some things more important than work, and this was one of them. It was a task he was going to leave until tonight, but depending on his talk with Fidelis Jes he might not have the opportunity. He crossed the street, taking the alleyway around to the back door, and was inside after slipping the lock with the blade of his knife.

The little house wasn't much to see. It had one room with a loft bed upstairs. The table and both chairs were covered in old penny novels. There was a rocker over by the window, empty, with a red shawl draped over the back. The air smelled strongly of lavender, likely to cover up the underlying scent of mildew. It took him only a moment to find the source of the latter—a pile of books in the corner, soaked through, with the telltale yellow streaks on the plaster above them that indicated a leaky roof.

Michel sighed and cleared away some of the books, making room for the box of food he carried under one arm. He made a quick circuit of the tiny house, noting cracks in the plaster, a second leak in the roof, and that one of the chairs was being held together by a length of tightly bound cord.

He bent over, rubbing his finger gently over a break in the front window pane, when he caught sight of a short, plump woman walking down the street. Her long, reddish-brown hair had begun to gray at the temples, and her dress was threadbare. She walked with a brisk, determined stride and held a sack stuffed with penny novels in one hand, smiling and waving at everyone she passed.

First of the month, Michel remembered. The day the bookstores put out their latest dreadfuls.

"You should say hi," he said to himself.

"To the pit with that. I don't have time."

"You're a terrible son."

"I know."

He ran to the back door, slipping out into the alley just as he heard his mother's loud greeting to her neighbors and the fumbling of a key at the front door.

He felt a wave of relief as he returned to the main road, the close call behind him. Visiting his mother inevitably led to a fight, and he didn't need that right now, not with a meeting with the grand master looming over his head.

A thought struck him. Perhaps his years of hard work had been noticed. Maybe he wasn't going to the grand master's office for punishment, but rather for a reward. He blinked through a drop of sweat that rolled into his eye, a brief fantasy playing through his head. He could be getting a promotion to Gold Rose. His friends would never buy another drink. His relations would live in big houses near the capitol.

He wouldn't have to slip his mother boxes of food because she spent her pension on penny novels.

He quashed the thought, not daring to hope, and decided to put on his best face. Whatever it was Fidelis Jes wanted, Michel would be a professional. The grand master could not be charmed or flattered. He respected power and competence. Michel couldn't offer the first. The second...well, Michel was very good at his job.

The not-so-secret headquarters of the Landfall Secret Police, known colloquially as the Millinery, was located just a few blocks down the road from the capitol building. The Millinery was an austere palace, a thoroughly modern construction of black granite with few windows on the first floor and castle-like battlements on the roof. It was the official face of the Blackhats, set up with barracks, holding cells, training yards, and offices that encompassed two whole city blocks. They even had a division just to take public complaints.

The resemblance to a regular police house was not, Michel suspected, accidental. The Lady Chancellor wanted people to trust the Blackhats.

Fat chance of that.

But public relations was not, thankfully, part of Michel's job. He entered through the wicket gate on Lindet Avenue, tipping his hat to Keln, the old gatekeeper standing just inside the door, before winding his way through the halls of the Millinery until he reached the northeast corner on the fourth floor. He dabbed the sweat from his face with a handkerchief, straightened his vest, and entered the offices of Fidelis Jes.

The grand master's offices consisted of two rooms—a small antechamber with a desk and waiting chairs, and a much larger office behind it, the double doors open to reveal a brightly lit room, decorated with colorful Kressian murals and furnished with mahogany furniture. The mahogany didn't surprise him—Fidelis Jes struck him as a mahogany sort of man—but the colors and light certainly did. Michel had expected something far more dour for the offices of a man who, among his many titles, was counted as the master of assassins.

"Michel Bravis here to see the grand master," he said to the secretary.

The secretary was a middle-aged woman with delicate, elfin features, short black hair, and excellent posture. She smiled at Michel from behind her desk and he sought to remember her name. Dellina. That was it. A Starlish who'd been with Fidelis Jes since just after the war. Jes's only confidante, other than the Lady Chancellor herself. Michel wondered how many state secrets Dellina had floating around in her head.

"You're his eight fifteen?" Dellina asked.

"That's right," Michel responded. "Michel Bravis."

"Of course." Dellina beamed in that warm but oddly condescending way that only secretaries could manage. "Agent Bravis. Thank you so much for coming in on such short notice. The grand master is running just a little bit late today, so if you have any morning appointments I can have a messenger at your disposal."

Michel frowned. "For what?"

"To delay any other appointments you may have. For your meeting with the grand master."

"Oh! Of course. No, that won't be necessary."

"Very good. You can have a seat just over there."

Michel had barely dropped into a chair and begun an examination of the room when the door burst open and Fidelis Jes strode through it. Michel leapt to his feet, hands behind his back, shoulders squared at attention. Jes didn't seem to notice. He was wearing a pair of formfitting trousers and a flowing white shirt, most of the buttons undone, his clothes soaked through with sweat.

"You're late, sir," Dellina said in a disapproving tone.

Jes flipped a hand dismissively. "Construction," he said. "My normal route has been blocked off by a new series of public tenements Lindet has going in. Make a note for me to skip Hawthdun Street tomorrow."

"Of course, sir. Your three eight o'clocks and your eight fifteen are all waiting, sir."

Fidelis Jes was often referred to as an ideal specimen of human fitness by the city's gossip columns and Michel could find no argument against it. Jes had a finely chiseled chest, shoulders and arms to match, and legs that would make an athlete weep. He was supposedly in his forties but didn't look a day over thirty, with refined cheekbones that gave him a haughty, memorable face. Rumor had it that Jes jogged around the base of the Landfall Plateau every single morning. Michel had never seen him jogging personally and assumed it was some kind of in-joke among the Gold Roses. Yet here he was, soaked with sweat, first thing in the morning.

Jes entered his office and closed the doors behind him. His voice came out muffled. "Who the pit is that?"

"That's your eight fifteen, sir. Michel Bravis. He's the Silver Rose you told me to fetch."

"Right." The following silence was punctuated by a muffled curse, then the doors sprang open. Jes's face was washed, dark brown hair slicked black, and he had changed into an identical, but clean, outfit. He buckled on a belt with a smallsword. "Where are my eight o'clocks?"

"In the courtyard, sir," Dellina answered.

Jes strode over to Michel, who found his throat suddenly very dry as the grand master examined him first from one side, then another. "Bravis," Jes said, emphasizing the "B." "Come with me."

Without another word, he strode out of the room. Feeling slightly alarmed, Michel glanced at Dellina, who gave him an apologetic smile and hurried after her master. "We're normally much more organized," she said as she passed. "But the Lady Chancellor's construction!"

Michel ran after the two, catching up as they descended to the third floor. Fidelis Jes walked with his head cocked to one side, only answering with a grunted yes or no while Dellina whispered in his ear. They reached the main floor and headed out into the courtyard, where Dellina hurried across to three men waiting in the morning sun. All three held smallswords, and Michel suddenly knew what Jes's eight o'clock appointments were. His stomach clenched.

"I'm so sorry," he heard Dellina saying to the three men. "There was construction this morning on the grand master's run and it's resulted in a delay. You have our deepest apologies." She left the three standing there, looking angry and perplexed, and returned to Jes. "The one on the right is the son of a wool merchant. Says you slept with his wife last week."

"Did I?"

"Yes. The one on the left says you ordered the execution of his brother. I can't find any records under the name but he claims it's true. I have no idea who the Palo in the middle is. Says he just wants a good fight."

In Michel's experience, everyone had at least one peculiarity. Powerful people tended to have more extreme peculiarities because of their wealth. Some of them were hidden, some out in the open. Fidelis Jes's was extremely public; even advertised. He had a standing invitation for anyone to try to kill him in single combat. No sorcery, no guns, no quarter. Michel forced himself to breathe slowly as he watched, feeling like he was in some kind of farcical play. He knew about the grand master's appointments, of course. He'd just never seen one personally.

Jogging aside, it was said that Fidelis Jes had not truly started his day until he'd had a cup of coffee and killed a man.

"Right," Jes said sharply. "I'm already behind schedule." Jes strode toward the three men, pointing at each in succession with his sword. "You first, you second, you third." The last word was barely out of his mouth when he leapt at the first combatant. They crossed swords once and Jes's blade tore out his throat. Jes was on the second combatant in two strides, and stabbed him through the heart before he'd even raised his sword.

The third combatant, the Palo, watched the other two fights, his eyes on Jes's footwork. He intercepted the grand master before the second fighter had even hit the ground and Jes fell back several steps. They crossed swords almost a dozen times before Jes disarmed him, stabbed him once in the stomach, then discarded his own sword and wrapped his fingers around his throat, driving the Palo to his knees. The Palo died of strangulation before he even had the chance to bleed out. Michel let out a sigh, not even realizing he'd been holding his breath, and hoped the queasiness he felt didn't show on his face.

Dellina handed Jes a handkerchief. "Well done, sir."

Jes dabbed his forehead, then cleaned his sword as a pair of men emerged from the other side of the courtyard and began loading the bodies into a wheelbarrow. "The Palo was pretty good."

"He held up well," Dellina agreed.

"Find out where the pit a Palo learned to duel like a Kressian. Those savages shouldn't have access to dueling lessons."

"Of course, sir."

"What time is it?"

Dellina checked a pocket watch. "Eight thirteen, sir. Here's your coffee," she said, taking a porcelain cup off the tray of a servant.

"Excellent. Ahead of schedule. Tell me when it's eight fifteen." Jes closed his eyes, head back slightly, and sipped his coffee with some relish.

Michel had no choice but to wait, still at attention, sweat trickling down the small of his back. He watched the third body—the one belonging to the Palo—as it was loaded onto the others on the wheelbarrow. The cobbles were slick with blood, and he couldn't help but wonder just how many men Fidelis Jes had murdered in such a fashion. Hundreds. Perhaps thousands. Was there a purpose to it, other than to show that he could?

Maybe he was going for a record.

Three murders in just a handful of seconds, and Jes seemed barely winded. *Everyone* feared Fidelis Jes. He was the Lady Chancellor's hand of vengeance, perhaps the most dangerous man in all of Fatrasta. And that was without even considering the secret police at his beck and call. Michel was used to the threat of violence hanging over his head; when he was undercover there was always the risk of being discovered, even tortured and killed. But there was almost always a way out, through charm or force or guile. Staring down the tip of Fidelis Jes's sword seemed as inevitable as a guillotine blade and that, to Michel, was infinitely more terrifying.

He said a little prayer to whatever god might be listening that he would never find himself in such a situation.

"It's eight fifteen, sir," Dellina said.

Fidelis Jes handed off his coffee cup. "Bravis, was it?"

"Yes," Michel said.

"Where do I know that name?"

"The Powder Mage Affair," Dellina said. "Two years ago."

Michel stiffened. Jes raised one eyebrow, and Michel felt like he'd just been reappraised. "That's right," Jes said. "Our informant. Did that end satisfactorily?"

"Very, sir," Dellina answered.

The wheelbarrow of corpses disappeared down a side path. Michel couldn't help but glance in that direction, and suddenly Jes was standing beside him, face close enough that Michel could feel his breath.

"Squeamish?" Jes asked.

Michel swallowed. "I'm a spy, sir. If I have to kill someone it means I haven't been careful enough."

"Have you ever had to?" Jes asked.

Michel hesitated. "No, sir."

"You will. What's your current assignment, Agent Bravis?"

"I'm training informants, sir."

"Cancel anything you have on your schedule." Jes snapped his fingers, and Dellina handed him a pamphlet, which he immediately passed to Michel. "Do you know what this is?"

The pamphlet was printed on the same cheap paper as a penny novel, but only a dozen or so pages thick. There was no printer's mark, nothing on the cover but the words SINS OF EMPIRE printed in large, blocky letters. It looked entirely unremarkable, like any of the hundreds of pamphlets filled with humor, news, gossip, or religion that circulated around Landfall on a daily basis. Michel flipped through it idly. "I'm familiar with the concept of a pamphlet, sir. But not this one in particular."

"You will be. My people tell me that within the next few days these are going to be everywhere. Over a hundred thousand of them were printed in the last week and we expect to see them flooding the streets."

Michel found himself holding his breath again. Pamphlets should be handled by the propagandists. He was a spy. "I'm not sure I understand, sir."

"It's the worst kind of garbage," Jes said, sneering at the pamphlet like it had just insulted his mother. "It claims to spell out all the crimes of our beloved Lady Chancellor, dragging her name through the mud. It puts forth that she is a dictator, a madwoman bent on forcing a new empire on this part of the world. Leftist drivel."

"Have we tracked down who printed them, sir?"

"We have. They were printed by a number of companies across Landfall, each of them believing they were working independently on a secret counterespionage project for the Lady Chancellor herself."

Michel could barely contain his shock. "It's antigovernment propaganda. How could they possibly think they were working for us?"

"In your line of work, Agent Bravis, how many people openly question the Blackhats?"

"None, sir."

"Yes, well. The companies were all hired at the same time, by different agents, each of them carrying an Iron Rose."

Michel's breath caught in his throat. The Roses were considered sacrosanct. As an organization, the Blackhats would tolerate all sorts of crime and corruption around the capital, as long as it didn't impede government business. But when it came to the Roses—nobody pretended to have a Rose who didn't earn it. "Does the public know about this?"

"We're burying the use of the Roses underneath our public investigation," Dellina said. "As well as providing plenty of our own propaganda. We've already lined up a scapegoat—a foreign businessman who will be shown to have printed the pamphlets as a badly timed prank. He'll be 'caught' within the week, fined, and deported, and then we'll gather all of the pamphlets as they hit the street."

"That seems wise."

"I'm glad you approve," Fidelis Jes said sarcastically. "I don't care much about the propaganda. As far as the fate of the nation goes, one piece of antigovernment propaganda, no matter how annoying, is not going to bring down the Lady Chancellor. However, I will not stand by and allow some leftist upstart to use Iron Roses to spread lies. That's why you're here, Agent Bravis. While our public investigation parades around a decoy, you're going to find out where those Iron Roses came from—fifteen in all. If they were forged, stolen, bought, or if they genuinely belong to one of our own people involved in a plot, I want to know and I want to know quickly."

Michel tried to wrap his head around all this information. The pamphlet, it seemed, was inconsequential. Fifteen Iron Roses, though... "Does the Lady Chancellor know?"

"I would rather she not," Fidelis Jes said. "You're no doubt wondering why I chose you, Agent Bravis. We have several skilled investigators within the Blackhats, but they all come from police backgrounds. They're used to operating in the public eye. Their actions are watched by the papers and enemy spies. Few people outside this office know how you rose to your rank. No one has their eyes on you. You can—and in fact are trained to—track down information without anyone else finding out."

Fidelis Jes exchanged a glance with his secretary and continued. "What's more, Dellina keeps a list. It contains the names of several young, ambitious Blackhats with bright futures. They must be intelligent, preferably self-taught, without many friends or family members. People whose loyalty is unquestioned, yet haven't risen high enough through the ranks that they aren't expendable. Your name is on that list and because your grandmother was a Palo you may be able to move in circles that our other agents cannot."

Michel flinched at the reminder about his heritage. Nobody liked a mixed-blood, and it wasn't something he advertised. "I see." Beyond his racial background, there were a lot of nice words in that statement. The only one that he really paid any mind was "expendable." And he didn't like it one bit. "I'll find the Iron Roses, sir."

"You had better." Fidelis Jes nodded to Dellina, who stepped forward to hand Michel a file.

"In the meantime," Dellina said, "we have another light assignment for you. We want as few people to know about our internal investigation as possible so this is something else that will let you snoop around without raising much suspicion. We've recalled a nearby mercenary company from work on the frontier in order to take care of some business in Greenfire Depths. Do you know about Lady Flint?"

"The powder mage?" Michel asked.

"Yes. It's her company. You'll be her Blackhat liaison."

Michel flipped through the file. Another powder mage. Just great. Two years ago he'd been an informant in central Landfall and had uncovered an assassination plot against the Lady Chancellor involving a Deliv powder mage. The discovery had earned him his Silver Rose, but now it seemed he'd been, what did the theater people call it? Typecast. Michel snorted. At least this time he and the powder mage were on the same side. "I've heard incredible things about her."

"She's an arrogant bitch," Fidelis Jes said, waving his hand in dismissal. "She thinks of herself as a principled mercenary, as if such a thing exists. Turn her loose on Greenfire Depths and we'll see how principled she feels after putting down a real Palo riot. The insurrections she's fought on the frontier will seem like a weekend stroll."

"Of course, sir."

"She'll be here this afternoon," Dellina said kindly. "Keep in touch with her, but remember your primary assignment."

Michel glanced down at the copy of *Sins of Empire* in his hand. "I'll get started right away."

"Very good," Fidelis Jes said. "Dellina?"

"Eight twenty-two, sir. You have breakfast with the Lady Chancellor in eighteen minutes."

Jes suddenly seemed to notice he was still carrying the bloody handkerchief he'd used to clean his sword. He discarded it, looking Michel up and down once more as if to assess whether he was really up to the job. His expression was not promising. "I have high hopes for you, Agent Bravis. If you succeed, you will have earned my gratitude. I'm sure you know how valuable that is. If you fail..." He trailed off and strode inside, followed by Dellina, leaving Michel in the courtyard with a bloody handkerchief and a small Palo janitor scrubbing crimson off the cobbles.

Michel closed his eyes, forcing himself to ignore the bald threat. "Think positive," he muttered, slapping the pamphlet against his open palm, reading the title over and over again. *Sins of Empire*. "Find the Roses and make my career."

"Or," he countered, "don't find them, and wind up a spot on the cobbles over there."

"He wouldn't actually kill me for a failure."

"You so sure of that?"

Michel didn't argue that point. "I could earn my Gold Rose."

"Maybe," he responded, his own voice a little too ominous.

He stuffed *Sins of Empire* into his back pocket and headed in the opposite direction across the courtyard, sidestepping the janitor and his work. "Well," he said to himself, "if I do fail, at least the consequences will be quick."

CHAPTER 5

Styke lay on his back on the floor, staring at the cracked plaster ceiling of the labor camp holding cell. Everything hurt. He rolled over with a groan, hacking up a wad of phlegm and blood and spitting it on the floor. He couldn't remember the last time he'd been given that good a working over. It had been three hours since they'd finished the beating and thrown him in here, but it felt like a lifetime.

Somewhere nearby, a frantically gathered group of labor camp officials would convene to decide what to do with him. They'd circulate that note from the Lady Chancellor's office, trying to read between the lines, wondering if they were supposed to keep him alive or if they could get away with finishing the job the military had started with a firing squad ten years ago.

Styke tried to remember if he'd killed anyone after the parole hearing. The whole fight was a bit hazy—screams, swinging truncheons, lashing fists. He'd kept his head enough not to draw his whittling knife—which they'd now confiscated—but he remembered breaking at least a few arms. He'd gone into the fight angry, and it was hard to keep his head when he was angry.

If he'd murdered a guard or two, he'd swing from the gallows by sunup regardless of whether the Lady Chancellor wanted him left alive or not.

He wanted to be angry with himself, but couldn't even muster the energy for that anymore. Five years since he'd last spoken back to a guard. Seven since he'd swung a fist, and eight since he'd tried to escape. All that in the vain hope that they'd let him walk after a parole hearing. He'd spend the next six months in the hole, for sure, and after that it would take years before he got any privileges back.

He sat up. To pit with sitting in the hole. What was going to happen to Celine? Her dad was dead, sucked under while digging ditches in the marshes. Styke was all she had. Without him, she'd be meat for the guards and inmates. She wouldn't last the season.

"Eight guards beat the piss out of you, and just a few hours later you're already sitting up."

Styke's head jerked toward the front of the cell, expecting one of the guards in their yellow frocks to be waiting for his turn with a truncheon. Instead, he found a man in a black suit and top hat, cane under his arm, wearing boots shined to a mirrorlike polish.

The man was tall and thin, with the lean shoulders of a duelist. He had a distinctive, hawkish face behind a black goatee and cold blue eyes. He looked to be in his thirties. Taking his cane in one hand, he tapped the cell bars. "Most people would never wake up from a beating like that. You really are damned near unkillable, aren't you?"

Styke regarded the stranger warily. Nobody dressed that well belonged in a labor camp, and certainly not standing outside the holding cells. "You see it happen?" he asked cautiously.

"I did, actually." A half smile danced across the stranger's lips.

"Did I kill anyone?" Styke asked.

"Cracked a few heads," the man said. "But they'll all survive.

It was impressive. I'm happy to see ten years of hard labor haven't taken the fight out of you."

Styke peered closer at the stranger, once again feeling like they should know each other. "You know who I am?"

"Does that surprise you?"

"I've been officially dead for ten years. My own parole judge thought I was 'some other Ben Styke.'"

The man paced up and down the hallway outside Styke's cell, then leaned against the wall as if the dust it would leave on his expensive suit was of little consequence. "Mad Ben Styke was a hero of the revolution. The Mad Lancers were a legend." He grinned. "Besides, we've met before."

Somehow, that didn't surprise Styke. There was something vaguely familiar about him, like Styke had seen his portrait over someone's mantel. "I don't remember you."

"Gregious Tampo, Esquire," the man said with a half bow.

"A lawyer?" Styke asked. "I haven't met many lawyers."

"Not back then," Tampo said. "I was a soldier. Dragoons attached to the Thirty-Second Regiment. Defected from the Kez foreign legion when the war started."

In any other country, the word "defector" was a curse. But among the Fatrastans it was a badge of pride. Just about everyone who fought in the revolution against the Kez was a defector of some sort. Styke searched his memory, trying to find some clue that would allow him to recall this stranger. But the name meant nothing. Maybe he'd remember something once his ears stopped ringing and the pain faded. "Doesn't ring a bell. No offense."

"None taken. We only crossed paths briefly."

There was a time Styke would have embraced a fellow soldier, offered him a beer, and spent the night trading stories. Not anymore. Ghosts from the past rarely boded well in the labor camps. New inmates meant another set of someone else's problems, and new guards meant more habits and mentalities to learn. But he found himself taken with this Tampo. Soldiers had an understanding with one another that most people couldn't grasp—a bond forged by victory, violence, and even defeat.

"Well," Styke said. He touched the side of his head gingerly, then tried to stand up. The guards hadn't managed to break any bones— it took more than truncheons to crack Ben Styke—but his head swam something fierce and it took a few moments to gain his feet without collapsing. He stretched his arms out, touching either side of the cell with his fingertips, working out the kinks in his back. "Thanks for the chat. It's good to hear someone remembers my name. But you'll want to get out of here before the guards return."

"They won't be bothering us."

"They make rounds pretty often."

"A handful of krana makes a strong impression."

Styke paused his stretching and blinked through the pain behind his eyes. "Are you here to see *me*?" he asked, incredulous. One of those guards must have landed a particularly strong blow to his head. In ten years he'd not had a single visitor.

"I actually came for your parole hearing," Tampo said. He tapped his cane against the ground a few times, fiddling with the end as if annoyed with himself. "Traffic held me up, so I was ten minutes late. Arrived just in time to see your scuffle with the guards."

This gave Styke pause. "I didn't even know when my hearing would be until this morning. How did you?"

"I have friends."

Styke took a half step toward Tampo, stopping just short of the iron bars. "You're not the one who gave my parole officer that note, are you?"

Tampo scowled. "What note?"

Styke thought about telling Tampo about the note from the Lady Chancellor's office, but everything he had to say sounded awfully whiny in his head. Besides, Tampo was a stranger, and Styke had already blabbed too much. It was best to clam up and wait for judgment from the camp administrators. He paced to the other end of the cell, then back. "So you bribed the guards to get to talk with me. I'm guessing it wasn't just to chat about the war."

"No," Tampo said matter-of-factly. "It's not."

"Then what could you possibly want from me?"

"I'd like to offer you a job."

Styke threw his head back and laughed. It was cut short by a strange clicking from his jaw, and the pounding headache that accompanied it. He winced, shaking his head, then met Tampo's eye. The lawyer was still leaning against the wall, and he looked slightly put out at having been laughed at. "By the pit, you're serious."

"Of course I'm serious. You don't think I'd come all the way down to the labor camp just to make a joke with a man the world thinks is dead, do you?"

"You going to offer me a job when I get out of here?" Styke retorted. "Because that's likely to be a very long time."

"On the contrary." Tampo checked a pocket watch. "If you accept my proposal, I expect you'll be standing outside the gates of the labor camp within fifteen minutes."

"Bullshit," Styke said. Any humor or comradeship he felt toward Tampo was gone, replaced by a cold anger. Was he being mocked? Played with? Was Tampo an agent of the Lady Chancellor's, come to toy with him? This was cruel, even by her standards.

"The work won't be easy," Tampo said, as if he didn't notice the dangerous glint in Styke's eyes. "There'll be fights, killing, maybe even full-fledged battles, but I expect those are all things you're used to. I'm guessing your old wounds from the firing squad have slowed you down a little, but based on the brawl with the guards, you're still more than capable. You're still Mad Ben Styke."

Styke felt a growl rise from the back of his throat. He resisted the urge to reach through the bars and squeeze Tampo's head between his hands until it popped.

Tampo's eyebrows rose slightly and he looked Styke up and

down like one might a newly purchased horse. "Yes, more than capable. Now then, I expect to use you as a tool—a blunt instrument for my own ends, some of which may be distasteful to you. That won't be a problem, will it?"

"Get me out of here," Styke said, "and I'll kill the bloody queen of Novi if you'd like."

"Excellent. Guards!" A pair of yellow-smocked guards appeared in the hallway. "Escort Mr. Styke outside the premises, if you will. Mr. Styke, I'll attend to a few items and then meet you outside. Try not to get into any fights on the way out."

The process was over as fast as a whirlwind. Styke was led through the holding cells, marched through the labor camp, and straight toward the front gates. He walked mechanically, in a stupor, unable to believe that this was really happening. Every step he expected this to be some kind of joke, a cruel attack on his psyche—a fleeting taste of freedom that would be pulled away at the last minute.

"Ben!" a voice called, pulling him out of his stupor. He turned to see Celine matching his pace, staying well out of reach of the guards. "Ben," she said, "they said you got in a fight. I thought you were a goner."

Styke felt a knot in the back of his throat. "Wait," he told the guards, stopping and turning toward Celine. He was yanked forward.

"No waiting," one of them said. "You leave now or you don't leave at all."

"Her," he said, pointing at Celine. "She comes with me." He let himself be pulled along, unable to stop his feet from walking him toward freedom.

"The girl wasn't part of the deal," the guard said.

"She's not a convict," Styke said, hearing a note of desperation reach his voice. "Her father was a convict. He died last season. She doesn't have to stay here, she's just stuck because she came along with him. Check the records, just let her out."

"Not happening," the guard said. Styke was shoved roughly

through the front gate of the labor camp, the gate shut behind him while the guards chased Celine away from the entrance. She stopped a safe distance back, staring openmouthed at Styke, a look of despair on her face. She was a child, but she was far from stupid. She knew what this meant—the fate his presence protected her from.

"Come on," Styke said. "I'm not a begging man, but please. Just let the girl go."

The guard checked the lock on the gate, then sneered at Styke. "You broke my cousin's leg earlier today. He won't work for months. Your kid back there"—he jerked his thumb toward Celine—"won't last the week."

Styke snatched at the guard through the bars, but the man skipped back with a laugh.

"You're nothing but a killer," the guard said. "You'll be back here in a few months, once that posh asshole is finished with you. And we'll have a welcoming committee waiting."

Styke smacked his fist against the bars of the gate and retreated a safe distance to pace, eyeing the guard towers above the palisade and the muskets they held at the ready. He would tear the whole bloody camp down to get to Celine.

Tampo returned and was allowed through the gate. He held up a piece of paper that Styke recognized as the note Raimy received from the Lady Chancellor's office. "Is this the note you referenced?" he asked.

"It is," Styke said.

Tampo produced a match, lighting the edge of the paper, and letting it burn down to his fingertips before brushing away the ash. "There," he said. "As far as anyone inside is concerned, no communication was received from the Lady Chancellor's office and you were released as a free man without parole based on your exemplary record." He dusted his suit jacket off and checked the polish on his shoes, looking pleased with himself, before gesturing toward a waiting carriage. "Shall we?"

Styke shook his head.

Tampo seemed taken aback. "You leave something inside?"

"Celine," Styke whispered. The girl had disappeared, probably hiding from the guards.

"Eh?"

"Celine," Styke said. "I'm not leaving without her. There." He caught sight of her near one of the administration buildings, peeking out from behind the corner. He'd always liked her independence— she could beat up any of the camp boys her age, and could outrun even the most determined convict—but she suddenly looked vulnerable and alone. He would *not* leave her in the camp. "She comes with me."

He waited for Tampo to say no. He could see the word on the lawyer's lips as he looked back and forth between the two. Then Tampo suddenly called for a guard to open the gate. A handful of coins changed hands, and a few minutes later Styke was riding in the carriage opposite of Tampo, an arm around Celine, the girl clinging to his side. His aches and bruises seemed far away, and even his knee didn't hurt as much as usual.

He looked down at Celine. She was clutching the canoe he'd carved her in one hand, the other grasping his. He glanced across at the lawyer, silently daring him to say something about his relationship with the girl. All of the convicts and guards certainly had.

"The two of you reek," was Tampo's only comment.

"So," Styke said. "Who do you want me to kill?"

"Have you ever heard of Lady Vlora Flint?" Tampo asked.

Styke recalled a newspaper article he read awhile back about the Adran-Kez War. "She's a general in the Adran Army, isn't she?"

"That's her," Tampo said. "But she's not with the Adran Army anymore. She left Adro a few years ago when the government decided to reduce the size of the military. Took the cream of the Adran Army with her and formed the Riflejacks, a mercenary rifle company about five thousand men strong." Tampo looked out the window while he spoke. "She's recently been recalled here to Land-fall to deal with the Palo riots. She arrives this afternoon. I want you to go join her company."

"What makes you think she would let me join?"

"She will when she finds out who you are. No general worth their salt would let Mad Ben Styke walk away. Besides, they had some losses putting down Palo revolts on the frontier and they'll want to come up to full strength."

"And if she lets me in?" Styke asked.

"Get close to her."

"You want me to kill her?" Styke was already working the idea through his head. Lady Flint was a powder mage, and Styke had never fought a powder mage before. He wasn't sure if he could manage one in a fair fight. Fair seldom came into play during an assassination, though.

Tampo grinned at Styke, but the smile never touched his eyes. "On the contrary," he said. "I want you to keep her alive. For now."

Styke thought he detected a sinister note to those last two words, but he shrugged it off. No more bars, no more hard labor. He didn't even have to report for parole. He laid his big, mangled hand on the back of Celine's head, gently patting her dirty hair. For the gift of his freedom—and Celine's—he'd kill any damned person Tampo asked.

CHAPTER 6

Michel waited by the docks of Lower Landfall, watching a procession of keelboats emerge from the Hadshaw Gorge and drift lazily toward their landing site near the market. The keelboats were flat, low-in-the-water crafts with peeling paint and a line of freestanding rowers on either side of their long, cigarlike frames. The decks of each boat were awash with dark red and blue—the uniforms of the mercenaries being transported on board.

Fatrasta had a long history of getting into bed with mercenary companies, from Brudanian soldiers carving land away from the Palo in the early decades of colonization, to the more recent Wings of Adom helping the Fatrastan Revolution against the Kez. The Lady Chancellor employed dozens of mercenary companies across the continent, in addition to Fatrasta's own military. Personally, Michel didn't trust anyone whose loyalty could be bought with a stack of krana notes.

"I'm not thrilled with this," he muttered to himself.

He rolled his eyes at the inevitable answer. "You're not thrilled with much of anything these days. Lady Flint has a great reputation. You should be happy they didn't assign you to some asshole."

"She might still be an asshole. Fidelis Jes said she was an arrogant bitch."

"Fidelis Jes is..." Michel paused, lest anyone nearby overhear his one-person dialogue. "...doesn't seem to have a great opinion of most people. Remember, this is just a light assignment. Take care of this and you can find those Iron Roses."

The keelboats drifted closer, their rowers occasionally dipping into the water to control their heading in the gentle flow of the river. The first keelboat finally pulled up next to the landing and a keelboater leapt onto the bank, securing the craft to land and running out the gangplank.

Soldiers almost immediately began to disembark, lifting their packs and rifles and coming onto the shore, stopping for a stretch, forming orderly groups in what Michel could only imagine were their companies. He stood with his hands behind his back, black cap pushed forward to shield his eyes from the glare of the afternoon sun, and remained, for better or worse, mostly ignored by the arriving mercenaries. He wore his formal uniform, with the black shirt with offset buttons, and silently cursed the man who decided that the Blackhats absolutely *had* to dress in black.

He eyed the first boat, then the second, and, with growing annoyance, the third. Dozens of them would be arriving throughout the rest of the day—the number it took to transport the whole brigade of mercenaries from the Tristan Basin—and he had no interest in waiting that long out in the heat.

Michel's waning patience was rewarded as the fourth boat pulled up to the landing. He recognized the first person to walk down the gangplank from the description in the dossier the Blackhats kept on her.

Everything about Lady Vlora Flint seemed to contradict her name. She was a short, slight woman of about thirty years of age with black hair tied back beneath her bicorn hat. She had a pretty face, worn by a decade of campaigning in the sun but looking little older for it, and blue, calculating eyes. Her uniform fit her like a second skin, sharply pressed despite several days on the keelboats. One hand rested comfortably on the grip of a pistol in her belt, while the other had a thumb hooked in her belt.

Someone less informed than Michel might laugh at such an unassuming woman at the head of a company of mercenaries. And they would be in for quite a nasty surprise.

Michel mentally considered Flint's Blackhat dossier, noting how little information it contained beyond the public record. Her life, after all, was almost entirely in the public eye—from her broken engagement to Adran and Fatrastan war hero Taniel Two-shot shortly before his death in the Adran-Kez conflict, to her exit from the Adran political arena just four years ago. As a powder mage, and the adopted daughter of Field Marshal Tamas, she was about the most dyed-in-the-wool soldier one was likely to find anywhere in the world.

Michel cleared his throat. "Good afternoon, General Flint."

Flint paused a few feet off the gangplank, twisting at the waist to elicit a series of loud pops from her spine and letting out a satisfied sigh. She eyed his black cap. "Good afternoon. Do I know you?"

He showed her his Silver Rose before tucking it back into his shirt. "Michel Bravis, of her Lady Chancellor's secret police."

Flint shook his hand, squeezing it just hard enough to let him know she was in charge of the conversation but not so much as to overcompensate. He wondered if she practiced her handshake. "A Blackhat, eh? To what do I owe the pleasure?"

"Not much of a pleasure, I'm afraid," Michel said, giving her his best sympathetic smile. "I've come from the Lady Chancellor's office. I'll be your government liaison while your company is stationed here in the city."

"I see," Flint said. "Here to keep an eye on me, are you?"

"That's the short of it," Michel said. "The long of it is that I'll give you your assignments, make sure you're paid, see to the comfort of your men, and offer you the assistance of the secret police when you're in need of it."

Flint raised one eyebrow. "That's... refreshingly honest."

"I try to keep these things painless," Michel said.

"Field Marshal Tamas always said a smiling spy was no different than a rug salesman," Flint said, sniffing. "But you don't smell like cheap pomade and cologne." A smile softened the remark.

Michel rocked back and forth on the balls of his feet, keeping the grin on his face, trying to get some sort of a read on General Flint. She was known as a hard one—hence the moniker of "Flint." But her sense of humor surprised him, which among high-ranking military types was about as common as a flying horse. She certainly didn't *seem* arrogant. He'd have to keep a close eye on her.

"Landfall smells like hot shit and sweat," Michel said. "Wearing cologne does very little to help. And I buy very expensive pomade, thank you. As much as I'd love to exchange witticisms with you all afternoon, I'm afraid I am here on government business."

Flint pointed to a young man dragging a trunk off the keelboat. "Just leave it over there, Dobri. Thank you." Her attention returned to Michel. "Of course. I was a little surprised at being urgently recalled, let alone being sent keelboats for my infantry. As far as I can tell the city hasn't been burned to the ground, so what's the hurry?"

"We're understaffed," Michel said, recalling the information he'd read in the file on Lady Flint's new assignment. "There have been several Palo riots in the last couple of months that our garrison is woefully unprepared to deal with, and the number of immigrants coming into the city means the Blackhats and the regular police are terribly overtaxed."

"You just need manpower?" Lady Flint asked, seemingly taken

aback. "And it couldn't have waited a few weeks for us to finish our work in the Basin?"

Someone, somewhere, had decided they wanted Lady Flint back in the city quickly. Michel wasn't about to question his superiors. "They decided that your presence here was more important."

A figure coming off the keelboat caught the corner of Michel's eye. He didn't recognize the face, but the man's bearing, the silver star on his lapel, and the familiar way with which he fell in beside Lady Flint told Michel that this was Colonel Olem. Another Adran war hero and, if rumors were to be believed, Lady Flint's longtime lover. Olem lit a cigarette, and breathed a long trail of smoke out his nostrils while he looked Michel up and down.

Flint didn't acknowledge Olem's arrival. "So what do you have for me?"

"An arrest." Michel handed over the file he'd been given that morning.

Olem choked on the smoke from his cigarette. "You brought our entire army down here to arrest someone?" He took the file from Lady Flint's hands and flipped it open, reading furiously.

Michel turned away, looking at the soldiers unloading the keel-boats, considering his words carefully. He was simply here to pass on orders. That didn't mean he had to *like* the orders. "The Palo used to be a disorganized collection of tribes and city-states scattered across Fatrasta. They fought among themselves more than they fought the Kressians, and were never more than a minor threat to Fatrastan colonies."

"That still seems to be the case on the frontier," Flint said.

"Not in Landfall. They've become organized; focused. Freedom fighters like the Red Hand send their agents here to stir up trouble. They strike and hold protests. Their riots are planned. The Palo in Landfall are in open sedition against the Lady Chancellor's government."

"I don't like where this is going," Flint said.

Michel held up a hand. "We're not asking you to slaughter any-one in the streets. The Lady Chancellor has no interest in making war against her own people. We just need you to arrest their local leader."

"A single person?" Flint asked flatly. "I would think such an act would be within the power of the Blackhats."

Michel met her eyes. "I wish it was that simple. No one knows where she is or what she looks like. Mama Palo is a ghost. Every attempt at arresting her has ended up either a dead end or a fiasco. All we know about her is that she's an old woman and that she's united the local Palo beneath her."

"You want us to bring in someone's grandmother so you can hang her?"

"Cut off the head of the snake," Michel said. "Once Mama Palo is dead, the Palo will go back to fighting each other and the Black-hats can bring stability to the city." *At least,* he added to himself silently, *that's the theory.*

Flint chewed on this for several moments, clearly uncomfortable with the idea. She exchanged a long glance with Olem, some silent communication passing between them.

"There's a reason you called us back with a whole brigade," Olem said.

"Yes," Michel admitted. "Do you know anything about Green-fire Depths?"

"Not really," Flint said.

"It's a pit. An immense, ancient quarry on the western side of the plateau. It's almost a mile across, stuffed with old tenements, filled to the brim with Palo. Palo homes, businesses, churches. No intel-ligent Kressian enters Greenfire Depths after dark, and Blackhats will only go there in force. Mama Palo is hiding somewhere in that rat's nest and it'll take an army to find her and bring her out." It *did* seem odd to him that Fidelis Jes would bring so many soldiers into the city to arrest one person. But the situation with the Palo had gotten bad and besides, it almost seemed like Jes was hoping Lady Flint *would* start slaughtering people in the streets. Not that Michel was going to tell *her* that.

"It sounds," Flint said, "like you're asking me to invade your own city."

"The Lady Chancellor leaves the details to you," Michel said, giving Flint a tight smile. He didn't like the whole idea, but he was certainly glad it wasn't his job. "She gives you full authority to operate within the Depths—short of burning the whole thing down, of course."

"That is, unfortunately, the best way to find a needle in a haystack," Flint muttered. "Assuming we agree, what kind of support can you give us?"

"Any intelligence we have on hand. We can provide logistical support for your men—food, lodging, ammunition, et cetera. We're also willing to pay you for an entire year's contract."

"That sounds fair," Olem commented.

His input seemed enough for Flint. "All right," she said. "How long do we have?"

"A month. But the Lady Chancellor would be very pleased if you found Mama Palo before that."

"I'll need every scrap of information you have on the Depths," Flint said. "Maps, information on factions, businesses. Everything you can give me."

"It'll be done," Michel said. "We have a few agents within the Depths. I'll make introductions." He produced a small square of stationery from his pocket, handing it to Flint. "Here's my card if you need to find me. I'll check in as frequently as I can. Is there anything else I can do for you?"

Flint ran her fingers over the embossed edge of the card, frowning. "I did have one question. Have you ever heard of a Palo wearing the skin of a swamp dragon and carrying bone axes?"

"No," Michel said after a moment's consideration. It sounded familiar—a story he'd been told as a child, perhaps—but nothing sprang immediately to mind. "I don't think I've heard of that before. Any reason you ask?"

"We ran into one of them putting down the uprising at Fort Samnan. Fought like a madman, killed or wounded nearly forty of my men. I've never seen anything like it short of a powder mage or a Privileged."

Michel shrugged. It sounded like nonsense. Stories from the frontier were frequently embellished, even by otherwise levelheaded people. He preferred to let them slide without any real scrutiny. Even if they were true, his territory was Landfall and its citizens—not whatever god-awful things were lurking out there in the swamps. "I should get back to work," he said, gesturing at the business card in her hand. "Call on me if there's anything you need."

He made his good-byes and drifted through the disembarking soldiers, then across the marketplace as he forced his mind to shift from one task to another, Flint and her men already put out of his mind by the time he reached the main thoroughfare.

Lady Flint would be, he decided, left to her own devices. Finding the Iron Roses, and doing so in a sufficiently short time so as to please Fidelis Jes, was going to take all his effort. And he might have to piss a few people off to do so.

Vlora watched the Blackhat retreat toward the market street before turning to Olem.

"What did you think of that?" she asked.

Olem puffed thoughtfully on his cigarette, reading the newspaper clipping that Michel had handed Vlora. "Not a bad fellow. For a spy."

Vlora frowned after Michel. "Seemed more like a bureaucrat to me. They wouldn't waste a real spy on us, would they?"

"Definitely a spy," Olem said. "You notice his face? Plain, clean-shaven, ordinary? Think you could describe him to me right now, even though he just walked away?"

"No," Vlora said after a moment's consideration. "I couldn't."

"Nobody with such a forgettable face works for the Blackhats as a regular old pencil-pusher," Olem said. "And the Silver Rose? That's middle management. Someone his age only gets a Silver Rose if he's distinguished himself."

"I didn't know Blackhats have ranks," Vlora said.

"Iron, Bronze, Brass, Silver, and Gold. But from what I understand their ranking system is skewed. The power belongs to the Gold Roses, and then there's everyone else. It's not that dissimilar from the Riflejacks," he added with a grin. "Lady Flint is in charge, then the rest of us poor sods."

Vlora took Olem's cigarette from him, taking a long drag and blowing the smoke toward the open sea. She got her first chance to really look around at their location. They stood on the slice of land between Landfall Plateau and the bay. Behind them the Hadshaw River wound through a gorge that split the Landfall Plateau in two. Before them, the river fed into a wide, tranquil bay protected from the ocean by a mixture of natural and man-made breakers. The smell of salt rode heavily on the air and gulls cried overhead.

Farther along the inlet from the keelboat landing was the proper dock, out in deep water with immense sailing ships at moor. Directly across from it was Fort Nied, an old fortress pitted and scarred by the Fatrastan Revolution.

"Find out more about him," Vlora said. "And dig up as much information as you can about Greenfire Depths and this Mama Palo. We can only trust the Blackhats as far as their own interests, which might include censoring whatever information they give us. I want the real story."

"On it," Olem said.

"Where are our cavalry?" she asked.

"I haven't heard anything from Major Gustar, but I doubt Landfall has the stables to house a thousand horses at the spur of the moment. I'll send word to them to camp north of the city, and we'll send them supplies. They'll be nearby."

Vlora wanted *all* her men here, but she'd have to make do with the infantry. She was suddenly nervous, the corner of her eye twitching like it did when an uncertain battle lay before her. "I don't want any surprises." She pressed a palm to her eye. "Also look into getting us a few hundred men to replace the losses we took in the Tristan Basin. I'd prefer Adrans."

"Will do."

"Thank you." She let a concerned look cross her face, feeling vulnerable, and turned toward Olem. "Tell me I haven't just put us on a powder keg and lit the fuse."

"You haven't just put us on a powder keg and lit the fuse," Olem said.

"Are you lying to me?"

Olem seemed thoughtful for a moment, turning himself away from the incoming sea breeze to light another cigarette. "More or less," he said.

"That's not at all reassuring."

CHAPTER 7

S tyke turned his face away from the street, studiously examining the table of trinkets in the market stall in front of him to avoid attracting the attention of a passing Blackhat. Styke remained hunched over, the brim of his hat pulled down to obscure his face, until long after the Blackhat disappeared into the crowd, before turning back and watching the Adran mercenaries unload their cargo off the keelboats.

Just an hour ago he'd managed to find an old newspaper article about the Riflejacks that gave him more information than Tampo's brief. The Riflejacks started off as Field Marshal Tamas's personal bodyguard during the Adran-Kez War, turning into a full brigade of picked men by the end of the conflict. When the Adran government decided to reduce the size of the army, General Flint offered them all a job working as mercenaries and they followed her out of the country, almost to a man.

Styke searched the faces of the Riflejacks, examining their body language, studying their uniforms and weapons, and found himself impressed. These were killers. Real soldiers. The men who spat in the Kez king's face and threw the Grand Army out of Adro ten years ago.

And Styke had to figure out a way to join them.

He remembered working with real soldiers. The feel of lances at his back, the smell of powder from a coordinated carbine volley, and then the rush as he dug his heels into Deshner's sides and three hundred armored cavalry slammed into an enemy flank. The enemy broke—they always broke—and the Mad Lancers had ridden their officers down like dogs.

He made a mental note of the two that the Blackhat had been speaking with and guessed they were General Flint and Colonel Olem. Even at this distance his nose twitched. Styke had a Knack—a minor sorcery—that allowed him to smell magic. It didn't help him one ounce in the work camp because anyone with useful sorcery tended to avoid being sent to the camps. The reek of sulfur about her told him she was a powder mage as clear as the smell of shit helped him find the outhouse.

Olem had a smell to him, too, though it was less pronounced. He smelled like rich, freshly turned soil. He, like Styke, also had a Knack. Styke would have to find out what it was.

"Hey," a voice said, "you just going to stand there blocking up my stall or you going to buy anything?"

Styke turned to find a red-faced man with a long beard and an apron looking up at him from behind one of the market tables. His stall was decked out with herbs, roots, mushrooms, and truffles. The sign over the stall said OPENHIEM'S APOTHECARY.

"Celine," Styke said absently, glancing over his shoulder. He found the girl two stalls down, eyeing a bin of apples, pacing back and forth in front of the fruit seller. She was wearing a new outfit: trousers and a shirt and hat. An old woman at the local bathhouse had scraped the grime from her face and arms. She almost looked like a real child now, and not that feral thing he'd adopted in the camp.

The fruit seller was watching her, too. He made a shooing motion with one hand, clearly expecting her to steal something. In response, Celine took a few steps closer to the apples, stuck her tongue out, and plucked a cloth doll off the table of the next vendor over. The fruit vendor seemed so surprised at the change in direction that Celine had already faded into the afternoon crowd before he could open his mouth.

"Hey, big man. You hear me?"

Styke's attention returned to the apothecary in front of him. He eyed the roots, then pointed at one of them. "Is that horngum?"

"It is," the apothecary said. His tone shifted from annoyed vendor to salesman in an instant as he looked over Styke's facial scars and obvious limp. "The best thing out there for pains and aches of all kind."

"Is it fresh?"

"Of course it's fresh!" the apothecary said indignantly.

Like Celine, Styke had cleaned himself up. His beard was gone, his hair cut, body washed and massaged. A new set of clothes clung tightly to his frame, the biggest the tailor had ready-made, and three more sets had been measured and marked out for him to retrieve later in the week. He felt like a new man—and at the same time vulnerable; a naked cur, ready to be called out by the city police at any moment and rushed back to the work camps.

He dug into his pocket for the roll of krana bills Tampo had given him. A few moments of haggling, and the apothecary handed him the entire root.

"Now then, you'll want to boil down a small portion into a tea..." the apothecary began.

Styke took a thumb-sized bite and began to chew. The horngum tasted sour, like a dozen lemons jammed into his mouth all at once.

He felt his cheek twitch and the right side of his jaw went completely numb. Slowly, his body began to have a pleasant tingle and he found that when he told his leg to move it obeyed him almost immediately. The apothecary looked on in horror.

"Yup," Styke said. "Definitely fresh."

He found Celine back around the side of the next stall over, eyeing a brand-new dress laid out by a seamstress. Styke took her by the arm, noting the pilfered doll in her pocket, and pulled her away from the seamstress's stall. "You can steal," he said quietly, "but if they catch you they'll put you back in the work camps. And I won't ask Tampo to go in for you."

Celine lifted her chin. "I don't get caught. My dad was the best thief in Landfall."

"And how did that work out for him?"

Celine cast him a sullen, sidelong glance. "He got sucked into the swamp at the work camp."

"Right. Remember that," Styke said. He put his hat on her, then grabbed her by the back of the shirt with his good hand and lifted her onto his shoulder, letting her settle in comfortably before he continued. He wondered briefly how they looked—a little girl in boy's clothing, balanced on the shoulder of a giant, her skinny arm wrapped around his scarred head.

"You remember this city?" he asked.

"Yes," Celine said matter-of-factly. "Dad was only in the camps for six months before he drowned. We used to go all over the boroughs, so I know each of them pretty well."

"Good. It's been a long time since I was here last. The city feels different...like an old saddle I sold long ago and have only now bought back. The market"—he gestured around him—"it's all the same." He pointed to the slanting, eastern face of the plateau. "That road there is new; so is that one. The main road over to the foundries has been widened. Everything is...wrong."

"My dad used to say it was progress. The Lady Chancellor ripping up the old buildings and putting in new ones, whole blocks at a time."

"Don't say that word."

"What word?"

"Progress. Say 'shit,' 'damn,' or 'pit' all you want, but 'progress' is a curse around me. Such a stupid bloody word." Styke shook his head, feeling Celine tighten her grip momentarily. "Lindet's trying to rebuild the city in her image, but it's all on the surface—the front half. She put any new tenements up in Greenfire Depths?"

"No," Celine said.

"Didn't think so." Styke pictured the map of the city he kept in his head. Landfall had started as a fort atop the cracked Landfall Plateau—an oblong chunk of rock that rose almost two hundred feet above the floodplains of Fatrasta's eastern coast. During the Kez reign, the town had overfilled the plateau and spread across the plains from Novi's Arm in the south to the labor camps in the marshes to the north. The "front half," as he liked to call it, included the bay, docks, industrial center, and the bourgeoisie tenements and government buildings up on the plateau. The "back half" consisted of several miles of slums, stretching toward the west, and including the old Dynize quarry known as Greenfire Depths.

Nobody cared about Greenfire Depths back during the war, and nobody cared about it now. Some things never changed.

Styke caught sight of a small building in the corner of the marketplace. Smoke belched from several stacks on the roof and a sign read FLES AND FLES FINE BLADES.

"You remember what you used to do in the camp?" Styke asked Celine.

"Keep an eye out?"

"Yeah. You're going to have to do that from now on, except this time it's going to be harder. We're not in the camp anymore, and not everyone is an enemy."

"Shouldn't that make it easier?"

"You'd think, but out here you don't know who your friends or enemies are. Every person you see has the potential to be either one, and you'll have to judge for yourself which they are."

"Dad always said never to trust anyone."

"Gotta trust some people some of the time. Otherwise what's the use of living?"

"So how will I know if someone is my friend?" Celine asked.

Styke lifted her off his shoulder as they drew closer to the sword vendor, setting her on the ground beside him. "For now, I'll let you know. But this is a big world. I won't be able to tell you all the time. You'll have to trust your instincts."

"I can do it," Celine said, lifting her chin proudly.

Styke patted her on the back of the head. "I know. Come on, we're going in here. I've got to see someone."

"Are they a friend or an enemy?" Celine asked.

Styke paused, considering this for a moment. "A friend. I hope."

The blade vendor had a long, narrow stall facing the market street, behind which several red-faced youths stood wearing smith's aprons, hawking swords and knives of all kinds to the passing crowd. Styke sidled up to the table and looked over it, eyeing the quality of the knives, looking for something that could fit his size. Nothing stood out to him. "Since when does Fles and Fles take on apprentices?" he asked.

Two of the boys behind the table glanced at each other. "Seven, maybe eight years now," the older one said.

And some things, Styke told himself silently, *change a lot.* "I'm looking for Ibana ja Fles."

"Ibana isn't here," the older boy said. "She went to Redstone a few weeks ago for an ore shipment."

Styke let out something between an annoyed groan and a sigh of relief. He wasn't entirely sure himself which it was. "How about the Old Man? He still kicking around here?"

"Mr. Fles is in the back."

"Right." Styke walked around the table and ducked into the building behind it, ignoring the protests of the apprentices. Celine followed on his heels.

The inside of the foundry was well lit by large windows and strategically placed gaps in the roof. Four bellows worked at once, feeding four fires, each of them attended by a trio of apprentices. The clang of hammers on steel was deafening as he passed through the center of the foundry and approached a curtain near the back. He pulled it aside to reveal a small workbench.

An old man, less than five feet tall with sagging cheeks and arms folded across his chest, sat rocking back in his chair, feet on the workbench, long mustache trembling as he snored loudly enough to compete with the hammers. Styke watched him for a moment, feeling an involuntary smile tug at the corner of his mouth.

There was a time he thought he'd never see Old Man Fles again.

Styke held his finger up to his lips, motioning to Celine to come inside the curtained-off workshop and close the curtain, then held his hands right next to the Old Man's left ear. He clapped them together as hard as he could, hard enough to make his crippled hand throb painfully.

Old Man Fles leapt halfway out of his chair, arms windmilling, and would have gone over backward had Styke not caught him.

"By Kresimir," Fles swore, "who the...what the...why are you back here? Can't you see important work is being done? I will summon my...I will summon...my..." Fles regained his composure slowly, his eyes focusing on Styke. He searched his apron pockets for a pair of spectacles and perched them on the bridge of his nose. "Benjamin?" he asked incredulously. "Benjamin Styke?"

"That's right," Styke said.

Fles blinked at him for several moments. His mouth opened, then closed, and slowly the surprised expression slid off his face, replaced by annoyance—like he was staring at a barely tolerated dog he thought had run off for good. "I thought you were dead."

"They tried," Styke said. "Twice."

"By Kresimir," Fles breathed. "Where have you been?"

"Work camps."

"Last we heard you'd been put up against the wall. You never wrote. Ibana is going to kill you." The three sentences came out in a quick tumble of words.

"I was. And they wouldn't let me."

"Won't matter to her, you know."

Styke sighed. "I know."

Fles's eyes went to Celine. "Who's this?"

"My associate, Celine. Celine, this is Old Man Fles. He's the best swordmaker in Fatrasta."

"Don't short me, boy," Fles said. "I'm the best in the world."

Celine seemed more than a little skeptical. "You're a blacksmith?" she asked.

"A blacksmith?" Fles huffed. "Do I look like I make horseshoes and trinkets? I deal death here, little lady. The finest death in all the lands. Here, take a look at this." Fles reached across his workbench, plucking a sword off the wall. It was a smallsword, simple and elegant, with a silver guard and gold rivets on the pommel. He held it beneath Celine's nose. "This is my latest. Took me eight months."

"It doesn't look very fancy," Celine said.

"Fancy has nothing to do with a good sword," Fles countered. "Doesn't matter if you're a child or seven feet tall—the balance on this sword is perfect. It weighs next to nothing, without sacrificing momentum. There's magic in this blade."

"It's also worth a prince's ransom," Styke said. "Three kings of the Nine all carry Fles blades."

"Two," Fles countered. "Field Marshal Tamas put Manhouch's head in a basket, in case you hadn't heard."

"Ten years ago," Styke said. "I did get the *occasional* newspaper."

"Just two kings now," Fles repeated with a sigh, putting the sword back on its peg.

Styke stared at the weapon for a few moments, barely hearing the clang of the hammers on anvils out in the foundry. He'd spent many years in this little workshop and his brain seemed to instinctively tune the hammers out. There were a lot of memories here, both good and bad. He steeled himself, forcing them all to the back of his head.

"So, you're out of the work camps and still alive? What are you doing here, then? Ibana's gone to Redstone, if you're looking for her."

"I need a blade," Styke said. "Something cheaper than that."

"As if I'd give you one of mine," Fles scoffed. "It'd be like a toothpick to you." He sucked on his front teeth for a moment, tapping the side of his head. "Ah, I seem to remember something…" He bent beneath the workbench, rummaging through several boxes before removing a long bundle. He withdrew the wrappings, tossing them on the workbench, and proudly held a knife out to Styke. "No idea why she kept it," he said. "It's far from her best work."

It was called a "boz" knife, after the inventor, but most people would find the "knife" part an understatement. It had a fixed blade and was thirty-two inches from the slightly hooked, double-bladed tip to the end of the worn, ironwood handle. It had a steel crosspiece, with a dried bit of something—probably a Kez officer's blood—still caught in the joint. Carved into the bottom of the handle was a craftsman's mark with the name "Fles." Styke removed the blade from its old leather sheath, examined it for rust or misuse—it was freshly sharpened and oiled—and kissed the craftsman's mark before fastening the sheath to his belt.

He swallowed a lump in his throat. It wasn't just an enormous knife, big even for the boz style. It was *his* knife.

Styke let Fles's complaint go by without comment and turned his attentions to the wrappings the knife had been stored in. On closer examination, it was a faded yellow cavalryman's jacket, with a colonel's star still pinned to one lapel. One of the pockets was heavy, and he turned out a silver necklace with a big, heavy ring hanging from the end—on the face of the ring was a skull the size of his thumb, run through with a lance, and a flag fluttering around it. The sigil of the Mad Lancers. Styke licked his lips, feeling a moment of reverence as he unhooked the chain and slid the ring over his right ring finger. Without a word, he folded his jacket and put it under his arm.

"Take it," Fles said. "Gets some of the junk out of my workshop. Ibana is going to throw a shit fit when she finds it missing." He grinned wickedly, then let the smile slide off his face.

"Thanks," Styke said.

"She's going to kill you," Fles reiterated.

Styke ignored the warning. "You still have your ear to the ground?" he asked.

"What do you mean?"

"Information."

"Bah," Fles said. "I haven't traded information since the war." He eyed Styke for a few seconds, his gaze lingering on the scars. "But I'm not deaf. What are you looking for?"

Styke considered his course of action, looking at the sword hanging on the wall behind Fles. The next words out of his mouth could have serious consequences. Bringing Old Man Fles into his vendetta could get him killed, and Ibana really would kill him if he did that. But Styke needed help.

"The Blackhats," he said, "they still as powerful as they were during the war?"

Fles snorted. "And then some, over and over again. They're one of the reasons I got out of the information business. If you work in Landfall, you work for the Blackhats, and I have no interest in them. During the war they were just a bunch of thugs and spies, but now..." Fles trailed off. "You don't want to get involved with the Blackhats."

"They give you any trouble?" Styke asked.

"I pay them off every few months with a box of castoffs. Gives their midlevel bureaucrats something to brag about, having a Fles blade, without watering down my image."

Styke couldn't help but grin. Fles was getting old, but he was still as sharp as any of his swords. The grin slipped off his face as he came to his next question. "And"—he took a breath—"Fidelis Jes?"

Fles looked like he'd bitten into a lemon. "Still runs the Black-hats. Still as cruel as ever. He's in the gossip columns every couple of months for killing someone important, and he seems to revel in it."

"Lindet lets him get away with open murder?" Styke was surprised by that.

"Not quite," Fles said. "He leaves space in his schedule for at least one duel every morning. Anyone can challenge him, as long as they don't use guns or sorcery. He's hated enough that his schedule is full weeks in advance, but he never loses."

Styke's grip tightened on the butt of his knife. "You mean I could just walk in there and challenge him to a fight to the death?" That sounded incredibly too easy.

"You'd be a fool." Fles snorted. "Never challenge someone in their own territory. Besides, you look like you got run over by an army's baggage train, while Jes is more dangerous than ever." Fles waved a finger under Styke's nose. "Don't you give in to that temptation or I'll tell Ibana, and she *will* desecrate your corpse."

"I'm not a fool." Styke said, though the prospect did tempt him. "I'd much rather enjoy the startled look on his face when he wakes up in the dead of night to my hands around his throat."

"Much better thinking," Fles agreed. "But getting that chance will be next to impossible. The Blackhats deal with any sort of threat with brutal efficiency. You should stay away from the Black-hats and stay away from Fidelis Jes."

Styke considered his mission from Tampo. "I will for now," he said. "But I can't ignore them for good."

"I hope you've got a damned good reason."

"Jes tried to sabotage my parole hearing. I don't know why, but if he knew I was in the labor camps then he might be the one who put me there in the first place. And if he's not, he'll know who did. I owe him for that. And," Styke said, gesturing with his mangled hand to the deep bullet scar on his face, "for this."

"What do you need?" Fles asked quietly.

"Everything about him. His habits, his friends. I want to know where he shits and where he eats. I want to know how tight Lindet has him on a leash."

Fles's face fell a little with every word Styke uttered. He stared at Celine for a few moments, then up at Styke. "I'll see what I can do."

"Thanks," Styke said.

"Is he going to come looking for you?" Fles said.

"I don't know," Styke replied. It wasn't something that had occurred to him, but the possibility made him swear inwardly. If Fidelis Jes wanted him kept in the camps, he'd be furious if he found out Styke was released. "Maybe."

"I'll keep an ear to the ground," Fles said, "but I'll have to be damned careful about it."

Styke looked around, the workshop feeling suddenly foreign to his eyes. It had been too long. "I appreciate the help. When Ibana comes back..."

"I'll tell her to find you."

"Thanks again." Styke took Celine by the hand and slipped out from behind the curtain and toward the front of the foundry. He was deep in thought, barely noticing the apprentices who stared at him as he went by.

"Ben!" Fles called out behind him.

Styke half-turned to the old swordmaker. "Yeah?"

Fles hobbled out into the middle of the market and peered up at him, face thoughtful, and said in a low tone, "Good to see you again. Is Mad Ben Styke back to give 'em the pit?"

Styke held his jacket out at arm's length, examining it for a moment before removing the pins from the lapels. He stuffed them in his pants pocket and slipped his arms into the jacket. It still fit him, even if it was a bit loose. He rolled his shoulders, feeling a knot that he'd not known he had, disappear from his stomach. He clenched one fist, feeling the heavy lancer's ring on his finger. "He is."

CHAPTER 8

Vlora sat in a wicker chair in the yard of Willem Marsh, one of Landfall's most popular outdoor coffeehouses. The sun had set but the Landfall boardwalk remained loud, well lit, and crowded. The docks creaked with the movement of the sea while sailors fought over dice and prostitutes. Vlora sipped her coffee and stared into the crowd, waiting for the inevitable knife fight to break out.

Pit, it was good to be back in a real city again.

She felt a hand briefly squeeze her shoulder, then Olem dropped into the chair beside her, his fingers rolling a new cigarette before he'd even settled.

"Well?" she asked.

Olem smiled at her from behind a sudden cloud of smoke. It was a cool, easy smile—one she hadn't seen for months—and it made her heart skip a beat. "I found us a room," he said. "At the Angry Wart in Upper Landfall. Running hot water, nightly pig roast, and a bed we could sleep head to foot across the width."

"I intend to do very little sleeping."

Olem leaned toward her, wiggling his eyebrows. "I don't intend on sleeping, either."

Vlora rolled her eyes.

"Because of my Knack," Olem explained in mock earnestness. "I don't need sleep."

"I know!" Vlora took the cigarette from him and took a drag before handing it back. She held the smoke in for a moment, then slowly exhaled it through her nostrils. "And you know exactly what I meant."

Olem smirked. Of course he knew what she meant, the prig. "The room costs a small fortune, but I think it'll be worth—"

Vlora punched him in the shoulder. "Report, soldier."

"Right," Olem said, rubbing his shoulder. "Michel was as good as his word. He's given us an old barracks on the edge of Greenfire Depths and sent over a few hundred boxes' worth of files the Blackhats keep on Greenfire Depths and the Palo activity in the city. I've got my sharpest boys reading through it all, but it'll take them days. Even then we won't know how much they held back."

Vlora nodded, pleased at how quickly Olem had organized the effort—as well as the idea of a hot bath and a large bed. They needed alone time that was hard to get in a mercenary camp in the middle of the swamp. "Have you gotten anything out of your contacts?"

"It'll take me weeks to set up any sort of intelligence network," Olem said, puffing out his cheeks and slowly letting them deflate. "I can't decide if the Blackhats will make it easier or harder. Practically everyone in the city sells information, but most of it goes directly to them."

"Do the best you can," Vlora said, reaching over and squeezing Olem's hand. "You ask anyone about Mama Palo?"

Olem snorted. "Yeah, and everyone has a different answer. She's either an enemy of the state, a freedom fighter, or a Palo god made flesh, depending on who you ask."

Vlora felt her skin crawl. "I've dealt with enough gods for one lifetime, thank you very much." She thought briefly about the Adran-Kez War, an involuntary chill creeping down her spine. "My entire family died killing the last one we encountered."

"Well," Olem said, shifting uncomfortably in his seat. He had his own memories from the war, his own ghosts—many of them the same as hers. "I don't think Mama Palo is a god. She's clever, though. Stirs up huge amounts of trouble without ever provoking an outright battle with the Blackhats. The Palo worship her, the Blackhats despise her, and the rest of Fatrasta just hopes to stay out of the way when she and Lindet finally come to blows."

Vlora forced a chuckle. "Is Lindet pissed someone is challenging her for queen of Fatrasta?"

"Wouldn't you be?"

"I've no interest in a queendom," Vlora said, dismissing the thought with a wave. "This Mama Palo...is she really that big of a threat?"

"I won't know for sure until I get my intelligence network set up." Olem held up a hand, signaling a passing waiter, and ordered coffee. He frowned at the dark night sky. "Nobody can challenge Lindet outright. It's not a winnable fight. But it looks like Mama Palo has no intention of fighting Lindet—simply annoying her to the point of giving up."

"Giving up what, though?" Vlora asked. "What does Mama Palo want?"

"Palo rights?" Olem speculated. "Palo independence? Land, money? What does anyone want?"

Vlora pointed at Olem's chest. "Find out. It sounds like the Blackhats want us to go through Greenfire Depths kicking down doors until we find her, but you catch more flies with honey than vinegar. If we can find out Mama Palo's goals we might be able to track her down." She ticked through half-formed plans in her head, examining each one briefly before discarding it—or storing it away for further consideration later.

"You see this guy watching us?" Olem asked, lifting his chin.

Vlora took Olem's coffee from the waiter, handing it across, before following Olem's gaze. She spotted the man quickly. He stood on the other side of the café, just inside the small partition between the coffeehouse and the boardwalk. He was big—no, enormous—with thick, broad shoulders and a bent back, his head held forward like a man used to hiding his height and still over six and a half feet tall. His left cheek had an old, pitted scar and his hair was gray, his jaw large and firm.

He wore a shirt and trousers that were slightly too small for him, and an old Fatrastan cavalry jacket slightly too big. His only weapon was hooked to his belt—a boz knife longer than Vlora's arm.

He stared openly at her and Olem, only pulling his gaze away to take a coffee and newspaper from a waiter, before heading in their direction.

Vlora tensed, not sure what to expect. She was a powder mage, faster and stronger than any four people in this café, but everything about the man, from his scars and limp to the casual way people moved out of his way as he walked through the crowded café, spoke of imminent violence. She found her heart beating a little faster.

Olem shifted in his chair, spreading his legs so that his pistol could be drawn easily. "I saw him down at the keelboat landing earlier today. I thought he was watching us, but I wasn't sure until now."

"Adom," Vlora breathed, "look at the size of that knife." She brushed her hand across the hilt of her sword.

The man slowed as he approached them, looking around with a frown, before reaching over to an occupied table and gently removing the coffee cup and handing it to the startled owner. "Pardon me," he said in a deep, quiet voice, dragging the table over between the three of them, then appropriating an empty chair and dropping into it, tucking his newspaper into one pocket.

He looked around as if he had misplaced something, then tilted his head back, calling over his shoulder, "Celine!"

A little girl detached herself from the café crowd, running between tables and chairs to join them. Without a word, he scooped her up and put her in his lap. His knee bounced her absently, and the girl laid her head on the big man's chest. It was a strange image, like a lamb curling up next to a bear. Vlora found the girl almost as interesting as the man—she was dressed as a boy, a shifty, watchful look in her eye that Vlora had seen in every mirror when she was that age. She was an orphan; a street child.

Vlora removed her hand from the hilt of her sword, but remained watchful. "Can I help you?" she asked.

"Good evening," the big man said. "My name is Styke. I'm looking for a job."

Vlora glanced at Olem, who seemed more than a little bemused by the whole situation. "I'm not entirely sure you're in the right place," Vlora said.

"You're General Vlora Flint," Styke said, nodding at her and then Olem. "You're Colonel Olem. You run the Riflejack Mercenary Company. I'm looking for mercenary work. Seems like the right place."

Vlora's first reaction was annoyance. Barely five minutes into a pleasant evening with Olem, and this brute had come out of the woodwork to interrupt it. Her second inclination was suspicion—if he really wanted a job, why hadn't he approached them down at the keelboat landing?

"Styke, you said?" she asked.

"That's right."

"If you'd like, Styke, I can give you the name of my quartermaster. Meet with him tomorrow and see if you're a good fit for the company. We are hiring a few more men. But I'll warn you, mercenary work isn't kind to a cripple."

A torrent of emotions flew across Styke's face, from confusion, to hurt, to anger, to rage, all in the course of a few seconds. Vlora would have been impressed if she wasn't so busy making a mental check that her pistol was loaded. Styke shifted in his chair, the wicker creaking dangerously, and straightened his jacket as he visibly regained control of himself, squeezing the girl gently as he did. "I'm sorry," he said, "but my name's Benjamin Styke, and I'm looking for a job."

Vlora stuck her chin out. If this was a Palo or Blackhat plot of some kind, it was daft as pit. "Is that supposed to mean anything to me?" she asked.

Styke frowned at her, his eyes hard, as if the scowl would jog her memory, then he suddenly sagged. "Been too long," he muttered. "Maybe it doesn't."

The girl, Celine, fidgeted in Styke's lap and scowled at Vlora. "Ben's a killer," she declared. Styke shushed her gently.

"I'm sure," Vlora said. "Look. I don't think the Riflejacks will be a good fit for you. You look like you can handle yourself in a scrap, but we're real soldiers, not…" She trailed off, a light going on in the back of her head at the same time Olem touched her arm. "Ben Styke. Why do I know that name?"

Styke perked up, but before he could answer Olem said quietly, "Taniel's letters." He leaned across the table, peering up into Styke's face, showing the type of interest that he normally reserved for a brand-new pack of tobacco. "You're Mad Ben Styke?" he asked.

"I am," Styke said.

"I thought you were dead."

"Most do," Styke replied.

Vlora noted that Olem wasn't just attentive. He was *very* interested, like he'd just noticed a half-price sign on a beat-up supply wagon. "You were watching us down at the keelboat landing earlier. Why?"

Styke seemed taken aback. "Was just down at the market and

saw you landing. Heard you were the best mercenary company on the continent and I recently became...unemployed. So I thought it was fortuitous."

Vlora spent Olem and Styke's short exchange searching her memories, looking for the name Ben Styke. Taniel's letters talked a lot about the people he'd met during his time fighting in the Fatrastan Revolution. She grasped on to one memory in particular, a letter regarding a battle in which Taniel had met a giant of a man, a lancer wearing enchanted medieval armor, who'd ridden into a torrent of enemy grapeshot, musket fire, and sorcery to save the battle and somehow come out on the other side.

His admiring descriptions of Ben Styke had seemed a silly fancy. Until now.

"You knew Taniel Two-shot?"

Styke raised his eyebrows, seeming pleased. "I fought beside him once," he said. "Pit of a fighter. He mentioned me?"

"Gushed about you, more like," Vlora said. She leaned back, reconsidering everything that had gone through her head the last few minutes. This wasn't just some big cripple looking for an excuse for rape and pillage. This was Mad Ben Styke, one of the heroes of the Fatrastan Revolution. Celine was right. He *was* a killer. "You still a lancer?" she asked, eyeing the leg he favored with his limp.

"No," Styke said, his face hardening. "They killed my horse after the war. Took my armor. And then all this, and..." He drifted off, averting his eyes.

There was a story behind that gaze, and Vlora felt the urge to ask him about it. But there were some wounds you could ask an old soldier about and others you had to wait for him to tell. She wanted to offer him a job here and now, but she couldn't for the life of her think of what to do with him. He was in no shape to hold a line, probably not even ride a horse.

She glanced at Olem, hoping for some levelheaded advice, but

Olem was still staring at Styke like a starstruck boy. "Did you really ride down a Privileged at the Battle of Landfall?" Olem asked.

"Put my lance through his eye," Styke said, prodding a finger at his own face. "Nothing better than watching a Privileged die. They always have the stupidest looks on their faces, like how dare I murder him before he could murder me."

Olem slapped his knee, guffawing, rocking back in his chair, and took one of his pre-rolled cigarettes from his pocket, offering it to Styke.

So much for levelheaded advice.

"You know they've written books about you?" Olem asked.

Styke snorted. "Probably a bunch of bullshit."

"We're soldiers," Olem said. "It's always a bunch of bullshit. Except when it's not." He turned to Vlora, with a face like a child asking to keep the puppy he'd just brought in off the street. "I'll give him a job if you don't," he said.

"We run the same bloody company," Vlora said.

"Pit," Olem said, "I'll put him on retainer just to sit around and tell war stories. The boys would love that."

Vlora glanced at Styke out of the corner of her eye. His face had soured at the mention of war stories, and he said in a pained voice, "I'd rather be a little more useful than that."

Vlora jerked her head at Olem, pulling him away from the table, and said quietly, "What the pit are we going to do with a big cripple? Even if he can fight, our boys are infantrymen. A guy like that is a brawler. No use putting him in a line."

"We can make use of him," Olem said. "Didn't you say earlier we needed some locals to do some dirty work?"

"I don't remember saying that."

"I'm pretty sure you did," Olem insisted.

Vlora sighed. Did she have a bad feeling about this Styke, or was she just avoiding saying yes because Olem was so insistent? "If you can figure out something to do with him, then we can..." Vlora stopped, holding up her finger, and looked at Styke. "You've been around a while?" she asked.

Styke nodded.

"Do you know anything about the Palo?"

"Probably a little more than the average veteran," Styke said. "A lot of them were our allies during the war. Before all this." He gestured at the city around them.

"Do you speak their language?"

"I'm a little rusty," Styke said. "But yes. I can write it, too, in a pinch."

"Useful," Olem observed, a little too eagerly.

Vlora shot him a look to be quiet. "All right, Ben Styke," she said. "I've got a task for you. It might sound stupid but if you can dig me up an answer you've got yourself a job."

The relief was plain on Styke's face. "Yes, ma'am."

"You know anything about a Palo warrior wearing swamp dragon armor and fighting with bone axes?"

Styke leaned back in his chair, regarding his coffee for the first time and downing it in a single gulp before wiping his mouth on his sleeve. He snapped his fingers, ordered another coffee and some spiced chocolate for Celine, then looked at a point of empty air between Vlora and Olem, considering. "Stories," he said.

"What kind of stories?"

"Sounds like a dragonman—Palo warriors descended from the Dynize emperors that used to rule these lands. The Kez wiped them out sixty or seventy years ago for being such a nuisance, and they haven't been seen since. They were a fairy tale when I was a kid. 'Eat your soup or the dragonmen will take you to the swamp.' That kind of thing."

Vlora felt the hair on the back of her neck standing on end. She knew all about old stories and fairy tales, and just how true they could end up being. "One of them inflicted almost forty casualties on my men at Fort Samnan," she said. "We killed him in the end, but I've never seen anything like that short of a powder mage or a Privileged."

Styke ran a hand through his short, gray hair. "Pit," he swore gently. "I didn't think they still existed."

"Yeah, well it sounds like they do." Vlora spat. The last thing she wanted was old fairy tales coming to life before she could finish her contracts and get out of this damned country. "I want to know if there are any more of them hanging out in the city. We're about to piss off the entire Palo population of Landfall and I'd rather not have more of these blasted dragonmen show up after we do it."

"I can take a look," Styke said. He took his new coffee and spiced chocolate from the waiter, offering the latter to Celine, but the girl had fallen asleep. Vlora resisted the urge to shake her head at the sight. A bloody lamb and a lion.

She reached across the table, offering Styke her hand. "Welcome to the Riflejacks, Ben Styke. I look forward to seeing what you can do."

CHAPTER 9

Michel waited outside the office of Captain Blasdell—the head of the public side of his investigation—his pocket watch ticking away the minutes, and made a mental note that he needed to call upon a handyman. The cracks in his mother's roof needed to be patched, as well as the chair fixed. He considered the fact that he'd been given an unlimited budget to find the Iron Roses and wondered if anyone was actually going to check his budget expenditures on the case, or if he could get away with paying the fixer with Blackhat money.

"Jes called me expendable. An investigation shouldn't need an expendable investigator," he said to himself quietly as he watched Captain Blasdell's door.

He answered with a cynical voice. "He did threaten to kill you if you fail."

"He did not."

"The man murders people for a morning workout, and those final words were awfully ominous."

"The Blackhats don't waste resources, and a Silver Rose like me is a resource. We're all in this shit together."

"Maybe you're expendable because he expects this to be dangerous." Michel forestalled replying to himself, considering the implications. Investigations *could* be dangerous. Someone willing to impersonate a Blackhat *had* to know the risks involved. Once they were found they would be tortured and executed, their friends and family sent to the labor camps. If they were willing to chance that, then they'd be willing to resort to violence.

"Or," he considered out loud, "expendable means that he could bury my career if this goes wrong for some reason." He couldn't foresee a way of this going wrong, but Michel readily admitted that Fidelis Jes was a smarter man than he. One didn't run the Landfall Secret Police without being able to see many possibilities for the future of every decision.

Michel took a deep breath. No need to waste his energy on worrying. He needed to focus on the task at hand, and to do so he needed to talk with Captain Blasdell.

The thought had barely entered his head when the door to Captain Blasdell's office opened. Blasdell was a thin woman in her forties, with a thoughtful, narrow face and a pair of armless spectacles balanced on the brim of her nose. A former police captain, she'd been brought into the Blackhats to help impose some sort of organization on their investigations. She was technically a Silver Rose, but everyone treated her like a Gold. She was the type of person Michel had heard referred to as the backbone of the Blackhats: incorruptible, unambitious, and competent.

She would never be promoted, yet never lose her rank. She was, in a few words, not going anywhere.

"You're Michel Bravis?" she asked, ushering him into her office.

"I am, ma'am. Thanks for seeing me." Michel had met the captain on several occasions but wasn't surprised that she didn't remember him. There were a lot of Blackhats, after all, and he was very good at blending into crowds. He could thank his late father for a face so plain most people forgot it within minutes.

"I didn't have much choice." Blasdell took a seat behind her desk and gestured to a few crates stacked on the corner. "Orders came straight from the grand master's office. I understand you are to have access to any information regarding my case."

"That's right, ma'am."

Blasdell drummed her fingers on the desk, fixing him with a look that said she would not be handing over information willingly. "Why?"

"I think that's classified, ma'am." Michel had no idea how much Blasdell had been told, and frankly he didn't want to have to explain everything to her.

"You think?"

"Pretty sure. All that matters is I need any information you've dug up in the last couple of days."

Blasdell leaned back, putting her boots up on her desk, the put-off look remaining fixed on her face. "The case is a farce," she said. "I've only got a skeleton crew working it, and in a few days we're going to trot out a scapegoat and put the whole thing to bed. Why do you need our information?"

Blasdell had an odd relationship with the Blackhats. She was one of them, and well regarded within the Millinery, but she never seemed to actually trust the people she worked with. Rumor had it Fidelis Jes found it amusing, but also that it made her difficult to work with. Michel didn't have time to deal with her mistrust. "Because, ma'am, the grand master is letting you do your job up until the scapegoat comes into play. Knowing your reputation, the skeleton crew has been working around the clock to come up with leads in the hope you'll solve this before Fidelis Jes makes the whole thing go away. Am I correct?"

She took her boots off the desk, eyes narrowed. "You are."

"Good. So what have you come up with in eighty hours?"

"The facts are," Blasdell said, drawing herself up and adopting a professional tone, "nine days ago fifteen messengers delivered fifteen orders to fifteen different printing companies. Each of them ordered ten thousand copies of *Sins of Empire* and swore the printer to secrecy by presenting an Iron Rose. The printers filled the order, and about eighty hours ago the first copy of the pamphlet hit the street. So far my investigation has cleared the actual printers of any wrongdoing. We're using descriptions of the messengers to try to round up some suspects, but so far we've got nothing promising."

"How about the Iron Roses?"

Blasdell tilted her head. "We were told not to approach the case from that angle."

Michel considered Blasdell's reputation. "But you have, haven't you?"

"I would never disobey a direct order."

Michel threw up his hands. "I don't really give a damn about orders. I need information, and anything you can tell me about those Iron Roses would make my life a hundred times easier."

"And what do I get out of it?"

Michel rolled his eyes. That mistrust that Blasdell was known for would be twice as annoying if it wasn't quite so warranted. People did things by the book in the Millinery or life could take a nasty turn. But what could he possibly give her in return? She was a hardworking bureaucrat who went to great lengths to avoid Landfall politics. What did she want?

"I could probably arrange a bonus."

"Not interested."

"How about for your men? This skeleton crew you've got working around the clock. What if I authorize time and a half for night work?"

"You can do that?" Blasdell seemed skeptical.

Michel considered his unlimited expense account. It was a risk, of course. Giving her some leeway with her men might give her the edge, letting her solve this case before they presented a scapegoat to the public. It wasn't the worst possible scenario—a solved case was a solved case, and it wouldn't ruin his career. But it wouldn't get him his Gold Rose, either. On the other hand, a bunch of grunts doing his work for him could be very useful. "Yes."

Blasdell considered this a moment. "All right, Agent Bravis. We have a deal. My men have discovered a few things. First of all, we know the Iron Roses weren't forged. We checked with every jeweler and metalworker in the entire city. No one would touch that kind of work."

"They could have been forged outside of the city."

"That's a possibility."

One that Michel couldn't do anything about. He wasn't going to travel all over Fatrasta on a wild goose chase, so he'd have to make the assumption that no one outside the city forged the Iron Roses, either. Michel tried to think like an investigator. He was a spy but, he supposed, a good spy should make a decent investigator. They always had their eyes open, following rumors, digging up traitors. "Stolen?" he asked.

"We're following up on that. No Iron Roses are missing within the Landfall city limits. We've sent messages to our sister precincts all over the country."

Nothing he could do about that but wait. "So it's possible they were originals?"

"Possible," Blasdell conceded.

"What do you think?" Michel asked.

Blasdell drummed her fingers on the desk. "I think they're most likely forgeries. They'd know we'd track them to their source, so they would have done the forgeries outside of our influence."

"The Nine?"

"It's what I would do, anyway. Puts a lot of distance between us and whoever did the forgeries, and we'll likely never know who did it. That's what I told the grand master two days ago, and in light of our investigation so far, I stand by it."

Something clicked in Michel's head. Fidelis Jes already suspected that the source of the Roses would never be found. *That's* why Michel needed to be disposable. If nothing came up from the investigation before they buried it, Michel might be forced on the goose chase he'd just decided to avoid. He might even have to sail to the Nine.

He was disposable in that the Blackhats could easily go on without him if he had a case that would take him a great deal of time.

The very thought of it made his stomach turn, and a panic seized his chest. He couldn't spend the next several years chasing ghosts. His career would stall, his mother would be left alone in Landfall, and he would never earn his Gold Rose. He needed to solve this thing, and fast.

"Have your men write up everything you have on the investigation so far and send it to my office. Keep them working. I'll authorize a fat bonus."

"Is there something you want them looking for in particular?" Blasdell asked.

Michel glanced at her sharply, but she didn't look suspicious. She just seemed glad to have something real for her men to work on. "Double-check with the local forgers. Keep digging around, and find out if any Iron Roses have been reported missing or stolen."

"Have it all sent to your office?"

"Yes, if you would. Thank you for your help, Captain." Michel left the captain's office, heading down the hall and toward the other side of the Millinery, where he had his own small, closetlike office. He rested there for a few moments, considering his meeting. He hadn't *intended* on taking over Captain Blasdell's investigation. In fact, he was fairly certain Fidelis Jes would be furious if he found out. Best to keep it quiet then, and hope that Blasdell didn't have occasion to bring it up before Michel could find the Roses.

Blasdell thought they were foreign forgeries. Michel had no way of testing that theory, so he thought it best to come at it from the opposite direction.

"What if they're originals?" he asked himself.

"Stolen?"

"Or misplaced?"

A thought occurred to him—one that made his jaw clench. "What if they weren't stolen? What if they were used by their rightful owners?"

"Are you suggesting fifteen Iron Rose traitors?"

"It's possible."

"Not likely."

He ran his hands through his hair, staring at the blank wall of his office. "I think," he said, "I'm going to look at a few bank accounts."

CHAPTER 10

Vlora went to meet Michel Bravis on the edge of Greenfire Depths the afternoon after her arrival in Landfall. The sun was scorching, and she fanned herself with her bicorn, a skin of warm beer hanging from her saddle horn as she rode at the head of the column snaking its way through the streets of the plateau. Olem rode at her side, with no comment but for the occasional complaint about the heat.

Around four o'clock Vlora called a halt as they reached a building that looked suspiciously large and fortlike. It was a long wall of rotten timbers, two stories high and punctuated every so often by a guard tower. Almost every inch of the wall was painted with graffiti in a dozen different languages or stuck with playbills advertising the latest ribald comedy. She looked up and down the street, ignoring the people who stopped and stared at her column of troops.

"This can't possibly be it."

Olem consulted a map spread out across his saddle horn and

then rode over to the nearest crossroads, peering up at the wooden placards. "This is it," he said. "Loel's Fort."

"That Bravis bastard promised me a barracks."

"Looks like a barracks to me," Olem said.

"It's a fort. A frontier fort, by the looks of it, old enough that it was built when this *was* the frontier."

"Doesn't look so bad," Olem responded with a halfhearted grin.

"This is supposed to be a modern city."

"Adopest still has a stone wall. The past sticks around."

Vlora cleared her throat. "Why can't we have the big fort out on the bay? What's it called, Fort Nied?"

"I think the garrison is stationed there." Olem rode his horse about half a block, then returned. "It looks cozy," he reported unconvincingly.

"You light a cigarette in that place and you'll kill us all."

Olem's look soured.

"This can't possibly be it," Vlora repeated.

"It is."

"How can you be sure?"

Olem jerked his chin. "Because our contact is right there."

Vlora turned to find Michel Bravis in the shade of a nearby awning, at ease in the heat, his collar sweat-stained and his lapel undone, wearing the black, offset-button shirt and ridiculous bowler hat, the Blackhat's trademark uniform. He gave Vlora a wave. Vlora resisted the urge to respond with a rude gesture.

"Good afternoon, ma'am," Michel said as he crossed the street to join them. He squinted up at the sun, as if it were the first time he'd noticed it today. "Bit warm out, isn't it?"

"Go to the pit," Vlora answered. "You promised me a barracks."

"This *is* a barracks," Michel said.

"It's a rotted ruin," Vlora snapped. "If I'm going to be weeding out your problems, potentially facing rioters, I want someplace my men can fall back to. A child throwing stones could break down those walls."

Michel walked over to the wall and kicked at one of the timbers. A splinter the size of Vlora's leg fell off. Michel stared at it for a moment, then turned to her with a salesman's smile. "Bit of paint. Some plaster. It'll be right as rain."

"I want something else," Vlora said.

"There *is* nothing else."

Olem cleared his throat. "It'll do, Agent Bravis. But we'll want supplies to get this fixed up, even if we have to replace every timber."

"I'll see what I can do."

Vlora shot Olem a look. Why didn't he ever let her give anyone a good chewing out anymore? "How is this place even still standing?"

"We used it during the war," Michel answered. He turned to walk along the wall and Vlora dismounted, handing Olem the reins and following Michel on foot. "I was just a kid at the time. I was one of the lucky ones that got out before the Kez arrived, so I didn't see it firsthand. It's said that Loel's Fort was the last defense at the Battle of Landfall, where we really turned the tide and fought the Kez back to the sea. Biggest battle of the whole war, tens of thousands dying on both sides. If it wasn't for the arrival of the Mad Lancers it would have ended here and I'd probably be speaking Kez."

Vlora exchanged a glance with Olem. It was the first time she'd heard of the Mad Lancers outside their meeting with Styke and Taniel's letters. "Who are the Mad Lancers?" she asked, hoping she didn't sound *too* casual.

"Were," Michel corrected. "Bunch of mean bastards who fought for us against the Kez. Ask around any pub in this town about Mad Ben Styke and I'm sure you'll hear a thousand stories. Especially around here. Lots of veterans in this part of town."

"Ben Styke?" Olem echoed.

"Everyone in Fatrasta knew his name. Damned near a legend." Michel shrugged. "We're not supposed to talk about him. He was executed at the end of the war for disobeying orders. Sullied name and all that. But you know how legends are."

"They refuse to die," Vlora said quietly.

"Right you are, ma'am." Michel reached the front gate of Loel's Fort and pushed open one of the big doors to reveal an overgrown muster yard, filled with lean-tos and a handful of dilapidated buildings. Michel's smile faltered for a moment, and Vlora swore under her breath. "Lots of paint," Michel said helpfully.

Vlora did a quick circuit of the premises. Nothing she saw changed her initial impression. The fort was a rotten dump. They must have thrown out hundreds of squatters to make room for her men. The least they could have done was clean the place up a little, too. "There's not enough room for five thousand men in here."

"There are two smaller forts within a few blocks of here," Michel said, turning around and indicating opposite directions. "Loel's Annex North and Loel's Annex South. Each of them has a proper barracks hall. That should give you enough space. We'll provide materials to repair any leaky roofs or broken windows. Until then, I assume you and your men have tents."

Vlora drummed her fingers against her leg and locked eyes with Olem. She formed a ring with her hands, pointed at Michel's neck.

Olem shook his head emphatically.

She mouthed the word *please*.

Olem rolled his eyes. Michel, examining the fort with a rueful look on his face, didn't seem to notice the exchange. He turned back toward them. "Have you seen the Depths yet?" he asked.

"No," Olem said, "we haven't."

Michel crossed the muster yard and took the steps gingerly up to the top of the western fort wall. "You should be able to..." He called down. "Yep, you can definitely see it from here." He beckoned for them to join him.

"I can't get a read on him," Vlora said quietly.

"Agent Bravis?" Olem asked.

"He's so...bland. Polite, but not too polite. Ready smile. Attentive, but almost distractedly so."

"I still think he's a spy," Olem said. "Think about it. That politeness is feigned. We've both been around enough politicians to spot it, but he's no politician. I caught his eye a couple of times when he didn't think I was looking. He's watching us carefully."

"Why would they assign a spy to us?"

"Because that's what the Blackhats do? Do you really think Lindet trusts a mercenary company in her capital city?"

"I suppose not." Vlora took a few deep breaths, forgetting the Blackhat and looking around at their surroundings. This wasn't how she wanted to start their latest assignment, but she knew she needed to cool her heels. If Olem was right, anything she said would likely be reported straight back to the people paying her commission. The last thing she needed to do was piss off an employer in a foreign city. "Promise me you can do something with this dump," she said quietly.

"It'll take some time," Olem responded, "but I'll put the men to work right away. We'll have a defensible barracks within a couple of weeks."

"Right about the time we get our own spy network in place."

"Should be about the length of it, yes."

"Remember," Vlora reminded, "we have just one month to find Mama Palo. We're going to have to work quickly."

Olem gave her a reassuring wink, and she left him to oversee the brigade's move-in and joined Michel on the west wall. "What do you have to show..." What she saw below took her breath away.

She'd heard the stories. She'd even gotten a glimpse at the Depths as they passed it on the keelboats in the gorge, but this... this was something else. It was as if a god had reached down and pressed his thumb against the Landfall Plateau, leaving a two-hundred-foot-deep mark a mile in diameter. The Depths wasn't just an old quarry; it was practically a crater, and it was jammed from one end to the other with tenements; roofs stacked with shantytowns and overgrown gardens, dilapidated construction that made Loel's Fort look structurally sound. The tallest roofs almost came within spitting distance of the Rim while the bottom—she couldn't even see the bottom beneath the chaotic hodgepodge of buildings.

Michel was looking at her with a strange smile on his face. Vlora closed her mouth, straightened her belt, and said, "This is something else."

"It is, isn't it?" Michel said, almost reverently. "I always like watching the expression on a newcomer when they first see the Depths. No one's ever ready for just how big it is. I've never been to the mountains, but I imagine it's like looking down on a valley that you didn't expect hidden away behind the peaks."

"I've never seen a valley packed with so much slum," Vlora said. "What did you say the population was?"

"Nobody knows for sure," Michel said, clearing his throat. His brief sense of wonder was replaced with helpful professionalism. "We suspect it's somewhere around two hundred thousand, though."

"All crammed in that hole?"

"Yes, ma'am. It's bigger than it looks, though. The tenements have whole road systems between floors, with cables that support hammocks and community spaces. There's even rumors that they've mined into the floor and gotten the old quarry pumps working again for subterranean space. They make use of every inch down there, going up and down. They have to."

"And it's all Palo?"

"Mostly," Michel said. "You get the occasional pocket of Kressian immigrants that don't know any better. Probably a few thousand old veterans that the Palo leave alone. But yes. Lots of Palo."

Vlora couldn't imagine such a thing. Even in Adopest, the worst slums tended to be no bigger than a few blocks, and they were scattered about the city. Here Landfall had managed to combine all of its slums and jam them into a literal hole in the ground. It was like a deep, festering sore on the Landfall Plateau, and the Lady Chancellor expected her mercenary company to sift through that to find a single Palo.

Well. No sense in waiting around. "I'm going to go take a look," Vlora said, heading back down the stairs without a backward glance. A few hundred men were already inside the fort, cleaning up the abandoned shantytown and inventorying supplies as the soldiers streamed through the gate. She passed Olem, got her sword and pistol from her horse, and fixed both to her belt. "I'm going for a walk," she told him.

Olem frowned. "You should have an escort."

"No need for that," she said firmly. This was often a prickly subject, and she had no interest in a fight. "I'm not Tamas, and I'd rather not attract attention."

Michel caught up with her just outside the fort. "Lady Flint!"

"Ah, Agent Bravis. Will you accompany me on my walk?"

Michel examined her with a mixture of horror and alarm. "It's just Michel, ma'am. You're not planning on going down *into* the Depths, are you?"

"I want to take a quick look around."

"Alone?"

"Yes."

"You go down there and you won't come back up."

Vlora peered closely at Michel. He was genuinely worried. The man seemed absolutely certain that Greenfire Depths was some sort of a death trap. Based on the construction alone she might agree, but... "You are aware I'm a powder mage?"

"Even powder mages can get lost. Or ambushed. Or overwhelmed."

Vlora knew that better than most. She remembered a campaign through the north of Kez, hunted by overwhelming numbers, cutting her way through enemy territory with the very men she eventually formed into her mercenary company. She'd survived that. She could survive a Palo slum.

"I think I can handle myself, Agent Bravis."

"I'm sure you can, ma'am, and I say this with the deepest respect—it's a maze. You won't be able to find your way out."

"Could you?"

"Of course, ma'am, but I've lived in Landfall my whole life, back before the Depths belonged to the Palo."

"Well, then," Vlora said with more than a little relish. "You should give me a tour." *And a real damned barracks next time.*

Michel froze. Vlora turned to face him, and could see him struggling to keep a lid on a torrent of emotions. "Ma'am," he finally said, "do you remember yesterday, when I said that Blackhats only go there in force? It's because they'll skin us alive if we get caught down there on our own."

Vlora wondered if he really believed that. She'd heard of slums in Adro where the police preferred to work in numbers, but they feared a robbery and a beating; nothing so savage as straight-up torture. She shrugged. "Suit yourself," she said, and continued to walk.

She heard a string of curses behind her, then Michel said, "Wait a moment, ma'am."

He disappeared into a nearby house and came back a moment later. His black jacket and hat were gone, replaced by a workman's brown jacket, the elbows patched and repatched, and a matching flatcap. Even the rose medallion, which the Blackhats seemed to wear like shields, was no longer hanging around his neck. Perhaps he really *did* fear being skinned alive. "A changing house," he explained. "It's always good to have a spare set of clothes lying around when you're a Blackhat near Greenfire Depths."

Michel led her down several side streets until they reached a thoroughfare that descended by way of switchbacks down the side of the quarry wall. Within two switchbacks they were equal to the tops of most tenements, and after six Vlora was more than a little disconcerted that she could not see the sky without looking straight up. The ground soon leveled out, and her boots splashed in a filthy morass of sludge.

"Welcome to the Depths," Michel said.

The air was damp, stifling, and dim. There were only glimpses of the sky, and most of the light was provided by well-placed mirrors redirecting the sun from the tops of the tenements. Michel noticed her examining one of the mirrors and said, "Courtesy of the Lady Chancellor, back before the Palo took over. It was a cheaper and safer way to light this place in the daytime."

"It needs it," Vlora said.

Michel pulled the brim of his flatcap forward. "We should keep moving," he said.

Vlora pulled herself away from examining the distressing construction of the tenements, with walkways and curtains running between them, whole buildings propped up by jacks and beams, and noticed that almost everyone within sight was staring at them. No, not at them. At her. Unlike Michel, she was still wearing her hat and uniform. She wondered if these people knew who she was, and that she'd spent the last year out in the frontier fighting their cousins for the government.

Perhaps this expedition was as ill-advised as Michel suggested.

Any sense of a real thoroughfare disappeared within a hundred paces. She could barely see the sky now, and after they'd gone just a hundred more she had to admit to herself that she was hopelessly lost. There was no sense of direction in this place, no recognizable landmarks. She was as good as underground.

She also noticed the sudden silence. A few moments ago there had been children playing in the streets, vendors haggling with old women, pedestrians strolling along the corridors. Now there were scarcely half a dozen people within eyesight and all of them heading the opposite direction. She couldn't help but feel the weight of watchful eyes between her shoulder blades. The silence seemed to make the stink worse, a noxious stench like rotten food and dead animals, and she now noticed the rats running every which way as they passed.

They took several twists and turns before Vlora said, "I think we're being followed."

"We're definitely being followed," Michel agreed. His mouth was a firm line, and they ducked down two more bends quickly. "It's pretty common down here. I told you, the Palo are organized. They keep an eye out for strangers—anyone with a Kressian face that they don't recognize. I wouldn't be surprised if we're being watched by Mama Palo's own spies right now."

The sense of helplessness that overcame Vlora as she tried to figure out which direction they were going was disconcerting, to say the least. Her eyes darted between doorways and windows but there were too many crannies to keep an eye on. An ambush down here, undertaken by a capable leader, could slaughter an entire brigade.

Her brigade.

"I think we should go," Vlora said.

"What do you think we're doing?" Michel's voice was on edge now, a little higher than usual, and before he'd finished the sentence they rounded one more bend to find the entrance to the switchbacks right in front of them. She thought she heard Michel give a quiet sigh, and then again once they'd reached the top of the switchbacks. She took a moment to catch her breath, looking back over the surreal slums below them.

"That," she said, chewing on her words and trying to work the smell out of her nostrils, "is not a pleasant place."

Michel gave her a tight smile, as if to say *I told you so*, but followed it up with a sympathetic nod. "That's putting it lightly. It used to just be a confusing slum. Get lost, ask for directions, you'll make your way back out by morning, perhaps with an empty purse. But now, with the Palo in charge, entire Blackhat squads go missing and are never heard from again."

"They really hate you, don't they?"

"Me?" Michel asked. "Ma'am, you seem like you prefer people to be honest with you, so I'll tell you this: They hate *us*. They may not know yet, but word will spread who you are and who you work for. When it does, your men will start disappearing."

The words felt like a punch in the gut. What the pit had she gotten herself into, coming to a place where her men couldn't be safe walking down the street? Surely, this kind of thing should be familiar? The swamps of the Tristan Basin were just as impenetrable and dangerous, yet it felt like a betrayal to come to a modern city and find the same kind of danger. But, she decided, they'd managed in the swamps and they'd manage here.

"Any advice I should give to my men if they get lost down in the Depths?" she asked. *If you say 'pray,' I will punch you in the face.*

Michel scrunched his nose, gazing down over the edge of the Rim, then checked his pocket watch. He swore to himself. "Advice? Yeah. Try to find a quarry wall, then stick with it until you find a switchback out. Don't leave the floor of the quarry until you find a switchback because if you go up one of those tenements, your maze has become three-dimensional." He checked his watch again. "I'm sorry, ma'am, but I have several more meetings today. Is there anything else I can do for you?"

Always running off. Vlora glanced toward Loel's Fort, where she could see the company flag being hoisted. It reached the top of the flagpole, jumped once, and the whole flagpole suddenly toppled over, raising a cloud of dust above the fort. *That doesn't bode well.* "Yes," she said. "I'm not going into that place without some sort of intelligence. You said you had agents in the Depths?"

"Yes. Well. Sort of. Here," Michel said, scribbling on the back of one of his business cards and handing it to Vlora, who read the words and address.

"The Ice Baron?" she asked.

"He's a businessman."

"Can he be trusted?"

Michel seemed to hesitate. "He's a man without guile so I guess in that sense, yes. He can be trusted. I'd suggest being discreet about your mission."

"What's our public reason for being stationed just outside the Depths?" Vlora asked. "People are going to ask questions, after all. We're a whole damned army."

"We haven't given one yet," Michel said. "The propagandists are working on it."

Vlora gave a derisive snort. Propaganda was a normal part of any government, but referring to their public relations office that way sounded damned cynical, even for Blackhats. "How about this," she suggested. "My men have been put on ice until the next mission. We've been recalled because of the recent riots, and we're here to keep the peace. While we wait for our next assignment I have several engineers who have offered to begin reconstruction around the rim of Greenfire Depths."

Michel cocked an eyebrow. "Do you have several engineers?"

"Very good ones," Vlora said. "And I like to keep my men busy when they're not fighting. I've noticed that the Lady Chancellor seems to love construction projects, so let us knock down and rebuild a few tenements and it looks like we're doing community good. Might even give us an excuse to snoop around the Depths."

Michel mulled it over. "It might work. I'll pass it up the chain of command."

"Let me know by tomorrow afternoon. People will begin asking questions, and I want an official answer to give them."

"Very good, ma'am." Michel tipped his hat and headed toward the building where he'd left his Blackhat uniform.

Back at Loel's Fort, Vlora stood in the doorway to watch the organized chaos of an army setting up a new headquarters. Olem noticed her after a moment and came by.

"How did it go? Is it as horrifying as they say?"

"No," she replied. "I'd like to build a summer home here. Retire. Let the grandchildren play in the streets."

"We'd have to have children first."

That was a conversation she wasn't having right now. "I'm being sarcastic. It's a bloody maze. Makes my skin crawl, and not just because of the sludge you have to walk through. I don't like it one bit. Oh, and I may have just set up a construction project for the engineers. Once they're done rebuilding the fort, that is."

Olem looked aggrieved. "I'll tell Whitehall. He'll be thrilled. Do we have a plan of attack for finding Mama Palo?"

"I'm not sure," Vlora answered, "whether the Blackhats thought they could trick us into using force, but I am *not* going to fight my way through that slum. We're going to finesse this thing. Agent Bravis gave me a card for someone called the Ice Baron. Know him?"

"Businessman," Olem said.

"I gathered. Sounds like he's our intelligence. Set up a meeting, and let's figure out how to get inside Greenfire Depths."

CHAPTER 11

S he has me chasing a fairy tale," Styke said, rolling the weight of his lancer's ring back and forth between thumb and fore-finger. It was barely past seven in the morning, and he stood at the far northern tip of the bay, squinting at the ships out past the breakers, sailing into the morning sun with the tide. His leg ached from the long walk, but he had a piece of horngum in the corner of his mouth and felt better than he had in years. To think, some-thing as simple as watching the ships go out could make his heart glow.

He'd spent his first and second nights of freedom at a sailor's hostel near the docks. The single room, not much wider than a closet, felt like a palace, and the bunk pallet like a four-corner bed. Celine slept on the top bunk, snoring through the early morning hours as Styke lay awake listening to the sailors break bread in the common room downstairs.

"A fairy tale," he repeated to himself, counting the eighth ship to leave port in just under fifteen minutes. He remembered a time when two ships a day was considered an event in Landfall. Pit, he could still see the docks burning in his mind's eye, set ablaze by the Kez navy, and wondering if they would ever rebuild. A lot of horrible things could be said about Lindet, but she had fulfilled her promise to turn Fatrasta into an economic power in just a single decade.

Styke glanced down at Celine, who sat on the rocks beside him with her head drooping sleepily into her lap. She could have stayed behind and slept, but had insisted on coming with him without a word of complaint. "You ever heard any stories of the dragonmen?" he asked.

Celine perked up, shaking herself awake. "No. Dad never told me stories. Taught me how to pick a lock and slip a pocketbook, but never any stories. Said stories were for babies and silly fools."

"Your dad was a prick," Styke said.

"I loved my dad." Celine sniffed. "And he loved me."

"Doesn't make him less of a prick. Listen—a thousand years ago, back when this land belonged to the Dynize, the dragonmen came out of the deepest swamps. They were the greatest warriors of a people who thrived on war, worth a hundred soldiers in any battle." Styke drew his knife, examining the blade in the morning sun before pointing it at Celine. "Dragonmen were trained from birth to be fierce, bold, and give no quarter. They proved themselves in their adolescence by killing the biggest swamp dragon they could find. They fashioned armor from its skin and axes from its bones and were blessed by the bone-eyes—the blood sorcerers. Made them damn near invincible."

Celine stared up at him, transfixed. "And?"

"And no one knows anything else about them," Styke said. "It's been lost in time. The Kez killed the last of the dragonmen decades ago, and the Dynize Empire hasn't been seen outside of Dynize in over a hundred years."

"Lady Flint said her men killed a dragonman."

"Maybe," Styke said. He had his doubts. Perhaps a fierce Palo warrior slaughtered some of her men. Perhaps that warrior even fought in the traditional dragonman garb. But the dragonmen were long gone.

He stared out at the rising sun. More was the pity. Few warriors—real warriors—existed anymore. This was a world of assassins and soldiers—people who killed in the dark or in formation. In his mind powder mages were the last true warriors and even they preferred to use their sorcery to kill at a distance. He briefly imagined Lady Flint dueling one of these fabled warriors, and it brought a smile to his face. That would be a fight to see!

"Lady Flint and that Olem fellow seemed to know who you were."

Styke reached down and tousled Celine's hair. "I thought they might not for a minute."

"But they did. Were you really as big a hero as they said? People in the labor camps called you a killer, but I didn't know you were a hero."

"In a time of war, killing makes you a hero, so . . ." Styke shrugged. "I guess I was, in a way."

"Have you killed a lot of men?"

"Hundreds."

She was silent for a moment as she absorbed the number. "Do you regret it?"

"Sometimes."

"My dad strangled an old woman once," Celine said. "She woke up while he was taking the family silver. But it wasn't during war, so I guess he wasn't a hero."

"Real piece of work, your dad." Styke tongued the bit of horngum in the corner of his mouth. "Why didn't he hang for it?"

"No one caught him. He was only sent to the camps later on for thieving. Why didn't you hang for all the people you killed?"

Styke looked down at her. It occurred to him he should be annoyed with all the questions, but he found they made him all the more fond of her. It reminded him of his little sister. Always asking questions, always trying to seek out the how and why. But that was decades ago. Before everything changed. "Because I was Mad Ben Styke," he said. "I killed for my country, so they slapped medals on my chest until I wasn't convenient anymore, then sent me to the camps."

"Could you kill a dragonman?" Celine asked.

"I haven't fought anything I couldn't kill," Styke said, testing the blade of his knife, then sucking the blood off the tip of his thumb. "But I was younger back then. Stronger. I'm pretty good at choosing my battles, and I wouldn't choose to fight a dragonman. Not one out of the stories anyway." He sighed, putting his knife away, and lifted Celine to her feet. "They don't exist anymore, so I'm not worried."

"If they don't exist anymore, what are you going to do?" Celine asked.

"I'll hunt around for a few days, chasing shadows, then I'll tell Lady Flint not to worry about them and hope she gives me something real to do." Styke frowned. He remembered the admiration on Olem's face, and the skepticism on Flint's, when they agreed to take him on. He had a nagging suspicion that they'd brought him on out of pity and the very thought almost made him sick.

He wasn't even sure why it bothered him so much. Tampo was his real employer, and his only job was to get close to Lady Flint. He was well on his way to doing it. "I want to be useful again," he muttered to himself.

"What?" Celine asked.

"Nothing." Styke took her by the hand. "We're going to see Old Man Fles. He might have a shadow or two for us to chase."

* * *

Old Man Fles sat out in front of Fles and Fles Fine Blades, a breakfast of milk and bread pudding balanced on his lap, watching as the early morning customers passed his booth to reach the food vendors farther into the market.

"Looks dead," Styke commented, sidling up next to the Old Man.

Fles tipped the brim of his flatcap back. "Nobody buys knives and swords at this hour. Our sales happen around midday, when the dandies and merchants' wives go shopping."

"Used to be a lot more morning traffic."

"Morning duels have gone out of fashion," Fles answered.

Styke remembered what Fles had told him about Fidelis Jes's habits. "Not with Fidelis Jes. You have any more information about him?"

"Pff." Fles shot him an irritated glance. "It's been what, forty hours? Have some patience, boy. If you think I'm going to go running to my contacts demanding answers about the Blackhat grand master, you're sorely mistaken."

"I thought you might work quickly. For old times' sake."

The irritated glance lasted twice as long this time. "I've always liked you, Ben, and I'm glad to see you're still alive even if you do look uglier than a skinned cat. But don't push it. I still fully expect my daughter to fillet you when she gets back, so what's the hurry?"

"I owe him," Styke said quietly.

"Oh, calm down. I've already put out some feelers and Fidelis Jes isn't going anywhere. What are you doing back here, anyway? I'll be mighty pissed off if you bring the Blackhats around."

"Have they come by to ask after me?"

"Not yet," Fles said. "But you better avoid the market. Me and Ibana can keep secrets, but I've got apprentices now and there's far too many eyes here. If you want to chat, come by the house."

"Do you still own the old place in Greenfire Depths?"

"Of course."

"I thought the Depths belong to the Palo now."

"They leave us alone," Fles said with a shrug. "The Fles name demands enough respect to get some distance. You think I've been sharpening Palo kitchen knives for free out of the kindness of my heart? Besides, I've never met a Palo who wants a piece of Ibana."

"Not the piece she'd give them," Styke said, smirking at the Old Man.

Fles rolled his eyes. "Yeah, well. Like I said, you shouldn't be seen around here."

"All right, all right. I'm going." Styke glanced over his shoulder, searching the crowd for Celine. "One last question. This is going to sound stupid, but have you heard anything about the dragonmen coming back?"

He expected a condescending grin and to be laughed out of the market. Instead, Fles removed his flatcap and scratched his head, looking thoughtfully up at Styke. "Funny you should ask that. There's been rumors about men in swamp dragon leathers down in Greenfire Depths. Nothing substantiated, and everybody thinks it's just Mama Palo playing with the Blackhats, but you're not the first person to mention dragonmen to me this week. And nobody has talked about them in more than hushed tones since I was a kid."

Styke scoffed. "Dragonmen *in* Landfall? That's ridiculous."

"I'm just telling you what I heard." Fles threw up his hands. "Sounded ridiculous to me, too, but everything's been crazy since the revolution. The Nine has gone to complete shit. The Adran king was put to death. People say Kresimir returned during the Adran-Kez War, gods fought and died, then Kez tore itself apart with their own civil war. The world's not right, Ben. The dragonmen returning? Well, anything could happen. If you want to find out about the dragonmen, though, you'll have to ask the Palo."

"Maybe I will." Styke left Old Man Fles muttering gloomily to himself by the front of the smithy and found Celine working her way through the shops. They left the market together, wandering south through the docks and then taking a hackney cab down through the industrial quarter and then to Upper Landfall, so Styke could get a look at the city he'd been absent from for so long.

And so he could think.

Everything he'd heard since being released told him that the Palo were a powder keg right now—not something he wanted to put his nose into. But Old Man Fles was right. If the dragonmen had returned, it was doubtful even the Blackhats would know. Only the Palo would be able to tell him.

He wondered if Flint knew exactly how dangerous it would be for Styke to hunt down answers regarding the dragonmen. Doubtful. She thought him a worthless cripple before she found out who he was—or rather, who he used to be. Searching Greenfire Depths for the most dangerous warriors in Palo history seemed far and above what she'd expected him to do.

But if he got her some real answers—if he had solid evidence that the dragonmen were, in fact, real and of what they were up to—he might wind up as part of her inner circle.

Exactly where Tampo wanted him.

Styke directed the carriage back around the western half of the plateau and through northern Landfall until he'd made a complete circuit of the city. It was well after noon when he found Old Man Fles back in his workshop, polishing his latest blade.

"I thought I told you not to come back here anymore," Fles said.

"I won't," Styke promised. "But I need you to do something for me."

"What?"

"Set up a meeting."

"With who?"

"A dragonman."

"That's the stupidest thing—"

Styke cut him off. "Just let it slip in the right places that the son of an influential Adran merchant wants to meet a dragonman. Say he'll pay a huge amount of money just to be able to talk to one for a few minutes. Say I'm a historian." Styke found a piece of paper and wrote down an address. "Set up a meeting at this pub, and let me know when to be there."

Fles fingered the paper. "You're going to attract all the wrong kinds of attention."

"That's the idea."

"You're mad."

Styke took Celine's tiny hand in his and turned to leave, throwing a crooked grin over his shoulder. "That's what they say."

CHAPTER 12

When Vlora knocked on the door to a large townhouse about half a mile east of Greenfire Depths, the last thing she expected to see when the door opened was a tall, stocky man with the dusty skin of a Rosvelean and a black bearskin draped over his shoulders. His face was red, sweat pouring from his brow, and he was dressed more like someone from the Adran Mountain-watch than a Landfall native. He looked from Vlora to Olem, then back to Vlora.

Vlora opened her mouth, but he spoke first. "Lady Flint?" he asked in a thick Rosvelean accent.

"Yes," she said slowly. "I'm looking for Baron Habba...Habber..."

The man grinned at her. "Baron Vallencian Habbabberden," he said proudly, throwing the door open. "Come in, come in. Agent Bravis said to expect you."

Vlora exchanged a glance with Olem, then followed the big man inside, through the hall, and into a sitting room on the left. She was surprised to find the foyer, hall, and sitting room entirely devoid of furniture. There were no wall hangings, decorations, or even lamps other than a few gas lanterns hanging from the walls. There also appeared to be no staff, despite the house being big enough to need a full retinue of servants.

The big man went to the mantelpiece, leaned against it, and produced a pipe from his pocket that he quickly puffed to life. "Lady Vlora Flint. Standing in my own home. What an honor!" He paused, looked around. "I have to apologize about the furniture. I was born in a tent smaller than this room and now I own four of these damned houses. I don't have the first idea what I'm supposed to put in them."

Olem cleared his throat and turned to one side to cough, clearly trying not to laugh.

"You're the Ice Baron?" Vlora asked, more than a little skeptical.

"I am. Don't try to say my name, nobody can. Just call me the Baron, or Vallencian to my friends. And you, Lady Flint, are my friend. I read your biography. It was very good."

What the pit is he talking about? "I don't have a biography."

"You do," the Baron assured. "It was written by a Rosvelean mercenary who served in the Kez Civil War. Excellent stuff. I'll have a copy translated and sent to you."

"Thank you? I think?"

"It is nothing. You must be Colonel Olem." Vallencian suddenly lurched forward, shaking both their hands warmly. "You like cigarettes, yeah? Try one of these." He removed a box from his jacket pocket and flipped it open with one hand to reveal a line of pre-rolled cigarettes.

Olem beamed. "Don't mind if I do."

Vlora waved away the offer as Olem lit his, trying to get a read on this Ice Baron. He was obviously a foreigner, obviously relished his status as such, wearing such a damned getup in this heat. "Forgive me if this is rude, but are you really a baron?"

"Are you a lady?" Vallencian shot back. He immediately threw up his hands. "I joke, I joke. I was born in a village in northern Rosvel, high up in the mountains. I bought a barony last year, but I've never been to it. A cousin manages the thing. Poorly, I understand. But I've been called the Ice Baron for far longer, just as you have been called Lady Flint for longer than you've had a title."

Vlora glanced at Olem. "I've never had a title. Lady Flint is just something that someone called me once, and it stuck."

Vallencian seemed to consider this, his brow furrowing. "That biography. I won't send it to you. It's shit."

Olem couldn't cover up his laugh that time, and Vallencian joined in with a chuckle. "Ah," he said, rubbing the back of his head, "I'm sorry for the state of this place. I'd say it's new, but it's been unfurnished for three years now. My footman just recently convinced me to buy a bed." He patted the bearskin on his shoulders. "All I need is Rangga here under my head and the saints sing me to sleep. And chairs? Ostentatious, I tell you."

"Don't you entertain?" Olem asked. "I mean, I've heard your name several times around the city. You run in prestigious circles."

"I am very entertaining," the Baron said, grinning in a way that made it obvious he knew what Olem had meant. "But I prefer to be a guest, rather than have guests. It feels more right to me. Gives me an excuse to give expensive gifts to my hosts, instead of just offering some wine and a bite of food. And with no hosting, I don't have to employ a bunch of assholes. Speaking of which, where is my damned footman?" He rolled his eyes. "Useless. I sent him out for dinner. I asked for lobster. Have you seen the lobsters here? I've never seen something so ugly, and when I first saw it I thought, I must kill it and eat it and now"—he smacked his lips—"I love it."

Vlora recognized when a man liked to talk, and it was already very clear that it was one of Vallencian's favorite hobbies. Talkers, she knew, could go on for hours if you didn't put a stop to it right away, so she coughed into her hand and said, "Baron, you said Agent Bravis had told you to expect us?"

"Yes, yes, of course. You want information about the Palo?"

"Greenfire Depths, specifically."

"Ah, the Depths." The Baron gazed at the ceiling, as if remembering a walk in a particularly striking park. "Have you ever seen anything like that before?"

"It's a rat's nest," Vlora responded bluntly.

Vallencian shook a finger at her. "There is beauty in a rat's nest; warmth, security, companionship. There is all of that and more in Greenfire Depths, and I try to tell that to the Blackhats but does anyone listen to Vallencian? No."

Vlora examined the baron's face. In some of the circles she'd traveled in Adro they would consider him a simpleton, but no simpleton amassed a fortune that would allow him to buy a barony after having been born penniless in a mountain village.

"Exactly how familiar are you with the Depths?" Olem asked. "And you must tell me where you got these cigarettes. This is terrific."

"I'll send you the name of my tobacconist. And I'm quite familiar. I meet with my business partners there every week. It's a very pleasant place once you get used to it."

Vlora shuddered, remembering the sense of dread she felt on just a short walk through the narrow corridors with Michel. "I'll take your word for it. You're telling me that you openly do business in Greenfire Depths, but you work for the Blackhats?"

" 'Work' is a strong word," Vallencian said. "I did not get this rich to work. The Blackhats come by every few weeks and ask me questions about what I've seen and heard in Greenfire Depths. I tell them. I also give them a substantial bribe and in return, they leave my ships alone. The Palo know of this, and they don't speak of anything within earshot that I might pass on. It's a good relationship. I try to operate my business without, how do you say, guile?"

"And you can travel freely in Greenfire Depths?"

"I avoid the bad neighborhoods."

"The entire thing is a bad neighborhood," Olem said.

Vallencian tilted his head at them. "Let me tell you something about Greenfire Depths. It has its own, what do the naturalists call it, ecosystem? It is its own world. It has its own economy, social classes, armies, even its own weather. To all the high and mighty in Upper Landfall the Depths looks like a shithole. But the Depths has its own slums, the worst of the worst, and its own palaces—places that would make you gasp upon sight. It is as varied as the city in which it resides."

Vlora rocked back on her heels, chewing on her lip. "That sounds complicated."

"It *is* complicated. It's taken me years to work it out myself."

"What," Olem asked, "is it you sell down there?"

"The only thing I do sell," Vallencian responded. "Ice."

"Ice?" Vlora echoed.

"When I was young, I made a small fortune in Rosvel in the beef industry. I came to Fatrasta, and the first thing I noticed was how damned hot it was. In Rosvel, they bring ice down from the mountains to keep food and drinks cool during the summer months."

"Same in Adro," Vlora said.

"Yes, and my family has done so for generations. Anyway, I spent my fortune on a ship to bring ice to Fatrasta."

"And people bought it?"

"The ice melted."

"Oh," Vlora said.

"So I packed it in sawdust, I did another trip." Vallencian scratched his chin. "The ice made it all the way here, and you know what I learned? No one wanted ice. Nothing here is cold, not even the mountains, and when no one knows of the cold they have no use for it. I lost everything. Then the war came. I smuggled guns for Lindet in the only thing I had left to my name: a rowboat. Smuggled some more guns, bought a yacht, smuggled some cannons, then the war ended. Spent my money on a new ship and brought more ice over to Fatrasta. Most of it melted before I could sell it, but then a funny thing happened."

"Yes?"

"The Palo decided they liked iced coffee. It caught on, and the Fatrastans and the Kressian immigrants began to ice their tea and now, about eight years later, here I am."

"You're very persistent," Olem observed.

"Persistence has earned me ninety-eight merchantmen and almost three hundred warehouses across Fatrasta and Rosvel. And," he said, looking around, "these big damned empty houses I don't know what to do with." Vallencian brought a hand to his chin. "Maybe I should bring more of my cousins over."

Vlora let out a low whistle. That had to make Vallencian one of the richest men in all of Fatrasta. Probably the Nine, too. And he didn't have a butler or a stick of furniture. What a strange man.

"So," Vallencian finished, spreading his hands. "That is who I am, and that is my relationship with the Palo. I'll help you how I can."

Vlora had thought long and hard about what information to share, and what not, and she decided for Vallencian's safety it was best to pare back even that. "My company has been assigned to the rim of Greenfire Depths. We're going to undertake some public works projects and act as a garrison."

"The Palo are not going to like that," the baron said, thrusting a finger at her. "They know who you are."

"That's what I need help with. I want to learn more about the Palo and find out how we can coexist. I don't want my men disappearing when they go out on patrol. I want a truce."

"And you think I can get that for you? Hah. Agent Bravis has exaggerated my place among the Palo. I'm just a businessman. An outsider."

"Bravis didn't tell me anything, actually. But it's clear that you've made it into the Palo inner circle. And that's what I want to do. For everyone's safety." Vlora chewed on her words for a moment, hoping they didn't sound disingenuous. This *was* for everyone's safety. But she was trying to capture the Palo's matriarch, and she found that leaving that out of the conversation made her feel a little guilty. She *liked* Vallencian. Lying, even by omission, felt distasteful. "Is there anyone I can meet to make that kind of deal with?"

The baron waffled on the question for a moment. "Perhaps I can introduce you to a few."

"What about this matriarch I've been hearing about? This Mama Palo? Is she the one who makes those decisions?"

Vallencian scoffed. "No outsiders talk to Mama Palo."

"Have you met her?"

"Haven't even seen her. I've talked to a few of her lieutenants, but never her."

"Is she a myth?"

"If she is, someone down there is playing the world's biggest joke on all of us, including the Palo. Mama is real. The Palo believe it. The Kressians believe it. Blackhats have been trying to catch her for years." Vallencian squinted at Vlora, but made no further comment on the matter. "If you want to make some sort of a truce with the Palo, you need to meet the right people. There is a gala in Greenfire Depths in a few days. I'll see if I can get you an invitation."

"A gala?" Vlora asked. She exchanged a glance with Olem, trying not to smirk.

"I told you," the baron said, "slums and palaces. Whole ecosystem. Where are you staying?"

"Loel's Fort," Olem said.

"Very good. I will get an invitation and send it to Loel's Fort. Hopefully I will see you at the gala then."

Vlora and Olem were shown out by the baron and returned to their waiting hackney cab, where they sat in puzzled silence.

"Did you know I had a biography written about me in Rosvel?" Vlora finally asked.

"Had no idea," Olem responded, crushing out his cigarette on the wall of the cab. "But these cigarettes are amazing."

"You're not helpful."

"He's a strange man," Olem said, answering her unspoken question, "but I think we can trust him. He's got an honest face."

"Yeah, so do a lot of horse traders."

"If you don't trust him, we won't use his help. I asked around before we came, though, and he's known as a fair, open businessman. Everyone seems fairly baffled by his success because he seldom takes opportunities to cheat anyone."

Vlora bit the inside of her cheek, mulling it over. "We'll see if he comes through on the invitation. I've been down into the Depths. There's no beauty there, and I'm not fighting through it to find this Mama Palo. We're going to have to do it"—she imitated Vallencian's accent—"with, how do you say, guile." Vlora switched benches, moving over next to Olem, and put her head on his shoulder.

"All right," Olem agreed, putting his arm around her, "but I'm not sending you down there without a whole damned regiment as an escort."

CHAPTER 13

Michel knew that the messengers who'd delivered *Sins of Empire* to the printers were his best bet at tracking down the Iron Roses. They *would* be discovered sooner or later. Fifteen people were fourteen too many to keep a secret, and the fact that so many were involved in a conspiracy and had still not been discovered almost two weeks later was damned impressive. He didn't have time to wait for someone to get dragged in off the street, though. He needed answers immediately, and that meant turning a direction in his investigation that few other Blackhats would be willing to go.

He spent two precious days following a hunch. He visited banks, ransacked a house and an apartment, and generally kept himself busy until he had all the information he needed and returned to the very place one shouldn't be looking for suspects in a plot against her Lady Chancellor's government.

The Millinery.

"Light" corruption ran deep among the Blackhats. Most, including Michel himself, considered it a perk of the job. Blackhats wound up with free meals or cups of coffee, or rushed to the front of the line in a government office. Neighbors might pitch in to pay your rent, because a Blackhat in the neighborhood generally discouraged the local gangs. Michel preferred to use his own leverage in places he couldn't afford normally—nice hotels, banks, tailors, high-end brothels.

But while that light corruption was tolerated, it was an unspoken rule that you never let your greed get the better of you. There was a line somewhere—though not strictly defined—and if you crossed it you'd be out on your ass, maybe even sent to a labor camp.

Which is why Michel felt a pang of sadness as he rounded a corner in the basement of the Millinery to find a hallway that dead-ended in a single counter. A cage was built in around the counter, like one might find in the back of a casino in a shady part of town, and the door to the right of it was reinforced with steel and locked from the inside. An older gentleman, balding and lean, sat behind the cage with his feet up on the counter. He had a book in one hand—the same kind of penny novels Michel's mother loved—and an apple in the other.

"Agent Bravis," he called before Michel had reached the counter. "What brings you down to the Treasury today?"

"Afternoon, Bobbin." Michel reached the cage and leaned against it, craning his head to get a look at the title of the book. He searched his pockets, wishing that he carried a flask. "New dreadful?"

Bobbin gave Michel an embarrassed smile and stashed the book under the counter. "Yeah. You know how it gets. Time crawls by down here."

"I bet," Michel said. He considered winding his way through the daily gossip—Bobbin managed to hear everything down here—but knew that would only be delaying the inevitable. "Bobbin, did you get your Gold Rose recently?"

"Me?" the treasurer scoffed. "I'm a Silver for life, Michel. Not much room for improvement down here. How about you? Ever get your Gold? I know you've been working for it for a while."

"No," Michel said, picking at his fingernails. "Not yet."

"I heard they gave you babysitting duty with those Adran mercenaries. Is Lady Flint as pretty as they say in the gossip columns?"

"She's like an old shoe," Michel lied. "Lost an eye a couple of years ago. Teeth falling out. Not a pretty picture."

Bobbin squinted at him. "You pulling my leg?"

"Might be." Michel scratched his chin. Pit, this was going to hurt. "Bobbin, have you heard about this thing with the *Sins of Empire*?"

"The pamphlet that's going around? I heard that Captain Blasdell is working around the clock on it, trying to find out who would order such damaging propaganda."

Bobbin didn't mention anything about the Roses, which meant Fidelis Jes had kept it out of the newspapers *and* out of the general gossip among the Blackhats themselves. Blackhats couldn't gossip to anyone but their fellows, but boy did they love to do just that.

"Did you hear about the Roses?" Michel asked.

"What about them?"

"Not many people know it, but that pamphlet got printed because the people who ordered them were all carrying Iron Roses."

Bobbin shifted in his chair. "That's insane. No one would impersonate a Blackhat like that."

"They definitely did," Michel said. "But you're right. It's insane. The propaganda is one thing—Captain Blasdell is all over that—but those Iron Roses are something else entirely. We've been trying to figure out where they came from."

The smile disappeared from Bobbin's face. He looked a little sickly.

"Now," Michel continued, "Captain Blasdell thinks they were forged by someone out of the country. It certainly makes sense. But me? I think they were originals. All the originals in Landfall have been accounted for—I believe you made that report yourself just a couple of days ago, right?"

"That's right," Bobbin said, licking his lips. "Every one of them is accounted for. You can even come back here and count them if you like."

"Of course, of course," Michel said. "I believe you. But I've got to follow my train of thought here. If the Iron Roses were originals, and haven't been stolen from the Millinery, that means they came from our own people. But it doesn't add up. Iron Roses are rarely reported as lost, and, thanks to the reputation of our grand master, are pretty much never stolen. And me? I think the idea that fifteen of our own Iron Roses were involved in an antigovernment plot seems a bit far-fetched."

"Michel," Bobbin said, his voice shaky, "I really should get some work done."

Michel ignored him. "So I thought to myself: Self, where does anyone get fifteen Iron Roses? And I answered: the Treasury, of course. And who's in charge of the Treasury? My old friend Bobbin."

Bobbin went red. His mouth flapped a few times, then his jaw tightened and he sat up straight. "I don't know what you're imply-ing," he said, "but you'd better watch your mouth, Agent Bravis. You know there's consequences for false accusations around here."

"I know," Michel said. "That's why I checked first. I went through your house this morning, and your apartment that's not on the books last night. I found the receipts from the Starlish Bank. Half a million krana is a *lot* of money. And you've been spending like a fool, too. Clothes, booze, women. I checked all your haunts and you're not being nearly as careful as you think you are. And before you start trying to come up with a story about me fabri-cating evidence, you should know I'm hunting around on private orders of the grand master. He's going to examine my report per-sonally and you know he'll find things that even I couldn't."

Bobbin's face went from red to white in the course of a few

moments. His breath was shallow, a sheen of sweat on his forehead. Michel hated seeing him like this. He was a trusted Blackhat, a Silver Rose with the only keys to the Treasury outside Fidelis Jes. He was supposed to be as inviolate as the Roses themselves, and what's more is that Michel *liked* Bobbin. Everybody did.

"I didn't know," Bobbin whispered.

"Know what?" This was the part, Michel knew, where everyone began to beg. They threw excuses, tried bribery, swore oaths.

But Bobbin knew that, and he didn't bother. "Fidelis Jes is going to skin me alive."

That seems pretty likely. "Know what?" Michel asked again firmly.

"I didn't know what they were planning."

Michel leaned against the counter and said in a gentle voice, "Tell me what happened."

"I was approached by a lawyer. He used the same brothel as me, over on the Wake. He told me he could pay me a huge sum if I lent him fifteen Iron Roses. I thought it was a joke at first. Nobody outside the organization knows that I'm the treasurer. But he kept insisting and by the time I decided to report him he had bought up all my debts. All of them. From the casinos, the brothels. Even the bookstores. Said he'd cancel all my debts *and* give me half a million if I lent him the Roses for one day. Insisted no one would even know they were gone."

Michel tilted his head to the side. It was a classic entrapment move, one the Blackhats themselves used when they needed to blackmail someone. Bobbin should have known better. "And did he give them back?"

"Yes. He took them from this door right here at nine o'clock at night and returned them again by six o'clock the next morning. Once I heard about this thing with the pamphlets, I suspected what had happened. But there was no official word about the Iron Roses having been used so I thought maybe it was just a coincidence."

A lawyer. The man behind this whole thing. Never mind those fifteen messengers with their Iron Roses. Michel now had the mastermind in his sights. Bastard walked right into the Millinery. What a pair of balls. "And there was no one you could ask to find out without implicating yourself?"

Bobbin nodded.

Pit. That was just basic self-preservation. Anyone stupid enough to admit to aiding in the misuse of Iron Roses—no matter how unknowingly—deserved what the Blackhat torturers did to them. Michel looked Bobbin over. He was trembling something fierce now, and looked like he might collapse at any moment. But he wasn't begging, and that was a pleasant surprise.

Michel hated the begging.

"I've been a wreck ever since," Bobbin said. "I knew deep down someone would find out, but I couldn't have my debts exposed. I would have lost everything."

"Out of the pot and into the fire," Michel said absently. He felt fantastic, pleased to have made a breakthrough like this in such a short amount of time. He'd solved this thing with the Iron Roses and though he didn't feel revealing Bobbin was going to earn him his Gold Rose, catching the perpetrator behind Bobbin's blackmail definitely would. This was big. He eyed Bobbin and made a decision—one he knew he was going to regret. "Tell me everything about who you worked for."

"I did," Bobbin said. "It was always the one guy. Tall, lean, but muscular. Had a soldier's build. Wore real fancy clothes and carried a cane. Said he was a lawyer."

"Did he give a name?"

"Nothing. Believe me, if I knew I would tell you. Pit, I'd help you track him down right now if I thought it would buy me a reprieve. But he was like a ghost."

Michel leaned forward, looking Bobbin in the eye, then nodded. "I do believe you. Right. Here's what's going to happen." He checked his pocket watch. "Don't get any funny ideas, because I've instructed Warsim to come down and check on me in two or three minutes, and I've left evidence of your little lending scheme with someone I trust."

Bobbin's brow furrowed. "What are you talking about?"

"I want you to open that door, punch me really hard in the face, and then I never want to see you again." Michel walked over to the door and stood patiently, hand at his sides. "And Bobbin, if they catch up to you, do me a favor and put one in your own head."

CHAPTER 14

A t midmorning, Vlora was summoned from her dingy, leaky headquarters in the old staff building at Loel's Fort. She came out to the muster yard expecting a messenger from the Lady Chancellor's office or one of her own scouts but instead found a small Palo man, hat in hand, standing beside a rickshaw. The man had a gaunt face and the characteristic ashen freckles and fiery red hair of a Palo. There were crow's feet around his eyes from too much squinting, and deep smile lines at the corners of his mouth. He ducked his head as Vlora approached.

"Lady Flint?" he asked in flawless Adran.

"That's me."

"Good afternoon. I am Devin-Tallis. I was sent by the Ice Baron."

Vlora's mind was elsewhere, churning over supply reports from her quartermasters, but she put them all out of her head at the mention of the peculiar baron. "Vallencian? What would he . . . Ah! Did he get me an invitation to the gala? When is that, tonight?"

"He did, my lady." Devin-Tallis smiled pleasantly, blinking at Vlora for several moments.

"Can I have it?" she asked.

"Ah, it does not work like that, Lady Flint. I *am* your invitation."

Vlora thought she understood immediately. The Depths was closed to outsiders. Of course she would need a guide to reach whatever "palace" this gala was being held in. She called toward the staff building for Olem, then turned back to the Palo. "When is it, exactly? Vallencian didn't give me any details."

"The baron seldom gives out details that don't have to do with one of his stories," Devin-Tallis said, speaking not as if he was a Palo peasant but rather a close friend of one of the richest men on the continent. "The celebration will take place at nine o'clock tonight, at the Yellow Hall. I'll take you there and bring you back."

Vlora looked over her shoulder, wondering where Olem had got himself to. "All right, what time do you want to leave?"

"Eight thirty should be fine. We're not all that far from the hall."

"Why'd you come so early?" Vlora asked.

"I work on the other side of town. I had a job over here, so I thought it seemed prudent. If it is pleasing to your ladyship, I'll wait here until you're ready to depart. I'll stay out of the way."

"Don't call me that," Vlora said. "Flint is fine, or General. All right, I'll have a guard ready by that time. Can horses maneuver through the Depths, or should I bring infantry?"

"Ah," Devin-Tallis said, clearing his throat, "I'm afraid horses would be a very bad idea. Besides, the invitation is for one."

Vlora paused. One? She couldn't even bring Olem with her? "They don't have to come inside. They're for protection. I've heard . . . things regarding the safety of the Depths." She half-expected the Palo to laugh at her, but instead his face grew solemn.

"One," he said, holding up a finger. "That is all I'm allowed to guide to the Yellow Hall. Lady Flint, or her appointee. No one else.

As long as you are with me, that is a guarantee of your safety as long as you do not start a fight."

"Even if I'm provoked?"

"Dueling is prohibited. You may bring your weapons, because you are a soldier, but if you draw them in anger your safety is revoked."

"Who, exactly, guarantees this safety?" Vlora asked. She didn't like anything about the arrangement. It sounded like a trap. Would Vallencian set her up?

"Everyone at the celebration will be a guest of Mama Palo." Devin-Tallis's face darkened slightly. "No one crosses Mama Palo. Should I wait, Lady Flint? Or have you reconsidered the offer?" He paused, considering, then added in a hushed tone, "Invitations like this are not extended often. The Ice Baron has vouched for you, and that allows you to enter Palo society this once. If you turn it down, you will not receive another opportunity."

Vlora had heard terms like this before, and it always led to one thing: a trap. Vallencian seemed genuine, and so did the Palo rickshaw driver. But she couldn't be certain. The implication here was that Mama Palo herself had approved her invitation, which could mean anything at all. She suddenly realized how little she knew of Mama Palo. Was she a malevolent force? Lindet and the Blackhats certainly seemed to think so. Did she scheme outside of Greenfire Depths and the Palo that she had united, or did she stay within a small area of influence? Was she the type to dare the ire of a dangerous mercenary company by harming their general?

As much as the situation made her leery, she felt like she had to take advantage of this. Blackhats didn't dare the Depths, yet she had been invited right to Mama Palo's doorstep. Perhaps Mama would even be there tonight in the flesh. Kidnapping her on her own would be impossible, but if Vlora could arrange another, less public meeting...

"All right," she said. "Eight thirty. I'll be here."

"Very good, Lady Flint. I'll wait."

"And I'll send someone out with some water," Vlora said over her shoulder, heading back toward the staff building. She found Olem on the other side of headquarters, helping a handful of soldiers pry an immense, rotted beam off the inside of the fort walls. The group leaned on a long pry bar, heaving and hoeing until the beam came loose in a shower of spongy wooden fragments. Olem saw Vlora and came to join her, dusting off his hands. "Don't you have anything better to do?" she asked.

"Yeah," Olem said reluctantly. "But they needed an extra body, so I pitched in. I like to get my hands dirty."

"That's why I like you," Vlora responded. She smiled at his rolled-up sleeves and the sweat on his brow, considering the things she'd like to do to him. But business came first. It always came first. "I just got my invitation to the gala."

Olem's face lit up and he gave her a wink. "Excellent! I'll get my dress reds and put together an honor guard."

"Yeah," Vlora said, drawing out the word. "That's a problem."

"How?" Olem asked, immediately suspicious.

"I'm the only one allowed to go. If I try to bring anyone else, the invitation is forfeit."

Olem looked nonplussed. "Well, we'll have to figure out something else, then." He paused, examining Vlora's face, then shook his head. "Oh, pit. You want to go in there alone, don't you? Absolutely not, I forbid it."

"You what?" Vlora said, her voice growing dangerously quiet. She grit her teeth, ready for a fight.

"I forbid it," Olem said, though with slightly less conviction. He knew he'd made a mistake.

"I love you dearly, but you do not forbid me anything," Vlora said in a low voice. "This is a once-in-a-million chance. I'm being invited straight into the den of our quarry, without a fight, without a risk to the lives of my men."

"The adder's nest, more like it," Olem spat.

"Have you known me to fear adders?" Vlora forced herself to rethink her anger. Olem wasn't coddling her. She knew this was a risk she was taking, perhaps foolishly. He was not in the wrong to question it. But she *was* the commanding officer.

"No," Olem answered after a few moments of silence. "I've never known you to fear much of anything."

"I'll have my weapons," Vlora said. "And my powder. I won't drink and I won't eat, and I'll keep a hand on my pistol. If anything happens I'll carve my way out of it."

Olem scoffed. "You're being pigheaded."

"Perhaps. It's a risk I'm willing to take."

"At least let me send Norrine or Davd with you."

Vlora lifted a finger like Devin-Tallis. "One invitation. No more."

"Shit," Olem said, pacing the space between her and the outer wall of the fort. "I wish Styke was here. He said he knows a bit about the Depths. If he was, I could at least have him shadow you."

"Well, he's not. Have you heard from him?"

"Stopped by earlier. Said he had a lead on those dragonmen. Said he'd know more tonight."

Vlora stood with her hands on her hips, drumming the butt of her pistol. She wondered if the big bastard was leading them on, or if he really had something. "All right. I'll meet with him when I get back. It might not be until tomorrow. It's a party, after all."

Olem's jaw tightened in a way she found endearing, and he finally said, "All right. Keep your sword loose, and don't trust anyone."

"Of course not."

"And," Olem added, "if anything happens to you, I will burn down Greenfire Depths, Lindet and Mama Palo be damned."

CHAPTER 15

Michel nursed a decent-sized bruise while Fidelis Jes stood over him, reading through his report on Bobbin's betrayal. Jes gave an occasional grunt or "hmm," but otherwise fumed silently at the papers in his hands. Michel could feel the grand master's anger almost as strongly as he could feel the throbbing just over his left eye.

"You're certain about this?" Jes asked finally, looking up.

Michel sat up straighter in his seat in the waiting room of the grand master's office. He glanced over at Dellina, whose sympathetic smile was reassuring but unhelpful, and nodded. "Yes, sir."

"Betrayed by our own treasurer," Jes spat, tossing the report across the room. Papers fluttered to the floor. "*And* he got away. Dellina, make a note to have our people in the port cities of Fatrasta keep an eye out for someone matching Bobbin's description. We don't have the time or resources to track him down right now, but we'll get him eventually." He looked down at Michel, eyes narrowed. "It seems, Agent Bravis, that you've exceeded my expectations by tracking down the Roses in just a few days, and then failed me by letting the traitor go. All at once. I'm impressed."

Not the good kind of impressed, the sardonic voice in the back of Michel's head said. "Sir, I don't think Bobbin matters much anymore. We need to hunt him down, of course," he added quickly, "but what we really want is the person who hired him. This lawyer. He's the real enemy here, and I'd like to request the chance to catch him." *And once I do, you're going to forget all about Bobbin and hand me a Gold Rose.*

Fidelis Jes's gaze did not falter. He stared at Michel, annoyed.

"I got a bit out of Bobbin before he attacked me," Michel went on. "He didn't know the name of the man who hired him. But we have a description. I can track him down *and* keep this thing quiet. With Bobbin gone our unknown enemy no longer has access to the Millinery."

"Unless he wasn't working alone."

Michel swore to himself silently. Bobbin was a loner—the single treasurer down on the bottom floor, always ready to share the office gossip but never really connecting with anyone. It hadn't even occurred to Michel that he might have an accomplice. "I think he was, sir." Michel tried to sound confident. "I'm fairly good at reading people. He gave me a full confession before he fled. I think he would have named names if there were any. He was mortified at his involvement in the scandal."

"Yes, you mentioned that in your report," Jes said sourly. He looked down at the report scattered around the room. "You're too easy on him, Agent Bravis. A traitor is a traitor."

"I understand, sir. I won't be taken by surprise so easily next time." Michel pointed to the bruise. "I'll have this to remind me to give him what for if I see him."

Jes snorted and walked into his office. He came out a moment later with his sword, making Michel's heart leap into his throat. Jes began to work through a series of thrusts and parries, fighting an invisible opponent, his sword sometimes coming within inches of Michel's face. Michel's hands trembled but he dared not move.

He does this when he's angry, Dellina mouthed.

Yes, Michel answered silently, *but he also murders people to get his blood going in the mornings.*

Almost a full minute passed before Jes set his sword across Dellina's desk and paced the room, finally turning to Michel with a soldier's snap and a more neutral expression on his face. "You're right," he said. "Finding where the Roses came from was your task, and you did manage to do that. But if you think you've earned my gratitude, you're sorely mistaken. You'll have your chance at redemption. Get this lawyer. Bring him in alive."

"Of course, sir."

There was a knock on the door, then it opened a few inches to reveal the young face of one of the office aides. His eyes widened at the state of the antechamber, and Dellina hurried over to speak with him in hushed tones. She conveyed the message to Fidelis Jes, whose eyes narrowed.

"Well," Jes said, clearing his throat, "it's your lucky day, Agent Bravis."

"Sir?"

"A random sweep brought a ruffian in off the street. She's confessed to being one of the messengers who used the Iron Roses, and given us a description of the lawyer matching the same one Bobbin gave you."

Michel let out a small sigh. This was fantastic news. A corroborating report gave him more credence in Jes's eyes, and someone else to question. "Did she have a name?" he asked hopefully.

"No," Dellina responded. "But there was an address."

Jes picked up his sword and pointed it at Michel, then toward the door. "Bring me this troublesome bastard, so I can flay him myself."

The lawyer's office was in the industrial quarter of Landfall, south of the plateau where the foundries and mills worked night and day, fed with raw goods by the keelboats constantly coming down the Hadshaw River. They turned out cigars for the Nine, spun wool for Brudanian colonies, canned fruit for Gurla, and processed a dozen other goods to ship all over the world.

Some enterprising landlord had constructed an office building right in the center of it all, renting rooms to the accountants and pencil-pushers who kept the surrounding mills running. The address given to Michel by Jes's aide was for the second floor, at the very end of the hall. The building manager described the lawyer— once again matching Bobbin's description—and said he never caught the man's name. His rent was paid in full every two weeks, in cash.

Michel left two Iron Roses by the main entrance to the office building and another two by the back—he wasn't letting anyone get the slip on him, even if the last time *was* intentional—then headed up to the second floor alone. He wore a nondescript tan suit jacket and matching pants, a flatcap held in one hand, and the collar of his white shirt sharply pressed. He walked up and down the hall of the second floor three times, looking through the windows of the offices, eyeing the suite at the end.

The suite matched the address Michel had been given, but nothing seemed out of the ordinary. He reached into his pocket, fingers curling around the heavy knuckledusters he kept for special occasions, and knocked with his free hand.

There was no answer. He knocked again, then gently put his ear against the door. Nothing but the sound of men comparing ledgers two rooms behind him.

He checked the door, finding it unlocked, and pushed his way in, adopting his best "clueless busybody" look, and was immediately arrested by the sight of a woman frowning at him from behind a secretary's desk. She was a young, severe-looking woman with her hair pulled into a tight bun behind her, a pencil in one hand, and a pile of papers in one corner of the desk.

"Hello!" Michel said happily in a slightly high-pitched voice he'd perfected back during his second stint as an informant. "Good afternoon, I'm so sorry... so sorry to barge in here but the door was unlocked."

The woman lifted her chin, her frown deepening. "May I help you, sir?"

Michel took the address out of his pocket. "Is this... this 214 Canal?"

"It is," she replied sharply.

"Oh, thank heavens. I was told there was a lawyer here. I can't... I can't remember his name but I was told he was very good and he might be able to help me."

"I think you have the wrong place," the secretary answered.

"I don't... I don't think so. I double-checked the address. I always... always do. This is a law office, is it not? The landlord said I had the right place."

The secretary looked like she'd sucked on a lemon. "It is," she answered, "but we don't practice publicly."

"Are you... you sure? Are you the lawyer, ma'am?"

"I am not. I am the secretary." She didn't offer her name.

Michel looked around the room. It wasn't large—just a reception area, with a door on the right and a door on the left, meant for a secretary to handle two separate offices. "The owner, is he in? I really must... really must speak to him. It's most urgent and I was told he could help me."

"He is not in."

Michel tried to judge whether she was telling the truth, but her obvious annoyance could mean anything. He swayed backward, as if he was about to step back into the hall, then grabbed for the door on his right, throwing it open. The office was bare, filled entirely with boxes, and not a person in sight.

"Sir!" The secretary leapt to her feet.

Michel crossed the reception area and opened the other door.

Inside was a desk with nothing but an oil lamp and several more boxes stacked in one corner. There were no other doors or entrances. This was the entire suite. The secretary had been telling the truth. Michel suppressed a frustrated growl.

The secretary snatched him by the arm. "Sir, I am afraid this is quite untoward. You cannot barge in here and—"

Michel cut her off with a wail. "I'm so sorry, ma'am! I just really need to speak with the . . . with the lawyer right away and I just want to see him and it's my wife and I just don't know where to turn!"

The secretary dragged him bodily toward the door, pushing him out into the hall. "Sir," she said sternly, straightening her skirt, "I am willing to let this impropriety slide because you are obviously not in your right mind. I just don't know who you think you are looking for, but this is not it. Mr. Tampo is not in and—"

"Tampo! Yes, that was his name. I must see him!" Inwardly, Michel cheered. He had a name now. And if he had a name, he had a scent. "When will he be in next?"

"Well, I never . . . hm. Mr. Tampo may be in tonight. He does not have regular office hours but if you come to call around sundown he likes to work when there's no one else around. I don't know what you want but I'll let him deal with you. Now if you will remove your hand, good day, sir!" She slammed the door, and Michel barely pulled his fingers out of the way in time.

He stared at the closed door for several moments, unable to help the feeling of elation. He had a name, he had an address, and he had a time. By tomorrow morning he'd have this whole *Sins of Empire* affair wrapped up, before the Blackhat propagandists even marched out their scapegoat.

Michel could practically feel the Gold Rose hanging from his neck.

CHAPTER 16

It took Old Man Fles three days to arrange a meeting for Styke. The information came in the form of a note, telling Styke that someone would meet him at Sender's Place in order to discuss the dragonmen. The note contained no other information about who, exactly, Styke was supposed to meet. But it would have to be good enough.

Sender's Place was an old pub on the Rim overlooking Greenfire Depths. It was in the basement below a proper gentleman's club and in Styke's day had been soldier-exclusive—a place where the infantry could drink away the horrors of battle while their officers smoked and played cards in their posh velvet couches just upstairs. It all took place under the watchful eye of Grandma Sender, who brooked no fights or pulling of rank. To the veterans of Landfall, it was a damned institution.

It wasn't the type of place anyone would try to start a fight.

It was about seven o'clock in the evening and Styke sat on a stoop across the street from the entrance to Sender's Place, his hands in his pockets, shoulders hunched and flatcap pulled down to cover his face. It seemed, from the look of things, that old Grandma Sender had fallen on hard times. The windows of the gentleman's club upstairs were boarded up, the paint peeling and the front stoop occupied by a beggar and his mutt.

"I've been here before," Celine told him.

"Oh yeah?"

"Yeah, my dad used to fence stuff here."

"To Grandma Sender?"

"No. A man he met in a back room. Grandma was nice, though. Always gave me a sweet."

"I always liked Grandma Sender," Styke commented. He was sad to see the ramshackle state of the place, and suspected it was held less sacred than it used to be. Oh well. Maybe it *hadn't* been the best place to set up a meeting. "All right. You stay out here. You see anyone suspicious head toward the stairs, you throw a pebble at that window there. If there's more than one, throw more than one pebble. Got it?"

"Right."

Styke headed across the street and put his hand on the iron handrail leading to the underground entrance.

"Ben!" Celine called.

He turned back.

"Be careful."

He nodded and headed down the stairs, ducking into the cool darkness. The pub was just as he remembered it—dimly lit, the faint smell of mala smoke hanging in the air, drunks sleeping off their afternoon hangovers on the corner benches, and old Grandma Sender herself, looking the same as she had ten years ago, standing behind the bar polishing glasses. Only the press of warm bodies and the sound of rowdy drinking songs were missing.

Styke let his eyes adjust to the dim light. He counted a dozen occupants, most of them drunk or on their way there, only a couple of them having dinner. None of them were Palo. He felt a smile tug at the corner of his mouth as the smell of the place brought back memories. He'd met Ibana here, more than fifteen years ago. She'd broken his nose, and Grandma Sender had thrown them both out for the night, so they'd bluffed their way into a card game upstairs and cleaned every krana out of two Kez generals.

"You just going to stand there eyeing the place or you going to have a drink?" Grandma Sender said, not looking up from her polishing. "Don't think about robbing us, we got nothing left."

Styke went to the bar. "Hard times?" he asked, laying down several banknotes. "Whiskey and a pipe."

Sender peered at him, scowling. "I know you?" She was a rough old woman, no doubt nearing seventy by now, skin wrinkled, leathery, and pale. She had one eye that seemed to perpetually squint.

"Doubt it," Styke said.

She shook her head. "Yeah, it's bad times." The money disappeared off the bar. "Used to be a veterans' pub. All the veterans either work down in the mills or been sent to the camps."

"No more veterans in Greenfire Depths?" he asked.

"Some," Grandma Sender admitted. "But not as many as you'd think. Taken over by the Palo these days and that lot is useless as far as I'm concerned. They won't drink a drop if the owner of the place isn't a Palo themselves so all I get is the rejects." She put a full glass in front of Styke, then packed a pipe with cherry-scented tobacco and handed it over. "You a veteran?" she asked. "You look familiar."

"Just another one of the weary dead, Grandma," he said. He laid another krana down and nodded to the corner of the bar farthest from the door. "Light. Over there."

Grandma Sender lit one of the myriad of gas lamps above the spot Styke had indicated and then left him alone with his whiskey and pipe. He produced the morning's newspaper and sat back with his feet up on a chair. There was a report on the front page about the Riflejack Mercenary Company taking residence in the old Loel's Fort and getting to work rebuilding a few nearby tenements. It would be the closest rebuilding project to Greenfire Depths in years and was stirring up a decent amount of support from the locals. Styke wondered what Flint was *really* there for—he hadn't been allowed that far into her good graces—but figured the positive press was some kind of red herring. It usually was in Landfall.

There was another story about a massive dig site south of the city. Thousands of laborers had been transported there to help excavate an old monolith. The site was closed to the public but rumor had it scholars were being brought in from the Nine. No one really seemed to know what for, though. Seemed like a lot of effort for an old stone.

Styke flipped through the stories, still pleased by the concept of getting a newspaper the day it came out instead of waiting weeks or months for it to be smuggled into the labor camps. It was all drivel, of course, but it was drivel about his city.

His head came up at the sound of a clink against the high window on the other side of the room. There was another clink. Then another. And another. Styke drew his knife and laid it on the table, casually setting the newspaper down on top of it, and spread his arms across the back of the bench.

The door opened. Even through the dim haze Styke could make out the pale, freckled skin of a young Palo man, followed by several companions. There were four of them all told, dressed in wool suits like any other city folk, no doubt trying to blend in as well as they could. Even during the war most Palo had stopped wearing their buckskins in the city limits. Too much bad blood between them and everybody else.

The four Palo fanned out just inside the door. One carried a pistol proudly on his hip, two others heavy boz knives like Styke's—though much smaller—while the fourth was already wearing a pair of iron knuckledusters. *Came looking for a bit more than talk, it seems.* Styke labeled the four of them in his head: Cheeks, Freckles, Soot, and Happy. Happy was the one with the pistol on his hip, wearing a big grin and looking around the pub like he planned on owning it by the end of the night.

"What do you four want?" Grandma Sender demanded. "Ain't got no time for the likes of you, not if you ain't drinkin'."

Happy gestured rudely. "Shut up, Grandma. Spoke when spoken to, or you'll get the back of my hand."

"Try it, you little runt," Grandma said, slamming the cup she'd been polishing down on the bar. "I'll..."

"Grandma," Styke called gently. "They're here to see me. Don't worry about them." With one foot he pushed the chair across from him out from the table and switched from Adran to Palo. "Sit down and leave the old lady alone. We have talking to do."

"No fighting!" Grandma Sender warned.

Happy narrowed his eyes at Styke and swaggered across the room, followed by the rest. He ignored the offered chair and stood across from Styke, arms folded. He wasn't a small man, as far as most were concerned. Lean, muscular, taller than average. Like most Palo he had bright green eyes and a bit of a squint that came from a thousand generations under the Fatrastan sun. He had the type of face and bearing that would put most women on their backs. If only, Styke mused, he had the charm to go with it.

"You the one who wanted to meet a dragonman?" Happy asked.

"I am," Styke said.

"You don't look like a historian."

"Funny. You don't look like a dragonman."

Happy spat on the floor. "As if a dragonman would bother with the likes of you. We're here to tell you to mind your own damned business. Nobody—scholars, historians, or whatever the pit you are—better come looking around for a dragonman unless you want your head staved in."

"Says who?" Styke asked.

Happy puffed out his chest. "Says me."

Styke eyed Happy's three companions. They weren't professionals, but they weren't fools, either. One of them examined the room, making sure Styke didn't have any backup, while the other two kept their eyes fixed firmly on Styke, their hands ready to move toward weapons. They expected to be meeting with some spectacled pipsqueak, but they had come ready for anything.

"Is there a dragonman in Landfall?" Styke asked, trying to sound only mildly curious.

"None of your damned business, you ugly bastard."

"Now, now. No need for name calling. I'm just asking questions. Asking questions never hurt nobody."

"It'll get you hurt real quick," Happy replied. He drew his pistol. "We're here to give you a message and it was supposed to be all gentle-like, but if you're gonna insist on being inquisitive I can give you a message you'll remember."

Styke sighed. Stupid kids. Too high on their own sense of... something... to look around them. There wasn't anyone to impress in this little place. It was neutral territory where they could have a frank discussion in private. Instead of taking a moment to wonder why a single old cripple seemed completely at ease being outnumbered four to one, Happy was posturing like an idiot.

In a slow, deliberate movement, Styke reached into his pocket and drew out a roll of krana notes. He peeled off a handful and laid them down on the table. "I'm just curious. Tell me a little bit about this dragonman and you can walk out of here with a pocket full of cash. I'll go on my merry way and nobody gets hurt."

Happy glanced over his shoulder at Soot incredulously, then toward a dark stall in the opposite corner of the room and back at Styke. "Who the pit do you think you are?"

"I'm just looking for a little information. Who's this dragonman? Why's he in Landfall now, when they haven't been seen for decades?" Styke spoke quickly to keep Happy on his toes. Five minutes ago he wouldn't have believed there was a dragonman in Landfall. But *someone* had sent these four.

Happy put one hand on the table and leaned forward, his pistol inches from Styke's cheek. "You don't get to ask questions, ugly. In fact, I think I'm going to ask them myself. Why do you want to know? Why do you care about the dragonmen? You better spit it out quick, because I'm losing my patience."

"You hear what I said?" Grandma Sender demanded from behind the bar. "I speak enough of your bullshit language to know you're getting your spirits up. No fighting in here! You five have trouble, take it out to the street."

"Shut up!" Happy yelled. His voice cracked. Something was off here and he knew it. Styke wasn't intimidated by four thugs or a pistol in the face, and that just didn't mesh with Happy's normal experience.

"Mind your manners," Styke snapped. "Answer my questions and you can walk out of here with two hundred krana and all your limbs."

Happy's finger twitched to the trigger of his pistol. "I will take that money and I'll shove this pistol up your—"

Styke snatched up his knife and bolted Happy's wrist to the table with the blade. "Never reach for the money first," he said, jerking the pistol out of Happy's hand.

Happy and his cohorts stared at the blade sticking out of Happy's wrist for several long seconds, then Happy began to scream. There was a mad scramble as the other three went for their weapons, and above it all Styke could hear Grandma Sender yelling, "No fighting, no fighting!"

Styke threw the table—and Happy along with it—at Soot. They both went down in a pile of limbs while the other two Palo leapt for Styke. He came off his bench and sidestepped a knife thrust from Cheeks, dropping the Palo with a punch to the temple.

Freckles managed to coldcock Styke in the jaw with the knuckledusters. Styke shook off the pain and leaned into another punch to his stomach. He grunted, then caught Freckles's arm and twisted hard. The sound of snapping bone was followed by Freckles's scream.

Cheeks recovered from Styke's punch and barreled back into the fight knife-first. Styke sidestepped the thrust and wrapped one arm around Cheeks's waist, pulling him close like a woman at a dance, and slammed his forehead against Cheeks's nose. The Palo slumped to the ground.

Styke strode over to where Soot and Happy were still caught under the heavy table. He righted it, then jerked his knife out of Happy's wrist. Soot scrambled toward his own knife, but Styke stepped on his arm. He leaned over Soot, taking him by the throat, and squeezed till he felt blood. Soot twitched several times and then was still, and Styke had to wipe the blood off his ring so it wouldn't slip from his finger.

The whole fight had taken less than twenty seconds, and Happy's face was frozen in terror as he crawled through a smear of his own blood, cradling his wrist, trying to reach the pistol Styke had taken from him. Behind them, Grandma Sender screamed obscenities at them all. Styke picked the pistol up and checked the pan. "It's not even loaded, you asshole." He raised his knife.

Happy rolled over. "By Kresimir, don't do it! I'm not the one you want. He is!" He thrust his finger toward a dark corner of the room. Styke hesitated, suspecting a trick. There was nobody in that corner.

The hairs on the back of Styke's neck suddenly stood on end as the very shadows themselves seemed to move. A man stood up, appearing as if he had emerged from nothing, adjusting the cuffs of his fine black suit. He was squat and muscular, with short, fire-red hair and a tuft of beard on his chin. Black tattoos snaked onto his wrists and neck but otherwise he might have been mistaken for a Palo businessman having a drink in the pub.

Grandma Sender, her arms thrown up over the mess of bodies on her floor, paused mid-tirade. "Where the pit did you come from?"

The stranger ignored her. "Why do you want a dragonman?" he asked. The words were strangely thick, like he had a mouth full of molasses, and it took several moments for Styke to realize why. He wasn't speaking Palo.

He was speaking a sister language, one so close they could be mistaken for the same; Dynize.

Styke forgot Happy on the floor beneath him. A killer knew a killer at first glance, and this one had a lot of blood on his hands. He held himself confidently, head slightly cocked, his body relaxed but his attitude screaming imminent violence. Styke turned toward this stranger—a dragonman—and held his knife out to his side.

"Just looking for answers."

"Well," the dragonman said. "You won't find them. Not here."

Styke had always been good at assessing a threat. He knew when to push and when to retreat and it had made him an unbeatable cavalry commander. But he couldn't read the dragonman at all, and that was disconcerting. "I think I will. Might have to pry them out of you, though." He gestured to the bodies of the Palo kids he'd just torn through. "These are yours, aren't they? Didn't even step in to give them a hand."

The dragonman's eyebrow twitched slightly, an arrogant tic that said it didn't matter much.

Styke felt a little bile in the back of his throat. These poor Palo kids were probably acolytes of some kind. In Styke's mind, that made the dragonman responsible, just like Colonel Styke had been responsible for every lancer under his command. "I don't like you," Styke said. "And I think I'm going to enjoy killing you."

The dragonman took a step forward, then stopped. His face reminded Styke of a cat, completely unreadable, eyes searching Styke for strengths and weaknesses. He seemed to hesitate and then, without warning, he suddenly went for the door, as quick and casual as a panther who'd decided not to fight a bear for its kill. He was out and gone in a flash, and Styke swore, limping after him. By the time he reached the street, the dragonman was already disappearing into the late afternoon crowd.

"Celine!" Styke jammed a new piece of horngum in his mouth, chewing violently to numb the spasm in his leg.

She joined him quickly, and Styke pointed after the dragonman. "Did you just see the Palo that came out of the door? The one in the black suit?"

"Yes."

"Follow him. Don't let him see you, but don't lose him. I'll be right behind you."

Celine took off into the crowd and Styke fell back, following at a leisurely pace. He wiped blood off his sleeve and face, grumbling under his breath. He didn't like being duped, or given the slip like that. He also didn't like getting answers that raised more questions.

Like what the pit a legend like a Dynize dragonman was doing alive and walking around in Landfall.

CHAPTER 17

V lora wore her dress uniform, sword and pistol at her belt, and met Devin-Tallis in the muster yard at eight thirty. It wasn't long until dark, and she boarded his tiny rickshaw with some trepidation. He immediately set off from Loel's Fort, heading down the street and toward the switchbacks that Michel had taken her down just two days earlier. By the time they reached the bottom all sign of daylight was gone, and she was surprised to see the narrow streets lit dimly by a handful of gas lamps she had not noticed earlier.

Within moments of reaching the floor of the Depths she was completely turned around. Devin-Tallis chugged onward, his legs working effortlessly as he pulled the rickshaw through a series of rapid, seemingly unnecessary turns, his feet splashing through the permanent layer of damp sludge that seemed to cover the streets. They traveled onward in silence for several minutes, and Vlora's heart beat a little faster with every passing moment and the realization that if Devin-Tallis left her suddenly, she had no hope of finding her way back to the plateau on her own.

She unwrapped a powder charge and sprinkled a bit on her tongue, relishing the sulfur taste, then snorting a bit more. The trance lit her mind like a fuse, letting her focus better, her vision sharpening so that she could see the dark spots between gas lamps as clear as if it were day.

Being able to see the sudden sharp angles and dubious construction of the overlapping tenements did very little to calm her. "You said this is a celebration," she said. "But Vallencian called it a gala. Which is it?"

Devin-Tallis spoke without turning his head. "Both, I suppose. It's a Palo celebration, the Day of the Two Moons."

Vlora tried to think of a festival that corresponded to today's date, but no harvests or astrological events came to mind. "What does that mean?"

"No idea," Devin-Tallis said. "I asked my father when I was a boy. He didn't know, either. It's a festival, and we celebrate."

"Usually a festival corresponds to something."

"Perhaps it once did," Devin-Tallis answered.

That wasn't much help. Vlora looked up, trying to get her bearings from the sky, but even the little slices of fading twilight that she had been able to see through the jumbled tenements were now gone, obscured by the masonry, boards, and cloth that stitched together the layers of Greenfire Depths. She took a little more powder to calm her nerves. "What kind of a name is Devin-Tallis?"

"A Palo one," he answered.

"I haven't met many Palo with two names."

"It's not actually two names," Devin-Tallis said. "Devin is my title. My given name is Tallis."

"No family name?"

"Some of us have them. It varies among the tribes. My tribe, the

Wannin, use a naming system that goes back to when the people you call the Dynize used to rule these lands. It's very old. We go by our title, and then our name."

Vlora thought of the way Kressian naming conventions went. The lower classes often only had a single name. They could buy or earn a second name—often an epithet like her "Lady Flint." Now that she thought of it, their methods were not dissimilar. "What does Devin mean?"

"One who serves."

"Is that a class thing, or..."

"Ah, no," Devin-Tallis said. "I pull a rickshaw, and I have since I was strong enough. It makes me good money, and allows me to keep a family. *One who serves* is a proud name. You might call it middle-class."

Vlora couldn't help but chuckle. So often it was easy to think of the Palo as savages—most Kressians did—but then she was reminded that most spoke Adran or Kez or some other Kressian language with little accent, and they grasped Kressian traditions better than Kressians grasped theirs. She wondered, if the Palo were not so divided, whether they would have any trouble pushing the Kressian immigrants into the sea.

It was most likely a possibility that haunted Lady Chancellor Lindet's dreams.

Vlora remembered someone she'd once known—the green-eyed girl Taniel brought back from his time in Fatrasta all those years ago, along with rumors of a scandal that had caused her no end of grief. "What does 'Ka' mean?" she asked.

Devin-Tallis slowed slightly, frowning over his shoulder. "I have not heard that before. I would have to ask. Ah, we are here." They rounded a corner and came to a sudden stop. Vlora glanced around. Nothing seemed out of the ordinary. There were no crowds, no arrival line of rickshaws. Just another side alley with a well-trodden street of stone and muck, ending in a well-lit door made of reeds.

"We're here?" Vlora asked.

"Yes."

"You're sure?"

"This is it," Devin-Tallis said. "The streets down here are narrow, so every house or hall has several entrances. The Palo don't care much for grand facades. It is, after all, what is inside that matters."

Vlora got out of the rickshaw and Devin-Tallis put it off to one corner, then led her to the door at the end of the alley and spoke his name. The reed curtain was pulled aside, revealing a narrow corridor and a pair of armed Palo. Vlora could smell the powder on them, and spotted their pistols a moment later. They gazed back at her stoically, and Vlora spread her senses, trying not to gasp when she felt hundreds of small caches of powder within fifty yards, each of them no doubt representing another armed guard.

Security, it seemed, was not a problem for the Palo.

Devin-Tallis waved her forward. "I will introduce you," he said, leading her down several narrow corridors, "and then I must return to my rickshaw."

"You're not coming in?"

"I am," Devin-Tallis said with a smile, "middle-class. The Palo have their own system, and only the elite are invited into the Yellow Hall. Ah. Here we are. I will come back and check on you in a few hours. If you wish to leave, simply send someone to find me."

Vlora had become increasingly aware of the low buzz of conversation at the edges of her powder trance, but a wave of voices suddenly burst upon her as if she'd entered a banquet hall. They passed two more guards in the gaslit corridor and then Devin-Tallis opened a heavy wooden door for her. What she saw nearly made her gasp.

They stood at the top of three steps leading down into an enormous room, easily a hundred paces across, with dozens of nooks and crannies. Chandeliers hung from the ceiling, and there were hallways and balconies above them that implied the building was much larger than this one hall. Light came from gas lanterns; food and drink, including wine and iced coffee and tea, were provided by smartly dressed servants. The walls and floor were made of the same dark yellow limestone from which the capitol building had been constructed, though the architecture here looked much older.

Guests filled the entire hall, dancing, speaking, lounging on couches along the walls. She had expected a sea of freckled faces with bright red hair, but instead found that only about half the people in the room were Palo. The others were Kressians from a variety of backgrounds, from white Adrans and Kez, to dusty Rosveleans, to black-skinned Deliv, and they all seemed to mingle freely.

"Welcome," Devin-Tallis said, "to the Yellow Hall."

Michel spent all day setting his trap. The grand master's office lent him Iron Roses to cover the entrance to the office building, to watch the windows, the back door, *and* the street. He had men follow the secretary home—which turned out to be just a few blocks away on the edge of the industrial quarter—and positioned people outside *her* door. This was his chance at wrapping up this investigation in just a few days. It would get him his Gold Rose.

He was not going to fail.

It was almost nine when Agent Warsim, Michel's sometime partner, scurried across the street and joined Michel in his hiding place beneath the shadow of a nearby factory. Warsim wore his Bronze Rose and carried a pistol and truncheon. "The boys think they've spotted Tampo," he said in a low whisper.

Michel bit nervously at his nails, eyes on the street, and headed out into the waning sunlight. He arrived a half a block from the office building in time to see a man in a sharp black suit and top hat, carrying a silver cane under one arm and an attaché case under the other, slip in the entrance.

Michel looked up and down the road, making fists to keep his hands from trembling. Pit, this was it. Tampo wasn't going to escape. He let himself inside and ascended the staircase, followed by Warsim and three Iron Roses. The building was quiet, most of the offices empty, and on the second floor there wasn't a single lantern lit except for the flicker of light coming from underneath the door of the suite at the end of the hall.

"Give me your pistol," Michel said, taking the weapon from Warsim. The five of them crept down the hall, careful not to make any noise, and came up against the suite door. He listened for a moment, then nodded to the biggest of the Iron Roses. "Open the door!"

Styke followed the dragonman through the city for almost two hours. He hung back—far back—so as not to draw attention, keeping his shoulders hunched and his hat pulled low. It was hard to follow anyone for a man of his size, but he kept Celine as a lifeline. She had her eyes on the dragonman, and Styke had his eyes on her.

The dragonman ranged all over. His path seemed random at first, and Styke was worried he knew he was being followed, but it soon became apparent that the dragonman was meeting with people. He stopped by a brothel in the industrial quarter, spent an hour in the Treasury building in Upper Landfall, then went down to the docks, where he visited three different ships in the course of fifteen minutes.

Styke got more than one good look at the dragonman in the light of day, and he was more convinced than ever that he was a Dynize. The Dynize were related closely to the Palo, both in looks and language, but there were subtle markers that someone with a good eye—and enough historical education—could see right away. The dragonman's eyes were slightly more oval, his cheeks a bit too gaunt, and his ears were pierced at the top of the ear instead of the lobe.

The mystery became to Styke not that the dragonman *was* a Dynize, but rather *why* he was a Dynize. Even before Styke's time at the labor camp the Dynize had been isolationists, the borders of their continent closed to outsiders—including merchants and missionaries. No one had seen them anywhere outside their country for more than a hundred years, even though Fatrasta lay practically on the Dynize doorstep. What were they doing here now?

Styke didn't even know the Dynize *had* dragonmen. The stories said the Palo developed their own warriors after the Dynize pulled out of Fatrasta. It seemed, though, based on the tattoos, that they'd taken their dragonmen straight from Dynize society. Which meant that the Dynize might have a whole nation's worth of dragonmen, and even if they were one in ten thousand, the prospect of an army of mythical warriors was... off-putting.

But all that seemed like a pretty huge assumption. Styke needed to stop getting ahead of himself and get the drop on the dragonman. It would be best to take him alive, but even tossing a dead body at the feet of Lady Flint would answer some questions. At the very least it would get her to trust him, which, Styke reminded himself, was his primary mission.

Styke pulled his head out of his own thoughts for a moment, looking around for Celine. He'd lost her a few times, but she wasn't hard to spot in her yellow shirt and boy's trousers. She kept well ahead of him and he didn't begin to worry until he'd gone almost a full block and saw no sign of her anywhere.

They were still down in the docks. This area was packed with warehouses and silos, half of them on the boardwalk, forming a myriad of alleys and switchbacks. It wasn't the ideal place to follow someone.

But it *was* a great place for an ambush.

Styke felt his heart beating a little faster. Celine would have called out if she ran into trouble, wouldn't she? She was a smart girl, more than quick enough to get away from most adults. But this was a dragonman, a killer as bloody and remorseless as Styke himself.

He found himself doubling his pace, head whipping back and forth as he rushed past alleys, looking for any sign of Celine. He kept one hand out in front of him, pushing dockworkers and sailors out of the way, the other hand on the hilt of his knife. She was here somewhere, he knew it, and he'd find her.

"Ben!"

Styke only needed to hear the sound once. He about-faced, backtracking through the evening traffic, even shoving a pack mule bodily from his path, his mind racing. His name had been yelled in desperation.

He checked the face of an alleyway and came up short.

The dragonman stood less than twenty paces away. His head was cocked, an expression of annoyance on his face, and he held a squirming Celine by the back of the neck. In his other hand was a polished bone knife, curved and wicked like a ceremonial dagger.

Styke felt his chest tighten at the sight of Celine. The dragonman was clearly hurting her, and he clearly didn't care.

"Ben, was it?" the dragonman asked casually. "You're going to answer some questions."

Styke drew his knife, knuckles white on the hilt, and took a step forward. "Like the pit I am."

The Iron Rose kicked in the door, cudgel in one hand, pistol in the other. His companions knocked in the two office doors of the suite, and Michel heard a string of protestations and a startled yell from one of them. He ran a hand over his mouth, trying to keep the enormous grin off his face.

He was a professional, after all.

He counted to ten seconds, then followed the Iron Roses inside suite 214, looking around. Tampo was in the office on the left, sitting behind the desk with Agent Warsim behind him. Tampo's jacket was pulled halfway down, trapping his arms so he couldn't move. Tampo would be feeling more than a little terror right now, and Michel was willing to let that last another couple of moments.

He did a quick circuit of the opposite room, using a knife to pry open one of the many crates that were stacked haphazardly around. He blinked down at the contents, frowning, before that big grin he'd been trying to suppress finally broke through his defenses. "Bring me that lantern."

One of the Iron Roses brought him the lantern from Tampo's desk. Michel held it over the crate, light spilling across the contents, to reveal stacks of *Sins of Empire*. With so many crates in this room and the next, there were probably thousands of copies here. There was now no doubt this was the man who'd arranged the printing of the pamphlet.

And Michel had him at gunpoint in the other room.

He suppressed the urge to dance over to Tampo's desk and instead walked, measuring his steps. He set down the lantern and leaned forward, gazing into Tampo's eyes. The lawyer was frozen in terror, his mouth working but nothing coming out. The trousers of his fine suit were soaked with urine. Sedition against the Lady Chancellor wasn't so clever now, was it? Michel found himself unsure of where to start. Was he supposed to question him? Take him straight to the Millinery?

"Looks like we're both in for a long night," Michel said, sitting on the edge of the desk. "Tell me, is your real name Tampo? Because I couldn't find it in any of the public records, and I had people searching all afternoon."

The lawyer's mouth continued to work. Michel frowned. He'd expected someone timid—revolutionaries often were once you took the piss out of them—but he hadn't expected someone so frozen by their own terror that they couldn't speak. He must realize how close to the end of his life he had come. Michel didn't particularly relish what was going to happen to Tampo. He didn't like torture, though it certainly had its uses, but he was exceedingly pleased to be the one to bring Tampo down. It was going to earn him his Gold Rose.

He leaned forward, smacking Tampo on the cheek gently. "Have anything to say?"

Tampo's jaw trembled, and he whispered something between his chattering teeth. Michel leaned forward to better hear it. "Speak up."

"I don't know who you think I am," the man said. "But I'm the janitor."

All the joy Michel had been floating on disappeared. This couldn't have been a mistake. Janitors didn't wear five-thousand-krana suits. They didn't carry canes. "Excuse me?"

"The lawyer who works here said he'd give me a hundred krana to come in tonight wearing his clothes."

Michel licked his lips. He snatched up the man's right hand, examining his fingers closely. They weren't the fingers of a law-yer. They were rough, burned, and blistered from years of manual labor, paint on his knuckles and dirt under his nails.

This was not Tampo.

"Son of a bitch!" Michel kicked over one of the crates, pointing at one of the Iron Roses. "Go get me the secretary. Now!"

CHAPTER 18

T he Lady Vlora Flint," Devin-Tallis announced loudly, as if he were a herald at a king's ball. He gave a half bow and withdrew, leaving Vlora at the top step, looking out over the array of faces that turned to look at her.

The normal conversation stopped, and the quiet buzz of whispered gossip replaced it. She could make out any of them if she focused, thanks to her powder trance, but she decided she'd rather not know what they had to say. Some faces seemed welcoming, others openly hostile, while even more were perplexed. Vlora resisted the urge to check the cuffs of her uniform and polish the crossed muskets of her brass Riflejack pin.

"Ah!" a voice boomed from nearby. "Lady Flint, my friend." Vallencian moved through the crowd like a bull through a herd of sheep, coming over and taking her by the arm and leading her down into the mingling guests, and to her relief the regular conversation immediately resumed. "I am so glad you took me up on the invitation," Vallencian said. "I know you military types. Don't like a place without a clear exit. But I tell you, it's worth it!"

"Thank you for arranging an invitation for me," Vlora said, ignoring the irony as she checked for exits and reached out with her senses to spot the guards. She passed familiar faces, though none with names she could remember, and caught more than one Palo staring at her. "I'm wondering," she confessed, "if this was such a good idea."

"It's fine," Vallencian declared. "Lady Flint has no need of an honor guard. You *are* an honor guard."

"I'm not sure what that means, but I'm beginning to think the biography you read of me may have greatly exaggerated my accomplishments," Vlora said. "I'm just a soldier." Which seemed an understatement right now. She had never liked this sort of crowd. Politicians always rubbed her the wrong way—one of the reasons she'd left Adro despite being a decorated general—and places like this were breeding grounds for the worst kind of petty politics. This had been a very bad idea indeed. "What is this place?"

"The Yellow Hall. Built by the quarry foreman back when the quarries here provided all the wealth in Landfall."

"It looks old."

"A hundred and fifteen years, I think. It's held up remarkably well for being buried underneath a dozen tenements. The yellow limestone is no facade—solid blocks." He led them near one of the walls and slapped it with one hand as if to demonstrate.

A whole villa, buried down here in the center of the Depths, long forgotten by the rest of Landfall. Surely the Blackhats must know about this place? "I thought there would be more Palo."

Vallencian led her through the press, past a table where he nabbed a glass of iced coffee and pushed it into her hands, and then toward the far corner. "Yes, yes. Usually more Palo, but it's a public celebration—as public as the Palo get—so they've invited everyone who does business down here." He pointed to a young woman in a sheer dress. "That is Lady Enna, she owns the biggest quarry in Greenfire Depths along with the Palo next to her, Meln-Dun. That old man with the glasses, that is Rider Hofflast. Owns ten thousand acres of sugarcane on an island off the coast, employs mostly Palo. There is a man who sells the lumber, a woman who trades furs. Everyone here does business with the Palo."

She wondered how so many Kressians could be down here, doing open business, while the Blackhats feared stepping foot in the Depths. It seemed preposterous and she wanted to ask Vallencian but it was a question she didn't want overheard. "I thought Lindet owned most of the businesses in Landfall."

Vallencian snorted. "She likes to think she does and," he said with a shrug, "she has a piece of every company in Fatrasta. It's the cost of doing business. Don't get me wrong, I respect Lindet. She's a smart, driven woman, even if she's as savage as a high-mountain bear. But she's overextended, and just one woman."

"You respect her?" Vlora echoed, looking around to see who might have overheard. This seemed poor company for such an utterance.

"Of course," Vallencian responded. "I never said I *liked* her. But she's a powerful, driven woman. There is a lot to admire."

Vlora glanced up at Vallencian. She found she was growing to like him more and more. "Even after the way she treats your... business partners?"

"I see the good in people," Vallencian said, matter-of-factly. "Even when it's hard to find."

"You see *too much* of the good in people," a voice suddenly said sharply. Vlora turned to find the woman in the diaphanous dress, Lady Enna, standing at her shoulder. Enna seemed just a little younger than she, well-endowed with long, brown hair and lips that most courtesans would kill for. She took Vlora's other arm, unasked, and leaned in conspiratorially. "Lady Flint, I am Lady Enna and I am absolutely honored to meet you."

"Thank you," Vlora said, giving her a tight smile. Enna's eyes were just a little too big, her expression just a little too forward, in a way that struck Vlora as artificial. Vlora opened her mouth to ask Vallencian a question, but the Ice Baron suddenly disengaged with an apology and disappeared into the crowd, leaving Vlora alone with Lady Enna.

The bastard.

Before Vlora could say a word, Enna leaned even closer. "Don't think I'm being too hard on Vallencian. We all love him to death, but he is a big stuffed bear, the mighty fool. He's too soft on Lindet and her blasted Blackhats. She is a terror and she must be stopped."

Vlora raised her eyebrows, startled to hear such a declaration. Was it *that* kind of party, full of dogmatic liberals? Or had Lady Enna had too much to drink? Vlora could smell the wine on her breath. She was tempted to say, *You know I work for her, right?* But she managed to keep her lips sealed. "I, uh...Do many other people feel the same way?"

"There are *thousands* of us," Enna assured. "Have you heard of the New Fatrasta movement?"

"I'm sure I have," Vlora said, though she definitely hadn't.

"Well, let me tell you, the New Fatrasta movement aims to put Lindet out of power, and to disband her group of legalized thugs." She leaned so close her head was practically on Vlora's shoulder. "Did you see the pamphlet that came out last week? *Sins of Empire?* Well, I have it on good authority that it was a high-ranking member of the New Fatrasta movement. There's whispers it was even the Red Hand. Wouldn't that be exciting?"

Vlora had dealt with agents of the Red Hand out on the frontier. "Exciting" was one word for it, but not one she would have chosen. He was one of the more effective Palo revolutionaries operating out of the wilds, and rumor had it his small guerrilla army drove Lindet to distraction. "This New Fatrasta, is it an organized thing?" she asked.

"Oh, no. We're not organized."

Doubtlessly.

"I'm sure you have a copy, but here, take this," Enna said. She paused to search her handbag until she found the pamphlet, thrusting it in Vlora's hands. It wasn't large, maybe ten or twelve pages, and when she turned it over the title *Sins of Empire* was printed on the front. "If you have not read it, you must immediately. It is an exposé on everything Lindet has done to this poor, helpless country. It tells us how her greedy, landgrabbing ways have destroyed the Palo people and raped Fatrasta's heritage. It speaks of the revolutions in Fatrasta and Adro and the changes that came from the Kez Civil War as a starting point to a whole new world that is led by the common people, for the common people."

Vlora opened her mouth several times through the tirade, but couldn't get a word in edgewise. She'd heard of this pamphlet—copies were given out all over Landfall the last couple of days, despite the Blackhats' efforts to censure them. It was a fascinating read with a few radical, naive ideas but a central premise that she basically agreed with. But as a necessity she kept her politics quiet, and out of her business. Politics had been the forte of Field Marshal Tamas, her mentor, a skill that had not rubbed off on her. Besides, mercenary generals didn't always get to choose who they worked for when their men had to be paid.

Which meant that, as a point, she refused to get pulled into political discussions. Especially with inebriated, well-meaning acolytes. "It sounds...interesting," she said, handing the pamphlet back.

"Keep it," Enna declared. "It will open your mind in ways you Will. Not. Believe. Say the word and I can get you more literature. As I said there are *thousands* of us, and though Lindet thinks she has the upper hand, the writers in this beleaguered city continue to work, churning out new manifestos every day that make me wonder why the world has not risen up to throw off their shackles."

Definitely drunk, Vlora decided. No one in their right mind shared this much politics in a city where such a thing could get you hanged, or worse. "You know," Vlora said, "it has been done."

Enna's eyes grew somehow larger. "It has?"

"Yes. That revolution in Adro. I was in it. We killed several hundred noble families and the king, sparking a war that ended over a million lives." *And wound up with more than one dead god.*

"That's right! It must have been glorious," Enna breathed.

"The Adran Coup was the most well-organized revolution in history, and even that turned into a shit show," Vlora said bluntly, immediately frustrated that she'd allowed her anger to seep through. Her involvement in the Adran Coup and the Kez Civil War had, she'd found, made her a bit of a celebrity among radical leftists. Which made her more than a little uncomfortable. "You don't want to live through a revolution," she added. "If you do survive to the end, half the people you've ever loved will be dead."

"Well," Enna said, her demeanor turning prickly, "you must break your omelet to use your eggs."

Vlora squinted at her. "What?"

"I think," a man said, slipping up beside Enna, "that she means you must break some eggs to make an omelet."

"Yes!" Enna exclaimed. "That's it!"

"Lady Enna, I think you should sit down," the stranger said. "Here, give me your arm, and come over here and speak with Vallencian. He has so missed your company." The man took Enna by the hand, leading her away, and returned a moment later with a rueful smile. He was tall, around Vallencian's height, but with the lean body of a duelist. He wore an expensive black suit, silver-headed cane under his arm, and had blue eyes that seemed to smile about something only he knew. He had no trace of an accent, suggesting he had grown up in Adro. He offered his hand. "Gregious Tampo," he said. "Esquire. It's a pleasure to meet you, Lady Flint."

Vlora immediately felt something off about the man. A sixth

sense made the hair on the back of her neck stand on end, and she half-expected his hands to be clammy and cold. She shook his hand. "You look familiar."

"We've never met," Tampo assured. "Though I'm told I have a soldier's face."

"You're a lawyer?" She studied his face. She'd seen it before, she was certain, and her first instinct was to try to remember any wanted posters she'd seen in local police stations. She opened her third eye, looking for any sign of sorcery about the man, but found nothing.

"I *was* a soldier, actually. Served in the dragoons during the Fatrastan Revolution. Lawyer now, though, that's true."

Vlora tried to ignore her initial misgivings. He seemed polite enough. And a fellow soldier, too. "Vallencian told me all the Kressians down here have business in the Depths. I assume yours is law?"

"I dabble in some politics. Try to protect the local Palo from time to time. But mostly I own a small newspaper that's printed in Palo. The only one in Landfall, in fact." He handed her a card. It said "The Palo Herald" on the front. There was no name or address printed on the back. "It's nothing too active. Just something to give the Palo people to help them keep up on news that matters to them."

Vlora froze, feeling as if she'd just been caught in some sort of trap. "What kind of news?" Tampo seemed just a little too comfortable; a little too pleased with himself.

"Oh," Tampo said pleasantly. "Everything we get our hands on. Intertribal politics, government policy, that sort of thing." He readjusted his cane, snatching a glass of iced tea from a passing servant and downing half of it in one go. "Sometimes we run stories about mercenary companies that have been putting down Palo revolts."

Vlora considered her words carefully, but all she could come up with was a high-pitched "hmm," followed by taking a sip from her own glass. She cleared her throat. "Are you a reporter, too, Mr. Tampo?"

"I am not," he said with a condescending smile. "Though my reporters have written several very detailed articles about you."

"And you wanted to meet me why?"

"Because the articles they write are fascinating. Something about you has the attention of my reporters. You've become a character study."

"I can't imagine you know enough about me to create a character study," Vlora said. She glanced around for Vallencian, hoping to make a polite escape from this conversation, but could not spot him.

"You'd be surprised," Tampo said. "Reporters dig up an awful lot. And they like to use it to paint a story. Tell me, were you really engaged to Taniel Two-shot?"

Vlora's stomach clenched. That was ancient history, more than a decade old and across the ocean. Yet it always seemed to rear its ugly head. "I was," she said coldly.

"Now, correct me if I'm wrong, but he broke off the engagement, did he not? Because he found you in the bed of another man?"

Vlora's fingers tightened on the hilt of her sword without having commanded her hand to move there, and she had to fight down the urge to run Tampo through without warning. She'd expected a conflict of some kind tonight—perhaps a confrontation with a Palo who knew someone her men had killed—but certainly not with a fellow Adran. "That one, childish decision ruined my life," Vlora said softly, "and I have spent the last decade putting it together. If you would like to step outside, I will kill you."

"No dueling, I'm afraid," Tampo said with a smug smile. "Mama Palo frowns upon it, and this is her residence. But you mistake my meaning. I'm not trying to twist the knife. I'm trying to help you understand something."

"What, exactly, is that?"

Tampo pointed at her chest. "Taniel Two-shot was a war hero in Fatrasta even before he became a war hero in his native Adro. He helped us win our War for Independence and he was a friend to the Palo. And now the woman who spurned him less than a year before his heroic death is here in Fatrasta putting down Palo revolts in the very location he tried to help both Fatrastans and Palo alike earn their freedom from the Kez. That, Lady Flint, makes you an absolutely perfect villain to my reporters."

"You think I'm a villain?" Vlora asked flatly. She'd been called far worse, but for some reason the accusation stung. She, a veteran fighter, a revolutionary by most standards, was an enemy? The very idea made her sick to her stomach.

"I don't write the narratives," Tampo said. "I just print them. I thought you should know how you stand in the consciousness of the Palo people."

"Then why am I here?" Vlora demanded loudly. More than one face turned toward her at the outburst. "Why was I invited to this gala if I'm nothing but a figurehead for what these people see as evil?" She'd had nothing to drink, yet her head felt foggy, her vision swimming.

"I don't know," Tampo said quietly. He seemed pleased by her reaction, and it made her bristle. "Perhaps not everyone here thinks you are a villain. But how can I know? Anyway, Lady Flint, it's been lovely meeting you. Have a wonderful evening and, if I may give you some advice, beware the Depths. They aren't kind to strangers."

Tampo disappeared into the crowd before Vlora could come up with a retort, leaving her to fume silently. She wanted nothing more at that moment than to *kill* something, and the little voice in the back of her head—which sounded suspiciously like Olem—told her to remove herself from a room full of civilians before someone said something stupid to her.

She managed to find a promising wing off the main hall with no occupants. It was dimly lit, and she could sense no patrolling guards as she slapped one hand against the yellow limestone and gave out an angry groan. Taniel *bloody* Two-shot. Eleven years since he severed their engagement—deservedly so—and destroyed her professional and personal reputation. Her life might have been over had not the Adran-Kez War started immediately, and Vlora's skills were needed so badly it gave her the opportunity to win back some friends.

Taniel had forgiven her—or so he said—before his death. But even after all this time it hung over her head, a specter of bad choices that haunted her bed, driving her to Olem, a man who never judged her even though she refused to marry him or have his children. She thought all the self-loathing of that choice was locked away in a cabinet at the back of her head, only visible to her, but now it was back to affect her professional life.

A villain.

She was half-tempted to head back inside and call Tampo out, Mama Palo's rules be damned. She slapped the rough stone wall again and again, until her hand ached and her palm bled. She was here with a job to do, people to charm, and now she didn't think she'd be able to focus again at all tonight. What a damned waste.

"Lady Flint?"

Vlora ran fingers through her hair, collecting herself, and hid her bleeding hand behind her back as she turned to find a Palo man standing behind her. He was only a little taller than she, with graying red hair and freckles so thick that his face might as well have been ash. He wore a fine tan suit that wouldn't be out of place in Adran high society, the collar flipped up. He must have been around fifty, and she recognized him as one of the men Vallencian had pointed out. Vlora cleared her throat. "Meln-Dun?"

"That's right," he said in slightly accented Kez. "I don't speak Adran. Is Kez all right?"

"Kez is fine," Vlora answered.

"Have we met?"

"No, I'm sorry. The Ice Baron pointed you out to me."

"As he did you to me just a few moments ago. I hope I'm not interrupting anything?"

Vlora could feel the limestone grit still stuck in her hand, her fingers slick with blood. "No, not at all. Is there something I can help you with?"

"Vallencian mentioned we might be able to help each other. It seems you're worried about the safety of your troops."

Vallencian has a damned big mouth. Vlora chose her words carefully. "That is true," she admitted. "But I don't want to give you the wrong idea. The Riflejack Mercenary Company is a stranger to Landfall and we've been placed here rather suddenly to act as a garrison. I've been told that Greenfire Depths, and the Palo who occupy it, have an understandable distaste for anyone who works for the Lady Chancellor. I'd hoped to figure out a way around that. It's why I'm here, actually, though I'm not doing a very good job at it." She looked at her bloody palm, certain Meln-Dun couldn't see it in the dim light. "You're the first Palo I've spoken to tonight."

"But not the last, I think," Meln-Dun said.

"Oh?"

Meln-Dun came up beside her, frowning down at her hand, which she hid once more behind her back. "We're all a little curious why you were invited here, Lady Flint. Mama Palo hasn't shared her reason with us, but we suspect that she wishes to have the same thing you do—a truce."

Vlora almost let out a sigh of relief, muscles relaxing throughout her body. "Is it possible?" she asked.

"Your reputation works against you down here," Meln-Dun said. "Some think of you as a butcher. But it also works for you, and even more of us consider you an honorable person with a dishonorable master. Vallencian has been telling anyone who will listen that you're here on a mission of peace—that you want to work with us, rather than kill us."

Interesting interpretation. "I would prefer that, yes."

"I read in the newspapers that your men will begin a new public works project. Vallencian claims the same thing. Is this true?"

"What? Oh, yes. It is. We're going to tear down some of the tenements up on the Rim and rebuild them with newer, safer materials and standards. We've already moved the occupants of two tenements to temporary lodgings."

"That's wonderful," Meln-Dun said warmly. "And this is where I think we can help each other. The Lady Chancellor has public works projects all over the city, but never in Greenfire Depths. I believe the tension between the Palo and the Blackhats has prevented this. But you could work as a bridge between us, and if you could change your project so that your men come down *here* and begin the monumental task of cleaning up the tenements in the Depths... well, I believe I could help you strike that deal, and grant you the protection you're after."

Vlora licked her lips. This was it. This was her way into the Depths, and it was being offered to her on a golden platter. There must be a catch—there was always a catch—but it seemed very straightforward. She had wanted to focus on the Rim, where she could keep her men safer, but if she could convince the Blackhats to give them the resources to begin a teardown in one corner of the Depths she could learn more about the people who live down here, meet their leadership—perhaps even find Mama Palo.

"That would be fantastic," Vlora said, trying not to sound too excited, "but I'm not sure I could convince the Blackhats to let me go through with it."

"I understand," Meln-Dun said. "The Blackhats and their bureaucracy are enemies even to their allies. But if you're willing to try, this would make great strides in mending the rift between our people."

Pit, Vlora realized, if this worked she might not even have to take down Mama Palo. This could end peacefully, without her having to betray Vallencian's trust or kill anyone. It seemed like the light at the end of the tunnel and she ran toward it full tilt. "I'll try."

"Thank you, Lady Flint. Now, if you'd like to accompany me back inside, I'll introduce you to some of the people who could help you make this happen."

Vlora took out a handkerchief and cleaned her hand, then took Meln-Dun's offered arm. She was no longer that scared, foolish girl she once was. She was Lady Flint, a decorated general, and she could not afford to feel sorry for herself.

She had work to do.

CHAPTER 19

Styke and the dragonman faced each other for an impossibly long moment as the world around them seemed to slow to a crawl. As far as Styke was concerned, there were only three people left in Landfall: the dragonman, Celine, and him. Celine fell quiet, continuing to wriggle helplessly in the dragonman's grip. Styke felt the handle of his knife slippery against the sweat on his palm. This was not a good situation. The dragonman had the upper hand, and Styke had always done his best not to fight when he wasn't confident of a win.

It would be better to retreat, let the dragonman slip away, and live to fight another day. That's what Colonel Ben Styke would have done, regardless of his reckless reputation. But the dragonman had Celine, and he didn't look like he wanted to "just slip away."

"Why are you following me?" the dragonman demanded. Styke remained silent, and the dragonman twisted his fingers. Celine let out a cry. Styke took half a step forward, but the dragonman twisted harder and Celine's eyes brimmed with tears.

"Orders," Styke said.

"From who?"

"Your mother."

"Funny. From who, big man? Who's asking questions about the dragonmen?"

"You think I care about the girl?"

"Of course you do. I can see it in your eyes."

"Do you know what will happen if you hurt her?"

The dragonman's eyes dropped to the knife in Styke's hand. He snorted, as if finding such a large weapon preposterous. Styke was easily a foot and a half taller than the dragonman and yet he seemed completely uncowed by Styke's height. It was annoying. "You're a cripple," the dragonman said. "You're fast. You're strong. But I saw all your tricks back at the pub. I'll slit the girl's throat and then I'll kill you, too. It won't be hard."

"Is that what they teach you in the Dynize army? To kill children?"

The dragonman's eyes tightened. "Children bleed as easy as anyone else, don't they? Why would they be spared? A child is nothing but a future enemy."

"Why are the Dynize in Landfall?" Styke demanded. "Why were they in the Tristan Basin? What do you want with Fatrasta?" He was getting angry, and fighting angry wasn't going to help him.

The dragonman allowed a small frown to cross his face. "You act as if you have the power here. Is this common among you Kressians? To make demands from a weaker bargaining position? Because it is foolish. Only the strong receive answers." As if to make his point he tightened his grip, and Celine let out a whimper.

"Ben..."

Styke ignored her. She wasn't part of this. She couldn't be part of this. Her survival did not matter right now. He had to focus all his energy on the dragonman, or he *would* lose the coming fight. Everything about the dragonman was getting on his nerves, from his acid calm to the way he didn't even sweat in the summer heat. He focused on that, allowing annoyance, instead of anger, to prepare him for a scuffle.

Styke put Celine out of his mind and looked the dragonman in the face. "Lady Flint. Her men killed one of you people up in the Tristan Basin. It was a rough fight, and she wanted to know if there were any more of you around." He felt a stab of satisfaction as the dragonman's mouth opened slightly, real surprise registering in his eyes.

"Sebbith is dead?"

"Yeah. Sebbith is dead. He died squealing like a helpless little girl. Begged for his mother like a green recruit, and shit himself as he bled out."

The dragonman stiffened. "That is a lie!"

Styke locked eyes with Celine in the moment the dragonman lost his calm. He made a chomping motion with his jaw, and Celine immediately twisted around, biting down hard on the dragonman's wrist. By the time her teeth closed on the dragonman's skin, Styke was already running, whipping his knife overhand as hard as he could.

Two things happened at once. The dragonman tossed Celine aside as easily as a doll, and he stepped to one side, snagging the knife out of midair as easily as if it were a ball. Styke slammed into him a moment later, not bothering with finesse, throwing all his weight at the dragonman's chest.

Both his knife and the dragonman's went flying. They crashed to the boardwalk, and Styke felt pricks like adder bites as the dragonman struck him flat-handed below the ribs. Styke ignored the punches and snatched the dragonman by the throat with his bad hand, drawing back his good into a fist. His heavy lancer's ring connected with the dragonman's nose, which broke beneath the blow, showering them both with blood.

They rolled through the alley trash, punching and kicking.

Styke took two quick blows to the head that left him seeing stars, and another to the jaw. He tried to get a solid grip on the dragonman but every time he did, the slippery bastard managed to get loose. They locked hands, and to his surprise the dragonman slowly forced Styke's arm away, then punched him twice below the arm. Styke tasted blood in his mouth, and spit it into the face of his opponent.

The dragonman managed to slip out of his grip again and was suddenly on his feet. Styke was too slow, coming up behind him and receiving a boot to his face for his troubles. The dragonman turned on Styke, seemingly to attack, before he looked up and suddenly fled, disappearing down the alley and into a nearby warehouse.

Styke remained on his hands and knees, blood dripping from his nose onto the boardwalk, and only looked up at the murmur of voices. A crowd had gathered, at least two dozen people, and someone was calling for the city police. The dragonman, it seemed, did not want to be seen by the public. Styke filed that bit of information away before getting to his feet.

Celine hid behind a nearby crate, sniffling and nursing an arm. Styke retrieved his knife, saw that the dragonman had dropped his own, and picked up that, too, before lifting Celine in one arm and pushing his way through the crowd. He was followed for about a block before people seemed to lose interest and he was able to disappear into the evening traffic.

He remained on the larger streets, ignoring the people who stared at his bloody clothes, until he was sure the dragonman hadn't doubled around to follow him. He found a quiet pub at the base of the plateau and ordered himself a beer and washbasin, then carefully checked Celine. She had bruises on the back of her neck, and when he touched her arm she did not cry out.

"Is it broken?" she asked.

"No," Styke replied. "Can you bend it?"

She bent it several times for him. Bruising, then. She probably caught herself on it when the dragonman threw her. She stared at her feet.

"Anything else hurt?" Styke asked.

"My neck."

"It'll heal."

"I know."

"You did good back there. Sorry I didn't find you sooner."

Celine sniffled, rubbing her nose on her sleeve. "I'm mad he caught me. Shouldn't have happened. Dad would have been furious."

"Shit happens," Styke said, finally allowing himself to sit down. He took a deep breath and drank his beer the moment the barmaid brought it over, then cleaned his face and hands in the washbasin they brought him next. When he finished he put one finger under Celine's chin, lifting her face so they looked each other in the eye, and he considered her for several moments. What a funny kid. She was a knife's stroke away from being a goner, yet she was disappointed in herself for getting caught in the first place. She probably didn't even know how close she'd come to dying.

Styke wasn't about to tell her.

"You did well," he repeated. He put one arm around her, pulling her against his chest. He considered the anger that had almost overtaken him when she was in danger, and wondered if this was what it was like having a flesh-and-blood kid. He'd been furious, protective. Like he was when one of his men had been in danger back in the war, but... more.

"I didn't do good. I lost him," Celine said, frowning.

Styke patted her on the cheek and drew the bone knife from his pocket. He held it up to the oil lamps of the pub. Swamp dragon bone, if the stories were true. Guess they had swamp dragons over in Dynize, too. The damned thing was bloody sharp. "Oh," he said, "I wouldn't say we lost him for good. I've got a feeling he'll come looking for this."

*   *   *

It took only a glance for Michel to realize that the secretary wouldn't be much help. Within minutes of arrival at Tampo's office building—probably about the time she figured out she was in Blackhat custody—she was a nervous wreck, and no one had so much as laid a hand on her. Michel sat on Tampo's desk, staring sullenly at the crates of *Sins of Empire*, wishing that he had it in him to beat on a helpless person.

He needed something to punch.

He got up and paced the room. Warsim had already confirmed with the landlord that the false Tampo was, indeed, the janitor, and it was agreed that the two had the same general hair color and build. Michel had the Iron Roses take all the hapless man's information and sent him home. The secretary they kept, sitting behind her own desk. She tried to put on a brave face in what she probably thought was her last night of freedom before a long stint in the labor camps.

Michel crossed to her desk. "What's your name?"

"Glenna."

"Glenna what?"

"Just Glenna. I don't have a family name."

"Right. Now, Glenna, tell me exactly what you do here."

Glenna's eyes were wide, her whole body trembling. "I'm so sorry, I didn't know you were a Blackhat. I didn't mean to do any—"

"Just," Michel cut her off, "tell me what you do."

"I'm Mr. Tampo's secretary. I don't really have a lot of work, but he employs me for sixty hours a week and pays quite well. I remain here and keep the office tidy, handle his mail, and deal with any visitors that might come by."

"Are there many?"

"No! There's an occasional workman, sometimes another attorney. I was ordered never to take any names—just introduce them if Mr. Tampo is in and take a brief message if he is out."

"How does Tampo know who the messages are from?"

"I give a brief description of the caller. Tall, fair-haired, smokes a pipe. That kind of thing. Mr. Tampo has always taken that as sufficient. He told me that no one will ever have this address that doesn't know his particular method of communication. That's why I was so suspicious when you came by today."

"What about the mail?" Michel asked, feeling his frustration deepen. Tampo was careful. Damned careful.

"Always outgoing," Glenna said. "Sometimes to Adro or Novi. Maybe Brudania. Redstone and Little Starland. I never see the letters themselves. I just drop them in the post."

"How does he pay you?"

"Cash. Every two weeks. Same time he has me pay the rent."

"When's the last time you saw him? Today?"

"No. Four days ago. He worked late one evening and told me he might come in tonight."

"But you didn't see him at all today?" Michel growled. This was getting him absolutely nowhere. Tampo *had* to have slipped up. No one was this thorough.

"After your visit this afternoon I sent him a message at our usual place—he keeps a box at the bank in Lindshire he checks every afternoon so I can contact him in an emergency—and told him that a strange man stopped by demanding to see him. I got a response by courier telling me to head home early and come in late tomorrow morning."

"Is Tampo always this cautious?"

"I never thought of it that way, but now that you mention it, yes."

"And you never considered it suspicious?"

"I thought he was an eccentric."

"Of course you did." Michel continued to pepper Glenna with questions for another half hour while Agent Warsim wrote down her answers. Michel's frustration only continued to increase as it became clear that Tampo didn't make the kind of mistakes that most people did. He didn't even make uncommon mistakes. His planning was damned perfect.

"What about the crates?" Michel asked. He reached down, picked up one of the copies of *Sins of Empire* that he'd knocked over earlier, and waved it under Glenna's nose. "Did you know what was in them?"

Glenna recoiled. "They were delivered just yesterday. I'm not a revolutionary! I'm a secretary and a good Fatrastan. If I'd known what was in them I would have reported it to the police immediately."

"You were never curious?"

Glenna lifted her chin. "Of course I was curious. Mr. Tampo left a message telling me not to look, so I didn't. I wouldn't jeopardize a good job like this, not in the current economy!"

Michel sighed, eyeing her for a few moments while he slapped *Sins of Empire* against one palm. "All right," he said. "You're free to go."

"Excuse me?"

Michel made a shooing motion. "Go on. Get out of here before I change my mind. If Mr. Tampo contacts you, you're to let us know immediately."

Glenna fled the room, a look of relief on her face. Michel waited until he could no longer hear her footsteps before he nodded to Warsim. "Have someone follow her. Watch her. Four men at all times. I want to know her every move." Warsim nodded and left the room, and Michel waved to the other two remaining Iron Roses. "Outside. I need a moment to think."

The room was soon empty, leaving Michel alone with all the crates of pamphlets. He pinched the bridge of his nose, staring at the floor, furious with himself. "You were sloppy."

"I did everything I could," he snapped back.

"You were sloppy, and you've lost your chance at a Gold Rose."

"I'm a spy, not an investigator. I shouldn't even be on this case."

"You're the one who offered to take it further. You've got two failures in a row to explain to Fidelis Jes."

Michel paced the room. This Tampo wasn't some careful academic. He knew how to hide, and how to protect himself from being discovered. He'd had experience in counterespionage, maybe back during the war or in the Nine. Pit, for all Michel knew he could be a rogue or retired spy from one of the cabals of the Nine. How perfect would that be?

There was a knock on the door and Warsim poked his head inside. Michel opened his mouth to snap at him but managed to rein in his temper. "What is it?" he said.

"I thought you'd want to know the grand master is on his way over here."

Michel felt a knot tighten in the pit of his stomach. *Shit.*

CHAPTER 20

Styke returned to Loel's Fort at almost two o'clock in the morning. He carried a sleeping Celine on his shoulder, his hips and knees hurting from walking halfway across the city, his ribs aching from his fight with the dragonman, and several tender spots on his chest and stomach that would be vivid bruises within a day or two.

He wasn't staying at the fort. He didn't quite feel like he was "one" of the Riflejacks yet, and the dilapidated barracks was still under construction, so he rented a cheap room a block away. He was looking forward to falling into bed and sleeping well into the morning, but first he wanted to leave a message for Lady Flint. It was with some surprise that he found a lantern still on at the staff office, and when he knocked on the door there was an immediate "Come!" from inside.

Olem sat on the other side of a round table in the middle of the staff office, four other officers clustered around it, cards and coins scattered on the table. Olem glanced up at Styke, then across the table at the pretty, middle-aged captain sitting directly across from him. "Your draw. What happened to you?"

"Got into a scrap," Styke said. He laid Celine down on a sofa in the corner, then stretched down to touch his toes, hearing his back pop in several places. The muscles of his bad knee twinged painfully. He dug a bit of horngum out of his pocket and tucked it into his cheek.

"Trouble?" Olem asked.

"Nothing I couldn't handle." Styke wondered when he'd last played cards. It was next to impossible to get a full deck in the labor camps. The camp guards thought it was funny to remove the same three cards from each deck you could buy at the camp commissary. It was annoying, but the convicts just came up with their own games to play that required three fewer cards.

"Heard someone busted up Mama Sender's earlier tonight," Olem said. "Some big beast of a guy killed three Palo and crippled a fourth. Took off chasing a fifth. Mama Sender swore he looked just like Ben Styke."

Styke scratched behind his ear. "Yeah, about that. I should probably send her a few hundred krana."

Olem threw a card down. "Already took care of it. Nobody in this city cares much about some dead Palo. Just try to clean up better next time. Any luck tracking down a dragonman?"

Styke examined Olem for a few moments. No tone of reproach. Just professionalism. He liked that. Olem seemed distracted, though, and despite everyone else in the room looking tired-eyed the silence at the card table was tense. What were they all doing up this late on a weeknight? Olem's Knack kept him from needing sleep, but the others doubtless had duties in the morning.

"I did," Styke said. "Was going to leave a message for Lady Flint and then head to bed. She's not awake still, is she?"

Olem reached over, plucking a cigarette from an ashtray on the

table and sucking on the end, discarding it with a disgusted look
when he realized it had gone out. "Lady Flint is down in Greenfire
Depths."

Styke froze mid-stretch. "Alone?"

"Yeah. Got invited to a gala at something called the Yellow Hall.
They wouldn't let her bring an escort or anything, and this is her
best shot at getting an in with the Palo."

"You let her go into Greenfire Depths alone?"

Olem looked up, an angry glint in his eye. "I don't 'let' Lady
Flint do anything. She can take care of herself better than anyone
in this room." *Including you,* his tone implied. Styke wasn't about to
argue with the sentiment, but he still didn't like it. Here he was, off
chasing mythical warriors, when his real purpose—Lady Flint—
was off in the most dangerous part of Landfall without a guard. If
she got herself killed right now, Tampo might very well sell Styke
back to the Blackhats.

Styke made a calming motion with his hands. "Agreed, but
Greenfire Depths. I don't like the sound of it." Not one bit. One
person, all alone in the Depths? This wasn't an invitation; it was a
damned death trap.

"What could we do?" Olem asked. "None of us knows this
place. Without her invitation, she wouldn't even be able to find the
Yellow Hall."

Styke rubbed the sleep out of his eyes. This was bad. He pointed
at Olem. "I can. But if she's meant to be alone there's no taking an
army down there. Let's go."

He expected an argument, or an indignant response about giving out orders. Instead Olem threw down his cards, scooped up a
pile of coins, and wordlessly buckled on his belt. "Any of you know
where Davd or Norrine is?" he asked the table. He was answered by
a round of headshaking and gave a frustrated grunt.

Styke went over to the sofa, nudging Celine awake. "You told me
that you know Greenfire Depths. Can you find the Yellow Hall?"

he asked gently. It took her a moment to wake up, then she was on her feet. "It's been a while," he added. "The Depths change, and I'm rusty."

"I can find it," Celine assured him.

Styke nodded to Olem. "Let's go find Lady Flint, and hope we're not too damned late."

Vlora spent hours mingling with the Palo elite and their Kressian business partners. She relaxed for the first time since entering the city, laughing at jokes, smiling, doing her best to drop the stony demeanor that had earned her her epithet. She was surprised to find most of the elite well educated, some of them even having gone to universities in the Nine, and by the end of the evening she could have been convinced that this was a whole different class of people from the insurrectionist tribes she'd put down in the swamps.

The guests retired one by one, leaving through the front door and down side halls, until only a handful remained. Vlora said her good-byes to Vallencian and Meln-Dun, pleased that Tampo was nowhere in sight, and found Devin-Tallis sleeping in his rickshaw outside. Water dripped through the tenements, and somewhere distant she could hear the patter of rain on the roofs well above them.

She woke Devin-Tallis, and they were soon heading down the narrow streets. "Was the celebration to your standards?" he asked.

Vlora settled into her seat, feeling more at ease and confident, slightly buzzed from one too many drinks. She had let her guard down, but now felt pleased to have done so. "I think I made some friends tonight," she said.

"Very good, Lady Flint. Ah, I found out what 'Ka' stands for while I waited for you."

"Oh?"

"'Ka' is *one who protects*. It's a Dynize epithet, meant only for bone-eyes from the royal family. None of the tribes use it."

Vlora tilted her head. "The Dynize haven't been here for a very long time. How could anyone possibly know it?"

"Our languages are similar. Besides, I asked one of the old-timers. The Palo, we have so little property that we pass down knowledge like you would family heirlooms."

"Sounds like it comes in handy."

"It does, Lady Flint." Devin-Tallis smiled over his shoulder at her. "See, Lady Flint. There is more than just fear in Greenfire Depths. There is knowledge, even friendship. I think that you..." He trailed off, suddenly slowing.

"Is there something wrong?" Vlora asked, leaning forward, her pleasant buzz dissipating like a morning fog.

Devin-Tallis looked one way, then the other, then turned toward her. He opened his mouth and let out a quiet groan, and it took her a moment to see the blood leaking from between his lips. Vlora scrambled from her seat, throwing herself forward to catch Devin-Tallis as he fell, lowering him into the rickshaw with one hand and jamming a powder charge into her mouth with the other. The power lit her veins and darkness became like day to her eyes, revealing two things at once.

First, that Devin-Tallis had a long, slender dart sticking out of his neck. Second, that they were not alone. The corridors around them were filled with shadows, at least a dozen Palo men and women holding cudgels, knives, and swords. They seemed confident that she could not see them and crouched in waiting while one of their number reloaded a blowgun.

Vlora drew her pistol and put a bullet between the culprit's startled eyes before he could bring the blowgun to his lips.

The crack and flash of the pistol seemed to freeze everyone in place. Vlora glanced at Devin-Tallis and could see he would be dead within moments. She tasted the powder on her tongue, rubbed the grit of it against the roof of her mouth, and reveled in the strength it gave her. "You've made a terrible mistake," she said, drawing her sword.

The words acted like a signal, and everyone seemed to fly into motion at once. Palo poured from the alleys, weapons raised, war cries on their lips. She let the first one run straight onto her blade and then jerked it with the strength of a powder mage, disemboweling him instantly, spraying gore into the eyes of his companion, whom she cut down as he tried to wipe away the blood. She flipped her pistol around in her left hand, ignoring the way the barrel burned her already wounded palm, and slammed the butt across the temple of another assailant while her sword worked in the opposite direction, opening the throat of a fourth.

The first four went down in as little time as it took them to reach her. She darted to the side, her footwork uncertain in the mucky street, and parried a sword that slashed at her face. She countered two more strokes and then ducked low, ramming her sword through the man's stomach and then shoving, skewering the woman behind him.

Without a powder trance, Vlora knew she would be considered a top-notch fighter among any company, and it became instantly clear that these attackers, while they had not been stupid enough to bring any powder with them, were not in any way prepared to fight a powder mage. She had trained her whole life as a soldier and a duelist. Her actions were cold and precise, the blade of her weapon aimed to kill or disable instantly, and she was fueled by the anger of seeing the innocent family man behind her die in his rickshaw.

She cut down two more before the concerted effort of four of the attackers managed to halt her forward momentum, presenting a wall of blades in a narrow corridor, forcing her to retreat lest she skewer *herself* upon their swords. She backed up, biding her time and checking her rear to be sure she wasn't being outflanked, waiting for one of them to make a mistake.

Behind them, she watched a fifth scramble for the blowgun that had been dropped by one of their companions, and she cursed herself for not bringing a second pistol. She fought a rising panic, knowing she needed to break through these blades and take them down or turn and flee, but fearing the possibility of running into even more attackers.

Vlora heard footsteps in the mud behind her and swore. She'd been outflanked. She pressed her back to a wall, holding her pistol in one hand and her sword in the other, trying to look in both directions at once.

She caught sight of a shadow behind the Palo who recovered the blowgun. The shadow grew so suddenly she thought her eyes were playing tricks on her until the hooked tip of a boz knife suddenly jutted from the Palo's chest. The Palo coughed, crying out, and was lifted into the air and thrown at his companions.

The shadow became Ben Styke, wearing his old yellow cavalry jacket, his face somehow uglier and meaner in the shadows of the gas lanterns. Behind her, footsteps became louder as Olem rounded the corner, his pistol raised. He shot one of her assailants in the chest. The dual distraction was all Vlora needed and she darted forward, dispatching the three remaining Palo in as many breaths.

Her chest heaved as she caught her breath, heart thumping from the adrenaline of the fight more than the effort. She nodded to Styke, briefly touched Olem's shoulder, then headed over to the rickshaw, where Devin-Tallis had already gone still. She plucked the dart from his neck, broke it between her fingers, and cast it aside. "Poisoned," she said, not bothering to hide the disgust in her voice.

"Pit," Styke breathed, surveying the line of corpses down the corridor. "You weren't kidding when you said she could handle herself."

Olem came up beside Vlora, putting one hand gently on her waist. She resisted the urge to lay her head on his shoulder, her body still trembling. "Are you all right?" he asked quietly.

"I'm fine," Vlora said.

Styke took two steps toward her, squinting in the dim light as he looked her over. "Didn't even get a scratch. Pit, remind me not to cross you."

"If they'd gone for me instead of my driver first, I'd be dead," Vlora said through clenched teeth.

"Your gala didn't go well tonight, I take it?" Olem asked.

"No, it went fantastic. Better than I could have hoped. I have no idea what provoked this." She kicked one of the corpses, letting out an angry grunt.

Beside her, Styke bent to clean his knife. He gestured to someone Vlora couldn't see, and Celine emerged from the shadows to join him, her eyes wide at all the carnage. "This," Styke told her gently, "is what happens when boys try to play with a woman like Lady Flint." He stood up. "We should go," he said. "If they're smart, they'll have a backup team in case they missed and your rickshaw made a run for it."

Vlora touched Devin-Tallis's forehead, then nodded. Whoever ordered this, she decided, had very little time left to live. She would make sure of that.

CHAPTER 21

Michel waited outside the office building for Fidelis Jes to arrive. His Iron Roses kept a cool distance, none of them eager to face a Silver Rose's foul mood, while Warsim had disappeared on another errand. Michel kept his eyes closed, his mind frantically working as he tried to come up with something—anything—to tell Jes about how his investigation wasn't a complete failure. He'd been handed the opportunity to catch Tampo red-handed, and he had failed. Sure, he'd done all the groundwork and set himself up for that possible success. But Fidelis Jes wasn't going to see it that way.

What was he doing wrong? Was he not considering all the angles? Was he out of his depth? In Tampo, he was clearly dealing with a professional. But wasn't he supposed to be a professional, too?

"I'm a spy," he muttered to himself. "Not a bloody investigator. This isn't what I'm good at."

"You're good at getting inside people's heads," he countered himself. "You're good at knowing what people will think, and why, and when. That's all the basic stuff an investigator needs to do, right?"

He made a frustrated sound in the back of his throat. "I am *not* an investigator. I know what people will think about *me*, and why and when. All that matters is keeping my cover. That's not the case here."

"So," he muttered back at himself, "what *is* the case?"

"I need to know the why and when regarding their relation to what they're doing. Not in regards to their relations with me."

Michel ran a hand through his hair, then tapped the side of his head with his fingers. That might be the key here. Michel was so focused on simply catching the guy that he hadn't considered his motives. Why was Tampo doing all this? He seemed awfully organized for a revolutionary. Revolutionaries tended to be high on passion and low on critical thinking and this was certainly not the case.

Could it be he *wasn't* a revolutionary? Did he have another motive for attempting to destabilize the country? Michel still had a copy of *Sins of Empire* in his pocket, and wondered whether the writing behind it was *calculated* to incite revolt, rather than a work of passion as he'd assumed.

It was an intriguing thought, and it gave him an entirely new outlook on this case.

The clop of hooves on cobbles brought Michel out of his reverie and he stiffened, watching as a carriage with a white rose on black curtains pulled up in front of him. The door was thrown open and Fidelis Jes emerged before the carriage had even come to a stop. The grand master was clearly in a foul mood, his jaw tight and eyes pinched, the collar of his immaculately pressed jacket undone. Michel knew Jes was a man of a strict schedule, and he wondered if this case was really important enough to have him out in the middle of the night like this.

Fidelis Jes stopped in front of Michel, glancing around as if to ask where the culprit was.

Well. No delaying the inevitable. "He slipped away, sir."

"Explain."

The one word made a bead of sweat trickle down Michel's spine. "He's a professional, sir. Someone with counterespionage training. He had several fail-safes in place so that we couldn't catch him, and tonight's raid has tipped our hand. I'm worried he'll go deeper undercover." Fidelis Jes opened his mouth, but Michel pushed onward with a sudden spike of confidence. "Sir, I think we've been going about this wrong. In light of this revelation, I don't think we're up against a revolutionary. I think we're up against someone who is dispassionately trying to take down the government. My first instinct is that someone is betting against us, against our economy, and I'd like permission to make a thorough search of wealthy foreigners who have traded against our market. It shouldn't take more than a few weeks, and all I have to do is see him in a place of business and then we'll catch him and bring him down."

Fidelis Jes stared at Michel for several moments, his eyes going out of focus as if his mind was elsewhere, and he gave a brisk nod. "Intriguing, Agent Bravis. I expect you to continue your investigation immediately."

Michel felt like a refreshing wind had just passed through his body. Every muscle relaxed. That was it? No death threats? No anger? Just a nod and "carry on"?

Fidelis Jes looked around at the Iron Roses and gestured for them to come closer. It was only eight or nine people, but the grand master addressed them as he might an army, with his hands clasped behind his back, chest out, sword at his side. "You're all to report to the Millinery immediately. Every Rose is on double duty for the next week."

No one gave voice to the groan they must have all been holding in, but several of them shifted uncomfortably.

Jes continued: "There has been an escape from one of the local labor camps. A dangerous war criminal by the name of Benjamin Styke. Every Iron and Bronze Rose is on alert until Styke is caught. When you report to the Millinery you will be given a description and an exhaustive report as to all his known associates. Find him. Catch him. He *must* be brought in alive. Dismissed."

The Iron Roses scattered, and Michel found himself alone with the grand master a few moments later. They remained standing in silence for several minutes while Jes looked up and down the streets, eyeing rooftops, as if considering where this dangerous criminal could be hiding.

Michel knew the name. Pit, everyone knew the name. Colonel Styke had practically surpassed "war hero" and gone straight to "folk hero."

"Sir," Michel finally ventured, "isn't Ben Styke..."

"He's alive. Forget everything you know about Benjamin Styke," Fidelis Jes said, his eyes still examining the surrounding buildings. "He is a crazed killer. He will murder anyone and anything, and he holds a grudge against the Lady Chancellor. I fear for her very safety."

"He's just one man, sir."

Jes whirled on him, forcing Michel to step back. "Styke is his own army. Do *not* underestimate him. He's older, crippled, but he will not be easy to take down." Jes took a measured breath, before going on in a calmer voice. "Styke has the loyalty of the city's veterans. The last thing I need is him stirring up trouble."

"Of course, sir. Am I...still on this investigation?"

"Yes. Why wouldn't you be?"

"Well, this Styke thing seems to be important."

"Oh, you'll be keeping your eyes open for Styke as well." Jes smirked. "Your failure to catch Tampo tonight has just made your job infinitely harder, Agent Bravis. I've been questioning the traitorous prison officials who allowed themselves to be bribed to secure Styke's release. It turns out they were paid off by a Mr. Tampo, Esquire. They even gave a description that matched that of your suspect."

All the relief felt at not having gained Jes's ire disappeared in a single instant. Michel sagged. Not only had he not managed to capture Tampo, but now he had to face the possibility of dealing with a dangerous war criminal. Michel wasn't an investigator, and he *definitely* wasn't a fighter. If he did manage to catch up with Tampo, and Styke happened to be with him, he'd be a goner.

He knew it, and from the smug look in Jes's eyes, the grand master knew it, too.

The very real prospect of a violent death was punishment for his failure.

"You've made great progress in such a small amount of time," Jes said, almost kindly. "I expect you to wrap this up quickly. Bring me Tampo and you will earn your Gold Rose. Bring me Styke as well, and I'll be in your debt."

Michel watched Fidelis Jes return to his carriage and drive away. The odds had just tipped significantly against him. But the rewards... he couldn't imagine many people had Fidelis Jes's favor. But if he was going to catch Styke before anyone else, he'd have to be fast.

CHAPTER 22

Celine led Styke and their small group out of the Depths and up to Loel's Fort, where the night was silent and all but a few Riflejack guards were in their beds. Styke followed Lady Flint into the temporary headquarters she'd set up in the old staff building and stood in the doorway, not entirely sure what to do as Flint pulled out a notepad and scratched something on it, handing it to Olem.

"Send a messenger to Vallencian. Tell him I was attacked and my escort killed."

Olem took the note and slipped by Styke, and Styke put a hand on Celine's shoulder, turning her toward the door. "Lady Flint," he said with a nod. "Glad you got out of there. I best be going."

"You," Flint said, giving him pause. "Stay." She snatched a bottle of wine from underneath the table in the center of the room and popped the cork with her knife. "You've earned a drink, I think."

Styke hesitated. For once, he was feeling less than confident about his position. His task was to keep Flint alive, at least until

Tampo gave the order, and now he wasn't entirely sure he *could* kill her. She'd been ambushed by more than a dozen men and walked away without a scratch. What hope would he have in his condition, even if he caught her unawares?

He'd have to cross that bridge when he reached it, he decided sourly. For now it was his job to get—and remain—close. He dragged a chair over to the table and sat down, pulling Celine up onto his lap.

Flint poured three glasses of wine. They drank in silence until Olem returned, nodding, and brought his own chair up to the table. He took his glass and raised it to Flint, then to Styke.

"My nerves are shot to shit," she said, the words clearly directed at Olem.

"The ambush?" Olem asked gently.

Flint drained her first glass and poured another, reaching under the table to get a second bottle of wine. "The ambush, the powder trance—I took a whole charge at once—and then the fight. I haven't had a call that close since the Kez Civil War." Her eyes were cast down, her voice quiet, and she seemed suddenly vulnerable. The moment passed quickly, and she looked at Styke with steel in her eyes.

"You looked like you were handling things fine," Styke said. He couldn't get those bodies out of his head. He was *used* to his own path of destruction. Even back during the war he rarely saw one that compared. But pit, he found himself *impressed* by Flint's. He thought about Taniel Two-shot, fighting out in the swamps, picking off Kez Privileged like they were bottles on a fence. "Powder mages," he said softly, a curse under his breath.

Flint leaned over, topping off Styke's glass. "Powder mages aren't invincible," she said, frowning. Styke noticed that her hand was still trembling, and remembered that she was barely thirty years old. He considered soldiers her age practically kids, even back when he was one. "We can be outflanked, overwhelmed, or taken by surprise. If you and Olem hadn't arrived they might have done all three and finished me off."

"We got lucky," Olem said. "We heard your pistol go off. We were only the next street over."

"Though I would have expected you to turn and run against so many men," Styke added.

Flint frowned. "They'd killed him. My escort. He was a good man—funny, clever, interesting. When something like that happens, instinct kicks in. I barely have control of myself. It feels like I blink, and then there are bodies." She met his eyes. "They call you Mad Ben Styke. Was it ever like that for you? The anger?"

Styke looked down at his glass. Pit, soldier talk. He was going to need more wine than this. He gave the glass to Celine. "Just a sip," he said, then drained the rest and pushed it over to the bottle. Olem refilled it.

Styke cleared his throat. "They say that some people are overtaken by a berserker rage in a battle. Their eyes mist and time seems to slow and they just kill everything that they see. I've heard people speculate that Field Marshal Tamas had that"—he nodded at Flint—"and that only his training kept him from being a true berserker." He twirled his lancer's ring with his thumb, listening to his chair creak under him as he shifted. "They called me Mad Colonel Styke because they thought a madness took me into battle. Because I made foolish charges against outrageous odds. But I've never had red mist. Sure, I lose my head sometimes, but when I kill, it's deliberate. I never—" He paused. "I rarely pick a fight I don't think I can win."

"Those charges," Olem said. "The two charges at the Battle of Landfall. You knew you were going to win those?"

Styke felt the memory flood him. He could almost taste the sweat and stench of the battle, the heat of burning buildings and racket of an artillery bombardment. He savored it. "Sounds arrogant when I say it out loud. But yeah, I knew I'd win. Nothing stood before me and my lancers. We wore enchanted armor, stuff that saw its heyday four hundred years ago, and it shrugged off bullets and sorcery like a parasol does rain."

"What happened to that armor?" Olem asked.

Styke could still hear his voice echo in the helmet and feel the reassuring weight of medieval plate on his shoulders. When he flexed his fingers he could almost imagine the lance back in his hand once more, the feel of his ring pressing against its wooden handle. "Lindet confiscated it after the war. Don't know what happened after that."

"Pity," Olem said.

Flint leaned back in her chair, glass dangling from her hands. Styke had heard it took a lot to make a powder mage drunk, and her eyes were barely foggy after a whole bottle of wine. "I want to know something," she said.

"Yeah?"

"Taniel Two-shot. Was he really a hero around here?" Before Styke could answer, she continued. "I mean, I've heard some of the stories, and I've heard his name spoken in conjunction with the war. But back then, when the whole thing happened, was he really as big of a war hero as they say?"

Styke tried to remember everything he could about Taniel Two-shot. It had been a long time. "People liked him. It was romantic. A young powder mage, out there avenging his mother's death against the Kez cabal almost two decades after the fact. That and fighting for Fatrastan independence to boot. The newspapers loved to write about him."

"Did the Palo take to him? I've heard rumors that they did, but I've never actually asked anyone."

"I think so," Styke said. "Like I said, I only actually met him once. We fought through the Battle of Planth together, and he saved my life by putting two bullets through a Warden's skull." He paused, trying to recall newspaper articles he'd read after his imprisonment. "Yes," he said more confidently, "the Palo did take to him. One became his guide and he took her back to Adro with him, and..." Styke trailed off, remembering who, exactly, he was talking to. He cleared his throat. "They say the two of them got married just before their death at the end of the Adran-Kez War."

Flint was entirely unreadable. "They never got married," she said.

"Ah." Styke wasn't going to push that subject.

"She wasn't a Palo, either," Flint said, looking away. "She was Dynize. Her name was Ka-poel, and she was a bone-eye sorcerer with enough power to . . . well. She was incredibly powerful."

Styke remembered her. He remembered her better than he remembered Two-shot, if he was being honest. He could smell the blood sorcery on her, and see the playful confidence that seemed so strange in the eyes of a Palo youth. "A Dynize," he echoed. "Didn't know there were any in the swamps."

"She was a refugee of some sort," Flint said. "Was adopted by a Palo tribe as a child. Taniel talked about her in his letters, and then I met her later, after he brought her back and—after things were over between the two of us. I hated her at first. Thought she had taken Taniel away from me. But then I realized that he was still mine when he got back, and that it was only after I did what I did that she claimed him for herself."

Styke glanced over at Olem, who remained silent through the whole thing. The two were obviously longtime lovers, and it couldn't be easy to live in the shadow of someone like Taniel Two-shot. But Olem just gave Styke a small, knowing smile, and rolled himself a cigarette. "You're getting drunk," Olem said softly to Flint.

"Yup," Flint answered. "Doesn't happen often. Feels kind of good to talk about it." Her eyes focused on Styke, and she said, "I like you. I have no idea why, but I do."

"Because we're both killers," Styke said before he could stop himself. He held his breath, but Flint just gave him a rueful smile.

"To killers," she said, raising her glass.

Styke clinked his against hers. He sensed it was time for him to leave the two of them alone, and stood up, finding that Celine was already fast asleep in his arms. He put her over his shoulder. "I saw a dragonman tonight," he said.

Some of the haze across Flint's face seemed to lift. "Really?"

"He's not a Palo. He's a Dynize."

Flint seemed to sober slightly. "What the pit is a Dynize dragonman doing in Landfall?" she mused, more to herself than to him.

"He knew of the other one. The one you killed. Said his name was Sebbith or something like that. If they knew each other, I'm guessing they were both Dynize. But I don't know why they're here."

"Find out," Flint said.

Styke sighed. He found himself liking—even respecting—Lady Flint more and more. If he did have to kill her it was going to be a challenge in more ways than one. But for now, they were on the same side. "I'll draw him out," he promised.

Vlora watched Styke carry Celine through the door. From the window she saw him cross the muster yard, and she was struck once again by the contrast of the man gently carrying a child that was not his own, and the killer she'd witnessed down in the Depths.

"Did you see him fight tonight?" she asked Olem.

"I didn't," Olem said. "I was too busy aiming at the assholes coming after you."

There might have been a note of reproach in his voice, though Vlora didn't know if she deserved it. She stood by her choice to attend the gala alone. "He came up behind one of the Palo silent as a ghost. He put that knife through the guy's sternum, then tossed him like a toy."

"The stories all said Ben Styke was the strongest man in Fatrasta."

"I wasn't confident it *was* Ben Styke until now," Vlora said. "But damn." She took another drink. The wine was loosening her lips, maybe a bit too much, but her heart rate had finally returned to normal. She looked at Olem, feeling a stab of regret. He was a soldier, and he was used to friends dying in battle, but she knew that he worried for her all the same. She suddenly felt all the things that she'd been unfair about over the years.

It was unfair to head off alone on a mission of unknown danger. It was unfair to pull rank. It was unfair to turn down his proposals for marriage when she had no intention of ever leaving him. It was unfair to put off having children, when they both wanted them.

It was unfair of her to lie.

"Olem," she said.

"Yes?"

"Do you remember after the end of the war? In the blood and the chaos when all those bodies were lost at Skyline Palace?"

"Quite well, yes." Olem's voice was flat, controlled, his lips clamped firmly around his cigarette. Vlora knew the pain the memory caused him, and was reluctant to add to it. No one had been closer to Field Marshal Tamas than Olem those last few months.

Her mouth tasted sour. She licked her lips, considering the secret she had kept for ten years. It had always felt like it wasn't hers to give, and yet now she knew it was foolish not to share it. "I've been telling myself and everyone else for ten years that Taniel and Ka-poel died during that fight. But they didn't. They survived the explosion and slipped away in the chaos."

Olem sucked on his cigarette, staring at her through the smoke. "I figured," he said.

"How?"

"You never grieved."

Vlora cleared her throat. Faithful, trustworthy Olem. The bastard knew all along. By Adom, he was the best present a commanding officer could ever get. "I love you," she said.

"I figured that, too." He handed her his cigarette, then said, "Why do you bring it up now?"

"Because they told me they were heading to Fatrasta. This was ten years ago, but I'm worried they're still here. I'm worried they're involved in all of this shit. I would have sensed his sorcery if they were in the city, but still... I'm worried. If they do get involved, I can't imagine it'll be on Lindet's side, and Olem? I can't fight Taniel or Ka-poel. Neither of them was quite human when they left, and they're out of my league." *And I don't want to fight them.*

"Well," Olem said, lighting a new cigarette, "we better hope they aren't still around then."

CHAPTER 23

Michel struggled through the early hours of the morning, unable to sleep and unable to work, trying to come up with some kind of plan for capturing the two enemies of the state that Fidelis Jes so desperately wanted brought in.

His first major decision was to discard his search for Styke. Half the Millinery was already looking for the old veteran, and Michel adding himself to that list would do little good. No, he needed to focus on his current goal, that of capturing Tampo. Tampo, if he could track the bastard down, would almost certainly lead him to Styke.

And if all the other sods searching for Styke managed to bring him in, Michel might be able to use that to find Tampo.

It was sound logic, but it didn't help him sleep.

He tossed and turned in his small attic apartment on the southern edge of the plateau before finally crawling out of bed and pulling on some clothes, heading unshaven into the first splash of morning light and taking a hackney cab a mile across town to the

Proctor market, where he stopped to fill a crate with breads and fruit before heading on foot through the still-sleepy streets.

Proctor was the kind of town in which, in those few moments he allowed himself to wonder what it would be like to settle down and have a family, he imagined himself living. It wasn't too clean, or too dirty, or too rich or poor. It was absolutely average in every way, and Michel loved that in a place like this he could be as friendly or anonymous as he liked.

In some ways he lived vicariously through his mother—idle days, reading books and chatting with neighbors, staying out of the sun.

The thought brought him up short next to a bookstore, and he stared through the front window as sellers carried crates of penny novels out onto the sidewalk to entice passersby. He chewed on his lip, trying not to think of everything he *should* be doing right now.

"Don't encourage her," he said softly to himself. "It only makes things worse."

"Oh, come on. I can be a good son once in a while."

"You can either be a good son by taking care of her, or you can be a good son by exacerbating her bad habits. You can't be both."

He rolled his eyes at himself. "Why not?"

"Because you don't get to be everything, Michel. You have to choose."

Michel ignored the raised eyebrows of one of the booksellers and told himself to shut the pit up before stepping inside and looking around for the more expensive, leather-bound novels in the back. He flipped through a few at random, remembering a time when he used to read almost as much as his mother, and then selected three adventurous-sounding titles and raised a hand for one of the clerks.

"Can I help you, sir?"

"I'll take these," Michel said.

"Thank you, sir," the clerk said. "We'll take care of the bill."

Michel blinked at the clerk for several seconds before realizing he was wearing his Blackhat uniform. Even though he kept his Silver Rose hidden on a necklace, it wasn't hard to tell what he was. He dug into his pocket for a wad of krana. "I don't mind paying," he said.

"It's all right, sir," the clerk said. "Thank you for your patronage."

Michel was rarely bothered by the perks that came along with his job. Free stuff was, after all, one of the best and he took advantage of it when he could. But the idea of buying books for his mother on Blackhat goodwill felt a little... off.

"Speaking of which," he muttered to himself, looking out the window at the crates of penny novels sitting on a table on the sidewalk. A familiar figure was already perusing the selection, even though the store had only been open for minutes. Michel sighed to himself, looking instinctively for the back exit, before turning back to the clerk. "Could you wrap these up for me, please? Also, I'd like to pay for anything that woman out there wants to buy." He thrust a ten-krana note into the clerk's hands before he could object, then stepped outside.

His mother stood by the penny novels, flipping through them thoughtfully, humming to herself and dancing slightly to the tune.

"Morning, Mother."

She jumped, turning to Michel with a look of surprise. "Michel! What are you doing here?"

Michel put on his most charming smile. "Just stopped in to pick something up for my mother," he said. "Was going to drop some food by your house on my way into work."

A torrent of emotions crossed his mother's face as he spoke. First she was surprised, then pleased, then her face fell to frustration and anger, all in the space of a few seconds. By the time he said the word "work" she looked downright furious.

She snatched him by the arm, pulling him around the corner of the bookshop and into the closest alley and then turning on him with a finger thrust up under his nose.

"What do you think you're doing, Michel?" she demanded.

Michel braced himself, his heart falling. "Shouldn't have bothered," he muttered to himself.

"What do you mean? Speak up, child!" She glared at his uniform, looking him up and down with the kind of disgust most mothers would upon finding their children naked in the streets. "Wearing that uniform? Coming around my neighborhood? What are the neighbors going to think? What are the bookshop owners going to think? I'm respected and liked around here!"

"I didn't even look to see what I was wearing," Michel said with a calming gesture, hoping that the shouting wouldn't attract attention. He didn't need this, not today.

"Hm!" his mother said, turning away from him. She fumed at the wall of the alley, looking at him sidelong.

"Look," he said, "I'm sorry. I know you don't like what I do for a living. I try not to complicate your life with it. But I was just trying to do something nice."

"Don't like what you...?" his mother sputtered. "It's not that I don't like it, Michel. It's that you're a Blackhat! My pappy—*your* grandpappy—was a full-blood Palo. Your *father* died fighting for our freedom against the Kez. What would they think to see you in that getup? Can't you see what you are, Michel? You're a thug! Every day you work for Lindet is another day you grind your birthright into the mud."

"Now wait just a minute," Michel said, feeling his own blood begin to rise. "That's going too far. I'm not a thug. I don't beat people up. I do some training, some liaison work. I'm respected doing what I do."

"It's not respect if it depends on fear."

"I meant to the people I work with."

"And I'm talking about the people you Blackhats tramp into the dust. I'm not a fool. I read the papers and listen to the gossip. Not even Lindet can keep a lid on all the news in this city. Did you know that just two streets down from my house a young woman was murdered by Blackhats for handing out flyers? Flyers, Michel!"

Michel glanced over his shoulder. "Please keep your voice down, Mother."

"Or what? You're going to drag me to the Millinery dungeons? Your own mother? I think Lindet's a downright bitch, and I don't mind who hears it. She's a tyrant, and you Blackhats are her bullies, and I don't want my son associated with them. Is that too much?" Her voice continued to rise in pitch till Michel was certain that people out on the street could hear her clearly.

"I'm not a . . . It's not . . . Mother, it's more complicated than that."

His mother took several deep breaths, her jaw quivering. He hadn't seen her worked up like this for years, and he wondered if it was the murder of the girl she mentioned. That kind of thing might be commonplace in Michel's world, but it would have shaken his mother deeply.

"You're a good boy," she said quietly. "And every time I see you in that outfit I'm reminded what you've gotten yourself into."

"I'm sorry," he said again. "It's just . . ."

His mother suddenly lifted her handbag, rifling around inside it for a few moments and then thrusting something in Michel's face. He took it from her absently, trying to finish his sentence, but when his eyes focused on the pamphlet he felt his heart fall. The now-familiar words *Sins of Empire* were printed on the front.

"Where did you get this?" he demanded.

"A nice young man was handing it out yesterday," she said. "You need to read it, Michel. It's the kind of truth you need to hear."

"Who?" he asked angrily. "What young man?"

His mother took half a step back, staring at him in shock, then raising her chin. "Don't think I'm going to tell you. *I'm* trying to help *you* now, and you need to listen to me for once. This pamphlet—"

"I know all about this pamphlet," Michel said, shoving it in his pocket and pushing her farther into the alley. He whispered urgently. "Mother, you can't be seen with one of these. They're cracking down on this very thing right now, and if they find one on you, they might..."

"They might what? Throw an old woman in prison?"

"They might!"

"Let them," she snapped. "I'm not the bumbling old fool you take me for. Your father and I protested the Kez in Little Starland. I loaded muskets for the Thirteenth during the war. I can handle prison."

"It's not just that, it's—"

She cut him off again. "Worried about your career? Worried that your old mom might ruin your chance of advancement?"

"Yes!" Michel hissed.

"Good! I don't want you advancing through that damned viper's nest anyway."

Michel gave an exasperated sigh and paced to the mouth of the alley and then back again. They'd had this same fight a dozen times, and it always came back to this. He'd try to keep her quiet, she'd threaten to purposefully tank his career, and then he'd avoid her for a couple of months and she'd go back to her reading.

"Did the handyman come around?" he asked gently.

"Hmph," she replied. "He did. I don't want you using Blackhat money to fix up my house."

Michel stopped, staring at her. "Your roof was leaking."

"I can handle a leak."

"It was destroying your books," he tried.

"I'll get more."

"You're being obstinate, Mother."

"I don't care. Blackhat money is soaked with the blood of my people. *Our people.*"

"You're only half-Palo, Mother."

"And I'm proud of that half!"

Michel paced back and forth, starting half a dozen sentences in his head and stopping each one before he said something hurtful. He finally took *Sins of Empire* out of his pocket and showed it to her. "Please, Mother, just do me a favor and avoid this particular pamphlet. It's not going to do anyone any good if the Iron Roses pick you up in a sweep." She harrumphed again, which was about as good an answer as he was going to get. Michel opened his mouth when he caught sight of the clerk from the bookstore peering around the corner. "What is it?"

"Sir," the clerk said, "your books are ready." He handed Michel a neatly wrapped package. Michel looked at the package in his hands, then at his mother.

"These are for you," he said softly.

His mother took the package. She could feel the weight of them, and he could tell by her face that she knew instantly what they were. He wondered when the last time she'd been able to afford leather-bound books was. She handed them back.

"I won't take books bought with Blackhat money," she said.

Michel wanted to shake her. "Just take them, Mother."

"No!"

The clerk gave a little cough, clearly embarrassed, and Michel turned on the poor man instead. "You," he said. "I want you to make sure she never pays for another book here. Understand? I'm going to check, and if I find out you've been charging her for even a single penny novel, I'll burn this damned place down."

The clerk's eyes grew wide, and Michel heard his mother's gasp as he strode from the alley. He tossed the package of leather-bound books onto a table and strode down the street, looking for the closest hackney cab. He was two blocks away before he found one and was soon inside, riding in welcome silence toward the Millinery.

"She doesn't understand," he said to himself angrily.

"You knew she wouldn't."

"I've always hoped she would. Someday."

"Does that make you a fool or an optimist?"

"Both."

It took him half the ride before he calmed down and realized he'd left her food sitting on a table in the bookstore. With the money she spent on penny novels, it was likely all she would have to eat for the next few days. He swore at himself and almost yelled for the driver to turn around.

One thought stayed him.

She'd gotten a copy of *Sins of Empire*. Not a week ago, but yesterday. The Iron Roses were meant to have rounded most of them up. Even if this was one young revolutionary who'd managed to hide a few stacks of the pamphlet, the fact that they were still being handed out *could* mean something. It could mean that they were still being printed.

But by whom? And where?

Michel climbed out of the cab at the Millinery and paid the driver extra to go pick up a basket of bread and deliver it to his mother's address. Inside, he found Agent Warsim at his desk in the corner, and tapped him on the shoulder.

"You busy?"

"No, sir."

"Good. I need you to make me a list of every printer in the city. Be thorough."

"Yes, sir. May I ask why?"

"Because I have just one idea, and I'm going to search every printing press from here to Redstone until I have a better one."

CHAPTER 24

S tyke broke his fast with an iced coffee and a thumb-sized piece of horngum just a few short hours after his late-night discussion with Olem and Vlora. He sat at a Palo-owned café on the northwestern side of the plateau—a prime spot on the ledge overlooking the Hadshaw River. Scarcely two paces and a hand-rail separated him and Celine from a hundred-and-fifty-foot sheer drop to the gently sloped foot of the plateau, then another fifty down to the floodplains on the bank of the Hadshaw where squat, wooden tenements sat upon stilts driven deep into the earth.

The land around the plateau that had once been nutrient-rich fields plowed by Kressian farmers was now suburbs of these stilted, flood-resistant tenements stretching for miles into the distance. It was a strange sight to Styke, a whole new part of Landfall that hadn't existed when he entered the labor camp scarcely a few miles from here. It made him feel like a stranger in his own city.

Celine stood at the railing, watching the people far below mill about the streets like ants, and swinging herself back and forth. She was a loose rail or a stiff wind away from tumbling over the side, but Styke remained quiet—and within easy reach.

His body ached from his brawl with the dragonman, and he could already feel the tenderness where the bruises would soon appear. His sleep had been restless last night, listening to Celine snore while the feather mattress, an unheard-of luxury for so long, felt lumpy and uneven beneath his back. As hard as he tried to keep his head down and just do his job, he couldn't help but wonder who had tried to kill Lady Flint, and what Tampo's ultimate interest in her was. Styke had never managed to be a blind follower—even back during the war he'd ignored half his orders—and playing by the rules now irked him like an ill-fitting saddle.

"What kind is that?" Celine asked, pointing.

Styke glanced over the edge, following Celine's finger to see a spotted horse far below them being led along the streets by its owner. "Palo Hotblood," he said.

"It looks the same as any other," Celine said, shooting him a suspicious look.

"The markings are Palo. Kressian horses rarely have that coloration. Look at the strong conformation, the hindquarters, the arched neck. That's a horse bred for agility and speed. Very sure-footed in the swamps and dense forests. Probably being brought into town for an auction. The roads down on the floodplain are soft, and the keeper is walking ahead so as not to risk a broken leg."

Celine pointed to another horse farther down the road, pulling one of the lighter, open-aired hackney cabs that were popular down there. "And that one?"

"Starlish Trunsin," Styke said. "Standard Kressian carriage horse. They cut the tail short to keep it from getting caught in the carriage, and in Starland they used to make wigs for the nobility out of it. Probably itched like a hat full of fleas, but there's no accounting for taste among rich people."

Celine pointed out almost two dozen more horses as Styke worked through a second cup of iced coffee, obliging her by naming the breed—or likely mix of breeds—and a few characteristics of each. He found the exercise relaxing, and the realization that he hadn't lost his touch even after ten years of rarely seeing anything but the old, worn-out mares they worked to death in the fens left him feeling pleased with himself.

He had just begun to smile, the horngum doing its work on his sore muscles, when a voice behind him said, "You know a lot about horses, Mr. Styke."

Styke turned in his seat to find Gregious Tampo standing a few feet back, top hat on his head, leaning on his cane. He looked like he'd been there for more than just a few moments, and Styke was annoyed he'd let anyone sneak up on him like that. "Had a few in my time," he said.

"You were a lancer. I'd imagine that was part of the job."

"You could say that. It's hard to find horses strong enough for a prolonged charge in plate armor. I had to keep my eye out all the time."

Tampo looked out over the floodplains, eyes squinted as if he could see all the way to the Tristan Basin. "I remember that horse you rode during the war. Biggest damn stallion I've ever seen."

Styke felt a pang of regret, picturing the big, black warhorse in his mind's eye. "Deshner," he said. "He was a Deliv draft horse. Mean bastard, but we got along well." *And some damn officer put a bullet in his head right before they put me up against the wall, just to spite me.* Styke fought down a surge of anger. He gripped his coffee cup and forced a smile. "Afternoon, Mr. Tampo. What can I help you with?"

"Good afternoon, Mr. Tampo," Celine echoed without turning away from the ledge.

"May I sit?" Tampo asked.

Styke gestured to Celine's unoccupied chair. Tampo took a seat and remained silent for several moments, studying Styke's face with an uncomfortable intensity. Styke studied right back, searching Tampo for any kind of a tell. What was his game here? What did he want with Lady Flint? Styke felt a surge of protectiveness for Flint and reminded himself he'd known her only for a few days and would more than likely end up having to kill her. She seemed a good officer—but Tampo had earned his loyalty by bringing him out of the labor camp.

"What happened last night?" Tampo asked. There was a hint of accusation in his voice, and Styke suspected he already knew about the attack on Lady Flint.

How he knew was another question. "Someone tried to kill Flint."

"I know. I trust you were there to protect her?"

"I wasn't," Styke said. No point in lying. Lying, in either the camps or the army, rarely made Styke's job easier. It just gave him one more thing he had to remember. "Not until the end."

"And why not?" Definitely accusatory. "I told you I needed her alive."

Styke shrugged. "You said you wanted me to get close to her. She's given me a task to do to get in her good graces. I'm not in the position to demand that she make me her bodyguard. Might be a bit suspicious if I did. Besides, from everything I've seen she can take care of herself pretty damn well." Tampo remained silent, twirling his cane absently where it lay across his knee. Styke continued: "I half-expected you to be behind the assassination attempt, to be honest."

To his surprise, Tampo smiled at that. "I appreciate the concern, but you *are* my plan regarding Lady Flint. She has powerful enemies in Landfall without even knowing it, and she may wind up being very useful to me in the future. I want her alive."

Now *that* was interesting. Styke wondered what kind of people had it out for a mercenary general. "And if she proves not to be useful?"

"Then I'll have you take care of the problem." Tampo hesitated. "Tell me, Mr. Styke, do you think you could kill a powder mage?"

Celine left her spot at the railing and came over and pulled herself onto Styke's knee, fixing Tampo with a flat stare. "Ben can kill anyone. Yesterday, he killed three Palo without breaking a sweat."

"Is that so?" Tampo tilted his head at Styke, looking from him to Celine with some significance.

"Some Palo kid got in the way of a job I was doing," Styke explained. "And Celine will keep her mouth shut around Lady Flint. Won't you, Celine?"

Celine folded her arms. "I like Lady Flint. But if Ben has to kill her, then..." She held her hands up as if to say "oh well!"

"Regular old pair of mercenaries here," Tampo commented. "Well, Mr. Styke, I'll ask again. Could you kill a powder mage?"

Styke considered the question for a few moments. "In my current state? Not in a fair fight. But I don't have a problem with fighting dirty. I'd probably be more worried about making my escape after killing Flint. I'd have to kill Colonel Olem, too, or risk him hunting me down, and those infantry seem pretty close to her, so it might get rough."

"I'm glad you're making plans for the eventuality, though I hope it does not come to that."

There seemed to be a genuine note of regret in Tampo's voice, and Styke wondered whether he was as cold a killer as Styke had originally pegged him to be. "Do I have a place in your plans?" Styke asked. "Beyond this thing with Lady Flint?"

"You're a killer, Mr. Styke," Tampo said matter-of-factly. "I always have use for a killer. Why do you ask?"

"Just wondering," Styke said, giving Tampo a tight smile. "Planning for eventualities."

Tampo sucked on his teeth, eyes narrowed, and returned to studying Styke in silence. Styke had to admit to himself that there was something unsettling in that gaze. Finally, Tampo said, "You're too clever, Mr. Styke. I think that's why they put you in the labor camp. You look like a thug, kill like a thug, but you think and talk like an officer. It confuses people—the looks and reputation give them expectations, and then you defy them all by being educated."

"Are you saying you regret plucking me from the labor camps?" Styke tensed. He did not particularly like Tampo, but Tampo had bought his loyalty along with his freedom. He would do nothing from his own end to jeopardize their relationship, but if Tampo turned on them Styke *would* gut him like a pig.

The smile Tampo shot back was actually warm. "On the contrary. I've gotten exactly what I was looking for."

"I thought you told me you wanted a blunt instrument."

"Ever seen an old-fashioned war hammer? They put a spike on the back for a reason." Tampo turned his attention suddenly to Celine, frowning, lifting the back of her hair gently to expose the red marks the dragonman had left on her neck. He gave Styke a sharp look.

"We ran into some trouble," Styke said.

"What kind of trouble?"

"It was a dragonman," Celine interjected, wiggling out of Styke's lap and returning to the railing. "He grabbed me by the neck, but Ben punched him in the face and took his knife."

Tampo's head jerked around. There was a tense moment of silence, all of the congeniality having gone out of Tampo. "Did you say a dragonman?" he asked quietly.

"She did," Styke answered.

"You saw one—you *fought* one?"

"More of a scuffle than a fight," Styke said, glancing at Celine. This was *not* something he wanted to discuss with Tampo right now. "I tried to draw him out, he sent some of his acolytes to get a feel for me, then he slipped away. Celine and I followed him across the city and there was a confrontation."

Tampo leaned across the table. Styke scooted his chair back

slightly, not entirely sure what was eliciting Tampo's intense response. Tampo said, "Back up and tell me everything."

Styke ran through Lady Flint's initial encounter with the dragonman in the Tristan Basin, her assignment, and then Styke's plan to get one to show his face. He told Tampo about following the dragonman through the city and, at Tampo's urging, listed all the places that the dragonman had visited on his errands. He finished with the scuffle, saying, "He ran when he saw the crowd. I suspect he's not eager to attract the wrong kind of attention."

"And you're sure he was a dragonman?"

"Same kind of black tattoos I've read about in the stories. Hard bastard, too. The only difference is...well, from the old stories you think of backwoods warriors straight out of the swamp."

"He wasn't?" Tampo asked.

"Too urbane. Wore a tailored suit, navigated the streets with ease. Another reason I think he was a Dynize, beyond the accent— he had the city written all over him and the only cities one might see a dragonman as commonplace these days are in Dynize."

"Agreed," Tampo said. "Palo dragonmen no longer exist. I knew the Dynize were scouting Landfall, but a dragonman..."

Celine swung just a little too far out on the railing, her feet slipping, and Styke snatched her by the back of the shirt and pulled her back without taking his eyes off Tampo. "Wait. You *knew* the Dynize were in Landfall? Does Lady Flint know that? Do the Blackhats know?"

"I can't think of a reason she'd keep it a secret if she knew." Tampo clicked his tongue, his expression annoyed, as if he'd let something slip that he hadn't meant to. "I'm not sure if the Blackhats know. They may have their suspicions, but...this isn't information you need to know." He held up a hand to forestall Styke's protest. "It's not that I don't think you can keep a secret, but rather that the more people who are aware of the Dynize, the greater chance they will disappear without a trace. They have proved, like your dragonman, to be skittish when made the center of attention."

This bit about Tampo already knowing about the Dynize made Styke return to his earlier question: What did Tampo want? It seemed that Lady Flint was only a small piece in a larger scheme, rather than the focus of his attentions. He had a stake in Landfall, though whether he was a revolutionary, a wannabe usurper, or simply a power broker of some kind, Styke could not guess. He was well connected and wealthy enough to know what was going on in Greenfire Depths *and* to get Styke released from Lindet's labor camps. That meant something.

Tampo gestured vaguely, as if to himself, and said, "Never mind all that. I want you to focus on Lady Flint for now. Track down this dragonman and get Flint her answers—I'll want to hear them as well—but try to stay as close to her as possible. She needs to stay alive for at least the next few months."

"Until?"

"Until I know if she'll be a help or a hindrance."

"You wouldn't happen to know where a dragonman might be hiding, would you?" Styke asked. "It would sure make my job easier."

"Unfortunately, I do not. You're on your own for now, but I'll pass on anything I can discover." Tampo got to his feet, gently brushing Celine's hair off the back of her neck to examine the red markings again. "Stay close to Mr. Styke," he told Celine. "The man who did that to you won't hesitate to go further if he catches you alone."

"Yes, Mr. Tampo."

Styke wondered if Tampo actually cared, or whether he was worried Styke wouldn't be able to focus if something happened to Celine. Tampo was right to worry, but the question intrigued Styke.

"One more thing," Tampo said as he turned to go. He held out a roll of banknotes. "Fidelis Jes knows that you've been released."

Styke twirled the ring on his finger, feeling along the lance with his thumb. Fidelis Jes could certainly complicate things. "How?"

"Seems one of the guards I bribed had instructions to let Fidelis Jes know if you happened to get out for any reason. We could do without the attention, but no helping it now, unfortunately."

Styke couldn't help but agree. He was already looking over his shoulder for this dragonman to come calling—now he had to figure out a way to navigate the streets without attracting the attention of the Blackhats. He was going to have to start taking hackney cabs everywhere. But something else was bothering him. "You have people in the Blackhats?"

"Local police, actually," Tampo said with a faint smile. "Seems Fidelis Jes has alerted most of the authorities that you're a mass-murdering war criminal that must be apprehended."

Styke felt a stab of anger. Being accused of being a murderer didn't faze him. But a war criminal? That was preposterous. "Does that amuse you?" he asked.

"A little," Tampo said. "I expect you to go ahead with your work. Just be warned that Fidelis Jes is coming for you. You'll want to keep a low profile."

"I'll be ready for it when he does," Styke said. He made a fist, imagining that it was around Fidelis Jes's throat. "If Flint finds out she'll hand me over without a fuss."

Tampo's smile broadened. "The garrisons haven't been told, so I suspect Lady Flint will not find out for some time. You probably have a week or two to make yourself indispensable. Once you do that—once you're one of her men—she won't let Fidelis Jes walk away with you." Tampo nodded to himself, as if satisfied with the meeting, and then turned and left the café as suddenly as he'd arrived.

Styke looked down at his third cup of coffee, the ice long melted, and then over at Celine. She was watching Tampo go, eyes sharp, and it struck him that she saw and heard more than most children her age. Good. It might just keep her alive to reach adulthood. Styke stood up, paid his bill, and took Celine by the hand. If Fidelis Jes knew he was out, he would stop at nothing to catch him. That meant looking in on old friends. Styke didn't have a lot of those left, so he thought it best he give them some warning.

CHAPTER 25

Vlora woke to the sound of a violent row outside the Loel's Fort staff room. She bolted upright, blinking sleep out of her eyes and fumbling for her pistol, only for the door to burst inward. She lunged for the sword beneath her cot but was snatched up by strong hands, lifted bodily to her feet, and thrust into the light of the single window in the center of the room.

"What the pit..." Vlora struggled, only to suddenly find herself free. She nearly collapsed, but managed to keep her balance, blinking at the big, bearded face in front of her. "Vallencian? What are you doing here? By Adom, Vallencian, I'm not dressed!"

The Ice Baron shushed her loudly and spun her around, examining her body in a way that might have been horrifying if it wasn't so clinical. Vlora tried to come to grips with what was happening, a hangover and far too little sleep keeping her head fuzzy. If there wasn't a good reason for this, she was going to kill him.

"Ach!" Vallencian exclaimed, snatching up Vlora's clothes from the chair she'd thrown them on last night and thrusting them into her hands. He turned away, as if suddenly embarrassed, his cheeks turning red, and began to pace furiously from one end of the room to the other as Vlora dressed. "I am sorry for this intrusion, Lady Flint, but I simply had to see that you were unharmed with my own eyes. If they had damaged a single hair on your head..." He let out a strangled exclamation.

Vlora's own anger died out as she managed to clear the sleep from her head and saw that Vallencian was physically trembling, his hands balled into fists, tears streaming down his face. "Vallencian? Are you all right?"

"My idiot footman waited until I awoke to give me your message, so I have just now found out you were attacked last night on your way home from the gala."

"Vallencian, calm down, or you'll give yourself apoplexy."

"You could have been killed!"

Vlora staggered over to the table, where she counted eight empty wine bottles. For who? Her, Olem, and Styke? Considering how hard it was for a powder mage to get a true hangover, most of that had gone in her. Pit, it was going to be a rough day. "I wasn't. I wasn't even hurt."

"Incredible. A testament to your skill, and to the favor of the god of your choosing. But Lady Flint, you were under *my* protection. You are *my* friend. I am mortified, and I hope you will accept any gift that is in my power to give."

Vallencian's solemn face, and perhaps a little leftover alcohol in her system, made Vlora giggle. She covered her mouth, mortified that such an un-general-like sound would come from her. Vallencian scowled. "I'm sorry," she said. "I'm so sorry, it's just...I've had so many people try to kill me. Vallencian, your apology is completely unneeded. I don't blame you in any way for what happened."

"I don't care! I blame myself." He looked away, brushed tears off his cheeks with his bearskin. "You could have been hurt, and I *did* lose another friend last night."

Vlora sobered up. "Devin-Tallis. His family..."

"They will want for nothing!" Vallencian declared. "His widow will be a countess! His children will attend the finest schools! I am not..." He choked on his words.

Vlora's cheeks burned with embarrassment. She'd never seen someone with so much passion before. For the first time she noticed a few of her soldiers standing just outside the door and shooed them away, wondering if they'd gotten an eyeful before she'd dressed. Oh well. No helping that now. Vlora stuck her head out the door. "Olem! Olem! Someone get the colonel, would you?"

"I'm right here." Olem rounded the corner at a jog, hand on the hilt of his sword. "Are you all right?"

Vlora jerked her head at Vallencian, who stood with his face toward the corner of the staff room, weeping openly. "Better than him," she muttered.

"Ah," Olem whispered back. "That's quite something. What's going on?"

"He claims he feels responsible for the attack on me last night, and the death of my guide. Pit, I can't..." She was cut off by an enormous crash. The sound made her jump, and she checked the window to find a cloud of dust riding over the walls of the fort. "What's going on?"

"The boys are taking down the first tenement," Olem answered.

"That was this morning? Pit, you need to remind me not to drink so much."

Olem cocked an eyebrow at her. "And I need to remind you what happens when I remind you of things."

"I only punched you in the face that one time."

"Twice, actually."

"I said I was sorry." Vlora looked over her shoulder at Vallencian, who seemed to be getting himself under control. "Can you...?" she said to Olem.

Olem pulled a handkerchief out of his pocket. "Vallencian," he said, "you wouldn't happen to have any more of those cigarettes?" The Ice Baron blew his nose loudly, and within moments the two of them were smoking up a storm in the corner of the staff room. Vlora stepped outside to get some fresh air, choked on the drifting dust from the demolition project the next block over, and went back inside.

By the time they finished their cigarettes, Vallencian seemed like his old self. He thumped Olem on the back and gave Vlora a sheepish look. "I am very sorry," he said. "I am known to get overly... protective of my friends."

"No need for the apology," Vlora said, realizing the irony that *she* had been the one attacked last night and *he* was the one in tears. "Vallencian, I do need something, though. Those assassins weren't there on their own volition, I'd stake my reputation on it. We need to know who had them waiting for me, and why, but the Riflejacks don't have the contacts in the city, and especially not in Greenfire Depths."

Vallencian discarded his spent cigarette and immediately produced his pipe, puffing it to life in moments. "I'm not sure I'll be much help in the Depths. But I can try. I'll give you all of my resources to discover who did this thing."

"Just a little help is all we ask."

"Nonsense! I may not have guile, but I have money and I know how to make it work for me. I'll find out who tried to have you killed, Lady Flint, I swear it. It's the least I could do for this mess that I've made of your room and for seeing you, um..." He cleared his throat.

"Let's forget that happened," Vlora suggested. She leaned over to Olem and whispered, "You need to remind me to get dressed after we..."

Olem chuckled. "Not a chance," he said under his breath.

"I will put pressure on my business partners to find answers for me," Vallencian said. "No answers, no ice. The Palo love their iced coffee."

"You don't have to put your business at risk," Vlora assured him. "One other thing, though. Can you tell me anything about Meln-Dun? I spent quite a lot of time with him last night, and he seems eager to help me make friends in the Depths. Does he have a good reputation?"

Vallencian considered the question for a moment. "He does, more or less. He owns one of the few remaining operating quarries in the city, and several hundred homes in Greenfire Depths."

"He's a landlord?"

"He is. Always buying up what he can from any Palo who go into debt. He's fair, though. Always gives them a chance to get back on their feet."

"I'm surprised that anyone owns anything down there," Olem said.

Vallencian shook his pipe at Olem. "Property is taken very seriously in the Depths! Most of the Palo own their apartments. It's a point of pride. I've tried to tell you, leave your expectations behind when it comes to the Palo! Meln-Dun, though..." He gave a shrug. "He's ambitious, but most seem to like him."

A landlord, with obvious plans to expand his holdings. That would explain why he wanted Vlora's help rebuilding a chunk of the Depths. Brand-new tenements would end up being prime real estate, and he'd no doubt put them in his pocket by the time construction was done. Vlora wondered how Meln-Dun's business came into play with Mama Palo's maneuvering against Lindet. Perhaps it didn't. Either way, it was something Vlora could use to infiltrate the Depths.

"About his partner," Vlora said.

"Lady Enna?"

"Yes, her. You may want to pass on a friendly warning. I'm not terribly interested in the politics of the city, but it's dangerous to be so loudly liberal in a place like Landfall."

Vallencian grimaced. "I know. I've tried, believe me. Lady Enna

is a sharp woman, but a little bit of wine in her brings out a bleeding heart. Meln-Dun does his best to make sure she doesn't go to
parties that aren't predominantly attended by people who either
agree with her or are ambivalent. My apologies for leaving you with
her—though you did seem to get along fine."

"Yes," Vlora said, drawing out the word. The events of last night
were coming back to her with more clarity as she gathered her
wits. "One last question. Do you know someone named Gregious
Tampo? He's a lawyer."

Vallencian's face brightened. "I do! Gregious runs a small mill
out beyond the fens. Lovely man, very friendly."

"A mill?" Vlora searched her pockets and came up with Tampo's
card, handing it to Vallencian. "He said he owned a printing press."

"First I've heard of it," Vallencian said. "He's only been around
Landfall for a few months but he seems to be in Mama Palo's good
graces. I understand he's going to set up a law firm in the city once
he's raised the funds. I do hope he finds success."

Vlora decided not to tell Vallencian about her interactions with
Tampo. She didn't need another passionate speech, or for him to
rush off half-cocked. Getting him to focus on finding whoever
hired those assassins was the most important thing. She paused
that thought, suddenly recalling a warning Tampo had given her
before leaving. *Beware the Depths,* he'd said. It had sounded vaguely
sinister at the time, and she wondered whether he had anything to
do with the attempt on her life.

Vlora jumped at a sudden boom, and then the following, prolonged crash. She reached for a sword that was not at her hip.

"The second tenement," Olem explained. "The engineers decided
to take them both down today."

"Could have warned me. Vallencian, thank you so much for
checking on me. I need to get to work but please, do not disrupt
your business on my account."

Vallencian waved off her protestation and stalked toward the door. "I will discover who hired your assassins, Lady Flint. I will also try to recover Devin-Tallis's body. It's Greenfire Depths, so the scene of your attack is probably already cleaned up, but I will still try." He turned, flourishing a bow. "For now, good afternoon!" He was gone a moment later, and Vlora let out a sigh of relief.

She ran her hands through her hair. "Is it really afternoon already?"

"One fifteen," Olem reported.

She mentally sorted through the long list of things she needed to get done, filing them in order of importance. She knew she should feel elation at the success she'd had last night at the gala, but the assassination attempt after left her wondering if this was all a terrible idea. She was getting mixed up in the petty politics of a slum exactly like she'd promised herself she wouldn't. "Let Agent Bravis know that I'm making progress," she told Olem. "But also tell him I'm going to need resources and permission to build in Greenfire Depths. Then set up a meeting with Meln-Dun. And," she said, handing him Tampo's card, "look into this. Find out who this guy is. He gave me the creeps."

CHAPTER 26

The Fles family home in Greenfire Depths had not changed much since Styke's last visit. It was located at the bottom of the quarry near the Greenfire Inlet, where the Hadshaw River Gorge and the Depths connected in a narrow corridor that allowed immense blocks of limestone to be floated up or down the Hadshaw River by barge. The house was an old stone manor, one of the few single homes left in the Depths, facing the inlet in such a way that it actually received a bit of sunlight every day. When Styke approached that time was well past, and the manor was cloaked in shadow.

Styke had expected the Fles family home to be a ruin by now, what with the current reputation of the Depths, but the street outside was devoid of the usual quarry grime, the stone facade of the house scrubbed clean. The big wooden sign that used to hang over the door declaring it FLES FINE BLADES had been replaced with a small bronze placard that said:

FLES FAMILY HOME

FOR BLADES SEE FLES AND FLES

AT HADSHAW MARKET

Styke watched the house for a few minutes while Celine did a circuit of the neighborhood to see if the Blackhats had managed to beat him here. He noted that the inlet was busy with Palo workers loading stone on barges, and there were truncheon-wielding Palo in pale green uniforms at regular intervals up and down the street. A Palo police force. He snorted. They really *had* taken charge of the Depths.

Celine returned, shaking her head. The Blackhats hadn't left anyone to watch the Fles home—at least anyone obvious—and Styke took that as a good sign. He went around to the side door, finding the spare key in the false knot halfway up the frame, and let himself and Celine into the old workshop.

Most of the manor had long ago been converted into a smithy for Fles's business, and then allowed to gather dust when the smithy moved to Hadshaw Market. The forge was now dark, the rooms quiet. Styke guided Celine through the dim light of the old smithy by memory until he reached the heavy oak door that separated the Fles home from the workshop. The door stuck, forcing him to put his shoulder against it, and he pushed his way inside.

The "home" portion of the manor contained several large rooms that all seemed to lead into one another, from the foyer, to the great hall, to the kitchen and larder. The mix of smells hit him first—the smoky scent left in clothes after all day at the forge, the corn oil and lime mix they used to rub the blades. Styke felt himself transported back twenty years, to a time when he was young and stupid, and without direction, hanging around the forge all day to flirt with Ibana while Fles worked his blades in the next room. There was still the old ironwood chair by the front door, atop the striped hide of a swamp-cat rug now worn thin.

Styke thrust aside all his old memories and stalked through the great room to the kitchen, following the smell of a woodstove and the whistle of a teakettle. He found Old Man Fles leaning against the counter beside the stove, snoring quietly, asleep on his feet.

Celine poked him gently. Fles stirred, swatting at an invisible fly, but continued to snore. "Why do old people sleep so much?" she asked.

"Fles has always been a napper," Styke said, taking the teakettle off the stove. "Fles. Fles!"

Old Man Fles jerked awake, nearly falling over. "I'm up! I . . ." He blinked and seemed to remember where he was before glancing from Styke to Celine. "What are you two doing here?"

"You said you didn't want me coming by the market," Styke answered.

Fles rubbed his eyes, stretched, then snatched the teakettle out of Styke's hand and poured himself a cup. He didn't offer any to Styke or Celine. "Right, right," he said, sniffing. "Surprised you're still alive. Thought the new city would eat you up by now."

"I'm a cripple, not an invalid," Styke said, growling. Bloody old man always liked to bait him.

"I hear you messed up a bar full of Palo kids up on the Rim."

First Olem, now Old Man Fles. "Word's getting around, huh?"

"Sure is." Fles poked Styke in the stomach with one bony finger. "Ow."

"Ow, nothing. You need to harden up, boy. The Blackhats are looking for you."

"I know."

Fles raised his eyebrows. "You know? Well look at you, getting your information before Old Man Fles. I just found out half an hour ago."

"They come by the market?" Styke asked, unable to keep the worry from his voice.

Fles waved him off. "Nah."

"Here?"

"Not yet. I fired up some of my old contacts this week. Turns out the Blackhats are quietly asking around about you. Nothing overt—nothing that gives away your name. Just telling people to be on the lookout for a scarred giant."

Styke nodded, feeling more than a little relieved. Maybe the Blackhats had forgotten about Styke's relationship with the Fles family. Not likely, but he could always hope. They hadn't started roughing up his old friends yet, at least.

"Don't touch that!" Fles said, swatting Celine's hand away from a knife on the counter. "You'll cut your damn fingers off."

"I can handle a knife," Celine said, sticking her bottom lip out at Fles.

"I keep mine sharp enough to shave with." Fles turned his attention back to Styke. "Boy, what happened with those Palo kids up at Mama Sender's? That's the place you had me setting up the meeting, isn't it? You really had to kill 'em?"

"Didn't want to," Styke replied. His initial feeling of joy at being back in the Fles home had soured, and he found himself scowling back at Fles. Everyone, even his friends, always assumed he *enjoyed* killing. Which he did, sometimes. But the assumption still hurt a little. "Damned kids came looking for a fight."

"Well, did you at least get the information you wanted? You find yourself a dragonman?"

"I did, actually."

"No kidding. What did he look like?"

"Like a Palo, but with black tattoos on his neck and arms." Styke reached to the sheath on the back of his belt and took out the dragonman's knife. "What do you think of this?"

Fles gave a low whistle and set down his tea to take up the blade. He handled it gingerly, turning it over and over again in his hands before taking it by the grip and giving a few experimental stabs. "Haven't seen one of these since I was a kid. Damn, would you look at that workmanship?" He held the blade up in front of his eyes, squinting at it for several moments. "Sharp as steel. There's sorcery in this knife. Lots of blood on it, too."

Styke didn't think there was any sorcery in the knife—his Knack would have sensed it—but one didn't argue with Fles when it came to blades.

Reluctantly, Fles handed the knife back to Styke. "Lots of stories around those weapons. Lots of history."

"Like?"

"Well, a dragonman's weapons are all made out of the bones of the swamp dragons they killed. That knife is from a back leg, I'd wager, but the axes they carry are the real prizes—carved from the jawbones, one from the top, one from the bottom. They say that each weapon is sanctified by a bone-eye, enchanted by a Privileged, and bathed in the blood of an innocent. It's probably all hogwash—Palo are a lot more civilized than we've ever given them credit for, and they haven't had their own Privileged for hundreds of years. Even their bone-eyes are pretty rare."

Styke sheathed the blade. "This one is a Dynize, not a Palo."

"That's preposterous. No one from the Empire has been seen here for over a hundred years."

"He was," Styke insisted. "And someone I trust told me the Dynize have been spotted in Landfall." He wondered if he actually *did* trust Tampo. He didn't have a lot of choice, he decided.

Fles rubbed his chin, scowling. "I would have heard about Dynize in town."

"So you don't know anything about it?"

"Not me."

"My source said that they were infiltrating Greenfire Depths, mixing in with the Palo."

"No, no. Can't be right." The Old Man sipped his tea, then topped it off and added a lump of sugar. "If it's true, and I'm not saying it is, the Palo might know more. But you'll need to ask one of them directly."

"That's what I've got you for."

Fles held up his hands. "My contacts got you a meeting with the dragonman. You missed your chance, and I have to live here. Palo favors are like gold, and you won't be using another of mine. Besides, asking after the Dynize could stir up a world of trouble."

Styke wondered if the Old Man was slipping. He'd already agreed to dig up information on the Blackhat grand master, but he wouldn't chase a rumor down here with the Palo? Strange. "All right. Then *I'll* ask. Who do I go to?"

"I think...no, not him. Not her." Fles went through an invisible checklist, talking to himself. "*Definitely* not her. Ah, got it. I'll send you over to Henrick Jackal. Old friend of yours."

Styke's mind was elsewhere, considering how he was going to approach the Palo directly. He'd always been evenhanded in his dealing with the Palo, and they'd always seemed to respect him for it, but it had been a long time. Those Palo kids and their dragonman overlord had proved that. He brought his thoughts back to the present. "Wait. Did you say Henrick Jackal?"

"That's what I said. I know you're a cripple, but I didn't think you were deaf, too."

Styke held a hand up to his eyes. "About yay high. Missing an ear and a pinkie?"

"Yeah, that's him. He's some kind of Palo spiritualist now."

"No," Styke said, snorting. "Not Mean Jackal."

"One and the same."

Celine tugged on Styke's sleeve. "Who is Mean Jackal?"

"Used to be one of my captains," Styke answered thoughtfully. "He was a founding member of the Mad Lancers, but was always a little crazy. Disemboweled the mayor of Little Starland for spitting on his shoe." Celine's eyes widened, and Styke frowned at the Old

Man. "You're *sure* Henrick Jackal is a spiritualist now? Is it some kind of a con?"

Fles shrugged. "Beats me. Heard he was the real deal. Teaches runaways to talk to river spirits or some such shit. Even the other Palo think he's a kook, but he's the only person who pays attention to the teenage castoffs so he's got his ear to the ground better than most."

"Well, I'll be damned," Styke said, searching his pocket for a bit of horngum and tucking it into his cheek. "Never would have pegged Jackal for getting religion." Styke's last memory of Jackal was watching him and Ibana attempt to fight their way, bare-handed, through a line of military police as their fellows led Styke up to the firing squad. He always figured Ibana got away with it—she had a family name, after all. But Jackal was a violent Palo, and Styke was surprised to hear he'd come out of that fight alive.

Old Man Fles wrote down the address—or a list of directions, which was as close to an address as one could get in the Depths— and handed it over. Styke tucked it in his pocket, gesturing to Celine toward the door. "When does Ibana get back?"

"A week," Fles answered. "Maybe two? Maybe less? Pit if you think I keep track of that girl. She's always off making new deals, bringing on new apprentices. Business head on her she got from her mother, but damn if I can keep up with it. Why? You hoping for some warning before she comes back and pincushions you?"

"Maybe," Styke replied. He wasn't quite sure himself. As much as he wanted to see Ibana, he knew it was going to hurt bad—both emotionally and physically.

"Right, right. Don't let the door hit you on the ass, et cetera," Old Man Fles said, waving them toward the foyer. "And go out the front. That damned workshop door keeps sticking and I don't want to deal with it tonight."

"Good-bye, Mr. Fles," Celine said.

"Bah!"

Styke and Celine headed toward the front door. Styke paused for a moment to look back at the great room, filled with a lifetime of knickknacks and furniture, a smile tugging at his ruined face. He opened the door behind him and turned toward the street.

Only to come face-to-face with a man in a black uniform, shirt buttoned up the left breast, truncheon and pistol at his belt. There were five more dressed identically just behind him, and the man in front had his hand raised as if he was just about to knock on the door. "Shit," the Blackhat managed, right before Styke buried his knife in his chest.

Styke shoved Celine back into the Fles house with one hand and twisted his knife with the other. He lifted, charging forward, using the Blackhat's body as a shield as his companions drew their pistols. The crack of gunfire erupted around him and Styke felt the bullets thump into his unfortunate Blackhat battering ram. He pulled his knife out and threw the body, cutting sideways with a wide arc to open the throat of the woman on his left.

A truncheon slammed across Styke's left shoulder. He took a second blow, ignoring the pain that erupted from his arm, and punched the Blackhat holding the truncheon hard enough to lift him off his feet. Styke grabbed the falling truncheon of another and brought his knife down hard, severing the man's hand at the wrist. He flipped the truncheon around, bloody hand and all, and slammed it across the face of its former owner, then let go to draw the bone knife from his belt and bury it in the eye of the last Blackhat.

The whole fight lasted less than twenty seconds. Styke's chest rose and fell from the effort, and he bent to finish off two survivors before they had a chance to start screaming. He glanced up, noting the Palo policemen still overseeing the quarry down the street. The Palo stared at him, unmoving, and the street was silent.

"By Kresimir, you made a damned bloody mess," Fles said, sipping his tea in the doorway, holding a kitchen knife in one hand. Celine hid behind him.

Styke looked down at the bodies and the growing pool of blood on the stone floor of the quarry. Some of the Palo down the street continued to stare, while others turned away. They saw the black uniforms and decided this wasn't their problem.

"Quit your bellyaching," Styke said, "and help me with these bodies. Celine, go get a bucket of water to clean up this blood. There should be some lye above the stove."

Fles sighed, downing his tea. "Friend with a pig farm owes me a favor," he muttered, "but we better move quick."

Two hours later, Styke had changed his bloody clothes and disposed of the six corpses. He walked into the only public post office remaining in Greenfire Depths and waited in line until he got to the front. A half-Palo, half-Rosvelean woman with brown, freckled skin greeted him. "Package or letter?" she asked.

"Package," Styke said. He opened his fist above the woman's desk, letting six Iron Roses clatter onto the wood. "I need the mailing address for the office of the grand master of the secret police."

CHAPTER 27

Michel stood outside a printshop in Middle Heights, a large, upper-class borough right in the center of the Landfall Plateau. He ran his eyes over the file in his hand—a comprehensive list of every single printer, both independent and government owned, in the entire city. "Huffin and Sons, Huffin and Sons," he murmured, running his finger along the edge to try to keep the letters from going in and out of focus. "Ah. Huffin and Sons." He put a mark through the center of the name and let his hand drop, looking up at the sun in the eastern sky.

He checked his pocket watch to find that it was well past nine in the morning and tried to remember if he'd slept. "No," he said quietly, "I definitely haven't slept for at least forty-eight hours now."

"You caught a few winks in that cab this morning," he reminded himself.

"Oh, right."

"And another cab last night."

"Okay. So I've gotten a good two and a half hours of sleep in the last forty-eight. Fantastic. That'll keep me on my feet all week."

He ran a hand through his hair and noticed a nearby shopkeep staring at him. "Probably shouldn't talk to yourself in public, either, Michel."

"Oh, shut up."

He flipped the shopkeep a wave and headed into the boulevard to catch a hackney cab and was soon heading back to his office at the Millinery. He checked his list again once he was inside. Two hundred and eighteen printers in the greater Landfall area. He'd covered roughly half in just twenty-four hours, which *he* found pretty damn impressive. But he hoped that Fidelis Jes didn't call him in anytime soon to discuss his use of time, because he was most definitely grasping at straws.

This Tampo fellow was no fool, Michel reasoned, looking out the hackney cab window at the passing faces going about their daily lives. *He printed all those pamphlets and then went into hiding. He won't resurface now that he knows we're looking for him. No way he's stupid enough to keep printing* Sins of Empire.

"But," Michel muttered to himself, "maybe he made a mistake. Or maybe he figures we're so wrapped up keeping the lid on the boiling kettle that is this city, we won't have the resources to check every single printshop."

Which they didn't, Michel reflected. Fidelis Jes had everyone looking for Ben Styke, a name out of Michel's childhood—Mad Ben Styke, hero of the revolution! Fancy that. That tough old bastard still alive after so many years.

Michel was drifting again. "Focus!" he said, looking down at the list. A little over a hundred printers to check. He could do that in another twenty-four hours or so—maybe forty-eight, if he took it a little easier. Some of these were way on the outskirts of town. Once he had that done he could get back to some real work, whatever the pit that meant, and maybe get some sleep.

"I thought this damn job was going to make my career. Now it's looking like it'll tank it."

The cab arrived at the Millinery, and Michel wondered if he shouldn't have just gone straight home. He was wobbly on his feet, and needed to get some sleep. Maybe he'd plant his face on his desk for a couple of hours, then get a cup of coffee and head back out.

Michel paid his driver and stepped outside, watching as three prison carriages pulled out of the street, followed by at least two dozen Iron Roses, all armed to the teeth. He blinked, wondering if he was seeing double, and wandered over to the old gatekeeper sitting on his chair just inside the double doors of the Millinery. "Hey, Keln, what's going on over there?"

Keln chewed slowly for a moment, then turned and spat a wad of tobacco into the street. "Six Iron Rose medallions just showed up on the grand master's desk."

Michel raised both eyebrows. *That* was news. "Shit. Where'd they come from?"

"Greenfire Depths," Keln said. "We're trying to keep it quiet, but..." Keln leaned over conspiratorially. "Word has it they came from the Ben Styke fellow that Fidelis Jes has everyone looking for. You didn't hear it from me, though."

"Cross my heart."

"Yeah, the boys are heading down to Greenfire Depths to try to recover the bodies."

"Any chance of that happening?"

"They sent word ahead to our Palo contacts. If the bodies are still in the Depths, the Palo will hand 'em over. They don't want no trouble."

And, Michel thought, *we'll make a public show of force and quietly pay them a few thousand krana per corpse.* "Best of luck to them."

"Yeah. The Depths are really causing us a headache lately, aren't they?"

Michel hoped his expression wasn't too clueless. He tried to run through all the problems originating from Greenfire Depths—aside from the usual Palo protests and riots—and came up short. "Eh?"

"Lady Flint," Keln prompted.

Pit. Michel had completely forgotten about Flint. He hadn't heard a word from her in days. Knowing his luck she was lying facedown in a gutter somewhere. "Right," he said. "Lady Flint." He paused, trying to come up with a not-so-obvious way to get the information out of Keln and gave up. "What happened with Lady Flint?"

Keln's eyebrows rose. "Aren't you her Blackhat contact?"

"What happened with Lady Flint?" Michel asked again, forcefully.

"A bunch of Palo punks tried to kill her."

Michel stared at Keln for a few moments while his tired brain tried to catch up with that information. "Well, shit," he said, and set off running for another cab.

Michel had the presence of mind to head back and get all the information he could about the attack—which wasn't much—before heading out to Loel's Fort. He arrived just an hour later and was surprised to find Lady Flint standing a few blocks down the street from the fort, overlooking a construction site while hundreds of her men cleared away rubble from a demolished tenement.

Michel leapt from his cab, heading over to stand beside Lady Flint, hoping he didn't look *too* panicked. An assassination attack on one of his wards and he didn't even find out for two days? He would have castigated anyone beneath him for such an oversight.

At first glance, he wondered whether Keln had been pulling his leg. Flint looked unharmed. There wasn't a scratch on her *or* her uniform, and she seemed to be in a pleasant mood while she discussed something quietly with another uniformed mercenary—an engineer, if Michel had to guess—who then went and began giving orders to the men down in the rubble of the tenement.

Michel watched for a few minutes, noting the way Flint's eyes roamed the surrounding streets in a constant, watchful vigil, and the way her hand rested on the hilt of her sword. He wouldn't say she was on edge, necessarily—her body language was fairly relaxed—but she was keeping an eye out.

Michel cleared his throat.

"Yes, Agent Bravis?" Flint asked without looking. "I was wondering how long you were going to stand there."

"Just taking in the scene, ma'am," Michel said jovially. "Looks like you're making great progress on these tenements."

"We are, thank you. We should begin construction of the replacement building within a day or so, and my engineers expect to have one finished by the end of the month."

"That's, ah, impressive." Michel had no idea how long it took to build a tenement, but that sounded awfully fast.

"It's a wonder what you can do with five thousand sets of hands and a few dozen competent engineers," Flint said. "My men build a palisade every night when we're on the march in enemy territory. Gives them a lot of experience with this kind of thing, and keeps them in shape."

Michel vaguely remembered reading something about the ancient Deliv legions doing the same. "Very good, ma'am. Has everything been going well on your"—Michel paused, glancing around to be sure they wouldn't be overheard—"other task?"

"Not as quickly as I'd like," Flint said. "But I believe I've made progress."

Flint had yet to actually look his direction, and Michel had the feeling she'd rather not give him the report he definitely needed to make to Fidelis Jes. Pit. He didn't have the time or energy for this. Perhaps it was best to just be direct. "I heard there was an attack."

"There was."

"What happened?"

Flint finally glanced in his direction. The look she gave him was somewhere between bemused and annoyed. "I thought you Black-hats knew everything that happened in the city."

"We have our...limitations. To be honest, all anyone at the Millinery knows is that a group of Palo attacked you. We don't know who, or why, or where the information even came from. It seems everyone's talking about it but no one has any better details. I was hoping I could get your side of the story and offer any assistance you might need in tracking down your attackers."

"The attackers are dead," Flint said bluntly.

"Ah." *And not a damn scratch on her. Did she defend herself, or had she bodyguards?*

"They ambushed me outside a gala I was attending at the Yellow Hall. I have not yet figured out who ordered the attack, or why, but I'm working on it. Does that satisfy, Agent Bravis?"

Michel grimaced. Flint was definitely annoyed—rightfully so. She was a general, after all, and it had taken her government contact two days just to check in on her after an attempt on her life. He decided to move past that as quickly as possible. "I haven't heard anyone mention the Yellow Hall for a long time. I understand that's the center of Mama Palo's power. And you were just invited in?"

"Vallencian got me an invitation."

Michel couldn't help but smile. In a city full of despicable, scheming, thieving people, the Ice Baron was one of the few he found truly pleasant. "I'll make a note of that, thank you. Were you able to meet with Mama Palo?"

"No. Seems no outsiders do. But the pretense of building these new tenements has given me an in among the upper crust of Palo society. I've talked with someone named Meln-Dun about beginning work like this"—she gestured to the construction site—"in the Depths itself. A community outreach program directly toward the Palo, if you will. I sent you information on the project just after the assassination attempt. Didn't you get my report?"

Michel considered the stack of unread folders on his desk at the

Millinery. "My apologies, Lady Flint, but I'm handling a hundred cases right now. Refresh my memory." He *had* to pay better attention. Maybe he could assign Agent Warsim to Flint indefinitely—though a Bronze Rose didn't befit a general.

Flint made a noncommittal noise in the back of her throat and Michel decided to ignore it. "You're using this construction project as a way to get closer to Mama Palo?" he asked. He found the prospect fascinating. The Blackhats had a heavy-handed approach to just about every facet of their involvement with Fatrastan society. He doubted it had ever even occurred to any of the Gold Roses that reaching out to the Palo—instead of beating them down—might actually gain them the cooperation they so bitterly sought.

"That's the idea," Flint answered. "I think it'll work, but I need your approval. And any information you have about Meln-Dun. Vallencian seems to trust him, but Vallencian seems to trust everyone."

Michel tried to remember what he could. "Meln-Dun is part owner of one of the few remaining quarries down there. I believe he's been cooperative with us in the past. One of the 'good ones,' I think my colleagues in the Millinery would call him."

"So I can trust him?"

"It's Blackhat policy not to trust any Palo."

"Your tone," Flint observed, "tells me you don't agree with that policy."

Michel cursed himself for being careless. He really did need some damned sleep. It was a small slipup, but if he accidentally criticized the Blackhats to anyone who actually cared, he might find himself on the wrong end of a long discussion with one of the less friendly occupants of the Millinery. "I should rather say, Meln-Dun can be trusted as far as any Palo. In my opinion, Palo are people the same as any other, so . . ." He let the implication hang in the air.

"Double-speak for 'it's up to you,' eh?" Flint asked.

Michel gave her what he hoped was a charming smile. Maybe he *should* just go home. A few hours in his own bed would do wonders more than the same time spent snoring into a file on his desk. "Meln-Dun is a respectable businessman," he said. "You should feel safe working with him. But he's also highly placed in Palo society, and we have no idea how close he is to Mama Palo."

"Too close," Flint said, nodding, "and I risk him getting wind of our plot on Mama Palo. Too far, and he's no good at all to me."

"Exactly." Michel couldn't help but wish there were more people like Flint in Landfall. Pit, in the Blackhats themselves. People who understood nuance, and were willing to take an unorthodox tactic to root out their enemies, were sorely lacking on the plateau. And the ones who did have that ability, like Captain Blasdell, were relegated to desk work. If he earned his Gold Rose, maybe he could change that.

If.

"I'll get you access to Greenfire Depths," Michel said, "and the supplies and money you'll need to begin a construction project down there. But you may have to convince Fidelis Jes you're making progress toward your real goal."

Flint waved the thought off, as if it were no real concern. "If Jes has any doubts he shouldn't have hired me. If he wants to question my tactics he can come down here and do so to my face."

Michel had to suppress a laugh. *That's* why people like Flint never rose to the top here in Landfall. If you want to be a Gold Rose or one of Lady Chancellor's inner circle, you had to be competent *and* subservient. Lots of smiling, nodding, and ass-kissing. He wondered if Lady Flint was capable of any of those.

His eyes fell to her sword, and he briefly wondered if she'd be able to out-duel Fidelis Jes. He was said to be the deadliest man in Landfall, but he made it a point never to fight anyone with sorcery. The fact that Lady Flint had walked away from a Palo ambush in the Depths told Michel a lot about her combat prowess. But she was a powder mage. Without her powder, was she any good?

"One other question," Flint said, bringing Michel out of his thoughts. "Are you familiar with someone named Gregious Tampo?"

All trace of exhaustion left Michel as quickly as if he'd been dunked in the bay. "Where'd you hear that name?" he asked, trying to keep his voice steady.

Flint must have heard some excitement in his voice, because she turned to him with a frown, looking him up and down. "You seem distracted today," she said.

"Never mind that. Tampo. Where did you hear the name?" *Gregious*. Michel had a first name now, and that *could* mean a lot.

"I met him," Flint said.

"Where?"

"The Yellow Hall. He was at the gala the other night."

"You're sure? Describe him to me!"

Flint hesitated. "He was tall and thin. He had black hair. A bit of a hawkish face. Seemed a bit off to me, like someone you wouldn't want to meet in a back alley, but I couldn't quite put my finger on it. He was incredibly rude to me at the gala, and I was wondering if he was someone I need to look out for."

Michel licked his lips, half-tempted to tell Flint about his alternate mission. But no, he needed to keep that information close. "What did he say? Did he tell you who he was, or where he lives?"

"He didn't offer a lot of information." Flint dug through her pocket and then handed Michel a card. All it said was "The Palo Herald" and "Gregious Tampo" in smaller letters underneath. Michel checked the back for an address, but there was nothing.

"Did he say where it was?"

"Not that I recall. He said it was a small newspaper that catered to the Palo. But when I asked Vallencian, he'd never heard of it."

"Can I keep this?" Michel didn't wait for an answer, but shoved the card in his pocket. He raised his hand toward the nearest cab. This was big. Huge, possibly. A small newspaper required a printing press, and printing presses could be traced. For the first time since he'd lost Tampo at his offices, Michel had another lead. "Thank you, Lady Flint. I'll get the permissions you require."

"Wait," Flint said. "What's going on with Tampo?"

A cab pulled away from the curb and headed toward Michel. "Tampo is an enemy of the state," he told Lady Flint. "If you see him again, you must arrest him and send for me—and only me— immediately. I must go. The Millinery," he ordered the cabdriver, leaping onto the running board.

Michel was going to find this *Palo Herald*, and this time he wasn't going to let Tampo get away.

CHAPTER 28

Styke entered a small Kresim church under the west rim of Greenfire Depths that matched the directions given to him by Old Man Fles. It was a dilapidated wood building; practically a disaster waiting to happen, long rotted through by the constant damp at the bottom of the quarry. The church was tucked up against the wall, a three-room construction with a steeple atop which Kresimir's Rope had long ago fallen off. The inside was well lit by gas lamps, the floor covered in rubbish, old pews long stolen or destroyed.

There was an orderly queue of people along one side of the chapel, and at the front, atop what had once been an altar to Kresimir, sat an immense soup pot and stacks of stale bread. Palo boys as young as Celine and all the way into their twenties either waited in line or already enjoyed their morning meal squatting by the wall or sitting cross-legged in the empty chapel. Styke was more than a little surprised to recognize the man standing behind the soup pot, dishing out bowls to the waiting youth.

Styke watched him work for a moment, remaining unnoticed, then pulled Celine to one side of the chapel and squatted down among the Palo, who gave him space without comment. He pointed at Jackal.

"Henrick Jackal," he told Celine, "was an orphan like you. Now look at him. Taking care of kids on the streets where he fought, killed, and stole. Funny how life works out."

Celine seemed more than a little impressed. "He looks like a killer."

Styke found a piece of horngum in his pocket and chewed thoughtfully for a few moments. A little girl solemnly proclaiming a man she'd never met as a killer made him chuckle, but she wasn't wrong. Jackal was missing an ear and the pinkie on his left hand, but even beyond the obvious war wounds he was an intimidating man. He was well muscled but lean, and held himself with the kind of confidence that tended to intimidate ordinary folks. He wore an old brown duster, parted in the middle to reveal a stomach hard enough to take a kick from a mule, and a pair of old buckskin pants. His red hair was long and braided off to one side, his shallow cheeks covered in the ashen freckles of a Palo.

A spiritualist, Fles had called him.

"Henrick isn't a Palo name," Celine observed.

"Neither is Jackal," Styke said. "But an orphan can call himself anything he wants."

They waited for almost thirty minutes for the line to die down, but more Palo teenagers entered the chapel to replace each that finished their breakfast and left. Eventually a pair of teens came through the front door lugging a new soup pot, letting everyone in line know they were out of bread but that they had enough gruel to go around.

Styke was just beginning to think this would go all day when a small Palo boy—probably no more than a year older than Celine—

suddenly approached them. He held two bowls of soup, and the last two loaves of bread from the platter, and offered them to Styke and Celine.

Styke took the soup, drinking it quickly and mopping the bottom of the bowl with the bread. It tasted awful, but Celine didn't seem to mind. The boy watched them through their meal, then said in broken Adran, "Jackal wants to see you."

Styke palmed a few pennies and slipped them to the boy, getting up and stretching his legs. He searched his pockets for more horngum and came up empty, making a mental note to stop by an apothecary.

Jackal had been replaced at his post by a pair of Palo teens, and Styke slipped past them to head into the vestry. It proved to be a dark, closetlike space, barely big enough for a sleeping roll and a small shrine comprised of a human skull, in front of which he found Jackal kneeling. Jackal's eyes were closed, and he faced the shrine with lips moving silently.

"You never struck me as the praying type," Styke said.

"I'm not praying. I'm talking."

"With?"

"A spirit."

Styke tried to remember what he could of Palo religion. With so many tribes scattered across Fatrasta there tended to be a wide array of beliefs. "I've never met a Palo who believed they could talk to spirits."

"That's because most Palo don't." Between sentences, Jackal's lips continued to move as if he were carrying on two conversations at once. Finally, he gave a slight nod and opened his eyes, smiling warmly at Styke. "Colonel Styke. When the spirits told me you were still alive, I thought they were playing a joke on me. The afterlife can get awfully boring, and spirits aren't to be trusted."

Styke snorted. He wondered if Jackal had finally lost the few marbles he'd started with. "Good to see you, too, Jackal. I thought once the military police were done with me they'd come after you."

"They did," Jackal said, his face not changing expressions. "Ibana held them off long enough for me to get away, and then her father pulled some strings to get her released from their custody."

"Smart," Styke said. "I appreciate you coming after me when they put me up against the wall."

"Little good it did." Jackal got to his feet, unfolding gracefully and stepping toward Styke. Before the war, he'd liked his space. He rarely closed within reach of another human being unless he was about to kill. Yet he reached out, running one finger boldly across the deep scar on Styke's face. "I'm sorry."

Styke wasn't sure he liked this new Jackal. He already seemed too gentle to be the same man he'd fought with in the war. "Wasn't your fault. Never mind that, anyway. Didn't mean to take you away from your . . . service. Just came by hoping you could help me out."

"The Dynize dragonman?" Jackal asked.

Styke scowled. "How . . . How did you know that?" he asked, hand falling to the hilt of his knife.

"Because I talk to spirits," Jackal said matter-of-factly. "Same way I know the little girl hiding behind you is named Celine, and her father was a thief who died in the camps. Same way I know you murdered six Blackhats today, and that you plan on learning Fidelis Jes's routine so you can murder him when he least expects it."

"Pit," Styke swore. There was no way Jackal could know all that just from whatever contacts he had among the Palo. Styke leaned forward a little and sniffed, but could sense no sorcery on Jackal. Spirits? Really?

Jackal's smile was a little condescending. "Think me a nutter. Everyone else does. But you'll take my information just like the boys outside will take my soup, won't you?"

Styke sucked on his teeth. Definitely not the same Jackal he'd once known. Did that mean he could no longer trust him? Had

Jackal turned into a Blackhat agent, or did he have his own agenda? "Yeah. I will."

"You're wondering if you can trust me," Jackal said. "And I wonder the same about you. You're serving two masters right now. Lady Flint, and..." Jackal's lips moved silently, and he tilted his head as if to listen to an unseen voice. "...someone the spirits won't even touch. Odd, that." He shook his head, as if suddenly confused. "I see Ben Styke before me. Broken, changed. Neither of us is the same man we once were, but I believe we once called each other friend. I would like us to do so again. To prove that, I'll tell you what I know about the Dynize. Come. Sit."

A few moments later Styke and Jackal sat at either end of Jackal's bedroll, cross-legged, Celine sitting in Styke's lap and listening to Jackal speak, enraptured.

"I've had to come about this information in the traditional way," Jackal said, removing a flask from beneath the skull shrine and handing it to Styke. "The spirits won't touch Privileged or bone-eyes. They don't particularly like powder mages or Knacked, either, but I can usually get them to take a closer look."

"Are you saying the dragonmen are bone-eyes?" Styke asked. He didn't think so—he would have smelled the sorcery on them.

"No, but some of the legends about dragonmen are true. They're anointed by bone-eyes, and it gives them some protection against sorcery."

"Anointed?"

"I'm not sure exactly what that means, but considering the bone-eyes use blood magic, it can't be anything good."

"Says the man who speaks to the dead."

"Speaking to the dead, and using the life-force of others in one's sorcery, are two very different things. Anyway, there are at least four dragonmen in Landfall."

"Four! Son of a bitch."

"At least. The Dynize have been here for over a year now,

infiltrating the various factions within Greenfire Depths. They have dozens of spies, and recruit the disaffected to their cause."

"Like those four Palo kids at Mama Sender's."

"Exactly."

"What's their cause?" Celine asked.

"That," Jackal said with a scowl, "is harder to say. They tell the youth stories of the glory of the Empire, of the wealth and decadence of their civilization, and promise them riches beyond belief in return for another set of eyes."

"For what?"

"For everything. The Dynize spies consume information the same way the Blackhats do."

"Are they preparing for some kind of invasion?" Styke asked. "The Empire has hidden behind closed borders for over a hundred years. Why move on Landfall now?"

"I think we're getting ahead of ourselves," Jackal responded. "They may be preparing to open their borders again. As far as we know, they've sent spies all around the world to find out how civilization has progressed since they were last a world power."

"The spirits don't tell you any more than that?"

"If you mock me, we won't discuss this any further."

Styke checked his sarcastic tone. "Sorry," he said. "It's a lot to take in."

"The spirits have a very difficult time penetrating Dynize," Jackal said after a moment of consideration. "Dynize Privileged protect the Dynize borders from any kind of sorcerous scrying, and it seems to work fairly well on the dead, too. I can't spy on them any easier than I can spy on Lady Chancellor Lindet behind the protection of her own Privileged."

"But you think the Dynize may just be feeling us out?"

"Perhaps," Jackal said.

"So where do the dragonmen come into this?"

"They appeared"—Jackal closed his eyes—"a couple of months ago and began making contact with their spies in the city."

"This is sounding more and more like the preparation for an invasion," Styke said. "It's what I'd do, anyway." He had a brief vision of whole hosts of dragonmen marching up the coastline on Landfall. Based on the one he fought two days ago, they'd cut through the Landfall garrison like a hot knife through butter.

"They're looking for something," Jackal said.

"What?"

"The godstones."

Styke frowned. A peculiar name. "What are those?"

"I'm not sure," Jackal said. "The name first came to me two days ago from the lips of one of those boys you killed at Mama Sender's."

Styke felt the hair on the back of his neck stand on end. "What does that mean?"

"It's much easier to wring information out of a spirit as they die—or are born, depending on your perspective—and I happened to catch one of your dragonman's acolytes as he entered the next world."

"Oh." This was all getting to be too much for Styke. Sorcery never bothered him; he could smell it a mile away, and the enchanted armor he wore in the war could shrug off Privileged magic as easily as grapeshot. But this business with spirits made his spine tingle. The dead were dead, and as a man who'd put plenty of them in their graves he preferred they stay there. But he *did* need information, and this was the best he was going to find. He tried to shrug off his discomfort. "Get anything else out of him?"

"Nothing useful. The dragonman's name was Kushel. He's middle-aged, from a city called Heaven's Pillar in Dynize. It seems he's been looking for the godstones for most of his life, and he's convinced he'll find them here in Landfall."

Styke leaned back on the bedroll and found himself considering the red marks on the back of Celine's neck. They, like those on his stomach and chest, had begun to bruise. The bruises would heal, but the thought of this dragonman manhandling a little girl—*his little girl*—made his blood boil. *I've killed a lot of people. But I've never so much as hurt a kid.* He remembered his thought about warriors, and how few of them remained in the world. It might be old-fashioned, but a warrior left the young and infirm in peace and protected those under their responsibility.

"I need more information," Styke said.

"I can try..."

"No. I need it straight from the dragonman. I need to draw him out again."

Jackal hesitated. His eyes dipped tellingly to the scar on Styke's face, then to his mangled hand. "We've both changed," Jackal said gently. "If it was the old Styke, I'd believe you could fight a dragonman, but in your state..."

"Yeah," Styke said, the words biting, "I know I'm a cripple. But I'm Mad Ben Styke, and I'm no fool. You can get word to him, can't you? Your spirits can tell you where he is, and your boys can deliver a message?"

"This isn't a good idea."

"You haven't even heard the idea," Styke said. "I want you to tell Kushel that I've got his knife, and he can take it from me at the muster yard in Loel's Fort."

Jackal pursed his lips. "That's an obvious trap."

"Of course it's an obvious trap. I'm not facing this bastard alone. If he's a legendary warrior, he can fight this old cripple for it on my own terms. And if I lose, at least I'll have the satisfaction of knowing Lady Flint will put a bullet in his head."

"He won't fall for it," Jackal said.

Styke removed the bone knife from his belt, as well as his own big knife, holding them side by side so Jackal could see. "The stories say these weapons are part of a dragonman's identity. If someone I hated had *my* knife, you bet your ass I'd cut my way through a brigade of infantry to get it back." He returned the knives, his eyes falling once more on the bruises on Celine's neck. "Just send the message."

CHAPTER 29

V lora stared at a smudge of blood on the slimy, limestone floor of Greenfire Depths and struggled to keep her anger in check. She could feel it at the edges of her awareness shoving and pushing like a creature trapped in a bubble of her mental making; a bubble that threatened to burst at any moment. She fought to keep her face stoic, her demeanor professional, even while a part of her reached out with her sorcerous senses to *feel* the black powder on the soldiers around her. Like standing on the edge of a cliff with the unnatural impulse to jump, she felt the urge to detonate every ounce of powder within the radius of her sorcery, killing her, her men, and no doubt hundreds of innocent Palo.

Perhaps some guilty ones, too.

"Please tell me," she said calmly, "that we know *something*."

Olem's Knack prevented him from needing sleep, but the redness in his eyes told her that he'd been pushing himself too far, not getting enough rest as he sought to gather all the information she needed from this city. He was frayed at the edges, smoking like a chimney, and the glint in his eye said he knew exactly what sort of self-destructive beast was rampaging through her head.

"All we know is this is the last place they were seen," Olem said. They stood about fifty yards into Greenfire Depths from the bottom of the Rim. The only light came from strategically placed reflective mirrors, and the dirty street—more like a corridor—was empty of Palo and eerily silent. Vlora had twenty soldiers with her and not a single one so much as muttered as they stared somberly at her and Olem.

They'd been with her long enough to know her moods.

The subject of their discussion, a single engineer and a squad of bodyguards that had come down here this morning to survey the destruction of a block of these spiderweb-like tenements, was missing. They'd been three hours late in reporting in when Vlora decided to lead an expedition to look for them, and in another three hours all she'd managed to find was this smudge of blood and a trail that went completely cold.

"This is where they were last seen?" Vlora echoed. "What were they last seen *doing*? Was there gunfire? Shouting? Screams? Damn it, Olem, I need *answers*."

Olem stared back at her, eyes narrowing slightly, and she immediately regretted raising her voice. "We've combed every tenement within a hundred yards. Not a single person reports anything out of the ordinary. That some of them mentioned our boys passing through at all is a miracle. *We're not wanted here*."

That's just too bad for them, isn't it? "Palo silence, huh?" Vlora remembered her talk with Gregious Tampo, along with the warning about her status among the Palo. She *was* their villain, and to think she could change that with a few handshakes and a now-well-publicized desire to rebuild a block of tenements was folly.

"Palo silence," Olem agreed.

"Expand our search area to two hundred yards. Bring more men down. I want our boys found." The orders were barely above a whisper, and Vlora could immediately see that Olem didn't like them.

"We shouldn't risk more men," Olem said reasonably.

"I won't abandon them."

"Every minute we're down here is another minute our enemies have to plan another attack."

"If this *was* an attack."

Olem looked pointedly at the smear of blood. "If we go kicking down doors, we'll be working against ourselves. We have to return to the fort and regroup."

Vlora closed her eyes. She knew Olem was right. She had a responsibility toward more than just the nine men who'd gone missing. The engineer, Petaer, was a particularly talented young man and his loss would be palpable, but the others were infantry. *Her* infantry, but infantry nonetheless. She needed to attend to the brigade. Not a single squad. But if she abandoned a squad, at what point would the men begin to wonder if they, too, would be abandoned?

"The order stands," she said, opening her eyes and locking them with Olem. His lip curled in a brief show of defiance, then he looked away, ashing his cigarette.

"All right," he said quietly.

"Two hundred yards. If they find anything, let me know immediately. No violence. Our men are to travel in groups of no fewer than twenty at any time. And tell them to begin mapping this area of the Depths in three dimensions. I want to know what this warren looks like. Search until eight, then call it off."

Olem perked up. "A map will be useful."

"That's why they pay me so well." Vlora slapped him on the shoulder with enthusiasm she didn't feel and turned back toward the entrance to the Depths that she could see through the dim light behind them. "Get me Meln-Dun. If I'm going to play his petty politics, I want him to protect my men."

*   *   *

Meln-Dun entered Vlora's office in Loel's Fort with hat in hand, a measured, sympathetic smile on his face. Vlora shook his hand and offered him a seat, and he spoke before she could begin.

"I'm very sorry to hear about the loss of your men," he said.

Vlora had to consciously keep her eyes from narrowing. How could he possibly know about the attack? "You know about that, eh?"

"Word spreads quickly in the Depths, and your men have been searching for hours."

Of course. A few hundred mercenary soldiers knocking on doors in one corner of the Depths surely would have attracted attention. This whole situation had her squinting at shadows, and Meln-Dun had done nothing to earn her distrust. "I'm sure it does. Which is why I was hoping for your help in finding my men."

Meln-Dun seemed to have expected the request, nodding before her sentence was even finished. "I already have my contacts looking into it, Lady Flint, and I'm honored that you'd ask my help." He hesitated a moment, then continued: "You have a reputation for respecting honesty, correct?"

"I do." Vlora didn't like the sound of that.

"Then, out of respect for that, I will not lie. I don't expect to find your men alive. Nine soldiers disappearing in the Depths suggests they did not simply get lost."

"I'm not a fool," Vlora responded, hoping it didn't come off too forcefully. "I'm aware they may already be long dead. But if there is a slight chance they're still alive, or of recovering their bodies, I'd like to do it as quickly as possible."

"Understood."

Meln-Dun studied Vlora's face, and not for the first time she found herself questioning his motives. She was so used to operating in the larger sphere of influence—with governors, generals, Privileged, and even kings—that she had to adjust her thinking to really understand the machinations of a local slumlord. Perhaps he was trying to improve his standing in the Depths, or perhaps he simply wanted to help usher in an era of reconstruction. She wondered if it was of any real importance. Once she found Mama Palo, her job here would be done and she could forget about the petty local politics.

Even as the thoughts went through her head, she mentally mocked her own arrogance. Did she really care so little for the people of Landfall? Would she be able to abandon these plans for new tenements and march off on the next mission? Her work here could inspire a new generation—perhaps a young politician or future general. It would be shortsighted of her to simply walk away from it.

What had Tamas always said? *The minutiae of the common man is the grease that slicks the gears of civilization.*

She wasn't a good enough thespian to *act* the part of a concerned foreign national. She *had* to care, and she *did*. Perhaps that's what Meln-Dun had sensed upon their first meeting. She pulled herself back to the present and smiled at Meln-Dun.

He smiled back and said, "Your concern for your men does you credit. The Blackhats simply write off their missing with barely more than a wave—their primary concern is getting back the Roses they wear around their necks."

"Does this happen often?" Vlora shifted sideways in her chair. "The disappearing?"

Meln-Dun hesitated. "Since Mama Palo came to power, it's become increasingly common. People go missing in the Depths, sometimes civilians, but mostly Blackhats. It's become a fact of life, and makes it very difficult for men like me to do business."

Vlora was surprised at the honesty of the answer. She'd assumed that the Palo were united in their hate of the current government, but Meln-Dun sounded almost regretful. There was something here. Something she could use. "Don't you hate the Blackhats?"

"Ah-hah, Lady Flint, you will not catch me so easily," Meln-Dun said, half-seriously. "I would never speak ill of the Lady Chancellor or her chosen servants."

Spoken like a true politician. A nonanswer was often more an answer than a definitive one. Meln-Dun didn't trust the Blackhats, but then Vlora hadn't expected him to. "And Mama Palo's policies? You don't agree with them?"

"I wouldn't say that, either," Meln-Dun said carefully. "I've just noted that the disappearances and the violence have increased since Mama Palo came into power. She supports violent revolutionaries like the Red Hand and offers succor to his agents. It's bad for business."

Vlora was beginning to see a picture of a man caught between two powers—the Blackhats who ran Landfall, and Mama Palo's goons who ran the Depths. She had wondered if his motives had extended beyond money and perhaps here they were—giving the people of the Depths a third choice for their loyalty. It took a brash, ballsy character to play both sides of the game like this. She needed to probe further.

Vlora said, "Forgive me if this comes across as rude, but do you consider yourself a businessman above a Palo?"

Meln-Dun raised his chin. "I am both, Lady Flint, and proud of it."

"Of course."

"That's like asking you if you consider yourself an Adran or a general first. It's a ridiculous notion."

Vlora noted the tightening of his eyes when he spoke, and the way he hunched his shoulders inwardly, like a cat wondering if it had been backed into a corner. He *was* playing both sides. She'd bet her sword on it. Vlora made a calming gesture. "My apologies. You're right, it is ridiculous."

Slowly, his shoulders relaxed and he leaned back in his chair. "I hope," he said, "that this partnership between us—building these new tenements in Greenfire Depths—will be the first step in something larger. I would like, in my own small way, to decrease the tensions between Palo and Fatrastans."

"Constructing new buildings would do that?" Vlora asked. She watched Meln-Dun's eyes, looking for any additional hint as to what he was thinking. This new realization—that he was making his own bid for power—could be very useful. But she would have to be careful.

"I believe it is a start."

"What's the end?"

"The end is obvious. Palo and Fatrastans working together to create a better world."

"That sounds like a laudable goal. What other steps do you foresee along the way?"

Meln-Dun leaned forward, as if surprised that Vlora was even interested. "Extending Lindet's modernization to the Depths, to start. More business between the Depths and the rest of Landfall. Perhaps over time, convincing Lindet to allow Palo to settle in some of the nicer areas of the city. The more Fatrastans are exposed to us, and us to them, the less we will have to fear each other."

"I wouldn't have pegged you as an idealist," Vlora said.

"I am not," Meln-Dun retorted. "I am pragmatic, and I pretend to be nothing more. Good relations create better business opportunities."

Vlora had to laugh at that. "You remind me of a friend of mine," she said. "Ricard Tumblar."

"I know that name," Meln-Dun said. "A prominent Adran, correct?"

"Very prominent. He's a businessman, and was the very first First Minister of Adro, elected by the people."

"Ah, yes," Meln-Dun said. "After your field marshal sent your king to the guillotine."

Meln-Dun butchered the pronunciation of "guillotine" and Vlora might have laughed had her memories not instantly gone back to the coup, and the Adran-Kez War that followed it. Those years, more than any others, had influenced who she was today. She had some fondness for them, but far more regret. So many unnecessary deaths, so many betrayals big and small. "That's right," she said. "And a whole different discussion. I'm glad that you're able to put your pragmatism to good use. So often pragmatics are tinged with cynicism."

"I think," Meln-Dun answered, "that is how I would describe Mama Palo. Cynical. An idealistic cynic, and…" He hesitated, glancing over his shoulder as if Mama Palo were right behind him.

Vlora gestured to the empty office. "Feel free to speak your mind. If you know anything about me, it's that I'm not a gossip."

"I really shouldn't," Meln-Dun said warily.

You really should. Vlora could feel her heart beating faster. "You don't have to say anything you don't want, but know you're among friends." There were several moments of silence before Vlora changed tactics. She quietly said, "Do you suspect that Mama Palo is behind the disappearance of my men?"

"I did not say that."

"You implied it." She leaned forward. "This is something I need to know, Meln-Dun. I do not like petty politics. If Mama Palo is behind the disappearance of my men, I need to know why. Was she behind the attempt on my life the other night? Was I invited to the gala only to be a target? Are you one of her agents? Is all of this"—she gestured at Meln-Dun—"just a way of getting me to lower my guard?"

Meln-Dun swallowed, beads of sweat appearing on his balding head.

"In my world," Vlora said, "wars are *declared*."

"Not in mine," Meln-Dun responded. "I am not your enemy. I

am not one of Mama Palo's agents, and I know nothing about the disappearance of your men."

Vlora watched his eyes for any sign of a lie. He met her gaze, unwavering.

Meln-Dun continued: "Mama Palo is crafty, striking from the shadows. She is an old woman, embittered toward the Kressian settlers who killed her husband, and the Blackhats who killed her son."

Vlora opened her mouth, surprised. "I did not know that."

"It's common knowledge in the Depths. We all have our own reasons for fighting our private wars. Mama Palo has taken hers public. As I said, she is an old woman, and old women are seldom direct. They achieved their age by being crafty, circumspect. Those Palo that attacked you outside the Yellow Hall may very well have been her men. They botched the job and now are trying to make up for it by whittling away at your forces."

"Inviting me to the party was a way to get me out on my own?"

"It could have been." Even now, Meln-Dun seemed loath to accept the idea as fact. "There are a thousand factions within the Depths, intertwined in ways that reflect your own political courts. It may have been someone else entirely, but know this: Few people act in the Depths without Mama Palo's say-so."

"Do you?" Vlora asked bluntly.

"I will not lie to you. Most of my business is approved—or not— by Mama Palo."

Another interesting bit of information. Mama Palo was bad for business in her encouragement of violence, *and* she could stifle Meln-Dun's entrepreneurship? Another reason for Meln-Dun to want her out of the way.

"And this thing that we're planning?" Vlora asked. "Beginning a modernization of the Greenfire Depths tenements?"

"She knows about our partnership."

Vlora wasn't surprised—they'd spent the last two days attempting to publicize her mercenaries' good intentions. No doubt

Meln-Dun had been involved in a similar propaganda campaign on the Palo side of things. The interesting part was that Mama Palo had approved of this whole endeavor. Perhaps the crafty old Palo was trying to draw Vlora out again, waiting for Vlora to make a mistake?

It was a game in which she couldn't see her opponent's face, or most of the pieces. Petty politics. *I've fought much worse,* she reminded herself.

Vlora wondered how much she truly trusted Meln-Dun. He was, after all, a Palo. Vlora tried to recognize that their reputation belonged mostly to a smear campaign by Lindet, but the Palo had also been her enemy in the swamps for over a year. She couldn't just ignore that because Meln-Dun was friendly. But she had to trust someone, and Meln-Dun seemed to be trustworthy as far as his own interests were concerned.

There was a knock on the door, and a messenger appeared with a note for Meln-Dun. The businessman looked it over with a scowl, then nodded to himself. "I must go, Lady Flint, but I will do what I can to stop these disappearances and find your missing men. The sooner things calm down, the easier it will be to begin to modernize the Depths."

He needs me more than I need him, Vlora realized suddenly. *Or at least, he thinks that's the case.* It was best to let him keep thinking that. She shook his hand and watched him go, called for Olem, and sat down to meditate on the conversation. She drew her sword, checking the balance, deep in thought.

Of all the people Vlora had met in Landfall so far, Meln-Dun was in the best position to comment on Palo politics. Until she learned otherwise, his guess was as good as a declaration: Mama Palo was waging a war on Vlora and the Riflejacks. Vlora couldn't be sure *why*: a grudge, tactical maneuvering, or even inside knowledge of Vlora's real task. But it meant that Vlora had lost the element of surprise.

She couldn't sit around waiting for Mama Palo to fall into her lap. She'd have to move quickly, or risk the disappearance of more of her men.

An attack on an enemy she knew so little about could very well get her and her men killed. It was risky. But Meln-Dun was Vlora's wild card, and she thought she already had a way to use him.

CHAPTER 30

I t took Michel the rest of the day and part of the next morning to find just two mentions of the *Palo Herald* in the Blackhat files at the Millinery. One referred to a junk Palo press that might or might not be printing propaganda. The second was just an address scribbled down in pencil. Based on the limited pieces of information, both of which were months old, no one had ever bothered following up on any rumors that may have spurred the first report.

He left the Millinery just after noon the next day, leaving the address of the *Palo Herald* with Agent Warsim in case he took longer than twenty-four hours to report back in. He briefly considered trying to deputize a few Iron Roses to keep an eye on him, but opted just to bring along his old knuckledusters. The Millinery was still on full alert looking for Ben Styke, and Michel didn't want to do anything that might bring on the grand master's attention before he was absolutely certain he had a line on Tampo.

The address was in a mostly Palo village called Landon Plain. About six miles northwest of the plateau, it was one of the many towns along the Hadshaw built almost entirely upon pylons that allowed the rickety wood houses to weather spring flooding. It appeared to be a small, but thriving trading center with a keelboat landing, three general stores, and even a theater. Michel left his cab near the city center and began walking down the hard-packed silt streets, muttering the address over and over again as he scanned the number plates above homes and shops—only about a quarter of which were actually marked.

Michel had opted to leave his black shirt and bowler cap at home, and instead wore a loose pair of rough wool workman's trousers and a cotton shirt, sleeves rolled up, flatcap pushed back on his head. A lone Blackhat in a Palo community tended to become a target; a poor Kressian day laborer might still get robbed, but would probably make it home in one piece.

A few eyes watched him as he passed, but no one followed him through the twisting streets. He was beginning to think the address was a dead end when he caught sight of a pair of number plates, the first two letters of which matched those on his card. He found a raised walkway and headed into a series of what looked like warehouses and industrial buildings, all constructed on the same batch of pylons. Palo workers moved bales of cotton and tobacco in and out of storage while foremen called out instructions. Michel was largely ignored.

He finally matched his address at the opposite end of the raised industrial park. There was a single door into a small shed of a building; a lean-to addendum to the warehouse next to it, with the words PALO HERALD stenciled in Palo on a sign next to the door. Michel peered in the window, then looked over his shoulder. There didn't appear to be anyone around.

Nor, he decided, did this little building look big enough to hold even a small printing press.

Michel opened the door and headed inside, one hand on the knuckledusters in his pocket and the other putting a cheap pipe in his mouth as he adopted a northeastern accent in his head. "Hallo?" he called. "Hallo?"

The *Palo Herald* was about as roomy as an outhouse. There were a few crates, newspapers spilling out the sides, and an old Palo man sitting with his back to the same wall the door was on. He wore an old buckskin jacket over a bare chest and a pair of cutoff wool trousers. His feet were bare, and he squinted up at Michel suspiciously.

"What can I do for you, sir?" he asked in broken Adran.

"Ah, hallo!" Michel said. "Is this the *Palo Herald*?"

The old man pointed above Michel's head. Michel took a step back and made a show of reading the sign outside. He switched over to Palo, hoping he wasn't too damn rusty to make a good impression. "Afternoon, friend. Looks like I came to the right place." He stepped over to one of the nearby crates and unobtrusively glanced inside. "My name's Fallon Marks and I'm an editor. A newspaper editor by trade, actually, and I'm looking for work. Just came down from Little Starland and was passing through, heard there was a newspaper in town."

"It's a Palo paper," the old man said, not unkindly. "Don't think it's your kind of thing."

"Well, it actually is my kind of thing. I've been editing a Palo newspaper up in Little Starland—the *Daily Basin*, you may have heard of it?—and to be honest, my friend, we ran out of funding and were forced to sell off all our equipment, wouldn't you believe it now? I'd hoped with Landfall being a big city there might be a Palo newspaper, or the chance to start one. Just as my luck ran out I was told about you. Is this where you print the newspaper?"

"Nope," the old man said. "Don't think we're hiring, either. Not a big operation. Just a few of the boys, working to spread the word of our land."

"Understood, understood. Right you are, my friend. Times are lean and hard, don't I know it, and to be fully honest I would work for a roof over my head and a bit of porridge in the mornings, if you catch my meaning. At least until I was able to secure some funding for a newspaper in Landfall."

The old man tilted his head to one side, seemingly bemused. "Ain't never heard of your..."

"The *Daily Basin*."

"...*Daily Basin*. Didn't know there was a Palo newspaper up in Little Starland."

"Not anymore, I'm afraid," Michel said with a sigh. "But you know, Landfall, I think maybe I can find some work down there. I guess I could look at the Kressian newspapers, but the Palo, well, the Palo are my passion, I've got to admit, don't you know. My granddaddy on my mother's side was a Palo and I'm proud of that."

"Ah," the old man said, his bemusement turning into a real smile. "Part brother, then?"

"Part brother indeed. Look, do you think you could see it in your heart to consider employment, good sir? I'd work for a roof for a few weeks, try to prove myself."

"Not my printshop," the old man said.

"Well, you think I could talk to the owner?"

"He's not around now. Rarely comes out."

"Well, could I get an address?"

"No." The old man gave a sympathetic smile. "No one talks to the owner. I could pass him your card, if you like."

"My card, yes! That would be perfect." Michel searched his pockets, letting a frown grow until he came up empty-handed. "It doesn't look like I have any on me right now. I sent my luggage on ahead to Landfall, don't you know, and to think I didn't keep a card on me. I could leave my cousin's address." Before the old man could respond, Michel snatched up a pencil and bit of paper and scribbled down the address of a Blackhat safe house, taking the opportunity to look closer at the crates of newspapers. They appeared to be just that—newspapers—most of them old and yellow, with a few recent issues on the very top. The latest was a couple of weeks old and had the words LADY FLINT BURNS FORT SAMNAN in bold letters. "Here you are, good sir, and thank you so much for taking the time to talk to me."

The old man took the paper without comment, rolling it like a cigarette and tucking it behind his ear. "Don't hold your breath," he said. "The big boss doesn't like Kressians very much."

"I understand," Michel said, wondering not for the first time if he'd followed a cold trail. No printing equipment on the premises, just some old newspapers, with no sign of any pamphlets. An absentee owner *could* indicate Tampo, but the fact that he "didn't like Kressians" suggested the owner was Palo. Michel couldn't think of a subtle way to ask if that was the case. "Pardon me, but just out of curiosity, where do you do your writing and printing? I could always drop in there and offer to lend a hand."

"No one's around today," the old man said. "Waste of time. Thanks for coming in."

It was an obvious dismissal, and Michel took the hint and tipped his cap to the old man. "Thanks again, good sir, have a blessed day."

He headed back out into the industrial park and took a look around, watching the Palo at work farther down the boardwalk. Most of the doors in the area were open to let air circulate and bring cargo in and out for transportation down to the keelboat landing. The only building with a closed bay door was the one immediately next to the *Palo Herald*. Michel checked the bay door gently to find it locked, then headed around to the back of the building to find a single door, the window blacked out, also locked.

Michel thought about jimmying the lock, but picking his way into a Palo warehouse in broad daylight seemed like a very bad idea. Instead, he went back to the street and waited until no one was looking before ducking *beneath* the industrial park.

Something he'd long ago learned about these towns built on

stilts on the floodplain is that almost every single house had a trap-door under it. Sometimes they were left unlocked so that no one could get trapped underneath during a flash flood. More often they were used to circulate cool air during the summer. A warehouse, he reasoned, would have several such entrances. He bent over double and picked his way through the refuse that had piled up under-neath the building until he reasoned he was directly under the *Palo Herald*. Then he headed another fifteen feet and found a trapdoor, right where he'd expected it.

He pushed up gently. Locked.

Applying a little more pressure, he was able to get the trapdoor far enough up to see that it was blocked by a simple wooden latch. Michel drew his belt knife and slid the latch, then lifted the trap-door to get a view inside the warehouse. It was dark and quiet, the only light coming from windows far up on the back side of the building. He listened for a few moments and then swung the door up and open, lifting himself inside.

He found himself less than three feet from a printing press. It looked like many of the others he'd seen, a loomlike contraption with two belts and a drum in the center, with a treadle on the other side to spin the belts. A machine like this could be operated rela-tively quietly, without attracting the type of attention that a steam press would.

Still, he wasn't convinced he had the right place. Keeping low, ready to make a run for the trapdoor, he crept the length of the warehouse. There was a narrow stairway up to a windowed office above him, not much larger than the storefront next door, and he found a second printing press. This one had a slightly differ-ent design, with what looked like some sort of a fold-and-thread mechanism—the exact sort of thing needed to print and bind a pamphlet. He turned his attention away from the printer and checked the nearest crates, going so far as to pry the lids off several using his knife and making far more noise than he was comfortable with.

It was on his fourth crate, just as he was beginning to think he had the wrong place, that he pried the lid to reveal a whole stack of *Sins of Empire.*

"Damn it all, Michel, you might make yourself an investigator yet."

"Careful," he whispered back at himself. "We're not out of this. You've got to set up a sting to catch Tampo. If he doesn't come down here much we might not be able to catch him quickly."

"But we have a building to trace for ownership records. More people to question who might know where he lives. You've got a damned good start. Now don't foul it up."

He carefully returned the lids to their spots, pressing down on the nails with the handle of his knife and hoping no one noticed they weren't hammered. He finished the last and crept quietly back toward the trapdoor, wondering how he was going to flip the latch back shut behind him.

A sudden noise made him jump, and his heart leapt into his throat at the realization it was the lock on the bay doors. He threw caution to the wind and ran toward the trapdoor, lowering himself down and pulling the door shut over his head just as he heard the bay open up and the old Palo man's voice say something muffled.

Michel let out a soft sigh. Well, that was that. Time to head back to his cab, and . . .

"We don't like snoops, mister," a voice said in Palo.

Michel spun awkwardly to find a Palo woman easily a foot taller than him with shoulders like an ox crouching just behind him. His feet scrambled for purchase in the soft, sandy peat beneath the warehouse, and he opened his mouth to let out a shout, only for her fist to connect hard with his jaw. His head jerked back and he caught himself on a pair of stilts, trying to grasp for his knuckledusters as the Palo woman's fist rose and fell one more time.

The blow knocked the sense out of him, throwing him to the ground, and he could only watch, stunned, as she grabbed him by the leg and pulled him back toward the trapdoor. "I got him!" she shouted up. "Here, come take him. We don't know if we're being watched."

Michel looked up into the faces of five Palo, including the old man, and felt himself lifted under the arms and handed up.

"Well," he said, his eyes going in and out of focus. "Shit."

CHAPTER 31

N o," Styke said.

He sat in the corner of the Loel's Fort mess hall, watching as more than a thousand soldiers cleaned away the remains of dinner and broke out dice, darts, cards, and beer. He found himself impressed by the orderliness of the process, and how it contrasted with normal military procedure—sending the men out on the town for their entertainment—in a way that focused their attention inward. For any other military company such a habit might drive the men mad with cabin fever, but here it just seemed to build the bonds between them.

Styke glanced up at the young soldier in front of him. Well, he thought of the woman as young, but she was probably in her thirties, thin as a rail and looking sharp in her crimson uniform with its dark blue cuffs and the crossed muskets and shako of the Riflejacks pinned to her breast. By the pins on her lapel, she was a sergeant. She held her hat in one hand, as if in supplication, and gave Styke an almost flirtatious smile.

"Are you sure?" she asked. "Word's been going around about you, Mr. Styke, and the boys are itching to hear about the time you fought beside Taniel Two-shot. Most of us served with him in the Adran-Kez War, you know. We don't know much about his time in Fatrasta."

Styke rolled his tongue around in his cheek, considering. There was a time when he liked telling stories—when he liked being the center of attention in a hall full of heroes. Not anymore. His eyes found Lady Flint, sitting at the other end of the hall with Colonel Olem and surrounded by soldiers of all ranks, and he wondered what she'd think of hearing about the heroism of her dead ex-fiancé. "I don't think—"

He was cut off by a tug on his sleeve. It was Celine, sitting beside him with her feet dangling from her chair, red sauce from tonight's spiced mutton all over her cheeks. "I want to hear about it, Ben."

Styke hesitated long enough for the sergeant to try again. "The rumor is you killed a Warden with your bare hands," she said. There was a bit of a challenge to her smile, as if she suspected such a rumor was nothing more than soldierly bragging taken to the extreme. "Taniel Two-shot aside, we'd damn like to hear about that Warden."

"Please," Celine said, drawing the word out.

Styke sighed. This felt a lot like he was being ganged up on. He wondered if he could safely get out of this without having to make a fool out of himself, but dozens of glances were being tossed in his direction. This sergeant wasn't acting alone. Word really *had* gotten around. He leaned over to Celine. "You get me that horngum I sent you out for earlier?" Celine handed him a package from a local apothecary, and he gratefully unwrapped it and broke off a bit of horngum root, tucking it into his cheek. Celine smiled up at him, and he wiped the sauce from the corners of her mouth with his sleeve. "All right," he conceded.

The sergeant beamed at him, then turned around and put two

fingers in her mouth, letting out a shrill whistle that brought silence on the hall. "Oi! We're gonna get a story, lads!"

Styke felt a flutter in his belly as all eyes suddenly turned toward him. "Right," he muttered to himself. "You've done this before, big man. Just tell it like it happened." He went to the center of the room and climbed onto the longest table, looking around at the sea of crimson uniforms and grizzled faces. These weren't green kids heading to war. These were veterans. And veterans were always harder to please. He fiddled with his ring—one of the few things that reminded him who and what he once had been—and locked eyes with Lady Flint from across the hall. She looked particularly unimpressed, and suddenly Styke decided he *wanted* to tell this story.

He drew his knife and pointed it at the sergeant, then raised his voice to be heard throughout the mess. "If you don't know who I am, I'm Ben Styke. I was a lancer back during the Fatrastan War for Independence."

"A Mad Lancer!" someone shouted from the back of the mess.

"Aye, that's right. A Mad Lancer. But this story isn't about them. It's about Taniel Two-shot."

There was a round of cheers, and the sergeant shushed everyone.

Styke continued. "I met Taniel Two-shot about a year into the war. I'd heard the rumors—some hotshot powder mage, the son of Field Marshal Tamas, making life miserable for the Kez army by killing any officer or Privileged to set foot in the Tristan Basin. I'll be honest, I expected a green-faced squirt dappered up in local buckskins, strutting around the Tristan Basin like he owned the place. Which he was."

A few chuckles rose from the back of the room.

"But by the time I got to him he was already a cold-blooded killer. I could see it in his eyes; smell the blood and powder on him from a mile away. He carried his father's reputation on his shoulders like a millstone, but gods be damned if he had to. They called him Two-shot, a ghost of the Basin, and he earned his reputation with the blood of his enemies. I wish I could say I knew him well. I would have liked to. We rubbed shoulders less than a week before and after the Battle of Planth. I bought him a beer, because the son of a bitch had lost his wallet in the swamp."

A few more laughs, these a little more enthusiastic.

"Some of you may have heard of the Battle of Planth, having spent time up in that neck of the woods yourselves. The official story spins a heroic last stand against all odds. What it doesn't tell you is that the people of Planth were abandoned by the interim government and only Two-shot's company decided to stay behind to give the people a fighting chance. It was going to be him and a few hundred of his irregulars against an entire brigade of Kez infantry. It was insane. He asked me to stay and"—Styke shrugged—"what could I say? They didn't call me Mad Ben Styke for nothing."

Styke could see he had everyone's undivided attention now. He might be bent and old, but he knew how much soldiers loved a good story. He turned around slowly, pointing his knife at the Riflejacks. "Taniel Two-shot spent three days evening the odds by putting a bullet in the head of every Privileged sorcerer in the Kez ranks. Took out a few officers, too. And a Warden, one of those sorcery-spawned killers. The day of the battle came and our little lot drew up in front of the city. The lancers took the center, the garrison took the wings, and the irregulars came down the river to flank the enemy." Styke looked at his knife, remembering the close fighting in the Basin, remembering the weight of the armor on his shoulders, the stirrups on his feet, the power of Deshner charging unchallenged across an open field. He felt tears in the corners of his eyes and blinked them away. His next words were quieter, and he could see the strain on the soldiers' faces as they leaned forward to hear them.

"You've never seen anything until you've witnessed three hundred lancers, wearing heavy plate you only hear about in legends, ride through enemy grapeshot like it was nothing more than rain. We hit them hard in the center and the garrison came in after us. I broke my lance on a Kez gunner and lost one of my swords fighting a colonel. It was as bloody a melee as I can remember, and we cut our way through to the general's bodyguard all the way to the rear.

"That's where I saw Two-shot. He'd brought his men around to flank and opened fire on the enemy rear, sowing confusion. The enemy general broke and ran, and me and a few of my lancers gave chase. What we didn't know was that we had pursuers of our own, and by the time we caught up with the general, two Wardens had caught up with us."

There was a chorus of boos. "Yeah," Styke said. "You know those sorcery-spawned assholes. I bet a few of you have lost friends to them. Well, I lost two of my best to those trash, and I would have gone down myself had Taniel not put a bullet in the head of one of those bastards. He saved my life that day, and for that I'll always be in his debt."

Silence lay over the mess hall for several moments before someone shouted, "He saved mine!"

"And mine, too!" someone else shouted.

The whole hall was suddenly filled with the sound of cheers and applause, and Styke felt a smile tug at the corner of his mouth. It was good to feel that kind of brotherhood again—the respect of soldiers. He turned to climb down from the table, but was stopped by a shout.

"What happened to the other Warden?"

"I once watched a Warden carve through thirty grenadiers before they took him down!" someone else said.

"I saw one get hit by straight shot from an eight-pounder and keep going."

"Shut up, everyone!" the sergeant shouted. "Yeah, Styke, what happened to him?"

Everything quieted down, the soldiers fixated on Styke. Styke's attention, though, was drawn toward the door, where a concerned-looking infantryman had rushed over to Lady Flint and was whispering in her ear. Flint stood up, gesturing to Olem, then said across the quiet hall, "There's a dragonman in the muster yard. He's looking for you."

Styke's hand fell to the handle of the bone knife at his belt, then he drew his own and got down from the table. "Celine," Styke said. "Stay here."

Styke joined Flint outside the mess, where the white-knuckled grip on her sword gave away the anger behind a stony, expressionless facade.

The dragonman sat in the dirt just inside the fort gates, ignoring the guards and their lowered bayonets like a cat might ignore squawking birds that he may later kill at his pleasure. He wore a heavy canvas duster, under which Styke could clearly see the rippled, dark green swamp dragon hide. A pair of bone axes lay on the ground beside him, discarded as if unimportant. Styke felt a tingle on his spine at the sight of the legendary gear, and wondered if he'd made an enormous mistake.

"So," Flint said through a clenched jaw, "you weren't spinning a yarn, were you? These bastards really are in Landfall."

Styke resisted the urge to let out an *I told you so* and instead nodded.

"What's he doing in my camp?"

Styke looked down at her grip on her sword. Unless he was mistaken, she was more than ready to handle this herself. "I invited him."

"You *what*?"

"I'm old. I'm crippled. I'm not chasing this bastard around Landfall. I told him if he wanted to get his knife back he had to come get it."

"What knife? You'll forgive me for being annoyed, but the last one of them I saw had just carved up forty of my men. I'm going to put a bullet in his head."

Styke put a hand gently on Lady Flint's arm. "This is…personal."

"You're damn right it is." Flint took a step forward.

"No," Styke said, pulling her back by the shoulder.

"If you lay a hand on—"

"If you try to keep me from doing my job," Styke growled, "you'll have to go through me and *then* the dragonman. You gave me a task. Let me finish it." He didn't wait for an answer, but turned and limped toward the dragonman, stopping in the middle of the muster yard. He rubbed his leg, hoping the horngum would keep him limber enough for a fight.

The dragonman watched him for a few moments, lounging on his elbow like he was having a country picnic. He finally got to his feet, shrugged out of his duster, and collected his bone axes. The swamp dragon armor comprised a breastplate, leaving toned arms bare, and a skirt of leather strips that went down to his knees. His legs and arms were crisscrossed with black tattoos, giving an outfit that might have looked silly on another man a particularly sinister effect.

Styke took the bone knife from his belt and held it up. "Kushel, was it?"

Kushel's eyes narrowed. "How do you know my name?"

"You have two ways to get your knife back," Styke said. "You can either tell me what these godstone things are that you're looking for, and what designs you Dynize pricks have for Landfall, or you can fight me for it."

Kushel openly scoffed. "You know a lot more than when we last spoke, Ben Styke. What makes you think I plan on letting anyone in this compound leave here alive?"

"Your friend up in the Basin only took out forty of Flint's men. Impressive for one man, I'll grant you, but you think you're going to handle their pissed-off friends?" Behind him, Styke could hear the soldiers pouring out of the mess hall and lining up to watch the confrontation. "Tell me what I want to hear and you'll walk out of here without a scuff on that pretty armor." Styke thought back on those Palo kids at Mama Sender's, about how they were too stupid to back down in the face of a man clearly unafraid of being out-numbered. He wondered if he was making the same mistake.

Probably.

Kushel's eyes made a slow, mechanical circuit of the yard, noting guards in their towers and up on the wall, and lingering on Lady Flint before finally coming to rest on Styke. Styke recognized the gears turning in Kushel's head. He'd made the same calculations on a thousand different occasions. *Can I walk out of this alive?* The slight upturn at the corners of his mouth said that he'd decided he could.

What an arrogant prick.

"Fight?" Styke asked. "You can pry this out of my old, crippled hand." He gripped the bone knife with his mangled hand and his boz knife with his good, and put his weight back on his right leg. He'd barely fallen into a stance when the dragonman suddenly leapt forward.

Styke had fought a lot of quick men in his time, from duelists to bona fide assassins. But he'd never seen someone cover twenty feet in the blink of an eye like that. Kushel's axes rose and fell, the left swinging down from overhead, the right swooping in for Styke's belly.

Styke surprised both of them by catching each blow on a knife blade, then blocking a second and the third. Kushel recovered quickly each time, pulling back to strike with the speed of an adder, each new attack coming with independent precision that would have marveled Styke had he the time to be impressed. All his focus went into reacting, catching, and redirecting, and for almost twenty seconds he fell back beneath a flurry of blows, unable to even manage a riposte. Kushel scored cuts across Styke's arms and chest, and Styke barely managed to keep them from biting deep.

Styke knew he was old and out of practice, but wondered if even in his prime he would have been able to match Kushel's speed. Only the weight of the weapons—Kushel's heavier, more cumbersome axes against Styke's knives—allowed him to keep up at all. The attacks came on relentlessly, each hit seemingly more powerful than the last, and Styke's crippled hand began to numb from the effort of blocking them.

That all changed when a twinge in his wrist fouled a block, and Kushel's ax bit into the bone of one of Styke's fingers. He released his grip on the bone knife with a yell of dismay, watching it fly into the dust ahead of an arc of blood.

The next strike came for his unarmed left. Styke snatched the ax by the haft and turned his fighting knife to pass beneath the blade of Kushel's other ax, allowing the blade to draw a long, crimson line down his arm. Kushel tried to stretch the advantage, pushing his ax into Styke's chest, but Styke did two things at once:

First, he slammed his forehead into Kushel's nose. Second, he twisted his knife and drew back. The blade slid along the polished bone haft of Kushel's ax and, with a final jerk, severed Kushel's thumb and four fingers.

The dragonman reeled back, stunned, but even with a destroyed hand managed to dodge Styke's next thrust. They each had one good hand and one weapon now, and Kushel jammed the stubs of his fingers against his side to try to stanch the blood, doing it all without comment or cry, which in itself was more than a little unnerving. He came on hard, ax crashing against Styke's knife, working inside Styke's guard with both blade and haft, leaving Styke's chin and chest bloody and bruised.

Styke's own crippled hand was slick with blood, and each time he tried to catch Kushel's ax it slipped out of his grip until he finally managed to hook it with his knife and pull back.

Kushel had learned that trick, and this time let the ax go instead of losing his fingers. He suddenly dropped low, kicking at Styke's knee. Styke grunted, unable to keep himself from toppling into the dust, trapping his knife hand beneath him as Kushel leapt on top of him. Kushel's bloody finger stumps were suddenly thrust in his face, the blood stinging his eyes, and Styke grasped blindly for something—anything—until he wrapped his fingers around the lip of Kushel's blood-slick armor.

He used the grip to roll Kushel beneath him, freeing his arm, and pressed the point of his knife firmly against Kushel's armor before using every bit of his strength to *shove* through the tough leather.

Kushel gave a choking sound as Styke pushed the knife to the hilt against his armor, yet still the dragonman fought on, weakening blows pounding against Styke's stomach and face. Styke let go of his knife and grit his teeth, grasping Kushel by the head and pulling him close. "Stop. Fighting." Kushel spat a mouthful of blood. Styke wiped it from his face and got to one knee, holding Kushel down with his crippled hand and drawing back the fist of his other.

"Wait!" Flint suddenly shouted. "We need him alive!"

Styke looked down at the knife in Kushel's bowels and the bloody, dusty ground around them. With the right attention Kushel might live a day, maybe two, in horrible agony. "You fought well," he said, "but a warrior doesn't threaten a little girl." He brought his fist down with all his might, caving in the top of Kushel's skull like an eggshell.

Styke knelt in the gore for several moments, his chest rising and falling, as he tried to gather himself. Blood and brains dripped from his fingers, a crimson smile in the empty eyes of the skull on his lancer's ring. Ten years since the last time he truly feared for his life in a fight. Ten years since anyone had matched him in strength. He was suddenly aware of the absence of sound, and lifted his head to see a thousand sets of eyes glued to him. Soldiers crowded the muster yard, watching him from the walls, and the roof of the staff office. A cigarette hung, unlit, from the corner of Olem's open mouth and Lady Flint regarded Styke with an appraising look, her mouth pressed into a hard line.

Slowly, feeling all the aches and twinges he'd ignored during the fight and several dozen cuts and bruises he'd received during it, Styke got to his feet. He collected one of the bone axes and walked over to Flint, holding it out. "For your men that died fighting this asshole's friend."

"Thanks." Flint took the ax, flipping it from side to side to examine the blade before lowering it. "He was our link to the Dynize in Landfall."

"There will be more," Styke said.

"Says who?"

"The spirits told me."

Flint didn't seem to be able to tell whether that was supposed to be a joke. Styke wasn't sure himself. "Tell me," Flint said, "what did you do to the second Warden? The one Two-shot *didn't* kill?"

"I punched his teeth in," Styke said, remembering the hot breath of the sorcery-twisted creature and the thick muscles that moved like snakes in his grip. "Then I broke his spine."

Styke limped toward the mess hall. He needed to get cleaned up, then find Celine. Part of him hoped she hadn't just seen that. The adrenaline began to subside and he felt sick from the absence of it and the overwhelming stench of death. But deep down, his heart sang.

He was still Mad Ben Styke, and he would not be trifled with.

Styke was halfway to the mess hall when a voice suddenly called out from the gate. "I'm looking for Ben Styke! Where is Ben Styke?"

"What the pit is it now?" Styke asked, turning around slowly. He came up short at the sight of a boy wearing a smith's smock with the words "Fles and Fles Blades" emblazoned in the corner.

"Are you Ben Styke?" the boy asked.

"Who wants to know?"

The boy licked his lips, his face white. "Jackal said I could find you here. It's Old Man Fles, sir. The Blackhats, they…"

Styke was already running past the boy, ignoring the hundred pains in his body, before the boy could finish the sentence. "Olem," he shouted over his shoulder, "keep Celine safe!"

CHAPTER 32

Vlora nudged the corpse of the dragonman with her foot and watched Styke's back as he ran—surprisingly spry for a cripple—out the front gate of Loel's Fort. "Where the pit is he going?"

"Want me to bring him back?" Olem asked.

"Yes. No. Shit." Vlora stewed in her own indecision. She needed answers about this thing with the Dynize, and the corpse at her feet wasn't going to give them to her. But after seeing what Styke did to a legendary warrior, she wasn't about to send any of her men after him to tell him to turn around. She'd learned long ago that there were certain people you didn't bother when they were in a hurry.

"Send someone to follow him. And get this asshole cleaned up."

"Right." Olem turned to the watching soldiers. "Fall out! Nothing more to see here, lads. You three, take care of the body. Bring Lady Flint the armor and weapons. Put the body on ice."

Vlora turned from her continued study of the dragonman to cock an eyebrow.

"Never know when a corpse will come in handy," Olem said with a shrug.

Vlora paced nervously as the muster yard emptied and the blood was cleaned up. Something about Styke's tale had her on edge, but she couldn't quite place it. Maybe she was bothered by the reminder of how much of an impact Taniel had on, not only her world, but everyone else's. Maybe it wasn't even the story itself, but his fight with the dragonman. Styke was no sorcery-enhanced powder mage. Normal men didn't have that kind of power. They didn't crush a skull with a bare fist or break a Warden's spine. She suddenly feared Styke, and she hadn't truly feared another person for years.

Maybe she didn't like remembering that there were still monsters in the world that even she couldn't comprehend.

The blood was just being scraped off the dirt of the muster yard when there was a sudden commotion at the front gate. Vlora stopped her pacing and turned around with a scowl, only to see a handful of Blackhats appear at the open doors of the fort. There were two riders with Bronze Roses hanging from their necks, and another six Iron Roses on foot gathered around them. Their ranks suddenly swelled as more joined them from the street. Ten, then twenty, then thirty Blackhats crowded into the space.

Vlora's heart was suddenly pounding. She checked her pistol and sword. "Someone get Olem," she ordered, striding toward the gate.

Her soldiers stood firm just inside the fort gate, while Blackhats shifted nervously, staring at the Riflejack guards like a pack of wild dogs waiting for a signal. For their part her guards were stone-faced, and their sergeant—a stubborn, flat-faced man missing an ear from enemy straight shot—was arguing with one of the Bronze Roses.

"Lady Flint's orders," Sergeant Jamenis insisted. "No one allowed inside Loel's Fort without being announced first. You wait until word comes back from the Lady and then—"

"It's all right, Jamenis," Vlora said, hurrying up behind him. "I'm right here. Stand down." Jamenis immediately stepped aside, saluting.

The Bronze Rose scoffed, urging his horse forward. Vlora grabbed the horse's bridle, holding up the whole mob. "I didn't say you could enter. Can I help you with something, Blackhat?"

"Your men are lucky you're here," the Bronze Rose responded. He tugged on his reins, but Vlora held firm. "Next time we won't be so accommodating. This is a surprise inspection, and I have full authority to search the premises on order of the grand master."

Vlora pursed her lips. Pushy Blackhats. This was the last thing she needed today. Was this Agent Bravis's idea of a joke? Or was this a screen for her cover—hoping the Palo would see she was being pushed around by the Blackhats and be more likely to trust her?

"No one inspects my men without my say-so," Vlora said.

"Grand master's orders," the Bronze Rose said again, as if the words were a magic password. "Surprise inspection. You do know what a surprise is, don't you?"

Vlora looked around at her gate guard, noting the tightening of fingers on rifles and the frowns on the faces of her men. She wondered what it would take to get the respect of the locals—Palo *or* Blackhats—and decided she'd have to live without it.

This could turn very ugly, very quickly. She tried to read the face of the Bronze Rose. He was sweating heavily, even for the heat, and he kept shifting the reins from one hand to the other.

"What's going on, Blackhat? I don't report to anyone except the Lady Chancellor herself, and I won't listen to the lip of a lapdog. Explain yourself before I shut the gates in your face." The Bronze Rose opened his mouth, but Vlora continued in a reasonable tone: "And before you throw threats and curses, remember that I have a brigade of the finest riflemen in the world within a whistle. Keep it civil."

The Bronze Rose chewed on his tongue for several moments, his face turning several shades of red before returning to a healthy, pink sheen. "We're looking for an escaped convict named Ben Styke. Witnesses say they've seen him entering this compound on at least two occasions. He is a dangerous war criminal and is to be remanded to our custody immediately."

"You're shitting me." The words slipped out before Vlora could stop herself, and she immediately bit down on her tongue, her mind racing. Styke was an escaped war criminal? A thousand little things clicked into place, every interaction with Styke suddenly making all the more sense. His disappearance from public life, his injuries, his desire to keep a low profile, his disconnect from the modern city.

The initial shock passed within moments, replaced quickly by an utter lack of surprise, and then a cold anger in the pit of her stomach. It must have all been plain to see on her face, because the Bronze Rose looked down from his saddle with a smug smile.

"If you'd just hand him over, we'll be gone in a few moments."

The Blackhats behind him all tightened their grip on their weapons. A little part of her realized they were *not* expecting an easy time of things, but the rest of her didn't give a damn. "Give me a moment," she snapped, spinning on her heel.

She found Olem coming toward her across the muster yard but snatched him by the shoulder and pulled him into the fort office, slamming the door behind her.

"He lied to us."

Olem pursed his lips. "Who?"

"Styke. There's a whole platoon's worth of Blackhats standing at our gate demanding we hand over Styke. He's a damned criminal. An escaped convict."

Olem paced to the other side of the room, took out a pouch of tobacco, and smoothed a rolling paper on the table.

"Olem..."

He held up his finger. "Hold on. I'm thinking."

Vlora flexed her fingers, gripping and ungripping the hilt of her sword. Everything was making her furious lately—it was like an angry cloud had descended on her the moment she entered Landfall, preventing her from sorting her thoughts clearly. She had to fight through it. She had to be cold, calculating. Before two weeks ago she didn't know Styke from a swamp dragon. She had no reason to trust anything he said—even if he had followed her orders and tracked down the dragonman. All she had was his reputation, Olem's admiration, and Taniel's letters.

Did she have any more reason to trust the Blackhats? They were notoriously two-faced and underhanded. They existed to lie and manipulate. But did they lie about this? Styke *was* dangerous, and it made perfect sense that he'd escaped from a labor camp. But why wasn't there a general alarm around the city? How was this the first Vlora had heard of it? Surely the newspaper would have reported something.

"He didn't lie to us," Olem suddenly said.

"What do you mean?"

"He just said he needed work. Never told us where he'd been, or why. And we never asked. So, technically, he never lied to us."

"What have I told you about using the word 'technically' to me?"

Olem finished rolling a cigarette and squinted at the ceiling. "That you'd kick my teeth in?"

"Right." Vlora ground her teeth. "I was just starting to like him. Pit, I was just starting to *trust* him."

"More than you trust the Blackhats?"

"Something I was wondering myself." The knot of anger still sat in her stomach, but it had diminished to a reasonable size and Vlora felt like she could approach the matter with a clear head. She took a deep breath. "There's nothing we can do for him," she said. "We're employed by the state. I could defy the Blackhats, but that mob out there means Fidelis Jes takes Styke *very* seriously. By the end of the night we could have an army outside our gates."

"The question, then," Olem said, "is whether we throw Styke to the dogs." He lit his cigarette and within moments had filled the room with a cloud of smoke. So much smoke was the best sign Olem was distressed, and Vlora didn't blame him. He liked Styke. After Styke's story about Taniel, then the fight in the muster yard, the men were beginning to take to him as well.

"I'm not sacrificing our footing here for one man," Vlora said quietly.

A pained expression crossed Olem's face. "I agree."

Vlora and Olem returned to the front gate, where the Blackhats were obviously getting antsy; horses pranced, men muttered, and the Bronze Rose grit his teeth as Vlora approached.

"He's not here," Vlora said.

Was that a bit of relief she saw in the Bronze Rose's eyes? "Where is he?" he demanded.

"Don't know. Ran off awhile ago. Didn't say where he was going. You have ten minutes to inspect the yard. I want Fidelis Jes to know that we were unaware of Styke's status. He's been cut loose and I'll give a public order that my men are to arrest him on sight. I don't like being lied to."

The speech seemed to satisfy the Bronze Rose, and he gave orders for his men to do a quick sweep of the fort. Vlora watched them enter, loathing herself for letting secret police have the run of her headquarters. Once they were all out of earshot, she turned to Olem.

"Where's the girl?"

"Celine? Styke left her behind when he took off. I think she's playing in the mess."

"Hide her. I won't let the Blackhats get their grubby hands on an orphan."

Olem dashed off a quick order to two of the nearby guards and then returned to Vlora's side. She watched as her men glared down the Blackhats rushing around the compound, and then said quietly, "Did you send anyone to follow Styke?"

"I sent one of my boys in plainclothes."

"Send another. I won't risk the brigade for one man—but for a few days at least, Styke was one of mine. The least we can do is give him some warning."

CHAPTER 33

Styke followed the Fles apprentice down into the Depths and through the warrenlike streets of the slum, straight toward the Fles family home. People stopped and stared, then headed in the other direction or slammed front doors shut as Styke passed, vacating the streets ahead of him like waves rushing before the prow of a ship. The dragonman's blood—and probably more than a little of his own—dripped from Styke's fingertips, leaving a steady trail, and he absently wiped his hand on his shirt from time to time.

The apprentice refused to say a word all the way to the Fles family home, and when they reached the front door he could only point in mute horror. The big oak door had been battered off its hinges and hung from a single hinge just inside the foyer. The house inside was dark, and Styke half-expected the apprentice to turn and flee, leaving Styke alone in some kind of a trap.

The apprentice remained close, as if loath to be alone, even if his only companion was a crippled, blood-covered giant.

Styke drew his knife and crept inside.

The destruction did not stop at the front door. Every scrap of furniture—every knickknack collected over a long life serving kings and commoners—had been reduced to scraps. A priceless grandfather clock lay on its side, broken apart by an ax; the collection of Brudanian porcelain on the mantelpiece had been smashed; Gurlish rugs were shredded and Kez vases crushed.

Styke squinted through the low light, taking in the wreckage. He knew immediately who had done it—the Blackhats—and he saw that they had been thorough. Even the walls had been attacked, hundreds of holes punched through the plaster in a hurried fury. The destruction could only have been more thorough if they'd set fire to the house, and only the fear of burning down the whole of the Depths would have stopped them. Somewhere within the house he could hear the sound of weeping, and that sound more than the ruin caused his heart to crack.

He felt his chest tighten, making it hard to breathe, and he croaked, "Where is the Old Man?"

"In the workshop," the apprentice said.

Fles's workshop had received the brunt of the damage. Workbenches were split, tools scattered, swords and knives bent and broken. In the center of it all huddled a small group—three apprentices, all of them gathered around a still form on the floor. The youngest of the boys, no older than Celine, wept openly while the other two had red eyes and trembling chins. Styke pushed them gently out of the way and knelt by the Old Man.

Old Man Fles was as beat up as his home. His face was a mess of blood and bruises, and one arm was bent at an odd angle under him. His shirt was soaked with as much blood as Styke's, and he clutched a broken sword in one hand. He lay where he'd fallen, the boys not daring to move him.

Styke's chest tightened further. He tried to speak, but satisfied himself with a gesture and a grunt. "Water," he ordered. He laid two fingers on the Old Man's neck, then put his ear next to his mouth. He could feel the faint pulse of the vein, the gentle touch of breath on his cheek. Old Man Fles was still alive.

Relief won out among all the other emotions swirling through Styke's chest. He forced them all down, clearing his throat, then clearing it again, when he noticed that the Old Man's eyes were open.

"Big, bloody idiot," the Old Man whispered.

"Shut up," Styke said. "Save your strength."

The Old Man tried to roll off his bent arm. He let out a high-pitched moan, then ceased his struggles. He managed to turn his head slightly, looking away from Styke, eyes searching the workshop. "A lifetime's work," he muttered.

"Because of me," Styke said. It was the only reason, of course. The Old Man paid his bribes, kept his nose clean. The Blackhats had no reason to attack such a highly regarded craftsman. Not unless they were trying to get to Styke. They must have found out the Old Man was passing him information somehow. Maybe one of the apprentices. Maybe a spy watching the house. Maybe the Old Man himself had slipped up.

"Of course it was cuz of you," the Old Man hissed. "Always knew you were bad luck." He tried to move his arm again, unsuccessfully.

Styke rolled the Old Man on his side gently, ignoring the protesting squeal, and pulled the arm around and laid it on his chest. It was definitely broken, and would probably need to be set. Styke could do it, but he had no idea if the shock of it would kill the Old Man. "You summon a doctor?" he asked the oldest of the apprentices.

"Just you," the apprentice responded. "He said no doctors."

"Well, he's an idiot. Go get the best surgeon in this half of the city, now."

"No doctors," the Old Man grunted.

"Shut your flapper," Styke snapped. The apprentice hesitated, looking from Styke to the Old Man and back. Styke bared his teeth. "Whatever you think he'll do to you if he gets better, I'll do worse right now. Surgeon. Go."

The apprentice fled, and Styke had the others light the lanterns and gather what was left of the Old Man's bed before carrying him to it. The Old Man cursed Styke's face and parentage throughout the whole process, then passed out once he'd been laid still again. Styke sat on the floor by the bed, back against the cold manor wall, while the remaining apprentices busied themselves cleaning up the workshop.

Styke stared at the ceiling, trying to remember the last time he had cried. Decades, probably, and the tears weren't coming now even if he wished they would. The Old Man had been the closest thing he ever had to a mentor. He was a national treasure, a craftsman on par with the gunmaker Hrusch, and he'd always been inviolate. No one touched him, because everyone wanted his blades.

"Right," Styke said to himself, the corner of his mouth lifting in a rueful smile. "Last time I cried was when I killed that old bastard who called himself my father."

"What are you going on about?"

"Awake?" Styke asked.

The Old Man groaned. "Barely." His voice was stronger now. "Thanks to you and your damned eyes. Things were going well, you know. Ibana been running the business for the last few years. Raking in the money. I was going to die a rich man. Now they've wrecked it all."

"Not all of it," Styke said.

"The shop at the market, too. They wrecked that last night. Found it a mess this morning, rushed home to find them tossing the house. There were thirty of the bastards, and they just kept asking where you were. Bastards. All of you."

"Them," Styke corrected absently. In his head, he was doing calculations, figuring out who he'd have to ask to track down thirty Blackhats, and how hard it would be to get rid of all those bodies. Jackal would probably help.

"All of *you*," the Old Man insisted, glaring at Styke. "I knew I should have told you to go stuff it the moment you walked through my door. You were always bad luck."

"Where's Ibana?" Styke asked.

"Still on her trip. She'll be back in a few…few days." The Old Man closed his eyes. He was fading, and Styke hoped he was going to pass out, and not away. "God, she'll be pissed. Gonna skin you alive."

"You already said that."

"Well, now I mean it. Pit. Have one of the boys wait on the edge of town to warn her. Don't want her messing with the Blackhats. I…" Fles trailed off, then sullenly said, "They took my sword. The latest I was working on. Didn't even have the dignity to smash it. Stole the bloody thing straight off." The flatness in his voice alarmed Styke more than any emotion, but the Old Man's eyes were closed against Styke's worrying glance.

"Rest," Styke said, climbing to his feet.

"Don't do it," Fles responded.

"Eh?"

"Don't do that fool thing you're thinking about doing."

"I'm not thinking about doing anything," Styke said. "Gotta make sure you're okay."

"Take me for a fool?"

In truth, Styke hadn't been considering much of anything. He wondered where the Blackhats would head next, and hoped Jackal was able to lie low. He considered sending one of the apprentices to Lady Flint to ask her to hide Celine, but he didn't want to get her involved in this. Whatever "this" was. Styke wasn't entirely sure, though a thought had crept into his head—the very one Fles was telling him not to consider—and he decided immediately on his course of action.

"No," he said quietly. "I never took you for a fool." When there was no answer he looked down to find Fles had passed out again.

He checked to make certain the Old Man's heart was still beating, then headed toward the workshop, only to stop in the great room, hand on the handle of his knife. A figure stood in the doorway, silhouetted against the lamplit street.

The figure turned his face toward the light. It was Colonel Olem, wearing plain frontiersman's clothes and a felt half hat. His usual cigarette was gone, replaced by a twig. He squinted through the dim light at Styke, then stepped outside and took a long, hard look at the placard beside the door.

"Friend of yours?" he asked.

Styke grunted an affirmative.

Olem chewed aggressively on the twig. "Blackhats do this?" he asked.

Styke felt his heart skip a beat. "How'd you know?"

"Gang of 'em showed up at Loel's Fort right after you left."

"Looking for me?"

"Looking for you," Olem echoed.

So much for not dragging Lady Flint into this. When it rained, his sister used to say, it poured. And shit was falling from the sky right now. "So she knows."

"Knows that you're a war criminal?" Olem said.

Styke took two strides forward, reaching for his knife, before he realized that Olem had staged it as a question, not a statement. Styke growled in the back of his throat. "I'm no war criminal. Not by any court in this land. Convicted of ignoring orders, yes. But any crime I've committed was for this country, and I'll ask you not to repeat that accusation."

Olem considered him, unflinching, looking him up and down. Styke thought of the Palo clearing the streets and slamming their doors as he passed and considered what he must have looked like—a giant, caked in blood, covered in a dozen nicks and cuts, his shirt sliced open. It all hurt; a fresh, wakeful pain that he'd ignored since the moment the apprentice had urgently called his name. Olem seemed suitably impressed, but unafraid, and Styke was struck by a random thought—the former bodyguard of the legendary Field Marshal Tamas was probably a son of a bitch to play against in cards.

"That seems fair," Olem said. "I've heard a lot about you. Read a few books. Talked to your old friends. You don't strike me as a war criminal."

"Then why are you here?" Styke asked. Olem wasn't stupid. If he was here to express Flint's displeasure, or to arrest Styke in the name of the Lady Chancellor, he would be in uniform, and probably backed by a whole regiment.

Olem held out his hand. "To give you this."

Styke took a stack of krana notes, rolling it between his fingers, inadvertently smearing them in blood. He handed them back. "I don't want it."

"Five thousand krana. It's your pay for two weeks' work."

"I didn't earn five thousand krana."

"And a little extra on the side," Olem admitted.

Styke swallowed a lump in his throat. Never mind that his purpose had been to infiltrate the Riflejacks. He was beginning to like them, and their commanding officer. He'd been beginning to fit in, feel like a real soldier again. "Flint is cutting me loose?"

"Sorry," Olem said, and sounded like he meant it. He held out the money again.

"Give it to Celine when she's old enough," Styke said, pushing past Olem. "Take care of her for me. Keep her out of the Blackhats' hands." It was a lot to ask, and he expected Olem to shake his head.

Instead, Olem said softly, "You're not taking her with you?"

"Not where I'm going." The Old Man was right. Styke was going to be an idiot. But it was the only route he could foresee, the only stratagem that didn't end with everyone he'd ever known tortured by the Blackhats. He paused in the street just outside the Fles manor and turned back to Olem. "I didn't escape from the labor camp," he said. "I only tried once, and halfheartedly at that."

"Why not?" Olem asked. "I saw what you did to that dragonman."

Styke looked at the blood on his fingers, remembering all the beatings he'd endured silently at the hands of the labor camp guards. He remembered every sleepless night from the ache of his old wounds, every day in the sun pulling sledges or mucking out trenches in the marshes. "Because I didn't want my life to end up like this. I'm a wolf, not a cur, and I won't flee for the rest of my life. Better to serve my sentence and be released on my own free will than to escape. Whatever they've done to me, I'm still Ben Styke, and I've got my pride.

"I didn't escape," he continued. "I was released. I thought maybe I was really free. That I could create a new life. But the Lady Chancellor only fears what she can't control, and so..." He shrugged, then began to trudge down the street. "I like Lady Flint. When you see her next time, tell her to be wary of a man named Gregious Tampo."

"You know Tampo?" Olem asked sharply.

"Not really," Styke said without turning around. "But he's the one who released me from the camps."

"Where are you going? What are you going to do?" Olem called after him.

"I'm going to make an appointment to kill a man."

CHAPTER 34

Michel was left alone in the tiny office above the *Palo Her-ald* printshop. His hands and feet were tied, his knife and knuckledusters taken by the big Palo woman, and the door to the office locked from the outside for good measure. His jaw ached and head pounded from the two blows to his head, and his ribs and chest hurt from a handful of kicks and punches they'd thrown in when he tried to talk his way out of...whatever it was they had planned for him. His bribery attempt had gone little better, earning him a cut over his ear.

He'd expected the beatings to begin immediately and continue until he broke down and told them who he was and what he worked for, but the moment they found his Silver Rose they trussed him up like a hog and carried him up to the office. He could see one of the Palo, a middle-aged man with a fierce scar beneath one eye, standing guard just outside.

He could probably pick through his ropes. He might even be able to jimmy the lock with something he found in the office. But he didn't think his chances of taking on a Palo guard—maybe even more than one—were very good with his head swimming.

If he lived through this, he was going to be *very* sore in the morning.

The hours crawled along as midday came and went, the tiny room heating up to an unbearable degree. Sweat poured from every pore, leaving him completely soaked through. He considered plan after plan, discarding each for the high probability of failure. He'd always been better at talking than running or fighting, and even though they'd discovered his Silver Rose he was still willing to do just that. If he couldn't bribe them or convince them to let him go, maybe he could get them to ransom him back to the Millinery.

Having to be ransomed back to the Millinery would send his career into a tailspin. Of course, a destroyed career was better than winding up in several pieces on Fidelis Jes's desk...

He considered every possible story he could tell his captors, and none of them seemed promising. His head continued to pound, his tongue dry. He was beginning to think he would faint when there was a brief commotion from downstairs and then slow, even steps on the stairs outside the office. He wasn't sure how long it had been since he'd been captured, but he hoped they were going to move him. Another minute in this heat would kill him sure as torture.

The door opened, and Michel looked up to see a man in a fine black suit, top hat in one hand and cane in the other. He was tall, thin, with black hair and a neatly trimmed mustache. Michel felt his heart drop into his stomach.

Tampo. Gregious Tampo. Michel noted the irony that after all this time and effort spent in hunting the bastard he had wound up on the wrong end of what would surely be a long and painful torture session. He licked his lips, wondering how long he would be able to hold out against questioning. Not long, probably. He'd always suspected that deep down, he was a coward.

Guess it was time to find out.

Tampo frowned at Michel, squinted in the low light, then pulled out a snuff box and took a pinch, holding his fingers delicately beneath his nose and sniffing. He looked again and sighed. "Get him some tea."

A few moments later Michel's arms were unbound and he gratefully chugged the contents of a waterskin, far too thirsty to care if it was poisoned. Tampo watched him drink, then turned and headed back downstairs, leaving Michel alone and unguarded. Hesitantly, not sure what kind of trap could be worse than his current predicament, Michel followed him down to the printshop.

The Palo made themselves scarce at a nod from Tampo, and Tampo turned to face Michel, leaning casually against the printing press in the center of the room. Michel glanced around furtively, trying to work out an escape route. The Palo were probably within earshot, but if Michel could get the drop on Tampo maybe he could make it back to his cab just outside the city.

If the cab was still waiting.

Fuzzy-headed and sore, Michel didn't like his chances of escape. Tampo's expression was neutral, even friendly, and Michel wondered whether he was going to get a chance to talk his way out of this after all.

"This is awkward," Tampo finally said.

"I imagine it is, isn't it?" Michel responded.

"Has it been you that's been after me all this time?"

Michel frowned at Tampo. This was the first time he'd actually seen him, but there was something awfully familiar about him, like he was a childhood friend long forgotten. "I've been on the case for about eight days," he responded.

"Shit," Tampo said. He picked his teeth with one immaculately clean fingernail, then knocked his cane against the base of the printing press. He seemed more annoyed than angry, and Michel was wondering when the other shoe would drop. "Well, I suppose there's really nothing we can do about it, is there?"

Michel was deeply confused. He'd half-expected Tampo to come in swinging that cane. Not for him to offer him tea and a double-helping of mild annoyance. Tampo shook his head, pinched the bridge of his nose, and remained that way for several seconds. Michel was just beginning to think something was wrong when Tampo's face...*changed*.

The change was not enormous. His eyes grew a little wider apart. His hair suddenly seemed to have some premature gray, and his mustache disappeared entirely. His nose became a little more hawkish, his cheekbones higher and haughtier, his lips thinner. In the course of about five seconds, Tampo became an entirely different man. The two men—Tampo, and the one that now stood before Michel—could have been cousins, but they would never have been mistaken for each other.

And Michel immediately knew why Tampo was so frustrated. He found himself sighing, too, partly in relief, partly at the stupidity of it all.

"Hello, Taniel," Michel said. "Why the pit didn't you tell me you were going to print a bloody pamphlet?"

CHAPTER 35

Styke entered the front gate of the Millinery, unopposed. A guard, slack-jawed, watched him limp through the archway, then yelled something unintelligible over his shoulder as Styke approached the old man sitting watch behind a counter just outside the gate. The old Blackhat snoozed quietly, slumped sideways in his chair, notebook slipping from his fingers.

"I understand Fidelis Jes takes appointments for fights," Styke said.

The old Blackhat snorted, rubbed his nose, and pushed himself upright in his chair while stifling a yawn. "Right, right," he said. "I'll take your name. Wait is a couple weeks. You can back out anytime before then if your blood cools."

"I'm going to fight him today."

The old Blackhat's eyelids fluttered and he scowled down at his notebook. "Don't you read the papers? The grand master only duels during the mornings, and he's all booked up. No exceptions."

"He'll make an exception for me." Styke picked at the dried

blood on his arms, watching it flake off and fall to the cobbles. He wondered if Old Man Fles would make it to the morning, and if it was cruel of him to allow the Old Man to die alone. But he wouldn't be alone, Styke reasoned with himself. Fles would die surrounded by friends. Unlike Styke, who wondered briefly if he'd always been destined to die surrounded by enemies.

"Hilarious," the old Blackhat said. "I'll take your name and address and we'll let you know when to keep your appointment."

"Benjamin Styke. Colonel. First Division, Third Cavalry, Mad Lancers."

"A soldier, eh? Usually you guys are smarter than…" The old Blackhat trailed off, his mouth working silently. From somewhere inside the Millinery came the sound of shouting, and the watchman finally looked up, mouth hanging open at Styke's appearance. "Oh," he said breathlessly. "It's you."

"It's me," Styke confirmed. "Tell Fidelis Jes I'm going to make a hand puppet out of his worthless corpse. I've told a dozen newspapers I'm on my way here, so if he tries to make me disappear the whole city will know him for a bloody coward." A lie, but a plausible one.

The guard lurched from his chair and backed away from Styke. "I'll, uh, give him the message. Give me just a few…moments." He bolted into the Millinery. The shouting got closer, and Styke was soon aware of the heavy tromp of feet. The narrow gate filled with faces as Blackhats crowded just inside, bristling with weapons from blunderbusses to cudgels. Feet shuffled and men jostled for position as they tried to look intimidating—while they stayed well out of arm's reach.

Styke leaned against the watchman's post, cleaning his nails and contemplating his mortality.

He did not expect to leave the Millinery alive. He didn't feel any real fear—he'd never desired death, but the prospect had never particularly phased him, either. He was here to die, and he suspected it would be by the hands of the very mob gathered just inside. He'd take a few of them with him, if he could, but his only real goal was to go down with bits of Fidelis Jes's brains on his shirt.

He pictured Fidelis Jes as he last saw him—thin, muscular, his neck a little too thick and his head a little too narrow, making him look like a nub of pencil stuck on a body, looking smug as he watched Styke's firing squad take aim. Styke froze that smile in his mind's eye and wondered what it would look like when he popped Jes's head between his palms like a ripe melon. The Blackhats would gun him down as soon as their leader expired, but Styke would die with a grin.

He had a few regrets. He wished he hadn't been forced to double-time Lady Flint. He regretted not saying he was sorry to Ibana. He wanted to know what Tampo's real plans were for Landfall.

He wished he could have watched Celine grow up.

"Colonel Styke?" a voice asked.

Styke came out of his reverie to find a woman of about thirty standing between him and the mob of Blackhats. "Who are you?"

"My name is Dellina. I'm the grand master's secretary. I understand you're here about personal combat with the grand master."

"I have no interest in waiting."

"Of course," Dellina said, smiling professionally. If she was put off by his bloody state, she didn't show it. "And we have no intention of keeping you waiting. The grand master is in a meeting right now but he left strict instructions to be summoned when you arrived. He should be here anytime."

Styke felt a knot form in his stomach. "He was expecting me."

"Yes, Colonel."

Styke felt the sudden kick to the ribs that accompanied the realization that he'd been manipulated. Of course. He'd played right into Jes's hands. Instead of forcing Jes to chase him around Landfall, Styke strode straight into the Millinery and offered himself up like a damned dunce.

That was the foolish thing Old Man Fles had been referring to.

No backing out now. Styke felt a little bit stupid, but he was not afraid. He was going to die, and Jes would die along with him. The feeling gave him some comfort, but he nonetheless kept his knife hand ready as Dellina parted the mob of Blackhats and led him through the Millinery. The mob dogged their heels, then disappeared as he was led into a small, nondescript courtyard toward the back of the building. The Blackhats reappeared a few moments later, gathered around the catwalk above the courtyard, watching him like so many vultures.

"May I offer you any fruit or wine?" Dellina asked politely.

"No." Styke shrugged out of his old cavalry jacket and handed it to Dellina, who took it without comment.

"And what weapons shall you be fighting with today?"

Styke looked around the courtyard. The cobbles showed regular scrubbing, but only in particular splotches, likely from cleaning up blood. He caught the glint of metal down one arched hallway, and spied a weapon rack with dozens of swords, knives, pistols, and muskets, all polished and on display. Styke tapped his knife.

"Knives it is," Dellina said.

This was where Fidelis Jes did his killing, and if the newspapers were any indication, he'd become damned good at it. Styke wondered if he should be feeling fear right about now, but dismissed the thought. He'd not felt it when he charged fifteen thousand infantry in the Battle of Landfall, nor when he charged a full brigade at Planth, backed only by Two-shot's irregulars and a small-town garrison. He'd not felt fear once during the war, and he refused to surrender to it now.

"Benjamin Styke," a voice called.

Styke felt his heart soar as Fidelis Jes strolled down a short run of steps at the far end of the courtyard. Seeing him approach was like witnessing the arrival of an old friend—if you planned on murdering him painfully—and Styke drummed the fingers of his good hand on the hilt of his knife, humming to himself.

This was it. A moment he'd dreamed about for ten years.

"Been a long time," Fidelis Jes said, falling into a soldier's stance about ten feet away.

"Too long," Styke said quietly. "And not long enough."

If Styke was a wreck of a human being, just a shadow of his former self, Fidelis Jes had done nothing but grow stronger and better-looking. His shoulders were wider than Styke remembered, his arms and thighs more massive, his skin pleasantly tanned. He still had that ridiculously thick neck and stupidly thin head, but they seemed less important when the rest of his body was a godlike specimen. Jes had not allowed himself to grow fat or lazy in his position. Styke hated him a little for that, but as far as hate went it was like throwing a glass of water into the ocean.

Jes grinned like he was about to carve up a particularly succulent turkey. "Pit, you're uglier than I remember. Bullet didn't help your face, did it? Or your back or knee." He clicked his tongue, shaking his head. "The years have not been kind to you, my friend."

"Were we ever friends?" Styke asked. For a moment, he genuinely couldn't remember.

"Allies."

"Not the same thing."

"I suppose that's true," Jes admitted. He squinted at Styke. "Decided you were ready to die, did you?"

Styke tapped on the hilt of his knife. "Everyone dies sooner or later." He studied Jes, searching his eyes and face. They had witnesses—dozens of Blackhats gathered on the catwalks above them—and Jes looked nothing but the confident blowhard that he'd always been. But Styke could see a crack in the armor; Jes's eyes were too inviting, his smile a little too wide. He bounced on his heels a little too eagerly.

He was nervous. As he should be.

"Knives, is it?" Jes asked. His voice cracked slightly, but he cleared his throat and repeated the question.

"Yes, sir," Dellina responded. She hurried down the side hall where Styke had spotted the weapon rack and returned with a fixed-blade knife just as big and heavy as Styke's. She offered it to Jes handle-first and he drew it with one swift motion. Styke expected him to look ridiculous with such a big knife, but Jes gave it a few comfortable, expert flourishes and then began to stretch his arms and legs, like a gymnast readying for a performance.

"I feel like there's so much to say," Jes said.

Styke jerked his knife from its scabbard and held it loosely in his good hand. "Not really."

"You don't want to ask about what I've accomplished while you were locked up? You don't want to hear about Fatrasta's wealth? Her glory? You don't want to ask after Lindet?"

"I see a rotten city with a fresh coat of paint," Styke said, considering his words carefully. "Lindet was always better at gaining power than she was at actually doing anything decent with it."

"Ripe words coming from you, Benjamin."

Styke shrugged. "I never claimed to do anything but destroy. You and Lindet talked the talk."

"Maybe if you'd given talk a chance you'd be something grand. Not a burned-out old cripple." The words were spoken in a gentle tone, but Styke could hear the dagger behind them. Jes's face smiled, but his eyes had begun to smolder, and Styke wondered if this performance was for the Blackhats watching them, or for Jes himself.

"You wanted me to kill kids," Styke said, loud enough the Blackhats could hear it.

"Everyone has to die," Jes responded without the slightest bit of remorse. "You just said so yourself. You made sure everyone knew that you were the monster Fatrasta needed, until it was inconvenient to you."

"Slaughtering children *is* inconvenient."

"Not to a *real* soldier," Jes shot back. "A real soldier follows orders."

"Like you? You've never been a soldier. Just Lindet's shadow, with no real substance of your own, wielding a stiletto in the darkness and killing fools every morning to try to convince yourself you're good enough. You're not. You never have been. One day your seams will loosen and the stink will escape and Lindet will toss you on the midden pile the same way she did me."

Jes's head snapped back, the smiling calm replaced by bared teeth. He swished his knife through the air in a figure eight and began to pace back and forth. The secretary made herself scarce, withdrawing to the edge of the courtyard.

"Benjamin Styke," Jes spat. "So clever. So strong. But you can't even protect your friends. Tell me, what drove you here? Burning down Gamble's bar? Smashing up Fles Blades? Wrecking Sunin's livery? Killing that old buzzard Hovenson? I wasn't sure what would get your attention, so I decided to do it all at once."

Styke forced his face to remain stony but felt a catch in his throat. Jes listed off a dozen more names and the ills his Blackhats had done to them, presumably that very morning. They were all old friends and officers, people who might have shown him succor in time of need. Styke's stomach tied itself in knots and he could only think of a handful of names that *weren't* on the list, Jackal among them. He hadn't even made contact with any of these people aside from Fles, to try to protect them from possible reprisal, but even that hadn't been enough.

All his lancers had suffered because of him.

"So," Jes asked, continuing to pace, "which was it?"

Styke rolled his wrist, loosening his knife hand. "Honestly, I didn't even know about any of that. I just woke up this morning and decided I'd turn your rib cage into a hat."

Jes did a little skip and jump. He wasn't playing anymore. His eyes had grown focused, studious, and they darted from Styke's face, to his bad hand, to his crippled leg. "Whose blood are you wearing?" he demanded.

Styke gave him a toothy grin. "Wouldn't you like to know?"

"No matter. I'll find out after I've cleaned this up."

Jes surged forward without warning, dropping into a knife fighter's stance and slashing at Styke's face. Styke heard the clang of their blades and felt the impact all the way up his arm. He stepped sideways, swiping with his left hand only to receive a shallow cut on his forearm for his efforts. They separated, clashed again, separated, then circled each other warily, Jes's eyes narrowed with concentration.

The dragonman had been furiously strong and fast, but he'd made one mistake: He'd let Styke grapple with him. Jes remained out of arm's reach, leading with his blade. He was cautious and measured, somehow seeming to watch Styke's legwork, knife hand, and eyes all at once. Jes's movements had the finesse of someone who killed for art, rather than survival, and he could read Styke's movements like a book.

They continued to circle for several moments. Styke sliced the air in figure eights in front of Jes's face, while Jes did the same to him, both attempting to convince the other of a feint. Styke managed to nick Jes's arm. Jes cut Styke's middle knuckle. The blades crashed and clanged off each other, and Styke noted the deep gouges forming in the blade of Jes's knife—and the lack of the same in his own.

Should have bought a Fles blade.

The errant thought cost Styke his focus, then his footing. He stumbled back to regain it, swiping erratically to keep Jes at bay. Jes followed closely, his knife taking a gouge out of Styke's left thigh before Styke could readjust himself and lash back, drawing a long, deep cut down Jes's arm.

To his surprise, Jes leaned into the cut and, unbelievably, dropped his knife. He caught it with the other hand, out of sight below Styke's own arm, and then slashed upward, catching Styke's chest with the hooked tip of his knife and then bringing it across below Styke's good hand. Styke felt his fingers go suddenly numb, the hilt slipping from his grip. He tried to catch it, leaning forward, only to feel a hard pinch on his thigh.

He looked down as Jes jerked the thick blade out of Styke's leg. Styke lost his footing, holding his wrist, and collapsed backward.

The whole sequence had taken just a few heartbeats. Styke felt tears in his eyes and his brain trying to catch up. He was on his back, the tendon of his good hand slit, his right leg on fire.

It wasn't supposed to happen this way. He was supposed to grab Jes, even if he took a knife to the gut to do it, and then choke the life out of him in a few moments. They were going to die together, and Styke was going to be happy to go out that way. Instead, he heard the clatter of his knife being kicked across the cobbles and then saw Jes's face hovering above him.

Styke snatched upward with his crippled hand. Jes batted it away brutally with the blade, nearly severing a finger, then reversed his grip and slammed his knife down into Styke's shoulder.

"Scream," Jes said quietly.

Styke grunted. He couldn't find any words, not now. He swallowed a sob, wishing Jes would lean over closely so he could bite his nose off. But Jes just lowered himself to one knee beside him, slowly twisting the knife deeper and deeper.

"I said scream!"

Every breath was ragged now. Styke could feel every little cut needle sharp, and his leg and arm refused to respond to any commands. He remembered the dying dragonman, and bit his own lip hard and spat the blood into Jes's face. Jes jerked the knife out of Styke's shoulder and pressed the pitted blade against his throat.

Styke felt the raw edge and silently urged Jes to slice deep.

"You gonna finish it?" he hissed.

And just like that, the blade was withdrawn. Jes stood up and left Styke's field of vision. Styke closed his eyes, forcing himself to swallow. *This is how it'll be, then? Jes is going to let me bleed out on the Blackhat cobbles?* Styke wrestled with the thought, trying to give his death some sort of value. This wasn't how it was supposed to happen.

But, he supposed, this was a soldier's death. Slowly, painfully, drop by drop on the battlefield.

A bad way to go. Somehow, though, a proper one.

"Pick him up," Jes suddenly ordered.

Styke's eyes shot open. Jes stood above him again, this time surrounded by his Blackhats. Hands reached down and grasped Styke, forcing him up to his feet, half-carrying, half-dragging him toward the edge of the courtyard before dumping him unceremoniously facedown in a wheelbarrow. He could smell rust, old blood, and rotten flesh.

There was a sudden silence, and then he heard Jes's voice right beside his ear.

"You once terrified me," Jes whispered. "But now that seems like a bad dream. I can't kill you. She won't allow it. But I *can* make sure that your legend dies before you do." Jes's presence withdrew, and Styke heard him say in a loud voice, "Take this piece of trash back to Sweetwallow Labor Camp. And make sure he stays there."

CHAPTER 36

Vlora stood at attention in the office of the grand master of Fatrasta's secret police and wondered when she'd last had to salute someone. Years, certainly, maybe even all the way back to the Adran-Kez War. That was the last time any general in the room had outranked her, and the last time Adro had a field marshal.

She certainly wasn't going to give a trumped-up spy that honor, no matter how annoyed he looked.

Fidelis Jes's brow was beaded with sweat. He wore a clean shirt, but she could see blood soaking through it in more than one place. He fidgeted in his chair, looking from her to the immense knife on his desk and back again as if she was expected to explain its presence.

She recognized that knife. Ben Styke had used it to kill a dragonman.

"You asked for me?" she said lightly.

Fidelis Jes swept the knife off his desk and deposited it in a drawer before clearing his throat. Vlora noted the enormous ring on the thumb of his left hand, worn over the glove so it wouldn't fall off. Styke's skull ring. "Lady Flint, I understand that you've been employing convicted war criminal Benjamin Styke. I want an explanation and I want it now."

"I'm not sure an explanation is warranted," Vlora responded coolly. She didn't like Jes's tone one bit, but she wasn't in a mood to get combative. She had too much on her plate right now to risk pissing off the Lady Chancellor's right-hand man. Though by the looks of things, she was already too late on that account.

Jes slammed his palm on his desk. Behind her, Vlora heard his secretary jump and made a mental note of the fact. Jes was not known for outbursts. "You have been employing an enemy of the state. If *that* does not warrant an explanation would you care to tell me what does?"

"I was employing an old, crippled soldier. He came to me asking for a job and with a name like that, who wouldn't hire him on?" Vlora had a sudden suspicion and voiced it. "Tell me, is it even public record that Styke is a war criminal? Because I don't hire on strangers without looking into their background and all my men could find was that he disappeared ten years ago."

"Don't get smart with me, General."

"Don't waste my time."

There was a slight intake of breath behind her and Fidelis Jes's eyes narrowed. Vlora ground her teeth, annoyed with herself. She was letting her temper get the better of her—but if there was one thing she wouldn't stand it was being condescended to.

"Before lecturing me on what I should or shouldn't know," Vlora said quietly, "consider your own practice of censorship and mis-information. I'm no stranger to propaganda but you Blackhats have taken it to an art. You shouldn't be surprised when someone is unaware of information you purposefully destroyed. Now, I've purged Styke's name from the books of my mercenary company and ordered my men to arrest him the moment he's spotted. He's one man. If you're unsatisfied with my efforts to reconcile the situation I'll exercise the withdrawal clause of my contract and my men will be out of the city by the end of the week."

Fidelis Jes looked like he'd swallowed something sour. He clenched and unclenched one fist on the desk, looking at the thick ring on his thumb, then said, "I don't think that's necessary."

"I'm glad to hear that. I've quite enjoyed working with the Fatrastan government and I like to keep a good thing going." It was a bald-faced lie, but Vlora had learned that a lie or two did wonders for professional relationships. Besides, she'd made her point: She would not be called in here and bullied like a schoolgirl.

"Then you'll tell me what you hired Styke for, and all of his actions while in your employ."

Perhaps her point hadn't been made clearly enough. Vlora wondered just what made Styke so important. He was incredibly dangerous; she'd seen that with her own eyes. But he was still just one man. And if Jes had his knife and ring, it must mean that Jes had him. Was Styke already dead? "We hired him to have an insider's view of the city; to keep someone on hand who could do dirty work for us if the need arose."

"And did it?"

"I sent him chasing ghosts. He was still working on that first assignment as of this afternoon."

Jes eyed her for several long moments. He seemed to have gotten control of himself, and he dabbed his forehead gently with a handkerchief before folding it and setting it aside. "Details."

"I sent him chasing after the Dynize," Vlora said. It was close enough to the truth. She had no interest in explaining the last two weeks to Jes. She had work to do, and she was itching to get out of this office.

"What?" Jes said sharply, his eyes snapping up to hers. "What do you know about the Dynize?"

The intensity with which he asked made Vlora raise her eyebrows. *Apparently not as much as you.* "Very little. Just that they've installed spies in Greenfire Depths."

"Preposterous."

You're either much worse at your job than I've been led to believe, or you're playing me for a fool. Either way I don't like it. "We don't know why or how many, but it's been interfering with my work, so I set Styke to the task of dealing with it. Now that he's out of the picture, I'll have to put some of my own men on the job."

"No," Jes said. "You're to ignore the Dynize. Whatever you do, do not engage them directly."

A bit late for that. And what happened to preposterous? "They're interfering with my work," Vlora repeated.

"You'll have to just deal with it," Jes said. "The Dynize are to be left unmolested."

Vlora wondered what kind of plans Jes had for the Dynize. Obviously he knew about their presence. Was he watching them? Trying to trap them? Were they here on the behest of the Blackhats to stir up trouble in Greenfire Depths? What the Blackhats had planned for the Dynize was just as murky as what the Dynize themselves were up to, but it made her plenty angry. "Even," she asked, "if dragonmen are stalking and murdering my soldiers?"

"Dragonmen?" Jes repeated quietly to himself. He sounded genuinely surprised, and Vlora felt a jolt of smug satisfaction. "No," he finally said. "Steer clear of them."

Vlora snorted. This was not how she wanted this conversation to go. She was not to be bait in some game being played out of her sight. "Why?"

"That's not your concern."

"It *is* my concern. My men are dying."

"They're soldiers," Jes said coldly. "That's what they do." Vlora opened her mouth, but before she could respond, Jes went on.

"What *is* your concern is the apprehension of Mama Palo. Your Blackhat liaison reports that you have your men tearing down and rebuilding entire tenements instead of searching for Mama Palo."

"In addition to searching for Mama Palo," Vlora corrected.

"Do you take me for an idiot?"

"No. I take you for someone who understands the nuance of a long-term plan." The words slipped out, and Vlora once again cursed herself for letting her temper get the better of her.

"You're trying my patience, Lady Flint."

"Should that bother me?" Vlora asked. "You gave me an assignment. You gave me two months. I'm less than two weeks in and you're demanding results. I'm not sure what you expect."

"I expect someone of your reputation to accomplish your work ahead of schedule. And yes, trying my patience should bother you. You act as if you own this place, Lady Flint. You act as if you're in Adro, among your friends and admirers. You are not. You're nothing but a cog in the wheel here, and I expect you to know your place."

"Are you threatening me, Fidelis Jes?"

"I don't threaten people, General. I just remind them who I am."

Vlora bit back a retort. The last thing she needed was a dick-measuring contest. Fidelis Jes was famous for his early morning duels, as well as his rule against using sorcery. She had no doubt that a fight between them without sorcery would be a close one. But she was a powder mage. A sniff of black powder and she would tear through his Blackhats like so much rabble. *Perhaps,* she thought to herself, *I've become too arrogant. Perhaps I need to be cautious.* She glanced at the ring on his thumb. "Is Styke still at large?"

"Styke has been dealt with."

Vlora reappraised the blood soaking through his clean shirt and the sweat on his brow when she first entered. Even now he was still flushed. She felt a moment of disquiet. Did he just fight Styke? After seeing what Styke did to the dragonman she couldn't imagine a normal man living through a fight with him, though Styke had been hurting pretty badly when he left. Whether or not it had been a fair fight, Fidelis Jes was still standing—and he had Styke's knife and ring.

He looked pretty smug about it, too, so maybe he did kill Styke himself.

"I'm moving the timeline up," Jes said suddenly. "Things have changed, and we need Mama Palo apprehended immediately."

"Excuse me?" Vlora didn't bother to hide her shock. "I have six more weeks."

"Not anymore."

"I've put plans in motion to take care of this peacefully."

"I don't care," Jes responded. "Bring in Mama Palo. You have three days."

"That leaves me no other option than to march in there with an army to try to find her. It'll be a bloodbath."

"As I said: You're mercenaries. You're paid to kill and die. Your illusions of solving this with a little community outreach may be laudable, but don't pretend to be something you aren't."

Vlora stiffened. "I'd like to speak with the Lady Chancellor."

"The Lady Chancellor has more important things to do than waste time with a mercenary commander. Your men will receive a bonus for the change in the timeline, but you're expected to fulfill your contract."

Vlora felt like she'd been slapped. Anger churned inside her, threatening again and again to come out in words she would doubtless regret more than what she'd already said. Jes thought he was putting her in her place, but he was only pissing her off. The problem was she could do little about it. If it were just herself she would call him out and cut him down. But she had responsibilities—she had men to keep safe. He was right—this was not Adro, and she was not among friends.

But marching into Greenfire Depths was not going to do her men any favors.

She pushed down her anger, trying to think clearly. Why was he moving up the timeline? Did it have something to do with the Dynize in Greenfire Depths? Jes was peeved, maybe even shaken. Perhaps from his fight with Styke—if that's indeed what happened—or perhaps from something else.

What wasn't he telling her?

"I'll see it done," Vlora finally said, wrestling the words out.

"Very good." Jes pointedly moved a file into the center of his desk, looking down at it in obvious dismissal. Vlora hesitated a moment, and then left.

Her honor guard—an insistence by Olem, who trusted the Blackhats almost as little as he trusted the Palo—stood just outside the Millinery. They had been joined by one of her men on horseback. The soldier tipped his cap. "Ma'am, message from Colonel Olem."

Vlora pulled herself into her saddle, sighing. "It's not good news, is it?"

"There's been another attack."

Shit. "Where?"

"Just inside Greenfire Depths. Meln-Dun was on a survey mission with a whole platoon."

Vlora tugged on the reins, turning her horse around toward Loel's Fort and urging it into a canter. Pit and damnation, Meln-Dun was the key to her entire strategy in the Depths. Even if her hand was forced to violence, she needed *some* kind of ally there.

The messenger kept pace. "We've thirteen casualties, but the platoon managed to pull out."

"And Meln-Dun?"

"Barely escaped with his life. One of our boys took a bullet for him."

Vlora bent over her saddle and urged her horse on harder, yelling for traffic to get out of her way.

*   *   *

Vlora swept through a report of the violence—an ambush by Palo insurgents in a narrow street in Greenfire Depths—and rushed into the fort administration office, where a shell-shocked Meln-Dun was having a gash on his face stitched up by a Riflejack medic.

The Palo businessman stared over her shoulder, frowning at nothing the first several times Vlora said his name. Finally he seemed to snap out of it, waving off the medic and meeting Vlora's gaze. He licked his lips, clearing his throat, but couldn't seem to be able to find anything to say. Vlora had seen this kind of thing before among green recruits or ordinary citizens caught in unexpected violence. Ambushes were terrifying no matter how experienced you were, and one in such a claustrophobic place like the Depths would be doubly so.

"It's all right," Vlora said, putting a hand on Meln-Dun's shoulder. "I already got the report. I know what happened."

"They attacked me," Meln-Dun responded, eyes wide. "I'm trying to help them. I'm one of them!"

"They attacked my soldiers," Vlora assured him.

"But I was there." Meln-Dun touched his chest. "I was standing right there in the open where they could easily see me. My own people were down there with us. They killed Seren-Tel and Eleuia."

"His surveyor and an assistant," the medic explained quietly.

"I've been working with Seren-Tel for twenty years. He's been a foreman at my quarry. I was going to..." Meln-Dun choked up, unable to speak any further.

Vlora exchanged a glance with the medic, who no doubt would like his patient left alone to collect himself. But Vlora didn't have time to leave Meln-Dun to grieve. Pushing him would be a risk, but Fidelis Jes had given her an ultimatum and Vlora saw a way to get what she wanted without marching her whole army into the Depths.

"Who do you think did this?" she asked gently.

Meln-Dun averted his eyes, like a child who doesn't want to tattle on a friend. Finally he said, "I believe it was Mama Palo's men. No, I know it was Mama Palo's men. I recognized one of her enforcers among the attackers."

"And you're sure they saw you in the crossfire?"

"I'm sure." Meln-Dun shifted and allowed the medic to finish the stitches. "Lady Flint, I don't think I should keep this from you."

"What?"

"I believe they *were* coming for me."

"Why would you say that?"

Meln-Dun waited until the medic had finished the stitches and Vlora had dismissed him. Once they were alone the Palo businessman seemed to gather his wits a little better, soaking the fresh stitches with a washcloth and cleaning the blood from his face. Vlora watched him the whole time, silently urging him to spit it out. She needed him to talk. This could be her opportunity to turn him against Mama Palo.

"I made a discovery this morning," he finally admitted. "Mama Palo is working with the Dynize."

Vlora circled around Meln-Dun and took a seat behind her desk. She leaned back in her chair, absorbing the information. Part of her wanted to be surprised, but it was the final piece of a puzzle that she didn't even know existed. *Of course* Mama Palo was working with the Dynize. They'd infiltrated the Depths, and Mama Palo ruled the Depths. If even the Blackhats knew about them then she must as well. It made complete sense that she was in cahoots with them.

"To what end?" Vlora asked, not caring if it revealed her previous knowledge of the Dynize.

Meln-Dun didn't seem to notice. "I'm not entirely sure. Some of us have suspected it for months, but I wasn't certain until this morning. I was at the Yellow Hall paying my respects when I took a wrong turn—the hall can be confusing even for those familiar with it—and entered a room with dozens of foreigners."

"You're sure they were Dynize?"

"Positive. Dynize and Palo may look the same to you Kressians, but to us the difference is as night and day. They didn't seem at all happy to be found, and I hurried from the place in fear of my life. I returned home, then came immediately here. I thought the safest place to be would be among your soldiers. At least until I could get word from my people whether I was in trouble with Mama Palo."

Vlora drummed her fingers on her desk, trying to decide what to do. Did she risk pushing him? "How can you be sure they came for you?"

"It would just be another reason," Meln-Dun said. "My deal with you... Well, to be honest, I haven't been entirely forthright. I told you Mama Palo knew about it, but I didn't say she disapproved. Her anger over my defiance, and my discovery of her Dynize allies... that ambush was meant for me."

So Meln-Dun had lied to her. The fact that he had been willing to work with her against Mama Palo's wishes had to be a good thing, didn't it? Vlora opened her mouth, then closed it again, rethinking her strategy. If she suggested an all-out coup against Mama Palo he might refuse. Some people could be mad about loyalty. But if *he* suggested it...

"I can offer you my protection while you're here at the fort," she said. "But beyond that I'm afraid there's little I can do. My soldiers are here to keep the peace and help with construction efforts, not interfere in the politics of the Depths."

"I appreciate it, but I—" Meln-Dun was cut off by a knock on the door. Vlora was surprised to find a Palo on the other side. "One of my assistants," Meln-Dun explained. "May we have the room for the moment?"

Vlora waited outside for almost five minutes, pacing the fort office and drumming her fingers on the wall. Her heart was beating double-time. She had a decision to make, and she couldn't hold Meln-Dun's hand through it all. She needed to either prepare her soldiers for an all-out invasion of Greenfire Depths, or figure out a way to get Meln-Dun's help in a coup against Mama Palo.

A sob broke her concentration. She crossed to her office door and listened for a moment, only for the door to open in her face. The messenger withdrew, leaving Meln-Dun looking pale and shaken. "I've just heard word from my quarry," he explained in a monotone.

"Yes?" Vlora urged gently.

"Mama Palo's men have seized my assets in the Depths. My quarry, my home, my family. You remember my business partner, Enna? She was found murdered in her home not a half-dozen blocks from here. To be so brazen!" Meln-Dun's expression hardened. "This has gone too far. Mama Palo must be stopped. I don't know what to do. I don't know which is worse—that I must flee my own people, or the prospect of going to the Blackhats for help."

This was exactly what Vlora had been waiting for. She leaned over Meln-Dun, trying not to appear too eager. "You know the Yellow Hall well?"

"Of course."

"Mama Palo's own chambers?"

"I do."

"Then," Vlora said, going to the door to summon a messenger, "I think we can help each other."

CHAPTER 37

Michel reached deep into the depths of his memory to find the tiny marble he'd stored there so many years ago. He handled it delicately, cracking it open like an egg and letting all of the thoughts, hopes, ambitions, and memories flood out into his mind. The outpouring of emotion was so sudden that, even though he knew it was coming, he lowered his head and began to weep.

It took him over an hour to regain control. He struggled to reconcile two different personalities with two very different sets of goals until, finally, they were one again and he remembered who he really was: Michel Bravis, a Son of the Red Hand and to his knowledge the only Palo to ever infiltrate the Blackhats to the rank of Silver Rose.

Taniel stood silently through the entire process, watching him curiously, a slight frown on his face. Michel used Taniel's face as a lifeline to his old self—the one he'd been before he joined the Blackhats—staring back into those cold blue eyes while his breathing normalized and his hands stopped shaking.

Michel dried the tears from his eyes and within moments found himself laughing. It began as a chuckle, bubbling up unbidden and escaping through his clenched teeth, and was soon a whole-hearted guffaw. He slapped his knees, bending over to try to catch his breath.

"What's so funny?" Taniel asked.

Michel, once again, regained control. "It's just I've barely slept in over a week trying to find the person who printed *Sins of Empire*, and after chasing him through the bloody streets I come to find out it's the very man I work for."

Taniel gave a sardonic smirk. "You almost caught me down in the Factory District. I would have felt a lot better about things if I'd known it was you on my tail." His face finally cracked into a smile and he seemed to relax, sitting down across from Michel and reaching for the skin of tea.

"If I'd caught you, it might have compromised my cover."

Taniel made a noncommittal sound. "Perhaps. Perhaps not."

Michel considered all the close calls and lucky breaks over the last two weeks, and then tried to think of them from Taniel's perspective. The whole thing had been a game of cat-and-mouse, only for them both to find out that there'd never actually been a mouse to begin with. It was a little humiliating, if he was being honest with himself, but he decided that if no one found out he could live with it in private.

"The face thing," he asked. "Sorcery?"

Taniel nodded.

"I didn't know that was possible. Can't other Privileged detect that kind of thing?"

"It's..." Taniel paused. "Very well done. Sorcery woven to cover sorcery. Not even another powder mage can detect me. Unfortunately, it's going to take a long time to reapply now that I've let it drop."

Michel winced. "Sorry."

"You had no way of knowing," Taniel reassured him. "Besides,

I thought it important for you to see my face." He suddenly leaned forward, peering into Michel's eyes. Michel tapped his foot with nervous energy. He didn't know everything about Taniel—there were a lot of rumors in the newspapers back during and after the Adran-Kez War, including the suggestion that he'd killed a god—but he did know that, at the very least, he was a powder mage not to be trifled with. "You do," Taniel asked, "remember your mission?"

Michel considered Taniel a friend, but no more than he might consider a friendly cave lion a pet. He nodded slowly. "Infiltrate the Blackhats. Gain their trust. Climb the ranks. Be indispensable."

"And?" Taniel asked.

"And wait," Michel said.

Taniel gave a satisfied smile. "Very good."

The waiting, Michel had decided, was the hardest part of being a spy. That's why he created the marble; that's why he stored the *real* him in a tiny corner of his mind and locked it away. If he could become someone else entirely, then the waiting no longer existed and he could carry on happily, untethered, until the moment it was time to change sides.

Becoming an actual spy for the Blackhats—a double agent working as a double agent—had been supremely difficult because he could not become someone else entirely. He was still Michel Bravis with a history and a family and friends and a heritage. He wanted nothing more than to make his mother proud of her Palo boy, working for a Palo cause, but instead he'd had to hurt her deeply by becoming the very thing she hated most—a member of the secret police.

Lucky for him, he was very good at compartmentalizing his emotions. But he wasn't perfect. "What am I waiting for?"

Taniel frowned. "You know better than to ask that."

Compartmentalize. *If I don't actually know my final goal, then I won't be able to spill it if my cover is blown and I'm tortured.* "I know," Michel said, taking a deep breath. "But sometimes..."

"You want to know that it's worth the trouble?"

Michel nodded.

"I won't fill your head with false promises," Taniel said.

"You've never claimed to."

Taniel reached over and placed his hand on the back of Michel's neck, grasping him in a brotherly embrace. He peered deep into his eyes, as if looking for something. There was a long, uncomfortable silence before Taniel pulled back, a thoughtful scowl on his face. "You're a Silver Rose now?"

Michel showed him the Silver Rose looped around his neck.

"Do you think you have a shot at becoming a Gold Rose?"

"I do," Michel said, then corrected himself. "Well, I did. Fidelis Jes is furious about the Iron Roses you stole. He promised to make me a Gold Rose if I brought you in."

"And if you fail to bring me in?"

"I'll be demoted." Michel didn't have to mention that a demotion would destroy years of hard work. The very thought made him anxious, tightening something deep in the pit of his stomach.

Taniel nodded, his thoughts seemingly far away. "We need you in the Blackhats more than ever right now."

Michel raised his eyebrows. He wondered briefly if Taniel was dedicated enough to the cause to hand himself over, but rejected the idea. Taniel *was* the Red Hand. Without him, the change that they wished to enact would never come about. "I might be able to string Fidelis Jes along for a couple more weeks. But he's already impatient, and something has him on edge. I can't guarantee that he won't pull me from the mission any day now."

"Do Silver Roses have access to Blackhat records?" Taniel asked.

He obviously had something in mind, but Michel needed to be careful in his questioning. If Taniel revealed too much, their whole effort could be at risk. "Some of them."

"Anything regarding sorcery?"

"No," Michel said. "Absolutely not. I know they exist—the Blackhats keep information on all the Knacked, powder mages, and Privileged in Fatrasta *and* the Nine. But that kind of information is only privy to the Gold Roses, Fidelis Jes, the Lady Chancellor, and Lindet's private cabal."

"Right," Taniel said, chewing his words like he had something sour in his mouth. "But a Gold Rose could find out about sorcerous artifacts?"

"I . . . think so?"

Taniel sat back, drumming his gloved fingers on the head of his cane. "I'm not sure if *think so* is good enough."

"If it's not . . ."

"It'll have to be," Taniel suddenly said, shooting to his feet and pacing the length of the room. "We need information, Michel. We think the Lady Chancellor is looking for something called the godstones, and we need to know how close she is to them."

Michel sat up straight. His assignment had always been so vague; this was the first time he'd been given any indication of a clear goal. It was electrifying. And frightening. "I can't find out that information as a Silver Rose."

"Then we'll have to get you your Gold," Taniel said, consulting a pocket watch. "Be back here in eighteen hours. Bring lots of friends."

Michel got to his feet, feeling slightly dizzy at the sudden changes to his mission. This was *happening*. "What am I going to find?"

"You," Taniel said, heading toward the door, "are going to find exactly what Fidelis Jes wants."

CHAPTER 38

Why am I still alive?

It was the foremost question in Styke's mind as he was pulled roughly from the back of the Blackhat paddy wagon and carried through the darkness. A dozen hands held him by the shoulders and legs, carrying him like a corpse, letting him swing and bump around every corner, his ass hitting every rock they crossed. The stink of the marshes filled his nostrils like the recurrence of a bad dream, and he knew from the creak of the gate, the cold breeze, and that horrid stench that he was back in the labor camp where he'd spent the last ten years of his life.

It wasn't supposed to happen this way. Jes was supposed to die, squealing like a pig, and Styke soon after him. What had gone wrong? Was Styke overconfident? Was he too wounded and worn out from his fight with the dragonman? Was he too crippled and old? Or was Fidelis Jes just that good?

Likely he'd never know.

His carriers constantly dropped him, their hands slipping on the slick blood that coated his body. Each scrape or jolt sent another lance of pain through his body. His once-good hand had gone completely numb, and the stab wound in his leg and shoulder both screamed out. He bit down on his tongue until he couldn't feel that, either, and wondered whether he'd bitten clear through it.

What did it matter if he did?

He kept his eyes closed—it was pitch-black but for the occasional lantern, so there wasn't much to see anyway—but he heard doors open and close, felt himself change directions a number of times, and when they finally came to a stop he guessed he was in the labor camp infirmary.

"On the count of three," a male voice said over his shoulder. "One, two, hup!"

Styke was half-lifted, half-thrown on a cold marble slab. He inhaled sharply, using all his focus not to scream. By the pit, this hurt. No, he decided, this had gone beyond hurt. He was cut up, humiliated, and his wrist...he'd never hold a knife again. He might not even hold a cup again.

"He's all yours," the voice said. "You, stitch him up. And the rest of you—the grand master wants him to heal for a few months, then you can do anything you want to him, short of killing him."

Styke heard the shuffle of feet leaving the room and finally opened his eyes. He found himself the focus of four guards and the camp doctor, a squirrelly little man by the name of Set. The infirmary had been cleared of patients and Styke was lying on one of the morgue slabs in the far corner.

The others gathered around him in a semicircle, and when he blinked one said, "Son of a bitch, he's still awake."

Styke let his head fall to one side and identified the speaker as Vladiar, a Rosvelean with a high-pitched voice and a neck as thick as a melon. He was the one whose cousin Styke had attacked after the parole hearing a few weeks ago. In fact, Styke recognized all four of the guards. They were Jeffron, Landral, and Zach, the most infamous guards in Sweetwallow.

"I can't believe he's still alive," Landral said. He had a wonky lip, and drool tended to slip out the side when he talked. He wiped away a rope of it with his sleeve.

"All that blood on him his?" Zach asked.

Vladiar grunted. "That's what the Bronze Rose said."

"Nobody bleeds that much and lives through it." That was put forward by Set, the doctor. Styke focused his eyes on the needle and thread clutched in one of Set's hands and the way they trembled. Set hadn't been a good doctor *before* he got the palsy. "Don't know how they expect us to keep him alive."

"Us? You, more like," Vladiar said. "We're just here to make sure he doesn't tear you in half."

Set paced from one side of the infirmary to the other, needle held in thumb and forefinger, the other hand on his chin. "Have you seen him? He's not going anywhere. The tendon is slit on that wrist—he'll never use it again—and that knife wound on his leg looks deep. Probably won't walk, either." He approached Styke and bent down to look him in the eye. Styke stared back, impassive, all his efforts going to keep himself from whimpering.

"We best get some straps," Set said. "Landral, fetch some of that rope they use for the sledges."

Landral scoffed, but headed out of the room.

Vladiar pushed Set out of the way and hunkered down at eye level with Styke. "You in there, big man?" He waved his hand over Styke's eyes. "Yeah, you're there. Kresimir, you're hard to kill. You remember what I told you a few weeks ago? I told you that you're nothing but a killer. Looks like you weren't even good enough at that, if what the rumors say are true." He harrumphed. "I must be a prophet, boys, because I told him he'd be back and look at that: He's back."

Styke closed his eyes. He knew the pain hadn't even begun. He'd take months to recover, and once he did the guards would make him wish he hadn't. It would be an endless cycle of beatings and hatred until the end of his days and he didn't even have one good hand left to fight back with.

The labor camp had never truly broken him, but this... this might.

"What happened to that kid you took out with you?" Vladiar asked.

Styke's eyes shot open. Vladiar was right there, close enough Styke could smell the cabbage on his breath. There was a shallow smile on Vladiar's lips, and he tapped the side of Styke's head. "I remember her. And I remember how you broke my cousin's leg. I'm gonna find that girl. I'll bring her back here, and I'll hand her over to the boys while you sit there and watch. I'll cut the tendons on the back of your legs and laugh when you try to crawl over to help her."

Styke bit his tongue again, suppressing the pain. He took a few breaths and felt every little cut react to the movement of his chest. He was tapped out. He had nothing left. "Good luck," he whispered.

"What the pit is that supposed to mean?"

Styke flopped his arm backward, nearly passing out from the pain of the stab wound in his shoulder. His hand might be useless, but he could still move, and he managed to wrap a forearm around Vladiar's neck and jerk him downward against the marble slab. There was a crunch, and Vladiar gave a whimpering cry and he collapsed.

"Holy shit!"

"Grab him."

The two remaining guards leapt into action, Zach going to Vladiar's side and Jeffron hammering a fist down into the wound on Styke's thigh. Styke gasped and rolled toward Jeffron, coming off the slab with more momentum than he'd expected. Jeffron caught him and almost kept his feet, but Styke slammed his forehead between Jeffron's eyes. The guard dropped like a sack of potatoes.

Styke slumped backward, the slab creaking on its frame. His breath came short and painful, and he put all his weight on his elbow. He got his leg beneath him and managed to fling himself around the slab and onto Zach, who was just getting up from his examination of Vladiar. The two went down in a heap, and Styke ground his chin first into one eye, then the other, ignoring the battering Zach gave his chest. He managed to get Zach's throat between the working fingers of his bad hand and squeezed until the other's cries were nothing more than a gurgle.

It took Styke several moments to gain his feet, but the knowledge that seconds were precious spurred him through the pain. There was nothing left of him—he was just meat on the move—and the only thought that kept him going was that he would kill every last guard in this blasted place until there wasn't anyone left to remember that he and Celine had left together.

Groans escaped his lips as he dragged himself up. This corner of the infirmary was a mess. Vladiar lay still, his head covered in blood, while Jeffron gave the occasional twitch and Zach gurgled quietly. Across the room, Set hid behind one of the infirmary cots. Styke swayed, caught himself on the slab with his crippled hand, and nodded at the doctor. "Stay there," he ordered.

Going was slow. Styke left the infirmary at a snail's pace, leaning against a wall when he could, putting the rest of his weight on the leg that *hadn't* been stabbed when he couldn't. He wondered, from time to time, what the pit he was doing. There was no escape from Sweetwallow. He certainly wasn't going to kill all the guards in his condition. They would find him in minutes. But those thoughts were fleeting and inconsequential. He was driven forward, leaving a trail of crimson behind him as he followed the long halls of the administration building past the guards' mess hall and the parole cells until he came out a side door near one of the fences.

With nothing to lean against he only made it a few steps before he fell. He caught himself on that crippled hand and lay still for several moments, listening for an alarm. The night was silent, even peaceful with the sound of crickets off in the marshes. Sweetwallow had a strict curfew, and the guards would slack off from time to time to play cards in their bunkhouse. Maybe Styke had gotten lucky. Maybe he could escape.

The pain was so bad as to cause a delirium. He remembered a time he'd been unhorsed in the middle of battle, hitting his head badly when he fell. He remembered the mud and the sound—the absolute chaos of the fight as he tried to get back to his senses. Hooves and feet had hammered the ground around him, and someone had bashed him from behind with the butt of a musket. His armor had taken the blow.

He couldn't remember what had happened next, but he could hear those hoofbeats pounding in his brain as loudly as if he were back in battle.

He squinted through the memories and focused on the cracked wooden fencing that surrounded Sweetwallow. The labor camp palisade was twenty feet tall and hardened in the sun. No breaking through and no going over the top—not in his condition.

"Ben, why did you leave me behind?"

Styke looked over his shoulder. Celine was behind him—or at least a vision of her—standing in the administration building doorway, legs planted to straddle the trail of blood he'd left. "I didn't," he managed. He forced himself up on his crippled hand, dragging himself toward the fence.

"You left me behind, Ben."

"I didn't," he insisted again, still dragging. "I took you out of this place. It was one of the only good things I've ever done, and you won't take it away from me. Ungrateful little shit." Something twinged in his shoulder and he bit down hard on his tongue before dragging himself forward another foot. "I didn't mean it," he muttered. "You've always been a good kid. I did leave you behind, but I left you with friends. Olem will take care of you. Send you to school. He's not a bad sort."

"I don't want to be with Olem. I want to be with you."

Styke reached the palisade and slapped his hand against the base. It was hard, firm. Might as well be iron. "Well," he said to the ghostly apparition of Celine. "That's too damn bad. I'm here forever, and you're out there."

"I'll get you out."

Styke raised his head, looking over his shoulder. The apparition was gone, but the voice he'd just heard sounded so real. He could feel tears in his eyes, and wondered if this was what it was like to go mad. He heard a yell somewhere inside the camp, and smiled softly as the alarm went off almost instantly. They'd find him any moment, and then...

Something warm touched his hand. It was so sudden and startling that he jerked away, gasping at the pain of the sudden movement. He peered at the base of the palisade, noticing a break in the thick wooden slats. Through the murk he thought he could see a tiny face. He blinked, cursing his eyes, then lowered his head to the cool dirt.

Brains, he decided, could play cruel jokes on their owners.

"Ben!"

Styke's head came up again. A tiny hand grasped his, tugging on his fingers.

"Ben, wake up!"

"Celine?"

"You don't look so good, Ben."

Son of a bitch. It *wasn't* a fever playing tricks on him. "Celine, you have to get away from here. They're searching the perimeter right now, and if you don't get out of here they'll find you and they'll—"

"Don't worry," Celine said, patting Styke's hand through the gap. "I brought friends."

Styke let out something halfway between a gasp and a laugh. "I don't have any friends, Celine. Get out of here."

"You do," Celine insisted. "And they're not very happy."

Styke heard a shout, and then a sudden crash farther down the camp palisade. The shouts escalated, and then pistol shots rang out, punctuated by the blast of blunderbusses and carbines. Celine was suddenly gone, and Styke reached forward weakly, grasping for her hand.

"He's down here!" he heard her shout. "On the other side of the fence!"

Styke listened, confused, to the clash of steel and the cries of the wounded. It was over in moments, and then hooves thundered toward him. He rolled onto his back, squinting at the hazy figures in the darkness. Who would possibly come for him? Was it Tampo? Was it Lady Flint?

Figures flung themselves off their horses and Styke felt himself lifted by strong but gentle hands, his back pressed against the base of the camp palisade. Torches were thrust in his face.

"Pit," a man's voice said, "he's pale as a ghost."

"Lost too much blood," another responded.

"Pit, would you look at him? I hardly recognize him."

"The blood should make it easier," someone else quipped.

Styke couldn't get his head around the voices—they were at once foreign and familiar, like a child's lullaby from the distant corners of his memory—and the sudden light of the torches blinded him. He tried to pull back as someone suddenly knelt in front of him and he could make out the unmistakable, runed gloves of a Privileged sorcerer.

Someone stood behind the sorcerer, silhouetted in the torchlight, pistol pressed against the base of the sorcerer's head.

"You have no idea who you're dealing with," the Privileged hissed.

Behind him, the silhouette responded in a husky female voice.

"We've been over this. I don't give a shit. Heal him, now. Any funny business and I'll clear your sinuses with a bullet."

"Look at him," the Privileged demanded. "This could take hours, and the process might kill him."

"I've got all the time in the world," the silhouette responded. "And you better hope it doesn't."

Styke took a ragged breath. He recognized that voice. Like the others, it was as if from a distant memory—but this one had haunted his dreams for ten long years. He felt tears running down his cheeks, his hands trembling. His eyes began to adjust to the torchlight, and he began to recognize faces standing in a semicircle around him.

Little Gamble. Ferlisia. Sunin. Chraston. Jackal.

Ibana ja Fles.

Ibana half-turned to the others, the pistol aimed at the head of the Privileged unwavering. "What the pit are you assholes waiting for? Set the inmates loose. Torch the admin buildings."

"The guards are held up in their bunkhouse," Ferlisia said.

Ibana grabbed Ferlisia by the collar, pulling her close. "Do you see what they've done to Ben? Our colonel? You set the guardhouse on fire, and shoot anyone who tries to escape. Shoot 'em in the legs and throw them back in. Pit-damned Blackhats have declared war on the Mad Lancers. They should have known better."

Styke jumped at the gentle touch of gloved fingers and felt his arm lifted to the light of the torch by the Privileged. The Privileged examined him clinically, then said quietly, "This is going to hurt. A lot."

The last thing Styke remembered was a blinding white light.

CHAPTER 39

T his is it?" Meln-Dun asked.

Vlora cocked an eyebrow at him as he stood in the doorway of the small pub back room she and a handful of chosen men had occupied on the rim of Greenfire Depths. There was some noise from the street outside, but for the most part things were quiet, peaceful. The Palo looked nonplussed, and she could see him counting the small group over and over again in his head until he finally turned to her with a pained expression. "This is not enough men."

There was a pregnant silence, only interrupted by the sound of Norrine dragging a whetstone across the blade of her sword. The scraping sound repeated twice before Vlora pointed to the man on her left. He was twenty-three and looked significantly younger with black hair and not a strand of beard on his chin. He was dressed just like her in dark green travel clothes, brown boots, high-collared shirt, and a slightly floppy tricorn that did well to hide his face. He carried a blunderbuss, nervously tapping the flared end against his boot.

"This is Davd. He was a drummer boy during the Adran-Kez War. Eleven years with the Riflejacks." She thrust a thumb to the woman on her right. "This is Norrine. She's been with the Adran Army for forty-two years. She was trained by Field Marshal Tamas himself." Norrine was an older woman with dirty-blond hair and an elfin-like face. She was nearly to her sixties, but a tight physical regimen made her look fifteen years younger. She continued to sharpen her sword, smirking at the fourth member of their group. Vlora introduced him. "Buden je Parst is Kez. Doesn't speak a word of Adran so don't bother. And Olem," Vlora finished, slapping Olem on the knee, "you've met."

Buden grinned at Meln-Dun, revealed six missing teeth. He was missing most of his tongue, too, but he preferred not to draw attention to that. Meln-Dun's pained expression deepened. "I understand your men are experienced," he said slowly, "but the Yellow Hall is guarded by the best the Palo have to offer. If the Dynize are there as I fear, there may even be dragonmen. You should take no fewer than two companies."

"Two companies," Vlora responded, "will just draw attention and slow us down. We're not going in there for a fight. We're there to smash in the door and bring in Mama Palo."

"Even still…"

Olem snorted. "Don't let her lead you on. This is the Riflejacks' dirty secret. Everyone in this room but you and me is a powder mage."

Meln-Dun's eyes widened and he swept his gaze across the small group once more. "I see. I had no idea the Riflejacks even *had* other powder mages."

"Hence the dirty little secret," Vlora said. She took a deep breath, trying to get in the right frame of mind for a night raid. She hadn't done anything like this for years, and the prospect both thrilled and scared her. Five men against a whole warren of Palo thugs was dangerous, even if four of them were powder mages. Mistakes could—*would*—be made. There would be surprises. Everything they planned could go awry the moment they stepped out the door of this pub.

Tamas had always said that a greater risk had better come with a greater reward. She was risking the very heart of the Riflejacks, but the reward was that she could accomplish the entire assignment in a single night—and she and her men walk away tomorrow with a full year's pay. Mama Palo's fall might even bring long-term stability to Greenfire Depths. The money was great, but her conscience allowing her to sleep at night was even better.

"Even with powder mages, I still don't see…" Meln-Dun began, but Norrine held up a hand.

"It'll be enough," she assured him.

The Palo finally entered the room and shut the door behind him, taking a seat. He seemed remarkably calm despite the attempt on his life earlier that day, and Vlora wondered if he'd been drinking to settle his nerves.

"Are you sure you're able to do this?" Vlora asked.

Meln-Dun gave a confident nod. "I am. I have to. They've killed my friends, taken my family and business hostage. If this does not happen tonight, I am finished." He scowled, then looked up at Vlora. "Something has been bothering me, Lady Flint."

"What's that?" Vlora mentally checked her kit, counting her powder charges, then making sure both her pistols were already loaded.

"Mama Palo told me something when we spoke last: that a known Blackhat was seen leaving your headquarters on more than one occasion."

Vlora exchanged a glance with Olem. "That is true," she said. "I've made no secret that we're employed by the state. In fact, I believe that's the reason you came to me in the first place."

"Yes, but this business with the rebuilding. Was it your main reason for being here?"

"Keeping the peace has always been our reason for being here."

Vlora swore inwardly. Was Meln-Dun getting cold feet? Did he suddenly realize how deep he was with the Palo's long-standing enemy? Surely this mustn't be news to him. She reminded herself how easy it was to be self-delusional when you had a passion.

"But," Meln-Dun pressed, "your purpose here. Were you assigned to bring down Mama Palo by the Blackhats?"

Vlora exchanged another glance with Olem, wondering if this would be a good time to lie. But, as she so often told her men, she hated a liar. "Yes."

Meln-Dun was silent for several long seconds, his tongue between his lips and his eyes on the floor. "All right. We can do this. I just wanted to know where you stood."

"Same place I've always stood," Vlora responded. "And I've never lied to you. I *do* have an interest in helping rebuild Greenfire Depths."

Meln-Dun looked away, unresponsive. Olem shrugged. Buden spat a wad of tobacco on the floor.

"It's well past time to get moving," Norrine warned.

"Agreed," Vlora said, getting to her feet. She checked her men, using her mage senses to be sure they had enough powder and their weapons primed. She took a spare pistol off the table behind Davd and held it out to Meln-Dun. "Have you fought before?"

"It's been many years," he said hesitantly.

"Take this just in case." She turned to face the others and said, "Remember, we're not here to conquer or fight or dilly-dally. We're grabbing Mama Palo and we're getting the pit out as quickly as possible. Keep your knives and swords handy. Firearms are to be kept in check unless it's absolutely necessary—if at all possible we want to be gone before they even know we've arrived. And only kill if we need to."

"There will be violence," Meln-Dun said with a frown. "Killing can't be avoided."

"I'm making as few enemies as possible tonight."

"Every one of Mama Palo's men you leave alive is another enemy on the morrow."

Olem inclined his head toward Meln-Dun in a way that said *he has a point*. Vlora shook her head at Meln-Dun. "We'll keep it as bloodless as possible, but make no mistake. We're all killers. This'll go painfully if it needs to. Let's get moving before it gets any later."

Davd led them out through the back of the pub and down a side alley, checking to be sure they weren't spotted, before motioning for Meln-Dun to go ahead. It was a quiet evening, a weeknight curfew in effect by order of Lindet, and they were nearly alone on the dark streets of the plateau.

Meln-Dun took a deep breath and stashed his pistol beneath his shirt before he led them along a series of winding streets. They crossed boulevards and back alleys running parallel to the Rim overlooking the Depths before finally taking a small, little-used path behind someone's house down into a narrow hallway cut into the very rock of the plateau.

They descended rapidly into the cool stone passage, the steps becoming impossibly steep, and only a quick pinch of powder snorted in each nostril gave Vlora enough night vision to see what she was doing. She heard the others preparing themselves likewise. At the front, Meln-Dun seemed to navigate confidently despite the pitch-black, and behind her Olem kept a hand on her belt, cursing from time to time as he stubbed a toe or bashed his elbow on the side of the quarry.

Their descent was arrested suddenly as Meln-Dun stopped to fiddle with a door, and a moment later they were on flat ground once again.

"Ground," Vlora corrected herself, wasn't the word for it. They had certainly not gone all the way to the bottom of Greenfire Depths, and as they walked down what appeared to be plastered hallways, their footsteps echoed like they were tramping along the scaffolding of a tenement construction site and felt only slightly more stable.

This appeared to be some sort of highway, and despite the twists and turns the corridor remained wide with small shop windows along either side and the occasional Palo family sitting along the walls with a gas lamp, taking a late meal or enjoying gossip with the neighbors. For the most part Vlora's small group was ignored, and when they reached the next junction she asked Meln-Dun about it.

"We're in what we call the Cobweb right now," he explained. "Suspended fifty feet above the floor of the Depths, some of these halls span the entire length of the quarry. It's much safer up here, but Kressians are never allowed." He put an emphasis on "never" and Vlora lowered the brim of her hat slightly, glancing over her shoulder.

They continued on for what felt like miles until Meln-Dun suddenly held up a hand. They came to a stop behind him. The Cobweb was much more active here, even more active than the streets up on the plateau, and the group had begun to receive more than one curious glance. Things were even better lit here, too.

"What's going on?" Vlora asked, gesturing for Olem to drop back with Norrine to watch their rear.

Meln-Dun pointed through an arched passage to a door a little farther on. "We're getting close to the Yellow Hall. Mama Palo's men patrol this area heavily. We're going to have to go down now, but we may encounter guards, starting just behind that door."

Vlora gestured to Davd, tapped her eyes, and pointed at the door. The young powder mage crossed the hall quickly, slinging his blunderbuss over his shoulder, and pressed gently on the door. Vlora counted to five, then followed.

Just inside lay a Palo man in a pale green uniform, slumped on his side. Davd tapped the side of the man's head. "He'll live, but he'll have a pit of a headache when he wakes up."

"Let's be in and gone before he does," Vlora said.

They were joined by the others, and Meln-Dun frowned at the unconscious Palo. "Those are the uniforms Mama Palo's personal guard wear. You shouldn't leave them alive."

"Yeah, you said that," Vlora responded, feeling a bit peeved. Meln-Dun was a businessman, but in her experience the strangest people could get overtaken by bloodlust when they had power over others. "There's no reason to kill him. Let's keep moving."

They descended two more levels down a narrow staircase, then a ladder, before Meln-Dun stopped them again. "We're here."

"Already?" Vlora asked.

"That was quick," Norrine commented.

Meln-Dun tossed aside a carpet to reveal a trapdoor. "We won't be able to come back this way," he said.

Vlora found out why a moment later. Below the door was a ten-foot drop to what appeared to be old clay shingles. She had a moment of confusion before she finally chuckled. "We're above the Yellow Hall. That's the original roof, isn't it?"

"It is," Meln-Dun answered. "The Cobweb was built above and around everything that existed in Greenfire Depths before, with the exception of some of the houses near the working quarries."

"Is that roof going to hold us?" Norrine asked.

Vlora glanced down into the darkness. "I hope so."

Davd went first, dropping down onto the clay shingles, scrabbling for purchase before getting a good footing. Vlora tossed down his weapons, then her own, and lowered herself down from the trapdoor by her arms before letting go. Davd caught her, helping her get her footing, before aiding the rest of the group down. Norrine came last, lowering the trapdoor gently onto her fingers before taking the drop.

They spread out across the roof, checking their weapons in the darkness before creeping along to the very edge of the shingles. Vlora could sense a steep drop below her—probably three stories or more—and wondered how they were going to get down. She and the other mages could make that jump without suffering damage, but Olem and Meln-Dun would break a leg.

Meln-Dun provided the answer a moment later, showing them to a small belfry that rose above the roof. Vlora joined them just as a few sharp words broke out.

"You've been planning this," Davd hissed.

Meln-Dun recoiled. Vlora shushed Davd and turned to Meln-Dun, only to find the Palo was not denying the accusation. "What does he mean?" she asked him.

"I mean," Davd answered, "all of this. The roof, the trapdoor, this belfry. He had to have planned this out well ahead of time."

"Don't mind me," Olem whispered. "Can't see a damn thing because I'm not a bloody powder mage. I'll just stand here in the dark until you've got this sorted out."

"He's been planning this," Davd insisted.

Vlora glanced quizzically at Meln-Dun before remembering that he couldn't see in the dark, either. He was doing all this by feel. "Well?" she asked.

"I..." There was an uncomfortably long pause, then Meln-Dun said in a defeated tone, "I've considered the need to remove Mama Palo for several months. She's been getting worse, more erratic, harder to negotiate with. I knew something would have to be done. I planned out this route several weeks ago, thinking I would be bringing Blackhats or Palo mercenaries in here to assassinate Mama Palo."

"Assassinate" was a dangerous word for a businessman. The idea bothered Vlora, but she thrust it aside. It turned out Meln-Dun was using them just as much as she was using him, and somehow that made her feel a little less guilty. "It's too late to quibble now. Get us through here."

"The belfry is boarded up from the inside. We'll have to break through it."

Davd thumped on the boards. "That feels pretty tight."

"It's going to make a pit of a lot of noise," Olem warned.

Vlora vacillated for a moment. She might be able to drop down and find another way in, then make her way back up to pry the boards off from the inside. But the Yellow Hall was an enormous house, and she could just as easily get herself lost and cornered. More important than staying silent was staying together.

"The belfry leads into the old master suite," Meln-Dun said. "It's where Mama Palo lives and holds court."

"We're above her court right now?" Vlora demanded.

"Yes."

"Making a damned racket. They probably already know there's someone up here." Vlora reached out with her senses, trying to find everyone within a hundred yards with the slightest bit of powder on them. She felt her other mages doing the same. Immediately below them there were concentrations of powder that amounted to three armed men. A fourth and fifth were coming up the stairs to the second floor of the Yellow Hall and beyond that... well, she lost count at thirty.

Mama Palo had a *lot* of bodyguards.

"Right," Vlora said, readying her pistol. "Davd, knock it in."

Davd backed up and took a running start, throwing himself against the boarded window of the belfry. There was a mighty crash and he disappeared in a swirl of dust. Vlora followed him through, helping him to his feet, while Norrine, Olem, and Buden rushed down the stairs with weapons at the ready. There was another crash as they forced a door below, and then a torrent of shouting in Adran, Palo, and Kez.

Vlora leapt down the stairs, blinking as she entered a brightly lit room. The walls were made of the same yellow limestone as the rest of the hall and decorated with candelabras and tapestries. The light came from lamps fed by haphazardly strung gas lines, and Vlora pulled up to find herself looking down the barrels of three pistols as well as the blades of another two swords.

There were five men, not three, and she suspected they would be joined by many more within a few moments.

The five Palo guards wore pale green uniforms and looked angry and startled, their faces red, fingers pulling triggers that wouldn't respond. Vlora could sense Norrine suppressing the powder in the pans, keeping the pistols from firing.

"Stop!" Vlora said, drawing her sword. "There's no need for bloodshed." She hoped to pit that they understood Adran, because her Palo was terrible. "We're here for Mama Palo. No one has to get hurt."

Behind the five men Vlora spotted an old woman lounging on a divan in the center of the room. She had a regal bearing, her chin held high, and she wore faded old buckskins and no jewelry like the Palo one might find deep in the Tristan Basin. She looked to be well into her seventies, hands shaking with rheumatism, and Vlora had a sudden pang of guilt.

This was who was causing so much trouble? *This* was who Vlora had come for? Could she bring herself to drag an old woman to the Blackhats and watch her hang?

The old woman seemed unafraid, even dismissive. "Kill them," she said in Palo.

That Vlora understood. "Keep the noise down!" Vlora hissed, sidestepping a sword thrust and drawing the tip of her own small-sword across a Palo's throat.

Mama Palo's bodyguards were good. *Very* good. Within moments Vlora could tell that they were trained fighting men, and the fact they lasted longer than half a breath against four powder mages was a miracle in and of itself. But they didn't last long, and only Buden wound up with a slice along his arm for their efforts and five dead or dying Palo soon lay on the floor.

"Davd, get the door," Vlora said, motioning toward the entrance. She could hear feet pounding in the hallways outside, and Davd and Olem reached it in time to throw their weight against several people trying to shove their way in. "Buden, clean yourself up. Norrine, secure the old woman. Wait, where…" Vlora's question was choked off in midsentence as she turned toward Mama Palo's divan.

Mama Palo knelt beside it, speaking frantically in Palo, hands in the air. Meln-Dun held his pistol against her head, and he pulled the trigger before Vlora could order him to stand down.

Vlora's instincts were faster than her tongue, and the powder in the pan of the pistol sizzled briefly but did not take as she reached out with her senses and suppressed the blast. She crossed the room in three strides and snatched the pistol away from Meln-Dun, tossing it to Norrine. "No! I made it clear we're taking her in."

She was surprised to see real hate in Meln-Dun's eyes. He sneered down at the old woman. "She deserves to die."

"Perhaps. But she's going to hang—this will be state justice, not ours."

"And that makes it better?"

"It has to," Vlora spat, "or else we're all just animals."

"The Blackhats will torture her. This is a kindness."

The statement brought Vlora up short as she realized he was probably right. She'd just been asking herself if she could hand an old woman over to face the noose, and she'd decided in a flash that she could. She had, after all, lost good men to Mama Palo's people. But to hand an old woman over to the Blackhat torturers? "I'm not here to do a kindness." She put herself between Meln-Dun and Mama Palo and helped the old woman to her feet. "Do you speak Adran?" She repeated the question again for Kez. Mama Palo ignored her.

"She speaks Adran and Kez just fine," Meln-Dun spat.

"You," Vlora said to him, pointing to the other side of the room. "Over there. And you, Mama Palo, are under arrest in the name of the Lady Chancellor for crimes against the state."

"Is it a crime to want to be free?" the old woman said in perfect Adran.

"In this country? Most definitely." Vlora handed the old woman over to Norrine, then joined Davd and Olem by the door. There was a steady thumping on the other side, and the latch had already broken. The wood itself would give way at any moment. "Hold!" Vlora shouted. "We've got Mama Palo. If you want her to see the dawn, you'll let us out of here peacefully!"

The thumping stopped, until Mama suddenly shouted something in Palo. There was an answering yell, and then the thumping redoubled.

"She told them to kill us no matter what happens to her," Meln-Dun reported.

"Norrine, keep her quiet!"

"Perhaps," Olem said, grunting as a particularly hard blow on the door almost threw him on his ass, "you shouldn't have told her we're handing her over to the Blackhats."

Davd began swearing colorfully when a jagged bit of the door splintered off and buried itself in his shoulder. "Here," Vlora said, taking his place. "Meln-Dun, what exactly was your plan to get out of here?"

"My plan was to kill Mama Palo and show her head to her guards. To take power."

"That actually works?" Davd asked.

"That's awfully tribal for a businessman," Olem said.

"Power is all they understand." Meln-Dun's voice was cold, angry, and for a moment he seemed like an entirely different person.

Vlora had a pang of doubt, wondering if she'd backed the wrong horse, before casting it aside. Too late now. "I think you underestimate your own people. You would have just gotten yourself killed very slowly."

"This door has seconds left," Olem hissed.

"All right. So much for not making any noise." Vlora closed her eyes, focusing on the powder that she sensed just outside the door. There were at least seven people out there, and she found their powder and, with a thought, ignited it. She used her sorcery to warp the blasts, containing it, focusing the explosions in small spaces to minimize the chance of starting a fire.

The blasts rattled the ceiling, causing plaster dust to sprinkle on their shoulders. The thumping stopped, and Olem immediately leapt away from the door, jerking it open, his pistol at the ready.

There were a lot more than seven people in the hall. At least nine had been killed by the blast, and another eight milled around, mouths open, fingers in ears as they tried to get back their hearing. The closest drew his sword, but Olem put a bullet in his chest. Vlora shot a second, and then Davd forced his way between them and a roar of his blunderbuss put the rest of the hall on their backs.

The hallway was a bloody mess of mangled bodies and crying, moaning wounded. Vlora forced herself to ignore the carnage. "Quickly," she said, leading her mages down the hall. She felt powder moving toward them and ignited it, using the same technique to warp the blast inward. She felt her energy ebb slightly with every effort, the sorcery bleeding away at her reserves in little jumps as she used it.

They cleared three more halls and made the ground floor, where Meln-Dun examined the latest carnage with an edge of disgust. "I thought you said no killing."

"I said I didn't want to kill," Vlora snapped back. "Maybe if you had a better exit strategy we wouldn't have to." She swore, furious with both Meln-Dun for his half-wit plan and with herself for agreeing to it so eagerly. She'd been too desperate to spare her men a fight.

Three men with swords faced them in the main hall where Vlora had attended the party less than a week before. She took them alone, snorting powder for a fresh trance before carving through them as quickly as she was able, making it as painless as possible. These men, unlike the ones upstairs, were clumsy and overenthusiastic. They never stood a chance.

She would have preferred to disable and move on, but her training was not in that kind of combat.

As Ben Styke had told her, she was a killer.

They fought through another six guards before getting out of the Yellow Hall. Meln-Dun led them down several side corridors before finding stairs to take them up, assuring them that the Cobweb gave them a far better chance of escape than being on the ground.

Vlora lagged behind, checking and rechecking her men with every step. Both Davd and Buden were wounded, and Norrine practically had to carry Mama Palo, but they were all present and accounted for. They reached the Cobweb, where Olem dispatched a Palo in a pale green uniform, and then they were running along the same corridor that had brought them to the Yellow Hall.

They made it all the way to their exit unopposed, and Vlora almost shouted with joy when she saw starlight overhead and they came out on the Rim. She looked back on the uneven lights of Greenfire Depths, her heart thumping hard.

They had made it. Six men in and six men out, and they had snatched Mama Palo from the very heart of her power. The old woman threw herself to the ground, forcing Norrine to lift her like a sack of potatoes and toss her over a shoulder. The sight angered Vlora, and she found herself wishing the old woman would go with some dignity.

It would certainly be more convenient.

Vlora didn't know how many Palo they had slaughtered on the way out. At least forty, she estimated. The poor bastards probably didn't know what hit them, and she wondered if there was any way to keep her name out of the entire affair.

A powder mage in Greenfire Depths? They would *have* to know it was her.

The Blackhats were waiting outside the gates of Loel's Fort. Vlora escorted Mama Palo into the back of the Blackhat prison wagon herself, and watched as a silent pair of Iron Roses locked the door. There was a whole company on guard, almost as many as they'd brought for Ben Styke. She searched their chests until she saw the dangling medallion of a Bronze Rose.

"Where's Michel Bravis?" she asked. "He was supposed to be here."

"Agent Bravis is busy," the Bronze Rose responded. "He'll be pleased about this, though. We've been working a long time to bring this bitch in."

Vlora bit her tongue, then couldn't help but ask, "What's going to happen to her?"

The Bronze Rose's eyebrows went up. "An example, that's what."

"Torture?" Olem asked, a dangerous note to his voice. He didn't like the prospect any more than Vlora did. She reached out in the darkness to gently touch his hand in warning.

"Nah," the Bronze Rose said with a note of regret. "She's going to hang within days. The grand master doesn't want any chance of a rescue attempt or riots. For the best, I suppose."

"For the best," Vlora echoed, allowing herself a silent sigh of relief.

The Blackhats were gone within moments, and Vlora found herself watching until the prison wagon was out of sight. She wondered about how quickly it had all gone. An hour ago Mama Palo had been challenging Lindet herself for control of a significant part of Landfall, and now she was just another criminal ready for the noose.

All thanks to Vlora and her mages. It soured her stomach a little, and she needed somewhere to spit, and a drink to get the bad taste out of her mouth.

"Lady Flint."

Vlora looked up to find Meln-Dun beside her. The anger and spite the Palo had shown during the kidnapping was gone, replaced with his normal placid calm. She wondered whether she'd seen a truer side to him, or if the stress of the mission had brought out something dark. The latter was not unheard-of.

"Well done," she told him.

"To you as well. I can't thank you enough, Lady Flint. It may take a week or two to calm things down in the Depths, but I'll have my people begin a purge of Mama Palo's followers immediately. I think a time of peace and prosperity is due in Landfall."

"I certainly hope so," Vlora answered. "And you'll be able to get your family back safe?"

"Yes, I believe so. I'll see to that tonight."

Vlora raised her eyebrows as Meln-Dun turned to leave. "Do you need an escort?"

"Ah," Meln-Dun said, "I don't think so. With the chaos of Mama Palo's disappearance I should be able to rally my own forces without trouble. Thank you again, Lady Flint. You have my gratitude."

The Palo businessman left by the main gate, leaving Vlora alone in the muster yard as her mages had gone to tend to their wounds.

Well, not quite alone.

Olem stood beside her, a weighing look in his eyes as he watched Meln-Dun leave. He wore a small frown, and tapped an unlit cigarette against his lip. The night was suddenly quiet within the fort, muted sounds of a city at sleep drifting over the walls. It was so peaceful that Vlora wondered if the entire raid had been a dream.

"This went off without a hitch," she said quietly. "Why do I feel shitty?"

"Having to kill a whole lot of people is a pretty large hitch," Olem answered. A match flared to life, and a moment later she smelled cigarette smoke.

"But I'm a bloody mercenary. I've killed hundreds of people. Maybe thousands. This shouldn't bother me."

"You're a killer," Olem agreed, "but you're a decent person."

The two statements seemed mutually exclusive to her. "Do you think about the people you've killed?"

"Seems like a pretty good path to madness."

There was a brief pause. "You didn't answer the question."

Olem sighed. "Sometimes. I try not to."

"Same here." Vlora looked out the gate, hoping that Mama Palo would make it to the noose unmolested. She may have been the enemy, but she was an old lady who had the guts to challenge the most powerful woman on this continent. That was something Vlora had to respect.

She intertwined her fingers with Olem's and said, "I'm sick of this place. Let's leave."

"I think," Olem responded, "we should get paid first."

CHAPTER 40

Michel returned to Landon Plain the next morning with three dozen Iron Roses, eight Bronze Roses, and two prison wagons. Taniel had told him that he'd get his Gold Rose today, but he wasn't entirely sure what to expect. Which, he reasoned, would make things more authentic.

He spent the entire ride trying to put his thoughts and memories back into the marble, but to no avail. He could feel himself slipping, mentally, thinking of the Iron Roses riding beside him in the wagon as his enemies instead of underlings. He caught himself worrying about Taniel—no, he corrected himself, Tampo—instead of champing at the bit to bring him in. It left him confused and irritable, and it took all his effort to keep from muttering about it under his breath.

Landon Plain was bustling when they arrived, but the moment the prison wagons with the white roses emblazoned on their sides and their accompaniment of Blackhats rolled onto a street the Palo scattered like a flock of geese, leaving goods, animals, and even rickshaws where they lay.

The *Palo Herald* was quiet as the Blackhats surrounded it, and Michel felt an anxious trepidation. What would he find inside? Bodies? Live Palo left as scapegoats? An ambush?

"All right," Michel said, getting out of the back of the prison wagon and pointing to two of the biggest Iron Roses he could find. "You two, take that door. You six, sweep under the docks. You four take the warehouse next door. Where's Warsim?"

"Here, sir," Agent Warsim responded, getting out of the next wagon.

"You take the lead."

Michel rounded to the far side of the prison wagon to watch the attack, a trio of Bronze Roses remaining close in case of a fight. He licked his lips, then nodded to Warsim as he and several big Iron Roses crept up beneath the sign that said PALO HERALD. As one, they kicked in the door and rushed inside while the rest of the group sprang into action.

Within moments Michel heard the crash of more doors being kicked in, and coordinated shouting from the crawl space beneath the warehouse. He listened to the tramp of feet, watching the open front door of the newspaper office with bated breath.

There was a long silence, broken only by the crash of something being knocked over, and then a single shout.

Warsim appeared in the doorway. "All clear!" he called.

Michel let himself breathe, jogging over to the building. "What's going on?" he demanded. "Where is everyone?"

"We've got nothing, sir," Warsim reported. "It's empty." He scowled, and Michel waited for the bad news.

"And...?" Michel prompted.

"There's a body upstairs."

Michel rushed into the warehouse and took the stairs two at a time up to the little room where, just yesterday, he'd spoken with Taniel. The room seemed dimmer than it had before, the walls closer together. And just inside, slumped beside a chair in the middle of the room, was a corpse lying facedown in a congealed pool of blood.

Michel slowly circled the body and waved away the buzzing flies. The corpse wore an expensive suit, now soaked through with blood, with a cane lying on the ground beside it. Michel picked up the cane and, using it and the toe of his boot, turned the body over. It held a spent pistol in one outstretched hand, and there was a bullet hole in the left temple. The wall behind the body was covered in blood and bits of brain.

The face, despite being covered in blood, belonged unmistakably to Gregious Tampo.

"Do we have a Knacked?" Michel asked, trying not to wretch.

"Sammlen, sir. He's downstairs," Warsim answered.

"Bring him up here."

Warsim returned with Sammlen a moment later, and Michel pointed to the body. "What is it you use to sense sorcery? Your third eye, right?"

"That's right, sir. It's not easy, but I can do it."

"Tell me if there's any sorcery here."

"Sir?" the Knacked asked, looking confused.

"Just look!"

The Knacked took a deep breath, closed his eyes, and then opened them halfway with an intent gaze on the corpse. He held it there for almost twenty seconds before shaking his head and blinking away a few tears. "No, sir. Can't see any sign of sorcery."

Michel circled the body one more time. This was definitely *not* Taniel. It definitely *was* Gregious Tampo. The height and weight looked right; the face was definitely his. Michel wanted to know exactly how this had been done—was that some other poor fool there, or had Taniel killed himself to give Michel an edge? It seemed impossibly unlikely. And besides, wondering wasn't Michel's job. His job was to get a Gold Rose.

"Did we find anything else?" Michel asked.

"No, sir."

"Do another sweep."

Michel let them search for almost an hour, tearing the printshop apart, before meeting Warsim outside next to a pile of everything of value they had found. The pile consisted of eighteen crates of *Sins of Empire*, eleven muskets, five pistols, ammunition, receipts from news distributors in Landfall, a whole library of antigovernment propaganda distributed by other revolutionaries throughout the last ten years, and a single handwritten diary belonging, apparently, to Gregious Tampo.

Down the street of the warehouse complex Michel spotted Palo faces in windows and peering around corners, no doubt curious as to what was going on. He ignored them, flipping through the diary while his Blackhats waited in silence. "I don't know if a corpse is going to be enough to get me my Gold Rose," he whispered to himself.

"Then you better have a damned good story to go along with it," he answered.

He read the last page of the diary and then flipped it shut, putting it in his back pocket and looking up at Warsim and the assembled Blackhats. "Take all of this to the Millinery," he said. "Inventory it and sell it."

"Even the pamphlets and propaganda?" Warsim asked.

Michel wondered how long it had taken Taniel to create the persona of Gregious Tampo—all the work that had gone into a false human being with an entire history. Tampo had written, published, and distributed a pamphlet that had, despite all the work, accomplished very little. Michel was sure it was not his only scheme, but it seemed like such a waste.

"No," he said. "Take the books and pamphlets outside the city and burn them. Gregious Tampo is dead, and this whole affair with him. Bring me his old secretary and landlord from the office building to identify the body."

"Right, sir. Anything else?"

"Yes. Let Fidelis Jes know I need to see him."

"You've brought me a body," Fidelis Jes said, his tone flat.

The grand master was having lunch at his desk, a napkin tucked into his pressed shirt, a bite of roast pheasant halfway to his mouth, orange sauce dripping onto the desk. He noticed the drip, swore and finished the bite, then wiped the desk with his napkin before tossing it on the half-finished meal and pushing his plate to one side. Jes did not look well—his eyes were bloodshot, his hair unkempt, and his shirt wrinkled. Michel, in the times he'd seen Jes around the Millinery, had never witnessed him so out of sorts.

Michel cleared his throat. "Yes, sir. That's right."

"What good is a corpse?" Fidelis Jes asked in a quiet voice. "What can I do with a body? I can't torture a body, can I? I can't squeeze it for secrets!" His voice rose in pitch until he finished by slamming a fist down on the desk, making Michel jump. Michel noticed a ring on his thumb—a heavy, silver ring with a lance through a skull. Had Jes worn that before today? Michel had not noticed, but Jes's fidgeting drew attention to it.

Michel grasped for something to say. "It's definitely him, sir."

"Excuse me?"

"I said..."

"I heard what you said," Jes snapped. "I want to know what you mean. How is that supposed to reassure me? It's definitely him. Bah! I'd rather it was a double, so I could send someone more competent out to bring the bastard in."

Michel was careful to let nothing show in his face. Not his rising certainty that Taniel was still out there, not his fear—and certainly not the deep loathing he felt for Fidelis Jes and everything he stood for. "Sir," he said in a reasonable tone, "that means it's over." He slipped the diary from his pocket and set it on Jes's desk. "With Tampo dead, it leaves no loose ends. Remember how careful Tampo was about bank records and rental agreements and witnesses? Well, he didn't have a perfect memory. He had to keep it straight somewhere, and it's right there."

Fidelis Jes looked at the diary with a vague air of disgust, as if Michel had plopped a dead groundhog on his desk. "You mean we have his organization?"

"*Everything,*" Michel emphasized. "There *was* no organization. There was only Tampo. He masterminded the entire *Sins of Empire* affair, using hired help every step of the way, most of which didn't even know his real name. He thought that he could overthrow the Lady Chancellor's regime through a sort of bloodless coup—by turning the populace against her and forcing her to step down."

"That's awfully shortsighted for someone so careful."

"Maybe. Maybe not. I checked with several of our propagandists and they said the theory is sound. Tampo wasn't going to stop with *Sins of Empire.* He planned dozens more pamphlets over the next few years. It's all in his diary. This was just the beginning, but we've managed to cut the head off the snake before it could multiply."

Michel leaned forward slightly as he spoke, putting excitement behind his words that he didn't feel. Jes had to *feel* this victory, *understand* its importance. The grand master had to be convinced that Tampo's suicide was not a fluke. Michel snatched up the diary, turning to the last few pages. "Look, sir. Tampo writes about the close calls he had with our Blackhats. We were *right* behind him, dogging him every step for the last week. He killed himself because he feared what we would do when we caught him. It doesn't matter that we don't have him, because all he worked toward was for naught."

Jes leaned back in his chair. He didn't look convinced, but he didn't look irate anymore, either. "I suppose you want to take credit for that, do you?"

"I was the one who dogged him."

Jes's eyes narrowed, and he watched Michel for a silence that stretched nerve-rackingly long before he got up, rounded the desk, and took the diary from Michel's hands. He paced the room, flipping through the pages. Michel stood at attention the whole time, sweat trickling down the small of his back while he waited for Jes to find some sort of mistake that would give away the entire game.

Michel had to admire Taniel's foresight. The journal was impeccable. It had been written in every week for almost three years, and illustrated the downfall of a disenfranchised Adran nobleman who'd escaped Field Marshal Tamas's coup in Adro ten years ago and come to Fatrasta, only to lose what remained of his family fortune on speculations. He had no friends or family to question, and this writing illustrated a paranoid mind that was convinced he could remove Lindet from power and then step into a role in whatever government rose from the ashes of hers.

The journal had not been written last night. It was a long, thoughtful work. Likely something Taniel had been keeping as some sort of kill switch for the whole persona of Tampo for the eventuality of being caught by the Blackhats.

But was it perfect?

Almost a half an hour passed before Fidelis Jes thoughtfully set the diary on the corner of his desk, then crossed the room to a small chest sitting above the fireplace. He palmed something, then turned toward Michel. "I'm not pleased by the conclusion of this problem, Agent Bravis," he said coldly.

Michel licked his lips.

"However," Jes said, "I *am* pleased that it's over. We have far more pressing items of concern going on right now. I consider your wrapping up of the *Sins of Empire* affair to have involved quite a lot of luck and blunder. But there is a place in the Blackhats even for that, so I will not demote you."

Michel suppressed a disappointed sigh. Not being stripped of his rank, he tried to tell himself, might have been the best possible out- come here. But it wasn't what he needed. It wasn't what Taniel had killed off Gregious Tampo for. He cleared his throat and mentally tossed the dice for a risky gamble.

"Sir," he said firmly, "I think I earned more than that. Without proper investigative training I tracked down Tampo and I ended the danger he presented toward the Lady Chancellor. I believe I've earned my Gold Rose."

Fidelis Jes crossed the room so quickly Michel threw himself backward, reeling. The grand master caught him by the front of his shirt, yanking him close, their noses almost touching. "You think you've earned the Gold Rose, do you?" Jes hissed.

Michel's throat felt like a desert. "Yes," he croaked.

"Luck and blunder aren't enough," Jes said. "But loyalty? Loy- alty, Agent Bravis, is a coin worth more than silver." He grasped Michel's shoulder, pressing something hard against Michel's skin, before releasing him and returning to his desk. Michel managed to catch the amulet before it fell, opening his fingers to reveal a Gold Rose. He let out a long, shaky sigh.

"Thank you, sir."

"I am short-staffed right now," Jes said. "But all my Gold Roses have a single objective. Benjamin Styke was captured last night and immediately escaped from Sweetwallow Labor Camp. The camp has been destroyed, and Styke is at large. You're to bring him in."

"What about Lady Flint?" Michel asked.

"What about her?"

"I'm her liaison."

"Not anymore. She's finished her current contract. If we give her a new one, I'll assign another Silver Rose. You've got work to do. Now get out of my sight."

Michel closed the door to Jes's office, leaving Michel in the antechamber with the secretary, Dellina. Dellina gave him a warm smile, as if he hadn't just about had his heart handed to him by the head of the secret police. "Congratulations," she said.

"Thanks," Michel replied in a daze.

"Go get a celebratory drink," she suggested. "It'll take the edge off."

"Good idea. First, I'm going to go change my pants."

CHAPTER 41

Vlora sat alone and watched the sun rise over the half-built foundations of the tenement that, until just last night, her men had been preparing to erect on the rim of Greenfire Depths. A sleepless night contributed to her sense of deep melancholy, and she wondered if anyone would come along and finish these tenements after she was gone.

It was an encouraging thought. Perhaps Meln-Dun would see them finished, or another Palo businessman. Maybe even the Blackhats. After all, they'd already allocated the funds. But she didn't know if it would happen, and she tried to tell herself she didn't care.

Feeling empathy for the Palo people was not new to her. She had tried to break their spirit on the frontier, but she had instructed her men to show mercy and compassion, and attempted to leave the survivors with the tools to better themselves. Her role out there had not been as a governor, but as a suppressor, and she wondered now if she would have found something more fulfilling out of the former.

Despite that preexisting empathy, something about Greenfire Depths made her feel more conflicted over the arrest of Mama Palo than she had over putting down any number of insurrections out in the swamps. She couldn't quite put her finger on why. Perhaps Vlora respected Mama Palo for her defiance. Perhaps she felt remorse over arresting an old woman.

She pushed the musings aside and picked herself off the street, walking through the tenement foundation and then over two blocks to look out on Greenfire Depths. She had more pressing things to worry about than rebuilding a city slum that held no real significance to her or any of her men. Far more important was how the Palo would react once they found out their leader had been taken by the Blackhats and sent to hang.

Vlora had tried to come up with a way to keep her name out of the story—she even considered making a personal request to Fidelis Jes—but she did not need to owe Jes a favor. Besides, they'd left too many witnesses and too much evidence behind. Everyone knew that the Riflejacks had the only powder mage in town, and all she could hope now was that no one figured out that she had three other mages with her as well. That was a trump card she preferred to hold on to.

No, the Palo would know exactly who had captured Mama Palo. Even if there weren't outright riots, the attacks against her men would escalate beginning as soon as today, and she had to consider their safety. Meln-Dun might be able to restore order. Or he might fail. Or he might use the Riflejacks as a point of unification to bring Mama Palo's former men under his control and turn all of Greenfire Depths against her. After last night, it wouldn't surprise her one bit.

Vlora wondered if it was time to get out of this place. Perhaps even to return to Adro and mend some old wounds.

She walked back to the tenement only to find Olem waiting for her, accompanied by a familiar face: Fidelis Jes. Vlora offered the grand master her hand, which he shook perfunctorily. Jes did not look entirely well; in fact, a second look told her he was still wearing the same shirt as yesterday, his hair mussed, his eyes bloodshot.

"He said it was an emergency," Olem said in a low voice, coming to her side.

"I see. I didn't know you left the Millinery, grand master," Vlora said.

"I do my best not to," Jes replied. "Hold the pleasantries, this isn't an honor, Lady Flint. I'm simply here to let you know that the Lady Chancellor is very pleased that you brought in Mama Palo so quickly. I myself am suitably impressed. I didn't think you could do it."

Vlora allowed herself to be pleasantly surprised. "Well, then. Thank you. I think."

If Jes had meant the compliment to be backhanded, he didn't show it. He turned away from her and Olem, studying the tenement foundation, clearly distracted.

"What will happen to Mama Palo?" Vlora asked.

"Oh," Jes said with a dismissive wave, "she's already been tried at a closed court this morning. I oversaw it myself. She'll be hanged in the public square outside the capitol building at noon tomorrow."

"I expected you to draw it out."

"I would have liked to. Mama Palo could have made an excellent example. But publicly torturing an old woman wouldn't have gained us much, and we're not entirely monsters, despite what you may think."

Could have fooled me.

Jes continued: "Noon tomorrow is enough time for the rabble to gather. Not enough time for them to organize."

Vlora watched him fidget with his sword for a moment and noticed that he was wearing Ben Styke's knife on his belt. Fidelis

Jes had struck her from the beginning as a man who kept trophies. He had not, however, struck her as a man who fidgeted.

It was Olem who voiced her next question. "This isn't just a congratulatory visit, is it?"

"No," Jes replied, his voice clipped. He clasped his hands behind his back, still looking away from her and Olem. "This is a matter of some personal embarrassment, but Benjamin Styke has escaped."

Vlora looked sidelong at Olem, who adopted a look that obviously said *good for him*, and shook her head. He scrunched up his face and dug in his pocket for his tobacco. "I assumed he was dead."

"He was not," Jes replied. "For reasons unbeknownst to me, the Lady Chancellor will not allow Styke to die. He was suitably chastised and returned to the labor camp in which he's been incarcerated for so many years."

"I thought he escaped that camp before."

"It was more complicated than that. Regardless, we thought it was a good place for him."

Vlora snorted. "But it wasn't."

"No," Jes snapped, finally turning toward her. "The Sweetwallow Labor Camp was destroyed last night, the buildings burned to the ground, the guards slaughtered, and the convicts released."

"You don't think that we did it, do you?" Vlora asked, incredulous.

"No. We believe it was the work of Styke's old comrades, the Mad Lancers."

The thought of a bunch of angry old veterans attacking a labor camp almost made Vlora laugh. She bit her bottom lip, glancing at Olem.

"Weren't they disbanded ten years ago?" Olem said.

Jes ignored the question. "I want Styke recaptured, and I want his accomplices hunted down and executed."

"And you want us to do it?" Vlora asked flatly. Even before he'd finished his sentence she began running numbers and logistics in her head, trying to decide how much work it would be to capture or kill a company of retired veterans. The Mad Lancers were legendary, but they were ten years past their prime. She didn't doubt her men could handle them. But she wasn't sure it was worth it.

"Your assignment regarding Mama Palo is over and we have paid you in a mix of bullion, bank notes, supplies, and letters of mark as requested."

Vlora gave a low whistle. "Already?"

"Yes," Olem confirmed. It was by far the fastest they'd ever been paid.

"I've even authorized a bonus, paid immediately, if you're willing to take on another assignment this very moment," Jes continued.

"Styke?"

"Yes, Styke."

Vlora continued to run through logistics, but suddenly put a stop to it. What was she doing? She hated Jes, didn't much care for Lindet *or* her government, and her men were about to have a significant population of the city turn against them purely by default. Besides, she liked Styke. He'd more than proved his mettle and she had no interest in chasing after him and putting him down like a mad dog.

She glanced at Olem. He'd managed to restore his card-playing face, but she didn't even need to ask his opinion on a matter like this. "Is this coming straight from Lindet?"

"From me," Jes replied.

"Not interested."

"I'll have Lindet on board with the idea by this afternoon."

"Still not interested."

Jes's face reddened slightly. Whatever he was expecting, an outright refusal was not it. "Is it because of your relationship with Styke?" He took a measured breath, then said, "We're rather low on manpower at the moment. I can provide you with a different assignment that will free up my own men to address this menace. We could have you continue your garrison of Loel's Fort to keep the peace against the Palo."

"My relationship with Styke, as I mentioned before, was as a sympathetic employer to an old crippled veteran. And no, I'm not interested in having my men picked apart by angry Palo for the next year. You can't fight what's going on in Greenfire Depths. You have to either make changes big enough to bring them around to your side, or burn the whole bloody place down."

"You could garrison Fort Nied..."

Vlora raised a hand to cut him off. She was surprised that Jes seemed so eager to keep her on the payroll. Her impression of him was that he didn't care one bit for her. "If I didn't know any better, I would think you're trying to keep me around."

"You're...valuable."

So are green-eyed vipers, but I don't let them have the run of my luggage. "No thank you, grand master. I expect to give my men some leave, and then we'll be departing Fatrasta entirely. Back to the Nine with us."

Jes ground his teeth. "And no amount of money would sway you?"

"Not any that comes to mind," Vlora replied.

"Well," Jes said. He fumed openly, his jaw thrust toward her. "I'm sorry to hear that. You'll understand that we don't want an unauthorized army on our soil. You have two nights to remove yourself from Loel's Fort and four to take your men out of the city. Good day, Lady Flint."

Jes strode away, fists clenched, and Vlora turned to Olem the moment he was out of earshot. "Did that seem strange to you?" she asked.

"Very," Olem said. "He is going to give himself an apoplexy."

"Over one man?"

"Well," Olem responded, "a whole company."

"It has to be something else," Vlora responded, though she couldn't for the life of her decide what. He probably *was* worried about Palo riots, and he did know about the Dynize, though they were hardly a threat contained as they were down in Greenfire Depths. "There's no way he's going that mad over the prospect of a single group of retired lancers running amok."

"The Mad Lancers were legendary," Olem said. "They broke whole Kez armies back in their day."

Vlora mulled that over. She'd witnessed legendary companies firsthand—some that lived up to their reputations, and more that did not. But even if every story was true, Jes's behavior didn't make any sense. Something else was on his mind. Something big. Styke was just the thorn that continued to prick him. "It's not our problem anymore. Looks like we've overstayed our welcome, both with the Palo and our former employer. Start chartering us passage back to the Nine."

"You were serious about that?" Olem asked.

Vlora hesitated. She had a lot of bad memories back home, some of which she'd been running from for more than five years. Perhaps it was time to head back and take those on. Or perhaps not.

"Check with the local chapter house of the Wings of Adom. See if they have any work for us. We'll head home for the winter, then re-form the company in spring. Maybe head to Gurla."

Olem touched the brim of his hat. "Right. Any specific action we're looking for?"

"I'm sick of oppressing people," Vlora said, glancing toward Greenfire Depths. "I'm sick of working for tin-pot dictators. Find me an underdog to fight for. As long as they can pay decently, of course."

"That's the kicker."

"It always is." Vlora took the cigarette out of Olem's mouth and drew on it deeply before handing it back. She had a feeling in her gut, a twisting of her bowels that made her want to look over her shoulder. Their need to be gone from Landfall was suddenly desperate, and she resisted the urge to run back to Loel's Fort that second.

"Something wrong?" Olem asked.

"Indigestion. I hope. Get the men ready to move out."

"Where are you going?"

"I'm taking a day off, then I'm going to see the fruits of our labor. I'll come find you after Mama Palo's hanging tomorrow."

CHAPTER 42

T he Privileged," Styke asked. "Did you kill him?"

He sat in bed in a rented room above a pub in one of the dozens of border towns that surrounded Landfall. It was the middle of the afternoon, and he could hear the hum of lunchtime conversation in the room below him and the clatter of traffic in the street outside. Ibana ja Fles, manager of Fles and Fles Fine Blades and second in command of the Mad Lancers heavy cavalry, sat on a chair beside the bed.

Few people would consider Ibana a beautiful woman. She had a tough, cracked face from years of working the forge, with a broad forehead and flat, pockmarked cheeks. She had dirty-blond hair tucked carelessly into a ponytail, with an easy smirk that brought back more than a few good memories. She towered over most men, just a few inches shy of Styke's height, and was strong as an ox. She used to entertain the lancers by cracking empty powder barrels between her thighs.

Ibana popped her knuckles one at a time, first working through one hand and then the other. Styke had been awake for several minutes, and she'd yet to say a word.

"No," she finally said. "I dumped him in a ditch on the other side of town."

"You're getting soft."

"I told him I'd let him go unharmed if he healed you. I keep my promises."

Styke looked down at his shoulder and traced a finger over a thin, pink scar—all that remained of the deep stab wound from Fidelis Jes's knife. He had seventeen other new scars of varying length over the rest of his body, each of them feeling tight and uncomfortable. He rotated his arm, surprised to feel only the slightest twinge. Everything felt as good as new—or at least as good as it was before his fight with Fidelis Jes. The Privileged had even taken some time on each of the old bullet wounds, and Styke found that he now had more, though not complete, use of his middle and index fingers on his left hand. "Healing Privileged are damned rare. Where did you find him on short notice?"

"He's one of Lindet's personal cabal. I actually nabbed him to take care of the Old Man, but then Celine showed up ranting about you going to the Millinery."

"Celine?"

"She's safe," Ibana said shortly.

"And the Old Man? Is he...?"

Ibana's eyes narrowed. "He'll live. No thanks to you. He's pissed as a pit about the house."

"I didn't want to involve him."

"But you did."

Styke chewed on his words, then decided a nod would suffice. "I had just got out. I needed someone I could trust."

"So you brought my elderly father into your personal vendetta?"

Styke scowled, confused. What was that supposed to mean?

"No," he finally said. "It wasn't about Fidelis Jes at all. At least, not from the start."

"I don't believe you."

"Have I ever lied to you?"

"On several occasions."

"About anything important?"

Ibana worked through her fingers again. Only one of them popped. "I don't want your excuses, Colonel."

Styke felt his stomach clench. Ibana only called him "colonel" when she was worried, or furious. She didn't look all that worried now. But he was done. He was whole and safe—at least temporarily—for the first time since before the war and he wanted to enjoy it for a few minutes. "What do you want, then?" he demanded.

"I want an apology."

"For what? Getting the Old Man's shop wrecked? Him beat up? Because if you don't think I'm bloody well sorry for that then you're a fool."

Ibana's jaw clenched. "No," she said quietly. "I expect you to apologize for leaving me alone the last ten years."

"Fine," Styke snapped. "I apologize. I apologize for making enemies with that psychotic horse's ass Fidelis Jes. For getting put in front of the firing squad. For getting hauled off and buried in a labor camp and then for trying to keep everyone else from getting my shit on them when I got out."

"I saw that camp. You could have escaped."

"I didn't want to."

"Why not?"

"Because I knew that this—your father, Little Gamble's pub, Sunin's apothecary—all the things they'd built would come crashing down the moment I escaped. I managed to get out without violence, and I was stupid to think that I was free. But I wasn't."

Ibana regarded him warily. "You knew about all that? Gamble's pub? People's homes and businesses?"

"Not until after my fight with Jes," Styke said, lowering his voice. "I went to fight him because I thought it would prevent all that. I wanted to keep him from hurting the rest of my friends. But he'd already done it, and he used it to taunt me when I was down." He let out a sigh, looking around the room, wondering what he was going to do next. Five minutes ago he'd felt like a new man, but the argument with Ibana had taken everything out of him. He felt drained and invalid, and when he tried to move his leg the old bullet wound reminded him that the Privileged hadn't been able to heal everything. "I'm sorry I left you alone."

Ibana stood up, stretching. "Here's the thing," she said, before suddenly snapping one fist forward, slamming it across Styke's face. Styke jerked back, knocking against the headboard, stars swirling before his eyes. He tasted blood and it took almost thirty seconds before he could see clearly. He found Ibana gone, the door left open behind her.

Styke rolled slowly out of bed, all the aches and twinges he thought he'd left behind suddenly catching up to him. He'd only had healing sorcery to this extent once before, and his body had felt like a new, slightly too-small glove for over a week. He tottered over to the washbasin and mirror on the other side of the bed and washed the blood off his face, checking his nose. It wasn't broken. Ibana had pulled her punch.

She *was* getting soft.

He checked all the new, pink scars again. Most he didn't remember getting, but he could still feel the slice along his left wrist that had left him unable to move his fingers. A bead of sweat rolled down the back of his neck and he quickly buried the memory, flexing his hand to remind him that it was working once again.

Ibana was back. The knowledge was both frightening and comforting at the same time. He'd always been the head of the Mad Lancers, she the backbone; in some ways not unlike the relationship between Lady Flint and Olem—though he guessed Ibana had a cruel streak that would make Olem blanch. None of that mattered now, though, he reminded himself. The Mad Lancers no longer existed. They were an idea, a memory—a shimmer on the distant horizon.

And his relationship with Ibana? He'd put her father in danger. He'd disappeared for ten years. He didn't know if she'd taken other lovers or pit, gotten married. He didn't want to ask. And even if she hadn't, ten years was an awfully large gap to cross.

"Pit, you're old," her voice said. Styke jumped. Ibana leaned in the doorway, eyeing his naked body. "I don't remember you being so wrinkly."

Styke didn't bother to look down at his scarred, pitted body. She was right. His skin looked like a tomato left out in the sun too long. He'd never really thought about the wrinkles before. "You still look good," he responded.

"Don't try to sweet-talk me."

"Just stating a fact. Everyone ages. You did it way better than me."

"Yeah," Ibana responded, "but you started off prettier."

"I guess we're even, then."

"On that account. Yeah." Ibana cleared her throat and hawked a wad into the chamber pot from across the room. "But you've got a lot of catching up to do on all the others. Now, you said this whole thing involving my father wasn't supposed to be about Fidelis Jes. You said you got out of the labor camp without violence."

Styke grimaced. He'd planned on telling her. Eventually. "I'd hoped you missed that."

"Not a chance. Tell me what's going on. All of it."

So Styke did. He started with the parole hearing, told her about Tampo, then joining the Riflejacks. He told her about the dragon-man, the Dynize, and the Palo. He talked until his throat was raw, and Ibana stood there unmoving through the whole thing. When he finished he looked around for his pants, only to find a new pair hanging by the washbasin.

"Is the girl yours?"

Styke froze, the pants around his ankles, one leg raised. "Celine?"

"Yeah. Her."

"I suppose so. She hasn't got anyone else." Styke didn't like the edge to Ibana's voice. He finished pulling the pants on and buckled the belt.

"But you didn't father her in the camps?"

"No. Her dad was a thief. Died mucking the marshes. Where is she?"

Ibana's tone softened. "She's downstairs playing with Gamble. He says she's just a few years younger than his daughters would have been if they survived the war, the sap."

Styke let out a soft sigh. The fact that, after all this, Celine was safe and close by was as comforting as waking up with a working hand. When he turned back Ibana had a strange half smile on her face. She uncrossed her arms and lifted her chin toward him. She seemed satisfied that Celine wasn't his by blood, and the fact she cared was somehow comforting to Styke.

"That's quite the story you told," Ibana said. "So what are you going to do now?"

"I'm not sure." Styke didn't trust that smile. It meant Ibana already knew how this conversation was going to end. It was unnerving. "I've got two masters right now. Tampo and Lady Flint."

"And do you owe either of them anything?"

"I owe Tampo my freedom. And I owe Lady Flint..." Styke frowned. He wasn't sure what he owed Lady Flint. She'd given him a job—a purpose—and the fact that he felt a modicum of guilt over the false pretenses he'd used told him all he needed to know. "I like Lady Flint. I like Olem and the Riflejacks. They warned me that the Blackhats were coming for me."

"You have obligations."

"I have obligations," Styke agreed. He was torn. He couldn't go back to Lady Flint. He didn't know how to contact Tampo and even if he did, was he any use to Tampo now that he was on the Blackhats' shit list? His best bet was to disappear. He could take Celine and head north. Catch a ship to Gurla or the Nine and be beyond Fidelis Jes's reach within a few weeks. Vanishing into thin air would be its own sort of vengeance. Jes would lie awake at night, wondering when the knife would come out of the dark, while Styke slept peacefully half a world away.

"You didn't mention your other obligations."

Styke raised his eyebrows. "You?"

"You bet your ass me. And everyone else."

"What do you mean?"

Ibana advanced into the room. "Have you forgotten the men and women downstairs? The Blackhats attacked your whole officer corps—everyone still alive, that is. They burned businesses, destroyed homes, beat some of our friends within an inch of their lives."

Styke's chest tightened and he looked away. "I...I've got nothing to offer them."

"Don't look away from me. I *will* break your nose, and then I'll go to work on your fingers. Those people would *die* for you, and all you can do is avert your eyes out of self-pity? You'll give them something, even if it's one last ride into glory and death. You're goddamned Mad Ben Styke."

"A ride?" Styke asked. "What would we ride against? There is no great empire battering down our doors this time."

"The Blackhats," Ibana suggested.

"The Blackhats," Styke said, nodding. He held up his hand, suddenly caught on his own words. He repeated his last sentence under his breath. "No great empire..." He looked Ibana in the eye. "The Dynize. Something is going on with the Dynize. I never found out what, but with dragonmen in the city they have to be planning something."

"Dragonmen." Ibana snorted. "Then we have two groups to ride against."

Styke's heart leapt at the idea. The Mad Lancers together again, prepared to fight through the teeth of whatever the world could throw at them. A week ago—pit, an hour ago—it would have seemed a silly thought, but now here it was. "Seems like a lot of enemies."

"Never bothered us before."

"What happened to our armor?" Styke asked. "Last I heard, Lindet was going to have it destroyed."

"Last I heard, too," Ibana said with a scowl.

"Enchanted armor is priceless. She wouldn't destroy it."

"It's Lindet."

Styke nodded. That was all Ibana needed to stay. He reached for his knife, his hand coming up empty, and remembered the sound of it clattering away across the cobbles after Jes's victory. Ibana's eyes followed the gesture, and Styke said quickly, "I'll get it back." He walked toward the door, then thought better of it, opening the window and looking down into the street. He wasn't ready to face his old officer corps. Not yet. He began to climb through the window.

"What are you doing?" Ibana demanded.

"Keep everyone here," he said. "If you have to move to avoid the Blackhats, leave word for me at Grandma Sender's."

"Where are you going?"

Styke remembered what Jes had whispered just before having him carted off. *I can't kill you. She won't allow it.* "It's long past time I had a talk with the one who holds Fidelis Jes's leash."

CHAPTER 43

Michel jogged up the steps to the Millinery courtyard, Gold Rose dangling from a chain around his neck, tapping gently against his chest. He shaded his face from the afternoon sun, realizing he'd left his hat on the desk of his new office. It was not, he decided, an auspicious start to his new command.

The word "command" felt foreign—so military and public, far from what he was used to—but after spending all night and most of the morning being briefed about his new responsibilities as a Gold Rose, he felt it was the most fitting word to use. Silver Roses were, technically, just one rank under a Gold Rose. But there were a lot of Silver Roses, and he'd always remained in the shadows, working alone, only taking advantage of his rank when he needed a couple of bodyguards or someone roughed up.

A few days ago the idea of bossing around a few dozen Iron and Bronze Roses had been a novel one, though ill-fitting. Now he was expected to take charge of more than six hundred Roses of all ranks and conduct a search for Benjamin Styke and a whole company of angry veterans.

"How hard will it be to find three hundred or so retired cavalry?" he asked himself.

"I don't know," he responded sarcastically. "How about you wander into the streets and ask around for the lancer unit that put the entire Kez army on edge?"

"That was ten years ago. They're all washed up."

"Tell that to the guards at the labor camp they set fire to last night."

Michel rubbed his eyes. He wasn't going to be alone in the search. Oh, definitely not. More than ten thousand Blackhats and twice that many in city police were currently combing the streets. He wondered how the pit *this* had been his first assignment, before remembering the wild look in Jes's eye when he demanded Styke's head. Every single Gold Rose—and everyone under them—had been told to look for Styke.

He wondered what his next assignment would be once Styke had been found and put down. His only real expertise was spycraft. Maybe Jes would allow him to organize the Blackhats' spies and let him set up a real training program. He'd daydreamed a hundred times what kind of changes he'd make if he were in charge, and now that looked like a real possibility.

Put him in charge of information, and he could bring the whole organization to its knees.

Michel slapped himself sharply, letting the pain bring him back to his senses. He still hadn't managed to put the real Michel back into his marble, and he could feel it slipping through. He needed to focus. He was a Gold Rose, and he needed to act and *think* exactly like one. He needed to blend in and do his job.

Except now he didn't just have to work and wait. He had an active assignment from Taniel to find these so-called godstones.

"Sir," a voice said. Michel glanced up to find Agent Warsim

approaching from down the fortifications. Warsim had been present for about a third of Michel's new briefing as he, too, had been promoted—to Michel's second in command. He wore his new Silver Rose proudly around his neck and nodded respectfully. "Didn't expect to find you up here, sir."

"Just, uh..." Michel glanced down into the courtyard, where Blackhats rushed back and forth, prison wagons being loaded down and sent out and men coming in with reports. He couldn't say he came up here to try to sort out the two different sides of his personality. "Watching the chaos for a moment." He shaded his eyes with one hand and wondered if he was ever going to get a good night's sleep again. He'd managed just two hours this morning after Dellina's briefing ended.

"I've assembled your Roses as you asked," Warsim said.

"I did? Oh, right. Very good. We're supposed to be looking for this Styke, correct?"

Warsim shuffled his feet nervously, a confused expression on his face. "That's right, sir."

"Okay, where?"

"Um, everywhere, sir."

"I meant us, specifically."

Warsim seemed to process this latest question. "Everywhere, sir."

Michel opened his mouth, then closed it again. "Hm." Warsim was by no means an idiot, but he'd never struck Michel as particularly smart, either. His advancement to Silver Rose was a fluke—or rather, Michel had requested it personally. Michel needed someone he knew reasonably well, who wouldn't ask questions, and took very little personal initiative. "Okay, where is everyone else searching? Let's start with eliminating those areas."

"I'm afraid that it's not very organized," Warsim said, producing a thick file from beneath his arm and flipping through it. "Controller Britt has his men searching all of Styke's old haunts and known associates. Other than that..." He ended with a shrug.

"It's a bloody free-for-all?"

"Yes, sir."

Michel turned away and rolled his eyes so hard it hurt. The most feared organization on this side of the planet, and the Blackhats fell to pieces once Fidelis Jes went out of sorts. Controller Britt was the seniormost Gold Rose, with two thousand men under his command, so he had claimed the easy stuff. Everyone else was now scrambling, hoping to be the first ones to find Styke and, probably, get some kind of favor with Jes and Lindet.

It was the first inkling Michel had that there was a pecking order even among the Gold Roses, and it did not please him. "Maybe I won't be getting to do as I like after all," he muttered to himself.

"What's that, sir?" Warsim asked.

"Nothing." Michel resisted the urge to give himself another slap. *Focus. You can be a Gold Rose and accomplish your real goal. If you can't, you'll have done all this work for nothing.* Michel turned his attention back to the chaos, trying to come up with some kind of plan. "You've got a military background, don't you?" he asked Warsim.

"I do, sir. Major in the infantry right after the war."

"You understand drilling, lines, grids, patterns. Correct?"

Warsim shifted. "I suppose so, sir?"

"Fantastic. Because I bloody well don't. Take our men down to the docks. Lots of places to hide down there. Search every ship at moor. I want reports on my desk every hour."

"Yes, sir!" Warsim turned to go, but Michel stopped him with a word.

"Oh, and Warsim?"

"Yes, sir?"

"How many men do you think we have left in the Millinery?" He watched as the last of the prison wagons left the courtyard, a lone Iron Rose crossing the cobbles in its wake.

"Practically no one, sir. Everyone's out looking for Styke."

"Right. Get going."

Michel chewed on the inside of his cheek as he watched Warsim sprint down the stairs and then through the Millinery gate and down the street.

Michel *could* go down and oversee the search himself. It's what all the other Gold Roses were doing. He *could* get some rest and try to digest everything that Dellina had briefed him on last night, including state secrets that he was sure Taniel would love to get his hands on—half of which he'd already forgotten.

He *could* bide his time, waiting for this Styke thing to blow over and securing his new place among the Gold Roses, becoming indispensable and trusted until he could just walk in and ask for any secrets he could possibly want to know.

The Millinery was all but empty. The chaos might be enough to conceal anything he got up to between now and whenever Warsim started to bring him reports.

And what the pit, Michel felt the need to do something really dangerous.

The Millinery archives had two sections. One was almost like a private library for the Blackhats. It contained criminal records, city ordinances, duplicates of police reports, and a hundred other useful types of information that anyone from Bronze Rose on up had access to at all times. It occupied three floors of the west wing of the Millinery and had a half dozen attendants, but Michel had often gone an entire day there without meeting another soul.

The second section of the archives was on the fourth floor of the west wing. It was accessible by a single stairway in one corner of the lower archives, which itself was blocked by a thick iron gate.

Michel entered the archives on the first floor and made his way up, careful to avoid the two attendants and three Blackhats he passed. By the time he'd reached the third floor his hands shook, and he wondered what he had gotten himself into.

"You're a spy, Michel," he muttered to himself. "Pull it together."

"I can be nervous if I want to."

"Oh, shut up. You're trembling like the first time you ever nicked a purse. You can do this."

"Can I? If I get caught it won't be for nicking a purse. I'll be tortured and killed."

"No you won't, you fool. You're a Gold Rose now. You're supposed to be here."

Dellina's briefing the night before had included a brief overview of the upper archives. Extremely brief. The upper archives were for necessary use only, and someone would give him the tour once this whole Styke mess was over.

"What if someone asks why you're here? What will you say then?"

"You'll come up with something. You always do."

"That's a terrible plan."

"Says you."

"You should wait," he whispered.

"Coward," he muttered back at himself, and headed toward the locked stairwell in the corner. He passed row after row of high shelves, stacked two rows deep with crates and paper boxes—all the secrets of Landfall. He reached the iron gate, checked over one shoulder, and knelt down in front of it to examine the lock.

It was not a basic keyhole. There was a slight, rounded indentation with seven wavy lines, each appearing to catch a separate mechanism. The lock itself was thick enough that blasting powder might not even be able to break it, and the mechanisms were protected behind polished steel.

He checked the hinges and the iron gate, noting that it didn't budge even in the slightest. "If I were a betting man, I'd say this is warded."

"You don't want anything to do with sorcery," he said back to himself.

"Right." He knelt down, turning his attention back to the lock before frowning. Those seven wavy lines looked awfully familiar. He touched them gently with one finger, frowning, until it dawned on him. Like the inverse of a Rose.

He drew the Gold Rose out of his shirt and looked at it closely, noting that there was a small raised portion in the center that his Silver Rose didn't have. Holding it in two fingers, rose out, he pressed the medallion into the lock and turned.

There was a series of clicks, then the sound of steel striking steel. The gate swung open at his touch.

"That," he whispered, "was too stupidly easy."

He left the gate slightly ajar and took the stairs to the fourth floor. As he entered the room he realized just how flawed his plan was.

The upper archives was as large as any of the floors beneath it. The long room had vaulted ceilings, and high windows cast lines of afternoon light through the swirling dust. Dozens of rows of files went on for at least a hundred feet, leaving him thousands of boxes, books, and files to look through. It would take months to search all of it.

All for a reference to these godstones Taniel needed found.

He searched the closest shelves for some kind of index, hoping that whoever kept the upper archives in order followed the same protocols as the attendants who took care of the lower archives.

Nothing.

He walked down the rows, tapping his fingers on boxes, hoping to find something that looked promising. He took out boxes at random, removing cloth-bound notebooks and single, apparently unrelated pieces of paper, leafing through them gently. One vellum manuscript appeared to be brand-new, while another note card crumbled to dust the moment his fingers touched it.

He sneezed, scattering the remains across two aisles.

"That's probably not good," he said under his breath, quickly heading to the next row of files. He was at once curious and terrified, listening to the steady thump of his own heart as he remained acutely aware of the open gate at the bottom of the stairs, and the unknown consequences if he was caught up here.

"Remember," he said to himself, "if someone finds you, pretend to belong here. People rarely question someone who looks like they know what they're doing."

He'd tested the theory on dozens of occasions, but somehow this place was far more taboo than any other he'd attempted to bluff his way through. The fact he didn't actually know if he *was* allowed to be here made his nerves all the worse.

He finally found an index at the far end of the hall. It took fifteen minutes to figure out how it was ordered, and another five to find what he was looking for, each of those minutes ticking by loudly on his pocket watch, precipitating dozens of nervous glances toward the stairs.

A long search provided him with a single volume labeled *Godstone*. He opened it eagerly, leafing through the pages for several seconds before his heart fell.

The whole thing was written in Old Deliv. He could recognize it, but not read a lick.

He flipped to the front page, wondering if he should try to steal the book and hand it over to Taniel, who could probably find a translator, or take the time to copy a couple of pages.

"Hello?" A voice drifted through the stacks, echoing off the vaulted ceilings. "Is someone up here?"

Michel took several deep breaths to calm himself. He knew where this was now. He could come back. Carefully, he went to close the book and put it back but his eye was caught by something written in pencil on the first page.

It was a number, not in Deliv numerals, but in Kressian. It looked like a street address. Beside it were the words, scribbled quickly, *I found it.*

He memorized the address, slid the book back in its place, and straightened his jacket.

"Hello?" The voice had an edge to it now. "You're supposed to check in when you come to the upper archives. I'm going to have to report this to the grand master."

Michel's initial thought to step out and flash his Gold Rose was immediately cast aside. He went to the end of his row and glanced around the corner, catching sight of an old woman wearing a deep frown, clicking along the marble floor with her cane.

Michel timed her steps before heading down a few aisles and making his way to the other end of the archives. He dashed for the stairs, hearing a voice call out behind him, "You there! Stop!"

He was down the stairs a moment later, then down two more flights and out of the archives, managing to avoid all of the archivists and patrons on his way out. Within minutes he was back in his office, heart thumping in his chest. He immediately found a pencil and paper and jotted down the address before he could forget, then sat down and stared at it for several minutes.

Could this be the location of the godstones? A warehouse, perhaps? Something for sorcerous items?

There was a knock on his door, causing him to jump so high he knocked the chair over, spilling him backward onto the floor. He recovered, rubbing the side of his head, and opened the door a crack.

To his relief, it was Warsim.

"Sir," Warsim said, "I've got the first report."

"Find anything?"

"Nothing, sir."

"Then why are you handing me a folder?"

"It's the report, sir."

"I thought you said we didn't find anything."

"We didn't."

Michel snatched the folder from Warsim, flipping it open to find a single paper with the words "Nothing to report" next to a time and date. Michel rolled his eyes. "By Adom, I hate bureaucracy. How about you tell me when we *have* found something." He shut the door in Warsim's face and righted his chair, collapsing into it. Several minutes passed before he was able to gather himself. He pulled the address out of his pocket and looked it over, muttering it under his breath.

Nothing to do but go find out what it meant.

CHAPTER 44

Styke tarried until dusk in a small town about seven miles due west of Landfall. The town was called Szada, and when he was a boy it had been distant and isolated from the Landfall Plateau, just a sleepy stopping point on the mail route to Redstone. Now it had tripled in size—though it still boasted a population of less than a thousand—and was practically a suburb of the Fatrastan capital.

He left town as the sun disappeared beneath the horizon and headed north across the marshes, picking his way through the dangerous, soggy grounds, relying on the experience of old memories to guide him. He wore a dark, mottled cloak with the hood up, and had borrowed a knife from Ibana. He wondered not *if*, but rather *how much* use it would get before the night was over.

The sky was almost entirely black when he finally spotted lights in the distance. He knew their source even before he made out the dark, brooding silhouette of the brick manor standing guard over the marshes. As he drew closer the light became well-defined candles placed at regular intervals in the windows of the sprawling manor.

Willowhaven House.

The soil eventually firmed, marking the edge of the manicured lawns around Willowhaven. Styke crouched low, moving between the shadows of the eponymous willows and the border of hedge-rows that surrounded the grounds. The bob of lanterns marked the path of the chancellorian guard. He waited and watched, counting out the rhythm of their patrol for more than an hour before finally making his final approach toward the manor.

Willowhaven was dark and foreboding. Even the candles in the windows seemed cold and distant, imbuing the house with a bleak loneliness. The lack of any movement inside, whether from servants or the Lady Chancellor herself, was disconcerting. Styke wondered if she'd chosen to spend this night in the city and decided it didn't matter.

He needed to send a message regardless.

He entered through the side door of the carriage house, pass-ing by the straw-filled stalls of the workhorses, running one hand absently along the warm noses that poked out to greet him. He patted the last one and stamped gently on the floor before reaching down and finding an iron ring by feel and memory.

Within moments he was ten feet below ground level, feeling his way through the dark, damp passageway that led toward the house. He emerged sometime later from behind a salt barrel in the manor's pantry, and slipped past the snoring form of the on-call chef. Styke felt his heart begin to hammer in his chest and slid the borrowed knife from his pocket.

Few people kept a chef on call in the middle of the night, but a midnight snack was one of the few joys Lindet had ever allowed herself.

She was most definitely home.

Styke crept up the stairs, light on his feet, avoiding all the worst creaks. The candles in the windows cast small, flickering amounts of light on the ironwood floors and banister, illuminating the art-covered walls and the old-style pillars with busts of long-dead philosophers and saints. The decoration was as it always had been in Willowhaven—rich, but demure—and Styke felt nostalgia tightening his chest.

He reached the master bedroom at the end of the hall and paused. The door was slightly ajar. He pushed on it gently, grip tightening on his knife.

The room was as he remembered it—obscenely large, with ironwood-paneled walls, an enormous four-poster bed with mahogany curtains, flanked on either side by a nightstand. There was a wing-back chair by the window, a lantern burning low beside it, and Styke could see the ember tip of a lit cigarillo. A shadow moved within the wings of the chair, and a delicate hand reached out to turn up the lamp.

"Hello, Ben."

Styke was immediately struck by how Lindet had lost the soft edges of her youth. She had grown gaunt over the years, and at thirty-three all the softness had been hammered out of her until only iron remained. She wore a pair of spectacles that cast shadows on her face. Her skin was naturally pale, her hair like strands of yellow silk. Her lips were thin, her chin strong, and even in her nightclothes she exuded a calm, dismissive air that gave Styke the urge to apologize for entering and back out of the room.

He stepped inside, slowly closing the door. "Lindet."

People always commented, privately, on Lindet's eyes. They were a steady blue like the sky on a clear day, and those who saw them often swore that an actual fire burned deep within. Some called it sorcery, some an embodiment of Lindet's ambition. The reflection of the lamp on the lenses of her spectacles cast a double likeness, one that seemed to dance independent of the flame that cast it. Styke noted something hanging over one arm of her wing-back chair.

It was his faded yellow cavalry jacket. The one he'd handed to

Fidelis Jes's secretary before he'd fought the grand master. Lindet's left hand clutched the jacket tightly, her knuckles white, the only break in her cool facade. Styke wanted to cross the distance between them. A single stroke, a splash of crimson for the ten years he spent alone in the labor camps after all he did to help her win Fatrasta's freedom.

Instead, he did a slow circuit of the room, checking the bed and closets for hidden assassins until he was satisfied he and Lindet were alone. Lindet's eyes followed him around the room, that perpetual flame beneath her spectacles her only movement save for the occasional rise and fall of her chest. The ash on her cigarillo grew long.

"You ordered my execution," he finally said.

Lindet took several moments to answer. "Who told you that?"

"Who else would have ordered it?"

"The way I understand it," Lindet replied, "you disobeyed a direct order. I didn't have to *order* anything. My officers simply carried out protocol by having a mutinous colonel put in front of a firing squad."

Styke's memories of the day were hazy. He remembered a lot of shouting, a skillful disarmament of his Mad Lancers under false pretenses before he was separated from them and forced up against a stake and tied in place. He hadn't fought back at first. Nobody expected to have to fight their own allies. When he finally realized what was happening, it was too late.

Fidelis Jes had been there, and he'd brought a *lot* of men.

"Nothing happens without your say-so," Styke said. "Certainly not my execution."

Lindet snorted. "I am not omnipotent. And you *did* disobey a direct order."

"So you didn't order me killed?"

"No."

Styke fingered his borrowed knife. "I don't believe you."

"That's not my concern."

"It should be."

Lindet's eyes dipped to the knife and she finally ashed her cigarillo over a pewter mug next to the lamp. She took a deep breath, as if this whole thing was quite troublesome, and said, "I received a message at two forty-seven that you had disobeyed a direct order and were to be shot. I dispatched a messenger at two fifty-six countermanding the order. My messenger arrived after the second volley. You were immediately taken down from in front of the firing squad and treated by the present physicians. They declared you dead and for three days you were left to rot." Lindet spoke in a monotone, as if she were reciting from a journal.

"But I didn't die."

"No," Lindet said. "I recovered what was left of you as soon as I was able—"

"Three days later," Styke interjected.

"I'd just won a war. It was a busy time. As I said, I recovered your body three days later and was rather startled to discover you still alive. You were treated and sent to the Sweetwallow Labor Camp with orders that your name be struck from the record and Colonel Benjamin Styke declared dead." Lindet's forehead wrinkled, and she dropped the cold monotone. "But you were not dead. I made sure of that. I never wanted you dead, Ben."

Styke turned away from Lindet, examining the room in the shadowing flicker of the lamplight. He remembered this room well. It still looked the same—it still smelled the same—and he wondered how she could bear to stay here.

"I believe," Lindet said, "that I am incapable of having you killed."

Styke heard the scoff escape his mouth. "I believe you're capable of having the gods killed if it suits your purpose."

"The gods have nothing to do with you and me," Lindet responded. "You've always been a pain in the ass. You've always flaunted orders, ignored your superiors, protected my enemies, and killed my allies. Everyone in my inner circle hated you—they hated you *so* much—but

I wouldn't let them touch you. I protected you until Fidelis Jes realized the same thing I did, that I was incapable of having you killed, and took the initiative."

"And you let him," Styke accused. "Even if I didn't die, you still killed me. No, I take that back. Sending me to Sweetwallow was worse than having me killed. You took everything away from me, even my name." His fingers tightened on the knife again.

"Sometimes kindness can be cruel."

"You like to think that, don't you? You like to think that your unbending will is all that stands between this country and oblivion, and that only you can see the way through. It's why you suppress the weak, marginalize the poor, crush the Palo, and crave control."

"I've seen the future, Ben," Lindet said quietly. "And I *am* the only one that can see the way through."

Styke walked over to Lindet's chair and put one hand on the wing-back, leaning close to look into her eyes. She stared back, coldly. The absence of even a tremble was more disconcerting than it would have been had she begged for her life. But that was Lindet. It always had been. It always would be. She believed every word she said.

"You could have had one of your Privileged heal me."

"To what end? The war was over. The Mad Lancers were an immediate liability. It was time to bury our monsters and move on."

"You didn't bury Fidelis Jes."

"I needed him. Same as I *still* need him. Had you remained free, you would have killed him for what he did to you."

"I still plan on it."

"And I find that incredibly inconvenient." A note of peevishness entered her voice, and Styke almost laughed.

"But you still let me in here." Lindet's eyebrows rose, and Styke continued: "I could smell the wards coming in. I could sense your Privileged. You keep this place locked down tighter than a king's asshole, and yet you still let me come here."

"I felt we needed to talk."

"You planning on having me killed on the way out?"

"As I said," Lindet responded, "I don't believe I'm capable of having you killed."

"Bullshit," Styke spat.

All this time he had remained leaning over her, their faces so close their noses almost touched. Lindet put out a finger and firmly but gently pushed him away. "Do you remember the night you killed our father?"

Styke turned away to hide his shock. He couldn't remember the last time either of them had acknowledged their kinship. Probably more than twenty-five years. "I try not to," he said, his voice catching in his throat. "It's not a happy memory."

"It is for me," Lindet shot back. "I was three and a half. You were what, twelve? Thirteen? I screamed when I found him standing over Mother's body. He came for me, that bloody knife still in his hand." Lindet's voice became breathy and animated, her eyes looking over Styke's shoulder as if she was witnessing a vision of the past. She gestured absently toward the door. "It was right down the hall. They've never been able to scrub all of Mother's blood out of that rug."

"You could have burned it."

"I keep it as a reminder of what cruel men do with power. Anyway, you put yourself between me and Father. To this day he is still the strongest, evilest man I've ever met and when he came for me you *broke* him. *That* is why I cannot have you killed, brother of mine."

Styke closed his eyes and forced himself to recall the past. They'd abandoned Willowhaven after their parents' deaths. They'd disappeared and changed their names, and eventually Styke had risen to power in the army, Lindet in politics. She'd bought this horrid place—though he never understood why—and kept it as her home though few living souls knew the significance of its history.

They'd gone their separate ways, but had always remained intertwined.

"You never told me you remembered that night," he whispered. "I thought you were too young."

"You never asked."

He could remember spotting the specter of his father standing over his mother's fresh corpse, smelling of whiskey at twenty paces. Lindet stood in the doorway to her room, a stuffed bear clutched to her chest, screaming so loud it would have awoken the servants had Father not sent them all away. He remembered Father advancing on Lindet, bellowing for silence, and him running to put himself between them.

One teenage kid against the giant of a man he'd inherited his size from. Styke still had scars from that fight.

He put Ibana's knife back in his pocket. "I'm not going back to Sweetwallow."

"I didn't think you would," Lindet said, as if the possibility had most certainly crossed her mind.

"But you won't call your dogs off."

He waited for her to say that she couldn't—that Fidelis Jes and the Blackhats were beyond her control, and that she could not bring them to heel if she wanted. Instead she shook her head and handed him his old cavalry jacket. For the first time he noticed that there was something else with the jacket—a bit of white cloth not much bigger than his palm. On it was a lance holding aloft a bare skull, flag swirling around them both; it was a scrap of flag, the emblem of the Mad Lancers.

"They found that flag in the remains of Sweetwallow Labor Camp. Jes is still trying to track down all the inmates that were released—including you—and he's been sending me messengers all day demanding I bring in the army. This morning he tried to deputize Lady Flint and her mercenaries to help find you."

The prospect gave Styke pause. He didn't want to fight the Rifle-jacks. He wouldn't win. "Did he?"

"Lady Flint's last contract is over. She would not accept another one. But if you and your lancers cause enough trouble, I *will* call in the army."

Styke suppressed a sigh of relief. Fatrastan soldiers he could deal with. "Where is my armor?"

Lindet lifted her chin. "I destroyed it."

"Three hundred sets of enchanted medieval armor, and you destroyed it? That was art."

"I believe you found it in a Kez art collection," Lindet said. "But yes, I destroyed it. Your lancers ran down whole *armies* in that armor, and proved that relics like that are too dangerous to be left intact."

Styke *definitely* didn't believe her this time. Lindet was not in the habit of destroying art—and she didn't destroy things that might still be of some use to her. For ten years he thought he was the exception to that rule, but if she was telling the truth about his execution, then there *was* no exception. He studied her face, considering pressing her further, but he knew her stubbornness reached even deeper than his.

"I could call off my dogs," she suddenly said.

Styke's eyes narrowed. "In exchange for...?"

"I could re-form the Lancers, make them my personal entourage. I'd restore all the personal property the Blackhats have destroyed this week and return your rank. You'd have uniforms, horses, pensions."

Styke scowled. Lindet had always been cold and calculating, ten steps ahead of her opponents, but since she was a child she would occasionally be struck by some ill-conceived fancy. This sounded exactly like that. It was a practical, win-win situation. But it wouldn't work. "Their lives have already been destroyed. You can't undo the past, no matter how much you try. And I *will* kill Fidelis Jes."

"It was just a thought," Lindet said, dismissing it with the flip of a wrist as she ashed her cigarillo. "Despite what you may think, I do, from time to time, try to make everyone happy."

"This doesn't end happily. For anyone," Styke warned.

"I know."

Lindet suddenly stood up, crossing the few feet between them and putting her hand against Styke's face, turning him first one way and then the other to examine the pitted scar where the firing squad bullet had bounced off his cheekbone. "In the morning," she said, "I have a country to run. I exist to instill order and protect this country—even from itself. Fidelis Jes will ask me to permit your death. I will, reluctantly, agree."

"I feel like this would go much more smoothly if you just had one of those Privileged hiding out in the bushes cut me apart with sorcery."

"We've been over that. I cannot have you killed."

"But Fidelis Jes..."

Lindet snatched the emblem of the Mad Lancers from his hand and thrust it in his face. She had nothing else to say, returning to her chair and gripping the armrests like a monarch on her throne. "Because I am weak, you and Fidelis Jes will destroy each other. Because I am weak, my Blackhats and the Mad Lancers will go to war. As I am weak, so shall this country be. You should go, before I find some inner strength."

Styke suddenly understood. There was a long way from ordering a man's death without his knowing—like what had been done to him ten years ago—and giving him the chance to fight back. She was allowing him that chance, even if the odds were stacked well against him. "One of us should finish this now and save Fatrasta the grief."

"Can either of us?"

Styke considered the knife in his pocket, and the little girl he saved so many years ago. "No."

"I didn't think so. All I ask is that you consider that which remains unseen." Lindet's voice dropped to a mere whisper. "A storm is coming, Ben, the likes of which this world has never seen. I have tried to prepare for it, but for all my efforts I remain... fearful."

Styke tried to imagine what could possibly scare the woman who'd faced down the Kez at the height of their empire. "The Dynize?" he asked.

"The Dynize. The Palo. Our enemies and our allies. Our very own machinations turned against us. I've tried to make Fatrasta strong enough to face what comes, but all our sins will be accounted for. I..." Lindet trailed off, shaking her head, and then treated Styke to one of her rare smiles. Despite her talk of fear, he could see the eagerness in her eyes. Whatever she saw in the future, she could not *wait* to face it. "I don't know enough."

"Well," Styke said, hearing a creak on the floorboards somewhere in the house below them, "let me know when you do." He wondered if it was a guard, or even the midnight chef. Regardless, he'd been here too long. "Good-bye, Lindet."

"Good-bye, Ben. Whatever happens, keep an eye on the horizon."

CHAPTER 45

Vlora loitered through the city for most of the day, finding a cheap but comfortable hotel that evening and taking breakfast the next morning in the sun at a cliffside café before finally wandering through the streets at random for several hours. It felt good to not be under contract, to not be in uniform. Back at the fort Olem would be getting the men ready to move out. She felt bad leaving all the logistical work to him, but she *needed* this.

She needed to be a civilian again, if only for a couple of hours.

The Landfall city square was several blocks of public park a stone's throw from the capitol building. There were mature ironwood trees, manicured shrubbery, cobble walking paths, and even a small pond. By the time Vlora arrived a little before noon, the area was almost entirely covered with people—several thousand at the very least. There was a volatile mix of angry Palo, wary Blackhats, and curious Kressians, all surrounding a high gallows in the middle of the otherwise pleasant park.

Vlora searched in vain for a vantage point from which to watch the execution before sniffing a bit of powder and scaling one of the ironwood trees, joining several rather surprised children on one thick, high limb. One of them, a boy of perhaps eleven, made a bit of space for her to perch on, eyeballing her sword and pistol.

The spot gave her a clear view of the gallows, as well as the crowd milling around it. Both the gallows and the crowd were absolutely crawling with Blackhats—easily one in every three people present—and it took Vlora only a few moments to realize why. Behind the gallows, flanked by a pair of white-gloved Privileged sorcerers and completely encircled in heavily armed Blackhats, was Lady Chancellor Lindet.

Vlora had never actually seen Lindet, but she'd read her description in the papers a number of times. The Lady Chancellor was a thin woman of medium height with blond hair and a pair of spectacles that she removed every so often to rub on her sleeve. The newspapers often described Lindet's eyes, and Vlora waited for some time for a good view before Lindet turned to face her. Vlora's light powder trance allowed her to see Lindet as if they were standing nose to nose.

Lindet's eyes did not disappoint. Deep-set, darkened by makeup, Lindet's gaze moved across the crowd again and again over the shoulders of her Blackhats. They were studious, critical, like a master craftsman checking her tools. Vlora remembered Taniel's letters mentioning how Lindet might easily be mistaken for a librarian if not for those eyes, and how they had made his throat go dry every time they lit upon him.

Like so many of Taniel's descriptions, Vlora had dismissed them as an exaggerated fancy, but when Lindet's gaze swept past her she felt a tangible presence and her heart skipped a beat, though she couldn't pinpoint why. It wasn't fear, or awe, or anything she could put her finger on. Vlora felt like a schoolgirl again, ducking to avoid the critical eye of the stern headmistress.

"Hey, lady," the boy next to Vlora said.

She shook her head, leaving her study of Lindet and letting her eyes refocus. "Yeah?"

"When is this thing supposed to start?"

"Noon," Vlora said.

The boy squinted at the sun, and Vlora checked her pocket watch. It was just a few minutes till. The boy bounced up and down on the branch, making the whole tree shake.

"I'd appreciate if you didn't do that," Vlora said.

"You scared of heights?"

Vlora craned her head to look at the other children lined up on the branch, then down at the twenty-foot drop. "Not really, but you're gonna ruin the pit out of my day if you knock someone else off."

"Oh, all right," the boy said glumly. His attention turned to her pistol and sword. "Hey, you think there's gonna be fighting? Da said that the Palo bitch was gonna hang high for stirrin' up trouble."

"Don't say bitch," the girl next to him said, elbowing him in the ribs.

"Well, that's what Da said! Anyway, I hope there's a fight." He leaned eagerly out from the branch. Vlora got herself ready to catch him if he fell. "Hangin's happen all the time, but Da always makes us go inside during the riots."

"Probably smart of him," Vlora commented absently. Her own attention moved to the Blackhats as a group of them shoved forward through the crowd, surrounding a prison wagon with white roses painted on the side. It came to a slow stop in front of the gallows and the Blackhats fanned out, pushing back the crowd, before opening the door. Mama Palo, looking rumpled and angry but no worse for the wear, was led out of the wagon.

There was a sudden cacophony, a shoving and shouting match

between Palo and the Blackhats nearest the wagon, then Mama Palo was led up to the gallows. Lindet, still flanked by her Privileged, climbed onto the gallows and waited patiently while the noose was draped around Mama Palo's neck.

Vlora could *feel* the protective sorcery surrounding Lindet. If she had opened her third eye she would have seen splashes of sorcerous color. The Lady Chancellor wasn't taking any chances with this crowd. Mama Palo would hang, and the Palo wouldn't be able to do a damn thing about it no matter how feisty they got.

"That's her, huh?" the boy said. "The ol' Palo bit—I mean, lady?"

"That's her," Vlora confirmed.

"She doesn't look like much."

Vlora couldn't help but agree. Mama Palo looked smaller, older, and more feeble in the light of day. Despite the pageantry and the obvious hopelessness of her situation, she managed to keep her chin up, her back straight. Once the noose had been tightened around her neck she gave a small smile.

For some reason, that smile made Vlora nervous.

Vlora scanned the crowd again, wondering if there would be a rescue operation of some kind. She had no intention of interfering—her work here was done—but anything the Palo mounted would be doomed to fail. She looked again and again, scanning for weapons among the crowd, or large groups of men, or anything that looked mildly organized. Nothing caught her eye.

She returned her gaze to Mama Palo. The old woman continued to smile, and Vlora wasn't the only person who'd caught on to it. Lindet eyed her warily while her Privileged searched the crowd with the same deftness as Vlora. They seemed satisfied with the absence of a threat, but remained vigilant.

Vlora's next check of the crowd caught sight of something peculiar, but it wasn't at all what she expected.

Standing near the edge of the park, leaning against a tree with his arms folded, lips pursed, was Meln-Dun. The Palo businessman smoked a cigarette, his eyes glued to Mama Palo, and Vlora couldn't help but wonder why he was here. He needed to be in Greenfire Depths, securing his power base—making sure his family and business were still intact. Had he already managed it? Was he here out of spite? To be sure that Mama Palo did, in fact, hang?

"Careful, lady, you're gonna fall," the boy next to Vlora warned.

She reached out to steady herself against the trunk of the tree and forced herself to settle down and watch the execution, though she couldn't keep from looking toward Meln-Dun. It would be wise, she decided, to check in with him, make sure everything had gone smoothly.

She was about to climb down from the tree when she spotted something that made her skin crawl: A pair of dragonmen stood less than fifteen paces behind Meln-Dun. They were powerful-looking Palo in gray, tailored suits and tinted spectacles, and they might have easily been mistaken for Palo businessmen but for the unmistakable black tattoos visible at their wrists and collars.

And behind them, almost close enough to touch the pair, was Gregious Tampo. Tampo was dressed to the nines and twirling a cane like he didn't have a care in the world. Vlora wasn't sure which she was unhappier to see—Tampo or the dragonmen—and then, like the final piece of a puzzle fitting perfectly, everything fell into place.

Tampo had been at the party. He was in Mama Palo's inner circle. Those dragonmen were there *with* him. And as she watched, they pushed through the crowd toward Meln-Dun.

Vlora almost knocked a pair of kids off the branch as she leapt from the tree. She landed in a crouch, the pain of the impact barely registering through her powder trance, and tried to shout a warning.

"Meln-Dun! Meln-Dun!"

Lindet had just begun to address the crowd, her voice amplified by Privileged sorcery, and Vlora's words were swallowed in the responding angry mutter of the mob. Vlora shoved her way through the crowd, tossing a powder charge into her mouth and chewing it into a mush of paper and grit, feeling the sorcery course through her veins.

She kicked and shoved, catching brief glimpses of Meln-Dun through the crowd. The dragonmen were almost upon him, and then she lost all sight of them as the crowd began to churn in response to Lindet's speech.

She arrived at Meln-Dun's tree, pistol drawn, only to spot him entering an alley with the two dragonmen. Gregious Tampo was nowhere to be seen.

She gave chase, her mind working desperately. Were the dragonmen *not* here to rescue Mama Palo? Were there more of them behind the gallows, preparing to spring a trap? Vlora hesitated, wondering if she should warn Lindet, but dismissed the notion. Lindet, after all, had two Privileged up there with her. Meln-Dun was unprotected.

Vlora dashed down several alleys, jumping to see over the heads of the sprawling crowd, catching glimpses of gray suits from time to time. She had gone nearly a block before catching sight of Meln-Dun walking into a small café followed by the two dragonmen. She charged along, her pistol held discreetly at her side, eyes scanning the traffic for any sign of Tampo or more of the Dynize.

She reached the entrance of the café, checked the pan of her pistol, and immediately ducked inside. Any moment she wasted might mean Meln-Dun's life.

The café was a long, narrow room. A handful of Kressians occupied chairs, sipping their noon tea. At the far end Meln-Dun and the two dragonmen slipped into a corner table while a Palo waiter brought them iced tea.

Vlora froze in the doorway. Meln-Dun didn't look like he was in danger.

Meln-Dun leaned over to one of the dragonmen and said something, to which the other chuckled. He slapped the dragonman on the back and lifted his gaze toward the doorway. Behind her, back in the park, Vlora heard the unmistakable sound of a trap-door opening, and the angry response of the crowd as Mama Palo was hanged for her crimes.

Vlora's breath felt as if it had been snatched away from her as she understood—or thought she did. Meln-Dun's family and business had never been in danger. The attacks on her men had been feints to lure her to Meln-Dun's side, and she had walked right into his trap, helping him take down Mama Palo to secure power in Green-fire Depths, taking advantage of her eagerness to carry out Lindet's task. The dragonmen weren't working for Mama Palo.

They were working for *Meln-Dun*.

All that passed through Vlora's head in an instant as Meln-Dun's eyes met hers. The Palo leapt to his feet, face turning red. Vlora hesitated, uncertain which of the three men across the café to put a bullet in. She'd come here thinking she would protect a friend, but she wasn't entirely sure if she could kill a single dragonman, let alone two. This was not a good fight.

"Kill her," Meln-Dun ordered.

The two dragonmen leapt from their seats. A café patron screamed, and Vlora spun toward the door, ready to run. She'd lose them quickly in the street, get back to the fort, and—

She collided with a man's chest, bouncing off it like she'd just run straight into a brick wall. She looked up to find Tampo in front of her, and snatched for her sword. His mouth opened, but she had no intention of letting him say a word. This was no coincidence; this was…

The thought was arrested as he snatched her by the wrist before she could fully draw her sword. She snarled at him, tugging, unable to so much as move.

"Sit down, Vlora," Tampo said calmly, shoving her to one side. She landed in a chair, almost tumbling to the floor, and was ready to come back up and at him in half a second only to find he had already stepped past her.

The cane in his hand clicked, and he drew the sword hidden within in a single, swift motion. The first dragonman moved impossibly quick, almost as fast as a powder mage, bone knife coming out and stabbing toward Tampo's chest.

Tampo was faster. Like a mongoose snatching a snake by the throat, Tampo skewered the dragonman through the center of the chest, picking him up and throwing him at his companion like he was no more than a rag doll. The second dragonman dodged the flying body only to have Tampo grab him by the wrist, producing an audible snap with a single twist, and driving the dragonman's head into the brick wall with the force of a draft horse's kick.

The whole fight was over in a handful of seconds. Meln-Dun fled out the back even before the dragonmen had reached Tampo, and Vlora moved to give chase only to have her arm caught by Tampo. The lawyer manhandled her out of the café and into the street before straightening his jacket casually and linking arms with her forcefully. She tried to pull away, but to no avail, and soon found herself walking briskly away from the scene of the crime.

Tampo whistled softly to himself, as if murdering a pair of legendary warriors without breaking a sweat was just another item on his to-do list, right next to a reminder to pick up a loaf of bread. Vlora stopped fighting him by the time they reached the next street over. She was in a daze, her mind tied in knots by what had just happened.

She knew of only one man capable of manhandling a powder mage, one man who might conceivably move so bloody fast. She'd not seen nor heard from him in ten years, and the last time they'd met he hadn't been entirely human anymore—and he'd had access to the kind of mysterious sorcery that might even be able to change his face and hide his sorcery.

Besides, after all this time she still knew that pleased whistle.

"Why are you here, Taniel?" she demanded.

Taniel Two-shot, wearing another man's face, lifted his hand to hail a hackney cab. "Because we need to have a talk."

CHAPTER 46

T his isn't a street address," the clerk said.

Michel stood at the front of a long line in the Landfall commissioner's office while a middle-aged clerk looked at him over the top of her spectacles. She held his paper in her hand, arm outstretched to one side as if the whole thing was a terrible inconvenience. Michel, wearing plainclothes instead of a uniform, resisted the urge to pull out his Gold Rose and reminded himself he was trying to be as circumspect as possible.

"You're joking," Michel said.

"Nope." She handed the paper back. "It's not an address."

He took it sourly, stuffing it in his pocket. "That explains why I couldn't find the damn place anywhere."

"Mm-hmm." The clerk made a show of looking around him at the line. "Next!" she shouted, waving him away dismissively. "It's not an address. It's a lot number. Probably south of the city."

"What do you mean, a lot number?" The next person in line

approached the desk and started talking, but Michel shoved himself back in front of the clerk. "Lot number?" he demanded.

"Public land. South of the city."

"That's the same as an address!"

"Good day, sir. Next, please."

Michel wasn't certain what to expect when he took a hackney cab two miles south of the outskirts of Landfall. There wasn't much out here but farmland—endless floodplains covered in tobacco, cotton, and wheat. What he *didn't* expect was to find a camp.

From a distance it resembled a labor camp. Acres upon acres had been cordoned off, a short palisade built to encircle countless rows of dirty tents. There were a few wooden buildings in the center, beside a number of man-made hills of soil, steaming in the summer heat like piles of shit. The camp had been plopped right in the center of a cotton field, plants crushed underfoot, muddy wagon ruts leading to and from the main road.

As he drew closer he caught sight of guards in yellow uniforms doing a frequent circuit of the camp, carrying Hrusch rifles instead of truncheons—a sure sign of a military presence. He vaguely remembered reading something in the newspaper about an archeology dig down here, but he hadn't read the whole article. The local colleges had half of Landfall dug up looking for Dynize relics, so one dig hadn't stood out to him.

The cab came to a stop near one of the muddy paths leading to the camp. Michel vacillated. Heading into camp didn't seem advisable, not with so many guards. But this was his best lead on the godstones. If he let it go, then...then what? The camp looked semipermanent. It would still be here in a week or two, and once the Blackhats were no longer on high alert Michel might get a chance to snoop around the upper archives with carte blanche. Hurrying now might betray his real purpose to Fidelis Jes.

He thumped on the roof of the cab. "Head back to the city," he called.

"Uh, sorry, sir," the driver responded. "A man wants to speak to you."

"A man . . . ?" Michel trailed off as a soldier rounded the side of the cab and came up to the window, opening the door with one hand while the other rested on the butt of his pistol. He wore a dark yellow uniform with the bar and star of a major in the Fatrastan army on one shoulder, and a stitched white rose on the other; a soldier working with Blackhat authority.

The major did not look pleased. His broad face was expressionless, his mouth pressed into a firm line and his back as stiff as a board. "Out of the cab," he said.

"I think there's been a misunderstanding," Michel responded.

The major reached inside and grabbed Michel by the front of his shirt, dragging him out of the cab as he protested. Michel managed to keep his feet, avoiding the indignity of falling in the mud, and soon found himself surrounded by a whole platoon of the Landfall garrison. He swallowed, closed his eyes, and let instinct kick in.

"You curious about what's going on here?" the major demanded, pointing at the camp behind him. "Didn't you see the signs? No stopping? The newspapers were told to stay out."

Michel cleared his throat, letting an irritated expression blanket his face, and snapped, "Are you paranoid, Major?"

The major leaned forward slightly, the corner of his mouth lifting in a sneer. "Am I what?"

Slowly, deliberately, Michel drew the Gold Rose from his shirt and let it dangle at the end of its chain. Somewhere in the back of the company someone muttered just a little too loudly, "The major messed up this time." He was quickly shushed.

"Surprise inspection, Major," Michel said, trying to sound as smug as possible.

The major somehow managed to straighten further, eyes snapping forward and hand coming up in a salute. "Sir!"

Michel didn't give the major any time to ask questions. He was in it now, and he needed to move quickly enough that he was gone before anyone could figure out that maybe he wasn't supposed to be here. He ran through a hundred questions in his head, trying to figure out how to ask what the pit this place was without looking like he didn't *actually* know. "State your name."

"Major Cole, sir."

"Major Cole, would you kindly have your men escort me to the camp?"

"Of course, sir. Fall in!"

Within moments Michel was squelching through the mud, wondering if his shoes would be completely ruined and resisting the urge to look back at his cab. This little excursion had either just gone very right, or very, very wrong.

They entered the camp through a guarded gap in the palisade. Convict laborers milled everywhere. Some stood by the palisade, taking their lunch of gruel and bread, while others hid from the heat beneath sagging tents. They stared at Michel with sunken, bleary eyes, and he wondered at the size of the workforce and the presence of the army for what appeared—from a distance, at least—to be a midsize archeology dig.

The major snapped another salute when they reached one of the buildings in the center of the camp. "Very sorry for the confusion, sir. I hope you'll understand I was just doing my job."

"Which is?" Michel asked, trying to look like he didn't actually care.

"Make sure no one takes too much interest in the camp, sir."

Michel bit his tongue to keep from asking why and gave a gracious nod. "Thank you, Major, I'll take your...zeal...into account on my report." He gave one last glance around, noting the direction from which the laborers were coming with their wheelbarrows and then stepping up to the door to the building in front of him. The major seemed to expect that Michel wanted to end up here, so there was nothing to do but duck inside.

He found himself in what appeared to be a hastily built office barely bigger than a frontier tent. It was startlingly cool inside; a block of ice packed in sawdust was positioned in the corner of the room, while a pair of convicts slowly fanned it to circulate the air. Most of the space was taken up by tables and chairs, covered in vast stacks of handwritten notes. Other than the convicts, there was only a single occupant: a man bent over a table in the center of the room, his attention so focused as he scribbled notes that he didn't even look up when Michel cleared his throat.

Michel picked his way through the papers, trying to avoid stepping on anything important with his muddy shoes. The man seemed completely oblivious to Michel's presence. He stopped scribbling for a moment to scratch his balding scalp and mutter to himself, then went back to work. Michel bent over the nearest table, examining the notes.

They meant nothing to him. Equations, long rambling paragraphs, geometry—there was even a star chart buried beneath a stack of reference cards. The notes appeared to be in at least four different handwritings, one of which looked awfully like the writing in the book where Michel had found the lot number for this camp.

He'd never been to an archeological dig, but he'd always imagined them far more orderly and severe—this looked like a professor's desk had just exploded. He cleared his throat again, loudly, and the man finally looked up, his eyes widening at the presence of another person in the room.

"Good afternoon," Michel said.

"Who are you?"

Michel pulled the Gold Rose out of his shirt and let it dangle for a moment before returning it.

"Ah." The man nodded happily, as if Michel's visit were as normal as the heat. He crossed the room, snatching Michel's hand and shaking it, leaving Michel's fingers covered in ink smudges. "Professor Cressel. So good to meet you. You're here to review our work?" He gestured across the seemingly endless stacks of paper. "I'm afraid it's a little unorganized, but I tell you this is all very exciting!"

"Professor," Michel said coolly, "I'm not here to review your work. Just the, uh, excavation site."

"Of course, of course," Cressel responded. "I'm afraid I'm not Privileged Robson, but the Privileged was called back to the city rather suddenly." Cressel squinted at Michel curiously, then waved it off as if what was going on back in Landfall was of no real consequence. "Things are going swimmingly here, however. The madness takes a few more people every day, but the monolith is almost entirely unearthed. We've been prepping the move for weeks and should be ready within days."

Michel tried to wrap his head around all the information and mentally ticked through what he knew: This was an archeological site of some kind; it was heavily guarded against outsiders; and something very important was located in the pit at the center of the camp. Michel's mouth was suddenly dry as he considered the implications.

"Where do you plan on moving it?" he asked faintly.

Cressel seemed surprised by the question. He tilted his head. "Dalinport, I believe. We need someplace better to conduct our experiments than the middle of farmland!" He scowled to himself, jotted a few things down on a scrap of paper, then smiled back at Michel.

Michel slowly sidled toward the window on the far side of the room, moving a box of papers out of his way before leaning to get a look outside.

About fifty yards away, perfectly framed by two mounds of excavated dirt, was an immense pit. In the center rose an obelisk, perhaps twenty feet above the ground and surrounded by scaffolding, with old men and women in suits clambering all over the face of it—taking impressions, writing down notes, and sometimes standing and staring as if they'd been overcome by something unseen.

Michel heard a whisper in the back of his head, like the sound of a curtain being drawn aside, and turned toward Cressel. The professor seemed oblivious, his nose back in his notes.

Michel licked his lips, squinting at the obelisk. He heard the whisper again, but ignored it. Was this the very godstone Taniel was looking for? For some reason Michel had envisioned something…smaller—something easily moved, like the size of a bread box. He remembered that Taniel had used the plural when he spoke of the godstones.

"Are there any others?" Michel asked.

Cressel looked up. "Hmm?"

"Any other go—" Michel caught himself. "Any other stones like this?"

"I don't believe so," Cressel said, though he seemed immediately caught up in the idea. "Could you imagine, though? We've already learned so much from this one, if there were more…" He trailed off, fiddling with his pencil, and turned back to his notes.

"Imagine," Michel murmured to himself, looking back out the window. The whispering grew louder, and he was certain now he wasn't imagining it. "Do you hear anything?"

"Oh, that's just the artifact. It talks sometimes."

Every hair on the back of Michel's neck stood up on end. He wanted to grab Cressel and shake him, demanding whether he really thought it was normal for an inanimate object to talk. He leaned closer to the window, pressing his nose against the glass, and stared. Whatever this *thing* was—it did not seem friendly. He scratched at his arm, feeling like the whispers were crawling beneath his skin.

"The madness?" he asked.

"Oh," Cressel said, unconcerned, "it just takes the laborers. We keep our researchers on a strict regimen. No more than two hours beside the monolith at any time."

Michel's eye twitched. This was not normal. Every sense screamed for him to flee, to get away from this thing. He focused on the laborers moving around beside the pit and noted the harried, sleepless looks on their faces, the wide-eyed stares. They felt it, too, but they had no choice but to work. Hence, he decided, the army.

"Would you like a tour of the excavation?" Cressel asked cheerfully.

"No thank you." Michel headed for the door. He had to tell Taniel about this. And he had to get as far from it as possible if he was ever going to sleep again.

CHAPTER 47

I don't know how you're doing it," Vlora said, "and I don't want to know. But I won't talk to you while you're wearing someone else's face."

She sat across from Tampo in the hackney cab, studying the unfamiliar face. This *was* Taniel; she knew it was. She *should* have known the moment they talked last week in the Yellow Hall but that face was too different and strange.

Over the years she'd seen sorcery the likes of which most Privileged could only dream, but she'd never witnessed anything like this. Her skin crawled, stomach turning. She should have been able to sense a fellow powder mage. She should have been able to feel the sorcery that hid his face in the Else.

She could do neither.

"Vlora," Tampo began in a gentle, reprimanding tone of voice that she'd heard a thousand times when they were teenage lovers.

"I'm serious," she snapped, trying not to throw up.

Tampo snorted, turning toward the window. "This isn't like putting on a mask," he said. "It takes hours to put back."

"I don't care."

"Damn it, Vlora…" Several moments passed before he finally put his face in his hands and drew them downward, like a man washing his face in the basin first thing in the morning. When his fingers withdrew his face had altered, a series of subtle changes to his eyes, cheekbones, chin, and nose that left him a different man; Taniel Two-shot, hero of the Fatrastan Revolution and Adran-Kez War. Godkiller.

Vlora opened the cab door and vomited onto the passing cobbles.

She straightened, wiping her mouth, the taste of bile on her tongue, then ran a hand through her hair to find she was sweating horribly. *That's out of the way,* she told herself. *You've seen strange things before. Why does this bother you so much?* She forced herself to examine Taniel closely, searching his face. This was definitely him.

"You haven't aged," she said.

"A side effect of Ka-poel's sorcery," Taniel said.

Taniel drew a pair of black gloves from his pocket and pulled them on over his fingers, drawing Vlora's attention to his left hand. The hand must have also been hidden behind this glamouring sorcery, because it was now smooth and hairless, the skin the color of fresh blood. Vlora snorted, hardly allowing herself to be surprised. "You're the Red Hand?" she asked.

Taniel gave her a wan smile.

With all the strangeness Vlora had just witnessed, she found herself especially drawn to the red skin. "How did that happen?"

Taniel put his hands in his pocket, pulling a sour face. "Also a side effect of Ka-poel's sorcery. I had a run-in with a very powerful Privileged. He almost won. The kickback from Ka-poel's protection turned him into a smear of blood and dyed my skin red. No idea why." He touched his elbow. "Goes all the way up to here."

Vlora shook her head in wonder. Taniel Two-shot was both the Red Hand *and* Gregious Tampo? A million questions went through her head, so many different things she wanted to say that it made her dizzy. Yet when she tried to speak, nothing important came out. "You've been busy."

"You could say that," Taniel agreed.

"So what? Are you immortal now?"

"Not that I'd like to find out." He pulled down the collar of his suit to show a healed scar beneath his neck. "Getting shot still hurts."

"Glad to hear some things never change, even when you ascend to . . . whatever it is you've become."

Taniel frowned, looking back out the window and not respond- ing. She could see the emotions leaping across his face, his lips twisting as he opened his mouth to speak, thought better of it, then tried to do so again with the same results. Vlora wanted nothing more than to reach across the space between them and punch him right between the eyes.

She managed to restrain herself. "You're a son of a bitch, you know that?" From the startled look on his face, that wasn't exactly what he was expecting her to say. She continued: "That shit you pulled on me in the Yellow Hall. Yapping at me from behind another's eyes about *our* past. Telling me that the Palo hated me because they loved you so much."

"None of that was a lie," Taniel said.

"That doesn't make it any less of a shitty thing to bring up after ten years."

Taniel rolled his tongue around in his cheek. "I'll admit, there was some old anger there."

"Get over it," Vlora said. "You're supposed to be dead. And now I find you here, half a world away, up to your neck in . . . I have no idea what you're up to your neck in. But I've been working for

Lindet for over a year and a little warning would have been nice. I've been *hunting* the Red Hand. It would have been nice to know it was you!"

"You've been working for Lindet killing the people I'm trying to protect."

"So I'm your enemy?"

Taniel pursed his lips.

Vlora went on. "You're a Palo now, then?"

"My wife is."

Vlora snorted. "Ka-poel—I assume you mean Ka-Poel—is Dynize. I remember that much. I've still got your letters. Been using them to navigate this stupid place and..." She let out a sudden laugh, unable to help herself. The irony of using Taniel's letters to aid in her campaign against people he was fighting for was just too much. She got herself under control, trying to get her mind to focus. A million questions, but only some of them were truly important. "The Palo getting organized. All the grief and worry they've been causing Lindet. That was you and Ka-poel?"

"Most of it," Taniel admitted. "And Pole considers herself Palo. She was raised here, you know."

"If that was the two of you, why didn't I run into more resistance when my Riflejacks were putting down uprisings in the swamps? Even you could organize the rabble better than what we faced."

If Taniel noticed the backhanded compliment, he did not acknowledge it. "By my count, there are over seven hundred Palo tribes stretched across the whole of Fatrasta. Probably more that we don't even know about. Uniting them is a giant pain in the ass. We barely have a line of communication to those out in the Tristan Basin, let alone the wilds beyond them."

"Just enough to get them riled up, eh?"

"Not intentionally," Taniel said.

One question down. "All right, so that wasn't you out in the

Basin. Then what the pit *are* you doing here? You say you're protecting the Palo? Uniting them? Why?"

"To give them a fighting chance against the Kressian incursion."

"You *are* Kressian," Vlora said. She could hear the anger in Taniel's words, and she felt her own rise to match it.

"I'm dead, remember?" Taniel said. "Besides, the Palo need all the help they can get. They're not stupid. They're not lacking in courage. They just don't have the training to stand up against Lindet."

"So you're fomenting a revolution?"

Taniel's face twisted. "It's more complicated than that."

"Indulge me."

"First of all, Lindet is brilliant, and I don't use that word lightly. In terms of planning, she's on par with my father."

"Everyone knows she's smart," Vlora conceded.

"No. She's brilliant. She has all of Field Marshal Tamas's ability to plan and none of his moral qualms."

"Tamas had moral qualms?" Vlora asked, half-joking.

"Compared to Lindet? Yes."

"You're Taniel-bloody-Two-shot. Why don't you just put a bullet in her head and be done with it?"

"That's what makes this complicated," Taniel said. "Lindet has contingencies for everything, including powder mages. She's accompanied by at least two Privileged at all times. Yes, I probably *could* kill her with Ka-poel's help, even though she's also got contingencies against blood magic. But this country is a tower of cards, and killing Lindet will make the entire thing fall down— she's made certain of that."

"I thought you're only worried about the Palo."

Taniel made a frustrated sound. "I'm worried about Fatrasta, both the Palo and the Kressians. The fates of everyone who lives here are tied together. I won't cut off my nose to spite my face.

Ka-poel and I have spent the last five years trying to figure out how to remove Lindet from power and the best we've come up with is outright revolution."

"And here I thought you were trying a peaceful route," Vlora said sarcastically. She wasn't sure what to make of this—any of it—but she didn't like it. It seemed almost funny that ten years ago she would have been on board with a coup in a heartbeat. She would have been idealistic, hopeful, determined—just like Taniel sounded. *She* was the one who'd changed, not him. No, not funny, she decided. Terrifying.

"I am," Taniel insisted. "Mostly. Uniting the Palo is the first step to a peaceful revolution. Our goal is to force Lindet into a corner. I've studied her moves for the last twelve years and I readily admit she's smarter than me. But I'm not an idiot, either. I can see patterns. Everything she does is for Fatrasta. Not the people, or the country, but the concept. She wants this country to *work* and so far it's done so by her will alone. If the whole of Fatrasta turns against her, she *will* abdicate."

Vlora was not convinced. Something was bothering her about this whole exchange, and she couldn't quite figure out what. "Was Mama Palo one of yours?" she asked.

"She was," Taniel said.

"You let her die."

Taniel's eyes tightened. "Technically, you killed her." He paused, blowing out softly through his nostrils. "I did not see you coming. Four powder mages accompanied by a Palo guide, right into the center of the Depths? That was ballsy, even for you. I would have stopped you if I had known it was coming."

"You could have rescued her from the gallows."

"To what end?" Taniel asked.

"To save an old lady's life! To rescue the one person who's been uniting the Palo against Lindet! To stop the Blackhats from having another victory. To..." Vlora trailed off, suddenly angry with

Taniel for his lack of action, and angry with herself for being complicit in Mama Palo's death. Taniel tilted his head to one side, and Vlora narrowed her eyes. "What?"

"The old woman who died wasn't Mama Palo."

Vlora opened her mouth, then closed it again. "You...son of a bitch, it's Ka-poel, isn't it?"

"Of course it is. The old woman who went to the gallows was named Cherin-tes. She's been a figurehead from the very beginning, and she knew it. And before you call me a monster for letting her die, a sickness in her blood would have seen her dead within the year anyway. She knew the risks."

"And Mama Palo?"

"It'll take Lindet a couple of months, but she'll eventually figure out that she missed."

"That *I* missed," Vlora corrected.

"Yup."

Vlora scowled. She didn't like the idea of leaving town and having rumors spread over the winter that she'd botched a job. It would be terrible for the Riflejacks' reputation. The intangible thing in the back of her mind was still bugging her. It was floating just outside her awareness, like a moth tapping against a windowpane. Suddenly, she reached out and snagged it. "The Dynize," she said. "Meln-Dun. The dragonmen. What's the connection?"

For the first time since their cab ride began, Taniel's face went stony, his eyes narrowing. "That's something entirely different," he said quietly.

"Is it a problem for you?"

"The Dynize are clever. They've been very subtle about their infiltration of the Depths. We've been watching them, keeping our distance, but if I've put the pieces together right, and Meln-Dun tricked you into helping him remove Mama Palo..."

"He did," Vlora growled.

"...and Meln-Dun has some sort of deal with the Dynize..."

"Seems little doubt of that," Vlora interjected.

"...then Ka-poel and I are going to move against them soon."

Vlora did not envy the Dynize who would be caught up in *that* purge. She knew what Ka-poel was capable of when she was angry, and if the sorcery disguising Taniel was any indication, she'd progressed even further since then. "Why are they here?" Vlora asked.

"We don't know."

"You don't know, or you won't tell me?"

"Both. We have our suspicions, but..."

Vlora waited for him to finish the sentence. He didn't. "You don't trust me," she finally said.

"You're working for Lindet."

"You just told me a lot more damning information than a few suspicions over Dynize spies."

"Compared to our suspicions, all of this is inconsequential. Besides, nothing I told you could help you fight us. The Blackhats have been trying to catch the Red Hand for years. The only way I survive is by making certain there's nothing to capture."

"Taniel Red Hand, huh?"

"Just Red Hand. Taniel's dead, remember?"

Vlora found herself troubled, wondering what suspicions Taniel could have about the Dynize that were even more sensitive than his war with Lindet. "The Riflejacks don't work for Lindet anymore."

Taniel's eyebrows rose. "Is that so?"

"We handed over Mama Palo. That was our job. I refused further employment."

"I'm glad to hear that," Taniel said, sounding genuine.

Vlora waited for a few moments, then said, "What are your suspicions?"

Taniel gave her a tight smile. "How would you like a job?"

The question shouldn't have taken Vlora off guard, but it did. She reeled mentally, taking a deep breath and leaning back in her seat to get her wits about her. She'd made up her mind to leave Fatrasta, maybe forever, and she was ready to board a ship by the end of the week. "What kind of a job?"

"I'm not sure yet. I might need an army sometime in the next couple of years. I could put you and the Riflejacks on retainer and have you wait around up north. Could come in handy."

It sounded like a mercenary's dream job. Be paid to wait around for pending orders. They wouldn't have to keep up appearances, manage a garrison, or anything. Her men wouldn't like the prospect of staying away from home for another two years—but they'd love the freedom of terrorizing the brothels and pubs of northern Fatrasta on someone else's krana.

"We're planning on heading home," Vlora said. She could hear the hesitance in her own voice, and Taniel pounced on it.

"I'll pay you whatever Lindet was paying you."

"You've got money?"

"Remember how we agreed to split the inheritance after the war? You got the domestic holdings, I got the foreign ones?"

"Yes," Vlora said slowly. She could have kept it all if she wanted. Despite their falling-out during the war, she was still Field Marshal Tamas's adopted daughter—and Taniel was technically dead. Legally, everything Tamas had before his death belonged to her.

"Did you ever bother to check those accounts?" Taniel asked.

"Not that I recall."

"Tamas was fabulously wealthy. He was the king's favorite for most of his life and didn't so much as buy himself a drink if he didn't have to. His foreign holdings could have bought him a sultanate in Gurla."

"Wish I'd known that before I became a damned mercenary commander," Vlora muttered. She ran through the logistics in her head, already drifting toward the problem of keeping her men sharp while on a sort of permanent leave, *and* avoiding Lindet's questions. Northern Fatrasta might be like a whole different country, but it was still ruled by Lindet. But there was one thing stopping her. "I can't," she finally said.

Taniel had the temerity to look hurt. "Why not?"

"I'm not getting involved in another revolution."

"It's not going to be a coup."

"I don't care," Vlora said. "A revolution is a revolution, and I've got no interest. I've seen the outcome of good intentions, and I'm not going to put either myself or my soldiers through any of it."

Taniel frowned, looking pensively at his gloved hands for some time. "Are you sure?"

"I'm sure."

The two of them sat in silence, eyes locked, studying each other. Vlora wondered what he was hiding—what he wasn't telling her. What did he know about the Dynize and the Palo and Lindet? What were his plans? Taniel had never been ambitious, and beyond the defense of Adro she had never witnessed him involved in a cause to which he was truly committed. To what lengths would he go to reach his goals? More important, what were Ka-poel's goals and motives in all of this?

A dozen more questions sat on the tip of her tongue, and a dozen times as many fears. Taniel was unreadable, but at least Vlora had once known him intimately; she might be able to foresee his intentions. Ka-poel was the truly terrifying one of the pair—both for her power, and her unpredictability.

Why were they here, struggling on behalf of a people who could not win a fight they did not want? Vlora guessed that the answer was in the question, that he and Ka-poel were the Palo's only hope. But was there something more?

Vlora realized suddenly that they hadn't moved for several minutes. Her throat went dry at the thought, her first instinct to be wary of ambush. "I'd like to return to the fort now."

Taniel gave a sad nod and thumped on the roof of the cab. "Loel's Fort," he commanded.

"Won't be going anywhere for a while, sir," the driver responded. "Traffic's all backed up."

Vlora stuck her head out the window, looking up and down the street and a long line of cabs, carriages, and wagons. Drivers were shouting at one another, some standing up in their seats to try to see what the holdup was. Urchins darted among the wheels, taking the opportunity to snatch goods out of the back of wagons before retreating to nearby alleyways.

"What's going on?" she asked.

"Not sure, ma'am," the driver said.

Vlora chewed on her bottom lip, reassuring herself that this was a coincidence. It had nothing to do with her or Taniel. It wasn't a trap of some kind. Her nerves were just strung too tightly. "Where are we?"

"Eastern lip, ma'am. Right above the bay."

More than two miles' walk back to Loel's Fort, and the heat of the afternoon was getting worse.

"I'll see what's going on," Taniel said, getting out of the cab. Vlora got out after him, paying the driver before running to catch up.

"I'm heading back to my men," she told him. "Olem will need help organizing our travel back to the Nine. You never really realize the logistics of moving a whole brigade until you're actually in command."

"Tamas loved that sort of stuff," Taniel said wistfully. He tapped his cane on the cobbles, frowning up at the rooftops as they wound their way through the crowd. A stiff breeze came in off the ocean, nearly taking Vlora's hat off. Taniel suddenly stopped and turned to her. "I'm not your enemy," he said.

"And I'm not yours." They stared at each other once again. They might not be enemies, Vlora thought to herself, but she couldn't exactly call them friends.

"I'm glad. Does Olem know I'm still alive?"

"He does."

"Tell him hello for me. Consult with him, if you're willing. Reconsider my offer."

Vlora bit her tongue. She knew that Olem would agree with whatever decision she wound up making. But as much as he hated ships and wouldn't be looking forward to the voyage home, he had to be aching to see the Nine again. "I'll talk to him."

"Thank you," Taniel said. He smiled to himself. "You know, sometimes I wish I had remained alive. That I'd just retired quietly and gone out into the world. That I could have stayed myself—I could have come back and visited, and Ka-poel and I could have taken dinner with you and Olem at a dockside club in Adro. I wish I could have lived a normal life."

"I don't think either of us would have been able to handle a normal life," Vlora responded.

"No. Probably not. I . . ." Taniel trailed off.

They'd continued walking, albeit slowly, as they spoke, and the eastern edge of the Landfall Plateau had come into view. A crowd had gathered in the street, all of them pointing and talking excitedly, looking at something down in the docks below.

No, Vlora realized. Not the docks. Farther out, beyond the edge of the bay. She pushed her way to the front of the crowd, craning her neck to see. There was a ship out there, easily half a mile from the shore. It was immense, a ship of the line with three decks of guns on either side and a forecastle that would have rivaled a tenement in height. The gray sails were drawn, and even at this distance she could make out tiny figures scrambling around the deck.

"Why are they stopped so far out?" she asked.

"Look at the flag," Taniel said flatly, stepping up to her side.

"What about it?" Vlora lifted her eyes, and it took a moment for the wind to catch the flag above the ship's highest sail, unraveling to reveal a black background with a cluster of red stars arcing across the center. "Oh," she whispered.

That flag did not belong to Adro or Kez or Brudania, or any of the countries of the Nine. It wasn't the emblem of a Gurlish province or any colonial power on the world.

It was the flag of the Dynize Empire.

"Take powder," Taniel said with a note of urgency.

"Why?"

"Just do it."

Vlora removed a powder charge from her pocket, cutting one end with her thumbnail and snorting a little in each nostril. She rubbed her nose and returned the rest of the charge to her breast pocket. Within moments her senses had sharpened, and she was able to pick out the details of the individuals on board the ship as if they were a few feet away. Men and women scurried across the decks, preparing longboats for lowering. It was strange to see a ship entirely manned by people with the red hair and ashen freckles of the Palo, and she had to remind herself that they weren't actually Fatrastan natives.

"What am I looking for?" she asked.

"The horizon."

Vlora lifted her gaze, and what she saw took her breath away. Far out beyond the closest ship, miles and miles from shore where even the best looking glasses would have trouble spotting them at the edge of the horizon, she could see more ships. There were dozens of them, perhaps forty or more, and each was capped by a tiny black and red dot that could only be the Dynize flag.

"Since when do the Dynize leave their home country?" someone beside her asked.

Vlora wet her lips and turned to Taniel, speaking in a low voice. "Since when do the Dynize have a fleet?"

"They don't," Taniel said, dumbfounded. "They shouldn't. This changes everything."

Vlora was running in a moment, not even bothering to hail a cab as she sprinted down the street, ignoring the shouts that followed her as with powder-enhanced speed she blew past people. She had to get back to the Riflejacks and Olem.

Taniel was right. This changed everything.

CHAPTER 48

Styke sat in one corner of Lady Flint's office in Loel's Fort, his borrowed knife in his lap, rocking on the back two legs of the chair, his face pointed at the ceiling and his eyes closed as he waited for Lady Flint to return from Mama Palo's execution. Across from him Ibana paced restlessly, thumbs hooked through her belt loops, repeating the same phrase every five minutes or so.

"This is a terrible idea."

"You mentioned that," Styke answered.

"Well, I'm mentioning it again. Couldn't you have just sent her a damned letter or something?"

Styke opened his eyes and kept them glued to the sagging plaster ceiling, listening to the chair beneath him creak in protest as he rocked himself gently with one foot. "I could have," he said. "But I didn't."

"I hadn't noticed," Ibana responded sarcastically.

Styke sucked in a mouthful of air, puffed out his cheeks, and slowly blew it back out. Ibana was right, of course. This *was* a terrible idea. Olem had told him before his fight with Fidelis Jes that he was no longer welcome here, and that the men had been ordered to arrest him on sight. The last thing he needed was for them to try exactly that and have this turn into a fight. He should have left Ibana with the other lancers. "Look," he said, "if you want me back, if you want me to take command of the Mad Lancers, then I'm going to set a few things to rest first."

Two things, to be precise. The first he'd taken care of not long after his conversation with Lindet by leaving a note for Tampo at the only address the lawyer had given him—a bank box on the western edge of the plateau. This was the second thing, and for some reason he'd decided it was far more important. He'd also, stupidly, decided to do it in person.

Ibana was about to respond, an argumentative look on her face, when Styke heard a commotion in the muster yard outside. They both froze, and Styke slowly lowered the front legs of his chair to the ground and got up, borrowed knife in hand.

"Where's Olem!" Lady Flint's voice demanded from somewhere outside.

Styke couldn't hear the answer, or make out Flint's barked order, but he could tell she was heading in his direction. He braced himself and gestured Ibana away from the door.

Lady Flint opened it a moment later, stepping inside while shouting over her shoulder, "Get everyone. Send a messenger to Fidelis Jes and Lindet telling them I want to see them."

"Which one?" someone asked.

"Either. Both. I don't care. I—" Flint cut herself off, pausing just inside the door at the sight of Ibana, eyes falling on Styke half a second later. Her pistol seemed to leap into her hand, and a shout on the tip of her tongue was arrested only by Styke barking one word:

"Wait!"

Styke stared down the barrel of Flint's pistol for an agonizing ten seconds, Ibana coiled as if ready to spring, hoping the whole time that nobody did anything rash. Slowly, bit by bit, Flint's finger came off the trigger. "What are you doing here?" she asked.

"We came to talk," Styke said, gesturing for Ibana to relax.

"Everyone wants to talk with me right now. It's getting bloody well old. How did you get in here?"

"Olem let us in."

Vlora whispered a litany of curses before finally lowering her pistol. "I still may shoot you. Who's this?"

Not a great start, Styke decided, but it was better than getting a bullet through the eye. "This is my second in command, Ibana ja Fles."

"The swordmaker?"

"That's right," Ibana said.

"I have one of your knives," Flint said. "It's some damn fine work. Pit, you're tall. Damn it, Styke, I thought I only had to deal with one giant." Ibana pursed her lips, but her shoulders relaxed and Styke gave a silent sigh of relief. Nothing like a little flattery to help cool the air. "Okay," Flint said, "if Olem let you in here he must think it's important. I'm a bit busy, so you have thirty seconds."

Styke took a deep breath, wondering why some words were so much easier to say than others. He chewed on them for a moment, glanced at Ibana—whose impatient look was no help at all—then said, "I came to apologize."

"For tricking me into hiring a convict and making me look like a fool in front of my employers?"

"No. Not for that."

Flint blinked. That wasn't what she'd been expecting. She closed the door behind her warily, putting her back to it, still holding her pistol. She was such a small thing, nearly two feet shorter than either him or Ibana. Her blocking the exit might have made him laugh if he didn't know what she was capable of. "Then what?" she asked flatly.

"You hired me under false pretenses," Styke said. "But not the ones you think. I did not escape from Sweetwallow like Jes told you. I was released." He'd considered long and hard what he wanted to tell Flint, and why. He'd decided that, while he owed Tampo his freedom, he owed Lady Flint his pride. After ten years in the camps, the latter was not something he'd ever thought to see again.

"I'm listening," Flint said.

"I was released from the camps by a lawyer named Gregious Tampo. He bribed the parole board, and as a condition for my freedom sent me to work for you. He wanted me to keep you out of trouble until he didn't need you anymore, and then kill you."

To Styke's surprise, Flint's face began to change the moment Styke mentioned Tampo's name. Her mouth dropped, then her brows lowered into a scowl, and then she threw her head back and let out an angry sigh. It was *not* the reaction Styke was expecting.

Flint scratched her head with the barrel of her pistol and then brandished it at Styke. "Did he actually tell you he wanted me dead?"

Styke looked at her askance. She was taking this awfully well for someone whose trust had been betrayed. "No," he said. "But that was obviously the end goal. He needs you for something. I never got the order to cut your throat, so I assume he still does. I'm here to warn you."

"Duly noted," Flint said.

"That's all there is," Styke said, getting to his feet and putting his knife away. "I thought you should know." He felt strange. Pleasant, but strange. He wasn't used to giving excuses or explaining himself to anyone. In his old life he'd never had to, and in the camps no one cared. The same went with apologizing. "You said you're busy, so we'll go now."

Flint's pistol came back up, wavering from Styke to Ibana. Styke tensed, glancing at Ibana, whose hand had gone to the sword at her hip. "Neither of you is going anywhere," Flint said.

"I told you," Ibana growled at Styke.

"Shut up," Styke responded. "I don't want to fight you, Flint. I came in good faith."

"I never offered any good faith," Flint snapped. "And if you think I'm not pissed as pit that I took a spy into my midst, you're dead wrong. But I'm not looking for a fight, either." She lowered her pistol, her mouth tightening into a straight line. "I respect the fact you came back. I should cut you to ribbons, but I'm not going to, and here's why: Tampo doesn't want me dead."

Styke exchanged a glance with Ibana. "How do you know?"

"Because Gregious Tampo isn't Gregious Tampo. He's a powder mage by the name of Taniel Two-shot, and he's been playing everyone in this damned city for fools."

"Uh," was all Styke could manage. He tried to wrap his mind around this information. Styke's memory wasn't great, but he'd fought beside Taniel during the war. Gregious Tampo was *definitely* not Taniel. "Two-shot is dead. You said so yourself."

"Taniel faked his death at the end of the Adran-Kez War," Flint replied. She finally stuffed her pistol into her belt, taking a small sniff of powder, removing the tremor from her voice. "He and the bone-eye you met back during the Fatrastan Revolution are here, now."

Styke scowled, licking his lips, thinking back over the meetings he'd had with Tampo. "No," he said. "I would have sensed it. My Knack can smell sorcery."

"Ka-poel's sorcery is stronger than anything you've ever encountered," Flint said, sounding almost resigned to the fact. "It fooled your Knack and it fooled my third eye. It's fooled a damn lot of people, but Tampo—or rather, Taniel—doesn't want me dead. If he sent you here to keep me out of trouble he probably thought he was protecting me."

This was a lot to take in. Ibana looked skeptical, and Styke himself echoed the sentiment. It was possible to hide from the Else using

Privileged sorcery, but it was incredibly difficult. Wearing someone else's face for long periods of time, and being completely undetectable? It would take a whole Privileged cabal to manage that.

Or, if Flint was telling the truth, a single powerful bone-eye.

Styke could think of no reason for Flint to lie. "So does this mean no hard feelings?" he asked slowly.

"I wouldn't go that far," Flint said, eyes flashing. "But a secret bodyguard is more palatable than a secret assassin." Her eyes suddenly widened. "Son of a bitch, I don't have time for this." She opened the door and yelled for Olem, then closed it behind her, eyes focusing on Styke. "Did you fight Fidelis Jes?"

"I did." Styke grimaced.

"And you lost?"

"He sent me back to the camps, crippled."

Flint looked him up and down. "You don't look crippled."

"The Mad Lancers rescued him," Ibana explained. "We may have, um, kidnapped a Privileged to heal his wounds."

"Kidnapped a Privileged..." Flint muttered. She shook her head. "Bloody madmen. Okay, so that is where we stand. Did you find anything else out about the Dynize before that whole debacle?"

Styke shook his head. He could see in her eyes that Flint had moved past the apology, the revealed betrayal, and all of that to something else. Her ability to compartmentalize was admirable, but he reminded himself not to make the mistake of assuming she would trust him again.

"So you know nothing about the Dynize fleet sitting out beyond the bay?" Flint asked.

"The what now?" Ibana asked, mouth falling open.

Styke managed to keep the shock off his face, but he felt like he'd been punched in the gut. "That's not possible," he said.

"Neither is Taniel Two-shot being alive," Flint responded. "But there it is. At least forty ships of war and I have no idea how many support frigates."

"The Dynize haven't left their country for over a hundred years."

"Tell me something I don't know."

"How do they even have a fleet?" Ibana demanded.

"I'd love to figure that out," Flint said, "but in the meantime I'd rather know *why* they're here."

There was a knock on the door and Styke jumped, only then realizing he'd been clutching the handle of his knife. Olem poked his head inside. "Vlora," he started, then saw Styke and Ibana. "Ah. You're still here."

"Yes, they're still here," Flint responded, acid in her voice. "And you and I are going to talk about this later."

"Sure," Olem said coolly. "After we talk about Fidelis Jes standing in the muster yard."

Styke was halfway to the door before he even knew he was moving. Flint threw out a hand, putting a surprisingly firm palm on his chest. "No," she barked.

Styke clenched and unclenched his fists. This was his chance. He was healed, fresh, angry, armed. He didn't care how many Blackhats Jes had with him out there, between him and Ibana they would carve through the lot and he'd pop Jes's eyeballs like pimples. He tried to step forward, but Ibana put an arm around his chest and hauled him back. He growled at her, and she slapped him across the face. It was enough for him to get control of himself, and he stalked to the other end of the room and glared at both Ibana and Flint.

"What does he want?" Flint asked. "Is it about the fleet?"

"It is," Olem answered.

Flint seemed to vacillate before pointing at Styke. "You, stay here. If you so much as put a finger outside this door I will put a bullet in your head. Olem, let Jes in the building."

She disappeared, leaving Styke and Ibana alone inside her office once more. Styke took several deep breaths, letting himself calm down before shrugging Ibana's hold off his shoulders. "I'm fine," he said quietly. He'd imagined a quick apology and a quicker exit, and now he was stuck here with his worst enemy on the other side of the door. He should have had a better exit strategy. Slowly, he crept over and put his ear against the door.

In the next room, he heard Fidelis Jes enter and a cold exchange of pleasantries between the two.

"What's going on?" Ibana whispered, joining him.

Styke listened carefully, only catching about half of the muffled conversation. "Jes is telling Flint about the fleet. Seems he wants to hire her."

"She's not working for him anymore?"

"No. That's what Lindet said. Their contract was for Mama Palo."

Ibana snorted. "You got lucky then. If she was still with him she would have handed us over. Or tried to."

"I don't think she would have," Styke answered. He shushed her, trying to catch more of the exchange, but to no avail. "What are we going to do about this?"

"About what? Jes?" Ibana asked. "We're going to kill him and use his skin to make you a new saddle."

Styke rolled his eyes. "And people say I have anger problems. No, about the Dynize."

"Sod the Dynize. We're riding against the Blackhats."

Styke stepped away from the door, taking Ibana by the arm and pulling her into the far corner, where they were less likely to be overheard. "If it's true, and there's a Dynize fleet out there, something is happening far bigger than you or I or the Mad Lancers." He remembered Lindet's warning to watch the horizon. Had she known this was coming?

Ibana lifted her face away from his, looking down her nose. "What are you thinking?"

"I'm thinking that we should lie low for a few months. See what happens. It may be that the Mad Lancers have more important things to do than slaughter Blackhats."

"You're going to let them get away with what they did to you?" Ibana hissed.

"Pit, no. I still want that saddle you promised me. But I formed the Mad Lancers to protect Fatrasta, not to avenge my own losses."

"You did it for both."

Styke chewed on the inside of his cheek. "Fair point. But something is happening." He paused, a thought occurring to him. He replayed the conversation with Lindet last night through his head. "Pit," he said breathlessly. "Lindet must have known they were coming."

"How?" Ibana asked.

"She told me to watch the horizon. She said Fatrasta would face its greatest threat and that she didn't think we would be prepared for it. I thought she was trying to throw me off the trail, but she was talking about the Dynize." He was certain of it now, and he silently cursed Lindet for it. "Damn it, she could have just bloody well told me."

"If she knew, why didn't she say anything?"

"She didn't think I needed to know," Styke said bitterly. "You know that I'm the only person in the world who knows her birthday? If it's not pertinent, she doesn't share it. Just some bloody cryptic warnings. I—"

His next sentence was cut off by the door swinging open. Styke snatched for his knife, but it was just Lady Flint. She was wearing a scowl, looking like she'd aged five years in the time since she left the room. "Is Jes gone?" Styke asked.

"Yes."

"What did he want?" Ibana demanded.

Flint crossed between them, rounding her desk and plopping down into a chair. Olem entered the room a moment later, taking up a spot just inside. Neither looked happy.

Finally, Flint said, "I need you and your Mad Lancers."

"Excuse me?" Ibana did not sound pleased.

Flint's tone was distant. "We'll outfit you with horses and kit. I want you riding north within the hour. We've got eight hundred cuirassiers and three hundred dragoons stationed in Jedwar. You're to take command of them and bring them back to the city."

Styke's chest was suddenly tight. "Why?"

"Because," Flint said, "I've just been deputized as a general in the Fatrastan army. That fleet outside is making Lindet twitchy. I've been given complete control over the garrison and defenses of Landfall."

"Is there going to be violence?"

"We don't know. Lindet isn't taking any chances, and I'm the best they've got."

"What about Jes?" Styke asked.

Flint's head turned, her eyes focusing on Styke with a single-minded determination that made him take half a step back. "You and the Blackhats are going to put aside your squabble until the danger outside has passed."

"Like pit we will." Ibana snorted.

"Like pit. *You will,*" Flint ordered.

Ibana scowled back at her, then said in a slightly chastised tone, "It's Jes you have to worry about."

Styke glanced between the two women, wondering if this would still come to blows. He'd never heard anyone speak to Ibana that way and live to tell the tale. But Ibana was still listening, so that was a good sign.

"Jes will stay the bloody pit out of my way while I am in command," Flint said, "or I'll put him in front of a firing squad before Lindet can so much as sneeze. You two can either follow my orders or get out of my office. I have real work to do."

Styke glanced at Ibana, then down at his own hands. It was right there at his fingertips, a new commission for him and his men, with horses and kit and a real purpose. All he had to do was reach out and take it. And put aside a decade of hatred.

Ten years since he last sat in a saddle. His balls were going to be so damned sore by the end of the night. "We'll leave at once," he said.

Flint nodded as if their joining her was a foregone conclusion. "Good. Major Fles. Colonel Styke. Welcome to the Riflejacks. Now go pick up the rest of your command."

CHAPTER 49

W hat's her name?"

Styke stood beside a dirt path in the center of a small town in the marshes north of Landfall, slowly stroking his thumb along the nose of the horse at his side. His attention was drawn to the south, head raised to watch for anyone heading this way from the city. Celine sat in the saddle astride the horse, gently running her fingers through his mane.

"*She* is a *he*," Styke said, glancing over his shoulder at Celine. She nodded at the correction, as if she'd been right all along. "He's a gelding, and I haven't named him yet."

"What kind is he?"

Styke glanced sidelong at the horse, continuing to run his thumb down the center of his nose. "Mix-breed. He's definitely a Bruda-nian draft horse, but…" He considered it a moment, running his hand down the length of the horse's back, enjoying the coarse feel of hair beneath his fingers. It had been too long since he'd last rid-den. He'd squeezed the reins so hard they had left an impression on his palm, and his inner thighs chafed like a bitch after just a couple of miles. But they were both good kinds of hurts.

Pain that reminded him he was a free man.

"His hindquarters are a bit sleeker than a regular draft horse," he said. "Look at the coloring. The black with a little brown mottle on the neck, with the white on his rump, is pretty rare. You find that on Gurlish racing horses."

"My dad bet on a Gurlish racing horse once," Celine said.

"How did that go?"

"Lost a few hundred krana. Said betting was for fools and threw his hat in the Hadshaw."

Styke snorted. "Everyone has to learn sometime." He ran his hand down the horse's neck again, enjoying the feel. Lady Flint's stablemaster said this was the biggest beast he had, and about the orneriest, but after a little heart-to-heart in the stables Styke felt like they had come to an understanding. He wasn't as big as Deshner, nor as strong, but he had some spirit. "Do you want to name him?"

"How about Precious?" Celine said.

"Absolutely not."

"Juggernaut!"

"Where the pit did you learn a word like that?"

"From…"

"Your dad," Styke finished for her. "Right, right. Regular ol' genius, wasn't he? How about we call him Amrec."

"Amrec is a boy's name."

"And Amrec is a boy." Styke leaned back to look at the gelding's hindquarters. "Or at least he used to be." He patted Amrec on the nose, fishing in his pocket for a carrot he'd grabbed from a merchant as he left town. "You like that, Amrec?" Amrec nearly took his fingers off taking the carrot, and Styke jerked down on the bridle gently. "None of that, hear me?"

He turned away from Celine and Amrec, looking back toward Landfall. They were a couple of miles out, and the plateau rose above the floodplains, hazy in the afternoon heat, while flies buzzed quietly around Amrec's swishing tail. Styke had picked one of the few rises in this area so he had a pretty good view of the road. He waited, watching, wondering.

Ibana had gone to tell the Mad Lancers that they had a new command, and that they wouldn't be tearing up the Blackhats—at least, not just yet. A little voice in the back of Styke's head whispered that he no longer had it. That the lancers would give up in anger and go home; that they weren't interested in his command, and just wanted to go out for blood.

He wouldn't blame them if they did. The Blackhats hadn't just beaten him; they'd broken the homes and businesses and, in some cases, bones of almost all the Mad Lancers veterans. Styke's body and the bones had been mended by Privileged sorcery. The rest was gone—ten years of trying to make something out of themselves, all down the drain because Styke had dared to leave the labor camp.

He wondered, if he'd known what he would ruin for the rest of them, whether he would have taken Tampo's offer.

Yes, he decided. He definitely would have. "No one else's suffering is ever as acute as your own," he muttered.

"What?" Celine asked.

"Nothing. Here." He reached in his pocket for his last carrot. "Feed this to Amrec. Talk to him."

"Will it make us friends?"

"Food, in my experience, is one of the few things that can cement a good friendship between strangers."

He watched a small group of riders leave the Landfall suburbs and head north along his path. He waited until he could clearly make them out as Blackhats before he took Amrec by the reins and led him around to the far side of the little village, hoping the patrol would pass through without stopping.

If the rest of the lancers backed out, would Ibana still follow him? She still seemed like her old self. But ten years was a long time, and she'd been furious after they left Lady Flint's. She'd cursed and yelled before storming off, and only a shout over her shoulder had given him any indication of where to expect her and the rest of the lancers to join him.

And now he was here. He had a girl, a horse, and the hope that a bunch of rowdy old veterans still thought of him as good enough to follow. By the position of the sun it was past seven in the evening. The others should have been here an hour ago. As it was, they'd have to ride well into the night to reach Jedwar and collect Flint's cavalry.

He kicked at a clump of dirt glumly, then put a hand on Amrec's flank—more to calm himself than the horse. Amrec suddenly stirred, snorting, and Styke reached for his knife and looked toward movement at the corner of his vision.

He let himself relax. It was just a Palo woman.

She was less than five feet tall, a slight thing with fiery hair, her skin spotted with the ashen freckles of her people. Her hair was cut short, just below the ears, and she wore a black duster that almost touched the ground when she walked. Her hands were lost in the sleeves, her face shaded by a matching, floppy-brimmed hat. Below the duster she wore weathered buckskins similar to those worn by Palo on the frontier.

Styke took a deep breath, deciding to just ignore her until she went away, when something pricked his senses.

He smelled rotten flesh and tasted copper on his tongue, but knew immediately neither of those senses came from this world. It was his Knack, warning him that there was sorcery nearby. Potent sorcery, belonging to a bone-eye.

Styke shifted warily, keeping his eyes on the Palo as she approached. He'd always found it hard to judge the age of Palo women, but she looked like she was in her late twenties or early thirties. She walked toward him slowly, calmly, her eyes sleepy and a half smile on her lips.

"Who is that?" Celine asked.

Styke shook his head. "Can I help you?" he asked in Palo.

The woman stopped about six feet away, her lips pursed, head tilting from side to side as she studied Styke. He felt tiny pinpricks along his skin, the smell of rotten flesh growing stronger. She removed her hands from her pockets and showed him that they were empty.

A Palo bone-eye. Fancy that. What could she possibly want with him? He gave her his best scowl. "Nothing here for you," he said. "Best move along."

She rolled the sleeves of her duster up, then went through a complex series of gestures. Styke found them almost impossible to follow, and he just shook his head at her and made a shooing motion with one hand. She snorted, then pointed at herself, then at him, and Styke inhaled suddenly, his nostrils flaring, as he remembered a Palo girl he met in the swamps back during the war. She was small, smelled of blood and sorcery, and she hadn't been able to talk.

She'd been accompanying Taniel Two-shot at the time and, if Flint was right, still was.

He took a step back, hand going instinctively to touch Amrec's neck. The big horse nipped at his ear, then bumped him with its nose. "It's you, isn't it?" Styke asked. "Taniel's girl. I remember you from Planth. Ka-poel."

Her smile widened.

Styke let out a shaky breath. Sorcery had never frightened him particularly. What unnerved him back at Planth, and here now, was Ka-poel's confidence. She held herself like someone seven feet tall, head high, shoulders squared, daring the world to try its worst. "What do you want?" he asked.

Ka-poel remained silent, studying him, then Celine, and finally Amrec.

"Did Taniel get my note?" Styke asked. "I guess I left it for Tampo, but the two of them are the same, aren't they?"

She stuck her bottom lip out, nodding as if impressed, spreading her hands toward him. *Very good.* She mimed writing, then reading, and pointed at him again with a nod.

"So he *did* get it."

Another nod.

"So he knows I quit? I appreciate what he did for me, but I've got other obligations now. If we cross paths again, I'll try to do him right, but for now..."

Ka-poel snorted. She folded her arms and shifted her stance, putting her weight on her back foot. It almost made Styke laugh, but he could still smell the rotting flesh of her sorcery.

"I suppose you think that's not good enough?" he asked.

She gave him a look that was less than impressed, then made a flat-handed gesture that he didn't quite understand. She reached into her duster pocket and removed an envelope, crossing the space between them to hand it over. Styke eyed her warily, breaking the seal with his thumb, then running his eyes across the writing. It was written in Adran, and said, *You still owe me a favor. I intend on collecting it.—T*

Styke handed the letter over his shoulder. "Put this in my saddlebags," he told Celine. Taniel still expected something, but seemed willing to hold on to that debt until later. "What's his game?" Styke asked Ka-poel. "He's playing long, isn't he? Huh. Never mind that. What's *your* game?"

Ka-poel gave him a cocky smile, chest rising and falling in a silent chuckle. Styke rubbed his nose, not enjoying the smell of her sorcery at all. She pointed at him, then at her palm, then at herself, lips moving silently. Styke didn't like the implication.

"What the pit is that supposed to mean?"

She pointed over his shoulder, and it took him a moment to realize she was pointing at the note he'd just handed to Celine.

"Are you saying I owe *you* a favor?"

She mimed shooting a pistol at him.

Part of him wanted to wring her neck, then boot her down the road. The other part, the part dedicated wholly to self-preservation, said that would be a very bad idea. "You're a funny little thing, you know that?"

She grinned and mouthed the words *I know*. She pulled her hand out of her pocket and, in a quick move, ran a knife across her left thumb. Styke shied away, but she was quicker than he'd expected and stepped over to him in a flash, reaching up on her tiptoes to smear the rising well of crimson across his forehead. He grabbed her by the shoulder, shoving her away, using the other hand to wipe at his forehead. She danced out of his reach, and he looked at the blood now on his hand and his face.

"What the pit was that for?" he demanded. "I don't like sorcery, girl, and I won't stand for—" His words were arrested by the sound of hoofbeats, and Styke took Amrec by the bridle, head tilted to listen to the approach of the riders. Blackhats? Or Mad Lancers?

Ka-poel gave him one last smile and slipped around the corner of the building. He considered going after her but had no interest in running headfirst into a group of Blackhats. Instead he hunkered in the shade of the building and rubbed at his forehead, trying to get all the blood off. He listened to the hoofbeats grow louder, and waited for them to pass him by.

They did not.

He forgot the blood. The hoofbeats were coming around the outskirts of the village, and it sounded like a lot of them. He pulled his knife, ready to throw himself at the first person to come around the corner, and bit off a yell as the first rider rounded it.

Ibana rode on a white stallion almost as big as Amrec, saddle weighed down with carbines, pistols, and cavalry swords. She was followed by others on horseback—Gamble, Sunin, Jackal—all his officers and then more, falling in as Ibana pulled up in front of him. They kept coming, rank upon rank, spreading out in a fan, until he could no longer count all of them. Well over two hundred cavalry, all heavily armed on stout warhorses and wearing the faded yellow cavalry jackets and black pants they'd been issued at the beginning of the Fatrastan War for Independence.

Sunin's uniform was too big, Gamble's too small, but each and every one of them had it. They even had their lances, tied to their saddles and waving yellow streamers in the air. The sight of it overwhelmed him, tears threatening his vision. He sheathed his knife, barely daring to breathe, mouth open like a gawking schoolboy.

Ibana dismounted, fetching a carbine, pistol, and heavy cavalry sword from her saddle and coming over to Styke.

"You came," Styke said, unable to think of any other words.

Ibana rolled her eyes, thrusting the bundle of weapons into his arms. "Of course I did, you big fool. We all did. You're Mad Ben Styke, and without you we aren't the Mad Lancers."

Styke looked over her shoulder at his old officers, and all the familiar faces gathered behind them. He remembered seeing some of them that night at Sweetwallow, but the memories were hazy and he hadn't truly believed they'd all come to rescue him. Yet here they were.

The faces stared back at him, expectant, and it took him several moments to realize they were waiting for him to say something. He shook his head and glanced at Ibana, wondering what she told them about their current mission. "We're not going to fight the Blackhats," he said, raising his voice.

He was greeted by silence. No mutters. No scowls. Just soldiers waiting for their orders.

"I never much fancied us as mercenaries," he said. "But the Mad Lancers always rode to protect Fatrasta, and Fatrasta, in case you noticed, doesn't really want us right now." Some of the riders exchanged looks, no doubt remembering what they'd lost at the hands of the Blackhats the last few days. "The only one who wants us is Lady Flint. She's been hired to protect Landfall from that Dynize fleet sitting out beyond the bay. It may come to a scrap. It may not. Regardless, she's going to pay us, feed us, and kit us up. She's also dead set on keeping us and the Blackhats from each other's throats. I've made my peace with that, and if any of you have a problem you can talk to me about it, or you can turn around and ride back to Landfall. That's up to you."

"We don't need any protecting from the Blackhats!" someone in the back shouted.

Styke searched for the source of the voice, but couldn't find it. "Like pit we don't," he said. "But I don't mind having them off our asses long enough for us to become the Mad Lancers again. We're old, we're rusty. Pit, I'm healed up a bit but I'm still a damn cripple. I'd rather ride a free man as part of the Landfall garrison than skulk around in the shadows waiting to get overwhelmed. Now, like I said, if you have a problem no one will hold it against you if you go. Ya hear?"

The gathered cavalry responded with a stoic silence. Leather creaked; horses shifted and whinnied. Sunin, looking almost ninety, her hair white and wispy, skin as wrinkled as a prune, leaned over in her saddle and spat a wad of chew into the grass.

"We don't ride for Lady Flint or Fatrasta," she said with her northern Fatrastan twang. "We ride for Ben Styke." The riders behind her nodded sagely, a mutter of approval going up. "If you want us working for Lady Flint, we'll work for Lady Flint. We'll follow orders. But don't think for a moment we'll forget the state we found you in the other night."

"That how you all feel?" Styke demanded.

A chorus of "yeah" and "bet we do" rose up over the lancers.

"Because you're all a bunch of fools," Styke grumbled. "Always have been."

"Yeah, but they're your fools," Ibana said.

"Suppose so. I guess that settles that." He thought of Ka-poel, and the crimson welling up from her thumb. He rubbed at his forehead. "Is there blood on my face?" he asked.

"No," Ibana responded.

Styke glanced down at his hand. There wasn't any blood there, either. He wondered if he'd imagined the whole thing—Ka-poel, Taniel's letter. He wondered if perhaps his mind was slipping. "Where's my banner?"

Ibana returned to her saddlebags, untying a long, oiled leather tube. She removed a bundle of cloth from the tube and, holding one end, let the rest unfurl. The banner was black on yellow with a crimson border, the center dominated by a grinning human skull spit upon a lance. Styke held out his hand, taking the banner for himself, rubbing the rough material between his thumb and forefinger.

"Jackal," he said. "Your lance."

He fixed the banner in place and then handed the lance back to Jackal with a nod.

"Bannerman," Styke said. "Lead us to Jedwar. We have a command to pick up."

CHAPTER 50

First thing in the morning, Michel left his small apartment in Fallen End and went to the local bank a few blocks over. He was on edge as he walked inside, his nerves still frayed from the visit to the monolith the day before, and was functioning on just a couple of hours of restless sleep. Whispers had filled his night, and none of them had been pleasant. He wondered how those researchers managed to stay near the godstone—and that more of them didn't go mad from exposure.

The bank was small, sleepy, with just two clerks, a single vault, and a row of lockboxes along the back wall behind the clerks. Michel hadn't been inside it in four years, and hoped he remembered the right number. He took bank stationery, wrote down the lot number of the monolith dig site—and specific directions that it was two miles south of Landfall—along with the word "CAUTION."

"Number 132," he said, handing the note along with a single krana over to the teller. Michel tapped the brim of his hat and left.

He had, no doubt, several folders on his desk with reports about how much nothing his new underlings had found in their search for Styke. He'd have to attend to those at some point. He should have done it last night, but the monolith had unnerved him enough to send him straight to home, a warm bath, and bed. Though none of that had helped him sleep.

Instead, he'd spent the disquieting hours putting his marble back together. His self—his real self—was safely stored away. With that note dispatched to Taniel, Michel could go back to being the good little Blackhat, heart and soul. He'd be a model Gold Rose, rooting out Fatrasta's enemies from a new place of privilege, worming his way up the ladder. Pit, in a few years maybe he'd be one of Fidelis Jes's confidants.

The higher he climbed, the easier it would be to help Taniel burn the whole thing down.

"No," he said to himself sternly as he walked, hands in his pockets, along the morning streets of Landfall. "You're Agent Bravis now. Not a whisper—not even a thought—of the man you were."

"Taniel," he answered in agreement, "is on his own with that... thing."

"And I'm going to forget it ever existed."

"Right."

Michel stopped by an early market, collecting several canvas bags of food, even stopping by a discount bookseller to grab a few penny novels at random. He found himself whistling, walking slow, ignoring the urgency he knew he should be feeling to get back to the Millinery and help find Styke. For the first time in a long time, he actually wanted to get to Mother's home *after* she returned from her usual perusal of the local bookstores.

He walked all the way to Proctor, a full forty minutes. He paused by the back alley to his mother's home and, still whistling, went around to the front, knocking once and letting himself inside. For once he was going to weather her lectures with a smile. For once he'd allow himself the small fantasy of telling her who he *really* was—though it would, of course, remain just a fantasy.

He immediately went to her small table, clearing away books and old canvas totes to set her food down, then turning toward her chair by the window. He froze, the whistled tune dying on his lips as he realized that the figure he'd spotted out of the corner of his eye in his mother's rocker was not, in fact, his mother.

It was Fidelis Jes.

Michel straightened, clasping his hands behind his back to hide their sudden tremble, and tried to act casual as he knocked a whole box of books off Mother's table. "Sir!"

Fidelis Jes rocked softly in her chair. He seemed back to his old self—hair slicked back, shirt pressed, face immaculately stoic. He gazed out the window down the street, a contemplative look on his face. His sword was unbuckled but still sheathed, lying across his knees, one hand resting on the hilt. Why the pit was he here? A thousand possibilities went through Michel's head, none of them good, but the grand master remained silent.

"Sir," Michel managed again, hoping he didn't stutter, "this is an unexpected honor. Is there something wrong? Has something happened with the Styke business?" He grimaced, telling himself to shut up. People went to Fidelis Jes. He did not come to them. This was unprecedented.

And the fact it was his mother's house was more than a little terrifying.

Michel took a step back and craned his head to look up into the loft. His mother wasn't there. Had she been taken away? Was she out running errands? Just as Michel's nerves were about to get the best of him, Fidelis Jes finally spoke.

"The Styke business has been called off. For now. The Dynize have our attention." Jes turned his gaze on Michel—stony, penetrating. There was no anger or pleasure in the grand master's eyes.

Michel could not read him in the slightest. "Tell me, Agent Bravis, how has your own search gone?"

"Ah, not well, I'm afraid," Michel said, speaking too loudly. "You see, there are a lot of reports on my desk I need to go through but Warsim will let me know as soon as we find anything and again let me tell you what an honor it is to have this..." Michel trailed off, licking his lips. Fidelis Jes remained expressionless.

"I'm not talking about that search," Jes said. "I meant the other one. The one you are conducting that gave you the strongest urge to search the upper archives within hours of receiving your Gold Rose."

Oh. Oh shit.

"I'm not sure what you mean, sir. Dellina didn't give me any instructions regarding the upper archives."

"No," Jes said. "She did not. But the man who was clever enough to work his way up to Gold Rose, even during a time of crisis, could figure out how to enter the archives. It's not difficult—which is why the archives are heavily warded. We keep records of when someone enters, and one of the archivists noted a man of your description fleeing just an hour after you entered."

Michel swallowed. Okay, this wasn't so bad. He could manage this. A plausible excuse was all he needed—information he craved, something that might get him into trouble, but not *too much* trouble. His mind raced, looking for the proper story to spin while keeping his face carefully neutral.

"Tell me, Agent Bravis. Why were you in the upper archives when we so dearly need everyone searching for Styke?"

"I thought..."

"You might find information there to help you track down Styke?" Jes finished, a slight smile touching his lips.

"...Yes, sir."

"A likely excuse, certainly. Then why did you visit Professor Cressel at the monolith dig yesterday afternoon? Was that some kind of wrong turn? A mistake? Or did you think you'd find Styke there, too?" Jes's tone turned mocking, and he suddenly slid to his feet, taking his sheathed sword in hand like a truncheon and doing a quick circuit around Michel the same way he'd done the first time Michel was called into his office. It reminded Michel exactly what he was to the grand master: a piece of meat.

"Think fast, Agent Bravis," Jes whispered into his ear. "I'm very interested in your excuses."

Michel tilted his head back slightly, Jes's whisper raising his hackles like nails on a chalkboard. It said, very clearly, that there weren't any excuses. Nothing would get him out of this. He tried to focus on something—anything—to get his mind around what was happening. He scrabbled mentally for some sort of bedrock.

"Where's my mother?" he croaked.

"Hm," Jes said, doing another circuit and stopping just behind Michel's left shoulder. Michel cringed inwardly, waiting for a blade or a fist or just about any kind of violence. "Tell me, Agent Bravis, why are you looking for the godstones?"

Michel cleared his throat. "Where's my mother?" he asked again.

"That's not important," Jes responded. "Who do you really work for, Bravis? Is it Brudania? The Deliv royal cabal? Adro? Well?" The last word came out a shout, and Michel finally flinched. Jes continued the circuit, coming back into Michel's frame of vision and stopping in front of him. He took the end of his sword, tapping Michel on the shoulder, then the elbow, then the side of his knee. They were the taps of a butcher checking for the tenderest spots of meat.

"You know this isn't going to go well for you, Agent Bravis. If you tell us everything it will...well, it'll still be very painful. But much, much shorter. I can assure you of that." Jes laughed to himself, as if this whole thing was really quite funny. "I'm genuinely impressed. You worked your way up to a Gold Rose only to betray yourself the very first day. I can't imagine how impatient you must have been to slip up so quickly. It's a combination of skill and stupidity that I haven't seen for a very, very long time."

Michel felt a tear roll down his left cheek. His fists were balled so tightly that his fingernails drew blood. He took several deep breaths, trying to come to some sort of acceptance that his life was over, but all he could think about were the books on the table behind him, and the fact that Fidelis Jes had sat in his mother's rocker. It was that unspoken threat that got to him worse than anything Jes was saying now, and it made his stomach twist into a knot.

"Where," he demanded, "is my mother?"

Jes turned around, stepping toward the door. "You should have worried for her health before you did all this, Agent Bravis. And to think, you were so promising..."

Michel dug into his coat pocket, fingers wrapping around the familiar brass of his knuckledusters. He took a quick step forward, drawing back with all his might and swinging his fist. His best bet was to make Jes kill him right now—end it quick, with the least amount of pain and maybe, just maybe, Jes would have no use for his mother.

But Jes didn't step out of the way, draw his sword, and run Michel through.

Michel's knuckledusters connected with the base of Jes's neck and the grand master dropped like a sack of potatoes. In half a breath, Michel found himself staring down at the unmoving form, mouth agape, unable to comprehend what had just happened. Then he did the only thing that came to mind:

He fled.

He was less than a block from the house when he rounded a corner and ran headlong into his mother. She screamed, books scattering in the street as the two of them went down in a heap. Michel regained his feet while his mother crawled around, swearing and grumbling, trying to stuff penny novels back into her satchels. He grabbed her under the arm, trying to help her up.

"You pillok!" she said, jerking her arm away. "Why don't you watch where you're going?"

"Damn it, Mother, we don't have time for this." He scooped her up bodily, depositing her on her feet. She squinted at him. "Michel? What are you doing here?"

"Saving your life," he said, dragging her along behind him.

"Wait, my books!"

"I'll buy you more!" He pulled her along until they were both running down the street, huffing and puffing. They made it less than a block before his mother stopped him, gasping for breath.

"What is going on?" she demanded. "And what is *that*?"

Michel looked down to see the Gold Rose had fallen out of his shirt. He stuffed it back, shaking his head. "Ignore that, I…" He paused. "Damn it! I should have damn well made sure he was dead." He took two steps back toward her house, stopped himself, then waved toward a nearby hackney cab. "Never mind. It's too late. Shit, shit, shit."

His mother slapped him on the shoulder. "Why are you cursing? And what's the meaning of this? I was going to spend the afternoon reading."

"You spend every afternoon reading!"

Her eyes suddenly widened as she caught up to what he'd said a moment ago. "And what do you mean, you should have made sure he was dead? Who?"

Michel leapt into the hackney cab as it pulled up beside the curb and shouted for the driver to head to Greenfire Depths. Once they were seated he let himself take a deep breath, wishing he had something to drink. He looked out the window, waiting for someone to come running after the cab, or a squad of Blackhats to burst from an alley. That arrogant bastard had come after Michel alone. There was no one to chase him down.

But there would be.

"Fidelis Jes," he said finally. "I left him lying on your floor. I might have killed him."

*   *   *

The Riflejack cavalry were having breakfast in their camp outside of Jedwar when Styke, Ibana, and Jackal rode through their tents and corrals, accompanied by one of their outriders.

Styke fell into old habits, glancing around at the equipment and state of the horses and men. Saddles were oiled, swords sharpened, and the carbines looked well cared for. The men lounged beside their morning cook fires, stirring pots and playing cards, their uniforms well worn but clean. He used the examination to focus on something other than how much his ass hurt.

"The corrals are sturdy," Ibana said approvingly.

"You bet they are," a man said, standing up beside Styke's horse. He was tall and lean, with the strong shoulders and bowed legs of someone who spent a lot of time in the saddle—and swinging a sword from one. He had light brown hair and mutton chops, and a clean-shaven face. He fetched his jacket from a nearby post and slid it on over his shoulders. "We're Adran cavalry. We don't screw around." He eyed the lancers' jackets, and the banner waving over Jackal's head. "You're Fatrastan military?" he asked.

"Who's in command?" Styke asked.

The soldier considered the question for a moment. "Colonel Olem. If you want to talk to him, you'll have to head to Landfall."

"Just came from there," Ibana responded. She leaned over in her saddle, handing the man a sealed letter. "Who's second in command?"

"I'm Major Gustar, so I guess that would be me," the man responded, taking the letter and frowning at the seal, which was stamped with the crossed rifles and shako of the Riflejacks. "What's this here?"

"New orders," Styke said. "My name's Colonel Ben Styke, and I've been ordered to take command of your cavalry." He bit his cheek, waiting for a fight. No one liked their command taken from them.

Major Gustar cast him a long, cool glance. Several of his men bristled openly, but Gustar simply said, "Sorry, Colonel, but we're Riflejacks. We don't take commands from foreign officers. Not unless Lady Flint tells us to directly."

"You might want to give those orders a read," Ibana suggested.

Gustar broke the seal and read through the letter, his eyes widening as he went. When he next looked up, his mouth was slightly agape. "You're *that* Ben Styke?"

"In the flesh," Styke replied. For the first time in a while, that little bit of awe in someone's voice didn't feel like a slap in the face for what he used to be. It felt good.

"And you're a Riflejack now?"

"We all are; we just don't have uniforms yet, so this old Fatrastan getup will have to do. This is Major Ibana ja Fles. She has direct command of the Mad Lancers. I'll leave you in charge of the Riflejack dragoons and cuirassiers. You both report to me."

Gustar snapped a salute. "Sir. Yes, sir. It'll be a pleasure serving under you."

"Say that again after I've ordered you to charge a pike line," Styke said. "We're needed in Landfall. Ibana will catch you up on the way. I want everyone ready to ride within a half hour."

"They'll be ready in fifteen minutes," Gustar said. "Up and at 'em, boys, we've got work to do!"

Styke took a deep breath, taking in the smoke of the cook fires, the smell of the horses, the sickly sweet scent of manure heaps, and the sour stench of unwashed soldiers at camp. His lungs yearned for all of it and more—for the corpses on the field and the fresh scent of crushed grass and powder smoke after a skirmish.

He pointed down at Gustar. "You. I think I'm going to like you."

CHAPTER 51

Vlora was shown into the foreign dignitary room of the capitol building the morning after accepting command of the
defenses of Fatrasta. She wore her parade uniform: Adran blues
with silver trim and crimson cuffs, the crossed rifles of the Riflejack
Mercenary Company emblazoned above her left breast opposite
two dozen medals for acts of valor she'd long forgotten.

The foreign dignitary room was a large, vaulted chamber decorated with yellow and white marble, lit by three enormous chandeliers and high banks of windows that looked out over the edge
of the Landfall Plateau and out to sea. Opposite the windows were
rows of tiered seating for the elite of Fatrasta, while an immense,
oval ironwood table occupied the very center of the room, surrounded by dozens of high-backed chairs.

The room had seating for hundreds of people and could probably fit more than a thousand, but the only occupants were Vlora
and Lady Chancellor Lindet.

Lindet sat at the table, a glass of iced coffee and a spread of papers in front of her. She looked up as Vlora's boots echoed across the marble floors and gave a brief, condescending smile. Vlora didn't take it personally. From what she understood, Lindet was condescending to everyone.

"Lady Flint," she said. "It's a pleasure to finally meet you."

The words were quiet, pleasant, pitched so as not to echo. Vlora rounded the table to be opposite of Lindet—likely where the Dynize delegation would sit in a short time—and leaned on one of the high-backed chairs. She inclined her head. "Lady Chancellor. Aren't we expecting the Dynize ambassador any moment?"

Lindet consulted a pocket watch. "Thirteen minutes," she said.

"Shouldn't this room be...full?" Vlora had passed Fatrastan dignitaries twittering away in the halls of the capitol building by the score, the whole lot practically seething nervous anticipation. The emergence of the Dynize Empire from isolation was the most exciting thing to happen here since Fatrasta declared their independence from Kez. To the businessmen and politicians waiting outside, the fact that the Dynize had arrived with a fleet of warships was barely worth a mention.

Unfortunately, that made those warships entirely Vlora's problem.

"I'll allow them in when I'm ready," Lindet said. She perused a page of stationery in front of her before signing the bottom and sliding it off to one side. "I'm so glad you took Jes's offer."

"It was enough money to let all of my men retire comfortably when this is over," Vlora responded.

"Purely mercenary," Lindet said with a small smile. "I can respect that."

The money hadn't been all of it, of course. Jes had pointed out, correctly, that if the city became blockaded the Riflejacks would not be able to leave. He also pointed out that an unattached mercenary company could easily be seen as an enemy of the state were the Dynize to prove antagonistic, and that his Blackhats would be forced to turn on her. More personally, Vlora relished the idea of *defending* the people of Fatrasta for once, rather than putting down their insurrections.

Vlora kept all of that in her head, instead answering Lindet with a nod. "If the Dynize have designs on Landfall, my men will hold it. I'll admit I'm surprised that you've put me in command of the entire city defense." Surprised didn't even cover it. She'd been handed command of a fourteen-thousand-man garrison, five forts, and another six thousand auxiliaries. Unless she was reading the politics wrong—which was a possibility—that made her one of the most powerful people in Landfall, answerable only to Lindet.

"You're the protégée of Field Marshal Tamas and the veteran of two wars and countless other engagements. Is there anyone else more qualified in the city?"

"No," Vlora admitted.

Lindet signed another paper. "The worst-case scenario," she said, "is that the Dynize are here to invade. In which case I've secured an extra brigade of riflemen and a decorated commander and removed the possibility of you being hired by my enemies. The best-case scenario is that the Dynize just happen to be out for a pleasure cruise with an entire fleet, and I've locked you into a four-year contract as defender of the shores of my nation. It seemed fairly win-win."

"You could have bought ten brigades for what you're paying us."

"I don't have ten brigades handy to buy," Lindet said. "Are you in the habit of telling employers that they've overpaid, Lady Flint?"

"No, ma'am. Forgive me for asking, but do you have any particular reason for thinking the Dynize are here for any other reason than peace?"

"Other than thirty-eight warships and a whole flotilla of support frigates?"

"Yes, other than those."

Lindet made a "hmm" sound that was neither an affirmative nor denial.

"Ma'am?"

Lindet looked at her over the tops of her spectacles, the brief smile returning. "I also understand that you've deputized the Mad Lancers into the Riflejacks. Is that correct?"

Vlora swallowed, noting that Lindet had dodged the question about the Dynize. She would have to come back to that. The subject of the Mad Lancers wasn't one she'd been looking forward to, but she hadn't hired them purely out of need. She'd also hired them because she knew it would cause an argument—an argument that would set the tone for her relationship with Lindet going forward. She braced herself for the coming fight. "Yes, ma'am."

"Good."

"Excuse me?" Vlora struggled to hide her surprise.

Another page was signed and set aside. "It makes Styke *your* problem, and if it keeps him and Fidelis Jes out of each other's hair for the time being, I consider that a bonus. I've instructed Fidelis Jes to steer clear of the Mad Lancers for now. I expect you to do the same for Styke. If you can. This Dynize fleet is more pressing a matter than internal squabbles."

Vlora exhaled the breath she'd taken in anticipation of a shouting match. "I'll keep Styke on a short leash."

"Good luck with that." Lindet checked her pocket watch again. "Eight minutes." She raised her voice. "You may allow everyone inside!"

Vlora didn't see any attendants, but the doors to the room were thrown open and a stream of people poured in. She recognized businessmen, politicians, Kressian ambassadors, and even the chief constable of the Landfall police. Within minutes the tiered seating was filled, as well as half of the chairs around the oval table. Vlora left the spot across from Lindet and rounded to stand beside her.

She spotted Vallencian off in one corner of the room, but when she raised her hand to greet him he looked away. The snub was not unexpected. The Ice Baron, she had assumed, would not be pleased that she had used his introduction to Palo society as a way to arrest Mama Palo. She didn't consider herself terribly vain, but the knowledge that he was no longer an enthusiastic fan made her a bit sad.

But she had more important things to think about. "Where *is* Jes, by the way?" she asked, casting about for the grand master.

"Personally overseeing security," Lindet answered. "The Palo have engaged in some light rioting since we executed Mama Palo. The last thing I need is some fool revolutionary taking a shot at the Dynize ambassador and causing an international incident." Lindet glanced up, a look of annoyance crossing her face. "Would you please stop hovering and have a seat?" She indicated the chair to her right.

Vlora took the spot hesitantly. No one had told her she'd be sitting *beside* Lindet during the meeting. She wondered whether her place was expedience, or flattery. Probably a little of both.

A light hand touched her shoulder, and she looked up to find Olem standing just beside her. She didn't realize that she'd been holding her breath before she let it out in a soft sigh. She gestured him closer. "I was not," she whispered, "ready to get back into politics."

"Really?" he asked. "Because you just dove in headfirst."

"I thought I was agreeing to fight. Why the pit am I at this table?"

"Defender of Fatrasta comes with a little more than just a combat role, I imagine," Olem commented.

"Pit. Will you be here through the whole thing?"

"I'll be seated just over there," Olem said, indicating a spot on the bottom row of seating behind her.

"Thank Adom. I feel like I'm sitting in a den of wolves."

"You are, love. You are."

The "love" was unexpected. Olem rarely got more informal than her first name in public, and she felt her cheeks redden. "Thank you," she whispered back.

"For?"

"Being here."

"Never want to be anywhere else."

"You have no idea how much that helps. By the way, just *how* mad is Vallencian about the Mama Palo thing?"

"I found out this morning that no café in Landfall will serve ice to a Riflejack, if that's any indication."

Vlora took a deep breath. That was going to be a hit to morale. Ice was about the only way the boys were getting through this stinking hot summer. "Send him a present. Something handsome, but practical. Dig through my sea chest to see if I have any old souvenir that might soften him up."

"I'll give it a try."

A messenger suddenly arrived, whispering something in Lindet's ear. Lindet stood up, turning to the door. The rest of the room, Vlora included, stood up with her, while Olem hurried back to his seat.

The messenger announced in a loud, clear voice, "The esteemed Ka-sedial, adviser to the throne of Emperor Janen I, Admiral of the Black Fleet and carrier of the imperial seal."

The man who entered the room was not, by any stretch of the imagination, impressive. He looked in his mid-sixties, with tufts of gray hair on the sides of a mostly bald head. His face was clean-shaven, a weak chin accentuated by a large nose and soft features. He wore a colorful gown of teal, purple, black, and yellow, raven's feathers dangling from each ear. He walked slowly, his hands clasped behind his back, taking in the room and assembly with a pleasant but slightly disdainful air.

Vlora's senses began to tingle, and she didn't have to open her third eye to tell that this man had sorcery. She immediately dismissed the idea that he was a Privileged, and then a Knacked. He definitely wasn't a powder mage. That left just one possibility, and it made her slightly ill.

He was a bone-eye, a blood sorcerer. The last time she'd met one of those had been Ka-poel. And she'd helped kill a god.

The bone-eye rounded the table, bowed briefly to Lindet, and then took a seat with the soft sigh of someone getting too old to spend much time on their feet. No one else came through the door, leaving Ka-sedial alone on the other side of the table, flanked by a dozen empty chairs. He didn't seem to mind.

Vlora glanced sidelong at Lindet, whose expression remained as placid as the bone-eye's across from her. She sat, and so did the rest of the room.

The room grew deathly still and silent. Someone in the hall outside sneezed. It felt as if the whole room was holding their breath, until Lindet lifted a single finger and one of her aides sprang to her side. "Where is his translator?" she asked. "We offered him one, didn't we?"

"I don't need a translator," the bone-eye said in clear, barely accented Adran.

Lindet dismissed her aide by lowering her finger and turned her entire attention to the bone-eye. Vlora leaned into the corner of her seat, fingers on her chin, marveling at the power dynamic here. Lindet was the most feared person in this part of the world, and yet this single bone-eye seemed to be trying to upstage her in every way.

"Well," Lindet replied, "that saves us the trouble. Ka-sedial, welcome to Fatrasta."

"Thank you, Lady Chancellor."

"It's tradition," Lindet said, "to ask guests about the news from their homeland, but I'm afraid that might take a while. We are a hundred years behind."

Ka-sedial tilted his head to one side, looking slightly bored. "Not at all. There was a civil war. Millions died to sword, famine, and sorcery. It has taken four generations, but the imperial family has retaken their rightful throne and brought peace to Dynize."

"Ah. Peace. I'm glad to hear it." Lindet did not sound at all glad to hear it.

"As are we."

Vlora noted that Ka-sedial did not reciprocate the question of news. He wouldn't, she decided. Not when the Dynize had been spying on Fatrasta for who knew how long. She wondered whether Lindet had sent her own spies into Dynize. The countries of the Nine had stopped bothering to approach the Empire over fifty years ago, but with access to Palo that would speak the Dynize language and look the part, Lindet might have actually gotten the chance to crack that nut.

It wasn't a great time to ask.

"I'm afraid," Lindet said, "that my next question might come off as rude, but it is the foremost on our minds and I would like to put my people at ease."

Ka-sedial smiled. "Why, you're wondering, is there a fleet of warships outside your harbor?"

"Precisely," Lindet said with a sour smile.

"It's an expedition," Ka-sedial said simply. "The Empire hasn't had a fleet to speak of since the last squadron was sunk off the Ebony Coast over seventy years ago. We've barred our borders to outsiders, kept ourselves and our problems isolated to our country. We've only been at peace with ourselves for about seven years now, and in that time we've had to rebuild so, so much—including our ships."

"And now that you've rebuilt them, what do you intend to do with them?"

Ka-sedial drummed his fingers gently on the table. "That depends on you, Lady Chancellor."

An audible gasp came from the assembly, and Vlora didn't blame them. The words were innocuous, but the tone held an unmistakable threat. The last person to publicly threaten Lindet, as far as Vlora knew, was the Kez governor who'd tried to relieve her of her post at the beginning of the Fatrastan Revolution. At the end of the war, his tongue was cut out as part of the peace settlement.

Vlora cleared her throat. "Ambassador, every expedition has a goal. What is yours?"

Ka-sedial turned his attention slowly toward her, like a lizard who's spied a particularly fat mealworm. She wondered if his spies had reported her to him.

"Lady Flint, I presume?"

That seemed to be a yes about the spies, she noted. "That is I."

"We've only come looking for what is rightfully ours."

The whole room hung on the sentence, tension thick enough to cut. "I'm curious," Lindet said, "what exactly you think that is." Her expression had not changed, but her voice had gone dangerously quiet. The assembly seemed to lean forward as one, straining to hear.

Ka-sedial didn't seem to have a problem hearing. "These lands belonged to the Empire at one time," he said, almost wistfully. "You've built your little nation atop the great ruins of our ancestors."

"And you expect to take that back?" Vlora asked flatly.

"No, no," Ka-sedial said. "It's been a very long century. My people are weary of war, and I understand that this is a modern age. We have no intention of conquering. We are only here for our rightful property, and once we have it we will be gone."

You're using the word "rightful" quite a lot. I don't think that means what it once did, not since Tamas beheaded the rightful king of Adro. Vlora glanced at Lindet, but the Lady Chancellor had sunk back in her seat, examining Ka-sedial through a hawk's narrowed eyes. She did not respond.

The silence dragged on for ten seconds, then twenty, then thirty. Ka-sedial finally leaned forward, his expression impatient. "We want the godstones returned to us."

There was a confused murmur from the gallery behind her, only cut off by Lindet's voice ringing out loudly. "Everyone out!"

The room was clear within a minute, leaving only the fifteen or so people at the oval table remaining. Everyone's eyes were glued on Lindet.

"What are the godstones?" Vlora asked. Ka-sedial stared at Lindet. Lindet stared back. Vlora leaned over to her and repeated her question quietly. Lindet ignored her, turning to whisper to the Privileged sorcerer sitting on her left. Vlora's attention was on Ka-sedial, but she caught the quiet response.

"We'll have it secured, ma'am."

Whether Ka-sedial heard their whispers, Vlora couldn't be sure. He looked from Lady Chancellor to Privileged and then back again. "We know you have them, and you know they belong to us. Hand them over and we'll leave these shores immediately."

"Or what?" Lindet said.

Vlora resisted the urge to glance back at Olem. This conversation had turned badly *very* quickly. "What are the godstones?" she asked again.

"Or we take them by force," Ka-sedial said.

"I thought you said your people are weary of war?" Vlora asked sarcastically. She wanted an answer about these godstones, and it was clear that everyone here was ignoring her questions.

"Hm. They are, Lady Flint. But some things are more important than a much-needed respite. We are weary, but we are also ready. If you think us broken by so much war, think again. Our armies are hardened veterans, raised on the taste of blood. I will let them drink again if I must."

Vlora looked at Lindet, but the Lady Chancellor still had not answered. Vlora wanted to reach over and shake her. "What," she demanded, "is so important about these godstones?"

"Everything," Lindet said. Her voice was barely above a whisper.

"Yes," Ka-sedial agreed. "Everything. The future of my very country depends upon their retrieval, and keeping them from us will be seen as an act of war."

Lindet suddenly stood. "You will have my answer by tomorrow. Good day, Ambassador." She left the table so quickly that the others scrambled to follow her, Vlora included. She glanced behind her as she left the room to find Ka-sedial still seated, with a determined expression that looked more like an avenging angel than a frail old man.

Vlora rushed to catch up to Lindet. "Are you going to explain to me what just happened?"

"Nothing that I had planned," Lindet responded. "You have until tomorrow to prepare the garrison for war. Send out messengers. Recall all my armies from the frontier, and raise levies from every city in Fatrasta."

Vlora's stomach tightened, twisting over itself in knots. That was not the command of someone who expected a blockade. That was the command of someone who expected a full-blown war. "What," she growled, "are these godstones?"

Lindet lifted her chin. "I believe you have work to do, General." She strode off, leaving Vlora standing alone, openmouthed.

Olem found her a few moments later, after pushing his way through the crowd of confused dignitaries. "What happened after she kicked everyone out?" he asked.

"I'm still not entirely sure." She looked at her hands, then up at Olem. "Have our men transitioned to Fort Nied?"

"Yes, but..."

"No buts. Send word that we have until morning to prepare for an invasion."

CHAPTER 52

Vlora arrived at Fort Nied an hour after the Dynize ambassador's visit came to a sudden end. The traffic had been almost impassable the entire way down the east slope of the Landfall Plateau, forcing her to walk the last quarter of a mile, listening to the gossip spread like wildfire among shopkeeps, pedestrians, and laborers. People wondered openly if the Dynize would invade, open trade routes, or simply resupply on a long journey toward the Nine. She could feel the city *pulse* with uncertain anticipation, and like a spring coiled too tightly the tension felt ready to snap.

Olem had gone on ahead on horseback, and by the time Vlora reached the fort her artillery crews stood at the ready and riflemen manned the battlements. An ensign brought her up to speed as she came in through the front gate: Riflejacks manned the fort, while the rest of the brigade had been distributed in patrol lines all along the length of the bay and docks, and messengers flooded in with news that the entire Fatrastan garrison was mustering at wooden forts both north and south of the city. Vlora turned the messengers right around with orders to have full troop reports by nightfall, then stopped to take stock of her new command post.

Fort Nied was not, thankfully, an ancient palisade like Loel's Fort. It was a modern star fortress directly on the bay, positioned to force all ships around it to reach the docks. It had open firing lanes on three points of the star to the ocean, and was protected by immense blocks of limestone enchanted by Lindet's Privileged to shrug off both cannon fire and sorcery.

The fort had survived a withering bombardment by the Kez fleet during the Fatrastan Revolution. It would, she assured herself, hold up again.

A messenger touched her arm. "Lady Flint, Colonel Olem says to tell you that the Dynize ambassador has returned to his ship."

"Right," Vlora said, jogging up the steps to the easternmost star on the fortress and standing on her tiptoes to look out to sea. She took a hit of powder, relishing the brief rush of sorcery and adrenaline before focusing on the ships. Sailors and soldiers stood stoically at attention. She was able to pick out Ka-sedial up on the forecastle of the flagship, speaking to what looked to be the captain. "I'd give my left arm to know what that asshole is saying right now."

"No," a voice said over her shoulder. "Maybe a little finger. Never an arm."

After everything that had happened, Vlora was still surprised to find Taniel standing behind her. Not Tampo the lawyer, but Taniel himself in the flesh. He wore a demure black coat and hat, his collar high. Just behind him stood a Palo woman, shorter even than Vlora and still as slight as she'd been ten years ago. She wore a black duster, her hands buried in the sleeves, and when Vlora locked eyes with her she winked.

"Hello, Ka-poel. Good to see you." Which might have been a stretch. Vlora had discovered long ago that being warm to the woman who wound up with her ex-fiancé was decidedly difficult, even if she did save Adro from a mad god.

Ka-poel dipped her head, giving a little wave.

"Still haven't figured out a way to talk with your sorcery?"

Ka-poel gave a tiny shrug, hands open, as if to say "what can I do?"

"She's experimented," Taniel said. "It's not easy to do, and even harder to sustain."

Vlora gave an involuntary shudder, wondering what "experimentation" entailed for a blood sorcerer, then looked around, suddenly alarmed. "You know, my men here were the core of the Seventh and Ninth, Tamas's own. There's a good bet plenty of them remember what you look like—and you're not the most inconspicuous pair."

"When people think that you're dead," Taniel said, "their eyes walk right past you. At least in my experience. Besides, Ka-poel's too tired to give me a new face on such short notice and it's worth the risk of being recognized. We have to talk."

Vlora growled under her breath. "I thought we already did that."

"Yeah, well, things have changed. I was hoping you'd reconsider my offer."

"It's a bit late," Vlora said. "The moment the Dynize arrived Lindet offered me a king's ransom to become defender of Landfall. I'm in command of the entire garrison."

Taniel glanced out to sea nervously. "Yes, I saw that."

"And I'm a bit busy." She stopped, squinting at Ka-poel. "I met my second bone-eye today. Cold bastard by the name of Ka-sedial. Stared down Lindet like she was a common strumpet. Do you know anything about him? Does he have the same kind of power you do?"

A short, silent communication passed between Ka-poel and Taniel before her hands began to move, firing off a rapid series of gestures that Vlora couldn't even hope to follow. Taniel watched them carefully before translating: "Ka-sedial isn't nearly as power-ful as she is, but he's in Lindet's class of cunning and ruthless. He's not to be trusted."

"I hadn't planned on it." Vlora wasn't particularly surprised that Ka-poel already knew who Ka-sedial was, but she made a mental note to ask later exactly *how* she knew. Taniel and Ka-poel were just a whole box full of useful information. If they bothered to share it.

The hand gestures, and the translation, continued. "Ka-sedial knows there's a bone-eye in the city. He's been trying to suss her out since the moment he landed. He's more experienced than she is, and it's taking all of her power to hide."

That, more than anything else, alarmed Vlora. Ka-poel was the strongest mortal sorcerer Vlora had ever encountered and she was *hiding* from Ka-sedial? Perhaps it was out of expedience more than anything else, but the fact that Ka-sedial was making it difficult on her did not reassure. "Is he going to cause problems?"

"Now?" Taniel said. "Bone-eyes are not Privileged. They don't have access to fire and lightning. Their sorcery is a slow burn, a patient gathering of resources. If it's a fight he wants, he won't be any real threat today. If he remains in the city, he will be an immense pain in the ass."

"So what you're saying is that even if we avoid a fight, and have some peace talks with the Dynize, he could eventually do some serious damage *without* his army?"

"Pretty much."

"Can you counter him?" she asked Ka-poel.

Ka-poel gave another one of those shrugs. "She'll try," Taniel said, "but she's self-taught. Ka-sedial is a trained bone-eye with sixty years of experience in blood sorcery."

Vlora rubbed her temples. None of this was information she wanted to hear. But, she reflected, important intelligence doesn't always come in the form of good news. She opened her mouth, only to have Taniel cut her off. "We're not just here about hiring you," he said, "or to feed you bits about the Dynize. We need information. What happened with the delegation?"

Vlora was half-tempted not to tell him. He'd made it clear before that he had his own agenda, and it was directly opposed to Lindet—who was, once again, Vlora's employer. "I should probably arrest you," Vlora said.

Ka-poel pointed at her and waved her hands flat in front of her as if to say "no."

"You're not going to," Taniel translated.

"Yeah, I picked up on that." He was right. She saw what he did to those dragonmen. She *should* be trying to get him on her side, just like she did with Styke—the Dynize might be a problem for both Lindet and the Palo, and she needed assets against a possible invasion—but a stubborn part of her whispered that she didn't *need* his help. She forced herself to look past her annoyance. "It didn't go well. Ka-sedial came in alone and as much as told Lindet that he wanted Dynize property back or he was going to take it by force."

"What kind of property?"

"Something called the godstones. Lindet wouldn't tell me what they are, but they sound like some kind of sorcerous artifact."

Taniel inhaled sharply, and Ka-poel pulled her top lip back. They exchanged a long look, before Taniel uttered one, drawn-out word. "Shit."

Vlora turned her attention briefly to the soldiers scurrying around in the fort yard below them, and the gun crews bringing powder and cannonballs up to the fixed guns, before turning back to Taniel. "What do you mean, shit?"

"You remember those theories I told you about—why the Dynize are here?"

"Yeah, I remember you wouldn't tell me about them," Vlora snapped.

"This is one of those theories," Taniel said with a grimace. "What did Lindet say?"

"She told him no, but that she'd think about it."

Ka-poel tapped her temple with one finger, shook her head, then made an expansive gesture. Taniel translated: "She's not going to give them to Ka-sedial. She's just buying time."

"For what?" Vlora demanded.

"For you to prepare for the invasion."

As much as Vlora had been fearing a Dynize landing, she didn't honestly believe that they'd actually do it. There were a thousand reasons, foremost among them that Fatrasta was still closely tied with the Nine. The fortunes of entire royal families were tied up in Fatrastan businesses and any war would bring the Nine into it in short order. "If the Dynize invade, they'll bring the Nine down on them. Surely their spies will have told them that."

"They don't care," Taniel said. "They're not interested in Fatrasta, just the godstones. The fact Lindet isn't handing them over means she knows exactly what they do, and that's almost as terrifying as the Dynize getting ahold of them."

"So," Vlora demanded, her patience wearing thin, "what do the bloody things do?"

Taniel tilted his head to the side. "What the pit does it *sound* like they do?"

"I don't know! Make gods? If I knew I wouldn't be...asking." The final word slipped out in a whisper, and Vlora found her mouth suddenly dry. "No. You must be joking."

"Have you ever wondered," Taniel asked, "where the gods came from?"

"I thought Kresimir made them."

"Where did Kresimir come from?" Taniel countered. "Where did the Gurlish gods that our cabals murdered during the occupation forty years ago come from? Gods are not born. They're made."

Dozens have come and gone in the history of our world. It's not public knowledge, but the cabals know. They've been looking for the godstones for centuries, and it just happened to be Lindet and her Privileged who found them."

Vlora didn't know what to believe. This seemed far-fetched, even for all the things she'd seen in her life, but she was talking to two living, breathing godkillers and all she knew was that she didn't *want* to believe them. She took a step backward involuntarily, sagging against a cannon. "So whoever has the godstones can create a god?"

"Do you think Lindet would trust anyone else to become a god?"

"She wants them for herself," Vlora breathed.

"And Ka-sedial wants them back."

"For himself?"

"Or his emperor. The Dynize civil war was sparked by the murder of their last god. The only way they ended their war was the promise to make a new one." Taniel leaned forward. "The Dynize are not motivated by greed or ambition. They are motivated by the desperation of dying faith, and that's more dangerous than anything else in the world."

Vlora looked back out past the breakers, at the masts on the horizon, her breath coming fast and short. "I saw what a god can do during the war. I'm not letting that happen again."

"Agreed," Taniel said, his face steely. Behind him, Ka-poel nodded.

"This is why you're here," Vlora said, voicing a sudden realization. "It's not about the Palo or Lindet or Fatrasta. You're here because of the godstones. To keep them out of Lindet's hands."

"To keep them out of anyone's hands," Taniel countered. "Don't get this wrong. We fight for the Palo because we believe in their cause. But the godstones are more important than any ethnic or political squabbles."

Vlora couldn't help but agree. This was bigger than her, or Lindet, or even the Dynize. The godstones could change the entire face of the world, and she feared—no, she *knew* that it would not be for the better. "I won't let them have them," she said, summoning all of her inner strength to stand up straight.

"The Dynize?" Taniel asked.

"Any of them," Vlora responded. She headed back down to the fort yard, calling for her horse and an escort of two hundred men. Employer or not, she and Lindet were about to have words.

CHAPTER 53

I t took several hours for Michel and his mother to reach Greenfire Depths.

He ditched his Blackhat uniform within minutes of making his
escape, and then they took cab after cab across the city, crisscross-
ing their own path, changing drivers, even walking a few blocks
along the Rim before reaching a thirty-unit, worn-down tenement
clinging to the cliffs on the western edge of the Depths.

Even after all his precautions to lose whoever might be pursuing
them, Michel did not feel safe as he jimmied the key in the lock of
his own personal safe house. His mother stood beside him, silent
after her initial outburst of questions in the first cab, staring down
the hall as if shell-shocked. Michel finally managed to knock the
rust off the lock of the apartment and kicked the door open.

"What is this place?" his mother asked.

"Inside," he said, glancing up and down the empty hall before
closing the door behind them.

The apartment was hot and stuffy, every surface coated in a

thick layer of dust. He coughed his way through the three bed-rooms and opened all the windows, checking the rooms for any sign of occupancy. No one had been here for a very long time.

About four years if he remembered right.

"Is this, what do the spies call it, a safe house?" his mother asked.

Michel was surprised she knew the word, then remembered that she spent all day reading penny novels. "Right," he said.

"Is this a Blackhat place?"

Michel barked a laugh, then shushed himself and crossed to a window that overlooked Greenfire Depths. He could smell smoke, and smoke in the Depths was never a good thing. He stuck his head outside and listened, hearing the distant sound of yelling and the crash of broken glass. The Palo were rioting, and he wasn't the least bit surprised—all the afternoon newspapers reported the hanging of Mama Palo.

This wasn't a safe time to be in the Depths, not for someone like him. He looked more Kressian than his one-fourth Palo, and that could be dangerous. But, he reasoned, it was far more dan-gerous to be *out* of the Depths right now. "Stay here," he told his mother, then went up two flights of rickety stairs and knocked on the fourth door on the left. He waited several minutes, knocking frequently, before a suspicious-looking Palo woman opened her door a crack. Michel held up a folded ten-krana note.

"I'm a Son of the Red Hand," he said. "I need a message taken to the Yellow Hall immediately."

The woman stared at him, stared at the krana note, then said, "There's rioting down at the Yellow Hall."

"I know. This is important. I live two floors down in the empty apartment."

She stewed on this information for a few moments. Michel's persona—his real persona, the one that had lived in the marble in the back of his head all these years—was just as careful as his Blackhat one. He and Taniel had a dozen backup plans, including safe houses, passwords, message chains, and bank boxes. He didn't remember half those plans, but he did know that he needed to get word to Taniel immediately that his cover had been blown.

When the woman didn't answer, Michel pulled out another twenty krana. She gave a perfunctory nod and said, "Meln-Dun's people have taken hold of the Yellow Hall, but I can get a message to the Red Hand." She snatched the money, and a moment later the door opened and a small boy ran into the hall and held out his hand expectantly.

Michel found a nub of pencil in his pocket and scribbled a note, handing it to the boy, who immediately took off down the hall.

He returned to find his mother sitting on the dusty sofa in the corner of the main room, staring at her hands. She looked up at him as he entered, a question on her lips, but remained silent. He looked out the windows one more time, listening to the distant shouts. The smell of smoke was getting stronger, and that didn't bode well at all. A fire in the wrong place and Greenfire Depths might go up entirely.

Michel sat down on the sofa beside his mother and stared at the wall. His life—the one he'd worked so hard to build the last four years—was over. There was a hole in his chest and he wondered if perhaps he'd gone in too deep with the Blackhats. He should be celebrating right now, ready to return to what he once was.

"Michel…"

"I met Taniel and Ka-poel seven years ago," Michel said without preamble. He didn't bother looking at his mother. He didn't want to see her face as she realized she'd been lied to for so long. "I bluffed my way into some politician's gala in Upper Landfall and went looking around for someone to con. Taniel and Ka-poel were supposed to be my mark—I was gonna rob them blind. But we got to talking, and there was something different about them."

He chuckled to himself, glad he'd not gone through with his plan to nick their wallets. Taniel would have probably turned him inside out. "Ka-poel saw through me right away, but instead of getting me kicked out of the gala they took me under their wing. They introduced me to people I had no right talking with, and over the course of a couple of hours I'd created a whole different persona. I was a disenfranchised young count from Starland trying to wrestle my fortune back from my duplicitous little brother. The idiots at that gala ate it up, and I left with ten thousand krana in donations to help me win back my title.

"I found out later that my new friends weren't who they said they were, either. They'd bluffed their way into the party just like I had, but they weren't there for money. They were creating a network of contacts that, I have to admit, were probably far more valuable to them than the ten thousand I left with were to me.

"I ended up working for them—petty thievery, forgery, that sort of thing." He ignored his mother's indignant snort and continued: "It wasn't long before I figured out that they weren't crime bosses or cons like I first suspected. They were playing a longer game, a bigger one. They were positioning themselves to take on Lindet. They championed the Palo, and I liked that because, well, because of Grandpappy."

He finally looked at his mother, wondering if the names Taniel and Ka-poel meant anything to her. Her memory tended to slip, so the chances of her remembering an old war hero—aside from her late husband—were slim. She peered at him cautiously through the dust, eyes narrowed as if seeing him for the first time.

"I don't know what you're saying, Michel," she finally said, "but it scares me."

"I'm saying"—Michel reached into his shirt and drew out his Gold Rose, letting it dangle from his fingertips as he stared at it— "that before I became this, I was something else. This," he said, bouncing the Gold Rose up and down by its chain, "is not me."

"What *are* you, then?"

There was a sudden knock on the door and Michel leapt to his feet, crossing the room as quietly as he dared and putting a finger to his lips. He approached the front door, palming his knuckle-dusters, and slowly moved the brass cover to the peephole to look out into the hall. He let out a soft sigh and stepped away from the door, pulling it open.

Taniel and Ka-poel stood in the hallway. Taniel was himself—not Gregious Tampo or any of the other faces he'd worn over the years—and Ka-poel hadn't aged a day in the years since Michel had seen her. Michel and Ka-poel exchanged a hug, and Taniel stalked into the room, giving it the same thorough inspection that Michel had when he first entered.

"How did you find me so quickly?" Michel asked. "I just sent a message minutes ago."

Taniel looked out the windows, then closed them against the increasing smokiness of the outside air. Michel's mother sat silently on the couch, as still as a frightened deer, eyeing the two new arrivals with something between suspicion and anger.

"We had someone watching your mother's home," Taniel said. "We were down at Fort Nied about an hour ago when we got the message that you attacked Fidelis Jes. We checked the home first, then came here hoping to find you. Your cover is blown, I assume?"

Michel nodded. "I slipped up."

Taniel gave a frustrated snort. "How?"

"I tripped a ward looking for some sign of the godstones in the Millinery upper library. Fidelis Jes came for me at Mother's home, and I was able to get the drop on him and escape."

Taniel and Ka-poel exchanged a glance, and Ka-poel shrugged as if it were of little consequence. Taniel seemed more annoyed. "It can't be helped, I suppose," he said. He reached into his pocket and pulled out the note Michel had left at the bank yesterday. "I haven't gotten the chance to check this yet. Care to explain?"

Michel quickly ran through his visit to the Millinery library and the dig site south of town, and as he spoke the irritation drained from Taniel's face until he was finally smiling.

"So we have it?" Taniel said.

"I think so. You'll want to be sure. I'm not sure if it's what you expected, though. It's huge—maybe eighty feet long; one of those big obelisks they dig up from time to time around the city."

Taniel crossed the room and sat down beside Michel's mother, his hand on his chin, seemingly without noticing she was there. His brow furrowed. "You're right, that's not what we expected at all."

"Michel." His mother finally spoke up, her voice an octave higher than usual. "Who are these people?"

Michel wiped his brow and glanced from Taniel to Ka-poel. Ka-poel gestured to herself, then to his mother, as if to say *go ahead and introduce us.* He hesitated for a long moment, wondering if his mother had fully grasped the importance of the story he'd told her just a few minutes ago. "Mother, this is Taniel and Ka-poel. They're the ones I work for."

"So you're not a Blackhat?"

"I am. Or rather, I was. I imagine Fidelis Jes is hunting for me now."

His mother leaned back from Taniel, taking him in. "Who are you?" she asked.

In answer, Taniel tugged at the fingers of his glove and removed it, revealing skin the color of fresh blood. His nails were long, his skin smooth, and he gave her a little wave.

Michel's mother inhaled sharply. "The Red Hand?"

"One and the same."

"He's a revolutionary. A guerrilla fighter."

"So is your son, Mrs. Bravis."

Michel gave his mother a tight smile. She blinked at him, and he could see the moment it all came together in her head. "You're a double agent," she said.

"I am."

She rose from the sofa, rushing across the room and throwing her arms around Michel before he could stop her. She clung to him, face buried in his neck, and he thought perhaps she was crying. He took her in his arms and gently patted her back, giving Taniel an apologetic smile. "It's okay, Mother."

"You're not a Blackhat, then. You're a good Palo boy, fighting against Lindet?"

"That's right."

"Why didn't you tell me?"

"I couldn't."

"I'm your mother!"

"That's why I couldn't," Michel said. He wondered if he should explain about being caught and tortured and all the risks and horrible things that could have happened to both of them if she'd known his true identity and slipped up. But that seemed like a bit much for her now. "I've been climbing the ranks from the beginning. Spying, informing, helping the Blackhats mop up the streets. A couple of years ago Taniel helped me catch a rogue powder mage. It earned me my Silver Rose, and I've just been aiming for my Gold ever since."

"Sorry to interrupt," Taniel said quietly. "But we have a problem."

Michel slowly extricated himself from his mother's grip and deposited her back on the sofa. She beamed at him, and he felt his cheeks color. "We have a lot of problems. Fidelis Jes wants my head."

"I don't think he's worried about you right now. That Dynize fleet out beyond the bay is threatening to attack. They want the godstones. I imagine all of Fidelis Jes's efforts are heading in that direction right now."

"You're joking."

"Not in the slightest. The Dynize want the godstones. My people tell me that their agents here in the Depths are the ones stirring up the rioters. I've already dispatched everyone I could to try to deal with them, but you, Ka-poel, and I are going to have to do something about that stone."

Michel drummed his fingers on the wall. "I'm not doing anything," he said. "Half the Blackhats in the city will be looking for me by now. I'm staying right here until I can get Mother safely out of the city. If the Dynize are going to attack, I don't want to be anywhere near this place."

"I don't think they are looking for you," Taniel responded coolly. "Jes survived your little attack, I can tell you that. But with this possible invasion he'll be rushing around trying to keep the Blackhats together. Besides, do you really think someone with his ego will have told anyone that a common spy got the drop on him? He'll keep that close to his chest until he has the time to find you himself."

Michel wasn't convinced. "Either way, I'm not a fighter."

"No," Taniel agreed. "You're not. But you've still got your Gold Rose, don't you?"

Michel touched the medallion under his shirt. "I'm going to get rid of it as quickly as I can."

"It might come in handy," Taniel said.

"It also identifies me as a Blackhat to all those rioters out there." Michel crossed to the corner of the room and folded his arms, trying to think. His primary worry was getting Mother out of the city. As far as he was concerned, Taniel was on his own from here on out. There was nothing more Michel could do to help, not now. He looked at Ka-poel, hoping for a little help. Both of them could be inscrutable at times, but Michel had always liked Ka-poel. She had a fantastic sense of humor.

Ka-poel fired off a rapid series of gestures at Taniel, and it took Michel a few moments to translate them in his head.

We need that stone, Ka-poel gestured.

"I know," Taniel said glumly.

If the Dynize manage to get it, that might be worse than letting Lindet keep it.

"I don't think we have a choice but to let them fight over it," Taniel responded. "We weren't ready for it to be that big."

We have to figure out something.

"Sure. But what are we going to do with eighty feet of solid rock? We can't just go down and steal it."

Michel pushed himself away from the wall and went to his mother's side, kneeling down beside the sofa. She was rocking back and forth gently, muttering to herself in Palo. "Are you all right?" he asked.

"All my books," she said mournfully.

Michel almost laughed out loud. The city was burning down around them, their whole world going to shit, and Mother could only think of the books she'd left behind at her house. He leaned over and kissed her gently on the forehead. "I'll get you out of the city, and then I'll buy you more. I promise."

"Can we even get out of here?" she asked. "Is it safe to get out through the riots and the Blackhats?"

Probably not, he said silently to himself. "We may have to hold tight for a while and risk the smoke. But I'll get you out." He bit one knuckle, scowling at himself, trying to think of something. If he risked a Blackhat contact, on the assumption that Taniel was right and Jes had not spread word of his betrayal, he might be able to smuggle them both out of the city before nightfall. But that was not a risk he was willing to take.

"Wait," he said, looking up at Taniel and Ka-poel. "What did you just say?"

"We're just trying to agree on a plan," Taniel responded.

"No. A moment ago," Michel said. "You said you couldn't just go down there and steal the godstone."

Ka-poel cocked her head.

"What if"—Michel held up a finger for their patience—"what if we *could* just go steal it?"

"I don't follow."

"How hard would it be to arrange a couple of barges to meet us upriver?" Michel asked. "Say, a mile north of Landfall? We'd want armed guards, barges, tow cables; the lot." He thought furiously, remembering what Professor Cressel had told him—that they'd be ready to move the obelisk within days.

Taniel exchanged a glance with Ka-poel. "It would be tight, but I think I could manage."

Michel took Taniel by the arm and nudged him toward the door. They stepped out into the hall, where the smoke was somehow even worse. Michel thought he heard a scream in the distance. "Could you get my mother out of the city? Immediately?"

"Certainly," Taniel said slowly.

Michel bit his lip. He had an idea. It was wild, insane, and more than a little bit stupid. But it just might work. "Okay," he said. "Get Mother out of the city and have your people ready with barges upriver. Do that, and we might just be able to steal the stone after all. Is that a deal?"

"So you're with me?"

"I'll have to be," Michel said. And it didn't make him happy at all. He stepped back inside. "We're going to get you out, Mother," he announced. "But you've got to go now."

"Michel," his mother said, a worried note in her voice, "aren't you coming with me?"

Michel gave his mother a hug. "Not yet. But we'll send you out with friends, and once this whole thing is over I'll come find you." He stifled her protests with another hug, then pulled her out into the hallway with him, linking her arm forcefully with Taniel's, while Taniel gave him a bemused look. "Time to go," he said to his mother. "I'll come find you, I promise." Over his mother's head he mouthed the words, *Get her out of here and meet me outside.*

Fifteen minutes later Taniel arrived in the street just outside of Michel's safe house tenement. Ka-poel stood on her tiptoes, eyes fixed on the end of the street. There was definitely screaming in the distance, and the smoke was so thick that a fire *had* to have caught several nearby tenements. It was going to spread fast, and he worried about everyone trying to get out of the Depths at once.

"All right," Taniel said. "Your mother's on her way. Now, what's your plan?"

"My plan," Michel responded, hoping he sounded more optimistic than he felt, "is to hope that Professor Cressel is ready to move the godstone. If he is, we're going to commandeer the damn thing."

CHAPTER 54

Olem caught up to her by the time Vlora's escort had plowed through the afternoon press and returned her to the capitol building. He rode up, catching her by the sleeve as she prepared to dismount.

"Let go," Vlora said, tugging off her riding gloves. "Norrine, Davd. Take vantages on the north and south points of the plaza." She watched the two powder mages dismount, rifles in hand, and disappear into the crowd.

Olem leaned over to her and in a low voice said, "I saw Taniel. You weren't kidding about the Red Hand. He said you were about to do something stupid. What's going on?"

"I'm about to do something necessary," Vlora responded, jerking her sleeve out of his grip and dismounting, handing the reins to a private. Olem was beside her in a moment, matching her pace as she strode up the capitol building stairs. People in the street stopped and stared, no doubt whispering over why an entire company of

Riflejacks had just arrived on Lindet's doorstep. Vlora didn't care what people thought was happening.

"Vlora…" Olem said in warning as they neared the doors. Blackhats on the top of the steps eyed her and her men nervously.

"No, Olem," Vlora responded. "I need you to trust me on this. It's important. I'll explain later, but this…" She couldn't find the words to express herself. What Taniel said echoed in her mind: *Gods aren't born. They're made.* She'd seen what happened when gods involved themselves in a modern world, and she wasn't letting it happen again. She brushed past the Blackhats on the top step and strode down the halls of the capitol building with three squads accompanying her. They reached Lindet's office, and Vlora turned one last time to Olem. "Tell me you're behind me on this."

"I'm not sure what *this* is," Olem replied, clearly unhappy. She braced herself for a fight, but he just nodded. "I'm with you."

"Bar the door," Vlora said. "Don't let any Blackhats inside."

The secretary outside Lindet's office tried to stop her, but Vlora strode through the antechamber and into Lindet's main room, where she found Lindet sitting on the front corner of her desk, listening while a dozen advisers all tried to speak at once. No one seemed to notice Vlora's arrival until she took a deep breath and, in her best officer's voice, bellowed, "Everyone out!"

The room fell silent, and twenty-some sets of eyes turned to stare at her. No one moved.

"Now!" she roared.

Lindet's staff fled the room, and within moments Vlora was alone with Lindet. The Lady Chancellor wore an irritated expression. "You'd better have a very good reason for this, General," Lindet said in a flat tone. Her eyes fell to the pistol and sword at Vlora's belt, then back up to her face.

"Very," Vlora said, crossing to the window and looking briefly down into the street. She could see the front steps and her soldiers standing at attention nearby. A squad of Blackhats had arrived and was arguing with Major Donevin. Across the street, Vlora saw a curtain flutter in a second-story window. There was a Privileged over there, well hidden from Vlora's sight. But not well enough.

She took a deep breath, reminding herself that this didn't need to escalate. This could all be solved very easily, very amicably. She just needed to communicate. "I would like to know what you're doing with the godstones," Vlora said.

"I don't answer to you," Lindet said, not moving from her spot at the edge of her desk. Her fingers drummed on the ironwood top.

"Let me rephrase that," Vlora said. "The godstones. I know what they are. I know you have them, and I know that *you* know what they are as well. What do you intend to use them for?"

"You've become very learned in the last two hours, Lady Flint. I wonder how."

"Don't dodge the question."

Lindet blinked several times. Vlora wondered how long it had been since someone took that tone with her—and what horrible fate had befallen them. "Who said I intend to use them at all?" Lindet asked.

Vlora felt a cold bead of sweat trickle down her spine and resisted the urge to rub it away. She did a circuit of the room, trying to walk away her own nerves, then stopped and took a sniff of powder. Lindet's eyes followed her the whole time.

"General, I assume you've considered the consequences of this outburst? I am your employer."

"I don't really give a damn, Lady Chancellor." Vlora stopped, turning to face Lindet. "We're talking about *making* gods. Do you really think a contract even crosses my mind on something as serious as this?"

"It should."

"Why?"

"Because you're treading very thin ice." Lindet's voice grew dangerously quiet. "I put you in an important place because I believe in your capabilities. Do you think I don't have plans to remove any person that I hand power to?"

"I believe you have plenty of plans," Vlora said. "That's what scares me. The godstones, where are they?"

"That's privileged information."

Vlora slammed a fist against the wood paneling on the office wall, making the wall rattle. "I don't give a shit! You have no idea what you're playing with. The Dynize just dropped an entire fleet in our laps because they want the godstones so badly, and you act as if they are of no consequence? *I know what they do.* That kind of power should not be handed over to anyone—nor kept."

Lindet rounded to the other side of her desk, her movements slow and smooth. She raised her hands as if to show she wasn't armed, then lowered herself into her chair. Vlora had never before occupied a room with an unarmed, not sorcerously gifted person who could make her feel like she didn't have the upper hand, and it infuriated her.

"I hope you have a proposal in mind," Lindet said, "and that your plan doesn't end with storming in here and shouting at me."

"Destroy them," Vlora said.

"Excuse me?"

"You heard me."

Lindet steepled her fingers below her chin. "First of all, I only have one. Let's pretend a moment that this ancient artifact can even *be* destroyed. We've had it in our possession for mere months and have learned immense amounts about the nature and history of sorcery. My Privileged tell me that they could study it for a dozen lifetimes and still not know all it has to offer. And you'd ask me to destroy it?"

"Yes," Vlora said.

"That, my dear general, is not happening."

"You'd risk it falling into the hands of the Dynize? Of a blood sorcerer and his hungry fleet?"

"That's why I hired you, in case you've forgotten."

Vlora wanted to spit. Lindet kept coming back to their relationship, as if a financial arrangement meant anything to Vlora. Perhaps Lindet didn't really grasp what Vlora had seen and experienced during the Adran-Kez War. Perhaps she didn't care. Perhaps Lindet's world was about contracts and control, and she just couldn't fathom anything outside those parameters. "And if I fail?"

"I'll consider destroying it as a last resort."

"You'd sacrifice the lives of my men and your whole garrison to keep this thing? Destroy it, and the Dynize have no reason to invade."

Lindet leaned across the desk, her eyes dancing with an otherworldly light. "I would sacrifice a million men to be a god, General. As would you. As would anyone in their right mind."

Vlora stared at Lindet, her frustration and anger turning to cold terror. This was not what she'd signed on for. She did not want this responsibility or this fight. But it *was* hers, if only because no one else would take it on. "I've met gods, and you're very wrong about that," Vlora said. She looked down, realizing that she was still wearing the parade uniform that she'd put on for the meeting with the Dynize ambassador. She tore off the strips of medals, one at a time, throwing them on Lindet's desk. "Lady Chancellor Lindet, as appointed defender of Fatrasta, I arrest you as a danger to the future of the country."

Lindet had the gall to actually look shocked. "You can't."

"I just did."

"I *am* Fatrasta."

"No. You're the steward of this country. You have responsibilities."

"Don't talk to me about responsibilities," Lindet snapped. "You bloody, ungrateful traitor. Guards!"

There was a brief scuffle outside, and then Olem stuck his head in the door. "Everything going well?" he asked.

"I'm arresting the Lady Chancellor."

Olem swallowed. "Right. Well, I guess that's happening." He retreated in the hall, where there was the sound of a further scuffle, then silence.

"I relieve you of your duty, General," Lindet said coldly. "Get out of my office."

"That's not going to work," Vlora responded. Her stomach flipped around, her guts tying themselves in knots. This was political suicide, and maybe more. She was conducting a coup. She could hear little but the hammering of her heart.

Lindet lifted her hand, and Vlora leapt forward. "Nuh-uh," she said warningly. "Give a signal and your Privileged die. I'm not so impulsive that I don't check the room when I enter, and I'm not the only powder mage in this city." Out across the rooftops she could sense Norrine and Davd hidden from prying eyes, weapons trained on Lindet's unseen bodyguards.

"I see," Lindet said, slowly lowering her hand. Her eyes narrowed. "You're making an immense mistake."

Vlora felt an overwhelming sadness take her, an exhaustion as if the weight of a mountain had just been pressed onto her shoulders. "I've made a lot of big mistakes, Lindet. This isn't one of them." She tilted her head, listening to a sudden chorus of shouts from out in the hall. A moment later Olem put his head back in the room.

"We've got a problem," he said.

"What is it?" Vlora asked, keeping one eye on Lindet.

"The Dynize have launched longboats."

"How many?"

Olem held up a finger, tilting his head. Half a second later, Vlora heard it, too. A distant, muffled thumping. *Boom. Boom-boom. Boom.* Vlora knew that sound well, unmistakable to any veteran officer. That was the music of a bombardment.

"All of them," Olem said. "It's a full-scale invasion."

Lindet lifted her chin, closing her eyes and taking a deep breath. "They didn't buy my gamble for time."

"It doesn't seem that way, does it?" Vlora responded. Her mind ran through a hundred scenarios as she tried to figure out what to do. She'd thrown herself into a fire trying to arrest Lindet, only to realize the fire was on a sinking ship.

"I think," Lindet said carefully, "that keeping the godstone out of Dynize hands is the most important thing we can do today."

"What, and forget this ever happened?" Vlora demanded.

"Oh, no. I never forget this kind of thing," Lindet responded coldly. "But I can overlook it until a future time. Why don't we finish this conversation *after* a foreign empire tries to kill us?"

Vlora considered the implications. She *had* Lindet right now. She should throw her in a cell. But doing so would have Fidelis Jes and the Blackhats breathing down her neck within hours. Lindet would be a formidable enemy once this was over—but Vlora needed an ally more than she feared the future consequences. "I agree," she said. "I'll need supplies and backup troops. Arm your Blackhats and send your Privileged to the coast. *All of them.*"

"You'll have them," Lindet promised.

Vlora left Lindet's office at a run. Olem was beside her in a moment. "What happened to arresting Lindet?"

"That's going to have to wait."

"You left her in power?"

"I don't think I have a lot of choice right now."

"And when she stabs us in the back?"

"We'll deal with that when it happens," Vlora said. "Send word to Norrine and Davd, we need them down at the fort. For now, we've got an invasion to stop."

CHAPTER 55

Vlora and Olem made it back to Fort Nied among a heavy bombardment of straight shot from the distant Dynize fleet. Cannon fire pounded the eastern slope of the Landfall Plateau, the blasts striking streets and buildings at random, forcing her and her men to shove their way through crowds of fleeing pedestrians, carriages, and carts. It was utter chaos as some sought the safety of the plateau, and others fled downhill toward the docks.

Everyone had turned out in their weekend best to gaze at the Dynize fleet and await news of the negotiations. No one expected a bombardment, and it showed in the terror of the faces of those running, fighting, or crying over the dead and wounded.

Vlora entered the fort, shouting over the whistle and impact detonations of the bombardment. "All guns open fire! Crews six and seven, sink that frigate off the point of the bay. Crews eight through eleven, load grapeshot and sweep the waters in front of the docks. I don't want any of their men getting close enough to torch the merchantmen at moor. The rest of you focus your fire on that ship of the line right off the southeastern star. Those ships will be inaccurate as pit but if they manage to get too close they'll be able to blast us to oblivion."

She took a deep breath, letting her senses soak in the sorcery woven throughout the walls of the fort. Fort Nied had survived the Battle of Landfall, holding out against the might of the Kez fleet. Its protective sorcery could shrug off a pit of a shelling, but she had no idea for how long.

She jogged up the stairs to the top of the eastern wall, gazing first out over the bay, then toward the open ocean, where puffs of smoke rose at regular intervals from every ship in the Dynize fleet. The fire was not focused—straight shot appeared to be landing everywhere from the industrial quarter all the way to the northern marshes—but Vlora doubted the Dynize cared. As far as she could tell, the sudden bombardment had a single purpose: to provide cover for the hundreds of approaching longboats by sowing chaos in Landfall.

"Where's Taniel?" she demanded of a nearby sergeant.

"Who?" the sergeant asked, looking confused.

"Damn it, nobody even knows..." She grunted in frustration, looking around, casting out her senses for another powder mage or a blood sorcerer. She found only her own three mages and nothing else. "So much for getting some help, you asshole," she muttered.

Vlora turned her attention to those longboats. They were each loaded with sixty or more Dynize soldiers, rowing hard for land, looking undeterred by the choppy waters that served to foul the aim of their capital ships. They would begin to land within fifteen minutes, and then it would be anyone's guess what happened next.

A brief terror seized her as she sought her memories and training. No one knew how the Dynize fought. Any engagements would have been more than a hundred years ago, fighting with wheel locks and early flintlocks. She didn't know if they fired in a line, preferred mass charges, or planned on simply bullying their way into a foothold by brute strength.

"Olem!" she shouted, waving to him from across the length of the fort wall. Olem raised his eyes, then ducked as a cannonball smashed into the top of the wall, ricocheting skyward with enough force to carry it over the entire fort and drop harmlessly into the bay. Olem ran toward her in a crouch. She grabbed him by the shirt, pulling him close enough to shout in his ear over the thunder of her own guns returning fire. "Those longboats are heading toward the north side of the bay. Who do we have out there?"

"Four thousand members of the garrison, and three companies of our own boys."

Vlora raised her head, looking out at the longboats. She took a sniff of powder, heightening her senses, peering at the Dynize soldiers and willing herself to read their strategy.

She'd never seen soldiers armed quite like this—outside of mannequins in a museum. They wore bright teal coats beneath angled, heavy-looking breastplates and folded steel helms. Their faces were stoic and hard, teeth clenched in gritty determination as they rowed closer and closer to land. A blast of grapeshot tore through one of the longboats, killing a third of the rowers and immediately causing the aft to dip into the water. The soldiers in the nearest boat threw lines to their bailing companions to try to keep them afloat in their heavy armor, but kept rowing hard for shore.

Their muskets looked mass-produced, each of them with the same flared, engraved stock a dozen decades out of fashion in the Nine. Vlora couldn't see enough detail to examine the flintlock mechanisms, but to her eye they looked just as modern as those of her men.

"Down!" Olem suddenly shouted, grabbing her by the shoulder and shoving them both to the ground behind the protection of the wall. Vlora's sorcerous senses flared, and a half a second later fire swept the top of the wall in a hot, angry column that scattered and charred two gun crews.

"Privileged!" someone shouted.

Vlora got to her feet, peering over the top of the wall, opening her third eye. She found the Privileged within moments—a woman, standing in the prow of one of the longboats about a quarter of a mile out from the shoreline. Her gloved hands waved over her head, fingers twitching and arms rising and falling like she was directing an opera.

Fire slammed into the north side of Fort Nied with the strength of a dozen cannonballs, engulfing crew eleven entirely. The Privileged suddenly jerked and toppled onto the soldiers behind her, crimson blossoming on her forehead. Farther down the wall, Vlora saw Norrine lower her rifle, blowing smoke from the end and immediately reloading. Vlora gave her an appreciative nod.

"There's more!" Norrine shouted.

Vlora sensed them, too. At least twenty Privileged, all of them out scattered among the longboats. Some of them were harder to get a fix on—obviously hiding themselves in the Else—while others seemed to note their fallen comrade and began to surround themselves with walls of hardened air.

"Olem, how many Privileged does the garrison have?"

"Two."

"Two?" Vlora demanded. "What good is two Privileged going to do against *that*?"

"We do have powder mages," Olem responded, gesturing to Norrine.

"Yeah, four of us. They have a whole bloody fleet. Send a message to Lindet. Tell her we need her personal cabal down here *now* or this fight might not last the evening."

As if to emphasize her point, there was a chorus of screams from the mainland as shards of ice appeared over the marketplace at the mouth of the Hadshaw, raining down among the civilians there. Vlora swore, turning to look back toward the longboats approaching the end of the bay. "Take Davd and an extra company. Reinforce the garrison out on the point. Tell Davd to focus his fire on the Privileged. Go!"

Vlora watched Olem spring down the stairs into the muster yard. He grabbed Davd from his spot at a gun port and within the minute he and a company of Riflejacks raced on foot down the causeway connecting Fort Nied to the land.

Vlora snatched the arm of a messenger. "Get replacement gun crews up here, and make sure one of our Knacked engineers is keeping an eye on the sorcery in these walls. I don't want the nasty surprise of their Privileged suddenly punching through this rock."

"Yes, ma'am!"

With her back to the wall, she lifted herself up to look sidelong out at the approaching longboats. The Privileged were gradually coming within range, raining sorcery down on the fort and bay. They, like the ships they were coming from, would get more accurate as they drew closer. She took a deep breath and reached out with her senses. Farther, farther, and yet farther still, stretching out over a thousand yards to one of the longboats with a Privileged on the prow.

With a thought, she detonated the powder of all the soldiers in the longboat. It exploded in a hundred smaller detonations, tossing flesh and wood for fifty yards in all directions. She felt the kickback from triggering powder deep in her bones, rattling her as if she was standing near the explosions.

It was an effective way to destroy a longboat, but she couldn't keep it up forever.

She wondered how many of the Dynize Privileged had ever encountered powder mages in a battle. She couldn't take them all out by igniting powder, but she didn't need to. "You!" she yelled, pointing at a nearby private. "Get me my rifle!"

CHAPTER 56

S tyke rode at the head of the column of a little over thirteen
hundred cavalry, the flags of the Mad Lancers and the Riflejacks flying in tandem from a pair of lances tied to the saddles of
Jackal and an Adran sergeant whose name Styke had forgotten.
Major Gustar and Ibana rode on either side of him—Ibana keeping her head tilted to one side, listening through her one good ear
as Gustar gave Styke a rundown on his new command.

Styke only half-listened, his eyelids drooping as a full night's ride
to Jedwar and back threatened to topple him from his saddle. His
legs were practically numb now, and he gripped his saddle horn
to remain steady, laying a calming hand on Amrec's neck. Behind
him in the saddle, Celine dozed peacefully, her arms wrapped
around Styke's stomach.

Gustar suddenly fell silent, and Styke looked up to find Ibana
nodding to the road in front of him. He felt an involuntary twitch
at the corner of his lip.

Blackhats. At least two hundred of them.

The Blackhats were heavily armed with blunderbusses and muskets. About half of them marched, the other half on horseback, with three heavy wagons among them. Styke looked over his shoulder at Jackal and jerked his head. Jackal grinned and rode past him.

"We going to call a halt?" Gustar asked.

"We don't halt for them," Ibana said, a note of disgust in her voice.

The column continued on as Jackal rode on ahead, reaching the Blackhats a hundred yards or so out. Styke could see one of the Blackhats look up at the banner, look back at Jackal, then take a good, hard gander at the approaching cavalry. He shouted something over his shoulder and slowly the Blackhats cleared the road.

By the time Styke reached the Blackhats they were waiting by the ditch, staring daggers at Styke and the banner that flew above Jackal's head. Styke directed Amrec off the side of the road, letting the rest of the column continue on as he approached the Blackhat with a Silver Rose dangling from his neck.

"You know who I am?" Styke asked.

The Silver Rose raised his chin in defiance. "Pretty good idea." He put on a good face, but Styke could see the fear in his eyes.

"Good. What are your orders?"

"None of your damn business."

"What are your orders regarding me?" Styke reframed the question.

Styke could see the "Sod off" on the tip of the Silver Rose's tongue, but a glance at the column of cavalry and he seemed to think better of it. "We've been ordered to ignore you. Bigger problems, it seems."

"Well," Styke responded, "glad your asshole of a boss can find something better to obsess over." He turned Amrec around and headed back toward the front of his column.

Behind him, the Silver Rose shouted out, "You have the road, lancer! But the grand master wants you to know this isn't over."

"No," Styke muttered to himself. "It isn't."

He caught back up with Ibana, blinking the sleep out of his eyes, resisting the urge to turn around and ride the Blackhats down. "Where are they going?" she asked.

"Didn't ask."

"Might have been a good idea."

Styke made a sour face. "They're Blackhats. They can go right to the pit for all I care."

The road carried them toward the distant Landfall Plateau, taking them over numberless marsh-fed rivers draining into the ocean and then up onto a rocky outcropping with thirty-foot cliffs plunging steep into the sea. They reached the top of these cliffs and Gustar suddenly turned over his shoulder, calling for a halt.

Ibana's head jerked around toward him. "Only the colonel calls a halt," she snapped.

Gustar ignored her. "Do you hear that?"

"Hear what?"

Gustar produced a looking glass, raising it to one eye and gazing toward the Landfall Plateau. He scanned the horizon, while Styke shared a puzzled glance with Ibana and strained to hear anything.

Then he caught it. The distant but unmistakable report of cannon fire.

Gustar thrust the looking glass at Styke. "To the east of Landfall," he said.

Styke let his eye focus, holding his hands steady to find the ships out beyond the harbor. Gray plumes of smoke rose above their gunports. He lowered the looking glass, wiped the eyepiece on his sleeve, then raised it again. The Dynize were definitely shelling the city. He'd expected to return with a thousand cavalry as part of a show of force. Not to defend Landfall. "We're under attack," he reported.

"That's insane," Ibana said. "They're supposed to have a diplomatic meeting today."

"It must have gone wrong," Gustar observed.

"Really damned bloody wrong," Styke said. He swept the horizon with the looking glass, taking in the full size of the fleet and the hundreds of longboats in the water between the ships and the shore. "Fort Nied is returning fire, and the Dynize are landing troops. Tell everyone we're in for a hard ride."

He heard Ibana shift in her saddle. "We've ridden all afternoon. Our men and horses are tired. Pit, the lancers rode all night, too."

"We've ridden all night to a fight before," Styke said.

"Yeah, when we were all ten years younger. We're old, fat, and out of shape. At least the rest of you are, anyway."

Styke was about to lower the glass when he spotted something else: more ships, far to the north of where the fleet had engaged with Fort Nied. There were at least a dozen transports emptying their decks of longboats, which plowed across the shallows to disgorge their troops with alarming swiftness. Styke quickly examined the lay of the land out from the beach—marshes and streams, with the odd village, and flat, drained suburbs at the base of the plateau.

He spotted a brigade in dark yellow jackets marching out of the suburbs, heading double-time for the landing Dynize. At a glance, the Dynize already outnumbered them and with the heavy armor they wore they looked more than an even match for basic garrison troops.

"Major Gustar, how do you feel about charging across sand?" he asked.

"Depends on the kind of sand," Gustar responded.

"I don't think you're going to get the chance to check." Styke handed the looking glass back and Gustar put it to his eye.

He frowned, and seemed to come to the same conclusion Styke had. "The garrison is badly outmatched. My cuirassiers will sink in that sand, but the dragoons might have a chance. You want me to hit them from behind?"

Styke grunted an affirmative and gently woke Celine, who rubbed her eyes and peered toward the distant enemies. "Sunin," Styke called.

He was joined by Major Sunintiel, her crooked yellow teeth framed in a broad grin. "Ordering a charge, Colonel? Been forever since I killed a man in battle, you know?" Sunin was old enough to be his great-grandmother, but looks were deceiving. She'd always been one of his meanest lancers—which didn't mean she'd survive the shock of a charge at her age.

"I am," Styke said, "but you're not in it. Take Celine."

"I'm not a nursemaid," Sunin objected.

"You can also barely hold a lance."

"Not true!"

Ibana snorted. "You're about a thousand years old, Sunin. Keep the girl safe."

Sunin grumbled, but she directed her horse up beside Styke. He took Celine by the back of the shirt, lifting and depositing her in front of Sunin. "Will you be all right?" Celine asked.

"Me?" Styke let Amrec prance below him. "I'll be fine. You take care of yourself. This is going to get bloody." He turned away from her. "Gustar, take your dragoons and sweep the beach. Ibana, draw up the Mad Lancers and the Riflejack cuirassiers on the road. We have killing to do."

CHAPTER 57

Michel, Taniel, and Ka-poel were forced to approach the dig site by horse, as the streets in and out of the city were all but impassable to cabs with pedestrians in a panic and the roads clogged by families and merchants fleeing the city. News that the Landfall bay was under attack by a Dynize fleet spread rapidly, and with it chaos.

They left the western plateau, forcing their way through the press of the industrial quarter, cutting across streams, parks, and yards, before finally rejoining the main highway just outside the city. It was a fraught ride, and Michel, who rarely, if ever, rode, felt like he was going to tumble from his saddle at any moment. His fear was only made worse when Ka-poel snatched his reins from him and led his horse in a gallop across the open floodplains.

He was only given a reprieve when they finally drew near the dig site and the three of them stopped a few hundred yards away, staring out across the farms at the cordoned-off, innocuous-looking excavation.

Taniel scowled in the direction of the monolith. Ka-poel raised her nose to the wind, as if trying to smell for something other than the smoke coming off Greenfire Depths. Michel, for his part, tried not to be sick from their ride and occupied himself with wondering what the other two were seeing.

He'd read a little about sorcery—it would be stupid to be a spy and not be aware of the ways he could be detected. But sorcery was as foreign to him as Gurla or Dynize, a distant concept that never really affected him in any significant way until he tripped those wards on the upper library and tipped his hand to Fidelis Jes. He thought of sorcery like he did politics: He knew it existed, and that it affected his life in deep, intrinsic ways, but he tried his best not to get any on him.

Yet here he was, leading a pair of godkillers to something that, if they were right, could actually *create* gods.

He lost his battle with his motion sickness, leaning over his saddle and vomiting noisily in the cotton field. Neither of his companions seemed to notice.

Taniel spoke up, his eyes still on the dig site, looking pensive and perplexed. "I wondered how it could have remained unnoticed for so long just outside the city, but even at this distance I can barely sense it." He glanced at Michel. "You're certain this is it?"

"I'm certain," Michel answered, spitting out the taste of sick and wiping his mouth. "I can't feel sorcery and that thing whispered in my head. I've never heard of anything that could do that. And even if I wasn't certain before, Fidelis Jes confirmed it this morning. They're digging up the godstone."

Ka-poel clicked her tongue to get Taniel's attention, then went through a series of hand motions too quickly for Michel to follow. Taniel watched carefully, nodding along. "What's going on over there?" he asked, pointing.

Michel followed his finger to see that part of the palisade surrounding the dig site had been torn down, and that hundreds of horses were being corralled by their handlers. Some sort of massive undertaking was under way, and it didn't take much for Michel to guess what.

"They're getting ready to move it," he said. "The professor in charge, Cressel, said they'd be ready within days. That was yesterday."

Ka-poel gestured quickly, and Taniel translated, "The arrival of the Dynize must have moved up their plans."

"Agreed," Michel said, though he wondered why he bothered. This wasn't his territory anymore. Taniel and Ka-poel were in charge, and he would let them have it.

Taniel removed a snuff box from his pocket and tapped a line of black powder out on the back of his hand before snorting it. He rubbed his nose and squinted toward the dig site. "There's a couple of Knacked down there," he said. "They'll be able to sense something off about Ka-poel. No telling how they'll react. They can't sense a powder mage, though."

"Any Privileged?" Michel asked, fearing the answer.

"None," Taniel said. "We actually passed one on our ride down here, beelining for the city. Probably recalled because of the attack."

Michel let out a sigh of relief. "Okay, so nothing down there but laborers, soldiers, and normal Blackhats. Right. This should be fine. Easy. No problem. We've got this. Can't think of a single thing that will go wrong. Just the easiest thing we've ever..." He trailed off when he noticed that both Ka-poel and Taniel were staring at him. "What?" he asked.

"You all right?" Taniel responded.

"I'm nervous."

"You'll do fine."

Ka-poel reached over and patted Michel on the shoulder, and he tried not to imagine that he was nothing more than a pet to these two. "Look," Michel said, "you two can fight your way out if this goes poorly. Me? I'm stuck."

Taniel reached over and slapped Michel on the back, almost knocking him out of his saddle. "We won't leave you behind."

"Thanks," he said, feeling less than reassured. He knew how this needed to go, and realized that he wasn't going to be able to cede control—and responsibility—over to Taniel. "Okay, let's get this over with. Ride behind me, and pretend I'm in charge."

"You're the boss," Taniel said.

"That's the worst thing you could say right now." Taking a deep breath, Michel headed toward the dig site.

Michel was met by the soldiers guarding the dig site about a hundred feet from the palisade. They looked tired and more than a little harried, casting glances toward the smoke rising above both the eastern and western ends of the Landfall Plateau. Michel didn't give them a chance to speak, drawing himself up in his saddle and pulling the Gold Rose out of his shirt, dangling it haughtily. "I'm looking for Major Cole," he said.

There were six of the guards, led by a sergeant, who immediately touched her cap at the sight of the Gold Rose. "Sir," she said, "Major Cole is overseeing the move, sir."

"Well, what are we waiting for? Take me to him!"

The sergeant glanced hesitantly at Taniel and Ka-poel before nodding. "Right this way, sir."

The dig site seemed to have transformed overnight. The wooden buildings had been ripped down, half of the tents were gone, and, with the exception of Professor Cressel, whom Michel immediately spotted scurrying around the lip of the excavation site, Michel didn't see anyone else who looked like they were from the college. This was no longer a dig, it seemed, but a military matter.

Soldiers and laborers swarmed the area, and several immense cranes had been erected to the north of the monolith, which itself was freestanding, the scaffolding removed, but now looped with hundreds of thick ropes of the kind they used to moor the biggest ships in port. To the north, positioned just beyond the two cranes, was the biggest wagon Michel had ever seen.

Calling it a wagon might have been an understatement. It was at least eighty feet long, with more sets of thick, wooden wheels than Michel could count, and hundreds of horses being led into position beyond it. The word "land-barge" immediately came to mind, and Michel had never seen anything like it.

"It sure is something, isn't it?"

The voice brought Michel out of his sense of wonder, and he looked down to see Major Cole standing beside his horse. "Back already, sir?" the major asked pleasantly.

The knot of stress between Michel's shoulders loosened ever so slightly. Apparently word of his treachery, or his attack on Fidelis Jes this morning, had yet to spread this far out. "It's quite the operation," he admitted, climbing down from his horse with less grace than he would have liked. He was quickly joined by Taniel and Ka-poel, the latter of whom Cole looked at with curious suspicion.

Michel pretended like they didn't exist and took on his most authoritative air. "You're really able to move this?"

"Professor Cressel has actually moved several monoliths this size or bigger," Cole said, pointing to the balding professor as he ran between cranes, pit, and labor foremen shouting for everyone to be careful. "He claims it's really quite simple—just a matter of levers and manpower. We have orders to get it moving by this afternoon, so only speed is going to be an issue now."

"But you can do it?" Michel asked.

"Landfall sent us four hundred more men, and Cressel says that'll do the trick."

"Good, good," Michel said. As he watched, there was a sudden shout, and the top of the monolith wobbled. Michel's heart leapt into his throat at the sight of something so solid and immense *moving*, and then it tipped without warning, falling several feet and causing him to gasp, before it came to a sudden stop at a sharp angle. Michel squeezed his eyes closed against a sharp pain, like nails on a chalkboard *inside his head*. "Kresimir," he swore, "that's insane."

Cole seemed less impressed. "I thought so, too. Are you all right?"

The pain was gone as suddenly as it arrived, and Michel couldn't help but stare at the monolith. "No, no. I'm fine," Michel said, noting that dozens of soldiers and laborers had touched their ears in pain. He glanced over his shoulder at Taniel and Ka-poel, who stood side by side stoically. Taniel's jaw was clenched, the veins on his face bulging, and Ka-poel seemed to tremble slightly.

With the monolith now at an angle, the workers swarmed down into the pit, tightening ropes, while others dug feverishly at the side of the excavation, causing the immense stone pylon to settle further onto its side. Michel could see their plan now with the mention of levers and manpower—they were going to get it at the proper angle and then pull it out of the pit.

"Major, who is in charge of the transportation?" Michel said, trying to sound casual.

"I am, sir."

"To Dalinport?"

"That's the plan."

"Not anymore," Michel said. "We've got a change of orders."

"Sir?" Cole said, turning his attention from the ongoing move entirely over to Michel. "We have everything lined up already. The road is clear, we have checkpoints in place. Our engineers have even smoothed out hills in the road to get this damn contraption along without a hitch."

"I know. I'm sorry, but things change. We found out just a few hours ago that the Dynize have designs on this very monolith."

"Why?" Cole asked, clearly surprised. "It's just an old rock."

Tell that to everyone who's been going mad from exposure to it. "I don't know, but we've got to get it as far from the coast as possible. The new plans are to take it across the plain to Herrenglade, where it'll be loaded onto a barge and pulled upriver." Michel glanced at Taniel. "I've not been told where it's going from there."

Cole looked suspiciously from Michel to Taniel to Ka-poel. "Are you sure, sir?"

"Quite." Michel tried not to hold his breath. His whole plan hinged on someone of Cole's rank not bothering to question the authority of a Gold Rose. Major Cole hadn't struck him as someone who asked questions, but he'd been wrong about people before.

"My apologies, sir," Cole said, "but do you have those orders in writing?"

Michel removed the Gold Rose from his shirt. "I have those orders in *me*. You think the grand master would send me down here on such short notice if it wasn't so damned important?"

Cole seemed uncertain. He backed away a couple of steps, glancing toward the excavation, and Michel tensed. Cole hadn't bought it. He'd summon his soldiers, and Michel, Taniel, and Ka-poel would be in a tight spot in moments. One he doubted he would be getting out of, even if the other two did.

"I'm going to have to send someone to confirm," Cole said. "The grand master's office made it clear that this thing is important to them, and I'm not interested in messing it up. No offense meant, sir, but I just can't change it without written confirmation."

Michel tried not to let his panic show on his face. It had almost worked, damn it. "Of course, Major Cole. But don't say I didn't warn you if the grand master is furious over the delay." He looked pointedly toward the smoke rising over Landfall, then turned around sharply, retreating twenty feet from Cole and his soldiers before whispering to Taniel and Ka-poel, "What do we do?"

Ka-poel lifted the satchel off her shoulder and began digging around inside, a frown on her face, while Taniel stared at the monolith. "That thing is a blight," Taniel spat.

"Tell me about it. I *felt* it when it fell," Michel said.

"It's like a knot of power, just lying out here in the middle of farmland, waiting for someone to come pick it up."

"And that someone is Lindet," Michel said. "We need to either come up with a new plan, or get the pit out of here."

Taniel nodded over Michel's shoulder, and Michel turned to find Major Cole approaching, an unhappy look on his face. "My apologies, Gold Rose," he said. "I've just got word that Dynize have landed farther south along the coast, cutting off our road to Dalinport. We don't have much time to get this moved, but we'll have it heading north as quickly as we can. You said it's bound for Herrenglade?"

"Yes, Major," Michel said, trying not to look relieved. He settled on smug. "And it's best we get moving quickly."

"Right," Cole said, snapping a salute. "We'll get things moving and I'll have my men arranged in a rear guard."

"How many soldiers do you have here?"

"About six hundred."

Michel glanced at Taniel, who gave a slight shake of his head. If the Dynize knew where the godstone was, and were headed directly here, six hundred men would not be enough. Michel said a silent prayer that the garrison would come out to help them.

CHAPTER 58

Styke grunted as his lance smashed through the breastplate of a Dynize soldier and ripped out the back of the soldier's uniform, dripping blood and gore. He leaned into the lance, trying to drag it free of the soldier's body, only for the corpse to catch on the belt of another Dynize. Styke let go of the lance with a frustrated shout so that the weight of it wouldn't knock him out of the saddle.

Beside him, Ibana's lance took a Dynize musketman through the eye, tearing the side of his head clean off, and then the Dynize front line was under their hooves.

The vanguard of the Mad Lancers spread out on the road, the thunder of their hooves almost drowning out the screams of men and horses at the impact of lances against bayonet-ready muskets. They swept forward, mowing down every Dynize that would not leap out of their way, while the Riflejack cuirassiers came on slowly behind, forming a fan that cleared the sides of the road of anyone who'd managed to escape the lancers' charge.

Styke drew up on a knoll, trying—but unable—to get a good

look at the beach several hundred yards to their left. A thick haze of smoke rose above the sand, and the sound of muskets and carbines exchanging fire drifted over the dunes.

He had a much better view of the road heading toward Landfall, where several regiments of Dynize soldiers had fallen into line and advanced swiftly into withering fire from the garrison.

"Do they even see us?" Ibana asked, reining in beside him.

"They see us," Styke confirmed, watching as messengers rushed between officers behind the Dynize lines. A few faces glanced back toward him and his lancers. "They just don't care."

"We've got cavalry coming up behind them, and they don't have anyone on horseback." Ibana leapt from her own horse, picking up a Dynize musket and giving it a quick examination. "These bayonets are not long enough to form an effective pike line against us."

"They're going to try and break the garrison before we can reach them."

Ibana stood on her tiptoes to look toward Landfall. "The garrison has gotten reinforcements. They outnumber the Dynize."

"And I'll give you ten-to-one that the Dynize troops are far better trained than the Landfall garrison. How thick are those breastplates?"

Ibana knocked the butt of the musket she held against the breastplate of a fallen Dynize, then turned it around and ran the bayonet through his neck. "Thick," she reported. "The angle on the front gives them a good chance of deflecting a musket ball at anything but close range."

"Shit." Styke stood in his stirrups, looking toward the beach. "You notice anything about these assholes?"

"Other than the fact we're outnumbered?" Ibana asked.

"Yeah, other than that. They don't give a shit. They're not running." He turned his horse around and rode back through the carnage to where he'd left his lance in the chest of a Dynize soldier. He dismounted, ripping his lance free, then climbed back into the saddle and rejoined Ibana. "Give the signal to re-form," he said, sweeping his eyes across the Dynize they'd just crushed. "We surprised two companies and they didn't so much as waver."

"They jumped out of our way," Ibana said, getting back in her saddle.

"Yeah, but they didn't break. What kind of infantry doesn't break in front of a surprise charge by twice their number in enemy cavalry?"

"Stupid ones?" Ibana suggested.

A nearby Riflejack cuirassier looked up from wrapping his blood-soaked arm. "Sir, infantry that doesn't break wins the day."

"Not all the time," Ibana said.

"But enough," Styke responded. He lifted his nose to the air, breathing in deep of powder smoke, getting hints of Privileged and powder mage sorcery like a vintner might test wine. There was something else beneath the more obvious scents, but it was so subtle that his Knack was at a loss to identify the source.

"That's the idea," the cuirassier confirmed. "Riflejacks don't break. That's how we win. It was the whole backbone of Field Marshal Tamas's tactics."

Styke could still hear fighting on the beach, and realized that the dragoons might have bitten off more than they could chew. Something was off about this Dynize army, and it wasn't just their sudden appearance. He felt the urgent need to get to Lady Flint and find out what was happening at the rest of the battle.

"All right," Styke said, "the garrison is on their own. Lancers! Carbines at the ready! Sweep down onto the beach and help our dragoons—once we clear the sand, we charge into the rear of the Dynize and keep going toward Landfall."

"What do you mean they're not running?" Vlora demanded.

"I mean they're not running," Buden slurred in Kez, next to impossible to understand with his half tongue.

Vlora stood up, looking out over the walls of the fort and tracking a Privileged with the sights of her rifle. He was half a mile out, hands raised as he directed sorcery toward the point of the bay where Olem, the garrison, and the Riflejacks fought to hold the shore against the longboats continuously landing in the shallows. She squeezed her trigger, detonating two extra powder charges with her mind and *pushing* them behind the bullet, willing it to fly longer and farther than any normal flintlock shot.

The bullet soared in a perfect arc, helped by the nudge of her sorcery, until it slammed into the Privileged's chest, knocking him into the foaming ocean.

She lowered her rifle and turned her attention toward the point of the bay. "They don't have anywhere to run," she said.

"No shit," Buden replied, thrusting one finger forward in a frustrated motion. "But a beach landing is the pit for anyone. Some of them should be running back into the water out of panic. Do you see a single soul turning around?"

Vlora watched as a longboat disgorged all but a handful of rowers, who immediately began heading back to the distant ships. The soldiers splashed through the shallows, muskets held over their heads, ignoring the continuous fire of Olem's soldiers with their hold on the beach. They reached dry sand and immediately fell to their knees, producing short, steel shovels from their packs and heaping up fortification in moments.

"They're not panicking," Vlora said.

"Yeah, that's what I'm trying to tell you."

Vlora turned her head toward the ocean, reaching out tentatively with her senses. The Else felt...confused. There were traces of sorcery everywhere from the attacking Privileged, not unlike streamers left behind by rockets. She could also feel the protective sorcery of the fort and...something else. It was subtle, like the barest hint of a foreign spice on a familiar meal.

She didn't know what it was, and that lack of knowledge terrified her.

There was a sudden clamor in the muster yard below, and a few moments later a familiar form appeared on the top of the wall, shaking off the two privates trying to tell him to keep his head down. Vlora didn't think anything could have made her smile in the middle of this, but somehow the sight of Vallencian did.

"Good afternoon, Lady Flint!" the Ice Baron boomed above the cannon fire.

"Vallencian, I don't think this is a good time."

He pulled himself up, standing well above the protection of the fort's walls, eyes a little wild from the cannon fire but too proud to admit it. "Nonsense! Lady Flint, I wanted to personally tell you that I've forgiven you for what you did to Mama Palo."

Vlora closed her eyes, resisting the urge to order her men to drag him bodily down into the safety of the fort. "Thank you, Vallencian," she said through gritted teeth. "I truly appreciate it. We are, however, fighting a battle here."

"It doesn't look too bad," Vallencian said, flinching as a cannonball smashed into the base of the fort a few dozen yards away and sent shattered bits of iron flying. A rifleman dropped his weapon, clutching his throat as he tried to scream through a mouthful of blood.

"It's bad, Vallencian," Vlora said firmly. "And it's not safe. You should leave. *Now.*"

Vallencian suddenly lurched toward her, grabbing her by the shoulders. "I have misjudged you, Lady Flint. I was evacuating my people from the city when I saw the uniforms of your men down here, manning the guns, and I could not leave you behind. Tell me what I can do to help with the defense."

"Nothing," Vlora said, waving him off desperately. She didn't have time for this. "Get out of here. Get your people to safety. I think we can hold the beaches, but I don't know how persistent the Dynize are going to be."

"The tide is going out," Vallencian noted.

"So?"

"So, that means that the longboats will have a harder time reaching shore."

"Small gifts," Vlora responded. Tide or no, the Dynize were still gaining ground.

"They have a beachhead," Buden said, garbling the last word so badly she almost didn't understand him.

"Vallencian, you are a good man. The best thing you can do is help evacuate your people and get safely out of the city. Get him out of here!" Vlora ordered her soldiers, who pulled Vallencian forcefully from the wall amid a torrent of protests. She couldn't spare Vallencian another thought. Buden was right. The point of the bay was covered in corpses floating in the shallows, more than she could count, but the Dynize seemed impervious to the deaths of their friends. They continued to leap from their longboats and now had a short fortification of sand a hundred yards long from which to return fire on Olem's troops.

"Buden," she said, "take one of the guns. Give Olem some support." She looked over her shoulder, eyes searching the smoldering wreckage on the eastern face of the plateau. "Where are our reinforcements?" she murmured. "Where are Lindet's Blackhats? We need everything we can get down here."

She continued to shoot at the Dynize Privileged, forced to get more creative with each shot as they formed hardened barriers of air to protect themselves. She overshot one Privileged, then angled the bullet down with the force of her mind, giving herself a headache in the process. Another she strengthened with half a kit's worth of powder, using brute strength to punch through the sorcerous shield, the Privileged, and four men behind him.

The roar of a cannon, much louder than normal, snapped her head around. Buden stood beside one of the big fort guns, steadying himself against one of the gunner crew, eyes narrowed and focused on the point of the bay. Vlora tracked the curve of the cannonball with her advanced senses, *feeling* the power that Buden had put behind it, and watched as it curved violently around the Dynize sand fortifications and then skipped along the ground, bowling through at least fifty men crouched just out of the waterline.

The Dynize scrambled to search for the source of the cannon fire, but even that didn't seem to deter them. More men landed and charged forward to take the places of their dead comrades.

"They should have run forever ago!" a nearby major shouted above the din, his looking glass focused on the point of the bay. "I've never seen anything like it. Why won't they break?"

Vlora shook her head and reloaded her rifle as a messenger reached the top of the fort wall and sprinted straight toward her.

"What news from Olem?" Vlora asked.

The messenger was pale, and for a moment Vlora feared the worst. But he gasped for breath and then said quickly, "I'm not sure about the colonel, ma'am. I just came from the capitol building!"

"Good! Where's our damned supplies and reinforcements?"

"I don't know."

"What the pit is that supposed to mean?" Vlora asked, snatching him by the collar of his jacket. "Where's the Blackhats Lindet promised me?"

"There's no one!"

Vlora released her grip, staggering back, and the messenger continued. "I've looked everywhere. The capitol building is all but abandoned, and I haven't seen a single Blackhat except from a distance. It's like they were never even there."

Vlora blinked in disbelief, feeling shell-shocked. Cannons roared around her, sorcery sputtering above the fort, her nostrils so thick with powder smoke that she thought the trance might overwhelm her. But none of that affected her like this news. Lindet had run. She'd sent Vlora down here to fight the Dynize, and she'd fled without so much as a warning.

"We've been betrayed," she whispered.

"What was that, ma'am?"

She grabbed the messenger by the shirt again, pulling him close to shout in his ear. "Colonel Olem is on the point of the bay. Tell him Lindet has betrayed us and the Blackhats won't be providing relief." She looked over the wall, seeing longboats rounding the breakers just a few hundred yards away. They'd reach the fort within minutes, or land and flank Olem.

"What do we do?" the messenger asked, a note of panic in his voice.

Vlora pushed him back, hating herself for fighting the urge to order a retreat. This wasn't her fight. These weren't her people or her city. "We do what we've been paid to do. We protect the city. Tell Olem... Tell him to hold the point of the bay."

CHAPTER 59

The Mad Lancers hit the Dynize infantry from behind with enough force to break even the strongest-willed soldiers, but the bastards refused to run. They remained locked in combat with the garrison, faces flat in steely determination while Styke and his cavalry rode up and down the length of the battle, grinding the Dynize to a pulp beneath hoof, lance, and saber until the garrison—which had looked on the verge of retreat—finally found their spines and finished off the outnumbered Dynize.

A cheer went up among the garrison as Styke re-formed the Riflejacks and lancers and rode through a gap in the Fatrastan lines. He reined in by the highest-ranking officer he could find—a lieutenant—and took a grim assessment of the garrison.

They'd almost been shattered by half their number of Dynize. Men had fallen out of rank, broken their weapons, and some had even fled only to now come crawling back sheepishly while everyone pretended they'd never left. The lieutenant snapped a salute. "Timely charge, sir!"

"You're not getting another one," Styke warned. "We're heading to the city. I lost hundreds of dragoons clearing that beach but more Dynize are on their way. I'll try to get Flint to send you help."

"We already requested more men," the lieutenant said.

"Right. Form up right and quick, and pull your wounded back behind the line." Styke gestured to the edge of the suburbs, some half mile behind them. "Pull back behind the marsh dikes and make it harder for them to reach you. The assholes don't have very good bayonets but that armor stops the better part of a good volley and they fight like sin up close."

"It's, ah, pretty terrifying, sir. The bastards wouldn't break, no matter how good we gave it to them."

"Nothing's more terrifying than death," Styke replied. "Make them pay for every step, and I'll make sure Flint sends you more men."

He peeled off, joining his cavalry on their ride toward the city. Styke felt his exhaustion dragging at him and could see it in the eyes of his lancers. After two quick, bloody engagements they were sagging, already used up from a full day's ride. They needed rest, and lots of it.

They weren't going to get it.

"Your lance is broken," Ibana said, slowing down to ride beside him.

Styke blinked at the shattered, bloody lance that ended just a few feet from his hand. He discarded it and leaned over Amrec, checking the horse's neck and chest for any damage. There were half a dozen nicks and cuts, but nothing major enough to cause concern. He gestured to Amrec's underbelly. "Legs?" he asked.

Ibana shook her head. "Good as gold."

He ran his eyes over her mount. "Deep cut on the left flank. Will need stitches. Where's Jackal?"

"Appropriating a horse from one of our fallen," she said. "His broke a leg and had to be put down."

Styke cringed. The death of men rarely bothered him, but the loss of a good horse always struck him as a tragedy. He turned Amrec around, standing in the stirrups, hoping the garrison looked in better shape from behind. They didn't.

"Another attack like that one and they'll break," Ibana observed, shaking gore from the tip of her lance and raising it above her head.

Styke couldn't help but agree. The garrison was slowly pulling itself together and drawing back in the lancers' wake toward the marsh trenches as he'd suggested. Styke dragged a sleeve over his nose, trying to get the smell of powder and death out of his nostrils so he could breathe properly. That strange hint of sorcery was still there, touching his senses, but not quite comprehensible. "I smell something," he said.

Ibana frowned. "Sorcery?"

"I don't know. It's there, just nothing I can identify. It feels like it's in us, around us."

"Bone-eye?" Ibana asked.

The thought hadn't occurred to Styke. "The Dynize are known for the bastards, aren't they?"

"And we have no idea what they're capable of."

Styke thought back to his encounter, real or imagined, with Ka-poel yesterday afternoon, and the blood that had disappeared from his face. He didn't realize it at the time, but he now felt distinctly marked. He tried not to think about it and drew his heavy saber, checking the blade with his thumb.

"Don't insult me like that," Ibana snapped. "I sharpened it myself."

"Just checking!" Styke assured her. "One of yours?"

"Dad's actually. He still makes a common blade from time to time, just to keep his edge."

"Is he . . . ?" Styke asked, letting the rest of the sentence waver off in uncertainty.

Ibana didn't meet his eyes. "When we left yesterday he was recovering. The Privileged healing almost killed him." She frowned into the distance. "Is that smoke over Greenfire Depths?"

Styke's whole attention had been on the coast until this point. He looked toward the plateau and was surprised to see thick black columns rising above the western half of the city. He felt his stomach clench. If Greenfire Depths went up in flame, they might lose the entire Palo quarter. Not that many Kressians would care, but that's where Old Man Fles was now. "I'm sure his apprentices will get him out," he said softly.

"I know they will," Ibana retorted. She checked the pan of her carbine and then began to reload. "The last thing anyone needs is a riot in Greenfire Depths while we're under attack."

"If the fighting just started a couple of hours ago, does anyone in the Depths even know?" Styke wondered aloud. He couldn't help but wonder how Lindet was dealing with all of this—she thrived under multiple pressures, and she had a *lot* of Blackhats in the city. She would probably draw them in close and use them only as a last resort. If the Dynize reached the suburbs the brutality of the fighting would make these engagements look like light skirmishes.

Styke pulled himself out of his thoughts and joined the vanguard, where he found Jackal now riding a blue roan beside a bloody-faced Major Gustar. The lance holding the Mad Lancers' standard had been broken, then mended with a belt, and now flew just a little lower and more crooked.

Somehow it seemed fitting.

"Orders, Colonel?" Gustar asked, trying to salute but only managing to bring his hand halfway to his face.

Styke admired the man's dedication but didn't show an ounce of pity. These Riflejacks were no Mad Lancers, but they definitely had guts. "Hug the coast. We've got flatland between here and the port, and the garrison's going to have their hands full with Dynize troops. We'll sweep the beach and report to Lady Flint for orders."

"Taking orders now, are we?" Ibana asked in a low, only slightly sarcastic voice. "Either you're getting old, or you actually think Flint has judgment worth a damn."

"Both," Styke replied. "But we'll find out for sure if we're still alive at the end of this." He cast his eyes around once again at the tired faces, the worn-out horses, and stood up in his stirrups, raising his saber into the air. "Ride for blood!" he ordered.

A fireball struck the ground with the force of a mortar shot just a dozen feet in front of Styke. Amrec went up on his hind legs, screaming in terror, and Styke—a sword in one hand and carbine in the other, his numb legs a poor purchase on Amrec's sides—was thrown from his saddle. He hit the ground, ears ringing, breath knocked out like he'd been hit by a boulder.

Horses thundered by on the rocky sand of the point of the bay, and his surroundings were almost entirely obscured by the thick pall of powder smoke, lit from time to time by sorcery and exploding mortars. The shore was pounded by enemy guns as if the Dynize cared little whether they struck their own men.

To Styke's right, crimson-coated Riflejacks and yellow-clad garrison soldiers fought like mad dogs against the never-ending, if inconsistent, tide of Dynize soldiers coming in from his left. Corpses of all three groups lay scattered on the beach.

Styke gained his feet, discarding the carbine that had snapped in half beneath him on his fall, and grabbed the hot muzzle of a charging Dynize soldier, redirecting the short bayonet over his shoulder and felling the soldier with a single blow to the neck from his saber.

"Amrec! Amrec, damn it!" Styke searched the bodies of nearby horses for Amrec, but none of them was nearly big enough. He heard a horse scream somewhere in the smoke but could not pinpoint the source. He threw himself toward the closest skirmish between Dynize and Fatrastan forces.

The Dynize breastplates, like a cuirassier's, were only armored on the front, held on by leather straps over the shoulders and around the back. Styke severed a Dynize spine from behind, laying about with the blade of his saber. A nearby Riflejack fell beneath a Dynize bayonet, and Styke grabbed the Dynize soldier by the back of the neck, squeezing until the woman went limp, then throwing her body onto the poor bastard she'd just skewered.

Another blast—a mortar—exploded nearby, and Styke felt the hot sting of shrapnel tear through his jacket, scoring his side and legs. He staggered from the force of the blast, nearly losing his head to a cannonball that glanced off the sand twenty yards away and bounced over his shoulder, blowing a hole clean through the breastplate of a Dynize musketman.

He continued fighting his way along the point of the bay, navigating by keeping the source of the sorcery to his left and the higher, rockier ground on his right. Occasionally a riderless horse ran through the smoke, bucking and crying, but none of them was Amrec.

The fighting grew more fierce, the more organized Riflejacks keeping the Dynize at bay at the end of their long bayonets. Styke found a uniformed body, crushed by the eviscerated corpse of a horse, and recognized the rider as one of his Mad Lancers, though the name escaped him after so many years.

A Dynize suddenly tore through the smoke, leaping bodies with the agility of a gazelle, a pair of bone axes in hand and torso protected by the now-familiar dark green leather of a swamp dragon. Styke coughed, spat up blood, and gave chase as the dragonman tore into a pair of Riflejacks, leaving them dead in his wake faster than either of them could raise a bayonet.

Styke caught up to the dragonman with long, painful strides, slashing with his saber. He missed, then leapt fully into the dragonman's side as the warrior reached a squad of Riflejacks, sending them both tumbling through the group of soldiers.

The dragonman came out of the tumble on top, spitting sand and blood, and slammed the haft of an ax into Styke's nose.

Styke, his saber lost, punched the dragonman in the jaw, causing the Dynize to lurch back, dazed, before he caught Styke's second punch and twisted his arm painfully to one side. Styke fought back, flexing, using every ounce of his strength, until the dragonman's head suddenly snapped back and the sound of a pistol being fired at point-blank range left Styke's ears ringing.

Styke shoved the body off him and got to his feet, only to find Olem—one arm bloody and bandaged, a deep slice along his left cheek, and his hat gone—standing with the smoking pistol among a squad of Riflejacks.

"I would have won it," Styke spat, half-joking, half-serious. Blood pounded in his ears, and he felt every tendon tight and ready for movement, his body like an oiled spring.

"I believe you," Olem said. "But we don't have time for their shit. One of those assholes already wounded Davd."

Styke didn't bother asking who Davd was. "I lost my horse," he said. "See a big bastard come through here?"

"I saw your second in command a few moments ago," Olem said. He suddenly lurched sideways, caught by a sergeant on his left. He shook his head, as if he wasn't sure where he was, then pointed. "Well timed on the cavalry, but you're useless in this smoke. If you can rally your men take them west. Flint will have use for you."

"You'll be able to hold the shore?" Styke asked.

Olem managed a smile, causing the deep gash on his cheek to weep blood. "We need infantry, not dragoons. I'm pulling my boys back before this gets any worse. Go on, get out of here."

Styke found Ibana less than fifty feet away. She was still on her own horse and held Amrec's reins in her teeth, forcing both horses to twirl, hooves flashing, battering at the Dynize infantry that stabbed at her with their short bayonets. Her saber rose and fell, dripping gore, and within moments she'd cleared the Dynize and stopped her spinning. She spotted Styke and raised her sword in a greeting.

Styke limped over and snatched Amrec by the bridle, the shrapnel from the mortar starting to sting. He grabbed the saddle horn and pulled himself up, just as Major Gustar emerged from the smoke. Gustar's horse had a definite limp, and his hand was bloody and hastily wrapped.

"This isn't going well," Ibana reported.

"We're to pull back," Styke said. "Get everyone out of this blasted smoke. Olem is letting the Dynize have the point of the bay."

Gustar just nodded wearily, riding into the smoke. A moment later an Adran bugle sounded.

"Try not to forget you're not wearing your armor anymore," Ibana said, appraising the cuts on Styke's side and arm.

"What's that supposed to mean?" Styke asked.

"It means you need to not ride into bloody sorcery and artillery fire, that's what it means. Sorcery and grapeshot are going to kill you as easily as any other man."

Styke looked at the blood soaking through his clothes. The pain was sharp, acute. It lit his senses like a fire. "I'll try not to do anything stupid."

"Letting the Dynize have any ground at all seems foolish."

"No choice," Styke replied. "They've paid for it in blood." He urged Amrec into a gallop, racing west, and within a minute the smoke had all but cleared. He watched over his shoulder as Riflejacks, the Fatrastan garrison, and his own cavalry emerged from the haze, clear relief in their eyes at being given the order to withdraw. The Dynize didn't seem to follow them out of the smoke, and he wondered if they'd finally used up all their men—or if they were just happy to take the beachhead and prepare for their next attack.

He ignored them all and set his sights on the causeway leading to Fort Nied.

CHAPTER 60

Messengers streamed in and out of Fort Nied, leaving Vlora with an increasingly uneasy feeling in the pit of her stomach. The garrison was under heavy fire from troops that had landed north of the city, while Olem faced heavy losses at the point of the bay, and the smoke from musket fire over his position continued to rise as fast as the breeze blew it away, making it next to impossible for Vlora, Norrine, or Buden to give Olem any support fire.

Greenfire Depths was in flames, and the Blackhats had been seen fleeing the city en masse. She ordered the garrison to bring any and all cannons from the old forts scattered around the city to the eastern edge of the plateau, and diverted two thousand men from the southern side of the city to reinforce the north, and another nine hundred to help Olem.

"All of them!" she shouted at a messenger in a yellow Fatrastan jacket. "We're not going to hold the bay, and I intend on making it next to impossible for the Dynize to take the plateau. Get me every weapon not nailed down inside the city. Raid Blackhat depots, I don't give a damn!"

"But the Blackhats…"

"Are gone! Damn it, I'll have my own men do it. Bloody pit, get out of my way!" She ran to the other end of the wall, taking a spare rifle from a wounded private she'd assigned to load her weapons. She searched the Else for a Dynize Privileged and, when she couldn't find one, put a bullet through the eye of what looked like a Dynize officer.

She paused, lowering her rifle, and returned to the Fatrastan messenger. "Wait!" she shouted. "I want this rioting put down, and the fires in Greenfire Depths extinguished. Anyone in the garrison who isn't dedicated to direct combat needs to do that. Get me newspapers, city criers, everything. If the rioters know the city is under attack by a foreign force, they might abate."

A cannonball slammed into the top of the wall, and Vlora ducked, and the sound that accompanied the impact put her on edge. A single glance confirmed her fear: Masonry had shattered. The Dynize attack had finally broken the sorcery holding Fort Nied together.

"I need engineers up here!" she shouted, glancing over the edge of the wall. Longboats drew near, too numerous for her smaller gun crews to pick out of the water with grapeshot. Men stood in the prows with grappling hooks, ready to scale the walls of the fort. "Does nothing scare these assholes?"

She took one step and sagged, her right leg refusing to obey her. She looked down to find a shard of limestone as big as her thumb and twice as long sticking out of her leg, blood soaking the pants around it. She jerked it out, so deep in a powder trance that she barely registered the pain, and quickly bound the wound with her handkerchief.

The pain she could drown out, but her muscles wouldn't respond.

She limped along the wall. "We can win," she whispered to herself. "We can win. We will not break in the face of our enemies. We will hold strong. We are the anvil. We are the stone." She reached the closest of her remaining gun crews and staggered over to the commander as he shouted orders.

"Distance, five hundred yards!"

"Distance, five hundred yards!" one of the crew repeated, helping the others adjust the aim of the gun. "Sir, ready to fire!"

"Fire!"

The cannon kicked back several feet, belching flame and noise. In the distance, the mast of a Dynize capital ship suddenly cracked, split, and with the slow momentum of a falling tree, toppled to the deck, scattering sailors and gunners.

"Report," Vlora demanded of the gun commander.

"Range, four-hundred and ninety yards. Reload, reload!" The gunner didn't bother looking or saluting. "We're almost out of straight shot, General," he shouted over the din. "We've got a few hundred rounds of canister left, but the boats will be here any moment."

"Major," Vlora shouted at an officer in the muster yard below, "I want riflemen lining the walls! Give everyone double ammunition and tell them to fix bayonets."

The gun commander continued: "The ships are getting closer. We've sunk at least eighteen of the warships and another thirty or so of the transports and small support, but there's just too damn many of them. We have"—he paused, scanning the walls, his lips moving as he counted—"just eight big guns left. Their ships of the line are getting close enough for some serious accuracy."

Vlora slapped the gun commander on the shoulder. "Keep giving them the pit," she ordered, limping over to another set of messengers. She was surprised to find one of them was a Palo, wearing one of the pale green uniforms she'd last seen on Mama Palo's men. Her heart leapt into her throat before she remembered that Mama Palo—the real Mama Palo—was on her side.

"You first," she said, pointing to the Palo.

"Message from the Red Hand," the Palo said, looking entirely unimpressed by the chaos of the battle raging around them. "He says that the Dynize infiltrators have started the fires and the riots in Greenfire Depths. He's dealing with that now."

Vlora let out a sigh. Finally, some good news. She'd forgotten entirely about Taniel and Ka-poel's Palo followers. If they could take care of the Dynize in Greenfire Depths and watch Vlora's back, it would let her commit the last of her garrison reserves to the fight—soldiers she desperately needed. "Does he have any men he could spare for this?" she asked, gesturing toward the ocean.

The Palo messenger shook his head. "The Dynize have landed more men south of the city."

Vlora let herself sag against the inner wall, letting out a soft sigh. *We are the anvil. We are the rocks upon which our enemy will shatter.* "I've just redirected all my men south of the city to reinforce the bay and the north."

"The Red Hand demands reinforcements to the south."

"He doesn't demand shit," Vlora snapped, suppressing the urge to take a swing at the Palo. "Don't shoot the messenger," she decided, was coined for this exact situation.

"The Red Hand wants you to know that the item in question is two miles south of the city. It needs to be protected from falling into Dynize hands."

"The item in..." It took Vlora a moment before she understood what that meant. "The godstone."

"That is what he called it, yes."

Vlora called down to the muster yard. "Major, do we have any-one else at all we can send south?"

The major opened his mouth to respond but was cut off by the sudden thunder of hooves as Styke, Ibana, and a half-dozen Mad Lancers—along with Major Gustar—rode through the open gates of the fort. Vlora's mind immediately changed directions and she waved off the major in the muster yard. "Styke!" she bellowed. "Report, now!"

Styke reined in just below her. "We've swept the beaches up north on our way in, and relieved Olem enough for him to with-draw from the point of the bay." Vlora swore. She *needed* him to hold that point. But Olem wouldn't pull back without damn good reason. "I've had about five hundred casualties," Styke went on. "Leaves me with a little over eight hundred able-bodied riders."

Vlora swore again. She'd hoped he'd arrive with full strength, but if he'd already been in two engagements, she should be impressed that he had anyone left at all. She looked toward the point of the bay, wondering how suicidal Styke *really* was to have ordered a charge into that smoky chaos on uneven ground.

"Two miles south of the city," she said. "There's an artifact down there. I don't know where, I don't know what the pit it looks like, but I need you to find it and secure it."

Styke and Ibana both frowned, exchanging a glance. "But the battle..."

"You'll get your battle," Vlora said. "The Dynize are coming up from the south, and they want that artifact. I don't know if they're heading for it specifically, but if they find it before you get there we'll have a pit of a time taking it back."

Styke nodded. "Right-o, General." Without another word he turned his big gelding back around and rode at the head of his men out of the muster yard. Vlora watched him go with a desperate longing. She needed Styke here, performing sweeps of the beach to relieve her defenders. But there was no one else to send, and the Dynize *could not have* the godstone.

"Ma'am," the gunner commander shouted, "we need those rifle-men up here now!"

"Major, get me those riflemen!"

"They'll be sitting ducks on that wall! The ships are too close."

Vlora grit her teeth, turning to look toward the ships of the line that were now just outside of the bay, broadside toward the fort, opening fire with fearless determination. "I'll take care of it," she said. "Just get your men up here."

Staggering forward, Vlora put both hands on the wall and then cast her senses outward until she found the powder magazine in the depths of the warship's hold. Hundreds of barrels of powder, all crowded together in one place. It took only a single thought to ignite it all, but she knew she'd feel a kickback strong enough to drop an elephant.

She touched off the powder and immediately felt like a wagon had run over her. She groaned, her head spinning, watching the ship blow apart through blurry vision, trying to breathe through a suddenly tight chest. It took her several moments to recover enough to have the presence of mind to duck as infantry in the Dynize longboats opened fire on the walls.

Within moments she was surrounded by her own riflemen, and the comforting cracks of Hrusch rifles returning fire.

CHAPTER 61

Michel watched, amazed, as the crews under Professor Cressel's direction managed to extricate the monolith from its sunken pit in the ground in less than two hours. Using a combination of ramps, cranes, and brute force, the stone column was pulled up and out onto a prepared soil shelf. The cranes were cleared away and the land-barge backed up beside the stage while laborers with shovels and pickaxes adjusted the contours of the land so that there was a gap of mere inches between the monolith and the land-barge.

It was a fascinating bit of engineering and, to Michel's eyes, went incredibly smoothly. A laborer's leg was caught in the spoke of the land-barge and had to be removed, but the man was carried off within minutes and the work continued, undistracted.

While Cressel prepared to move the monolith onto the land-barge, Michel caught sight of Ka-poel up on top of the horizontal monolith. She squatted, fingers tracing shapes on the monolith's exterior like a child playing in the sand.

"What's she doing up there? You up there, get down!" Professor Cressel waved his arms at her, but she ignored him. "Major Cole!" he shouted.

Major Cole lifted his head from a discussion with his troop, pointing Cressel toward Michel, who glanced at Taniel as the professor stormed toward them. "What *is* she doing?" Michel asked.

"Don't ask me," Taniel said. "We've been together almost eleven years, and I still don't understand her half the time."

"She knows that people have gone mad from being too close to that thing, right?"

"She knows," Taniel confirmed.

Professor Cressel approached, pointing over his shoulder. "Gold Rose, would you be so kind as to remove your companion from the specimen?"

"Why?" Michel asked. "Is she bothering anything?"

"It's quite unsafe! I've dismissed all the researchers from the site aside from myself. The move is very dangerous. The fact we haven't lost anyone yet today is a miracle!"

Michel leaned over to Taniel. "Does she need to be up there?"

"Pole!" Taniel said, cupping his hand around his mouth. "Pole!"

She waved her hand dismissively, and Taniel gave Michel an unapologetic shrug. "She's working. Nothing but force is going to get her down. You're welcome to try, but I'm not going to."

"Does she know that the entire monolith could shift or slide?" Professor Cressel demanded, tugging at the last wisps of gray hair on his head. "It could take an arm, or a leg, or crush her completely!"

"She's aware of the danger," Michel assured him. "Your men can work around her."

Cressel retreated to his dig, fuming silently, and Michel chewed on the inside of his cheek. Every so often he glanced toward Landfall. The smoke from Greenfire Depths had gotten worse, and he hoped that his mother had managed to escape the city by now. His primary concern, however, had shifted to the eastern side of the plateau, where fire and powder smoke rose in alarming amounts from over the bay. The sound of bombardment was near constant, and he could see the pinprick lights of shells bursting high over the ocean. It seemed so distant and unimportant, but it wouldn't be for long.

"Major Cole," Taniel said loudly, "any word from your men on the approaching Dynize?"

Cole finished speaking to his officers and then crossed to them, a grim look on his face. "There's four regiments just finished landing about six miles from here. At best we have a few hours until they get here. I've sent runners back to Landfall with requests for reinforcements. No idea if we're going to get them or not. One of my boys from the city just arrived, and he said the fighting there is bad."

Michel exchanged an alarmed glance with Taniel. None of that was good news. If the Dynize reached them, they wouldn't stand a chance. But the news that Cole was actively sending messages to Landfall meant that Michel's trickery might be discovered.

"Can this be hurried along?" Michel asked.

"Cressel assures me he's hurrying the best he can without risking damage to the obelisk."

"Good, good," Michel said. He started to pace, counting out ten paces, then walking back to Taniel before repeating the route several times. Major Cole watched him do it once, then returned to his officers, barking out orders. Michel stopped his pacing to watch the chain of command as officers passed orders to enlisted men, and the soldiers began to slowly shift to the southeast of the dig site, forming themselves into a protective cordon around the excavation.

A loud creaking brought Michel's attention back to the monolith, and he turned just in time to see Ka-poel ride the immense stone off the dirt shelf upon which it rested to slide down thick, flattened timbers and crunch onto the land-barge. The monolith came to a stop, the land-barge and its load settling almost a foot closer to the ground. Michel let out a breath he didn't realize he'd been holding in, and Taniel shook his head.

Ka-poel flashed them both a grin, then returned to studying the side of the monolith.

Michel approached Professor Cressel, clapping his hands. "Well done, Cressel, well done. Are we ready to move?" He could hear the desperation in his tone and tried to suppress it.

The professor adjusted his glasses, squinting at an open folder in his hands. "The engineers are checking the axles and securing the load. We should be ready to move out in half an hour."

Michel grimaced. "Make it fifteen minutes."

"Sir!" Cressel protested.

Michel waved his finger under Cressel's nose with a confidence he didn't feel. "Fifteen minutes, unless you want your eyeballs to wind up as Dynize trophies."

"Dynize don't take eyeballs as trophies." Cressel snorted.

"Whatever. Make it quick, Professor, time is running out."

A tap on his shoulder brought Michel around to find Taniel standing beside him. Taniel's attention was no longer on the monolith or the soldiers, and he took an indiscreet snort of powder and pointed north. "You see that?"

Michel squinted. "I don't see anything."

"Riders coming in. Cole should spot them in a few minutes."

"Is it relief from Landfall?"

"Maybe," Taniel said. "Maybe not." He peered into the distance like a big cat warily protecting its kill, then said, "They're Blackhats."

"Shit. We've got to go," Michel said, already heading toward the corral where Cole had stashed their horses. He turned to find Taniel not following him, then ran back and snatched him by a sleeve. "It's not worth the risk," he said. "If the Blackhats know that

I attacked Fidelis Jes they'll snatch me the moment they see me, and you and Ka-poel a few seconds after. We've got to get out of here while we still can."

Taniel suddenly smiled, shaking his head. "We wait."

Michel resumed his pacing, doing two quick rounds before returning to Taniel's side. "You're sure you want to do this?"

"Go if you want," Taniel said. "But Ka-poel and I will stay."

Michel swore to himself. Every instinct told him to run. The Blackhats would skin him alive over the course of a very, very long time if he was found here by anyone aware of who he really was. Fidelis Jes might be alive or dead, but it didn't matter—he would have told *someone* about Michel's betrayal, if only his secretary, and they'd be out for Michel's blood. "Is this it?" he asked.

Taniel looked at him in surprise. "Is what it?"

"This godstone? Is this the culmination of all my work? Is this what I toiled for years to discover? Was this my true purpose in joining the Blackhats?"

Taniel seemed to consider the question for several moments before answering slowly. "This was one of many perceived purposes. It would have been preferable to leave you among them, but yes...the discovery of the godstone was the most important thing we had in mind when we sent you to work for the Blackhats."

The revelation gave Michel a sense of peace that he hadn't expected. It felt as if a great weight had been lifted from his shoulders and he mentally examined the marble that he'd kept his *real* self in for so many years before discarding it with an almost giddy laugh.

"What's so funny?" Taniel asked.

"Nothing," Michel said. "I'll stay."

As Taniel predicted, Major Cole's scouts saw the Blackhats just a few minutes later, and Michel himself noted the dust cloud a little after that. Like Michel, Taniel, and Ka-poel, the Blackhats didn't bother with the road, riding instead straight across the farmland directly toward the dig site. By the look of things, there were a damned lot of them, and as they drew closer Michel could see that they were heavily armed.

His decision to see this whole business with the godstone through to the end seemed less and less like a good one.

And then it got worse.

"Major Cole!" one of the guards shouted across the din of laborers preparing the land-barge for moving. "We've got a thousand Blackhats coming in, with Fidelis Jes himself! They say he wants a report from you personally!"

Michel's mouth tasted of ash. He looked at Taniel.

"You're right," Taniel said with a low whistle. "Time to go. Get Ka-poel, I'll fetch the horses."

Waiting until Major Cole's attention was elsewhere, Michel made his way over to the side of the land-barge. "Ka-poel!" he hissed, repeating her name three times before she finally looked up from her studies with a frown. She tried to wave him away. "No," he replied. "Fidelis Jes will be here any moment. We have to go *now*."

Ka-poel gestured rudely at him before smacking her fist against the monolith in frustration, then heading toward the other side. Michel threw himself under the land-barge, crawling on all fours beneath the creaking, weighty axles, sweat pouring down his face by the time he made it to the other side. Ka-poel was already down, and she helped him to his feet and the two ran for Taniel.

They met him at the corral as he brought out their horses. They were mounted a few moments later, and riding out of the camp when a guard waved them down. "Sir! Major Cole wants to know where you're going!"

"We're heading out to meet the grand master," Michel threw over his shoulder, not bothering to look back.

"But you're going in the wrong direction!"

"No," Michel muttered to himself. "We're definitely going in the right direction." They broke out of the camp and had gone about a hundred yards when he said, "Wait. No, we're going in the wrong direction. Taniel, where the pit *are* we going?"

"East," Taniel responded over his shoulder.

"I can see that! But east is the ocean. East is the Dynize!"

"We hug the coast and head north back to Landfall. Vlora will need the help, and if we can get any of her men we'll be able to come back and take the godstone from Fidelis Jes."

Michel wanted to shout how stupid an idea that was, and how much he wanted to head *away* from the burning city, but his words turned into a strangled shout as he spotted a number of Blackhats peel off the main contingent and head to cut them off. "Taniel!"

"I see them."

Ka-poel rode close and snatched Michel's reins and then bent over her own horse, urging her onward. The three practically flew across the plains, Taniel and Ka-poel riding like the wind while Michel just clung to his saddle horn, hoping he didn't fly off and break his neck when they leapt a ditch. The Blackhats drew closer and closer, and Michel's certainty they would be caught grew deeper until Taniel suddenly veered northwest.

"Why are we heading *toward* them?" Michel asked.

"I have a plan," Taniel said. Michel spared a look up from the back of his horse's neck to see that Taniel's eyes were on Landfall, not the approaching Blackhats.

"Focus!" Michel shouted. He squeezed his eyes closed and heaved, wondering if he had anything left in his stomach to throw up. Their gallop suddenly slowed, and he opened his eyes again to find the Blackhats upon them, Taniel's hands held in the air. Michel felt a sudden sinking feeling, dizziness threatening to pitch him from the saddle. "We're surrendering?" he managed.

"We're surrendering," Taniel confirmed. "For now."

Michel's bowels felt like water, and he tried to seek a way out of this to no avail. There were about thirty Blackhats to the three of them. Michel was useless in a fight, and he knew that most of Ka-poel's sorcery depended on preparation. That would leave thirty men to Taniel, which, he considered optimistically, might not be that difficult if they were all carrying powder.

He decided that must be Taniel's plan, and gritted his teeth, waiting for Taniel to detonate their powder, killing the lot of them. The moment never came.

"Agent Bravis," a voice called out.

Michel didn't think he could feel any sicker. The voice disproved him. "Grand master," he answered, staring at his saddle horn like a sullen child.

Fidelis Jes rode to the front of his column of Blackhats, head held high, face flushed from a hard ride. "Gutsy," he said, a small note of admiration in his voice. "We intercepted a message from Major Cole that you were in the camp about twenty minutes ago. Imagine my delight when you tried to run."

"Delight imagined, sir," Michel said. He wondered if he should just get this over with now—he could charge the grand master, weaponless, and hope that Fidelis Jes's bodyguards gunned him down in the process. It was the best idea he could come up with on the spur of the moment, and it didn't sound all that appealing.

Better than dying slowly in a torture chamber, though.

Jes rubbed the back of his neck, which was covered by his collar, and Michel allowed himself the fantasy of a dark purple bruise back there. How the bastard had managed to survive being punched in the spine by knuckledusters was beyond him, but when it came to Fidelis Jes his survival seemed almost a given. Jes cast a curious glance at Taniel and Ka-poel, his gaze lingering on the latter. "You have a lot of explaining to do, Agent Bravis. You'll be coming with us to Dalinport, where you'll have plenty of time to do so."

"The road to Dalinport is blocked," Taniel said. "The Dynize have landed."

"I've brought enough men to put down the Dynize in our path," Jes said.

Ka-poel gestured at Taniel, then tapped the backs of her hands and held up four fingers. "Privileged, eh? That will certainly help."

"Who the pit is this?" Fidelis Jes demanded.

Michel gave him a wan smile, but did not answer.

"Who are you?" Jes spat at Taniel.

Taniel sighed, as if annoyed that it had come to this, and then tugged on the fingers to his left glove. He pulled it off, revealing the blood-red skin of his hand.

Jes's perpetual sneer deepened. "The Red Hand? Bah. I expected better of you, Agent Bravis. A cabal spy; a Kez nationalist; I expected you to be better than working for a common rebel."

"Not terribly common," Michel said, watching as Taniel slowly got off his horse and drew his sword from his saddlebags.

"Fidelis Jes," Taniel said, "I've wanted to kill you for a very long time."

"Sir," one of Jes's officers warned, "we don't have time for this."

Fidelis Jes seemed to vacillate between getting to the dig site and a good fight. Michel was less than surprised when his baser instincts won out and he slid gracefully from his saddle and grabbed his sword, walking toward Taniel. "Who are you?" he asked. "I expected the Red Hand to be Palo, but you're obviously Adran."

"Michel's tale of an Adran expatriate was closer than you'd think," Taniel said, running two fingers down the length of his sword as if to test the blade. Michel thought he heard the sound of distant hoof-beats, but his eyes were glued to the scene in front of him. He silently urged Taniel to just kill the bastard and stop screwing around.

Fidelis Jes stretched lightly, bending one way, then the next, his eyes never leaving Taniel. "I expect this to be quick," he said. "So if you have anything else to tell me, do it now."

Taniel closed his eyes halfway, holding his sword out in front of him in both hands, tip pointed toward the ground as if he were praying. He remained that way for almost thirty seconds before Fidelis Jes lost his patience.

"Your time is up," the grand master snapped, stepping forward.

Taniel's sword came up, tip pointing over Jes's shoulder, and he barked the words, "I'm not here to kill you."

Jes sneered. "You're right about that."

"*He* is."

Taniel leapt out of the way of Jes's thrust, moving so quickly Michel could barely follow him. Taniel grabbed Jes by the back of the hair, kicking one leg to make him stumble, and turned him around, shoving him forward. Michel lifted his eyes, surprised to see more riders coming in just behind the Blackhats.

The man at their head was the biggest, ugliest man Michel had ever seen. He wore a faded Fatrastan cavalry jacket and rode a black warhorse with a black and brown mottled neck. His face was pitted and scarred, his back slightly bent in the saddle, and he rode ahead of a standard flying an image of a lance through a skull. The same skull that was on the ring that Fidelis Jes wore.

Michel didn't have to ask who that was.

"Jes!" Ben Styke roared, throwing himself from the saddle before his horse had even come to a complete stop. "You're a dead man!"

CHAPTER 62

Styke strode toward Fidelis Jes, chest heaving from the ride,
every bit of tiredness that had threatened to make him call
a halt on the journey south of the city now gone from his mind.
He gripped his saber in one hand, his other balled in a fist, and he
ignored the startled shouts of the Blackhats around him. Behind Jes
stood Taniel, sword drawn, and behind him Ka-poel and another
Blackhat were still on horseback.

Jes looked between Taniel and Styke as if unsure from which
direction the fight was coming, but Taniel stepped back and gave a
slight bow. Jes turned his attention entirely to Styke.

"I've already killed you twice," Jes said. "I'm going to make sure
the third time is more permanent."

Even Styke had to admit Jes cut a fine figure. He wore the Blackhat uniform, black on black with the buttons up the side of his
jacket, tailored to hug his muscled chest and legs. He wore a thin
white scarf around his neck and a Platinum Rose pinned to his left
breast, with Styke's lancer's ring on his thumb and boz knife at his

belt. Styke spared a glance for Jes's horse, saddlebags weighed down for a long journey. Flint was right—the Blackhats had abandoned the city.

Styke discarded his saber and drew Ibana's knife, forcing himself to breathe evenly. At the sight of this, Jes let out a barking laugh. He sheathed his own sword and pulled Styke's big knife out of his belt, brandishing it mockingly.

Styke's mind flashed through all the mistakes he'd made last time—coming into a fight wounded, overcome with anger, letting his emotions overrule his senses. He tried to expel all of that. He knew he was hurting, tired, but something felt righter about this fight. The Privileged that Ibana had kidnapped had partially healed Styke's crippling wounds. He was Colonel Ben Styke again, the Mad Lancer of Landfall. He wouldn't be put down like a dog. He looked at his knife in Jes's hand, the ring that touched the handle. "Those are mine."

"Not anymore." Jes spat the words as he came at Styke at a run. His knife flashed high in a feint, then plunged low for Styke's belly.

Styke tossed Ibana's knife aside and grabbed the blade of his stolen weapon, stopping Jes dead in his tracks. He ignored the sharp blade biting through his flesh, scraping the bones of his fingers, and brought his right fist around to connect with Jes's nose. The Blackhat grand master's head snapped backward.

"This isn't about revenge," Styke said. "This is because you're an asshole." Styke let go of the knife blade, snatching Jes's sleeve with his bloody, slippery fingers, and jerked him forward. He slammed his fist once more into the bridge of Jes's nose and the grand master dropped into a heap at his feet.

Styke leaned over and slid the ring off Jes's thumb and over his own finger, relieved to feel the familiar weight of it. He took his knife out of Jes's lifeless hand, and then with two quick strokes severed his head. He lifted it by the hair, ignoring the blood that soaked his shirt and trousers, and stared into the dead, faintly surprised eyes. He sighed, wishing he had more than a few moments to relish the corpse at his feet, and looked up to find Ibana on horseback, pushing her way to the front of the assembled Blackhats. He tossed her the head, which she caught easily in the crook of her arm. "We don't have time to make a saddle," he said.

Behind him, the Blackhat with Ka-poel was noisily ill.

Ibana held the head at arm's length, examining it, then nodded. "This will do."

"Taniel," Styke said with a nod, noting the blood-red color of his hand. He remembered reading something about a rebel named the Red Hand years ago. Funny that it should be the infamous Ghost of the Tristan Basin. "You've got a lot of secrets, don't you?"

"We all do," Taniel responded, sheathing his sword.

Styke eyed Jes's Blackhat bodyguards. They were silent, shifting wordlessly in their saddles, staring at the headless body of their grand master. "Who's in charge here?" Styke demanded.

"Technically he is," Taniel said.

Styke turned to look at the Blackhat still mounted beside Ka-poel. The man was green-faced, wiping the corner of his mouth with his sleeve. He gave a sickly smile and waved at Styke. "Gold Rose Bravis at your service, Mr. Styke."

"Colonel Styke," Styke corrected, letting the word roll off his tongue. Pit, he never thought he'd enjoy saying that so much.

One of Jes's bodyguards, openly wearing his Silver Rose on his uniform, pointed at Bravis. "Jes said he was a traitor."

To Styke's surprise, Bravis slipped from his saddle and staggered over to the headless body of Fidelis Jes, nudging it with his toe. He whispered to Styke, "I'm working on the fly here, so just go with it." He looked up at the bodyguards and in a loud voice said, "What did this shitheel tell you was going to happen to your families?" The uncomfortable silence continued, and so did Bravis. "Did he tell you they'd be evacuated from the city in due time? That there were more of us ready to help your friends and relatives make their way away from Landfall should the garrison fall?

"Or," Bravis went on, "did he try to tell you that the Riflejacks would hold the city on their own while you all got as far as possible from the fighting?" He shook his head theatrically. "I can see those saddlebags. Thousands of you are packed for a journey, coming down to escort some ancient relic instead of protecting your homes. That sounds a lot like fleeing."

The Silver Rose from earlier spoke up. "We're not fleeing. We're on the Lady Chancellor's business."

"The Lady Chancellor's business is protecting Landfall," Bravis snapped back. He reached down to Jes's body, looking for a moment like he might vomit again, and plucked the Platinum Rose from Jes's chest before dancing back just a little too quickly. He thrust his finger at Styke. "Fidelis Jes has been telling you this man—this hero of Fatrasta—is a dangerous criminal. Jes has been lying to you, just like he was lying to me, and this next lie will lose us the city we love, the city full of our friends and families."

"And what would you have us do?" the Silver Rose demanded.

"A thousand heavily armed Blackhats? I'd have you protect the city. You see these flags?" He pointed behind the Blackhats, where the Mad Lancers had gathered up, and Jackal and the Riflejack bannerman rode side by side. "Ride with them. Ride with Ben Styke, hero of the Fatrastan Revolution. Ride with the Riflejacks, defenders of Landfall as appointed by the Lady Chancellor herself. What would I have you do? Fight. Now get back to the main column, gather the rest of the Blackhats, and ready yourselves for a fight."

Three Blackhats, all of them wearing Silver Roses, conferred among themselves. They turned to Bravis. "Who's in command of the Blackhats?" one of them asked.

Bravis drew himself up and pinned the Platinum Rose to his chest. "I am."

There was a brief pause, and for a moment Styke thought they might laugh in Bravis's face. But the Silver Rose grimaced, then nodded. "As you command, grand master." He turned, leading the rest of Jes's bodyguards through the Mad Lancers and galloping back toward where the main body of the Blackhats had formed up about half a mile away.

Styke joined Taniel beside Michel Bravis and took a long, hard look at him. The Blackhat had forgettable features—a weak chin, round face, and light brown hair mussed from a long ride. He was also trembling like a leaf. Compared to the corpse at their feet, he wasn't a terribly convincing grand master. But, Styke supposed, he did have a head.

"Did you just convince them to protect the godstone by convincing them not to protect the godstone?" Taniel asked, tongue-in-cheek.

"Yeah," Bravis said shakily. "I think I did." He looked between Styke and Taniel. "I take it you two know each other."

Styke looked at Taniel. Taniel wore a small smile, eyes very clearly saying that he was not yet done with Styke. Styke ignored it. "Yeah."

"And you're down here to intercept the Dynize that are south of us?" Bravis asked.

"Right on that account, too."

Bravis looked about ready to faint. "Oh, thank Adom I got it all right. Whew."

Styke eyed Bravis, not sure he was ready to trust a Blackhat with anything, even if he was obviously with Taniel. In fact, he realized, that might make him *less* trustworthy. "The godstone, is this the artifact Lady Flint sent me down here to protect?"

"It is," Taniel confirmed.

"Do we know anything else about the Dynize we're going to face?"

"Only that there's at least four regiments." Taniel lifted his chin in the direction of the Blackhat army. "And that, with the Black-hats, you've got an extra thousand men and two Privileged."

Styke went and found the knife he'd borrowed from Ibana and put it in his saddlebags, taking a few moments to clean the deep gash along his fingers and bind it with a handkerchief. It stung badly, and it would hurt his ability to fight, but he could still flex his fingers.

He checked the blade on his own knife and cleaned the blood off it on Jes's jacket. "Blackhats are little more than a bunch of thugs. They're not going to be much good against four regiments of these Dynize. The bastards are *tough*, and they do not break."

"Make them break," Taniel said.

Styke weighed the odds in his head. A thousand Blackhats. Eight hundred Riflejack and Mad Lancer cavalry. A few hundred Fatrastan soldiers already guarding the godstone. Two-to-one numbers in favor of the Dynize did not please him. "I've had worse odds," he said, heading for his horse. "But you're coming with me, Two-shot, and I want you to scatter the brains of any Privileged those bloody Dynize have with them."

By the time Michel returned to the dig site, the land-barge and its cargo had already begun to move, creeping at a disappointing speed across the fields while horses pulled and the whips of team-sters rose and fell. Laborers helped push from behind, or rushed on ahead to smooth the ground with hands and shovels.

The monolith was moving, but Michel could already see it was going nowhere quick.

He forced himself to ignore the murmurs of the Blackhats behind him and rode up to Major Cole, who stared for a long time at the Platinum Rose on Michel's chest. For better or worse, Michel was in charge now. He was not, however, confident of a command that began with the bloody murder of the *last* grand master. If he survived the day wearing this Platinum Rose, he promised himself, he'd be a very happy man.

"Sir," Major Cole finally said, saluting.

Michel put as much bluster as he dared behind his voice. "Major

Cole, we've received almost two thousand riders as backup from Landfall. Colonel Styke is taking command of the defense of the monolith. I asked him to keep the fight as far from us as possible, but I'm going to keep your soldiers in reserve here with the land-barge in case the Dynize make it past them."

"With the what?"

"The land-barge." Michel felt his cheeks redden. "I just thought it looked like..."

"A barge on land," Cole said with a reluctant nod. "Yeah, I get it. It fits. We've all just been calling it the big wagon."

"Mine is much better. Keep your men nearby, Major Cole." Michel slowly trailed off, watching as orders were shouted, some confusion about the chain of command was cleared up, and then the Blackhats rode off behind Styke's cavalry. He looked around, realizing that Cole had already gone to see to his own men, and found that his only companion was Ka-poel. "Did Taniel go with Styke?" he asked.

Ka-poel nodded.

"Right. That doesn't leave us with much if the Dynize manage to break through the Mad Lancers."

Another nod, this one slightly more solemn.

Michel's horse suddenly lurched under him, nearly knocking him from the saddle, and he decided he'd had enough. "To the pit with this," he said, climbing down once the animal had calmed. "I am not riding on that thing any longer. Horses were meant to pull carriages, not be ridden."

Ka-poel didn't look terribly impressed. She turned her own horse around to face the south, then pulled out her rucksack and began to rummage through it again while Michel approached the land-barge, dodging laborers and ropes. He pulled himself onto the platform, then walked alongside the horizontal monolith, doing his best not to touch it, until he reached where Professor Cressel stood at the very front of the land-barge.

The professor pushed his spectacles up, looking to the south. "Are we going to outrun the Dynize?" Cressel asked.

Michel looked pointedly at the ground, moving past at nearly a snail's pace. He should be grateful they were moving at all, but he fought down his own rising panic and replied, "I'm afraid not, Professor."

"Do we have enough men to protect the monolith?" Cressel asked.

Michel opened his mouth, thought better of his answer, and changed his "no" to a "maybe." "Landfall sent a couple of Privileged. That should even the odds." *Unless they have Privileged of their own.*

"Ah, excellent." Cressel patted the monolith affectionately. "We absolutely cannot let this fall into enemy hands. It's too important."

Michel leaned on the monolith without thinking, jumping as a spark of static seemed to leap from the stone to his shoulder, then rubbed his hands together to try to get rid of the distasteful feeling the spark had left behind. The whispering in the back of his head had returned, no longer drowned out by the excitement of the move. He wondered if maybe coming up here had been a stupid idea, and looking up found that Ka-poel was riding slowly alongside, the reins of his horse tied to her saddle. She seemed to sense his discomfort and gestured to the horse.

"I'll stay here," Michel said. "Less of a chance of breaking my neck, thank you." The land-barge suddenly lurched, nearly pitching him to the ground and beneath the wheels. He grabbed Cressel to steady himself.

"Are you all right, Gold Rose?" Cressel asked.

"It's grand master now," Michel said absently, pointing to the Platinum Rose pinned to his chest. "And no. I hate myself, I hate this stupid monolith, and I hate the bloody Dynize for the fact that I can now see them and—oh shit, Ka-poel, I can see them!"

Ka-poel raised her head, looking toward the south, where a dust cloud now enveloped the sky not a mile away. The distant report of musket fire reached them and Ka-poel went back to digging in her satchel.

"Did you say Ka-poel?" Cressel asked curiously. "Ka is a Dynize title. Is she a Dynize? Are you a Dynize?" Cressel's eyes suddenly widened. "That's a Dynize *bone-eye* title. That woman is a blood sorcerer?"

"I wouldn't worry about it too much," Michel said.

"Blood sorcery! That would explain so much. It could be the key to what we've been missing, I..." His ramblings dropped in tone to a mere mutter, and Michel was content to let them stay that way. Nervously he watched the dust cloud, quickly becoming black from powder smoke, and silently willed the teamsters to move the land-barge a little bit faster.

A Silver Rose rode up beside Styke, eyeing him and the banner flying from Jackal's lance before giving a nervous salute. "Sir, we're not trained cavalry. I'm not sure how effective we're going to be against the Dynize."

"You'll be plenty effective," Styke replied, not trusting himself to look the Blackhat in the eye. He considered the irony of him, here, giving orders to a contingent of Blackhats instead of grinding their bones to dust, and then forced himself to think of the much happier fact of Jes's head now in a sack hanging from Ibana's saddle.

"We haven't exactly trained for this."

"No," Styke said, "but you'll manage anyway. Can your men shoot from horseback?"

"Most of them, yes."

"Good. Split into two groups. I'm not going to bother throwing you at their center—your men aren't capable of such a charge, and your horses don't deserve it. I want each group to peel off from our main column and circle the enemy flanks. You'll act as light skirmishers. Hit them from the sides, and hit them hard with everything you have. Fire at will and all that. Put one of your Privileged on either side and tell them to focus on any Privileged the enemy may have, and *then* to turn on the infantry."

The Blackhat seemed relieved not to be participating in a charge. "I think we can do that," he said.

Styke reached over and snatched the Blackhat by the arm, nearly yanking him out of the saddle. "You'll *know* you can do it," he growled. "You bastards have been gunning for me for two weeks, and if you don't show some spine and make these Dynize *bleed*, I'll hunt you down personally when I'm done with this and put your head in the same sack I put Jes's. Understand?"

"Yes, sir," the Blackhat managed to choke out.

Styke pushed him right back in his saddle and gave him a toothy grin. "And if you keep their flanks off my ass for long enough to win this battle then maybe, just maybe, we can be friends. Now go make sure your men understand all that very clearly."

The Blackhat rode off, and Styke focused on the approaching Dynize. The infantry were coming on at a double march, arranged in four solid columns that, as Styke drew closer, gradually slowed and fanned out into rows. Styke blinked through sweat dripping into his eyes and pushed back against the niggles of dread and doubt that exhaustion let permeate his brain.

Outnumbered two to one. Cavalry against infantry—infantry that, it seemed, refused to break in the face of superior enemy action. Routing an enemy was the best chance cavalry had against such odds and Styke did not like their prospects one bit.

"Taniel!" he called, turning in his saddle to look for the powder mage. He discovered Taniel about twenty feet behind him, standing in the stirrups, a rifle held to his shoulder, sighting down the barrel as Ibana held his reins. "What is he doing?" Styke shouted.

"His job," Ibana responded. "They have six Privileged and—"

Taniel's rifle jumped, the crack making Ibana flinch slightly and then rub one finger in her ear. Taniel watched the horizon, focused, rifle still raised, his lips moving as he counted silently. Several seconds later he lowered his rifle and immediately began to reload. "They have four Privileged," he reported.

Styke laughed despite himself. "Jackal, relay orders. I want every one of ours with an unbroken lance to form a spearhead. Behind them, the Riflejack cuirassiers, then after them the dragoons. Line us in a column tight and hard, narrow like a flared lance. Six rows of four, then six rows of five, six rows of six, and on. Wedge formation."

"Do I have to remind you," Ibana called, "that we don't have our bloody armor anymore?"

"And the Dynize don't have sword bayonets."

"Knife bayonets aren't a joke."

"To the pit with them," Styke said. "If the bastards won't route, we'll cut through their center and then tear them apart from behind. They won't know what hit 'em."

Taniel raised his rifle to his shoulder, aimed, then looked over at Styke. "You really are a bloody madman."

"Everyone keeps telling me that," Styke said. "Jackal, get me a new lance. I'll tip the wedge."

Styke's people were outnumbered two to one. The Dynize, he decided, should have brought more men.

CHAPTER 63

Vlora used her sorcery to ignite a tiny bit of powder almost a mile away. It detonated, and chain reaction was almost instantaneous as the rest of the powder in the ship of the line's magazine went up with it, tearing the ship in half and hurling the entire mast so far through the air that it almost struck dry land.

The kickback was also instantaneous. Vlora felt it deep in her bones, the force of the explosion like a wine barrel knocking her down a flight of stairs. She nearly fell from her perch on the edge of the wall, fingers gripping the stone with all the strength she could manage. Her head pounded, the wound in her leg, a graze on her shoulder, and a dozen other scrapes and bruises threatening to break through her powder trance as she was overwhelmed with the sensations thrown at her from every direction.

A hook suddenly clattered over the wall immediately beside her, and she spared a glance to find a longboat at the base of the fort, a Dynize infantryman already a quarter of the way up the rope by the time she could pull her knife and cut it. There was a startled scream, then a splash, and three Riflejacks suddenly joined her position and fired down into the longboat while grappling hooks continued to be flung over the wall.

The same was happening all up and down the wall. For almost half an hour the Dynize had tried to gain purchase. The fort was surrounded by corpses and the wreckage of longboats, but more persisted in their attempts. Over on the land, Olem's men had been driven all the way back to the causeway, where they had now dug in, refusing to budge, fighting in fierce hand-to-hand with the Dynize.

"Colonel coming in!" a voice yelled.

Vlora forced herself off the ramparts, barely able to hold her own weight on the railing as she made her way down into the muster yard. The main gate was opened briefly and Olem staggered in, supported on either side by a pair of privates. His face was covered in blood, his jacket was gone, and one arm was in a sling. She hurried over to him, grabbing him around the neck and pulling him into an embrace.

"Report," she whispered.

"Still alive," he grunted. "I left Major Supin in command with orders to hold the causeway at all costs. Pit, I need a cigarette. Whole bloody tobacco pouch is soaked with Dynize blood."

"At least it's not your own," Vlora said, choking back a sudden, unbidden sob. She wasn't sure where it came from—fear of seeing him like this, or joy that he seemed to be in better shape than he looked.

"No," Olem replied, "*my* blood ruined my rolling papers." He took his arms off the privates and waved them away, testing one foot tentatively before limping over to a bench along the inner wall and sagging into it. Vlora sat down beside him, allowing herself a moment's rest.

"You look as bad as I feel," she said.

Olem looked up sharply. "Those ships out there. That was you?"

Vlora nodded.

Olem suddenly turned, grasping her by the face and forcing her to look him in the eye. He studied her for several moments before letting go. "You're in shock," he said.

"I'm fine," she tried to assure him. Distantly, she was aware that he was probably right. Detonating so much powder had consequences, even for someone experienced like her. "Okay, maybe I'm not fine."

"Don't do that again," he warned. "The kickback could kill you."

"You know," she said, trying to give her voice a joking tone, "I'm the powder mage here."

"And, when you were thinking more clearly, you told me in no uncertain terms not to let you pull this kind of shit. An entire magazine going up is no joke."

Vlora turned away, wishing he didn't worry so much. This was the time for fighting, not concern. Regrets could be had later. "I'm still alive," she said. "And I wouldn't have done it if we didn't need the help. How's it going out there?" She flinched as a Dynize cannonball tore through the northeastern wall, sending bits of masonry and bodies flying. Within moments there were Dynize at the breach, but the Riflejacks beat them to it, filling the space with a wall of bayonets.

"Not great," Olem said. "The Riflejacks are holding together, but the garrison has taken a massive pounding. They're wavering, and I don't blame them. The bloody Dynize should have conceded the fight an hour ago, but they just keep coming."

Vlora watched as a Dynize threw himself over the wall, musket in hand, only to be pincushioned by Riflejack bayonets. "It's sorcery," she said.

"You're certain?"

"It has to be. No one is that brave, or that stupid—no one. Norrine said she hasn't seen a single Dynize turn and run. I think it's the bone-eye."

"Have you been able to find him?"

"Believe me, I've tried. Ka-sedial's ship is three miles out. Taniel could make that shot. I can't."

Olem grimaced. "Well, we don't have Taniel. Is Ka-sedial working alone?"

"I've sensed a few other bone-eyes. Managed to kill two. Still looking for the third. Unless we break the will of these bastards, they're going to overrun us."

"They don't have much left," Olem said hopefully. "Half their fleet is at the bottom of the ocean or on its way, and there aren't many longboats left in the water."

"All they have to do is overrun us," Vlora said. "And they're real damned close."

Another Dynize managed to gain the top of the wall. Vlora's heart leapt in her throat as she realized this wasn't a normal foot soldier, but a leather-clad dragonman. He was a big, brutish man with a long, delicate-looking white sword, and he cut through several Riflejacks before Vlora could even reach for her pistol. By the time she had it out and loaded, the dragonman had gone down beneath a hail of close-range rifle fire, but he'd done more damage than twenty Dynize soldiers.

"I need to be back up there," Vlora said, getting to her feet.

Olem grabbed her hand. "You're not in any shape to do anything but get in the way."

"Commanders aren't just there to fight. They're to be seen." She limped back toward the stairs, only to come up short at the sound of an inhuman groan that echoed across the bay. The sound sent a shiver down her spine, and she ignored her pain, snorting an extra charge of powder, forcing herself up the stairs to the ramparts. What she saw there took her breath away.

Across the bay, half the ships at port were on fire, smoke billowing high and black into the sky. But that wasn't what caught her attention. Several of those burning ships were no longer moored, and were actively being pulled out to sea by the departing tide. She rubbed her eyes, uncertain she could trust them as she saw tiny figures running along the decks, untangling rigging, and trying to put out the fires.

"What the..." Vlora stared, openmouthed, as a ship belching black smoke from two sails, with the flames quickly spreading, creaked and groaned in a savage turn, sweeping through the bay waters, coming within spitting distance of the walls of Fort Nied. Its prow crashed through dozens of longboats, forcing the occupants to leap into the water, where they were quickly dragged under by the weight of their armor.

A handful of sailors worked frantically to keep the ship steady, while the familiar figure of Vallencian stood on the aft-castle, legs planted, laughing madly as he fought the wheel.

The merchantman was quickly past the fort, heading at an alarming speed out past the breaker walls. Another merchantman followed suit, then another, while a fourth was quickly abandoned by the sailors trying to keep it under control as the flames grew too perilous. It drifted madly, crashing into breakers.

"What the pit are they doing?" a soldier behind Vlora asked.

Vlora watched, awed, trying to find words. "The Ice Baron is sacrificing his fleet to save this battle." She remembered his comment about the tide going out, then balled her hands into fists. There was no way he was coming back from this—even if he abandoned ship, he wouldn't be able to swim back, not against the tide. It was a suicide mission for his ships and him and his sailors, and they had to know it.

The remaining Dynize ships quickly turned their cannons on Vallencian's merchantmen, but to little effect. The merchantmen were already ablaze, nothing more than floating battering rams, and Vallencian's ship collided full-on with a ship of the line that had managed to avoid Fort Nied's guns all afternoon. The sound was terrible, a horrible screech like a hundred demons clawing their way from the pit. Both Dynize and Vallencian's sailors leapt into the water, abandoning the wreckage as both ships began to sink.

The second of Vallencian's merchantmen crushed the forecastle of another warship, while the third cut behind yet another Dynize ship, destroying the rudder and crushing the rear windows of the aft-castle.

Fighting seemed to grind to a halt as men from both sides stopped to watch the terrible collisions. Vlora gained the edge of the wall, firing her pistol at an officer in a longboat below her, then shaking her head as she felt something *snap* within her.

At first she thought it was something physical within her—a bone, or a ligament, or just about anything that could go wrong. When she didn't feel any pain, she looked around her, searching for the source of that snap. It took her several moments to realize that something had changed.

The Dynize, for the first time all afternoon, suddenly wavered.

It wasn't immediate. Slowly, like a flame exposed to a gradually stiffer breeze, the Dynize offensive seemed to flutter and flex. Their shouting became uncertain, their momentum stalled. Minutes passed as the fighting grew more desperate and then, across the water where Olem's troops still barely held the end of the causeway, Vlora saw a Dynize soldier throw down his musket and flee back toward the beach.

He was joined by others and then, like a candle being blown out, the entire Dynize army routed.

The Riflejacks and garrison seemed to get a second wind, redoubling their efforts and giving chase. The Dynize soldiers reached the water, some of them clamoring into the few remaining longboats while others realized the hopelessness of trying to swim away and turned to organize a defensive. It was too late, and Vlora's men hit them from behind, forcing them back into the ocean.

Vlora watched Dynize soldiers in their heavy breastplates drown by the score, unwilling to comprehend the horror of such a fate.

She looked toward the wreckage of Vallencian's ship, knowing it would be days before she would be able to mount a rescue, and took a deep breath.

Somehow, some way, they had managed to win the day.

Styke drew his carbine one-handed, sighting along it for half a second before pulling the trigger. He was past the puff of smoke a moment later, and accompanied by the crack of a hundred other carbines as the lancers and cuirassiers opened fire on the front line of the Dynize infantry.

The Dynize, falling into a defensive formation, fired back a single volley. Styke felt a bullet slam into the meat of his left shoulder and pushed away the sharp, sudden pain, rotating his arm to make sure it would still work. Behind him horses screamed and fell, and he holstered his carbine without looking back and took his lance in hand, lowering it at the now-reduced Dynize front line.

Amrec leapt a wounded infantryman and Styke lowered his lance, tearing out a Dynize throat with the tip and driving it into the face of the next Dynize. He kept his grip tight, aiming true until the lance was snapped just past the haft. He threw the useless weapon at an infantryman trying to bring his bayonet to bear on Amrec's chest, then drew his heavy saber, swinging it with enough force to decapitate a Dynize officer.

He spurred Amrec forward, unwilling to give up his momentum, and plowed through the front eight rows of infantry until he was among the Dynize who had not yet been ordered to lower their weapons. The Dynize scrambled to defend themselves, officers shouting and swearing while they attempted to halt the vicious charge.

Styke hazarded a glance over his shoulder. Jackal was still right behind him, along with the Riflejack bannerman, but Ibana and a huge number of his remaining lancers had disappeared in the chaos. He gritted his teeth and bent from his saddle, slashing beneath the arm of an infantryman, then waved his sword. "Forward, you dogs!" he roared. "Forward!"

His cavalry continued to plow onward. Styke caught sight of a Dynize Privileged, white gloves raised above his head, a scarf wrapped around his face to protect his nose from the powder smoke. Styke angled Amrec toward the Privileged, determined to run him down before he could do any real damage, only to watch him tumble from his saddle with a bullet wound through his chest.

Two-shot, it seemed, was still hard at work.

Styke forced his way through the press, Amrec leaping and kicking with the nimbleness of a Gurlish racing horse. They plowed through three more lines and then suddenly he was free, riding across open farmland behind the Dynize position. He pulled Amrec around and watched as a few hundred of his cavalry managed to extricate themselves from the tangle.

He spared a glance in either direction, satisfied to see the flash of fire and lightning, along with the bloom of powder smoke, as the Blackhats and their Privileged tore into the Dynize flanks. The strategy, it seemed, had worked. The Dynize attention was split between both cavalry and skirmishers, and they didn't appear to have any Privileged left to answer those accompanying the Blackhats.

Styke counted to forty to allow enough of his cavalry to emerge from the Dynize ranks before waving his sword over his head. "Form up!" he bellowed, and spurred Amrec back into the fray before the Dynize officers could turn their lines around to face him.

He rode roughshod through the confused Dynize columns as they attempted to fight both riders and the sorcery on their flanks. Halfway through he spotted Ibana, jacket bloody with a broken lance in one hand and a smallsword in the other, having formed up several dozen unhorsed cavalry into a loose circle, which was in danger of being overrun by the Dynize. Styke led his remaining cavalry straight to them.

A Dynize bayonet caught Styke on the thigh just as he reached Ibana's men. The pain came quick and hot, and he snatched the musket out of the startled soldier's hands and swung it around, cracking it across the man's head with enough force to break the stock. Another bayonet was thrust toward his face, barely missing his eye, and then a musket stock, swung like club, slammed into his cheek. He reeled back, seeing stars, and swung his saber blindly.

Lightning struck so close that it almost turned Styke and Amrec into a pillar of ash. Fire followed it a moment later in a column as thick as a man, crashing down from the heavens, zigzagging its way through the Dynize ranks. Infantry cooked instantly in their armor, and Styke's nostrils were filled with the smell of burned flesh and hair. As suddenly as he'd been close to overwhelmed, the field around him was empty of enemies.

He wheeled Amrec around, looking wildly. The Blackhats, their numbers greatly reduced, had managed to make it all the way around the Dynize flank and come up behind them. One of their Privileged was bleeding from a gunshot wound, but the fingers of them both continued to twitch and gesture, raining death among the Dynize. The fire and lightning spread outward from Styke's position in the center, bringing ruin to the entirety of the Dynize infantry with startling speed.

Styke slid from his saddle, watching the Privileged work, and limped over to Ibana. She knelt by the side of a Riflejack whom Styke did not recognize, holding the man's hand as he writhed in pain. The better part of the Riflejack's left arm had been taken off by an enemy sword, and the rest would have to be amputated.

Styke looked around at the carnage, wondering if he would be sick from the sudden feeling of elation that rose within his chest. The smell of the dead, the wind in his hair, the blood on his steel: It made him feel vibrant and alive like nothing in the world had ever done for him. He thought about the guards at the labor camp and all the men he'd allowed to beat and belittle him just to try to reach parole.

"I shouldn't have stayed," he said, breathing deeply of the smell of sorcery and burned corpses. "I should have fought my way out years ago."

"What are you going on about?" Ibana demanded.

Styke lifted his chin to the chaos, watching as Taniel Two-shot, no longer on horseback, used a bayoneted rifle to tear through a whole company of Dynize infantry on his own. It reminded him of the grace with which Lady Flint fought, though somehow quicker and more terrifying. "If you can't break them," he said.

"Grind their bones to dust beneath your hooves," Ibana finished, not lifting her eyes from the wounded Riflejack. "Did we win?"

Between the Blackhat Privileged, the remaining cavalry, and Taniel, they were mopping up the last of the Dynize. It was a stark reminder of just how quickly sorcery changed the tide of battle, and how easily it could have been Styke's bones turned to ash from a Dynize Privileged, if not for Two-shot to even the odds.

"Yeah," he said, drawing his knife and kneeling down beside the Riflejack and sizing up the arm that needed to be amputated. "Bite down on your belt, son. This is gonna hurt, but it'll be a cleaner cut. We won."

CHAPTER 64

Vlora stood in the prow of a longboat as it did a circuit through the water surrounding Fort Nied. The slow strokes of the rowers left barely any wake behind them yet still managed to stir corpses to the top of the water, their bloated forms face-down, bobbing gently, their teal uniforms stained by the blood still seeping from their bodies. Somewhere off her port side the water suddenly exploded in movement as sharks emerged to fight over a corpse. Riflemen behind her stood, took aim, and shot into the water. The foaming frenzy increased for several seconds and then died down to leave the bay placid, gentle waves lapping bodies toward the shore.

Vlora's own body was a collection of aches, sharp pains, and developing bruises. She wondered if this was what it felt like to be trampled, and dug in her pocket for a powder charge, pinching just the slightest bit off the top and snorting it from between her fingers. The stitches in the shrapnel wound in her leg stopped throbbing.

"It's a complete waste," a voice said behind her.

"I disagree," a second voice responded. "We can rebuild this wall without lessening the structural integrity of the fort."

"Are you mad? We don't have access to the kind of sorcery that made this fort as strong as it was. I say we level the whole thing and bring in the best stonemasons money can buy. We'll build something better. With modern techniques we don't even *need* sorcery to make the walls nearly impervious to straight shot."

"You've been reading too much of that idiot Yaddel," the second voice said. "Modern construction is incredible, but it can't beat sorcery."

"Yaddel is a visionary!"

"Yaddel is a quack."

Vlora eyed the walls of Fort Nied, noting three complete breaches and at least fifteen spots of heavy damage. No doubt the engineers behind her saw more damage with their experienced eye. She gave a soft sigh at their arguing and tuned it out, glancing over the bay as some thirty or more longboats just like hers traversed the waters, fishing out corpses with hooks and nets, riflemen shooting every shark that surfaced.

Beyond the bay, well past the range of her few remaining cannons and the flotsam of what used to be their flotilla, the rest of the Dynize fleet sat at anchor, swarming with sailors making repairs. She counted just eight capital ships and two times that number in support frigates.

Since the Dynize army had finally routed last night, she hadn't heard a word from Ka-sedial. No white flags. No suit for peace. Not even a request to barter for the dead and wounded. The Dynize fleet simply waited, and Vlora didn't mind admitting to herself that their silence was unnerving.

She tried to forget it, at least for the moment. She and her men had won a damned hard battle last night, and she allowed a smile to creep onto her face. The melancholy that gripped her now would be gone in a few days' time, and her head would be back to the logistics of running an army—providing food, shelter, and pay, and bringing their numbers back to a full brigade.

She scowled at the Landfall docks and the smoke still rising from several destroyed ships. Only a few remained untouched by the fires, while dozens were a complete loss, no doubt representing the imminent bankruptcy of several shipping companies. Fortunately, none of that was her problem.

Vlora's absent-minded inspection of the fort and environs suddenly focused on a body washed up on the shore not far from the causeway that attached Fort Nied to the mainland. She turned to her rowers. "Over there," she ordered.

"But ma'am," an engineer said, "we're not done with our inspection of the fort."

"You can finish after you drop me off," Vlora said. "I want a full report by the end of the evening—one from each of you." Conscious of the sharks prowling beneath the layer of flotsam and bodies, she waited until the longboat had reached the shallows, then she leapt into the water. She waded ashore and fell on her knees beside a body.

It belonged to an enormous man with a dark, soaked beard, colorful clothes, and the thick tatters of a bearskin still clinging to his shoulders. His face was pale as death, his chest still.

"Damn it, Vallencian," Vlora muttered, feeling the first real pang of horror that had struck her through the sea of bodies. "You were about the only decent person in this whole damned city." She called to a nearby squad from the garrison that was sorting corpses by uniform on the rocky beach. A sergeant with a squat, ugly face and shaved head waddled over, hooked spear thrown over his shoulder.

"What can I do for you, ma'am?"

"This is one of mine," she said. "I want him put in the morgue with the other Riflejack officers."

The sergeant scowled appraisingly at the body. "Right you are, ma'am, but it doesn't seem like a good idea to put him in the morgue."

"Why not?"

The sergeant produced a mirror from his pocket and knelt down, thrusting the mirror up in front of Vallencian's nose. A thin film of fog appeared. "Because he's not dead."

Vlora felt a wave of relief sweep over her. Finally, some good news. "He's half-drowned. Get me a surgeon. Go!"

The sergeant scurried off, and Vlora bent over Vallencian, searching his chest for the barest hint of movement. If she held very still, and squinted, she could see it. "Crashed one of your ships into the Dynize and then managed to swim all the way back against the tide. You're a damned workhorse, you know that?"

One of the garrison doctors soon arrived with assistants. He pumped Vallencian's lungs carefully with glass tubing, then they carried him back toward Fort Nied on a stretcher. Vlora remained out on the beach, telling herself that she should accompany Vallencian until she knew whether he was going to survive, but unwilling to watch him die if it came to that.

The shadows began to grow long, and Vlora smelled the familiar scent of tobacco before she heard the crunch of boots on gravel. She turned to find Olem picking his way gingerly over the rocky terrain, his head bandaged and his arm in a sling.

"Glad to see you're up and walking," Vlora said.

"I'm not glad to see you are," Olem replied. "You should be resting."

"There's work to be done."

"Like standing out here, staring at the bodies?"

Vlora snorted. She wanted to reach out and take Olem by the hand, retire to a hotel room up on the plateau, and spend the next two weeks with him recovering in each other's arms. "I went with the engineers to examine Nied's fortifications from the water."

"And?"

"Doesn't look great. Any news from the Dynize?"

"Not a peep. I'd hoped you saw some sort of indication that they were ready to talk."

Vlora turned back toward the ocean. The Dynize ships remained, quietly menacing, as if daring any of the unburned ships in port to make a run for it. "Not that I've heard. Do we have casualty reports?"

"Thirty-five hundred wounded, seven hundred dead."

Vlora perked up. "That's far better than I expected."

"It's only Riflejack numbers," Olem responded sourly.

"Oh." Vlora fought the sinking feeling in the pit of her stomach. That meant that only a few hundred of her soldiers had escaped the battle unharmed. Recovery would be weeks at best, and they'd lose a number of the wounded to disease, infection, or blood loss. "The garrison?"

"The garrison," Olem said slowly, "was hit hard. They've got fewer wounded than us, but about eight thousand dead. They're not used to this kind of fighting."

"Nobody is used to this kind of fighting," Vlora responded, shaking her head. "I've never seen anything like it—soldiers that just would not break, no matter how many dead we piled in front of them. I saw Ka-poel a couple of hours ago. She told me that it was definitely blood magic, spread out across half a dozen bone-eyes. The ship Vallencian plowed into must have contained one of the more powerful practitioners, and his death shattered their concentration."

"At least that's a mystery solved."

"I'm not sure I like knowing," Vlora said. "All my training—pit, all Adran strategy—is based off breaking a less-well-trained enemy. If the enemy will not break, then how do we win?"

"We won yesterday."

"Barely."

"Can Ka-poel replicate the Dynize sorcery?"

"She's powerful enough, that's for sure. But she's not formally trained. Everything she can do is self-taught, and she says providing a backbone to ten thousand men is a challenge she's never even considered before. All her attention right now is focused on the godstone."

"And?" Olem asked, ashing his cigarette and lowering himself with a groan to the sand beside Vlora.

"And what?" Vlora said with a frustrated shrug. "None of us are Privileged. The two remaining Privileged that the Blackhats left behind don't want to go near the thing. We don't know exactly what it is or how it works. I don't even want to think about it." She put her head in her hands and rubbed her eyes. "Speaking of the Blackhats…"

"We don't know where they are," Olem answered. "I sent out riders. Best guess is Lindet retreated to a safe distance and, once she finds out we've won, she'll return to the city."

"And bring thousands of angry, armed men with her." Vlora gritted her teeth, wondering if she was strong enough for a power struggle so soon after the end of this battle. "I'll kill her before I let her take control of the godstone."

"Does she know that?"

"I told her as much when I threatened to arrest her."

"So much for the element of surprise." Olem flicked a cigarette butt toward the water. "I saw them carrying Vallencian toward the fort. They said he's still alive."

"For now," Vlora responded.

"I'm going to go check on him. Come find me when you decide to stop watching them collect the bodies."

Vlora helped Olem to his feet, then watched him head back toward Fort Nied, before attempting to collect herself emotionally. Seven hundred men dead. Too many names to memorize, but she'd read through the lists before they were laid to rest. She wondered if they had died hating her for putting them in front of the Dynize.

"They knew the risks. They signed up for the coin," she told herself. "You didn't bring a bunch of greenhorns out into the wild. You brought the best damned riflemen in the world, and it's the only reason most of us are still alive today."

Somewhere down the beach, members of the garrison had started a driftwood bonfire. Fire for the Dynize dead. Earth for the Riflejacks and garrison. The price of victory.

The price of saving a city of a million people.

CHAPTER 65

S tyke lay on his back in the long grass of a Fatrastan floodplain and stared up at the blue, cloudless sky, meditating on
the events of the last two weeks. Somewhere off to his left Ibana
was yelling at *someone*, though he couldn't imagine who because
the rest of the Mad Lancers were either laid up in the surgeries
or off in the city looting Blackhat munitions depots. In his head,
he imagined the look on Fidelis Jes's face when he realized how
much shit the lancers had managed to steal before the Blackhats
returned to the city, and then he remembered that Fidelis Jes's face
was attached to a head in a bag, quite possibly still tied to Ibana's
saddle.

The thought brought a smile to Styke's face. Jes's corpse was
probably already burning on a mass pyre, anonymous, with a thousand others south of the city. A fitting end for a man who dedicated
his life to making sure everyone knew and feared him.

"What are you grinning about?"

Styke turned his head to find Ibana standing over him, hands on her hips, looking nonplussed. "Thinking about Jes."

"Of course you are. By the way, that head is starting to stink. What do you want to do with it?"

"Would it be crass to ram it on the end of my lance and ride through Landfall all day tomorrow?"

"Sounds perfectly suitable to me. We have a problem, though."

Styke sat up, fighting a brief dizzy spell. "What is it?"

"The Mad Lancers always ride with three hundred. We started off with two hundred and forty-three yesterday, and now we're down to a little over a hundred and fifty. Where are we going to find more men?"

"That's your job."

"Like the pit it is," Ibana said. She stalked away, then stalked back. Her pacing continued for a few moments before she stopped. "You know, those Riflejack cavalry were quite good."

"I'm not sure what Flint would do to you if she found you recruiting from her ranks, but I wouldn't blame her."

"As if," Ibana scoffed.

"You want to fight her?"

"...No."

Styke turned, feeling the crack and pop of his spine, then lay back down on the soft grass. He took off his ring and rolled it over his fingertips, examining the scuffs and nicks in the silver, most of them too deep to polish out. "Didn't think so. Find them somewhere else. In fact, what about those Blackhats that rode with us against the Dynize? Go round them up, see if a few have a spine." He put his ring back on.

"I could try for one of those Privileged," Ibana mused. "We haven't had a Privileged with us since...I forget her name."

"Jain? Jaim?" Styke asked. "I don't remember, either. Pit, she was good-looking, though."

Ibana kicked him in the ribs. He clutched at them, laughing, until it felt like the movement had burst a couple of stitches on his shoulder. He checked his shirt, noting a new splotch of blood, and went back to staring at the sky.

"Why the pit are you down there?" Ibana asked.

"Can't smell the burning corpses," Styke answered. Which was true. But he also liked the peacefulness of it, and the way that not a single cloud marred the sky and he was allowed, for the first time in more than a decade, just to lie there and do nothing. Besides, he was cut to pit, and it hurt to move.

"Ben!" a voice called.

Styke tried to sit up, but he was tackled back to the ground by Celine, who wrapped her arms around his neck and pinned him, squeezing until her face turned red. Styke put one arm around her, squeezing back, before picking her up by the back of her trousers and depositing her on his chest. "You survived the fight," he observed.

"I did!" Celine said. "Sunin let me kill a man."

Styke sat up, sending Celine tumbling to the grass. "What?" he asked flatly.

Celine righted herself, then nodded emphatically. "I held the lance and everything. I put it through his freckled cheek and watched his brains come out the other side. It was gross."

Styke got to his feet, ignoring Ibana's chortle, and searched around for Sunin. He didn't have to look far. She was a stone's throw away, tending to her horse. "What the pit, Sunin!" he shouted. "You took her into battle? You let her *kill* someone?"

"She has to learn to fight someday," Sunin said over her shoulder, not bothering to turn around.

"Yeah, when she doesn't need help holding a lance. Damn it, Sunin, you were supposed to keep her safe."

"I had men to kill. Besides, she's safe, isn't she?"

Styke growled, looking at Ibana, who was now bent over, shaking with laughter. Styke lifted a foot and planted it on her shoulder, shoving her backward. She fell into the grass laughing, face red. When he turned back to Celine she was staring at him with her chin lifted, like she was expecting something.

"You," he said, pointing a finger at the little girl, "I'm not happy with you. You shouldn't be killin' anyone, not at your age."

"Yes," Celine replied haughtily. "Well, I did, and you can't undo that. I'm a hero now."

"By whose standard?"

"Yours! I killed a man during wartime. You told me that makes you a hero. I wanted to be one, and now I am."

Ibana, now lying with her limbs splayed in a gasping heap, let out a barking laugh. "She's got you there, Benjamin."

"Damn it, I—" Styke cut himself off. He gritted his teeth, wondering what her dad would have done to punish her for something like this. Probably buy her a pint and take her to a drug den, the stupid git. Styke leaned over, searching through the grass for one of the tiny red wildflowers that were common this time of year. He plucked it, tying the stem in a knot, then deposited it behind her ear. "All right," he said quietly. "You're a hero. But don't you go into battle again, you promise?"

Celine stared at her feet glumly.

"And no taking pointers from that old witch over there. Sunin can't even hold a lance straight anymore. I'll teach you to fight myself—by the time I'm done with you, you'll be able to gut someone twice your size without breaking a sweat." Celine looked up, beaming, and angled her head toward him to show off the flower. Styke surprised himself by leaning over and kissing her on the cheek. "Now go kick Sunin in the shins *really* hard for me."

She ran off, and Styke glanced at Ibana to find her staring at him, a strange smile on her face. The moment he turned his head it disappeared, and she climbed to her feet with all trace of laughter gone. "I suppose this is gonna be like it was back during the war, isn't it? I go do all the work, and you lounge around waiting for the next battle?"

"That was the plan."

Ibana rolled her eyes. "What *is* the next battle?"

"Not sure," Styke said, considering. "We'll stick with Lady Flint. She needs good cavalry, and she pays well."

"Rumor has it she tried to arrest Lindet right before the Dynize attacked."

Styke had heard that rumor as well. It made hitching his horse to her wagon a riskier move, and removed the protection she'd originally promised against the Blackhats. But it also made him like her twice as much. "Then she definitely needs more cavalry, and the lancers might get to kill some Blackhats after all." He frowned, recalling the ships still anchored out beyond the breakers and the piles of dead being burned all around the city. "The Dynize don't have just one army," he said quietly. "I don't give a shit about this godstone thing, but they've invaded my country, and that pisses me off. They'll be back, and I intend on being there to punch them in the face."

"You don't think Flint's going to just up and off to the Nine?" Ibana asked.

"I don't," Styke said. "Even if she finds an open port at a nearby city with enough ships to transport her men...no, I think she's found something she's not willing to budge on. That obelisk." He lifted his head, looking east to where the godstone still lay where it had fallen during the Dynize attack. "Something about it, and the fact that both Lindet and the Dynize want it so badly, sets her off. We'll stay with her for now." He was suddenly tired, feeling the weight of a battle on his shoulders, and he gave a brief thought for the dead left behind.

"Are you Colonel Styke?"

Styke raised his eyes to find a man on foot, wearing the sharp, clean uniform of a Blackhat with a Silver Rose pinned to his chest. He definitely wasn't one of the men who'd gone into battle with them yesterday. Styke reached behind him, touching the handle of the knife at his belt. "I am."

"Message for you," the Blackhat said, handing over a sealed note. The paper was blank, the wax seal without distinguishing marks. Styke sniffed at the paper, smelling the faintest hint of sorcery. He broke the seal with his thumb and read the contents.

Brother, I understand you have survived the battle. I give you my congratulations and my thanks. The nation owes you and the Riflejacks a great debt. One which, unfortunately, will never be paid. Lady Flint has decided we are enemies, and therefore will have to be removed.

The Dynize will not stop—another fleet, as big as the one that attacked Landfall, has dropped their soldiers about eighty miles south of the city. I beg that you abandon Flint and ride to find me in Redstone. I have summoned my armies back from the frontier and instituted a conscription. We will crush these Dynize invaders and take back what is ours before something worse can come of this.

If you see Fidelis Jes, do not kill him. I have use for you both.

It was signed with a simple "S."

Sister.

Styke rolled the paper between his thumb and forefinger thoughtfully, then started when it suddenly burst into flames. Within moments the letter was consumed by a sorcerous fire.

"What just happened?" Ibana asked.

Styke brushed the ashes off his fingertips and sniffed them. "A ward," he said. "Likely triggered to burn the message within a few minutes of my breaking the seal."

"What did it say?"

Styke ignored her, looking at a black smudge of ash on his palm. "Will you take a return message?" he asked the Blackhat.

"Yes, sir. The lady expects it."

"Good. Ibana, fetch this nice young man the sack you have tied to your saddle."

CHAPTER 66

S o you're saying this isn't over?" Michel asked.

Styke shook his big head and spread his hands. "According to Lindet, there's a whole other army headed this way. We have less than a week."

Michel stood on the plain south of Landfall, just a few hundred yards from the remains of the land-barge. The big wagon had been struck by errant sorcery during the battle—lightning that almost fried Michel where he stood, and destroyed enough of the big wheels that it wouldn't be going anywhere without being entirely rebuilt.

He waited with a group consisting of Styke, Lady Flint, Taniel, and Ka-poel and wondered what had gone so terribly wrong in his life to throw him into such company. He shouldn't be here with warriors, sorcerers, and officers, trying to make decisions that would affect hundreds of thousands of people. He should be watching from the shadows, causing the tiny ripples that kept the government running.

He did not, he decided, like the stage, even if it was so far a small one, because he knew that somewhere was a boardroom filled with the mayor and the city elders, waiting for some sort of response from Vlora regarding the battle with the Dynize. Somewhere was the Lady Chancellor, wondering where her ancient Dynize relic and her Blackhat grand master had gotten to.

"We can't defend the city," Flint said. "Not without heavy reinforcements. Fort Nied cannot withstand another shelling, and we're down well over half of our forces. Did Lindet indicate if she was willing to contribute to the war effort?" She seemed annoyed that it had been Styke, and not her, who received a communiqué from Lindet.

Styke grimaced. "She's pulling back all the way to Redstone and gathering her armies. Sounds like she's written off Landfall. She'll let the Dynize take it, then return with a bigger army—presumably before they manage to use the godstone."

"Do they know how to use it?" Michel asked. He didn't belong here with the others, but the least he could do was add to the conversation.

"We're not sure," Taniel said, his eyes on Ka-poel, who gave an exaggerated shrug. "The godstone has been buried beneath the dirt outside of Landfall for over a thousand years. The knowledge may be lost, but we don't know how good the Dynize record-keeping is."

"They knew it was here," Flint pointed out.

"Because of their own records, or because their spies told them Lindet had unearthed it?" Taniel responded. "We don't know enough about the Dynize, but I suspect that's going to change far quicker than we'd like."

Flint seemed distant and withdrawn, and stared across the plain toward the godstone. "They're coming for that," she said.

"I'm tempted to just give it to them." Styke snorted.

"Absolutely not," Flint snapped back. "Not while I'm still breathing. They want a new god, and I've seen the damage gods do. I will not allow it to fall into their hands."

There was a flurry of gestures from Ka-poel, and Taniel translated. "Given enough time, we could reconstruct the land-barge. I imagine Professor Cressel will help us. He's obsessed with the thing."

"To what end?" Flint asked, glancing sidelong at Taniel and Ka-poel. "Where would you take it?"

"We take it to the Hadshaw River, put it on a couple of barges, and bring it north. There's more than one Palo stronghold we could send it to where it would be safe, and give us time to study it."

"It should not be studied," Flint insisted.

Ka-poel pursed her lips, tilting her head in a very clear message. *Why?*

"Because we're toying with something we don't understand. Ka-poel is powerful, but that... *thing* can make gods. I wouldn't trust myself to toy with it. I certainly don't trust you."

Ka-poel glared openly at Flint, who seemed unaffected. Taniel sighed. "So what do you suggest? Burying it back in the ground and hoping the Dynize can't figure out where it was?"

Michel couldn't help himself. He was surrounded by some of the most famous people in the world, and all they could do was bicker. He let out a laugh, and then found everyone staring at him. He cleared his throat. "It's simple, isn't it?"

"What is?" Styke asked.

"We destroy it. Blow the damn thing to the pit. I read somewhere that black powder is caustic to Privileged, and can even have dampening powers on sorcery. Just strap it with all the powder barrels you can find and set it off."

There was a long, awkward silence. Ka-poel snorted. Taniel sighed unhappily, while Styke looked indifferent. Flint gave an emphatic nod. "All right," she said. "We destroy it. If you won't, then I will. Are you going to fight me on this, Taniel?"

Ka-poel launched into a silent tirade, her hands moving quickly, angrily. Taniel watched it go on, then finally turned to Flint with a resigned sigh. "No, we won't fight you on it. We'll help you destroy it."

Flint was off a moment later, yelling for powder kegs, while Taniel and Ka-poel conferred among themselves. Styke seemed untalkative, so Michel found himself alone, wandering off across the cotton fields with no real direction in mind. In the distance, Landfall still smoldered and he wondered if the rioting had finally died down. According to Taniel, his Palo had flushed out the Dynize agents, then rallied the rioters to put out the flames. It sounded too good to be true, but so did the fact that he was still alive after such a vicious battle.

Michel walked toward Landfall slowly, feeling sick to his stomach. So many deaths over such a stupid thing, this godstone. He cheered silently for Flint to blow it to the pit, even if it made Taniel and Ka-poel angry. After so many years as their spy, he realized that he no longer knew their goals.

He realized that, even worse, he no longer knew his own goals. His mission had been accomplished, his cover betrayed. By all the rules of espionage he should disappear—maybe even flee the continent altogether. He wondered if he could use the Platinum Rose to withdraw a king's ransom from a bank and vanish before anyone noticed, and if Mother would enjoy someplace with a cooler climate. Maybe he'd head in the opposite direction of Taniel and Flint, and go to Adro.

"Sir," a voice said, and Michel was startled to find himself no longer alone. It was one of the Blackhats, a young woman with a torn jacket, a Silver Rose on her breast, and a crutch under one arm. "Agent Hendres reporting, sir."

Michel blinked back at her for several moments before he remembered that the Platinum Rose was still pinned to his chest. "Right," he said. "What do you have to report?"

Hendres looked slightly bewildered for a moment, looking first at Michel and then toward Landfall. "Sir, I...have nothing to report. But I just wanted to know: I overheard Lady Flint talking to one of her men. Has the Lady Chancellor really abandoned Landfall to the Dynize?"

Michel sighed, cursing Flint and her military-loud voice. "I hope not," he replied, hoping it didn't sound too much like a bald-faced lie.

"Thing is, sir, you spoke to us yesterday before the fight about our friends and families. There's not many of us left, but we'd like to head back to help them get out of the city."

"Then what are you waiting for? Why are you standing here yapping at me?"

"Orders, sir."

Michel looked down at the Platinum Rose. He unpinned it, lifted it over his head to throw it into the cotton fields, then thought better of it and slipped it into his pocket. "I'm nobody to be giving orders," he explained. "I just said the things I did because they needed to be said."

Hendres's face fell, and she nodded slowly, looking down at her boots. The sight of her disappointment made Michel think of all the times his mother had given him that same look, not knowing that he—the real him—was working for the very things she valued.

"If you need orders," Michel said, removing the Platinum Rose from his pocket and holding it up, "then you have them. Get the men back in the city. Tell them to find their families. They can help rebuild if they like, or abandon Landfall. I don't know if the Dynize are planning on burning it down or occupying it, but you'd better make it quick." He put the Rose back in his pocket, then walked over to offer Agent Hendres his arm. She leaned against it gratefully, and the two of them began the long walk toward Landfall.

There was a series of loud shouts, and Michel turned around to look back in the direction of the monolith. He realized that he'd wandered quite far away, and squinted to see people running away from the wrecked land-barge.

"Duck," he said, helping Hendres into a crouch.

The sight of the blast reached them several moments before the sound and shock wave did, making his ears ring and nearly knocking him flat on his ass. A giant ball of flame rose up around the godstone, and he felt a deep stab of satisfaction. That, as it went in the storybooks his mother so liked to read, was that. He kept his eyes on the smoking ruin in the distance for some time before turning back to Landfall.

"What are you going to do, sir?" Hendres asked.

Michel considered this for a moment, then replied, "I'm going to do what I do best. I'm going to find my mother, be certain she's safe, and then I'm going to make sure that Landfall keeps running in fair weather or foul."

EPILOGUE

Taniel's ears rang from the sound of the blast, despite the globs of wax he'd stuffed in them. He watched the fireball from the explosion die down and fought the headache that came along with controlling the detonation of so much powder. He, working in tandem with Vlora, had used his sorcery to warp the entire power of the blast of almost a hundred barrels of powder directly toward the center of the monolith.

It was enough explosive power to destroy a small city.

"It didn't work," he said, digging the wax out of his ears.

"Thank you for that observation," Vlora replied sourly as she and Ka-poel did the same. Together, the three of them walked to the monolith, picking their way through the charred grasses and the matchsticks that remained of the land-barge. The explosion had stained the limestone black, quite effectively cleaning the remaining dirt from its cracks and crevices, but appeared to have not so much as scratched the surface.

Ka-poel ran her hand along the ancient runes on the godstone's side, then shook her head. *Nothing.*

"That explosion should have ground this stupid block to dust— or at least cracked it," Vlora said.

Taniel walked up and down the length of the godstone twice, reaching out gingerly with his senses, wishing that he had Ka-poel's ability to read the Else. A Privileged would be far more useful here than either him or Vlora, and Ka-poel was learning about this thing on the fly, so he wasn't at all confident in his own senses.

Besides, he didn't *like* feeling the godstone in the Else. It made the backs of his eyeballs itch and gave him a feeling like spiders crawling up his spine. He'd seen a lot in this world—pit, he'd killed *two* gods—but this godstone made his skin crawl in a way that facing Kresimir in person had never done.

"I'm not letting you take it," Vlora said emphatically.

Taniel raised his hands in surrender. "You made your position very clear. But the Dynize are on their way, and unless you've got any better ideas..." He trailed off, and glanced at Ka-poel, who was now standing back, one hand on her chin, mouth pressed into a thoughtful line.

She gestured to him. *I think I have something.*

"To destroy it?" he asked.

No. It might take me a long time to destroy it. But there may be something else. She explained her plan, and Taniel found himself nodding along.

"Ka-poel wants to try something," he said to Vlora. "The wards in the godstone are like nothing any of us has ever seen before. They won't just succumb to brute force. All that powder we piled on didn't even cause a dent in them."

"So," Vlora asked suspiciously, "what do you want to try?"

Taniel was annoyed at her suspicion, but admitted to himself that she was right to be. In a way, he agreed with Lindet. The godstone needed to be kept and studied. He just didn't trust either Lindet or the Dynize to do so. And unlike Vlora, he *did* trust his wife to do it.

Ka-poel didn't answer Vlora. Instead, she searched her satchel for a knife, then bent over, cutting a thin furrow in the dirt. She walked backward, working a line into the ground, slowly around the entire monolith. Vlora watched the process with her lips pursed. "Is this something that's going to get me killed?" she asked.

"When Ka-poel works," Taniel said, hoping his own worry didn't show in his tone, "it's often something likely to get *her* killed." He tilted his head. He thought he had *some* idea as to what she was up to, but after eleven years as companions she still managed to surprise him more often than not. Blood sorcery was far more an art than a science, and it always seemed to his eyes that Ka-poel made up her own rules.

When she'd finished her furrow she stepped back, then back farther, then a little farther, gesturing for Taniel and Vlora to get behind her. Vlora snorted impatiently, but followed her instructions.

"Give her time," Taniel asked, retreating to a safe distance.

Ka-poel took a deep breath, squaring her shoulders and holding her hands with palms pointed downward. There she remained as the seconds, then minutes, ticked by.

"What's she doing?" Vlora finally whispered.

Taniel responded honestly, "I have no idea."

It was some time before he got the strange impression that the ground was moving. He ignored it at first, and then realized it wasn't the ground at all. Something was creeping over the soil through the stalks of the cotton plants. He looked down at his feet and all the hair on the back of his neck stood on end.

The ground was covered in blood. Not soaked with it, but literally covered, like red ink spilled on an impermeable surface. It flowed, black and thick, bringing the smell of rotten corpses with it, toward the godstone. Vlora didn't seem to notice until the blood reached the stone and began to climb up it, and then she let out a gasp.

The blood continued to come. There were ample amounts, after all. Thousands of gallons soaked into the dirt, and it all moved along at her whim.

"Is this something she does often?" Vlora asked, obviously unnerved.

"I've never seen this before."

The blood worked its way up and around until it completely covered the monolith in a thick black sludge, and then it disappeared slowly, like water going down a drain. It took Taniel a moment to realize the blood had soaked *into* the godstone.

"That," Vlora said, awe in her voice, "is one of the most terrifying things I've ever seen."

Taniel eyed the side of his wife's face, wondering what was going through her mind. Even on the best of days, she could still be inscrutable. She was a mystery, through and through, and sometimes it scared him. But then again, that mystery was why he loved her as much as he did.

Ka-poel suddenly let out a sigh and sagged, and Taniel rushed forward to catch her before she fell. She felt so small in his arms; weak. He remembered that someone had once described her as a teapot full of gunpowder—powerful but fragile—and he thought the description as apt as ever. "You'll need to rest tomorrow," he told her.

She nodded in agreement.

"What has she done?" Vlora asked, walking up to the monolith and placing her hand hesitantly on the side.

Taniel reached out with his own senses. He could no longer feel the sorcery of the monolith, or the dark whispering in the back of his mind. It was, it seemed, nothing more than stone. Ka-poel spoke with her hands, and he translated: "She's sealed it. The sorcery is still there, buried inside, but she used the..." He frowned, watching as she repeated her hand motions, then he continued. "She's used the blood of the fallen to create a barrier. She says the Dynize bone-eyes probably will be able to pick it apart, eventually." He laughed at the final two gestures, her bold confidence amusing him. "But," he said, "she's far more powerful than any of them. It'll take them forever to access the stone."

"So we have time," Vlora said flatly.

"That's all we can offer," Taniel responded.

Vlora paced back and forth, and Taniel hoped she understood. Ka-poel was dangerous, but she was not infallible or omnipotent. If she said breaking the godstone was beyond her ability, he believed her. "How long?" Vlora asked.

Ka-poel shrugged, and Taniel said, "Months? Years? Who knows? It depends on how clever Ka-sedial is."

Vlora was clearly unhappy with the answer, but she walked across the field to a number of her aides standing farther back. She returned a moment later, a scowl on her face. "It's done," she said.

"What?" Taniel asked.

"I've ordered the evacuation of the city."

"Ah."

Vlora suddenly closed her eyes, and Taniel wondered if he spotted tears there. "Why," she asked in a whisper, "does it feel like I lost?"

"You didn't," Taniel said.

"I didn't?" she echoed.

"No. Without you and the Riflejacks, the godstone would be in Dynize hands now. They'd have a tool to make a monster."

"They'll still get it," Vlora said. "We're leaving the city. Withdrawing. I can't defend it without Lindet's help, and she now wants my head. The Dynize will take Landfall *and* the godstone."

"We'll be back," Taniel said confidently. He nodded to himself, hoping he was right. The fate of the entire continent rested on the idea. "It'll take some time, but I'll give you an army of Palo that can match the Dynize."

"And what about Lindet?" Vlora asked.

"We'll have to deal with her when it comes to that. In the meantime, we need to worry about the other two godstones."

Vlora inhaled sharply. "Excuse me?"

Taniel felt tired—more tired than he'd felt at any time since his father died. But he also felt good. This was the first step in a plan he and Ka-poel had been working on for the better part of a decade. He glanced around, noticing that some of the Riflejacks were staring at him and Ka-poel. They were beginning to suspect who he was, and he didn't much care. In fact, there was a freedom in being alive to the world again. "Two more godstones," he said, holding up his fingers. "Don't worry. I'm sure Lindet is already well on her way to finding them. We just have to make sure we get to them before she does."

ACKNOWLEDGMENTS

I can never say enough about my awesome editor, Devi Pillai, and the guidance she gives to my books. She was especially patient with this one, and it's ten times better than it would have been without her ability to make me do my best. The usual thanks go out to my agent, Caitlin Blasdell, who runs interference for me when I'm behind schedule, and gives me pep talks when I need them.

Thanks to my wife, Michele, for reading the drafts of this book into the early hours of the morning to help me get it done. Her advice is an invaluable part of my writing.

Special thanks to my beta-readers, including David Wohlreich, Peter Keep, Mark Lindberg, and Justin Landon. A good beta-reader is often an unsung hero of the editing process, and mine are no exception.

The biggest appreciation goes out to all the people at Orbit who take these stories from my head and put them on the shelf, including (but not limited to) Lauren Panepinto, James Long, Alex Lencicki, Ellen Wright, and Laura Fitzgerald. None of this would happen without the whole team doing their jobs—a fact that is often overlooked by the fans who love these books.

And of course, thank you to everyone for reading. You're the best fans a writer could hope for. I'm blessed to have a place on your shelves, and hope to continue to deserve that honor for many books to come.